OXFORD WORLD'S CLASSICS

# THE DUKE'S CHILDREN

THE DUKE'S CHILDREN is the last in Trollope's six-volume sequence of novels known as the Palliser series. They chart the career of Plantagenet Palliser, and his troubled marriage to Lady Glencora. The novels depict the social milieu of the aristocracy and upper middle-class of mid-Victorian England, with occasional forays into low life and the criminal underworld. They combine the machinations of politics with an intimate exploration of personal relationships to paint an unparalleled portrait of an age. The novels can be read independently and as part of a linked whole. They are:

> *Can You Forgive Her?* (1865)
> *Phineas Finn* (1869)
> *The Eustace Diamonds* (1872)
> *Phineas Redux* (1873)
> *The Prime Minister* (1876)
> *The Duke's Children* (1880)

KATHERINE MULLIN is Senior Lecturer in English Literature at the University of Leeds. Her book, *James Joyce, Sexuality and Social Purity*, came out in 2003. She is currently working on a literary and cultural history of typists, shopgirls, and barmaids, *Working Girls: Literature, Labour, and Sexuality 1880–1920*.

FRANCIS O'GORMAN'S recent publications include *Victorian Literature and Finance* (2007), *The Cambridge Companion to Victorian Culture* (2010), and an edition of Arthur Conan Doyle's *The Hound of the Baskervilles* (2006). He is now writing a history of worry, and is Professor of Victorian Literature at the University of Leeds.

## OXFORD WORLD'S CLASSICS

*For over 100 years Oxford World's Classics have brought readers closer to the world's great literature. Now with over 700 titles—from the 4,000-year-old myths of Mesopotamia to the twentieth century's greatest novels—the series makes available lesser-known as well as celebrated writing.*

*The pocket-sized hardbacks of the early years contained introductions by Virginia Woolf, T. S. Eliot, Graham Greene, and other literary figures which enriched the experience of reading. Today the series is recognized for its fine scholarship and reliability in texts that span world literature, drama and poetry, religion, philosophy and politics. Each edition includes perceptive commentary and essential background information to meet the changing needs of readers.*

OXFORD WORLD'S CLASSICS

ANTHONY TROLLOPE

# *The Duke's Children*

Edited with an Introduction and Notes by
KATHERINE MULLIN and FRANCIS O'GORMAN

OXFORD
UNIVERSITY PRESS

# OXFORD
## UNIVERSITY PRESS

Great Clarendon Street, Oxford OX2 6DP

Oxford University Press is a department of the University of Oxford.
It furthers the University's objective of excellence in research, scholarship,
and education by publishing worldwide in

Oxford New York

Auckland Cape Town Dar es Salaam Hong Kong Karachi
Kuala Lumpur Madrid Melbourne Mexico City Nairobi
New Delhi Shanghai Taipei Toronto

With offices in

Argentina Austria Brazil Chile Czech Republic France Greece
Guatemala Hungary Italy Japan Poland Portugal Singapore
South Korea Switzerland Thailand Turkey Ukraine Vietnam

Oxford is a registered trade mark of Oxford University Press
in the UK and in certain other countries

Published in the United States
by Oxford University Press Inc., New York

Biographical Preface, Introduction, Select Bibliography, Chronology, Explanatory Notes
© Katherine Mullin and Francis O'Gorman 2011
Appendix © Nicholas Shrimpton 2011

The moral rights of the authors have been asserted
Database right Oxford University Press (maker)

First published as a World's Classics paperback 1983
Reissued as an Oxford World's Classics paperback 1999, 2008
New edition 2011

British Library Cataloguing in Publication Data

Data available

Library of Congress Control Number: 2011934702

Typeset by Glyph International, Bangalore, India
Printed in Great Britain
on acid-free paper by
Clays Ltd, St Ives plc

ISBN 978-0-19-957838-2

4

# CONTENTS

# BIOGRAPHICAL PREFACE

ANTHONY TROLLOPE was born on 24 April 1815 in London. He was the fourth surviving child of a failing barrister and gentleman farmer, Thomas Anthony Trollope, and his wife Frances (née Milton), who became a successful novelist and travel writer. Trollope's childhood was dominated by uncongenial schooling. He was sent to Harrow, the boys' public school in north London, as a day boy, then to Sunbury, Surrey, while awaiting a place at his father's former school, Winchester College. Trollope was admitted to Winchester in 1827, but his father's embarrassing inability to pay the fees became known to fellow pupils. He was moved back from Winchester to Harrow in 1830 for two further years, which he later described as 'the worst period of my life'.[1] Unsurprisingly, he did not shine academically, and when, in 1834, the whole family fled to Bruges in Belgium to avoid imprisonment for debt, he obtained a clerkship in the London headquarters of the newly-created Post Office through his mother's connections.

The beginning of Trollope's long Post Office career was not encouraging. He soon became known for unpunctuality, and was, by his own account, 'always on the eve of being dismissed'.[2] His scanty salary led him into debt, and travails with money-lenders would later inform the scrapes of many fictional characters. Trollope was sustained by a habit of imagination that was first acquired during his unhappy adolescence. Daydreaming not only allowed him 'to live in a world altogether outside the world of my own material life';[3] it served as an apprenticeship for fiction. Yet it took a change of scene from London to rural Ireland to persuade Trollope to express his imagination in writing.

In July 1841, aged 26, Trollope was appointed deputy postal surveyor's clerk, based in Banagher, King's County (now Co. Offaly). His new-found professional success helped him to grow in social confidence. Ireland prompted his lifelong enthusiasm for hunting with hounds, too. That enthusiasm was never far from his writing, and sometimes it made life difficult for him at work, not least because hounds and horses were an expensive pastime. Within a year, he became engaged to Rose Heseltine, the daughter of a Rotherham banker who was holidaying in what is now Dun Laoghaire. Trollope proposed after barely a fortnight's acquaintance. The wedding was, for

---

[1] Anthony Trollope, *An Autobiography* (Oxford: OUP, 1980), 11.
[2] Ibid. 46.                                    [3] Ibid. 43.

financial reasons, postponed for two years until 11 June 1844. Marriage
and the birth of two sons, Henry Merivale in 1846 and Frederick James
Anthony in 1847, helped Trollope to find what he called the 'vigour
necessary to prosecute two professions at the same time'.[4] His first
novel, *The Macdermots of Ballycloran* (1847), sold far fewer than the
400 copies printed. But it was favourably reviewed and was followed
by a second Irish tale, *The Kellys and the O'Kellys* (1848). Both kept an
uneasy silence on the Famine, to which Trollope was a horrified witness, but his recollections of the famine years would inform the later
*Castle Richmond* (1860). The failure of *La Vendée* (1850), on the French
Revolution, together with the increasing demands of his Post Office
career, conspired to deflect Trollope from fiction for some years.

In 1851, he was sent to the south-west of England to investigate
ways of expanding the rural postal system. His successful development
of the pillar box, which he first tried out in St Helier in the Channel
Islands in 1852, led to the spread of post boxes throughout the UK.
The project won Trollope promotion to the surveyorship of the north
of Ireland in 1854, and his family settled in Donnybrook. During these
years, he composed the first novel to bring him real recognition, *The
Warden* (1855). The first of six 'Chronicles of Barsetshire', *The Warden*
was set, like its successors, in a fictional county, based on the south-
west England Trollope knew. Although they dramatized changes in the
ecclesiastical world, the 'Chronicles' were also secular in their interests.
While *The Warden* brought him less than £10, Trollope 'soon felt it
had not failed as the others had failed',[5] and began work on *Barchester
Towers* (1857). It was warmly reviewed. But it was not until the publication of *Dr Thorne* (1858) that he met with unmixed success. The novels
following—*Framley Parsonage* (1861), *The Small House at Allington*
(1864), and *The Last Chronicle of Barset* (1867)—established his reputation, his popularity, and his fortune.

During the twelve years between *The Warden* and *The Last Chronicle*,
Trollope published seventeen novels, numerous short stories, and several collections of travel writing. This extraordinary scale of production was sustained by his habit of rising at five each morning to allow
three hours of writing—250 words each quarter of an hour, he boasted
in *An Autobiography*—before leaving for the office at nine. Other celebrated writers have written to a similar schedule, but Trollope's pride
in his achievement has never been entirely admired by critics. His
schedule made him an invaluable contributor to the *Cornhill Magazine*,
founded in 1859 by the novelist, William Makepeace Thackeray. The

---

[4] Ibid. 69.        [5] Ibid. 98.

serialization of *Framley Parsonage* in the *Cornhill*'s first issues did much to secure the magazine's and Trollope's reputation. Through the *Cornhill*, he made lasting friendships with major literary and artistic figures. By 1859, he was living in the north London suburb of Waltham Cross, after a promotion to Post Office surveyor of the eastern district. He was soon elected to the Garrick and Athenaeum Clubs, and became a stalwart of the Royal Literary Fund. These were marks of serious literary success. He also, in 1860, met a young American woman, Kate Field, with whom he fell in love. The nature of *that* relationship is known almost as little as Trollope's relationship with Rose. But Kate mattered to him—and would do till the end of his life.

Trollope concluded the Barsetshire Chronicles on a high note, considering *The Last Chronicle of Barset* to be his best novel. Following the model of Honoré de Balzac's *Comédie humaine*, Trollope saw realist fiction as capable of depicting a complex culture through a multivolume series. The Palliser volumes, beginning with *Can You Forgive Her?* (1865) and ending with *The Duke's Children* (1880), were his other major sequence. These novels, like the Barsetshire Chronicles, could be read separately and in different orders without irrecoverable loss—but they formed a continuous whole all the same. In the story of the Pallisers, Trollope developed one of his strongest themes—the difficult marriage and its negotiations. He also explored great political issues, including the 1867 Reform Bill and the disestablishment of the Irish Church, while inviting readers to map the Conservative leader Daubeny onto Disraeli, and the Liberal Gresham onto Gladstone. His portrayal of democratic politics has remained consequential for generations. The novels' political appeal, nonetheless, was carefully balanced against other enticements: 'If I wrote politics for my own sake, I must put in love and intrigue, social incidents, a dash of sport, for the sake of my readers',[6] he said, with characteristic pragmatism.

Trollope resigned from the Post Office in 1867. His earnings from writing had long outstripped his salary. The following year, feeling that 'to sit in the British Parliament should be the highest object of ambition to every educated Englishman',[7] he stood as the Liberal candidate for Beverley in the 1868 General Election. He was unsuccessful. That failure haunted his fiction as it must have haunted his private life. Trollope interspersed the Palliser series with other novels and studies. He was by this stage a professional writer whose commitment was broken significantly only by field sports and travel. Trollope's international voyages included Australia, where Frederick, his younger son, was a sheep

[6] Ibid. 317.    [7] Ibid. 290.

farmer: *Australia and New Zealand* (1873) was a result. Trollope and
Rose left London in 1880 for South Harting in Sussex, hoping country
air would ease his persistent asthma. This was no retirement: the last
two years of his life saw a further six books, including *Mr Scarborough's
Family* (1883), a study of parental domination, and the unfinished *The
Landleaguers*, a return to Irish matters (published posthumously, 1883).

In early November 1882, Trollope suffered a stroke, and, on
6 December, he died in London at the age of 67. He had written forty-
seven novels, five volumes of short stories, four travel books, three
biographies, an autobiography, and two translations from the classics,
together with uncollected pieces of journalism. His prodigious output
included a biography of Thackeray, and a study of Cicero whose political judiciousness was often a silent model behind his admirable fictional
politicians. Few who knew Trollope could avoid commenting on his
loud and bluff persona in public: at 5 ft. 10 in., and around 16 stones, he
struck those who met him as burly—a man of bodily appetites. It was
difficult for many to imagine him dissecting the emotional complexities
of his characters with such delicacy and sympathy.

Trollope's posthumous *An Autobiography* (1883) startled a large
number of readers. Its dry discussion of how much money his fiction
made denied any Romantic model of authorship. Here was no account
of the creative flash of inspiration. Writing fiction was more like a trade,
the result of well-applied skill and labour. But, knowing at first hand the
cost of his father's failure, it was important to Trollope to demonstrate
to his family, if to no one else, that he had made such a success of his
life. He had no university degree, and was without the much-coveted
honour of a seat in Parliament. He wished to demonstrate too, in a culture less familiar with the notion of a professional writer than ours, that
writing could indeed be a life. His estate was valued at the huge sum of
£25,892 19s. 3d.

Biographies of Trollope are always to some degree doomed to follow the sparse facts laid out in *An Autobiography*. The nature of his
marriage, his feelings for Kate Field, his relationship with his sons,
let alone the secrets of his inner life, are among the topics on which it
is impossible to write with certainty. Trollope had no commitment to
privacy—but private he remains. Declining to reveal himself in correspondence, he is, perhaps, only glimpsed in the astonishingly fertile
novels about human lives, desires, and choices, which were his enduring bequest to English literature.

*Katherine Mullin*
*Francis O'Gorman*

# INTRODUCTION

*[Readers who are unfamiliar with the plot may prefer to treat the Introduction as an Afterword.]*

*The Duke's Children* (1879–80) is the final published novel of Anthony Trollope's Palliser series, which had begun in 1864 with the first volume of *Can You Forgive Her?*[1] A story of generational conflict, of loyalty, of problems with principle, of the capacity of love to harm those who are loved, *The Duke's Children* invokes the great trope of romance: reconciliation. It has the shade of Shakespeare's *The Tempest* about it. Yet this is no easy romance, as Shakespeare's was not.[2] Ostensibly, this is the happy ending for the great narrative of the Pallisers (though it is possible that Trollope, leaving the ending open, was allowing the possibility of *another* Palliser novel: there is certainly no farewell at the end like that which concludes *The Last Chronicle of Barset* (1867), the final novel of the Barsetshire series). It is true that Lady Glencora lies dead as *The Duke's Children* opens. But, by the end, friendships have been restored, the Duke has returned to the service of his country, the Palliser children have married those whom they desired to marry, and they are back on good terms with their father. Harmony, it seems, has been re-established.

Yet not quite so. For the reconciliation achieved here—that to which the whole story moves—is so double-edged that it invites the hardest questions about Trollope's sense of the world, and about the consolations fiction can offer. If it is easy to think of Trollope as a defender of the status quo, as somehow a 'comfortable' novelist, *The Duke's Children* is a provocative reminder, beneath its surface, of the difficult, uncertain, and decidedly uncomfortable world that in truth he envisages. Recognizing that discomfort means realizing that the unsaid of this novel is as important as the said.

Trollope was not quite the man he used to be when he began to issue *The Duke's Children* in parts in *All the Year Round* from October 1879 to July 1880. In his last years, as his son Henry Merivale Trollope said, 'my father continued his work. He would not otherwise have been happy'.[3] But there were reasons why he was not entirely happy

---

[1] On the appropriateness or otherwise of calling the Pallisers a 'series', see the Appendix to this edition, pp. 507–17.

[2] For a full account of Trollope's use of 17th-cent. drama in another of the Palliser novels, see Nicholas Shrimpton's Introduction to *The Prime Minister* in the same series.

[3] Anthony Trollope, *An Autobiography* (Oxford: Oxford University Press, 1980), p. xxiii.

despite that. Certainly, *The Prime Minister* (1876) had been, at least in his eyes, a failure. 'It was worse spoken of by the press than any novel I had written', he would say bravely in *An Autobiography*, published posthumously in 1883.⁴ With the new novel, first written in the same year as *The Prime Minister*, he decided to make accommodation with his readers, or at least *one* reader, more plainly than before. *The Duke's Children* began as a four-volume work (see the Note on the Text), but Trollope was willing to cut it down to three for the printed version. It was not something he had done before. Perhaps, in fact, he saw some wisdom or opportunity in his editor's suggestion to prune, since he was perfectly capable of saying no. He had, after all, plainly refused, even as an unknown novelist, to cut *Barchester Towers* (1857) by a volume, as he proudly recalled in *An Autobiography*.⁵ But, privately, he would soon tell his son that he would be content enough simply writing, even without publication. 'I finished on Thursday', he said in a letter in December 1880, 'the novel I was writing [*Kept in the Dark*], and on Friday I began another [*The Fixed Period*]. Nothing really frightens me but the idea of enforced idleness. As long as I can write books, even though they be not published, I think that I can be happy.'⁶ There was a time when few English publishing houses would have contemplated *not* issuing a Trollope novel.

As it happens, *The Duke's Children*, in the end, was quite well received by critics. Among the most penetrating reviews was that in *The Spectator*, 12 June 1880, where the reviewer thought this 'dramatic essay, if we may so term it, upon the aristocratic principle, in its relation to politics, society, and morality, possesses an interest which few or none besides Mr. Trollope could have imparted to it; it is the thoughtful and sensible judgment of an able and comparatively impartial mind on one of the quaintest of modern problems [i.e., the problem of aristocracy's role in politics]'.⁷ Trollope could neither have been dismayed by that, nor by *The Athenaeum*'s more affable certainty that the novel 'seize[d] the attention of his readers by interesting and amusing them'.⁸

But some of Trollope's more private difficulties enter the substance of the text. Trollope is no plainly autobiographical writer, though he

⁴ Ibid. 360 n.

⁵ Ibid. 103–4.

⁶ *The Letters of Anthony Trollope*, ed. N. John Hall, with the assistance of Nina Burgis, 2 vols. (Stanford: Stanford University Press, 1983), ii. 886.

⁷ From *The Spectator*, 53 (12 June 1880), 754–5, repr. in Donald Smalley (ed.), *Anthony Trollope: The Critical Heritage* (London: Routledge, 1969), 470.

⁸ From *The Athenaeum* (29 May 1880), 694; repr. in Smalley (ed.), *Critical Heritage*, 467.

certainly was not averse to using incidents from his life in his fiction—
*The Three Clerks* (1858) straightforwardly narrated his job interview
for his first clerkship at the Post Office, for example.[9] His inner life,
however, so notoriously impenetrable, is always hard confidently to
associate with the psychological histories of his fiction. Yet *The Duke's
Children* perhaps brings into *some* dramatic form important issues from
that inner life in the few years before Trollope's death in 1882.

Trollope's sense that his two sons had not entirely distinguished
themselves may lurk in the Duke's initial disappointments in his two.
The elections at Silverbridge and Polpenno more obviously echo with
Trollope's discontent about failing to win Beverley in 1868 (even if he
was somewhat awry in thinking he *could* win it). Canvassing in that
election, the novelist said, was the 'most wretched fortnight of my
manhood'.[10] The success of Lord Silverbridge and Frank Tregear are
moments, perhaps, of imaginative recompense. (If readers wonder why
Trollope left it as late as he did to try to enter Parliament, they will
need to know that, as a civil servant in the Post Office, he was ineligible
to vote, let alone stand for election to the Commons.) And it is hard not
to think, more daringly, that the romantic life of Lord Silverbridge is
revealing of Trollope too. Silverbridge is ready to take Lady Mabel
as his wife, but falls in love with Isabel Boncassen, the beautiful,
self-possessed daughter of the New World. Trollope's own mysterious
emotional life was centred on a long marriage, about which he said in
*An Autobiography* almost nothing, except, airily, that it was 'like the
marriage of other people, and of no special interest to any one except
my wife and me'.[11] But there was also, later, the—mysterious—romantic
friendship with the American, Kate Field (1838–96). Certainly,
Trollope's biographer, N. John Hall, had no hesitation in saying that
Isabel 'is based in part on Kate Field'.[12] But what might that imply? Is
that trio of Kate, Rose, and Trollope a shadowy presence here in the
story of Mabel, Isabel, and Silverbridge, a story that, perhaps, hints at
*Trollope's* guilt and pleasure and desire? When the novelist wrote to
Kate on 17 January 1881 to say of George Eliot, who had died only
a few weeks before, that 'in truth she was one whose private life should
be left in privacy,—as may be said of all who have achieved fame by
literary merits',[13] he could not have reported to a more appropriate

[9] See *Autobiography*, 35–6.
[10] Ibid. 300.
[11] Ibid. 71.
[12] 'Anthony Trollope', *Oxford Dictionary of National Biography* (*ODNB*), electronic edn.
[13] *Letters of Anthony Trollope*, iii. 892.

person what he wished for his own life, and not least as it concerned Kate.

The novel may look inwards, and it tempts readers to make connections with the author's life while knowing they can never be sure. But *The Duke's Children* points outwards more plainly. Trollope continues to read so well into the twenty-first century partly because of his capacity to ask enduring questions in engaging romantic plots that, while they belong to particular moments of history, exceed them. He reads well still in part because politics to him is a matter of real life, of flesh and blood. *The Duke's Children* was once thought perfunctory in its dealings with politics, and Steven Armarnick still thinks it is only the original manuscript that can properly be described as political.[14] It is true that the published novel has hardly any explicit account of Parliament or policies, of committees or manifestos, of public life at all. But it is immersed in politics for all that, for it dramatizes major political themes about the nature of conservatism; about liberalism, compromise, principle, progress, and coalition; about obedience and authority, representation and democracy. And it does so by not dealing with them directly. The political questions, which are as much ours as they are the Victorians', are made meaningful by being made domestic.

*The Duke's Children* meditates on the meanings of the words 'liberal' and 'conservative'. Central to both in political terms is a question of how to deal with change. And those themes are examined in the life of a single family. Lord Silverbridge, in spurning his father's Liberal traditions, becomes a Conservative in an act of 'rebellion'. But should the house of Omnium as a whole accept change or remain the same? That is the dominant question of the Duke's life in this novel, and it is a personal and a political one. Should, more precisely, the Duke accept the newcomers—in political and social terms—Frank Tregear and Miss Boncassen into an old and distinguished family? What kind of change can be reasonably expected from a man of principle? And how can change be effected? Lady Mary is absolutely determined in her commitment to Frank Tregear: they will not compromise. The reader can see they will succeed from the start. The compromise, then, must come from others. The novel invites its reader simultaneously to admire the unshakeable loyalty of Frank and Mary, and to wonder if such unshakeableness is wholly admirable. It is, after all, only the

Duke's readiness to adapt and accept that means such stubbornness does not become disastrous, unredeemable conflict. The dangers of refusing to change can only be defused when they are not met with an equal refusal. This is a political issue, but understood here as a domestic one. It is the novel's most characteristic way of looking at public topics.

Plantagenet Palliser served as Prime Minister in a coalition government. But at the end of *The Duke's Children*, over what kind of coalition must he preside at home? It is partly a political and partly a social alliance, and it includes the determined. Tregear, the Duke's son-in-law, is staunchly Conservative; Mary has defied him to live on her own terms; Silverbridge, though less than steadfast in political party affiliation, has refused to marry as his father hoped and is united to a woman whose grandfather had been a 'poor labourer who earned his bread among the shipping at New York' (p. 313).[15] Gerald could hardly be said to be determined in anything, but is hardly making a triumphant success of his life. Will *this* 'coalition' work? It will require distinctive qualities to hold such diversity together, and pragmatism rather than principle may be needed to support it. But *The Duke's Children* is stacked against the Duke. He gets his way in nothing, and at the end, we are crucially deprived the knowledge of whether he was in any way wise, in any way right. We are not permitted, through the closure of this great narrative, to judge the success of the final coalition with which the novel so intriguingly leaves us.

Uncertainty arises, in part, from Trollope's profound ambivalence about the nature and limits of authority. The Duke may seem the personification of power—as paterfamilias, as head of the house of Omnium, as a former Prime Minister who, during the novel's course, agrees to return to his country's service. To the Boncassens, looking in from outside, he is properly the lord of Isabel's fate, and submission to his will is required by both social and seemingly natural laws. Yet the novel queries the Duke's authority not through these incomers from a new republic, but through those who know him best. Rebellion takes place within the Palliser circle. Notwithstanding 'the quiescence of her manner' (p. 41), it is Lady Mary—'she who is of all the dearest' (p. 58)—who mounts the most devastating challenge to the Duke's will.

---

[15] *All the Year Round*, while issuing *The Duke's Children*, included the article 'A Night-Cruise in New York Harbour' (10 Apr. 1880), 468–71, as well as the historical piece, 'Married Beneath Her', 471–5, the title of which might have seemed an ironic comment on Trollope's story.

Lady Mary, Trollope reminds us, belongs to 'these very free days' (p. 152)—that is to say, an age of mounting agitation around what was termed 'the woman question'. *Can You Forgive Her?*, describing the unhappy early marriage of Mary's parents, was published in the wake of the 1857 Matrimonial Causes Act that established civil divorce. Written between the two Married Women's Property Acts of 1870 and 1882, *The Duke's Children* is similarly politically aware. The Duke's suspicions that Tregear is little better than a fortune-hunter (as the manuscript version had initially implied more clearly), and Tregear's own uneasy consciousness that Mary's money will help him, underline that, in part, it is property that is at stake. Before the Married Women's Property Act of 1882, a wife's property automatically passed to her husband on marriage. Although heiresses were normally partly protected through prenuptial legal settlements, Lady Mary attempts to refuse her own commodification as an heiress—a process sharply exposed when Lady Cantrip explains to Lord Popplecourt that Mary will bring her husband 'A large portion of her mother's money' (p. 223). Mary's insistence on choosing her own husband, irrespective of his fortune or social position—and with her mother's posthumous support—is both a romantic and a political act.

Mary's resolute autonomy is underlined in Chapter 24, which ironizes through its title the Duke's words about his daughter, 'She must be made to obey'. Obedience is one of the novel's most unstable and contested concepts, as the more it is insisted on, the more resistant it becomes to precise and practical definition. 'Say that you will obey me', the Duke demands in Chapter 8 (p. 58), insisting his daughter is bound 'to rely upon those to whom your obedience is due'. But although Mary concedes in Chapter 11 that 'she would obey her father', she also 'had a strong idea that she would ultimately prevail' (p. 74). Obedience, in this context, means not absolute submission, but an ostensible compliance in uneasy coexistence with a muted and unshakeable resistance. While 'He had his power to which she must submit [...] she also had hers,—to which it was possible he might be made to submit' (p. 187). Mary 'obeys', if she obeys at all, partially, contingently, and on her own terms. She decides for herself the shape and the limits of her acquiescence. It is her sense of scruples and honour, rather than the Duke's authority, which really keeps the lovers apart.

Mary 'would obey her father to the letter', we learn in Chapter 29 (p. 187). And Trollope's own sympathy with her is, perhaps, slyly indicated in the chief point of contest through which the struggle between father and daughter is expressed. Obedience 'to the letter' is ironic, because what Mary will not do is stop writing letters. The novel is punctuated by correspondence sent by, delivered to, or withheld from Mary, much scrupulously shown to third parties as an outward sign of her conformity. Her freedom, we are reminded, is facilitated by a recent innovation, the postbox. This was an idea that Trollope (who took the concept from France) recommended for use in the Channel Islands, and it spread during his career at the Post Office across the United Kingdom (previously, letters could only be left at post offices). When Mary writes to Tregear against her father's wishes and announces to a dismayed Lady Cantrip that 'I put it myself into the pillar letter-box', the novel tells us more than that Mary is 'a very self-willed young lady' (p. 153). Suggestively, it hints at her creator as her accomplice.

Mary's commitment to this decorous yet steely form of self-assertion is most explicitly voiced when, briefly liberated from the seclusion of Richmond, she travels with her brother to meet Lady Mabel Grex. 'How I do wish I were a man!' (p. 188), she declares. Silverbridge's dismayed reply, 'You are not going to take up woman's rights, I hope' (p. 188), is answered with: 'What would papa say if he heard that I was going to give a lecture at an Institute?' (p. 189). These words prepare the ground for what is to follow. Mary is no platform feminist, but her breach of propriety in Mabel's drawing room is none-theless a powerful statement about the woman question. For the most prominent woman lecturer of the 1870s was Josephine Butler (1828–1906), whose campaign against the state regulation of prostitution urged women to break a 'conspiracy of silence' and speak out about sexuality. When Frank Tregear unexpectedly bursts in on Mabel and her guests, Mary is initially 'stricken dumb by the presence of her lover' (p. 191). But her reticence is replaced with boldness when she 'threw herself into his arms and put up her lips to be kissed' (p. 192). The critic Juliet McMaster observes that 'Mary as immovable object does not have much dramatic interest', but that is misleading.[16] The embrace, a dramatic act indeed, is an eloquent declaration of erotic freedom, both embarrassing and unanswerable, silencing even Tregear himself. Like Josephine Butler, Mary flouts proprieties in the name of a greater justice, risking her own reputation for the sake of a nobler cause. Mary's staunchest supporter in this scene is, inevitably, Lady Mabel, who despite her own buried love for Tregear, recognizes and envies her rival's courage. Mary's unladylike, reckless kiss casts into

[16] Juliet McMaster, *Trollope's Palliser Novels: Theme and Pattern* (London: Macmillan, 1978), 133.

relief Mabel's own strategic disingenuousness, necessitated by her awareness that 'A girl unless she marries becomes nothing' (p. 491). Reluctantly renouncing the penniless Tregear, she intends instead to marry money, but the cost of her decision is revealed in Chapter 73. 'A dozen men have asked me to marry them', she explains to Silverbridge: 'And though they might be nothing till they made that request, then they became—things of horror to me' (p. 464). Her ellipsis is a baulking driven by sexual disgust, a revulsion peculiarly exposed against the honest openness of Mary's desire.

Honesty and openness are, however, balanced against the novel's sustained fascination with gambling and risk. *The Duke's Children* muses on the capacious theme of the home as place where great public and political issues are worked out in domestic situations. But it also reflects on how gambling in the public world of horse racing can be a suggestive language for understanding romantic choice. The pleasures and dangers of speculation are most obviously introduced through the subplot about Silverbridge's catastrophic adventures on the turf. The sabotaging of his St Leger favourite, Prime Minister, and the shady dealings of Major Tifto foreshadow the novel's wider concern with the vagaries and consequences of fortune. Games of hazard touch the lives of almost all of the major characters, as Trollope once described the start even of his own career as a novelist as a gamble on the likelihood of success, a flirtation with the hope that 'if the one chance in twenty did turn up in my favour, then how much might I win!'[17] Lady Mabel condemns gambling as ungentlemanly, and her own inheritance is compromised and ultimately eroded by the gambling of her father and brother Lord Percival. Their recklessness is one reason why her beloved family home, Grex, is in such disrepair—and it is probable that the vast sum Silverbridge loses overnight on Prime Minister would have done much to restore it. No youth, Trollope said of his novels in *An Autobiography*, 'has been taught that in falseness and flashness is to be found the road to manliness'.[18] And they are 'taught'—if that is quite what fiction does—by dramas of failure. Percival is responsible for another gambling crisis in the house of Omnium when Gerald loses £3,400 to him at cards. Gambling is not confined to the racecourse, nor to Major Tifto's immediate circle, despite Silverbridge's attempts to keep Tifto and racing away from the more serious aspects of his life. Such efforts at quarantining are futile. And, anyway, chance and risk seep into the wider moral fabric of the novel, informing the most intimate of relations.

[17] *Autobiography*, 79.        [18] Ibid. 146.

For Trollope, marriage is the biggest gamble of all. The risky pursuit of a fox in the novel's hunting scenes is a dim analogy for the risky pursuit of a partner, but the romance plots are more obviously replete with the language of the racecourse. *The Duke's Children* opens with two prizes—Lady Mary and Silverbridge—and two gamblers—Frank Tregear and Lady Mabel—who are willing to risk everything and each other in hopes of success. They are not only motivated by money, of course. But they cannot pretend it is irrelevant. As an impoverished younger son of staunch Conservative principles, Tregear is a hundred-to-one outsider, yet he is nonetheless first past the winning post (in the manuscript version, the reader is more doubtful at the beginning whether Frank would be a worthy winner).[19] Lady Mabel, however, is 'a horse of another colour' (p. 302), who is unsettlingly compared with Major Tifto himself as one who bets all and loses (though he ends more happily in the manuscript version). Tifto—coarse, male, 'on the wrong side of forty' (p. 43), but still faintly likeable—seems initially worlds away from the fragrant, sophisticated, vibrant, and witty Mabel. Yet the curious rumour about Tifto, 'the common assertion that he painted' (p. 43), or used cosmetics to retain the illusion of youth, suggests another who is conscious of youth and beauty as depreciating assets. Both Mabel and Tifto intend to exploit their friendship with Silverbridge for their own advancement, but both draw back, too squeamish to pursue their advantage. In hobbling Prime Minister on the eve of the St Leger, then only accepting a meagre £2,000 as his share of the fraud, Tifto ruins his chances, just as Mabel is partly to blame herself for the collapse of her hopes to become Silverbridge's wife. As the novel in its published form draws to its close, both Tifto and Mabel become increasingly abject, pleading, and pitiable. Despite her disapproval of gambling, Mabel slips into the language of the turf when confessing her pursuit of Silverbridge. 'I craned at the first fence' (p. 488), she admits, failing to seize success even when 'the cup had come within the reach of her fingers' (p. 346). Marriage becomes, in these moments, like a game of chance, where all is staked on shifting, risky desires. It is a game Isabel Boncassen plays too, in hazarding both that a three months' separation will increase Silverbridge's ardour, and that her insistence on the Duke's consent will secure his favour. Tregear and Isabel are the winners of this matrimonial sweepstake, but Mabel is the loser, left financially and emotionally impoverished.

Although *The Duke's Children* bears witness to the seductions and catastrophes of risk, it is also alert to the pitfalls of certainty.

[19] See Armanick, 'Trollope at Fuller Length', 200–1.

Through the intergenerational conflict between the Duke and his children, it nuances the moralizing voice that might condemn Silverbridge
for losing the staggering sum of £70,000 during one drunken evening,
or castigate Mabel even more severely. For against the glamour and
charisma of Mabel or Frank Tregear is balanced the exemplary fixity of
Lord Popplecourt: a stable, earnest, dreary dullard who could never
hope to charm Mary for a dinner party, far less a lifetime. The willing-
ness to gamble and speculate has an attendant allure that the novel is
not afraid to recognize. The Duke chooses Lord Popplecourt as his
daughter's suitor partly because he sees in him a version of his younger
self—one of many moments where it is clear that the father's feelings
about his children's romantic alliances are overshadowed by his own
anxious memories. The Duke's union with Glencora was no risky
romantic plunge, but, as he confesses, 'a matter of sagacious bargaining' (p. 77). It is only through his attempt to impose just such a bargain
on his daughter that he comes to think more seriously about the consequences of his own act. Glencora is a haunting presence, and Mary is
both physically and morally an echo of her. As Mary vows never to
forget Tregear, the Duke 'reflected whether his own wife, this girl's
mother, had ever forgotten her early love for that Burgo Fitzgerald
whom in her girlhood she had wished to marry' (p. 79). The story of
that blighted romance, and the marriage that superseded it, is the story
of the first of the Palliser novels. Perhaps when bargaining replaces
gambling, it means that human passion is always less; trouble, worry,
and something like guilt always more.

  Published two years before Trollope's death, about a man looking
back on a long and distinguished career, the reader might expect *The
Duke's Children* to validate the wisdom arising from longevity, perspec-
tive, the passing of time. What it actually offers is something less
secure. The presence of modernity supplies much of the background to
the novel. Characters are whisked from the moors of Crummie-Toddie
to Polpenno, or even from Egham to Newmarket in the space of a day,
on trains that are increasingly fast (though not, alas, fast enough to get
Lord Gerald back to Cambridge on time). Coming out in instalments,
the novel was involved literally in the reader's waiting: anticipation, the
passage of real and of fictional time are natural subjects of the reader's
contemplation. The words of the novel in its serialized form must
be waited for, and so must the letters in the novel itself. A highly
efficient modern postal service, with many deliveries a day, sends
letters speeding around the country—and, *in extremis*, telegrams (*All
the Year Round* for 10 January 1880, printing Chapters 26 and 27 of

*The Duke's Children*, included a topical article on 'Postal Improvements', looking back to the achievements of Rowland Hill who had died in August 1879).[20] This sense of acceleration is mapped onto the bodies of the younger generation—bright young things possessed of restless energy summarized in Isabel's lively performance on the tennis court at Killancodlem.

Time passing is marked by the speed of travelling letters, but also by the meaning of words themselves. The novel marks the difference between one way of looking at the world and another through the slang of the younger generation, as perceived by the Duke. Both the Duke and Silverbridge have, characteristically, different uses for the word 'awful'. When Silverbridge employs the modern sense (as in 'awfully hungry', p. 160) against his father's sense that it refers to 'awe', two people are divided by the same language. Of course, the larger division by the same language in the novel is that of Great Britain and the United States. And that, on a much broader scale, is a matter of modernity as well. The 'international theme' of the American in Europe is easily thought the property of Henry James in the nineteenth-century novel. But Trollope, author of *The American Senator* (1877), shares similar ground. James's most ample early exploration of the relations between the Old World and the New was *The Portrait of a Lady* (1880–1), which James was finishing as he read *The Duke's Children*.

The Duke and the Boncassens are both worried about a marriage that will unite them. The Pallisers are one of the most celebrated families in Great Britain, and the Boncassens—though their name almost insists they too come from a good house—are the children of a new nation. They possess neither noble ancestry nor a conviction that those with noble ancestry should rule. In Silverbridge's courtship of Isabel there is all the subdued tension between aristocratic government and republican; between a country with a strong conviction in class as an organizing principle of society and one that puts its faith in the possibility of any worthy individual making their name. (Trollope may well have had the real marriage, on 15 April 1874, of Lord Randolph Churchill, third son of the seventh Duke of Marlborough, and Miss Jeanette Jerome, of New York City, in mind: they were the parents of the future British Prime Minister, Winston Churchill.) James was fascinated by the charms Europe worked on Americans, and Trollope is a chronicler of that too. His mother, Frances Trollope, had

[20] Elsewhere, while issuing *The Duke's Children*, the periodical showed an interest in new communication technologies: see, e.g., 'Solar Telegraphy' (11 Oct. 1879), 400–3 and 'Telephonic Reporting for the Press' (13 Dec. 1879), 65–8.

established her career as a writer with *Domestic Manners of the Americans* (1832), and that title (though not Mrs Trollope's views, which her son thought 'somewhat unjust'[21]) would serve a portion of *The Duke's Children*. 'At New York', Trollope says of Miss Boncassen,

> she would dance, as she had said, with bank clerks. She was not prepared to admit that a young London lord was better than a New York bank clerk. Judging the men on their own individual merits she might find the bank clerk to be the better of the two. But a certain sweetness of the aroma of rank was beginning to permeate her republican senses. (p. 214)

She looks to a future relationship in which republican and aristocratic sentiment can live together. That leads to a question about the unknown future of her marriage. But beyond that, characteristically, Trollope's acceptance that Silverbridge and Isabel *can* marry is full of the modern moment.[22]

The future governance of Great Britain may need to work with the United States and tomorrow will test whether there really can be a functioning union between what was once a colonial power and its colony. That is an alert political implication of Trollope's final Palliser novel. When the text declines to let us know how the strange domestic coalition of the Duke's family will work out, it is declining to let us know whether this gamble in international relations will pay off too, with all its implications. Anthony Trollope, perhaps, could hardly have been more prophetic when thinking that the future of British governance (the elected rather than the hereditary rulers of the land, at any rate) would in part depend on government's relationship with America.

There is a buzz of the modern in *The Duke's Children*. But modernity is matched in the novel with older ways of framing narrative, and some curious throwbacks to much earlier ideas. There is a hint of romance in this story of a noble Lord and his children, and a young Knight growing into his proper place; a hint of the *Bildungsroman* in the moral education of Lord Silverbridge (that was more prominent in the manuscript version of the novel); more than a hint of the fairy tale of the American girl being swept away by a British Lord. And there is even just a little of a ghost story here. Lady Glencora is dead as this novel begins and one of the most forceful of Trollope's creations is lost. But the fact that her story lingers over the narrative gives her more than a faint presence in the dealings of others. Her early love for Burgo, as already said, looms uncomfortably in the Duke's mind. His realization

[21] *Autobiography*, 161.
[22] *All the Year Round* was generally interested in this topic: see Theo Gift's 'That American Girl: A Table d'hôte Romance' (22 Nov. 1879), 42–9.

that Glencora knew about Frank and Mary but did not tell the Duke is a realization of another one of her failings that, loyally, he cannot admit aloud, however much it is at the heart of his problems with Mrs Finn. The Duke keeps coming back to his wife's past, and his past with his wife, and fretting. Lady Glencora is more than just a memory, too. 'Lady Mary was very like her mother,' Trollope says in Chapter 2, 'especially in having exactly her mother's tone of voice' (p. 15). Glencora is dead, but in listening to Lady Mary, she is almost heard again.

The presence of the past to which the reader may be most alert in this novel is not the local matter of Glencora's doings, but the whole complex mixture of narratives from the previous Palliser novels as a whole. *The Duke's Children* is a story with a substantial amount of fiction behind it, though what exactly to do with that history is always an intriguing question: Nicholas Shrimpton, in the Appendix to this edition, sensibly enumerates some of the issues in imagining the Palliser novels as coherently sequential. But *The Duke's Children* certainly looks backwards *in some ways* to predecessors, and out to new, unwritten plots that start rather than finish here. Afterlives press on the reader at the end of a group of novels that have held a readership from the middle of the Victorian period to the present. Their *genre* has its own imaginative afterlife too, for Trollope's conception has proved reinventable. John Galsworthy's *The Forsyte Saga* (1906–21) reinterpreted the Victorians and the form of the Trollopian political-romantic novel for a new generation. But the idiom of the multi-part political drama now belongs to a different medium, to the screen not the page. The Palliser novels, as it happens, were themselves made into television in Hugh David and Ronald Wilson's 1974, twenty-six-part series, called simply *The Pallisers*, which grew from the success of the still-admired 1967 BBC version of *The Forsyte Saga*. Not merely the text, but Trollope's suggestive genre could be adapted. The multi-part episodic political novel metamorphosed into the multi-part episodic political serial drama: in America, *The West Wing* (1999–2006), or *Commander in Chief* (2005–6); in the UK, *House of Cards* (1990) among them. There have been sustained parodies and comedic versions of the political serial, too. Trollope would hardly have recognized the distant ripples of his own explorations of the private and public lives of men and women in and around government in these new, creative versions. Yet there he is, all the same.

Trollope's popularity was in decline as he finished the Palliser novels, though he did not stop writing. 'The cruel, hard-hearted, indifferent public must be the judge [of worth],'[23] he told an aspiring writer in 1881. He was looking back to his long courtship of Victorian readers from his first work of fiction, *The Macdermots of Ballycloran* (1847), but also recollecting his recent, dispiriting experience with *The Prime Minister*. Readers, and later viewers, were not, though, to prove in the long term cruel, hard-hearted, or indifferent. They remain entranced by the whole story of the Duke of Omnium, his friends, enemies, and his family, even if N. John Hall is nearly right to say that 'Trollope has two distinct reputations, one with critics, another with readers'.[24] The Palliser novels, vigorous, energetic, and moving to the end, ask searching questions of public life in the most engaging and accessible of domestic narratives, in which *decency* is elevated to the guiding principle of human affairs. There is still nothing quite like them in English fiction.

[23] *Letters of Anthony Trollope*, ii. 908.          [24] *ODNB*.

# NOTE ON THE TEXT

*The Duke's Children* was written in its first form between May and October 1876: it was destined for the weekly periodical *All the Year Round*, founded in 1859 by Charles Dickens and, by this stage, owned and edited by his eldest son, Charles Dickens Jr (1837–96). After editorial advice, Trollope cut the manuscript by about a quarter. This work was done during April and May 1878. Readers will want to know that it was a fixed principle with Trollope—unlike, for instance, Dickens—to complete the entire novel before publishing it in serial form.

The shorter version of *The Duke's Children* appeared in weekly instalments in *All the Year Round* from 4 October 1879 to 24 July 1880. For the serialization, Trollope was contracted to receive £400. Ironically, this was exactly the same amount he had calculated in *An Autobiography* that he earned in his second job at the Post Office (as a surveyor's clerk in Ireland back in August 1841): that was, he said, 'the first good fortune of my life'.[1] A partial clue to the sums involved is Trollope's statement that, in Ireland in 1858, he 'could keep a good house over my head, insure my life, educate my two boys, and hunt perhaps twice a week, very comfortably on £1400 a-year'.[2] On 13 June 1878, Chapman & Hall agreed to pay £1,000 for the copyright to the book edition, which was published on 15 May 1880 in three volumes. A single-volume version came out later that year. In August 1880, Trollope saw the accounts for the book's sale ('the first account I have ever seen of one of my own books'[3]) and discerned that, to date, the company had lost £120, which he promptly offered to pay back.[4] Despite that, the critical reception of the volume had been relatively good (see the Introduction, p. xi).

The autograph manuscript of *The Duke's Children* was offered by Henry M. Trollope, Trollope's son, on 11 February 1918 to a British Red Cross sale, and is now in the Chauncey Brewster Tinker

---

[1] *Autobiography* (Oxford: Oxford University Press, 1980), 59.

[2] Ibid. 127.

[3] *The Letters of Anthony Trollope*, ed. N. John Hall, with the assistance of Nina Burgis, 2 vols. (Stanford: Stanford University Press, 1983), ii. 880.

[4] Financial information about *The Duke's Children* from *Letters of Anthony Trollope*, esp. ii. 871 n. Trollope left an estate worth £25,892 19s. 3d. in his will (probate details from *ODNB*).

manuscript collection at the Beinecke Library, Yale University, catalogued as series 1, box 14, folder 590.

   The text used in this edition is that established for the Oxford
Trollope, first published under the general editorship of Michael
Sadleir and Frederick Page in 1954, with a few obvious errors silently
corrected.

### *Acknowledgements*

The editors wish to thank Dinah Birch, Simon Dentith, Judith Luna,
and Jane Wright for their help with this edition.

# SELECT BIBLIOGRAPHY

*Biographical*

Trollope, Anthony, *An Autobiography* (1883; Oxford: Oxford University Press, 1961).

—— *The Letters of Anthony Trollope*, ed. N. John Hall, with the assistance of Nina Burgis, 2 vols. (Stanford: Stanford University Press, 1983).

Glendinning, Victoria, *Trollope* (new edn., London: Pimlico, 2002).

Hall, N. John, *Trollope: A Biography* (Oxford: Oxford University Press, 1993).

Mullen, Richard, *Anthony Trollope: A Victorian in His World* (London: Duckworth, 1990).

Sadleir, Michael, *Trollope: A Commentary* (London: Constable, 1927).

Super, R. H., *The Chronicler of Barsetshire: A Life of Anthony Trollope* (Ann Arbor: University of Michigan Press, 1988).

Terry, R. C. (ed.), *Trollope: Interviews and Recollections* (Basingstoke: Macmillan, 1987).


*General (but with relevance to* The Duke's Children*)*

apRoberts, Ruth, *Trollope: Artist and Moralist* (London: Chatto & Windus, 1971) [in America, *The Moral Trollope*].

Cockshut, A. O. J., *Anthony Trollope: A Critical Study* (London: Collins, 1955).

Dames, Nicholas, 'Trollope and the Career: Vocational Trajectories and the Management of Ambition', *Victorian Studies*, 45 (2003), 247–78.

James, Henry, 'Anthony Trollope', in *Partial Portraits* (1888; Ann Arbor: University of Michigan Press, 1970).

Jones, Vivien, 'James and Trollope', *Review of English Studies*, 3 (1982), 278–94.

Letwin, Shirley, *The Gentleman in Trollope: Individuality and Moral Conduct* (London: Macmillan, 1982).

MacDonald, Susan Peck, *Anthony Trollope* (Boston: Twayne, 1987).

Michie, Elsie, 'The Odd Couple: Anthony Trollope and Henry James', *Henry James Review*, 27 (2006), 10–23.

Polhemus, Robert M., *The Changing World of Anthony Trollope* (Berkeley and Los Angeles: University of California Press, 1968).

Smalley, Donald (ed.), *Anthony Trollope: The Critical Heritage* (London: Routledge, 1969).

Super, R. H., *Trollope in the Post Office* (Ann Arbor: University of Michigan Press, 1981).

Turner, Mark W., *Trollope and the Magazines: Gendered Issues in Mid-Victorian Britain* (Basingstoke: Macmillan, 2000).

—— '"Telling of my Weekly Doings": The Material Culture of the Victorian Novel', in Francis O'Gorman (ed.), *A Concise Companion to the Victorian Novel* (Oxford: Blackwell, 2005), 113–33.

## *On* The Duke's Children *in particular*

Butte, George, 'Ambivalence and Affirmation in *The Duke's Children*', *Studies in English Literature 1500–1900*, 17 (1977), 709–27.

Franklin, J. Jeffrey, 'The Victorian Discourse of Gambling: Speculations on *Middlemarch* and *The Duke's Children*', *ELH: Journal of English Literary History*, 61 (1994), 899–921.

Hagan, John, '*The Duke's Children*: Trollope's Psychological Masterpiece', *Nineteenth-Century Fiction*, 12 (1958), 1–21.

Halperin, John, *Trollope and Politics: A Study of the Pallisers and Others* (London: Macmillan, 1977).

McMaster, Juliet, *Trollope's Palliser Novels: Theme and Pattern* (London: Macmillan, 1978).

Pei, Lowry, '*The Duke's Children*: Reflection and Reconciliation', *Modern Language Quarterly*, 39 (1978), 284–302.

Tracy, Robert, *Trollope's Later Novels* (Berkeley and Los Angeles: University of California Press, 1978).

## *On the text of* The Duke's Children

Armanick, Steven, 'Trollope at Fuller Length: Lord Silverbridge and the Manuscript of *The Duke's Children*', in Margaret Markwick, Deborah Denenholz Morse, and Regenia Gagnier (eds.), *The Politics of Gender in Anthony Trollope's Novels: New Readings for the Twenty-First Century* (Aldershot: Ashgate, 2009), 193–206.

Bailey, J. W., '*The Duke's Children*: Rediscovering a Trollope Manuscript', *Yale University Library Gazette*, 57 (1982), 34–8.

Birch, Dinah, 'A Note on the Manuscript', in Anthony Trollope, *The Duke's Children*, ed. Dinah Birch (Harmondsworth: Penguin, 1995), 507–10.

## *Useful websites*

http://www.trollopesociety.org/
http://www.anthonytrollope.com/
http://www.trollope.org/

# A CHRONOLOGY OF
# ANTHONY TROLLOPE

(Selected publications are noted here only; volume publication is given in all cases.)

| *Life* | *Historical and Cultural Background* |
|---|---|
| 1815 (24 April) AT born in London. | Battle of Waterloo and final defeat of Napoleon. |
| 1823 Enters Harrow Boys' School. | Monroe doctrine formulated to protect American interests in relation to Europe. |
| 1825 At school in Sunbury. | Stockton and Darlington Railway, first public railway, opens. |
| 1827 Admitted to Winchester College. | |
| 1830 Back at home in poverty then to Harrow School again. | Accession of William IV in Britain; in France, rioting sees overthrow of the Bourbons and accession of Louis Philippe. |
| 1832 | First Reform Act increases electorate to *c*.700,000 men. |
| 1834 Trollope family flee creditors to Bruges; AT takes up clerkship at London Post Office; a period of poverty and an unpromising start to work. | 'New Poor Law'; Tolpuddle martyrs (early example of, in effect, trade union membership). |
| 1839 | First commercial telegraph in UK. |
| 1841 After much misery, AT is offered the post of deputy postal surveyor's clerk at Banagher, King's county, Ireland; begins to hunt. | British occupation of Hong Kong; Robert Peel becomes Prime Minister. |
| 1843 Begins *The Macdermots of Ballycloran.* | Wordsworth becomes Poet Laureate. |
| 1844 Marries Rose Heseltine from Rotherham (d. 1917). | Factory Act shortens working day, increases minimum hours of schooling. |
| 1845 | Great Famine begins in Ireland (–1850). |
| 1846 Henry Merivale Trollope born (d. 1926). | Repeal of Corn Laws, major achievement for free trade; Lord John Russell becomes Prime Minister. |
| 1847 Frederick James Anthony Trollope born (d. 1910); *The Macdermots of Ballycloran.* | Ten Hours Factory Act (cuts working day to 10 hours for women and children). |

| *Life* | *Historical and Cultural Background* |
|---|---|
| 1848 *The Kellys and the O'Kellys.* | European revolutions; second Chartist petition. |
| 1850 *La Vendée*, a failure. | Tennyson becomes Poet Laureate; restoration of Catholic ecclesiastical hierarchy. |
| 1851 Working for the Post Office in England. | Great Exhibition, evidence of British dominance in trade. |
| 1852 Suggests the new pillar box for post on the Channel Islands. | Opening of new Palace of Westminster; Earl of Derby becomes Prime Minister followed by Earl of Aberdeen. |
| 1853 | Crimean War (–1856). |
| 1854 Post Office surveyor for the north of Ireland: family in Donnybrook. | |
| 1855 *The Warden*, first of the 'Chronicles of Barsetshire'; thereafter, he sets himself writing targets (usually 10,000 words a week). | Abolition of final newspaper tax leads to growth of new journalism and newspaper titles; Palmerston becomes Prime Minister. |
| 1857 *Barchester Towers*, a success. | Indian Mutiny; Matrimonial Causes Act extends availability of divorce. |
| 1858 *Doctor Thorne* (Barsetshire). | Jewish Disabilities Act; abolition of property qualification for MPs; Earl of Derby is Prime Minister, then Palmerston again. |
| 1860 Beginning of instalments of *Framley Parsonage*; moves to London as Post Office surveyor; meets Kate Field, an American woman, in Florence, with whom he forms a strong attachment. | Wilberforce–Huxley debate on evolution. |
| 1861 | American Civil War begins. |
| 1862 Elected to Garrick Club. | London Exposition; Lincoln's Emancipation proclamation. |
| 1864 Elected to the Athenaeum. *The Small House at Allington* (Barsetshire, but introduces Plantagenet and Glencora Palliser). | |
| 1864–5 *Can You Forgive Her?* (first of the Palliser novels; vol. 1, Sept. 1864; vol. 2, July 1865). | |

| *Life* | *Historical and Cultural Background* |
|---|---|
| 1865 | Abolition of slavery in North America; Earl Russell becomes Prime Minister. |
| 1866 | Success with commercial transatlantic cable; Earl of Derby becomes Prime Minister. |
| 1867 *The Last Chronicle of Barset*. Resigns from the Post Office to edit *Saint Pauls: A Monthly Magazine* with illustrations by Millais. | Second Reform Act (further extension of franchise to about 2 million electors). |
| 1868 Defeated as Liberal candidate for Beverley in the General Election. | Trades Union Congress formed; Disraeli becomes Prime Minister followed by Gladstone. |
| 1869 *He Knew He Was Right*; *Phineas Finn* (Palliser). | Suez Canal opened; first issue of *Nature*. |
| 1870 *The Vicar of Bullhampton*. | Forster's Education Act, widely extending provision of primary education; first Married Women's Property Act, granting married women the right to their own earnings and to inherit property in their own name. |
| 1871 Travels in Australasia. | Paris Commune; legalization of Trade Unions. |
| 1872 *The Eustace Diamonds* (Palliser). | |
| 1873 *Phineas Redux* (Palliser); *Australia and New Zealand*. | Financial crisis begins US Long Depression. |
| 1874 | First Impressionist Exhibition (Paris); Disraeli becomes Prime Minister. |
| 1875 *The Way We Live Now*. | Third Republic in France; Theosophical Society founded. |
| 1876 *The Prime Minister* (Palliser). | The telephone patented. |
| 1877 *The American Senator*. | |
| 1878 *Is He Popenjoy?*; *South Africa*. | Exposition Universelle (Paris), including arts and machinery. |
| 1879 *Thackeray* in the English Men of Letters series. | |
| 1880 Moves to South Harting, Sussex. *The Duke's Children* (Palliser); *Life of Cicero*. | First Anglo–Boer War (–1881); Gladstone becomes Prime Minister. |
| 1881 *Dr Wortle's School*. | Assassination of US President James Garfield. |

| Life | Historical and Cultural Background |
|---|---|
| 1882 *Lord Palmerston*; *The Fixed Period*, a futuristic novel. Suffers a stroke; (6 Dec.), dies in nursing home. Buried in Kensal Green (his grave reads: 'He was a loving husband, a loving father, and a true friend'); leaves estate worth £25,892 19s. 3d. | Phoenix Park Murders; Egypt now British protectorate; second Married Women's Property Act allowing married women to own and control their own property. |
| 1883 *Mr Scarborough's Family*; *An Autobiography*. | Death of Richard Wagner. |
| 1887 Publication of AT's brother, Thomas Adolphus Trollope's *What I Remember*, with alternative account of the family upbringing. | |

# THE DUKE'S CHILDREN

# CONTENTS

**VOLUME III**

# VOLUME I

## CHAPTER 1

### WHEN THE DUCHESS WAS DEAD

No one, probably, ever felt himself to be more alone in the world than our old friend,* the Duke of Omnium, when the Duchess died. When this sad event happened he had ceased to be Prime Minister. During the first nine months after he had left office he and the Duchess remained in England. Then they had gone abroad, taking with them their three children. The eldest, Lord Silverbridge, had been at Oxford, but had had his career there cut short by some more than ordinary youthful folly, which had induced his father to agree with the college authorities that his name had better be taken off the college books,—all which had been cause of very great sorrow to the Duke. The other boy was to go to Cambridge; but his father had thought it well to give him a twelvemonth's run on the Continent, under his own inspection. Lady Mary, the only daughter,* was the youngest of the family, and she also had been with them on the Continent. They remained the full year abroad, travelling with a large accompaniment of tutors, lady's-maids, couriers, and sometimes friends. I do not know that the Duchess or the Duke had enjoyed it much; but the young people had seen something of foreign courts and much of foreign scenery, and had perhaps perfected their French. The Duke had gone to work at his travels with a full determination to create for himself occupation out of a new kind of life. He had studied Dante,* and had striven to arouse himself to ecstatic joy amidst the loveliness of the Italian lakes.* But through it all he had been aware that he had failed. The Duchess had made no such resolution,—had hardly, perhaps, made any attempt; but, in truth, they had both sighed to be back among the war-trumpets. They had both suffered much among the trumpets, and yet they longed to return. He told himself from day to day, that though he had been banished from the House of Commons, still, as a peer, he had a seat in Parliament;* and that, though he was no longer a minister, still he might be useful as a legislator. She, in her career as a leader of fashion, had no doubt met with some trouble,—with some trouble but with no disgrace; and as she had been carried about among the lakes and mountains, among the pictures and statues, among the counts and countesses, she had often

felt that there was no happiness except in that dominion which circumstances had enabled her to achieve once, and might enable her to achieve
again—in the realms of London society.

Then, in the early spring of 187–, they came back to England, having persistently carried out their project, at any rate in regard to time.
Lord Gerald, the younger son, was at once sent up to Trinity.* For the
eldest son a seat was to be found* in the House of Commons, and the
fact that a dissolution of Parliament was expected served to prevent
any prolonged sojourn abroad. Lady Mary Palliser was at that time
nineteen, and her entrance into the world was to be her mother's great
care and great delight. In March they spent a few days in London, and
then went down to Matching Priory.* When she left town the Duchess
was complaining of cold, sore throat, and debility. A week after their
arrival at Matching she was dead.

Had the heavens fallen and mixed themselves with the earth, had the
people of London risen in rebellion with French ideas of equality,* had
the Queen persistently declined to comply with the constitutional
advice of her ministers, had a majority in the House of Commons lost
its influence in the country,—the utter prostration of the bereft husband could not have been more complete. It was not only that his heart
was torn to pieces, but that he did not know how to look out into the
world. It was as though a man should be suddenly called upon to live
without hands or even arms. He was helpless, and knew himself to be
helpless. Hitherto he had never specially acknowledged to himself that
his wife was necessary to him as a component part of his life. Though
he had loved her dearly, and had in all things consulted her welfare and
happiness, he had at times been inclined to think that in the exuberance
of her spirits she had been a trouble rather than a support to him.* But
now it was as though all outside appliances were taken away from him.
There was no one of whom he could ask a question.

For it may be said of this man that, though throughout his life he
had had many Honourable and Right Honourable friends,* and that
though he had entertained guests by the score, and though he had
achieved for himself the respect of all good men and the thorough
admiration of some few who knew him, he had hardly made for himself
a single intimate friend—except that one who had now passed away
from him. To her he had been able to say what he thought, even though
she would occasionally ridicule him while he was declaring his feelings.
But there had been no other human soul to whom he could open
himself. There were one or two whom he loved, and perhaps liked;
but his loving and his liking had been exclusively political. He had so

habituated himself to devote his mind and his heart to the service of his country, that he had almost risen above or sunk below humanity. But she, who had been essentially human, had been a link between him and the world.

There were his three children, the youngest of whom was now nearly nineteen,* and they surely were links! At the first moment of his bereavement they were felt to be hardly more than burdens. A more loving father there was not in England, but nature had made him so undemonstrative that as yet they had hardly known his love. In all their joys and in all their troubles, in all their desires and all their disappointments, they had ever gone to their mother. She had been conversant with everything about them, from the boys' bills and the girl's gloves to the innermost turn in the heart and the disposition of each. She had known with the utmost accuracy the nature of the scrapes into which Lord Silverbridge had precipitated himself, and had known also how probable it was that Lord Gerald would do the same. The results of such scrapes she, of course, deplored; and therefore she would give good counsel, pointing out how imperative it was that such evildoings should be avoided; but with the spirit that produced the scrapes she fully sympathised. The father disliked the spirit almost worse than the results; and was therefore often irritated and unhappy.

And the difficulties about the girl were almost worse to bear than those about the boys. She had done nothing wrong. She had given no signs of extravagance or other juvenile misconduct. But she was beautiful and young. How was he to bring her out into the world? How was he to decide whom she should or whom she should not marry? How was he to guide her through the shoals and rocks which lay in the path of such a girl before she can achieve matrimony?

It was the fate of the family that, with a world of acquaintance, they had not many friends. From all close connection with relatives on the side of the Duchess they had been dissevered by old feelings at first, and afterwards by want of any similitude in the habits of life. She had, when young, been repressed by male and female guardians* with an iron hand. Such repression had been needed, and had been perhaps salutary, but it had not left behind it much affection. And then her nearest relatives were not sympathetic with the Duke. He could obtain no assistance in the care of his girl from that source. Nor could he even do it from his own cousins' wives, who were his nearest connections on the side of the Pallisers. They were women to whom he had ever been kind, but to whom he had never opened his heart. When, in the midst of the stunning sorrow of the first week, he tried to think of all this, it seemed to him that there was nobody.

There had been one lady, a very dear ally, staying in the house with them when the Duchess died. This was Mrs Finn,* the wife of Phineas Finn, who had been one of the Duke's colleagues when in office. How it had come to pass that Mrs Finn and the Duchess had become singularly bound together has been told elsewhere. But there had been close bonds,—so close that when the Duchess on their return from the Continent had passed through London on her way to Matching, ill at the time and very comfortless, it had been almost a thing of course, that Mrs Finn should go with her. And as she had sunk, and then despaired, and then died, it was this woman who had always been at her side, who had ministered to her, and had listened to the fears and the wishes and hopes she had expressed respecting the children.

At Matching, amidst the ruins of the old Priory,* there is a parish burying-ground, and there, in accordance with her own wish, almost within sight of her own bedroom-window, she was buried. On the day of the funeral a dozen relatives came, Pallisers and M'Closkies,* who on such an occasion were bound to show themselves, as members of the family. With them and his two sons the Duke walked across to the graveyard, and then walked back; but even to those who stayed the night at the house he hardly spoke. By noon on the following day they had all left him, and the only stranger in the house was Mrs Finn.

On the afternoon of the day after the funeral the Duke and his guest met, almost for the first time since the sad event. There had been just a pressure of the hand, just a glance of compassion, just some murmur of deep sorrow,—but there had been no real speech between them. Now he had sent for her, and she went down to him in the room in which he commonly sat at work. He was seated at his table when she entered, but there was no book open before him, and no pen ready to his hand. He was dressed of course in black. That, indeed, was usual with him, but now the tailor by his funereal art had added some deeper dye of blackness to his appearance. When he rose and turned to her she thought that he had at once become an old man. His hair was grey in parts, and he had never accustomed himself to use that skill in managing his outside person by which many men are able to preserve for themselves a look, if not of youth, at any rate of freshness. He was thin, of an adust* complexion, and had acquired a habit of stooping which, when he was not excited, gave him an appearance of age. All that was common to him: but now it was so much exaggerated that he who was not yet fifty might have been taken to be over sixty.

He put out his hand to greet her as she came up to him. 'Silverbridge,' he said, 'tells me that you go back to London to-morrow.'

'I thought it would be best, Duke. My presence here can be of no comfort to you.'

'I will not say that anything can be of comfort. But of course it is right that you should go. I can have no excuse for asking you to remain. While there was yet a hope for her——' Then he stopped, unable to say a word further in that direction, and yet there was no sign of a tear and no sound of a sob.

'Of course I would stay, Duke, if I could be of any service.'

'Mr Finn will expect you to return to him.'

'Perhaps it would be better that I should say that I would stay were it not that I know that I can be of no real service.'

'What do you mean by that, Mrs Finn?'

'Lady Mary should have with her at such a time some other friend.'

'There was none other whom her mother loved as she loved you— none, none.' This he said almost with energy.

'There was no one lately, Duke, with whom circumstances caused her mother to be so closely intimate. But even that perhaps was unfortunate.'

'I never thought so.'

'That is a great compliment. But as to Lady Mary, will it not be as well that she should have with her, as soon as possible, someone,— perhaps someone of her own kindred if it be possible, or, if not that, at least one of her own kind?'

'Who is there? Whom do you mean?'

'I mean no one. It is hard, Duke, to say what I do mean, but perhaps I had better try. There will be,—probably there have been,—some among your friends who have regretted the great intimacy which chance produced between me and my lost friend. While she was with us no such feeling would have sufficed to drive me from her. She had chosen for herself, and if others disapproved her choice that was nothing to me. But as regards Lady Mary, it will be better, I think, that from the beginning she should be taught to look for friendship and guidance to those—to those who are more naturally connected with her.'

'I was not thinking of any guidance,' said the Duke.

'Of course not. But with one so young, where there is intimacy there will be guidance. There should be somebody with her. It was almost the last thought that occupied her mother's mind. I could not tell her, Duke, but I can tell you, that I cannot with advantage to your girl be that somebody.'

'Cora wished it.'

'Her wishes, probably, were sudden and hardly fixed.'

'Who should it be, then?' asked the father, after a pause.

'Who am I, Duke, that I should answer such a question?'

After that there was another pause, and then the conference was ended by a request from the Duke that Mrs Finn would stay at Matching for yet two days longer. At dinner they all met,—the father, the three children, and Mrs Finn. How far the young people among themselves had been able to throw off something of the gloom of death need not here be asked; but in the presence of their father they were sad and sombre, almost as he was. On the next day, early in the morning, the younger lad returned to his college, and Lord Silverbridge went up to London, where he was supposed to have his home.

'Perhaps you would not mind reading these letters,' the Duke said to Mrs Finn, when she again went to him, in compliance with a message from him asking for her presence. Then she sat down and read two letters, one from Lady Cantrip,* and the other from a Mrs Jeffrey Palliser,* each of which contained an invitation for his daughter, and expressed a hope that Lady Mary would not be unwilling to spend some time with the writer. Lady Cantrip's letter was long, and went minutely into circumstances. If Lady Mary would come to her, she would abstain from having other company in the house till her young friend's spirits should have somewhat recovered themselves. Nothing could be more kind, or proposed in a sweeter fashion. There had, how-ever, been present to the Duke's mind as he read it a feeling that a proposition to a bereaved husband to relieve him of the society of an only daughter, was not one which would usually be made to a father. In such a position a child's company would probably be his best solace. But he knew,—at this moment he painfully remembered,—that he was not as are other men. He acknowledged the truth of this, but he was not the less grieved and irritated by the reminder. The letter from Mrs Jeffrey Palliser was to the same effect, but was much shorter. If it would suit Mary to come to them for a month or six weeks at their place in Gloucestershire, they would both be delighted.

'I should not choose her to go there,' said the Duke, as Mrs Finn refolded the latter letter. 'My cousin's wife is a very good woman, but Mary would not be happy with her.'

'Lady Cantrip is an excellent friend for her.'

'Excellent. I know no one whom I esteem more than Lady Cantrip.'

'Would you wish her to go there, Duke?'

There came a wistful piteous look over the father's face. Why should he be treated as no other father would be treated? Why should it be supposed that he would desire to send his girl away from him? But yet he felt that it would be better that she should go. It was his present purpose to remain at Matching through a portion of the summer. What could he do to make a girl happy? What comfort would there be in his companionship?

'I suppose she ought to go somewhere,' he said.

'I had not thought of it,' said Mrs Finn.

'I understood you to say,' replied the Duke, almost angrily, 'that she ought to go to someone who would take care of her.'

'I was thinking of some friend coming to her.'

'Who would come? Who is there that I could possibly ask? You will not stay.'

'I certainly would stay, if it were for her good. I was thinking, Duke, that perhaps you might ask the Greys* to come to you.'

'They would not come,' he said, after a pause.

'When *she* was told that it was for her sake, she would come, I think.'

Then there was another pause. 'I could not ask them,' he said; 'for his sake I could not have it put to her in that way. Perhaps Mary had better go to Lady Cantrip. Perhaps I had better be alone here for a time. I do not think that I am fit to have any human being here with me in my sorrow.'

## CHAPTER 2

### LADY MARY PALLISER

IT may as well be said at once that Mrs Finn knew something of Lady Mary which was not known to the father, and which she was not yet prepared to make known to him. The last winter abroad had been passed at Rome, and there Lady Mary Palliser had become acquainted with a certain Mr Tregear,—Francis Oliphant Tregear. The Duchess, who had been in constant correspondence with her friend, had asked questions by letter as to Mr Tregear, of whom she had only known that he was the younger son of a Cornish gentleman, who had become Lord Silverbridge's friend at Oxford. In this there had certainly been but little to recommend him to the intimacy of such a girl as Lady Mary Palliser. Nor had the Duchess, when writing, ever spoken of him as a probable suitor for her daughter's hand. She had never connected the two names together. But Mrs Finn had been clever enough to perceive that the Duchess had become fond of Mr Tregear, and would willingly have heard something to his advantage. And she did hear something to his advantage,—something also to his disadvantage. At his mother's death this young man would inherit a property amounting to about fifteen hundred a year.* 'And I am told,' said Mrs Finn, 'that he is quite likely to spend his money before it comes to him.' There had been nothing more written specially about Mr Tregear; but Mrs Finn had feared not only that the young man loved the girl, but that the young man's love had in some imprudent way been fostered by the mother.

Then there had been some fitful confidence during those few days of acute illness. Why should not the girl have the man if he were lovable? And the Duchess referred to her own early days* when she had loved, and to the great ruin which had come upon her heart when she had been severed from the man she had loved. 'Not but that it has been all for the best,' she had said. 'Not but that Plantagenet has been to me all that a husband should be. Only if she can be spared what I suffered, let her be spared.' Even when these things had been said to her, Mrs Finn had found herself unable to ask questions. She could not bring herself to inquire whether the girl had in truth given her heart to this young Tregear. The one was nineteen and the other as yet but two-and-twenty! But though she asked no questions she almost knew that it must be so. And she knew also that the father, as yet, was quite in the dark on the matter. How was it possible that in such circumstances she should assume the part of the girl's confidential friend and monitress? Were she to do so she must immediately tell the father everything. In such a position no one could be a better friend than Lady Cantrip, and Mrs Finn had already almost made up her mind that, should Lady Cantrip occupy the place, she would tell her ladyship all that had passed between herself and the Duchess on the subject.

Of what hopes she might have, or what fears, about her girl, the Duchess had said no word to her husband. But when she had believed that the things of the world were fading away from her, and when he was sitting by her bedside,—dumb, because at such a moment he knew not how to express the tenderness of his heart,—holding her hand, and trying so to listen to her words, that he might collect and remember every wish, she had murmured something about the ultimate division of the great wealth* with which she herself had been endowed. 'She had never,' she said, 'even tried to remember what arrangements had been made by lawyers, but she hoped that Mary might be so circumstanced, that if her happiness depended on marrying a poor man, want of money need not prevent it.' The Duke suspecting nothing, believing this to be a not unnatural expression of maternal interest, had assured her that Mary's fortune would be ample.

Mrs Finn made the proposition to Lady Mary in respect to Lady Cantrip's invitation. Lady Mary was very like her mother, especially in having exactly her mother's tone of voice, her quick manner of speech, and her sharp intelligence. She had also her mother's eyes, large and round, and almost blue, full of life and full of courage, eyes which never seemed to quail, and her mother's dark brown hair, never long but very copious in its thickness. She was, however, taller than her mother, and very much more graceful in her movement. And she could already assume a personal dignity of manner which had never been within her mother's reach. She had become aware of a certain brusqueness of speech in her mother, a certain aptitude to say sharp things without thinking whether the sharpness was becoming to the position which she held, and, taking advantage of the example, the girl had already learned that she might gain more than she would lose by controlling her words.

'Papa wants me to go to Lady Cantrip,' she said.

'I think he would like it,—just for the present, Lady Mary.'

Though there had been the closest possible intimacy between the Duchess and Mrs Finn, this had hardly been so as to the intercourse between Mrs Finn and the children. Of Mrs Finn it must be acknowledged that she was, perhaps fastidiously, afraid of appearing to take advantage of her friendship with the Duke's family. She would tell herself that though circumstances had compelled her to be the closest and nearest friend of a Duchess, still her natural place was not among dukes and their children, and therefore in her intercourse with the girl she did not at first assume the manner and bearing which her position in the house would have seemed to warrant. Hence the 'Lady Mary.'

'Why does he want to send me away, Mrs Finn?'

'It is not that he wants to send you away, but that he thinks it will be better for you to be with some friend. Here you must be so much alone.'

'Why don't you stay? But I suppose Mr Finn wants you to be back in London.'

'It is not that only, or, to speak the truth, not that at all. Mr Finn could come here if it were suitable. Or for a week or two he might do very well without me. But there are other reasons. There is no one whom your mother respected more highly than Lady Cantrip.'

'I never heard her speak a word of Lady Cantrip.'

'Both he and she are your father's intimate friends.'

'Does papa want to be—alone here?'

'It is you, not himself, of whom he is thinking.'

'Therefore I must think of him, Mrs Finn. I do not wish him to be alone. I am sure it would be better that I should stay with him.'

'He feels that it would not be well that you should live without the companionship of some lady.'

'Then let him find some lady. You would be the best, because he knows you so well. I, however, am not afraid of being alone. I am sure he ought not to be here quite by himself. If he bids me go, I must go, and then of course I shall go where he sends me; but I won't say that I think it best that I should go, and certainly I do not want to go to Lady Cantrip.' This she said with great decision, as though the matter was one on which she had altogether made up her mind. Then she added, in a lower voice: 'Why doesn't papa speak to me about it?'

'He is thinking only of what may be best for you.'

'It would be best for me to stay near him. Whom else has he got?'

All this Mrs Finn repeated to the Duke as closely as she could, and then of course the father was obliged to speak to his daughter.

'Don't send me away, papa,' she said at once.

'Your life here, Mary, will be inexpressibly sad.'

'It must be sad anywhere. I cannot go to college, like Gerald, or live anywhere just as I please, like Silverbridge.'

'Do you envy them that?'

'Sometimes, papa. Only I shall think more of poor mamma by being alone, and I should like to be thinking of her always.' He shook his head mournfully. 'I do not mean that I shall always be unhappy, as I am now.'

'No, my dear; you are too young for that. It is only the old who suffer in that way.'

'You will suffer less if I am with you; won't you, papa? I do not want to go to Lady Cantrip. I hardly remember her at all.'

'She is very good.'

'Oh yes. That is what they used to say to mamma about Lady Midlothian.* Papa, pray do not send me to Lady Cantrip.'

Of course it was decided that she should not go to Lady Cantrip at once, or to Mrs Jeffrey Palliser, and, after a short interval of doubt, it was decided also that Mrs Finn should remain at Matching for at least a fortnight. The Duke declared that he would be glad to see Mr Finn, but she knew that in his present mood the society of any one man to whom he would feel himself called upon to devote his time, would be a burden to him, and she plainly said that Mr Finn had better not come to Matching at present. 'There are old associations,' she said, 'which will enable you to bear with me as you will with your butler or your groom, but you are not as yet quite able to make yourself happy with company.' This he bore with perfect equanimity, and then, as it were, handed over his daughter to Mrs Finn's care.

Very quickly there came to be close intimacy between Mrs Finn and Lady Mary. For a day or two the elder woman, though the place she filled was one of absolute confidence, rather resisted than encouraged the intimacy. She always remembered that the girl was the daughter of a great duke, and that her position in the house had sprung from circumstances which would not, perhaps, in the eyes of the world at large, have recommended her for such friendship. She knew—the reader may possibly know*—that nothing had ever been purer, nothing more disinterested than her friendship. But she knew also,—no one knew better,—that the judgment of men and women does not always run parallel with facts.* She entertained, too, a conviction in regard to herself, that hard words and hard judgments were to be expected from the world,—were to be accepted by her without any strong feeling of injustice,—because she had been elevated by chance to the possession of more good things than she had merited. She weighed all this with a very fine balance, and even after the encouragement she had received from the Duke, was intent on confining herself to some position about the girl inferior to that which such a friend as Lady Cantrip might have occupied. But the girl's manner, and the girl's speech about her own mother, overcame her. It was the unintentional revelation of the Duchess's constant reference to her,—the way in which Lady Mary would assert that 'Mamma used always to say this of you; mamma always knew that you would think so and so; mamma used to say that you had told her.' It was the feeling thus conveyed, that the mother who was now dead had in her daily dealings with her own child spoken of her as her nearest friend, which mainly served to conquer the deference of manner which she had assumed.

Then gradually there came confidences,—and at last absolute confidence. The whole story about Mr Tregear was told. Yes; she loved Mr Tregear. She had given him her heart, and had told him so.

'Then, my dear, your father ought to know it,' said Mrs Finn.

'No; not yet. Mamma knew it.'

'Did she know all that you have told me?'

'Yes; all. And Mr Tregear spoke to her, and she said that papa ought not to be told quite yet.'

Mrs Finn could not but remember that the friend she had lost was not, among women, the one best able to give a girl good counsel in such a crisis.

'Why not yet, dear?'

'Well, because——. It is very hard to explain. In the first place, because Mr Tregear himself does not wish it.'

'That is a very bad reason; the worst in the world.'

'Of course you will say so. Of course everybody would say so. But when there is one person whom one loves better than all the rest, for whom one would be ready to die, to whom one is determined that everything shall be devoted, surely the wishes of a person so dear as that ought to have weight.'

'Not in persuading you to do that which is acknowledged to be wrong.'

'What wrong? I am going to do nothing wrong.'

'The very concealment of your love is wrong, after that love has been not only given but declared. A girl's position in such matters is so delicate, especially that of such a girl as you!'

'I know all about that,' said Lady Mary, with something almost approaching to scorn in her tone. 'Of course I have to be——delicate. I don't quite know what the word means. I am not a bit ashamed of being in love with Mr Tregear. He is a gentleman highly educated, very clever, of an old family,—older, I believe, than papa's. And he is manly and handsome; just what a young man ought to be. Only he is not rich.'

'If he be all that you say, ought you not to trust your papa? If he approve of it, he could give you money.'

'Of course he must be told; but not now. He is nearly broken-hearted about dear mamma. He could not bring himself to care about anything of that kind at present. And then it is Mr Tregear that should speak to him first.'

'Not now, Mary.'

'How do you mean not now?'

'If you had a mother you would talk to her about it.'

'Mamma knew.'

'If she were still living she would tell your father.'

'But she didn't tell him though she did know. She didn't mean to tell him quite yet. She wanted to see Mr Tregear here in England first. Of course I shall do nothing till papa does know.'

'You will not see him?'

'How can I see him here? He will not come here, if you mean that.'

'You do not correspond with him?' Here for the first time the girl blushed. 'Oh, Mary, if you are writing to him your father ought to know it.'

'I have not written to him; but when he heard how ill poor mamma was, then he wrote to me—twice. You may see his letters. It is all about her. No one worshipped mamma as he did.'

Gradually the whole story was told. These two young persons considered themselves to be engaged, but had agreed that their engagement should not be made known to the Duke till something had occurred, or some time had arrived, as to which Mr Tregear was to be the judge. In Mrs Finn's opinion nothing could be more unwise, and she said much to induce the girl to confess everything to her father at once. But in all her arguments she was opposed by the girl's reference to her mother. 'Mamma knew it.' And it did certainly seem to Mrs Finn as though the mother had assented to this imprudent concealment. When she endeavoured, in her own mind, to make excuse for her friend, she felt almost sure that the Duchess, with all her courage, had been afraid to propose to her husband that their daughter should marry a commoner* without an income. But in thinking of all that, there could now be nothing gained. What ought she to do—at once? The girl, in telling her, had exacted no promise of secrecy, nor would she have given any such promise; but yet she did not like the idea of telling the tale behind the girl's back. It was evident that Lady Mary had considered herself to be safe in confiding her story to her mother's old friend. Lady Mary no doubt had had her confidences with her mother,—confidences from which it had been intended by both that the father should be excluded; and now she seemed naturally to expect that this new ally should look at this great question as her mother had looked at it. The father had been regarded as a great outside power, which could hardly be overcome, but which might be evaded, or made inoperative by stratagem. It was not that the daughter did not love him. She loved him and venerated him highly,—the veneration perhaps being stronger than the love. The Duchess, too, had loved him dearly,—more dearly in late years than in her early life.* But her husband to her had always been an outside power which had in many cases to be evaded. Lady Mary, though she did not express all this, evidently thought that in this new friend she had found a woman whose wishes and aspirations for her would be those which her mother had entertained.

But Mrs Finn was much troubled in her mind, thinking that it was her duty to tell the story to the Duke. It was not only the daughter who had trusted her, but the father also; and the father's confidence had been not only the first but by far the holier of the two. And the question was one so important to the girl's future happiness! There could be no doubt that the peril of her present position was very great.

'Mary,' she said one morning, when the fortnight was nearly at an end, 'your father ought to know all this. I should feel that I had betrayed him were I to go away leaving him in ignorance.'

'You do not mean to say that you will tell?' said the girl, horrified at the idea of such treachery.

'I wish that I could induce you to do so. Every day that he is kept in the dark is an injury to you.'

'I am doing nothing. What harm can come? It is not as though I were seeing him every day.'

'This harm will come; your father of course will know that you became engaged to Mr Tregear in Italy, and that a fact so important to him has been kept back from him.'

'If there is anything in that, the evil has been done already. Of course poor mamma did mean to tell him.'

'She cannot tell him now, and therefore you ought to do what she would have done.'

'I cannot break my promise to him.' 'Him' always meant Mr Tregear. 'I have told him that I would not do so till I had his consent, and I will not.'

This was very dreadful to Mrs Finn, and yet she was most unwilling to take upon herself the part of a stern elder, and declare that under the circumstances she must tell the tale. The story had been told to her under the supposition that she was not a stern elder, that she was regarded as the special friend of the dear mother who was gone, that she might be trusted to assist against the terrible weight of parental authority. She could not endure to be regarded at once as a traitor by this young friend who had sweetly inherited the affection with which the Duchess had regarded her. And yet if she were to be silent how could she forgive herself?* 'The Duke certainly ought to know at once,' said she, repeating her words merely that she might gain some time for thinking, and pluck up courage to declare her purpose, should she resolve on betraying the secret.

'If you tell him now, I will never forgive you,' said Lady Mary.

'I am bound in honour to see that your father knows a thing which is of such vital importance to him and to you. Having heard all this I have no right to keep it from him. If Mr Tregear really loves you'—Lady Mary smiled at the doubt implied by this suggestion—'he ought to feel that for your sake there should be no secret from your father.' Then she paused a moment to think. 'Will you let me see Mr Tregear myself, and talk to him about it?'

To this Lady Mary at first demurred, but when she found that in no other way could she prevent Mrs Finn from going at once to the Duke and telling him everything, she consented. Under Mrs Finn's directions she wrote a note to her lover, which Mrs Finn saw, and then undertook to send it, with a letter from herself, to Mr Tregear's address in London. The note was very short, and was indeed dictated by the elder lady, with some dispute, however, as to certain terms, in which the younger lady had her way. It was as follows:

'DEAREST FRANK,

'I wish you to see Mrs Finn, who, as you know, was dear mamma's most particular friend. Please go to her, as she will ask you to do. When you hear what she says I think you ought to do what she advises.

'Yours for ever and always,

'M. P.'

This Mrs Finn sent enclosed in an envelope, with a few words from herself, asking the gentleman to call upon her in Park Lane,* on a day and at an hour fixed.

## CHAPTER 3

### FRANCIS OLIPHANT TREGEAR

MR FRANCIS OLIPHANT TREGEAR was a young man who might not improbably make a figure in the world, should circumstances be kind to him, but as to whom it might be doubted whether circumstances would be sufficiently kind to enable him to use serviceably his unquestionable talents and great personal gifts. He had taught himself to regard himself as a young English gentleman of the first water, qualified by his birth and position to live with all that was most noble and most elegant; and he could have lived in that sphere naturally and gracefully were it not that the part of the 'sphere' which he specially affected requires wealth as well as birth and intellect. Wealth he had not, and yet he did not abandon the sphere. As a consequence of all this, it was possible that the predictions of his friends as to that figure which he was to make in the world might be disappointed.

He had been educated at Eton,* from whence he had been sent to Christ Church;* and both at school and at college had been the most intimate friend of the son and heir of a great and wealthy duke. He and Lord Silverbridge had been always together, and they who were interested in the career of the young nobleman had generally thought he had chosen his friend well. Tregear had gone out in honours, having been a second-class man.* His friend Silverbridge, we know, had been allowed to take no degree at all; but the terrible practical joke by which the whole front of the Dean's house had been coloured scarlet in the middle of the night, had been carried on without any assistance from Tregear. The two young men had then been separated for a year; but immediately after taking his degree, Tregear, at the invitation of Lord Silverbridge, had gone to Italy, and had there completely made good his footing with the Duchess,—with what effect on another member of the Palliser family the reader already knows.

The young man was certainly clever. When the Duchess found that he could talk without any shyness, that he could speak French fluently, and that after a month in Italy he could chatter Italian, at any rate without reticence or shame; when she perceived that all the women liked the lad's society and impudence, and that all the young men were anxious to know him, she was glad to find that Silverbridge had chosen so valuable a friend. And then he was beautiful to look at,— putting her almost in mind of another man* on whom her eyes had once loved to dwell. He was dark, with hair that was almost black, but yet was not black; with clear brown eyes, a nose as regular as Apollo's, and a mouth in which was ever to be found that expression of manliness, which of all characteristics is the one which women love the best. He was five feet ten in height. He was always well dressed, and yet always so dressed as to seem to show that his outside garniture had not been matter of trouble to him. Before the Duchess had dreamed what might take place between this young man and her daughter she had been urgent in her congratulations to her son as to the possession of such a friend.

For though she now and then would catch a glimpse of the outer man, which would remind her of that other beautiful one whom she had known in her youth, and though, as these glimpses came, she would remember how poor in spirit and how unmanly that other one had been, though she would confess to herself how terrible had been the heart-shipwreck which that other one had brought upon herself;

still she was able completely to assure herself that this man, though not superior in external grace, was altogether different in mind and character. She was old enough now to see all this and to appreciate it. Young Tregear had his own ideas about the politics of the day, and they were ideas with which she sympathised, though they were antagonistic to the politics of her life. He had his ideas about books too, as to manners of life, as to art, and even ethics. Whether or no in all this there was not much that was superficial only, she was not herself deep enough to discover. Nor would she have been deterred from admiring him had she been told that it was tinsel.* Such were the acquirements, such the charms, that she loved. Here was a young man who dared to speak, and had always something ready to be spoken; who was not afraid of beauty, nor daunted by superiority of rank; who, if he had not money, could carry himself on equal terms among those who had. In this way he won the Duchess's heart, and having done that, was it odd that he should win the heart of the daughter also?

His father was a Cornwall squire of comfortable means, having joined the property of his wife to his own for the period of his own life. She had possessed land also in Cornwall, supposed to be worth fifteen hundred a year, and his own paternal estate at Polwenning* was said to be double that value. Being a prudent man, he lived at home as a country gentleman, and thus was able in his county to hold his head as high as richer men. But Frank Tregear was only his second son; and though Frank would hereafter inherit his mother's fortune, he was by no means now in a position to assume the right of living as an idle man. Yet he was idle. The elder brother, who was considerably older than Frank, was an odd man, much addicted to quarrelling with his family, and who spent his time chiefly in travelling about the world. Frank's mother, who was not the mother of the heir also, would sometimes surmise, in Frank's hearing, that the entire property must ultimately come to him. That other Tregear, who was now supposed to be investigating the mountains of Crim Tartary,* would surely never marry. And Frank was the favourite also with his father, who paid his debts at Oxford with not much grumbling; who was proud of his friendship with a future duke; who did not urge, as he ought to have urged, that vital question of a profession; and who, when he allowed his son four hundred pounds a year, was almost content with that son's protestations that he knew how to live as a poor man among rich men, without chagrin and without trouble.

Such was the young man who now, in lieu of a profession, had taken upon himself the responsibility of an engagement with

Lady Mary Palliser. He was tolerably certain that, should he be able to overcome the parental obstacles which he would no doubt find in his path, money would be forthcoming sufficient for the purposes of matrimonial life. The Duke's wealth was fabulous, and as a great part of it, if not the greater, had come from his wife, there would probably be ample provision for the younger children. And when the Duchess had found out how things were going, and had yielded to her daughter, after an opposition which never had the appearance even of being in earnest, she had taken upon herself to say that she would use her influence to prevent any great weight of trouble from pecuniary matters. Frank Tregear, young and bright, and full of hearty ambitions, was certainly not the man to pursue a girl simply because of her fortune; nor was he weak enough to be attracted simply by the glitter of rank; but he was wise enough with worldly wisdom to understand thoroughly the comforts of a good income, and he was sufficiently attached to high position to feel the advantage of marrying a daughter of the Duke of Omnium.

When the Duchess was leaving Italy, it had been her declared purpose to tell her husband the story as soon as they were at home in England. And it was on this understanding that Frank Tregear had explained to the girl that he would not as yet ask her father for his permission to be received into the family as a suitor. Everyone concerned had felt that the Duke would not easily be reconciled to such a son-in-law, and that the Duchess should be the one to bell the cat.*

There was one member of the family who had hitherto been half-hearted in the matter. Lord Silverbridge had vacillated between loyalty to his friend and a certain feeling as to the impropriety of such a match for his sister. He was aware that something very much better should be expected for her, and still was unable to explain his objections to Tregear. He had not at first been admitted into confidence, either by his sister or by Tregear, but had questioned his friend when he saw what was going on. 'Certainly I love your sister,' Tregear had said; 'do you object?' Lord Silverbridge was the weaker of the two, and much subject to the influence of his friend; but he could on occasion be firm, and he did at first object. But he did not object strongly, and allowed himself at last to be content with declaring that the Duke would never give his consent.

While Tregear was with his love, or near her, his hopes and fears were sufficient to occupy his mind; and immediately on his return, all the world was nothing to him, except as far as the world was concerned with Lady Mary Palliser. He had come back to England somewhat before the ducal party, and the pleasures and occupations of London life had not abated his love, but enabled him to feel that there was something in life over and beyond his love; whereas to Lady Mary, down at Matching, there had been nothing over and beyond her love— except the infinite grief and desolation produced by her mother's death.

Tregear, when he received the note from Mrs Finn, was staying at the Duke's house in Carlton Terrace.* Silverbridge was there, and, on leaving Matching, had asked the Duke's permission to have his friend with him. The Duke at that time was not well pleased with his son as to a matter of politics, and gave his son's friend credit for the evil counsel which had produced this displeasure. But still he had not refused his assent to this proposition. Had he done so, Silverbridge would prob- ably have gone elsewhere; and though there was a matter in respect to Tregear of which the Duke disapproved, it was not a matter, as he thought, which would have justified him in expelling the young man from his house. The young man was a strong Conservative; and now Silverbridge had declared his purpose of entering the House of Commons, if he did enter it, as one of the Conservative party.*

This had been a terrible blow to the Duke; and he believed that it all came from this young Tregear. Still he must do his duty, and not more than his duty. He knew nothing against Tregear. That a Tregear should be a Conservative was perhaps natural enough—at any rate, was not disgraceful; that he should have his political creed sufficiently at heart to be able to persuade another man, was to his credit. He was a gentle- man, well educated, superior in many things to Silverbridge himself. There were those who said that Silverbridge had redeemed himself from contempt—from that sort of contempt which might be supposed to await a young nobleman who had painted scarlet the residence of the Head of his college*—by the fact of his having chosen such a friend. The Duke was essentially a just man; and though, at the very moment in which the request was made, his heart was half crushed by his son's apostasy, he gave the permission asked.

'You know Mrs Finn?' Tregear said to his friend one morning at breakfast.

'I remember her all my life. She used to be a great deal with my grandfather.* I believe he left her a lot of diamonds and money, and that she wouldn't have them. I don't know whether the diamonds are not locked up somewhere now, so that she can take them when she pleases.'

'What a singular woman!'

'It was odd; but she had some fad about it. What makes you ask about Mrs Finn?'

'She wants me to go and see her.'

'What about?'

'I think I have heard your mother speak of her as though she loved her dearly,' said Tregear.

'I don't know about loving her dearly. They were intimate, and Mrs Finn used to be with her very much when she was in the country. She was at Matching just now, when my poor mother died. Why does she want to see you?'

'She has written to me from Matching. She wants to see me——'

'Well?'

'To tell you the truth, I do not know what she has to say to me; though I can guess.'

'What do you guess?'

'It is something about your sister.'

'You will have to give that up, Tregear.'

'I think not.'

'Yes, you will; my father will never stand it.'

'I don't know what there is to stand. I am not noble, nor am I rich; but I am as good a gentleman as he is.'

'My dear fellow,' said the young lord, 'you know very well what I think about all that. A fellow is not any better to me because he has got a title, nor yet because he owns half a county. But men have their ideas and feelings about it. My father is a rich man, and of course he'll want his daughter to marry a rich man. My father is noble, and he'll want his daughter to marry a nobleman. You can't very well marry Mary without his permission, and therefore you had better let it alone.'

'I haven't even asked his permission as yet.'

'Even my mother was afraid to speak to him about it, and I never knew her to be afraid to say anything else to him.'

'I shall not be afraid,' said Tregear, looking grimly.

'I should. That's the difference between us.'

'He can't very well eat me.'

'Nor even bite you;—nor will he abuse you. But he can look at you, and he can say a word or two which you will find it very hard to bear. My governor is the quietest man I know, but he has a way of making himself disagreeable when he wishes, that I never saw equalled.'

'At any rate, I had better go and see your Mrs Finn.' Then Tregear wrote a line to Mrs Finn, and made his appointment.

## CHAPTER 4

### PARK LANE

FROM the beginning of the affair Tregear had found the necessity of bolstering himself up inwardly in his great attempt by mottoes, proverbs, and instigations to courage addressed to himself. 'None but the brave deserve the fair.'* 'De l'audace, et encore de l'audace, et toujours de l'audace.'* He was a man naturally of good heart in such matters, who was not afraid of his brother-men, nor yet of women, his sisters. But in this affair he knew very much persistence would be required of him, and that even with such persistence he might probably fail, unless he should find a more than ordinary constancy in the girl. That the Duke could not eat him, indeed that nobody could eat him as long as he carried himself as an honest man and a gentleman, was to him an inward assurance on which he leaned much. And yet he was conscious, almost with a feeling of shame, that in Italy he had not spoken to the Duke about his daughter because he was afraid lest the Duke might eat him. In such an affair he should have been careful from the first to keep his own hands thoroughly clean. Had it not been his duty as a gentleman to communicate with the father, if not before he gained the girl's heart, at any rate as soon as he knew he had done so? He had left Italy thinking that he would certainly meet the Duchess and her daughter in London, and that then he might go to the Duke as though this love of his had arisen from the sweetness of those meetings in London. But all these ideas had been dissipated by the great misfortune of the death of Lady Mary's mother. From all this he was driven to acknowledge to himself that his silence in Italy had been wrong, that he had been weak in allowing himself to be guided by the counsel of the Duchess, and that he had already armed the Duke with one strong argument against him.

He did not doubt but that Mrs Finn would be opposed to him. Of course he could not doubt but that all the world would now be opposed to him,—except the girl herself. He would find no other friend so generous, so romantic, so unworldly as the Duchess had been. It was clear to him that Lady Mary had told the story of her engagement to Mrs Finn, and that Mrs Finn had not as yet told it to the Duke. From this he was justified in regarding Mrs Finn as the girl's friend. The request made was that he should at once do something which Mrs Finn was to suggest. He could hardly have been so requested, and that in terms of such warm affection, had it been Mrs Finn's intention to ask him to desist altogether from his courtship. This woman was regarded by Lady Mary as her mother's dearest friend. It was therefore incumbent on him now to induce her to believe in him as the Duchess had believed.

He knocked at the door of Mrs Finn's little house in Park Lane a few minutes before the time appointed, and found himself alone when he was shown into the drawing-room. He had heard much of this lady though he had never seen her, and had heard much also of her husband. There had been a kind of mystery about her. People did not quite understand how it was that she had been so intimate with the Duchess, nor why the late Duke had left to her an enormous legacy, which as yet had never been claimed.* There was supposed, too, to have been something especially romantic in her marriage with her present husband. It was believed also that she was very rich. The rumours of all these things together had made her a person of note, and Tregear, when he found himself alone in the drawing-room, looked round about him as though a special interest was to be attached to the belongings of such a woman. It was a pretty room, somewhat dark, because the curtains were almost closed across the windows, but furnished with a pretty taste, and now, in these early April days, filled with flowers.

'I have to apologise, Mr Tregear, for keeping you waiting,' she said as she entered the room.

'I fear I was before my time.'

'I know that I am after mine,—a few minutes,' said the lady.

He told himself that though she was not a young woman, yet she was attractive. She was dark, and still wore her black hair in curls, such as are now seldom seen with ladies. Perhaps the reduced light of the chamber had been regulated with some regard to her complexion and to her age. The effect, however, was good, and Frank Tregear felt at once interested in her.

'You have just come up from Matching?' he said.

'Yes; only the day before yesterday. It is very good of you to come to me so soon.'

'Of course I came when you sent for me. I am afraid the Duke felt his loss severely.'

'How should he not, such a loss as it was? Few people knew how much he trusted her, and how dearly he loved her.'

'Silverbridge has told me that he is awfully cut up.'*

'You have seen Lord Silverbridge then?'

'Just at present I am living with him, at Carlton Terrace.'

'In the Duke's house?' she asked, with some surprise.

'Yes; in the Duke's house. Silverbridge and I have been very intimate.* Of course the Duke knows that I am there. Is there any chance of his coming to town?'

'Not yet, I fear. He is determined to be alone. I wish it were otherwise, as I am sure he would better bear his sorrow, if he would go about among other men.'

'No doubt he would suffer less,' said Tregear. Then there was a pause. Each wished that the other should introduce the matter which both knew was to be the subject of their conversation. But Tregear would not begin. 'When I left them all at Florence,' he said, 'I little thought that I should never see her again.'

'You had been intimate with them, Mr Tregear?'

'Yes; I think I may say I have been intimate with them. I had been at Eton and at Christ Church with Silverbridge, and we have always been much together.'

'I have understood that. Have you and the Duke been good friends?'

'We have never been enemies.'

'I suppose not that.'

'The Duke, I think, does not much care about young people. I hardly know what he used to do with himself. When I dined with them, I saw him, but I did not often do that. I think he used to read a good deal, and walk about alone. We were always riding.'

'Lady Mary used to ride?'

'Oh yes; and Lord Silverbridge and Lord Gerald. And the Duchess used to drive. One of us would always be with her.'

'And so you became intimate with the whole family?'

'So I became intimate with the whole family.'

'And especially so with Lady Mary?' This she said in her sweetest possible tone, and with a most gracious smile.

'Especially so with Lady Mary,' he replied.

'It will be very good of you, Mr Tregear, if you endure and forgive all this cross-questioning from me, who am a perfect stranger to you.'

'But you are not a perfect stranger to her.'

'That is it, of course. Now, if you will allow me, I will explain to you exactly what my footing with her is. When the Duchess returned, and when I found her to be so ill as she passed through London, I went down with her into the country,—quite as a matter of course.'

'So I understand.'

'And there she died,—in my arms. I will not try to harass you by telling you what those few days were; how absolutely he was struck to the ground, how terrible was the grief of the daughter, how the boys were astonished by the feeling of their loss. After a few days they went away. It was, I think, their father's wish that they should go. And I too was going away,—and had felt, indeed, directly her spirit had parted from her, that I was only in the way in his house. But I stayed at his request, because he did not wish his daughter to be alone.'

'I can easily understand that, Mrs Finn.'

'I wanted her to go to Lady Cantrip who had invited her, but she would not. In that way we were thrown together in the closest intercourse, for two or three weeks. Then she told me the story of your engagement.'

'That was natural, I suppose.'

'Surely so. Think of her position, left as she is without a mother! It was incumbent on her to tell someone. There was, however, one other person in whom it would have been much better that she should have confided.'

'What person?'

'Her father.'

'I rather fancy that it is I who ought to tell him.'

'As far as I understand these things, Mr Tregear,—which, indeed, is very imperfectly,—I think it is natural that a girl should at once tell her mother when a gentleman has made her understand that he loves her.'

'She did so, Mrs Finn.'

'And I suppose that generally the mother would tell the father.'

'She did not.'

'No; and therefore the position of the young lady is now one of great embarrassment. The Duchess has gone from us, and we must now make up our minds as to what had better be done. It is out of the question that Lady Mary should be allowed to consider herself to be engaged, and that the father should be kept in ignorance of her position.' She paused for his reply, but as he said nothing, she continued: 'Either you must tell the Duke, or she must do so, or I must do so.'

'I suppose she told you in confidence.'

'No doubt. She told it me presuming that I would not betray her; but I shall,—if that be a betrayal. The Duke must know it. It will be infinitely better that he should know it through you, or through her, than through me. But he must be told.'

'I can't quite see why,' said Tregear.

'For her sake,—whom I suppose you love.'

'Certainly I love her.'

'In order that she may not suffer. I wonder you do not see it, Mr Tregear. Perhaps you have a sister.'

'I have no sister as it happens.'*

'But you can imagine what your feelings would be. Should you like to think of a sister as being engaged to a man without the knowledge of any of her family?'

'It was not so. The Duchess knew it. The present condition of things is altogether an accident.'

'It is an accident that must be brought to an end.'

'Of course it must be brought to an end. I am not such a fool as to suppose that I can make her my wife without telling her father.'

'I mean at once, Mr Tregear.'

'It seems to me that you are rather dictating to me, Mrs Finn.'

'I owe you an apology, of course, for meddling in your affairs at all. But as it will be more conducive to your success that the Duke should hear this from you than from me, and as I feel that I am bound by my duty to him and to Lady Mary to see that he be not left in ignorance, I think that I am doing you a service.'

'I do not like to have a constraint put upon me.'

'That, Mr Tregear, is what gentlemen, I fancy, very often feel in regard to ladies. But the constraint of which you speak is necessary for their protection. Are you unwilling to see the Duke?'

He was very unwilling, but he would not confess so much. He gave various reasons for delay, urging repeatedly that the question of his marriage was one which he could not press upon the Duke so soon after the death of the Duchess. And when she assured him that this was a matter of importance so great, that even the death of the man's wife should not be held by him to justify delay, he became angry, and for awhile insisted that he must be allowed to follow his own judgment. But he gave her a promise that he would see the Duke before a week was over. Nevertheless he left the house in dudgeon, having told Mrs Finn more than once that she was taking advantage of Lady Mary's confidence. They hardly parted as friends, and her feeling was, on the whole, hostile to him and to his love. It could not, she thought, be for the happiness of such a one as Lady Mary that she should give herself to one who seemed to have so little to recommend him.

He, when he had left her, was angry with his own weakness. He had not only promised that he would make his application to the Duke, but that he would do so within the period of a week. Who was she that she should exact terms from him after this fashion, and prescribe days and hours? And now, because this strange woman had spoken to him, he was compelled to make a journey down to the Duke's country house, and seek an interview in which he would surely be snubbed!

This occurred on a Wednesday, and he resolved that he would go down to Matching on the next Monday. He said nothing of his plan to anyone, and not a word passed between him and Lord Silverbridge about Lady Mary during the first two or three days. But on the Saturday Silverbridge appeared at breakfast with a letter in his hand. 'The governor is coming up to town,' he said.

'Immediately?'

'In the course of next week. He says that he thinks he shall be here on Wednesday.'

It immediately struck Tregear that this sudden journey must have some reference to Lady Mary and her engagement. 'Do you know why he is coming?'

'Because of these vacancies in Parliament.'

'Why should that bring him up?'

'I suppose he hopes to be able to talk me into obedience. He wants me to stand for the county*—as a Liberal,* of course. I intend to stand for the borough as a Conservative, and I have told them so down at Silverbridge. I am very sorry to annoy him, and all that kind of thing. But what the deuce is a fellow to do? If a man has got political convictions of his own, of course, he must stick to them.' This the young Lord said with a good deal of self-assurance, as though he, by the light of his own reason, had ascertained on which side the truth lay in political contests of the day.

'There is a good deal to be said on both sides of the question, my boy.' At this particular moment Tregear felt that the Duke ought to be propitiated.

'You wouldn't have me give up my convictions!'

'A seat in Parliament is a great thing.'

'I can probably secure that, whichever side I take. I thought you were so devilish hot against the Radicals.'*

'So I am. But then you are, as it were, bound by family allegiance.'

'I'll be shot if I am. One never knows how to understand you now-adays. It used to be a great doctrine with you, that nothing should induce a man to vote against his political opinions.'

'So it is,—if he has really got any. However, as your father is coming to London, I need not go down to Matching.'

'You don't mean to say that you were going to Matching.'

'I had intended to beard the lion in his country den; but now the lion will find me in his own town den, and I must beard him here.'

Then Tregear wrote a most chilling note to Mrs Finn, informing her with great precision, that, as the Duke of Omnium intended to be in town one day next week, he would postpone the performance of his promise for a day or two beyond the allotted time.

## CHAPTER 5
### 'IT IS IMPOSSIBLE'

DOWN at Matching Lady Mary's life was very dull after Mrs Finn had left her. She had a horse to ride, but had no one to ride with her. She had a carriage in which to be driven, but no one to be driven with her, and no special places whither to go. Her father would walk daily for two hours, and she would accompany him when he encouraged her to do so; but she had an idea that he preferred taking his walks alone, and when they were together there was no feeling of confidence between them. There could be none on her part, as she knew that she was keeping back information which he was entitled to possess. On this matter she received two letters from Mrs Finn, in the first of which she was told that Mr Tregear intended to present himself at Matching within a few days, and was advised in the same letter not to endeavour to see her lover on that occasion; and then, in the second she was informed that this interview with her father was to be sought not at Matching but in London. From this latter letter there was of course some disappoint-ment, though some feeling of relief. Had he come there she might possibly have seen him after the interview. But she would have been subjected to the immediate sternness of her father's anger. That she would now escape. She would not be called on to meet him just when the first blow had fallen upon him. She was quite sure that he would disapprove of the thing. She was quite sure that he would be very angry. She knew that he was a peculiarly just man, and yet she thought that in this he would be unjust. Had she been called upon to sing the praises of her father she would have insisted above all things on the absolute integrity of his mind, and yet, knowing as she did that he would be opposed to her marriage with Mr Tregear, she assured herself every day and every hour that he had no right to make any such objection. The man she loved was a gentleman, and an honest man, by no means a fool, and subject to no vices. Her father had no right to demand that she should give her heart to a rich man, or to one of high rank. Rank! As for rank, she told herself that she had the most supreme contempt for it. She thought that she had seen it near enough already to be sure that it ought to have no special allurements. What was it doing for her? Simply restraining her choice among comparatively a few who seemed to her by no means the best endowed of God's creatures.

Of one thing she was very sure, that under no pressure whatsoever would she abandon her engagement with Mr Tregear. That to her had become a bond almost as holy as matrimony itself could be. She had told the man that she loved him, and after that there could be no retreat. He had kissed her, and she had returned his caress. He had told her that she was his, as his arm was round her; and she had acknowledged that it was so, that she belonged to him, and could not be taken away from him. All this was to her a compact so sacred that nothing could break it but a desire on his part to have it annulled. No other man had ever whispered a word of love to her, of no other man had an idea entered her mind that it could be pleasant to join her lot in life with his. With her it had been all new and all sacred. Love with her had that religion which nothing but freshness can give it. That freshness, that bloom, may last through a long life. But every change impairs it, and after many changes it has perished for ever. There was no question with her but that she must bear her father's anger, should he be angry; put up with his continued opposition, should he resolutely oppose her; bear all that the countesses of the world might say to her;— for it was thus that she thought of Lady Cantrip now. Any retrogression was beyond her power.

She was walking with her father when she first heard of his intended visit to London. At that time she had received Mrs Finn's first letter, but not the second. 'I suppose you'll see Silverbridge,' she said. She knew then that Frank Tregear was living with her brother.

'I am going up on purpose to see him. He is causing me much annoyance.'

'Is he extravagant?'

'It is not that—at present.' He winced even as he said this, for he had in truth suffered somewhat from demands made upon him for money, which had hurt him not so much by their amount as by their nature. Lord Silverbridge had taken upon himself to 'own a horse or two,' very much to his father's chagrin, and was at this moment part proprietor of an animal supposed to stand well for the Derby.* The fact was not announced in the papers with his lordship's name, but his father was aware of it, and did not like it the better because his son held the horse in partnership with a certain Major Tifto, who was well known in the sporting world.

'What is it, papa?'

'Of course he ought to go into Parliament.'

'I think he wishes it himself.'

'Yes, but how? By a piece of extreme good fortune, West Barsetshire is open to him. The two seats are vacant together. There is hardly another agricultural county in England that will return a Liberal, and I fear I am not asserting too much in saying that no other Liberal could carry the seat but one of our family.'

'You used to sit for Silverbridge, papa.'

'Yes, I did. In those days the county returned four Conservatives. I cannot explain it all to you, but it is his duty to contest the county on the Liberal side.'

'But if he is a Conservative himself, papa?' asked Lady Mary, who had had some political ideas suggested to her own mind by her lover.

'It is all rubbish. It has come from that young man Tregear, with whom he has been associating.'

'But, papa,' said Lady Mary, who felt that even in this matter she was bound to be firm on what was now her side of the question, 'I suppose it is as—as—as respectable to be a Conservative as a Liberal.'

'I don't know that at all,' said the Duke angrily.

'I thought that—the two sides were——'

She was going to express an opinion that the two parties might be supposed to stand as equal in the respect of the country, when he interrupted her. 'The Pallisers have always been Liberal. It will be a blow to me, indeed, if Silverbridge deserts his colours. I know that as yet he himself has had no deep thoughts on the subject, that unfortunately he does not give himself much to thinking, and that in this matter he is being talked over by a young man whose position in life has hardly justified the great intimacy which has existed.'

This was very far from being comfortable to her, but of course she said nothing in defence of Tregear's politics. Nor at present was she disposed to say anything as to his position in life, though at some future time she might not be so silent. A few days later they were again walking together, when he spoke to her about herself. 'I cannot bear that you should be left here alone while I am away,' he said.

'You will not be long gone, I suppose?'

'Only for three or four days now.'

'I shall not mind that, papa.'

'But very probably I may have to go into Barsetshire. Would you not be happier if you would let me write to Lady Cantrip, and tell her that you will go to her?'

'No, papa, I think not. There are times when one feels that one ought to be almost alone. Don't you feel that?'

'I do not wish you to feel it, nor would you do so long if you had other people around you. With me it is different. I am an old man, and cannot look for new pleasures in society. It has been the fault of my life to be too much alone. I do not want to see my children follow me in that.'

'It is so very short a time as yet,' said she, thinking of her mother's death.

'But I think that you should be with somebody,—with some woman who would be kind to you. I like to see you with books, but books alone should not be sufficient at your age.' How little, she thought, did he know of the state either of her heart or mind! 'Do you dislike Lady Cantrip?'

'I do not know her. I can't say that I dislike a person whom I don't think I ever spoke to, and never saw above once or twice. But how can I say that I like her?' She did, however, know that Lady Cantrip was a countess all over, and would be shocked at the idea of a daughter of a Duke of Omnium marrying the younger son of a country squire. Nothing further was then said on the matter, and when the Duke went to town Lady Mary was left quite alone; with an understanding that if he went into Barsetshire he should come back and take her with him.

He arrived at his own house in Carlton Terrace about five o'clock in the afternoon, and immediately went to his study, intending to dine and spend the evening there alone. His son had already pleaded an engagement for that afternoon, but had consented to devote the following morning to his father's wishes. Of the other sojourner in his house the Duke had thought nothing; but the other sojourner had thought very much of the Duke. Frank Tregear was fully possessed of that courage which induces a man who knows that he must be thrown over a precipice, to choose the first possible moment for his fall. He had sounded Silverbridge about this change in his politics, and had found his friend quite determined not to go back to the family doctrine. Such being the case, the Duke's ill-will and hardness and general severity would probably be enhanced by his interview with his son. Tregear, therefore, thinking that nothing could be got by delay, sent his name in to the Duke before he had been an hour in the house, and asked for an interview. The servant brought back word that his Grace was fatigued, but would see Mr Tregear if the matter in question was one of importance. Frank's heart quailed for a moment, but only for a moment. He took up a pen and wrote a note.

'MY DEAR DUKE OF OMNIUM,

'If your Grace can spare a moment, I think you will find that what I have to say will justify the intrusion.

'Your very faithful servant,

'F. O. TREGEAR.'

Of course the Duke admitted him. There was but one idea in his head as to what was coming. His son had taken this way of making some communication to him respecting his political creed. Some overture or some demand was to be preferred through Tregear. If so, it was proof of a certain anxiety as to the matter on his son's part which was not displeasing to him. But he was not left long in this mistake after Tregear had entered the room. 'Sir,' he said, speaking quite at once, as soon as the door was closed behind him, but still speaking very slowly, looking beautiful as Apollo as he stood upright before his wished-for father-in-law—'Sir, I have come to you to ask you to give me the hand of your daughter.' The few words had been all arranged beforehand, and were now spoken without any appearance of fear or shame. No one hearing them would have imagined that an almost penniless young gentleman was asking in marriage the daughter of the richest and greatest nobleman in England.

'The hand of my daughter!' said the Duke, rising from his chair.

'I know how very great is the prize,' said Frank, 'and how unworthy I am of it. But—as she thinks me worthy——'

'She! What she?'

'Lady Mary.'

'She think you worthy!'

'Yes, your Grace.'

'I do not believe it.' On hearing this, Frank simply bowed his head. 'I beg your pardon, Mr Tregear. I do not mean to say that I do not believe you. I never yet gave the lie to a gentleman, and I hope I never may be driven to do so. But there must be some mistake in this.'

'I am complying with Lady Mary's wishes in asking your permission to enter your house as her suitor.' The Duke stood for a moment biting his lips in silence. 'I cannot believe it,' he said at last. 'I cannot bring myself to believe it. There must be some mistake. My daughter!

Lady Mary Palliser!' Again the young man bowed his head. 'What are your pretensions?'

'Simply her regard.'

'Of course it is impossible. You are not so ignorant but that you must have known as much when you came to me.'

There was so much scorn in his words, and in the tone in which they were uttered, that Tregear in his turn was becoming angry. He had prepared himself to bow humbly before the great man, before the Duke, before the Crœsus,* before the late Prime Minister, before the man who was to be regarded as certainly one of the most exalted of the earth; but he had not prepared himself to be looked at as the Duke looked at him. 'The truth, my Lord Duke, is this,' he said, 'that your daughter loves me, and that we are engaged to each other,— as far as that engagement can be made without your sanction as her father.'

'It cannot have been made at all,' said the Duke.

'I can only hope,—we can both of us only hope that a little time may soften——'

'It is out of the question. There must be an end of this altogether. You must neither see her, nor hear from her, nor in any way communicate with her. It is altogether impossible. I believe, sir, that you have no means?'

'Very little at present, Duke.'

'How did you think you were to live? But it is altogether unnecessary to speak of such a matter as that. There are so many reasons to make this impossible, that it would be useless to discuss one as being more important than others. Has any other one of my family known of this?' This he added, wishing to ascertain whether Lord Silverbridge had disgraced himself by lending his hand to such a disposition of his sister.

'Oh yes,' said Tregear.

'Who has known it?'

'The Duchess, sir. We had all her sympathy and approval.'

'I do not believe a word of it,' said the Duke, becoming extremely red in the face. He was forced to do now that which he had just declared that he had never done in his life,—driven by the desire of his heart to acquit the wife he had lost of the terrible imprudence, worse than imprudence, of which she was now accused.

'That is the second time, my Lord, that you have found it necessary to tell me that you have not believed direct assertions which I made you. But, luckily for me, the two assertions are capable of the earliest and most direct proof. You will believe Lady Mary, and she will confirm me in the one and the other.'

The Duke was almost beside himself with emotion and grief. He did know,—though now at this moment he was most loath to own to himself that it was so,—that his dear wife had been the most imprudent of women. And he recognised in her encouragement of this most pernicious courtship,—if she had encouraged it,—a repetition of that romantic folly by which she had so nearly brought herself to shipwreck in her own early life. If it had been so,—even whether it had been so or not,—he had been wrong to tell the man that he did not believe him. And the man had rebuked him with dignity. 'At any rate it is impossible,' he repeated.

'I cannot allow that it is impossible.'

'That is for me to judge, sir.'

'I trust that you will excuse me when I say that I also must hold myself to be in some degree a judge in the matter. If you were in my place, you would feel——'

'I could not possibly be in your place.'

'If your Grace were in my place you would feel that as long as you were assured by the young lady that your affection was valued by her you would not be deterred by the opposition of her father. That you should yield to me, of course I do not expect; that Lady Mary should be persistent in her present feelings, when she knows your mind, perhaps I have no right to hope; but should she be so persistent as to make you feel that her happiness depends, as mine does, on our marriage, then I shall believe that you will yield at last.'

'Never!' said the Duke. 'Never! I shall never believe that my daughter's happiness can be assured by a step which I should regard as disgraceful to her.'

'Disgraceful is a violent word, my Lord.'

'It is the only word that will express my meaning.'

'And one which I must be bold enough to say you are not justified in using. Should she become my wife to-morrow, no one in England would think she had disgraced herself. The Queen would receive her on her marriage. All your friends would hold out their hands to us,—presuming that we had your goodwill.'

'But you would not have it.'

'Her disgrace would not depend upon that, my Lord. Should your daughter so dispose of herself, as to disgrace herself,—which I think to be impossible,—your countenance could not set her right. Nor can the withdrawal of your countenance condemn her before the world if

she does that with herself which any other lady might do and remain
a lady.'

The Duke, when he heard this, even in the midst of his wrath, which
was very violent, and in the midst of his anger, which was very acute,
felt that he had to deal with a man,—with one whom he could not
put off from him into the gutter, and there leave as buried in the mud.
And there came, too, a feeling upon him, which he had no time to
analyse, but of which he was part aware, that this terrible indiscretion
on the part of his daughter and of his late wife was less wonderful than
it had at first appeared to be. But not on that account was he the less
determined to make the young man feel that his parental opposition
would be invincible.

'It is quite impossible, sir. I do not think that I need say anything
more.' Then, while Tregear was meditating whether to make any reply,
the Duke asked a question which had better have been left unasked.
The asking of it diminished somewhat from that ducal, grand-ducal,
quasi-archducal, almost godlike superiority which he had assumed,
and showed the curiosity of a mere man. 'Has anybody else been aware
of this?' he said, still wishing to know whether he had cause for anger
against Silverbridge in the matter.

'Mrs Finn is aware of it,' answered Tregear.

'Mrs Finn!' exclaimed the Duke, as though he had been stung by an
adder.

This was the woman whom he had prayed to remain awhile with his
daughter after his wife had been laid in her grave, in order that there
might be someone near whom he could trust! And this very woman
whom he had so trusted,—whom, in his early associations with her,
he had disliked and distrusted, but had taught himself both to like and
to trust because his wife had loved her,—this woman was the she-
Pandarus* who had managed matters between Tregear and his daughter! His wife had been too much subject to her influence. That he had
always known. And now, in this last act of her life, she had allowed
herself to be persuaded to give up her daughter by the baneful wiles of
this most pernicious woman. Such were the workings of the Duke's
mind when the young man told him that Mrs Finn was acquainted
with the whole affair. As the reader is aware, nothing could have been
more unjust.

'I mentioned her name,' said Tregear, 'because I thought she had
been a friend of the family.'

'That will do, sir. I have been greatly pained as well as surprised by
what I have heard. Of the real state of the case I can form no opinion till

I see my daughter. You, of course, will hold no further intercourse with her.' He paused as though for a promise, but Tregear did not feel himself called upon to say a word in one direction or in the other. 'It will be my care that you shall not do so. Good-morning, sir.'*

Tregear, who during the interview had been standing, then bowed, turned upon his heel, and left the room.

The Duke seated himself, and, crossing his arms upon his chest, sat for an hour looking up at the ceiling. Why was it that, for him, such a world of misery had been prepared? What wrong had he done, of what imprudence had he been guilty, that, at every turn of life, something should occur so grievous as to make him think himself the most wretched of men? No man had ever loved his wife more dearly than he had done; and yet now, in that very excess of tenderness which her death had occasioned, he was driven to accuse her of a great sin against himself, in that she had kept from him her knowledge of this affair;— for, when he came to turn the matter over in his mind, he did believe Tregear's statement as to her encouragement. Then, too, he had been proud of his daughter. He was a man so reticent and undemonstrative in his manner that he had never known how to make confidential friends of his children. In his sons hitherto he had not taken pride. They were gallant, well-grown, handsome boys, with a certain dash of cleverness,—more like their mother than their father; but they had not as yet done anything as he would have had them do it. But the girl, in the perfection of her beauty, in the quiescence of her manner, in the nature of her studies, and in the general dignity of her bearing, had seemed to be all that he had desired. And now she had engaged herself, behind his back, to the younger son of a little county squire!

But his anger against Mrs Finn was hotter than his anger against anyone in his own family.

## CHAPTER 6

### MAJOR TIFTO

MAJOR TIFTO had lately become a member of the Beargarden Club,* under the auspices of his friend Lord Silverbridge. It was believed, by those who had made some inquiry into the matter, that the Major had really served a campaign as a volunteer in the Carlist army* in the north of Spain. When, therefore, it was declared by someone that he was not a major at all, his friends were able to contradict the assertion, and to impute it to slander. Instances were brought up,—declared by these friends to be innumerable, but which did, in truth, amount to three or four,—of English gentlemen who had come home from a former Carlist war, bearing the title of colonel, without any contradiction or invidious remark. Had this gallant officer appeared as Colonel Tifto, perhaps less might have been said about it.* There was a little lack of courage in the title which he did choose. But it was accepted at last, and, as Major Tifto, he was proposed, seconded, and elected at the Beargarden.

But he had other points in his favour besides the friendship of Lord Silverbridge,—points which had probably led to that friendship. He was, without doubt, one of the best horsemen in England. There were some who said that, across country, he was the very best, and that, as a judge of a hunter, few excelled him. Of late years he had crept into credit as a betting-man. No one supposed that he had much capital to work with; but still, when he lost a bet he paid it.

Soon after his return from Spain, he was chosen as Master of the Runnymede Fox-Hounds, and was thus enabled to write the letters M.F.H.* after his name. The gentlemen who rode with the Runnymede were not very liberal in their terms, and had lately been compelled to change their Master rather more frequently than was good for that quasi-suburban hunt; but now they had fitted themselves well. How he was to hunt the country five days a fortnight, finding servants and horses, and feeding the hounds, for eight hundred pounds a year, no one could understand.* But Major Tifto not only undertook to do it, but did it. And he actually succeeded in obtaining for the Runnymede a degree of popularity which for many years previous it had not possessed. Such a man,—even though no one did know anything of his father or mother, though no one had ever heard him speak of a brother or a sister, though it was believed that he had no real income,—was felt by many to be the very man for the Beargarden; and when his name was brought up at the committee, Lord Silverbridge was able to say so much in his favour that only two blackballs* were given against him. Under the mild rule of the club, three would have been necessary to exclude him; and therefore Major Tifto was now as good a member as anyone else.

He was a well-made little man, good-looking for those who like such good looks. He was light-haired and blue-eyed, with regular and yet not inexpressive features. But his eyes were small and never tranquil, and rarely capable of looking at the person who was speaking to him. He had small well-trimmed, glossy whiskers, with the best-kept moustache, and the best-kept tuft on his chin which were to be seen anywhere.

His face still bore the freshness of youth, which was a marvel to many, who declared that, from facts within their knowledge, Tifto must be far on the wrong side of forty. At a first glance you would hardly have called him thirty. No doubt, when, on close inspection, you came to look into his eyes, you could see the hand of time. Even if you believed the common assertion that he painted,*—which it was very hard to believe of a man who passed the most of his time in the hunting-field or on a race-course,—yet the paint on his cheeks would not enable him to move with the elasticity which seemed to belong to all his limbs. He rode flat races and steeple chases,*—if jump races may still be so called; and with his own hounds and with the Queen's did incredible things on horseback. He could jump over chairs too,—the backs of four chairs in a dining-room after dinner,—a feat which no gentleman of forty-five could perform, even though he painted himself ever so.

So much in praise of Major Tifto honesty has compelled the present chronicler to say. But there were traits of character in which he fell off a little, even in the estimation of those whose pursuits endeared him to them. He could not refrain from boasting,—and especially from boasting about women. His desire for glory in that direction knew no bounds, and he would sometimes mention names, and bring himself into trouble. It was told of him that at one period of his life, when misfortune had almost overcome him, when sorrow had produced prostration, and prostration some expression of truth, he had owned to a friend his own conviction that could he have kept his tongue from talking of women, he might have risen to prosperity in his profession. From these misfortunes he had emerged, and no doubt, had often reflected on what he himself had then said. But we know that the drunkard, though he hates drunkenness, cannot but drink,—that the gambler cannot keep from the dice. Major Tifto still lied about women, and could not keep his tongue from the subject. He would boast, too, about other matters,— much to his own disadvantage. He was, too, very 'deep',* and some men, who could put up with his other failings, could not endure that. Whatever he wanted to do he would attempt round three corners. Though he could ride straight, he could do nothing else straight. He was full of mysteries. If he wanted to draw Charter Wood he would take his hounds out of the street at Egham* directly in the other direction. If he had made up his mind to ride Lord Pottlepot's horse for the great Leamington handicap,* he would be sure to tell even his intimate friends that he was almost determined to take the 'baronet's' offer of a mount. This he would do even where there was no possible turn in the betting to be affected by such falsehood. So that his companions were apt to complain that there was no knowing where to have Tifto. And then, they who were old enough in the world to have had some experience in men, had perceived that peculiar quality of his eyes, which never allowed him to look anyone in the face.

That Major Tifto should make money by selling horses was, perhaps, a necessity of his position. No one grumbled at him because he did so, or thought that such a pursuit was incompatible with his character as a sporting gentleman. But there were some who considered that they had suffered unduly under his hands, and in their bargains with him had been made to pay more than a proper amount of tax for the advantages of his general assistance. When a man has perhaps made fifty pounds by using a 'straight tip'* as to a horse at Newmarket,* in doing which he had of course encountered some risks, he feels he ought not to be made to pay the amount back into the pockets of the 'tipper,' and at the same time to find himself saddled with the possession of a perfectly useless animal. In this way there were rocks in the course through which Tifto was called on to steer his bark. Of course he was anxious, when preying upon his acquaintances, to spare those who were useful friends to him. Now and again he would sell a serviceable animal at a fair price, and would endeavour to make such sale in favour of someone whose countenance would be a rock to him. He knew his business well, but yet there would be mistakes.

Now, at this very moment, was the culmination of the Major's life. He was Master of the Runnymede Hounds, he was partner with the eldest son of a Duke in the possession of that magnificent colt, the Prime Minister, and he was a member of the Beargarden. He was a man who had often been despondent about himself, but was now disposed to be a little triumphant. He had finished his season well with the Runnymede, and were it not that, let him work as he would, his expenses always exceeded his means, he would have been fairly comfortable.

At eight o'clock Lord Silverbridge and his friend met in the dining-room of the Beargarden. 'Have you been here before?' asked the Lord.

'Not in here, my Lord. I just looked in at the smoking-room last night. Glasslough and Nidderdale were there. I thought we should have got up a rubber,* but they didn't seem to see it.'

'There is whist here generally. You'll find out all about it before long. Perhaps they are a little afraid of you.'

'I'm the worst hand at cards, I suppose, in England. A dash at loo* for about an hour, and half-a-dozen cuts at blind hookey,*—that's about my form. I know I drop more than I pick up. If I knew what I was about I should never touch a card.'

'Horses; eh, Tifto?'

'Horses, yes. They've pretty good claret,* here, eh, Silverbridge?' He could never hit off his familiarity quite right. He had my-Lorded his young friend at first, and now brought out the name with a hesitating twang, which the young nobleman appreciated. But then the young nobleman was quite aware that the Major was a friend for club purposes, and sporting purposes, and not for home use.

'Everything of that kind is pretty good here,' said the Lord.

'You were saying—horses.'

'I dare say you do better with them than with cards.'

'If I didn't I don't know where I should be, seeing what a lot pass through my hands in the year. Anyone of our fellows who has a horse to sell thinks that I am bound to buy him. And I do buy 'em. Last May I had forty-two hunters on my hands.'

'How many of them have you got now?'

'Three. Three of that lot,—though a goodish many have come up since. But what does it amount to? When I have anything that is very good, some fellow that I like gets him from me.'

'After paying for him.'

'After paying for him! Yes; I don't mean that I make a fellow a present. But the man who buys has a deal the best of it. Did you ever get anything better than that spotted chestnut in your life?'

'What, old Sarcinet?'*

'You had her for one hundred and sixty pounds. Now, if you were on your oath, what is she worth?'

'She suits me, Major, and of course I shouldn't sell her.'

'I rather think not. I knew what that mare was, well enough. A dealer would have had three hundred and fifty pounds for her. I could have got the money easily if I had taken her down into the shires, and ridden her a day or two myself.'

'I gave you what you asked.'

'Yes, you did. It isn't often that I take less than I ask. But the fact is, about horses, I don't know whether I shouldn't do better if I never owned an animal at all but those I want for my own use. When I am dealing with a man I call a friend, I can't bear to make money of him. I don't think fellows give me all the credit they should do for sticking to them.'

The Major, as he said this, leaned back in his chair, put his hand up to his moustache, and looked sadly away into the vacancy of the room, as though he was meditating sorrowfully on the ingratitude of the world.

'I suppose it's all right about Cream Cheese?' asked the Lord.

'Well; it ought to be.' And now the Major spoke like an oracle, leaning forward on the table, uttering his words in a low voice, but very plainly, so that not a syllable might be lost. 'When you remember how he ran at the Craven with 9 st. 12 lb. on him, that it took Archbishop all he knew to beat him with only 9 st. 2 lb., and what the lot at Chester* are likely to be, I don't think that there can be seven to one against him. I should be very glad to take it off your hands, only the figures are a little too heavy for me.'

'I suppose Sunflower'll be the best animal there?'

'Not a doubt of it, if he's all right, and if his temper will stand. Think what a course Chester is for an ill-conditioned brute like that! And then he's the most uncertain horse in training. There are times he won't feed. From what I hear, I shouldn't wonder if he don't turn up at all.'

'Solomon* says he's all right.'

'You won't get Solomon to take four to one against him, nor yet four and a half. I suppose you'll go down, my Lord?'

'Well, yes; if there's nothing else doing just then. I don't know how it may be about this electioneering business. I shall go and smoke upstairs.'

At the Beargarden there were,—I was going to say, two smoking-rooms; but in truth the house was a smoking-room all over. It was, however, the custom of those who habitually played cards, to have their cigars and coffee upstairs. Into this sanctum Major Tifto had not yet been introduced, but now he was taken there under Lord Silverbridge's wing. There were already four or five assembled, among whom was Mr Adolphus Longstaff,* a young man of about thirty-five years of age, who spent very much of his time at the Beargarden. 'Do you know my friend Tifto?' said the Lord. 'Tifto, this is Mr Longstaff, whom men within the walls of this asylum sometimes call Dolly.' Whereupon the Major bowed and smiled graciously.

'I have heard of Major Tifto,' said Dolly.

'Who has not?' said Lord Nidderdale,* another middle-aged young man, who made one of the company. Again the Major bowed.

'Last season I was always intending to get down to your country and have a day with the Tiftoes,' said Dolly. 'Don't they call your hounds the Tiftoes?'

'They shall be called so if you like,' said the Major. 'And why didn't you come?'

'It always was such a grind.'

'Train down from Paddington every day at half-past ten.'

'That's all very well if you happen to be up. Well, Silverbridge, how's the Prime Minister?'

'How is he, Tifto?' asked the noble partner.

'I don't think there's a man in England just at present enjoying a very much better state of health,' said the Major pleasantly.

'Safe to run?' asked Dolly.

'Safe to run! Why shouldn't he be safe to run?'

'I mean sure to start.'

'I think we mean him to start, don't we, Silverbridge?' said the Major.

There was something perhaps in the tone in which the last remark was made which jarred a little against the young lord's dignity. At any rate he got up and declared his purpose of going to the opera. He should look in, he said, and hear a song from Mdlle Stuffa.* Mdlle Stuffa was the nightingale of the season, and Lord Silverbridge, when he had nothing else to do, would sometimes think that he was fond of music. Soon after he was gone Major Tifto had some whisky-and-water, lit his third cigar, and began to feel the glory of belonging to the Beargarden. With Lord Silverbridge, to whom it was essentially necessary that he should make himself agreeable at all times, he was somewhat over-weighted as it were.* Though he attempted an easy familiarity, he was a little afraid of Lord Silverbridge. With Dolly Longstaff he felt that he might be comfortable,—not, perhaps, understanding that gentleman's character. With Lord Nidderdale he had previously been acquainted, and had found him to be good-natured. So, as he sipped his whisky, he became confidential and comfortable.

'I never thought so much about her good looks,' he said. They were talking of the singer, the charms of whose voice had carried Lord Silverbridge away.

'Did you ever see her off the stage?' asked Nidderdale.

'Oh dear yes.'

'She does not go about very much, I fancy,' said someone.

'I dare say not,' said Tifto. 'But she and I have had a day or two together, for all that.'

'You must have been very much favoured,' said Dolly.

'We've been pals ever since she has been over here,' said Tifto, with an enormous lie.

'How do you get on with her husband?' asked Dolly,—in the simplest voice, as though not in the least surprised at his companion's statement.

'Husband!' exclaimed the Major; who was not possessed of sufficient presence of mind to suppress all signs of his ignorance.

'Ah,' said Dolly; 'you are not probably aware that your pal has been married to Mr Thomas Jones for the last year and a half.' Soon after that Major Tifto left the club,—with considerably enhanced respect for Mr Longstaff.

## CHAPTER 7

### CONSERVATIVE CONVICTIONS

LORD SILVERBRIDGE had engaged himself to be with his father the next morning at half-past nine, and he entered the breakfast-room a very few minutes after that hour. He had made up his mind as to what he would say to his father. He meant to call himself a Conservative, and to go into the House of Commons under that denomination. All the men among whom he lived were Conservatives. It was a matter on which, as he thought, his father could have no right to control him. Down in Barsetshire, as well as up in London, there was some little difference of opinion in this matter. The people of Silverbridge declared that they would prefer to have a Conservative member, as indeed they had one for the last session.* They had loyally returned the Duke himself while he was a commoner, but they had returned him as being part and parcel of the Omnium appendages. That was all over now. As a constituency they were not endowed with advanced views, and thought that a Conservative would suit them best. That being so, and as they had been told that the Duke's son was a Conservative, they fancied that by electing him they would be pleasing everybody. But, in truth, by so doing they would by no means please the Duke. He had told them on previous occasions that they might elect whom they pleased, and felt no anger because they had elected a Conservative. They might send up to Parliament the most antediluvian old Tory they could find in England if they wished, only not his son, not a Palliser as a Tory or Conservative. And then, though the little town had gone back in the ways of the world, the county, or the Duke's division of the county, had made so much progress, that a Liberal candidate recommended by him would almost certainly be returned. It was just the occasion on which a Palliser should show himself ready to serve his country. There would be an expense, but he would think nothing of expense in such a matter. Ten thousand pounds spent on such an object would not vex him. The very contest would have given him new life. All this Lord Silverbridge understood, but had said to himself and to all his friends that it was a matter in which he did not intend to be controlled.

The Duke had passed a very unhappy night. He had told himself that any such marriage as that spoken of was out of the question. He believed that the matter might be so represented to his girl as to make her feel that it was out of the question. He hardly doubted but that he could stamp it out. Though he should have to take her away into some further corner of the world, he would stamp it out. But she, when this foolish passion of hers should have been thus stamped out, could never be the pure, the bright, the unsullied, unsoiled thing, of the possession of which he had thought so much. He had never spoken of his hopes about her even to his wife, but in the silence of his very silent life he had thought much of the day when he would give her to some noble youth,—noble with all gifts of nobility, including rank and wealth,—who might be fit to receive her. Now, even though no one else should know it,—and all would know it,—she would be the girl who had condescended to love young Tregear.

His own Duchess, she whose loss to him now was as though he had lost half his limbs,—had not she in the same way loved a Tregear, or worse than a Tregear, in her early days? Ah yes! And though his Cora had been so much to him, had he not often felt, had he not been feeling all his days, that Fate had robbed him of the sweetest joy that is given to man, in that she had not come to him loving him with her early spring of love, as she had loved that poor ne'er-do-well? How infinite had been his regrets. How often had he told himself that, with all that Fortune had given him, still Fortune had been unjust to him because he had been robbed of that. Not to save his life could he have whispered a word of this to anyone, but he had felt it. He had felt it for years. Dear as she had been, she had not been quite what she should have been but for that. And now this girl of his, who was so much dearer to him than anything else left to him, was doing exactly as her mother had done. The young man might be stamped out. He might be made to vanish as that other young man had vanished. But the fact that he had been there, cherished in the girl's heart,—that could not be stamped out.

He struggled gallantly to acquit the memory of his wife. He could best do that by leaning with the full weight of his mind on the presumed iniquity of Mrs Finn. Had he not known from the first that the woman was an adventuress? And had he not declared to himself over and over again that between such a one and himself there should be no intercourse, no common feeling? He had allowed himself to be talked into an intimacy, to be talked almost into an affection. And this was the result!

And how should he treat this matter in his coming interview with his son;—or should he make an allusion to it? At first it seemed as though it would be impossible for him to give his mind to that other subject. How could he enforce the merits of political Liberalism,* and the duty of adhering to the old family party, while his mind was entirely pre-occupied with his daughter? It had suddenly become almost indifferent to him whether Silverbridge should be a Conservative or a Liberal. But as he dressed he told himself that, as a man, he ought to be able to do a plain duty, marked out for him as this had been by his own judgment, without regard to personal suffering. The hedger and ditcher must make his hedge and clean his ditch even though he be tormented by rheumatism. His duty by his son he must do, even though his heart were torn to pieces.

During breakfast he tried to be gracious, and condescended to ask his son a question about Prime Minister. Racing was an amusement to which English noblemen had been addicted for many ages, and had been held to be serviceable rather than disgraceful, if conducted in a noble fashion. He did not credit Tifto with much nobility. He knew but little about the Major. He would much have preferred that his son should have owned a horse alone, if he must have anything to do with ownership. 'Would it not be better to buy the other share?' asked the Duke.

'It would take a deal of money, sir. The Major would ask a couple of thousand, I should think.'

'That is a great deal.'

'And then the Major is a very useful man. He thoroughly under-stands the turf.'

'I hope he doesn't live by it?'

'Oh no; he doesn't live by it. That is, he has a great many irons in the fire.'

'I do not mind a young man owning a horse, if he can afford the expense,—as you perhaps can do; but I hope you don't bet.'

'Nothing to speak of.'

'Nothing to speak of is so apt to grow into that which has to be spoken of.' So much the father said at breakfast, hardly giving his mind to the matter discussed,—his mind being on other things. But when their breakfast was eaten, then it was necessary that he should begin.

'Silverbridge,' he said, 'I hope you have thought better of what we were talking about as to these coming elections.'

'Well, sir;—of course I have thought about it.'

'And you can do as I would have you?'

'You see, sir, a man's political opinion is a kind of thing he can't get rid of.'

'You can hardly as yet have any very confirmed political opinion. You are still young, and I do not suppose that you have thought much about politics.'

'Well, sir; I think I have. I've got my own ideas. We've got to protect our position as well as we can against the Radicals and Communists.'*

'I cannot admit that at all, Silverbridge. There is no great political party in this country anxious either for Communism or for revolution. But, putting all that aside for the present, do you think that a man's political opinions should be held in regard to his own individual interests, or to the much wider interests of others, whom we call the public?'

'To his own interest,' said the young man with decision.

'It is simply self-protection then?'

'His own and his class. The people will look after themselves, and we must look after ourselves. We are so few and they are so many, that we shall have quite enough to do.'

Then the Duke gave his son a somewhat lengthy political lecture, which was intended to teach him that the greatest benefit of the greatest number* was the object to which all political studies should tend. The son listened to it with attention, and when it was over, expressed his opinion that there was a great deal in what his father had said. 'I trust, if you will consider it,' said the Duke, 'that you will not find yourself obliged to desert the school of politics in which your father has not been an inactive supporter, and to which your family has belonged for many generations.'

'I could not call myself a Liberal,' said the young politician.

'Why not?'

'Because I am a Conservative.'

'And you won't stand for the county on the Liberal interest?'

'I should be obliged to tell them that I should always give a Conservative vote.'

'Then you refuse to do what I ask?'

'I do not know how I can help refusing. If you wanted me to grow a couple of inches taller I couldn't do it, even though I should be ever so anxious to oblige you.'

'But a very young man, as you are, may have so much deference for his elders as to be induced to believe that he has been in error.'

'Oh yes; of course.'

'You cannot but be aware that the political condition of the country is the one subject to which I have devoted the labour of my life.'

'I know that very well; and, of course, I know how much they all think of you.'

'Then my opinion might go for something with you?'

'So it does, sir; I shouldn't have doubted at all only for that little. Still, you see, as the thing is,—how am I to help myself?'

'You believe that you must be right,—you, who have never given an hour's study to the Subject!'

'No, sir. In comparison with a great many men, I know that I am a fool. Perhaps it is because I know that, that I am a Conservative. The Radicals are always saying that a Conservative must be a fool. Then a fool ought to be a Conservative.'

Hereupon the father got up from his chair and turned round, facing the fire, with his back to his son. He was becoming very angry, but endeavoured to restrain his anger. The matter in dispute between them was of so great importance, that he could hardly be justified in abandoning it in consequence of arguments so trifling in themselves as these which his son adduced. As he stood there for some minutes thinking of it all, he was tempted again and again to burst out in wrath and threaten the lad,—to threaten him as to money, as to his amusements, as to the general tenure of his life. The pity was so great that the lad should be so stubborn and so foolish! He would never ask his son to be a slave to the Liberal party, as he had been. But that a Palliser should not be a Liberal,—and his son, as the first recreant Palliser,—was wormwood to him! As he stood there he more than once clenched his fist in eager desire to turn upon the young man; but he restrained himself, telling himself that in justice he should not be angry for such offence as this. To become a Conservative, when the path to Liberalism was so fairly open, might be the part of a fool, but could not fairly be imputed as a crime. To endeavour to be just was the study of his life,* and in no condition of life can justice be more imperatively due than from a father to his son.

'You mean to stand for Silverbridge?' he said at last.

'Not if you object, sir.'

This made it worse. It became now still more difficult for him to scold the young man.

'You are aware that I should not meddle in any way.'

'That was what I supposed. They will return a Conservative at any rate.'

'It is not that I care about,' said the Duke sadly.

'Upon my word, sir, I am very sorry to vex you; but what would you have me do? I will give up Parliament altogether, if you say that you wish it.'

'No; I do not wish that.'

'You wouldn't have me tell a lie?'

'No.'

'What can I do then?'

'Learn what there is to learn from some master fit to teach you.'

'There are so many masters.'

'I believe it to be that most arrogant ill-behaved young man who was with me yesterday who has done this evil.'

'You mean Frank Tregear?'

'I do mean Mr Tregear.'

'He's a Conservative, of course; and of course he and I have been much together. Was he with you yesterday, sir?'

'Yes, he was.'

'What was that about?' asked Lord Silverbridge, in a voice that almost betrayed fear, for he knew very well what cause had produced the interview.

'He has been speaking to me——' When the Duke had got so far as this he paused, finding himself to be hardly able to declare the disgrace which had fallen upon himself and his family. As he did tell the story, both his face and his voice were altered, so that the son, in truth, was scared. 'He has been speaking to me about your sister. Did you know of this?'

'I knew there was something between them.'

'And you encouraged it?'

'No, sir; just the contrary. I have told him that I was quite sure it would never do.'

'And why did you not tell me?'

'Well, sir; that was hardly my business, was it?'

'Not to guard the honour of your sister?'

'You see, sir, how many things have happened all at once.'

'What things?'

'My dear mother, sir, thought well of him.' The Duke uttered a deep sigh and turned again round to the fire. 'I always told him that you would never consent.'

'I should think not.'

'It has come so suddenly. I should have spoken to you about it as soon as——as soon as——' He had meant to say as soon as the husband's grief for the loss of his wife had been in some degree appeased, but he could not speak the words. The Duke, however, perfectly understood him. 'In the meantime, they were not seeing each other.'

'Nor writing?'

'I think not.'

'Mrs Finn has known it all.'

'Mrs Finn!'

'Certainly. She has known it all through.'

'I do not see how it can have been so.'

'He told me so himself,' said the Duke, unwittingly putting words into Tregear's mouth which Tregear had never uttered. 'There must be an end of this. I will speak to your sister. In the meantime, the less, I think, you see of Mr Tregear the better. Of course it is out of the question he should be allowed to remain in this house. You will make him understand that at once, if you please.'

'Oh, certainly,' said Silverbridge.

## CHAPTER 8

### 'HE IS A GENTLEMAN'

THE Duke returned to Matching an almost broken-hearted man. He had intended to go down into Barsetshire, in reference to the coming elections;—not with the view of interfering in any unlordly, or rather unpeerlike fashion,* but thinking that if his eldest son were to stand for the county in a proper constitutional spirit, as the eldest son of so great a county magnate ought to do, his presence at Gatherum Castle,* among his own people, might probably be serviceable, and would certainly be gracious. There would be no question of entertainment. His bereavement would make that impossible. But there would come from his presence a certain savour of proprietorship, and a sense of power, which would be beneficial to his son, and would not, as the Duke thought, be contrary to the spirit of the constitution.* But all this was now at an end. He told himself that he did not care how the elections might go;—that he did not care much how anything might go. Silverbridge might stand for Silverbridge if he so pleased. He would give neither assistance nor obstruction, either in the county or in the borough. He wrote to this effect to his agent, Mr Morton;—but at the same time desired that gentleman to pay Lord Silverbridge's electioneering expenses, feeling it to be his duty as a father to do so much for his son.

But though he endeavoured to engage his thoughts in these parliamentary matters, though he tried to make himself believe that this political apostasy was the trouble which vexed him, in truth that other misery was so crushing, as to make the affairs of his son insignificant. How should he express himself to her? That was the thought present to his mind as he went down to Matching. Should he content himself with simply telling her that such a wish on her part was disgraceful, and that it could never be fulfilled; or should he argue the matter with her, endeavouring as he did so to persuade her gently that she was wrong to place her affections so low, and so to obtain from her an assurance that the idea should be abandoned?

The latter course would be infinitely the better,—if only he could accomplish it. But he was conscious of his own hardness of manner, and was aware that he had never succeeded in establishing confidence between himself and his daughter. It was a thing for which he had longed,—as a plain girl might long to possess the charms of an acknowledged beauty;—as a poor little fellow, five feet in height, might long to have a cubit* added to his stature.

Though he was angry with her, how willingly would he take her into his arms and assure her of his forgiveness! How anxious he would be to make her understand that nothing should be spared by him to add beauty and grace to her life! Only, as a matter of course, Mr Tregear must be abandoned. But he knew of himself that he would not know how to begin to be tender and forgiving. He knew that he would not know how not to be stern and hard.

But he must find out the history of it all. No doubt the man had been his son's friend, and had joined his party in Italy at his son's instance. But yet he had come to entertain an idea that Mrs Finn had been the great promoter of the sin, and he thought that Tregear had told him that that lady had been concerned with the matter from the beginning. In all this there was a craving in his heart to lessen the amount of culpable responsibility which might seem to attach itself to the wife he had lost.

He reached Matching about eight, and ordered his dinner to be brought to him in his own study. When Lady Mary came to welcome him, he kissed her forehead and bade her come to him after his dinner. 'Shall I not sit with you, papa, whilst you are eating it?' she asked; but he merely told her that he would not trouble her to do that. Even in saying this he was so unusually tender to her that she assured herself that her lover had not as yet told his tale.

The Duke's meals were not generally feasts for a Lucullus.* No man living, perhaps, cared less what he ate, or knew less what he drank. In such matters he took what was provided for him, making his dinner off the first bit of meat that was brought, and simply ignoring anything offered to him afterwards. And he would drink what wine the servant gave him, mixing it, whatever it might be, with seltzer water.* He had never been much given to the pleasures of the table; but this habit of simplicity had grown on him of late, till the Duchess used to tell him that his wants were so few that it was a pity he was not a hermit, vowed to poverty.

Very shortly a message was brought to Lady Mary, saying that her father wished to see her. She went at once, and found him seated on a sofa, which stood close along the bookshelves on one side of the room. The table had already been cleared, and he was alone. He not only was alone, but had not even a pamphlet or newspaper in his hand.

Then she knew that Tregear must have told the story. As this occurred to her, her legs almost gave way under her. 'Come and sit down, Mary,' he said, pointing to the seat on the sofa beside himself.

She sat down and took one of his hands within her own. Then, as he did not begin at once, she asked a question. 'Will Silverbridge stand for the county, papa?'

'No, my dear.'

'But for the town?'

'Yes, my dear.'

'And he won't be a Liberal?'

'I am afraid not. It is a cause of great unhappiness to me; but I do not know that I should be justified in any absolute opposition. A man is entitled to his own opinion, even though he be a very young man.'

'I am so sorry that it should be so, papa, because it vexes you.'

'I have many things to vex me;—things to break my heart.'

'Poor mamma!' she exclaimed.

'Yes; that above all others. But life and death are in God's hands, and even though we may complain we can alter nothing. But whatever our sorrows are while we are here, we must do our duty.'

'I suppose he may be a good Member of Parliament, though he has turned Conservative.'

'I am not thinking about your brother. I am thinking about you.' The poor girl gave a little start on the sofa. 'Do you know— Mr Tregear?' he added.

'Yes, papa; of course I know him. You used to see him in Italy.'

'I believe I did; I understand that he was there as a friend of Silverbridge.'

'His most intimate friend, papa.'

'I dare say. He came to me, in London yesterday, and told me——! Oh Mary, can it be true?'

'Yes, papa,' she said, covered up to her forehead with blushes, and with her eyes turned down. In the ordinary affairs of life she was a girl of great courage, who was not given to be shaken from her constancy by the pressure of any present difficulty; but now the terror inspired by her father's voice almost overpowered her.

'Do you mean to tell me that you have engaged yourself to that young man without my approval?'

'Of course you were to have been asked, papa.'

'Is that in accordance with your idea of what should be the conduct of a young lady in your position?'

'Nobody meant to conceal anything from you, papa.'

'It has been so far concealed. And yet this young man has the self-confidence to come to me and to demand your hand as though it were a matter of course that I should accede to so trivial a request. It is, as a matter of course, quite impossible. You understand that; do you not?' When she did not answer him at once, he repeated the question. 'I ask you whether you do not feel that it is altogether impossible?'

'No, papa,' she said, in the lowest possible whisper, but still in such a whisper that he could hear the word, and with so much clearness that he could judge from her voice of the obstinacy of her mind.

'Then, Mary, it becomes my duty to tell you that it is quite impossible. I will not have it thought of. There must be an end of it.'

'Why, papa?'

'Why! I am astonished that you should ask me why.'

'I should not have allowed him, papa, to go to you unless I had,—unless I had loved him.'

'Then you must conquer your love. It is disgraceful and must be conquered.'

'Disgraceful!'

'Yes. I am sorry to use such a word to my own child, but it is so. If you will promise to be guided by me in this matter, if you will undertake not to see him any more, I will,—if not forget it,—at any rate pardon it, and be silent. I will excuse it because you were young, and were thrown imprudently in his way. There has, I believe, been someone at work in the matter with whom I ought to be more angry than with you. Say that you will obey me, and there is nothing within a father's power that I will not do for you, to make your life happy.' It was thus that he strove not to be stern. His heart, indeed, was tender enough, but there was nothing tender in the tone of his voice or in the glance of his eye. Though he was very positive in what he said, yet he was shy and shamefaced even with his own daughter. He, too, had blushed when he told her that she must conquer her love.

That she should be told that she had disgraced herself was terrible to her. That her father should speak of her marriage with this man as an event that was impossible made her very unhappy. That he should talk of pardoning her, as for some great fault, was in itself a misery. But she had not on that account the least idea of giving up her lover. Young as she was, she had her own peculiar theory on that matter, her own code of conduct and honour, from which she did not mean to be driven. Of course she had not expected that her father would yield at the first word. He, no doubt, would wish that she should make a more exalted marriage. She had known that she would have to encounter opposition, though she had not expected to be told that she had disgraced herself. As she sat there she resolved that under no pretence would she give up her lover;—but she was so far abashed that she could not find words to express herself. He, too, had been silent for a few moments before he again asked her for her promise.

'Will you tell me, Mary, that you will not see him again?'

'I don't think that I can say that, papa.'

'Why not?'

'Oh papa, how can I, when of all the people in the world I love him the best?'

It is not without a pang that anyone can be told that she who is of all the dearest has some other one who to her is the dearest. Such pain fathers and mothers have to bear; and though, I think, the arrow is never so blunted but that it leaves something of a wound behind, there is in most cases, if not a perfect salve, still an ample consolation. The mother knows that it is good that her child should love some man better than all the world beside, and that she should be taken away to become a wife and a mother. And the father, when that delight of his eyes ceases to assure him that he is her nearest and dearest, though he abandon the treasure of that nearestness and dearestness with a soft melancholy, still knows that it is as it should be. Of course that other 'him' is the person she loves the best in the world. Were it not so how evil a thing it would be that she should marry him! Were it not so with reference to some 'him', how void would her life be! But now, to the poor Duke the wound had no salve, no consolation. When he was told that this young Tregear was the owner of his girl's sweet love, was the treasure of her heart, he shrank as though arrows with sharp points were pricking him all over. 'I will not hear of such love,' he said.

'What am I to say, papa?'

'Say that you will obey me.'

Then she sat silent. 'Do you not know that he is not fit to be your husband?'

'No, papa.'

'Then you cannot have thought much either of your position or of mine.'

'He is a gentleman, papa.'

'So is my private secretary. There is not a clerk in one of our public offices who does not consider himself to be a gentleman. The curate of the parish is a gentleman, and the medical man who comes here from Bradstock. The word is too vague to carry with it any meaning that ought to be serviceable to you in thinking of such a matter.'

'I do not know any other way of dividing people,' said she, showing thereby that she had altogether made up her mind as to what ought to be serviceable to her.

'You are not called upon to divide people. That division requires so much experience that you are bound in this matter to rely upon those to whom your obedience is due. I cannot but think you must have known that you were not entitled to give your love to any man without being assured that the man would be approved of by—by—by me.' He was going to say, 'your parents,' but was stopped by the remembrance of his wife's imprudence.

She saw it all, and was too noble to plead her mother's authority. But she was not too dutiful to cast a reproach upon him, when he was so stern to her. 'You have been so little with me, papa.'

'That is true,' he said, after a pause. 'That is true. It has been a fault, and I will mend it. It is a reason for forgiveness, and I will forgive you. But you must tell me that there shall be an end to this.'

'No, papa.'

'What do you mean?'

'That as I love Mr Tregear, and as I have told him so, and as I have promised him, I will be true to him. I cannot let there be an end to it.'

'You do not suppose that you will be allowed to see him again?'

'I hope so.'

'Most assuredly not. Do you write to him?'

'No, papa.'

'Never?'

'Never since we have been back in England.'

'You must promise me that you will not write.'

She paused a moment before she answered him, and now she was looking him full in the face. 'I shall not write to him. I do not think I shall write to him; but I will not promise.'

'Not promise me,—your father!'

'No, papa. It might be that—that I should do it.'

'You would not wish me so to guard you that you should have no power of sending a letter but by permission?'

'I should not like that.'

'But it will have to be so.'

'If I do write I will tell you.'

'And show me what you write?'

'No, papa; not that; but I will tell you what I have written.'

Then it occurred to him that this bargaining was altogether derogatory to his parental authority, and by no means likely to impress upon her mind the conviction that Tregear must be completely banished from her thoughts. He began already to find how difficult it would be for him to have the charge of such a daughter,—how impossible that he should conduct such a charge with sufficient firmness, and yet with sufficient tenderness! At present he had done no good. He had only been made more wretched than ever by her obstinacy. Surely he must pass her over to the charge of some lady,—but of some lady who would be as determined as was he himself that she should not throw herself away by marrying Mr Tregear.

'There shall be no writing,' he said, 'no visiting, no communication of any kind. As you refuse to obey me now, you had better go to your room.'

## CHAPTER 9

### 'IN MEDIAS RES'*

PERHAPS the method of rushing at once 'in medias res' is, of all the ways of beginning a story, or a separate branch of a story, the least objectionable. The reader is made to think that the gold lies so near the surface that he will be required to take very little trouble in digging for it.* And the writer is enabled,—at any rate for a time, and till his neck has become, as it were, warm to the collar,—to throw off from him the difficulties and dangers, the tedium and prolixity, of description. This rushing 'in medias res' has doubtless the charm of ease. 'Certainly, when I threw her from the garret window to the stony pavement below, I did not anticipate that she would fall so far without injury to life or limb.' When a story has been begun after this fashion, without any prelude, without description of the garret or of the pavement, or of the lady thrown, or of the speaker, a great amount of trouble seems to have been saved. The mind of the reader fills up the blanks,—if erroneously, still satisfactorily. He knows, at least, that the heroine has encountered a terrible danger, and has escaped from it with almost incredible good fortune; that the demon of the piece is a bold demon, not ashamed to speak of his own iniquity, and that the heroine and the demon are so far united that they have been in a garret together. But there is the drawback on the system,—that it is almost impossible to avoid the necessity of doing, sooner or later, that which would naturally be done at first. It answers, perhaps, for half-a-dozen chapters;—and to carry the reader pleasantly for half-a-dozen chapters is a great matter!—but after that a certain nebulous darkness gradually seems to envelope the characters and the incidents. 'Is all this going on in the country, or is it in town,—or perhaps in the Colonies? How old was she? Was she tall? Is she fair? Is she heroine-like in her form and gait? And, after all, how high was the garret window?' I have always found that the details would insist on being told at last, and that by rushing 'in medias res' I was simply presenting the cart before the horse. But as readers like the cart the best, I will do it once again,—trying it only for a branch of my story,—and will endeavour to let as little as possible of the horse be seen afterwards.

'And so poor Frank has been turned out of heaven?' said Lady Mabel Grex to young Lord Silverbridge.

'Who told you that? I have said nothing about it to anybody.'

'Of course he told me himself,' said the young beauty. I am aware that, in the word beauty, and perhaps, also, in the word young, a little bit of the horse is appearing; and I am already sure that I shall have to show his head and neck, even if not his very tail. 'Poor Frank! Did you hear it all?'

'I heard nothing, Lady Mab, and know nothing.'

'You know that your awful governor won't let him stay any longer in Carlton Terrace?'

'Yes, I know that.'

'And why not?'

'Would Lord Grex allow Percival to have his friends living here?'
Earl Grex was Lady Mabel's father, Lord Percival was the Earl's
son;—and the Earl lived in Belgrave Square.* All these are little bits of
the horse.

'Certainly not. In the first place, I am here.'

'That makes a difference, certainly.'

'Of course it makes a difference. They would be wanting to make
love to me.'

'No doubt. I should, I know.'

'And therefore it wouldn't do for you to live here; and then papa is
living here himself. And then the permission never has been given. I
suppose Frank did not go there at first without the Duke knowing it.'

'I dare say that I had mentioned it.'

'You might as well tell me all about it. We are cousins, you know.'
Frank Tregear, through his mother's family, was second cousin to
Lady Mabel; as was also Lord Silverbridge, one of the Grexes having,
at some remote period, married a Palliser. This is another bit of the
horse.

'The governor merely seemed to think that he would like to have his
own house to himself—like other people. What an ass Tregear was to
say anything to you about it.'

'I don't think he was an ass at all. Of course he had to tell us that
he was changing his residence. He says that he is going to take a back
bedroom somewhere near the Seven Dials.'*

'He has got very nice rooms in Duke Street.'

'Have you seen him, then?'

'Of course I have.'

'Poor fellow! I wish he had a little money; he is so nice. And now,
Lord Silverbridge, do you mean to say that there is not something in
the wind about Lady Mary?'

'If there were I should not talk about it,' said Lord Silverbridge.

'You are a very innocent young gentleman.'

'And you are a very interesting young lady.'

'You ought to think me so, for I interest myself very much about you.
Was the Duke very angry about your not standing for the county?'

'He was vexed.'

'I do think it is so odd that a man should be expected to be this or
that in politics because his father happened to be so before him! I don't
understand how he should expect that you should remain with a party
so utterly snobbish and down in the world as the Radicals. Everybody
that is worth anything is leaving them.'

'He has not left them.'

'No, I don't suppose he could; but you have.'

'I never belonged to them, Lady Mab.'

'And never will, I hope. I always told papa that you would certainly be one of us.' All this took place in the drawing-room of Lord Grex's house. There was no Lady Grex alive, but there lived with the Earl a certain elderly lady; reported to be in some distant way a cousin of the family, named Miss Casseway,* who, in the matter of looking after Lady Mab, did what was supposed to be absolutely necessary. She now entered the room with her bonnet on, having just returned from church. 'What was the text?'* asked Lady Mab at once.

'If you had gone to church, as you ought to have done, my dear, you would have heard it.'

'But as I didn't?'

'I don't think the text alone will do you any good.'

'And probably you forget it.'

'No, I don't, my dear. How do you do, Lord Silverbridge?'

'He is a Conservative, Miss Cass.'

'Of course he is. I am quite sure that a young nobleman of so much taste and intellect would take the better side.'

'You forget that all you are saying is against my father and my family, Miss Cassewary.'

'I dare say it was different when your father was a young man. And your father, too, was, not very long since, at the head of a government which contained many Conservatives.* I don't look upon your father as a Radical, though perhaps I should not be justified in calling him a Conservative.'

'Well; certainly not, I think.'

'But now it is necessary that all noblemen in England should rally to the defence of their order.' Miss Cassewary was a great politician, and was one of those who are always foreseeing the ruin of their country. 'My dear, I will go and take my bonnet off. Perhaps you will have tea when I come down.'

'Don't you go,' said Lady Mabel, when Silverbridge got up to take his departure.

'I always do when tea comes.'

'But you are going to dine here?'

'Not that I know of. In the first place, nobody has asked me. In the second place, I am engaged. Thirdly, I don't care about having to talk politics to Miss Cass; and fourthly, I hate family dinners on Sunday.'

'In the first place, I ask you. Secondly, I know you were going to dine with Frank Tregear, at the club. Thirdly, I want you to talk to me, and not to Miss Cass. And fourthly, you are an uncivil young—young,— young,—I should say cub if I dared, to tell me that you don't like dining with me any day of the week.'

'Of course you know what I mean is, that I don't like troubling your father.'

'Leave that to me. I shall tell him you are coming, and Frank too. Of course you can bring him. Then he can talk to me when papa goes down to his club, and you can arrange your politics with Miss Cass.' So it was settled, and at eight o'clock Lord Silverbridge reappeared in Belgrave Square with Frank Tregear.

Earl Grex was a nobleman of very ancient family, the Grexes having held the parish of Grex, in Yorkshire,* from some time long prior to the Conquest. In saying all this, I am, I know, allowing the horse to appear wholesale;—but I find that he cannot be kept out. I may as well go on to say that the present Earl was better known at Newmarket and the Beaufort,*—where he spent a large part of his life in playing whist,—than in the House of Lords. He was a grey-haired, handsome, worn-out old man, who through a long life of pleasure had greatly impaired a fortune which, for an earl, had never been magnificent, and who now strove hard, but not always successfully, to remedy that evil by gambling. As he could no longer eat and drink as he had used to do, and as he cared no longer for the light that lies in a lady's eye,* there was not much left to him in the world but cards and racing. Nevertheless he was a handsome old man, of polished manners, when he chose to use them; a staunch Conservative and much regarded by his party, for whom in his early life he had done some work in the House of Commons.

'Silverbridge is all very well,' he had said; 'but I don't see why that young Tregear is to dine here every night of his life.'

'This is the second time since he has been up in town, papa.'

'He was here last week, I know.'

'Silverbridge wouldn't come without him.'

'That's d—— nonsense,' said the Earl. Miss Cassewary gave a start,—not, we may presume, because she was shocked, for she could not be much shocked, having heard the same word from the same lips very often; but she thought it right always to enter a protest. Then the two young men were announced.

Frank Tregear, having been known by the family as a boy, was Frank to all of them,—as was Lady Mabel, Mabel to him, somewhat to the disgust of the father and not altogether with the approbation of

Miss Cass. But Lady Mabel had declared that she would not be guilty of the folly of changing old habits. Silverbridge, being Silverbridge to all his own people, hardly seemed to have a Christian name;—his godfathers and godmothers had indeed called him Plantagenet;—but having only become acquainted with the family since his Oxford days he was Lord Silverbridge to Lady Mabel. Lady Mabel had not as yet become Mabel to him, but, as by her very intimate friends she was called Mab, had allowed herself to be addressed by him as Lady Mab. There was thus between them all considerable intimacy.

'I'm deuced glad to hear it,' said the Earl when dinner was announced. For, though he could not eat much, Lord Grex was always impatient when the time of eating was at hand.* Then he walked down alone. Lord Silverbridge followed with his daughter, and Frank Tregear gave his arm to Miss Cassewary. 'If that woman can't clear her soup better than that, she might as well go to the d——,' said the Earl;—upon which remark no one in the company made any observation. As there were two men-servants in the room when it was made the cook probably had the advantage of it. It may be almost unnecessary to add that though the Earl had polished manners for certain occasions he would sometimes throw them off in the bosom of his own family.

'My Lord,' said Miss Cassewary—she always called him 'My Lord'—'Lord Silverbridge is going to stand for the Duke's borough in the Conservative interest.'

'I didn't know the Duke had a borough,' said the Earl.

'He had one till he thought it proper to give it up,'* said the son, taking his father's part.

'And you are going to pay him off for what he has done by standing against him. It's just the sort of thing for a son to do in these days. If I had a borough Percival would go down and make radical speeches there.'

'There isn't a better Conservative in England than Percival,' said Lady Mabel, bridling up.

'Nor a worse son,' said the father. 'I believe he would do anything he could lay his hand on to oppose me.' During the past week there had been some little difference of opinion between the father and the son as to the signing of a deed.

'My father does not take it in bad part at all,' said Silverbridge.

'Perhaps he's ratting himself,'* said the Earl. 'When a man lends himself to a coalition he is as good as half gone.'

'I do not think that in all England there is so thorough a Liberal as my father,' said Lord Silverbridge. 'And when I say that he doesn't take this badly, I don't mean that it doesn't vex him. I know it vexes him. But he doesn't quarrel with me. He even wrote down to Barsetshire to say that all my expenses at Silverbridge were to be paid.'

'I call that very bad politics,' said the Earl.

'It seems to me to be very grand,' said Frank.

'Perhaps, sir, you don't know what is good or what is bad in politics,' said the Earl, trying to snub his guest.

But it was difficult to snub Frank. 'I know a gentleman when I see him, I think,' he said. 'Of course Silverbridge is right to be a Conservative. Nobody has a stronger opinion about that than I have. But the Duke is behaving so well that if I were he I should almost regret it.'

'And so I do,' said Silverbridge.

When the ladies were gone the old Earl turned himself round to the fire, having filled his glass and pushed the bottles away from him, as though he meant to leave the two young men to themselves. He sat leaning with his head on his hand, looking the picture of woe. It was now only nine o'clock, and there would be no whist at the Beaufort till eleven. There was still more than an hour to be endured before the brougham* would come to fetch him. 'I suppose we shall have a majority,' said Frank, trying to rouse him.

'Who does "We" mean?' asked the Earl.

'The Conservatives, of whom I take the liberty to call myself one.'

'It sounded as though you were a very influential member of the party.'

'I consider myself to be one of the party, and so I say "We."''

Upstairs in the drawing-room Miss Casseary did her duty loyally. It was quite right that young ladies and young gentlemen should be allowed to talk together, and very right indeed that such a young gentleman as Lord Silverbridge should be allowed to talk to such a young lady as Lady Mabel. What could be so nice as a marriage between the heir of the house of Omnium and Lady Mabel Grex? Lady Mabel looked indeed to be the elder,—but they were in truth the same age. All the world acknowledged that Lady Mabel was very clever and very beautiful and fit to be a Duchess. Even the Earl, when Miss Casseary hinted at the matter to him, grunted an assent. Lady Mabel had already refused one or two not ineligible offers, and it was necessary that something should be done. There had been at one time a fear in Miss Casseary's bosom lest her charge should fall too deeply in love with Frank Tregear;—but Miss Casseary knew that whatever danger there might have been in that respect had passed away. Frank was willing to talk to her, while Mabel and Lord Silverbridge were in a corner together.

'I shall be on tenterhooks now till I know how it is to be at Silverbridge,' said the young lady.

'It is very good of you to feel so much interest.'

'Of course I feel an interest. Are not you one of us? When is it to be?'

'They say that the elections will be over before the Derby.'

'And which do you care for the most?'

'I should like to pull off the Derby, I own.'

'From what papa says, I should think the other event is the more probable.'

'Doesn't the Earl stand to win on Prime Minister?'

'I never know anything about his betting. But,—you know his way,—he said you were going to drop a lot of money like a—— I can't quite tell you what he likened you to.'

'The Earl may be mistaken.'

'You are not betting much, I hope.'

'Not plunging. But I have a little money on.'

'Don't get into a way of betting.'

'Why:—what difference does it make,—to you?'

'Is that kind, Lord Silverbridge?'

'I meant to say that if I did make a mess of it you wouldn't care about it.'

'Yes, I should. I should care very much. I dare say you could lose a great deal of money and care nothing about it.'

'Indeed I could not.'

'What would be a great deal of money to me? But you would want to get it back again. And in that way you would be regularly on the turf.'

'And why not?'

'I want to see better things from you.'

'You ought not to preach against the turf, Lady Mab.'

'Because of papa? But I am not preaching against the turf. If I were such as you are I would have a horse or two myself. A man in your position should do a little of everything. You should hunt and have a yacht, and stalk deer and keep your own trainer at Newmarket.'

'I wish you'd say all that to my father.'

'Of course I mean if you can afford it. I like a man to like pleasure. But I despise a man who makes a business of his pleasures. When I hear that this man is the best whist-player in London, and that man the best billiard-player, I always know that they can do nothing else, and then I despise them.'

'You needn't despise me, because I do nothing well,' said he, as he got up to take his leave.

'I do so hope you'll get the seat,—and win the Derby.'

These were her last words to him as she wished him good-night.

## CHAPTER 10

### 'WHY NOT LIKE ROMEO IF I FEEL LIKE ROMEO?'

THAT'S nonsense, Miss Cass, and I shall,' said Lady Mabel.* They were together, on the morning after the little dinner-party described in the last chapter, in a small back sitting-room which was supposed to be Lady Mabel's own, and the servant had just announced the fact that Mr Tregear was below.

'Then I shall go down too,' said Miss Casseway.

'You'll do nothing of the kind. Will you please to tell me what it is you are afraid of? Do you think that Frank is going to make love to me again?'

'No.'

'Or that if I chose that he should I would let you stop me? He is in love with somebody else,—and perhaps I am too. And we are two paupers.'

'My lord would not approve of it.'

'If you know what my lord approves of and what he disapproves you understand him a great deal better than I do. And if you mind what he approves or disapproves, you care for his opinion a great deal more than I do. My cousin is here now to talk to me,—about his own affairs, and I mean to see him,—alone.' Then she left the little room, and went down to that in which Frank was waiting for her, without the company of Miss Casseway.

'Do you really mean,' she said after they had been together for some minutes, 'that you had the courage to ask the Duke for his daughter's hand?'

'Why not?'

'I believe you would dare do anything.'

'I couldn't very well take it without asking him.'

'As I am not acquainted with the young lady I don't know how that might be.'

'And if I took her so, I should have to take her empty-handed.'

'Which wouldn't suit;—would it?'

'It wouldn't suit for her,—whose comforts and happiness are much more to me than my own.'

'No doubt! Of course you are terribly in love.'

'Very thoroughly in love, I think, I am.'

'For the tenth time, I should say.'

'For the second only. I don't regard myself as a monument of constancy, but I think I am less fickle than some other people.'

'Meaning me!'

'Not especially.'

'Frank, that is ill-natured, and almost unmanly,—and false also. When have I been fickle? You say that there was one before with you. I say that there has never really been one with me at all. No one knows that better than yourself. I cannot afford to be in love till I am quite sure that the man is fit to be, and will be, my husband.'

'I doubt sometimes whether you are capable of being in love with anyone.'

'I think I am,' she said very gently. 'But I am at any rate capable of not being in love till I wish it. Come, Frank; do not quarrel with me. You know,—you ought to know,—that I should have loved you had it not been that such love would have been bad for both of us.'

'It is a kind of self-restraint I do not understand.'

'Because you are not a woman.'

'Why did you twit* me with changing my love?'

'Because I am a woman. Can't you forgive as much as that to me?'

'Certainly. Only you must not think that I have been false because I now love her so dearly.'

'I do not think you are false. I would do anything to help you if there were anything I could do. But when you spoke so like a Romeo of your love——'

'Why not like a Romeo, if I feel like a Romeo?'

'But I doubt whether Romeo talked much to Rosaline of his love for Juliet.* But you shall talk to me of yours for Lady Mary, and I will listen to you patiently and encourage you, and will not even think of those former vows.'

'The former vows were foolish.'

'Oh,—of course.'

'You at least used to say so.'

'I say so now, and they shall be as though they had been never spoken. So you bearded the Duke in his den, and asked him for Lady Mary's hand,—just as though you had been a young Duke yourself and owned half a county?'

'Just the same.'

'And what did he say?'

'He swore that it was impossible.—Of course I knew all that before.'

'How will it be now? You will not give it up?'

'Certainly not.'

'And Lady Mary?'

'One human being can perhaps never answer for another with perfect security.'

'But you feel sure of her?'

'I do.'*

'He, I should think, can be very imperious.'

'And so can she. The Pallisers are all obstinate.'

'Is Silverbridge obstinate?' she asked.

'Stiff-necked as a bull if he takes it into his head to be so.'

'I shouldn't have thought it.'

'No;—because he is so soft in his manner, and often finds it easier to be led by others than to direct himself.'

Then she remained silent for a few seconds. They were both thinking of the same thing, and both wishing to speak of it. But the words came to her first. 'I wonder what he thinks of me.' Whereupon Tregear only smiled. 'I suppose he has spoken to you about me?'

'Why do you ask?'

'Why!'

'And why should I tell you? Suppose he should have said to me in the confidence of friendship that he thinks you ugly and stupid.'

'I am sure he has not said that. He has eyes to see and ears to hear. But, though I am neither ugly nor stupid, he needn't like me.'

'Do you want him to like you?'

'Yes, I do. Oh yes; you may laugh; but if I did not think that I could be a good wife to him I would not take his hand even to become Duchess of Omnium.'

'Do you mean that you love him, Mabel?'

'No; I do not mean that. But I would learn to love him. You do not believe that?' Here he smiled again and shook his head. 'It is as I said before, because you are not a woman, and do not understand how women are trammelled. Do you think ill of me because I say this?'

'No, indeed.'

'Do not think ill of me if you can help it, because you are almost the only friend that I can trust. I almost trust dear old Cass, but not quite. She is old-fashioned and I shock her. As for other women, there isn't one anywhere to whom I would say a word. Only think how a girl such as I am is placed; or indeed any girl. You, if you see a woman that you fancy, can pursue her, can win her and triumph, or lose her and gnaw your heart;—at any rate you can do something. You can tell her that you love her; can tell her so again and again even though she should scorn you. You can set yourself about the business you have taken in hand and can work hard at it. What can a girl do?'

'Girls work hard too sometimes.'

'Of course they do;—but everybody feels that they are sinning against their sex. Of love, such as a man's is, a woman ought to know nothing. How can she love with passion when she should never give her love till it has been asked, and not then unless her friends tell her that the thing is suitable? Love such as that to me is out of the question. But, as it is fit that I should be married, I wish to be married well.'

'And you will love him after a fashion?'

'Yes;—after a very sterling fashion. I will make his wishes my wishes, his ways my ways, his party my party, his home my home, his ambition my ambition,—his honour my honour.' As she said this she stood up with her hands clenched and head erect, and her eyes flashing. 'Do you not know me well enough to be sure that I should be loyal to him?'

'Yes;—I think that you would be loyal.'

'Whether I loved him or not, he should love me.'

'And you think that Silverbridge would do?'

'Yes, I think that Silverbridge would do. You, no doubt, will say that I am flying high?'

'Not too high. Why should you not fly high? If I can justify myself, surely I cannot accuse you.'

'It is hardly the same thing, Frank. Of course, there is not a girl in London to whom Lord Silverbridge would not be the best match that she could make. He has the choice of us all.'

'Most girls would think twice before refusing him.'

'Very few would think twice before accepting him. Perhaps he wishes to add to his wealth by marrying richly,—as his father did.'

'No thought on that subject will ever trouble him. That will be all as it happens. As soon as he takes a sufficient fancy to a girl he will ask her straight off. I do not say that he might not change afterwards, but he would mean it at the time.'

'If he had once said the word to me, he should not change. But then what right have I to expect it? What has he ever said about me?'

'Very little. But had he said much I should not tell you.'

'You are my friend,—but you are his too; and he, perhaps, is more to you than I am. As his friend it may be your duty to tell him all that I am saying. If so, I have been wrong.'

'Do you think that I shall do that, Mabel?'

'I do not know. Men are so strong in their friendships.'

'Mine with you is the older, and the sweeter. Though we may not be more than friends, I will say that it is the more tender. In my heart of hearts I do not think that Silverbridge could do better.'

'Thanks for that, Frank.'

'I shall tell him nothing of you that can set him against you.'

'And you would be glad to see me his wife?' she said.

'As you must be somebody's wife, and not mine.'

'I cannot be yours, Frank; can I?'

'And not mine,' he repeated, 'I will endeavour to be glad. Who can explain his feelings in such a matter? Though I most truly love the girl I hope to marry, yet my heart goes back to former things and opens itself to past regrets.'

'I know it all,' she whispered.

'But you and I must be too wise to permit ourselves to be tormented by such foolish melancholy.' As he said this he took her hand, half with the purpose of bidding her good-bye, but partly with the idea of giving some expression to the tenderness of his feelings. But as he did so, the door was opened, and the old Earl shambled into the room.

'What the deuce are you doing here?' he said.

'I have been talking to Lady Mabel.'

'For about an hour.'

'Indeed I do not know for how long.'

'Papa, he is going to be married.' When she said this Frank Tregear turned round and looked at her almost in anger.

'Going to be married, is he? Who is the fortunate woman?'

'I don't think he will let me tell you.'

'Not yet, I think,' said Frank gloomily. 'There is nothing settled.'

The old Earl looked puzzled, but Lady Mabel's craft had been successful. If this objectionable young second-cousin had come there to talk about his marriage with another young woman, the conversation must have been innocent. 'Where is Miss Cassewary?' asked the Earl.

'I asked her not to come down with me because Frank wished to speak to me about his own affairs. You have no objection to his coming, papa?'

There had been objections raised to any intimacy with Frank Tregear; but all that was now nearly two years since. He had been assured over and over again by Miss Cassewary that he need not be afraid of Frank Tregear, and had in a sort of way assented to the young man's visits. 'I think he might find something better to do with his time than hanging about here all day.' Frank, shrugging his shoulders, and having shaken hands both with the daughter and father, took his hat and departed. 'Who is the girl?' asked the Earl.

'You heard him say that I was not to tell.'

'Has she got money?'

'I believe she will have a great deal.'

'Then she is a great fool for her pains,' said the Earl, shambling off again.

Lady Mabel spent the greater part of the afternoon alone, endeavouring to recall to her mind all that she had said to Frank Tregear, and questioning herself as to the wisdom and truth of her own words. She had intended to tell the truth,—but hardly perhaps the whole truth.* The life which was before her,—which it was necessary that she should lead,—seemed to her to be so difficult! She could not clearly see her way to be pure and good and feminine, and at the same time wise. She had been false now;—so far false that she had told her friend that she had never been in love. But she was in love;—in love with him, Frank Tregear She knew it as thoroughly as it was possible for her to know anything;—and had acknowledged it to herself a score of times.

But she could not marry him. And it was expected, nay, almost necessary that she should marry someone. To that someone, how good she would be! How she would strive by duty and attention, and if possible by affection, to make up for that misfortune of her early love!

And so I hope that I have brought my cart in to its appointed place in the front, without showing too much of the horse.

## CHAPTER 11
### 'CRUEL'

FOR two or three days after the first scene between the Duke and his daughter,—that scene in which she was forbidden either to see or to write to her lover,—not a word was said at Matching about Mr Tregear, nor were any steps taken towards curtailing her liberty of action. She had said she would not write to him without telling her father, and the Duke was too proud of the honour of his family to believe it to be

possible that she should deceive him. Nor was it possible. Not only
would her own idea of duty prevent her from writing to her lover,
although she had stipulated for the right to do so in some possible
emergency,—but, carried far beyond that in her sense of what was right
and wrong, she felt it now incumbent on her to have no secret from her
father at all. The secret, as long as it had been a secret, had been a
legacy from her mother,—and had been kept, at her lover's instance,
during that period of mourning for her mother in which it would, she
thought, have been indecorous that there should be any question of
love or of giving in marriage. It had been a burden to her, though a
necessary burden. She had been very clear that the revelation should be
made to her father, when it was made, by her lover. That had been
done,—and now it was open to her to live without any secrecy,—as was
her nature. She meant to cling to her lover. She was quite sure of that.
Nothing could divide her from him but his death or hers,—or falseness
on his part. But as to marriage, that would not be possible till her father
had assented. And as to seeing the man,—ah, yes, if she could do so
with her father's assent! She would not be ashamed to own her great
desire to see him. She would tell her father that all her happiness
depended upon seeing him. She would not be coy in speaking of her
love. But she would obey her father.

She had a strong idea that she would ultimately prevail,—an idea
also that that 'ultimately' should not be postponed to some undefined
middle-aged period of her life. As she intended to belong to Frank
Tregear, she thought it expedient that he should have the best of her
days as well as what might be supposed to be the worst; and she therefore resolved that it would be her duty to make her father understand
that though she would certainly obey him, she would look to be treated
humanely by him, and not to be made miserable for an indefinite term
of years.

The first word spoken between them on the subject,—the first word
after that discussion,—began with him and was caused by his feeling
that her present life at Matching must be sad and lonely. Lady Cantrip
had again written that she would be delighted to take her;—but Lady
Cantrip was in London and must be in London, at any rate when
Parliament should again be sitting. A London life would perhaps, at
present, hardly suit Lady Mary. Then a plan had been prepared which
might be convenient. The Duke had a house at Richmond, on the river,
called The Horns.* That should be lent to Lady Cantrip, and Mary
should there be her guest. So it was settled between the Duke and Lady
Cantrip. But as yet Lady Mary knew nothing of the arrangement.

'I think I shall go up to town to-morrow,' said the Duke to his daughter.

'For long?'

'I shall be gone only one night. It is on your behalf that I am going.'

'On my behalf, papa?'

'I have been writing to Lady Cantrip.'

'Not about Mr Tregear?'

'No;—not about Mr Tregear,' said the father with a mixture of anger and solemnity in his tone. 'It is my desire to regard Mr Tregear as though he did not exist.'

'That is not possible, papa.'

'I have alluded to the inconvenience of your position here.'

'Why is it inconvenient?'

'You are too young to be without a companion. It is not fit that you should be so much alone.'

'I do not feel it.'

'It is very melancholy for you, and cannot be good for you. They will go down to The Horns, so that you will not be absolutely in London, and you will find Lady Cantrip a very nice person.'

'I don't care for new people just now, papa,' she said. But to this he paid but little heed; nor was she prepared to say that she would not do as he directed. When therefore he left Matching, she understood that he was going to prepare a temporary home for her. Nothing further was said about Tregear. She was too proud to ask that no mention of his name should be made to Lady Cantrip. And he when he left the house did not think that he would find himself called upon to allude to the subject.

But when Lady Cantrip made some inquiry about the girl and her habits,—asking what were her ordinary occupations, how she was accustomed to pass her hours, to what she chiefly devoted herself,— then at last with much difficulty the Duke did bring himself to tell the story. 'Perhaps it is better you should know it all,' he said as he told it.

'Poor girl! Yes, Duke; upon the whole it is better that I should know it all,' said Lady Cantrip. 'Of course he will not come here.'

'Oh dear; I hope not.'

'Nor to The Horns.'

'I hope he will never see her again anywhere,' said the Duke.

'Poor girl!'

'Have I not been right? Is it not best to put an end to such a thing at once?'

'Certainly at once, if it has to be put an end to,—and can be put an end to.'

'It must be put an end to,' said the Duke, very decidedly. 'Do you not see that it must be so? Who is Mr Tregear?'

'I suppose they were allowed to be together.'

'He was unfortunately intimate with Silverbridge, who took him over to Italy. He has nothing; not even a profession.' Lady Cantrip could not but smile when she remembered the immense wealth of the man who was speaking to her;—and the Duke saw the smile and understood it. 'You will understand what I mean, Lady Cantrip. If this young man were in other respects suitable, of course I could find an income for them. But he is nothing; just an idle seeker for pleasure without the means of obtaining it.'

'That is very bad.'

'As for rank,' continued the Duke energetically, 'I do not think that I am specially wedded to it. I have found myself as willing to associate with those who are without it as with those who have it. But for my child, I would wish her to mate with one of her own class.'

'It would be best.'

'When a young man comes to me who, though I believe him to be what is called a gentleman, has neither rank, nor means, nor profession, nor name, and asks for my daughter, surely I am right to say that such a marriage shall not be thought of. Was I not right?' demanded the Duke persistently.

'But it is a pity that it should be so. It is a pity that they should ever have come together.'

'It is indeed, indeed to be lamented,—and I will own at once that the fault was not hers. Though I must be firm in this, you are not to suppose that I am angry with her. I have myself been to blame.' This he said with a resolution that,—as he and his wife had been one flesh,—all faults committed by her should, now that she was dead, be accepted by him as his faults. 'It had not occurred to me that as yet she would love any man.'

'Has it gone deep with her, Duke?'

'I fear that all things go deep with her.'

'Poor girl!'

'But they shall be kept apart! As long as your great kindness is continued to her they shall be kept apart!'

'I do not think that I should be found good at watching a young lady.'

'She will require no watching.'

'Then of course they will not meet. She had better know that you have told me.'

'She shall know it.'

'And let her know also that anything I can do to make her happy shall be done. But, Duke, there is but one cure.'

'Time, you mean.'

'Yes; time; but I did not mean time.' Then she smiled as she went on. 'You must not suppose that I am speaking against my own sex if I say that she will not forget Mr Tregear till someone else has made himself agreeable to her. We must wait till she can go out a little into society. Then she will find out that there are others in the world besides Mr Tregear. It so often is the case that a girl's love means her sympathy for him who has chanced to be nearest to her.'

The Duke as he went away thought very much of what Lady Cantrip had said to him;—particularly of those last words. 'Till some one else has made himself agreeable to her.' Was he to send his girl into the world in order that she might find a lover? There was something in the idea which was thoroughly distasteful to him. He had not given his mind much to the matter, but he felt that a woman should be sought for,—sought for and extracted, cunningly, as it were, from some hiding-place, and not sent out into a market to be exposed as for sale. In his own personal history there had been a misfortune,—a misfortune, the sense of which he could never, at any moment, have expressed to any ears, the memory of which had been always buried in his own bosom,—but a misfortune in that no such cunning extraction on his part had won for him the woman to whose hands had been confided the strings of his heart. His wife had undergone that process of extraction before he had seen her, and his marriage with her had been a matter of sagacious bargaining. He was now told that his daughter must be sent out among young men in order that she might become sufficiently fond of some special one to be regardless of Tregear. There was a feeling that in doing so she must lose something of the freshness of the bloom of her innocence. How was this transfer of her love to be effected? Let her go here because she will meet the heir of this wealthy house who may probably be smitten by her charms; or there because that other young lordling would make a fit husband for her. Let us contrive to throw her into the arms of this man, or put her into the way of that man. Was his girl to be exposed to this? Surely that method of bargaining to which he had owed his own wife would be better than that. Let it be said,—only he himself most certainly could not be the person to say it,—let it be said to some man of rank and means and fairly good character: 'Here is a wife for you with so many thousand pounds, with beauty, as you can see for yourself, with rank and belongings of the highest; very good in every respect;—only that as regards her heart she thinks she has given it to a young man named Tregear. No marriage there is possible; but perhaps the young lady might suit you?' It was thus he had been married. There was an absence in it of that romance which, though he had never experienced it in his own life, was always present to his imagination. His wife had often ridiculed him because he could only live among figures and official details; but to her had not been given the power of looking into a man's heart and feeling all that was there. Yes;—in such bargaining for a wife, in such bargaining for a husband, there could be nothing of the tremulous delicacy of feminine romance; but it would be better than standing at a stall in the market till the sufficient purchaser should come. It never occurred to him that the delicacy, the innocence, the romance, the bloom might all be preserved if he would give his girl to the man whom she said she loved. Could he have modelled her future course according to his own wishes, he would have had her live a gentle life for the next three years, with a pencil perhaps in her hand or a music-book before her;— and then come forth, cleaned as it were by such quarantine from the impurity to which she had been subjected.

When he was back at Matching he at once told his daughter what he had arranged for her, and then there took place a prolonged discussion both as to his view of her future life and as to her own. 'You did tell her then about Mr Tregear?' she asked.

'As she is to have charge of you for a time I thought it best.'

'Perhaps it is. Perhaps—you were afraid.'

'No; I was not afraid,' he said angrily.

'You need not be afraid. I shall do nothing elsewhere that I would not do here, and nothing anywhere without telling you.'

'I know I can trust you.'

'But, papa, I shall always intend to marry Mr Tregear.'

'No!' he exclaimed.

'Yes;—always. I want you to understand exactly how it is. Nothing you can do can separate me from him.'

'Mary, that is very wicked.'

'It cannot be wicked to tell the truth, papa. I mean to try to do all that you tell me. I shall not see him, or write to him,—unless there should be some very particular reason. And if I did see him or write to him I would tell you. And of course I should not think of—of marrying without your leave. But I shall expect you to let me marry him.'

'Never!'

'Then I shall think you are—cruel; and you will break my heart.'

'You should not call your father cruel.'

'I hope you will not be cruel.'

'I can never permit you to marry this man. It would be altogether improper. I cannot allow you to say that I am cruel because I do what I feel to be my duty. You will see other people.'

'A great many perhaps.'

'And will learn to,—to,—to forget him.'

'Never! I will not forget him. I should hate myself if I thought it possible. What would love be worth if it could be forgotten in that way?' As he heard this he reflected whether his own wife, this girl's mother, had ever forgotten her early love for that Burgo Fitzgerald whom in her girlhood she had wished to marry.

When he was leaving her she called him back again. 'There is one other thing I think I ought to say, papa. If Lady Cantrip speaks to me about Mr Tregear, I can only tell her what I have told you. I shall never give him up.' When he heard this he turned angrily from her, almost stamping his foot upon the ground, when she quietly left the room.

Cruel! She had told him that he would be cruel, if he opposed her love. He thought he knew of himself that he could not be cruel,—even to a fly, even to a political opponent. There could be no cruelty without dishonesty, and did he not always struggle to be honest? Cruel to his own daughter!

## CHAPTER 12

### AT RICHMOND

THE pity of it! The pity of it!* It was thus that Lady Cantrip looked at it. From what the girl's father had said to her she was disposed to believe that the malady had gone deep with her. 'All things go deep with her,' he had said. And she too from other sources had heard something of this girl. She was afraid that it would go deep. It was a thousand pities! Then she asked herself whether the marriage ought to be regarded as impossible. The Duke had been very positive,—had declared again and again that it was quite impossible, had so expressed himself as to make her aware that he intended her to understand that he would not yield whatever the sufferings of the girl might be. But Lady Cantrip knew the world well and was aware that in such matters daughters are apt to be stronger than their fathers. He had declared Tregear to be a young man with very small means, and intent on such pleasures as require great means for their enjoyment. No worse character could be given to a gentleman who had proposed himself as a son-in-law. But Lady Cantrip thought it possible that the Duke might be mistaken in this. She had never seen Mr Tregear, but she fancied that she had heard his name, and that the name had been connected with a character different from that which the Duke had given him.

Lady Cantrip, who at this time was a young-looking woman, not much above forty, had two daughters, both of whom were married. The younger about a year since had become the wife of Lord Nidderdale, a middle-aged young man who had been long about town, a cousin of the late Duchess, the heir to a marquisate, and a Member of Parliament. The marriage had not been considered to be very brilliant; but the husband was himself good-natured and pleasant, and Lady Cantrip was fond of him. In the first place she went to him for information.

'Oh yes, I know him. He's one of our set at the Beargarden.'

'Not your set, now, I hope,' she said laughing.

'Well;—I don't see so much of them as I used to do. Tregear is not a bad fellow at all. He's always with Silverbridge. When Silverbridge does what Tregear tells him, he goes along pretty straight. But unfortunately there's another man called Tifto, and when Tifto is in the ascendant then Silverbridge is apt to get a little astray.'

'He's not in debt, then?'

'Who?—Tregear? I should think he's the last man in the world to owe a penny to any one.'

'Is he a betting man?'

'Oh dear no; quite the other way up. He's a severe, sarcastic bookish sort of fellow,—a chap who knows everything and turns up his nose at people who know nothing.'

'Has he got anything of his own?'

'Not much, I should say. If he had had any money he would have married Lady Mab Grex last year.'

Lady Cantrip was inclined from what she now learned to think that the Duke must be wrong about the young man. But before Lady Mary joined her she made further inquiry. She too knew Lady Mabel, and knowing Lady Mabel, she knew Miss Cassewary. She contrived to find herself alone with Miss Cassewary, and asked some further questions about Mr Tregear. 'He is a cousin of my Lord's,' said Miss Cass.

'So I thought. I wonder what sort of a young man he is. He is a good deal with Lord Silverbridge.'

Then Miss Cassewary spoke her opinion very plainly. 'If Lord Silverbridge had nobody worse about him than Mr Tregear he would not come to much harm.'

'I suppose he's not very well off.'

'No;—certainly not. He will have a property of some kind, I believe, when his mother dies. I think very well of Mr Tregear;—only I wish that he had a profession. But why are you asking about him, Lady Cantrip?'

'Nidderdale was talking to me about him and saying that he was so much with Lord Silverbridge. Lord Silverbridge is going into Parliament now, and, as it were, beginning the world, and it would be a thousand pities that he should get into bad hands.' It may, however, be doubted whether Miss Cassewary was hoodwinked by this little story.

Early in the second week in May the Duke brought his daughter up to The Horns, and at the same time expressed his intention of remaining in London. When he did so Lady Mary at once asked whether she might not be with him, but he would not permit it. The house in London would, he said, be more gloomy even than Matching.

'I am quite ashamed of giving you so much trouble,' Lady Mary said to her new friend.

'We are delighted to have you, my dear.'

'But I know that you have been obliged to leave London because I am with you.'

'There is nothing I like so much as this place, which your father has been kind enough to lend us. As for London, there is nothing now to make me like being there. Both my girls are married, and therefore I regard myself as an old woman who has done her work. Don't you think this place very much nicer than London at this time of the year?'

'I don't know London at all. I had only just been brought out when poor mamma went abroad.'

The life they led was very quiet, and must probably have been felt to be dull by Lady Cantrip, in spite of her old age and desire for retirement. But the place itself was very lovely. May of all the months of the year is in England the most insidious, the most dangerous, and the most inclement. A greatcoat cannot be endured, and without a greatcoat who can endure a May wind and live? But of all months it is the prettiest. The grasses are then the greenest, and the young foliage of

the trees, while it has all the glory and all the colour of spring vegeta-
tion, does not hide the form of the branches as do the heavy masses of
the larger leaves which come in the advancing summer. And of all villas
near London The Horns was the sweetest. The broad green lawn swept
down to the very margin of the Thames, which absolutely washed the
fringe of grass when the tide was high. And here, along the bank, was a
row of flowering ashes, the drooping boughs of which in places touched
the water.* It was one of those spots which when they are first seen
make the beholder feel that to be able to live there and look at it always
would be happiness enough for life.

   At the end of the week there came a visitor to see Lady Mary. A very
pretty carriage was driven up to the door of The Horns, and the servant asked for Lady Mary Palliser. The owner of that carriage was
Mrs Finn. Now it must be explained to the reader that there had never
been any friendship between Mrs Finn and Lady Cantrip, though the
ladies had met each other. The great political intimacy which had
existed between the Duke and Lord Cantrip had created some intimacy also between their wives. The Duchess and Lady Cantrip had been
friends,—after a fashion. But Mrs Finn had never been cordially
accepted by those among whom Lady Cantrip chiefly lived. When
therefore the name was announced, the servant expressly stating that
the visitor had asked for Lady Mary, Lady Cantrip, who was with her
guest, had to bethink herself what she would do. The Duke, who was
at this time very full of wrath against Mrs Finn, had not mentioned this
lady's name when delivering up the charge of his daughter to Lady
Cantrip. At this moment it occurred to her that not improbably
Mrs Finn would cease to be included in the intimacies of the Palliser
family from the time of the death of the Duchess,—that the Duke
would not care to maintain the old relations, and that he would be as
little anxious to do it for his daughter as for himself. If so, could it be
right that Mrs Finn should come down here, to a house which was now
in the occupation of a lady with whom she was not on inviting terms, in
order that she might thus force herself on the Duke's daughter?
Mrs Finn had not left her carriage, but had sent in to ask if Lady Mary
could see her. In all this there was considerable embarrassment.
She looked round at her guest, who had at once risen from her chair.
'Would you wish to see her?' asked Lady Cantrip.

   'Oh yes; certainly.'

   'Have you seen her since,—since you came home from Italy?'

   'Oh dear, yes! She was down at Matching when poor mamma died.
And papa persuaded her to remain afterwards. Of course I will see her.'

Then the servant was desired to ask Mrs Finn to come in;—and while this was being done Lady Cantrip retired.

Mrs Finn embraced her young friend, and asked after her welfare, and after the welfare of the house in which she was staying,—a house with which Mrs Finn herself had been well acquainted,—and said half-a-dozen pretty little things in her own quiet pretty way, before she spoke of the matter which had really brought her to The Horns on that day.

'I have had a correspondence with your father, Mary.'

'Indeed.'

'And unfortunately one that has been far from agreeable to me.'

'I am sorry for that, Mrs Finn.'

'So am I, very sorry. I may say with perfect truth that there is no man in the world, except my own husband, for whom I feel so perfect an esteem as I do for your father. If it were not that I do not like to be carried away by strong language I would speak of more than esteem. Through your dear mother I have watched his conduct closely, and have come to think that there is perhaps no other man at the same time so just and so patriotic.* Now he is very angry with me,—and most unjustly angry.'

'Is it about me?'

'Yes;—it is about you. Had it not been altogether about you I would not have troubled you.'

'And about——?'

'Yes;—about Mr Tregear also. When I tell you that there has been a correspondence I must explain that I have written one long letter to the Duke, and that in answer I have received a very short one. That has been the whole correspondence. Here is your father's letter to me.' Then she brought out of her pocket a note, which Lady Mary read,—covered with blushes as she did so. The note was as follows:

'The Duke of Omnium understands from Mrs Finn's letter that Mrs Finn, while she was the Duke's guest at Matching, was aware of a certain circumstance affecting the Duke's honour and happiness,—which circumstance she certainly did not communicate to the Duke. The Duke thinks that the trust which had been placed in Mrs Finn should have made such a communication imperative. The Duke feels that no further correspondence between himself and Mrs Finn on the matter could lead to any good result.'

'Do you understand it?' asked Mrs Finn.

'I think so.'

'It simply means this,—that when at Matching he had thought me worthy of having for a time the charge of you and of your welfare, that he had trusted me, who was the friend of your dear mother, to take for a time in regard to you the place which had been so unhappily left vacant by her death; and it means also that I deceived him and betrayed that trust by being privy to an engagement on your part, of which he disapproves, and of which he was not then aware.'

'I suppose he does mean that.'

'Yes, Lady Mary; that is what he means. And he means further to let me know that as I did so foully betray the trust which he had placed in me,—that as I had consented to play the part of assistant to you in that secret engagement,—therefore he casts me off as altogether unworthy of his esteem and acquaintance. It is as though he had told me in so many words that among women he had known none more vile or more false than I.'

'Not that, Mrs Finn.'

'Yes, that;—all of that. He tells me that, and then says that there shall be no more words spoken or written about it. I can hardly submit to so stern a judgment. You know the truth, Lady Mary.'

'Do not call me Lady Mary. Do not quarrel with me.'

'If your father has quarrelled with me, it would not be fit that you and I should be friends. Your duty to him would forbid it. I should not have come to you now did I not feel that I am bound to justify myself. The thing of which I am accused is so repugnant to me, that I am obliged to do something and to say something, even though the subject itself be one on which I would so willingly be silent.'

'What can I do, Mrs Finn?'

'It was Mr Tregear who first told me that your father was angry with me. He knew what I had done and why, and he was bound to tell me in order that I might have an opportunity of setting myself right with the Duke. Then I wrote and explained everything,—how you had told me of the engagement, and how I had then urged Mr Tregear that he should not keep such a matter secret from your father. In answer to my letter I have received—that.'

'Shall I write and tell papa?'

'He should be made to understand that from the moment in which I heard of the engagement I was urgent with you and with Mr Tregear that he should be informed of it. You will remember what passed.'

'I remember it all.'

'I did not conceive it to be my duty to tell the Duke myself, but I did conceive it to be my duty to see he should be told. Now he writes as though I had known the secret from the first, and as though I had been concealing it from him at the very moment in which he was asking me to remain at Matching on your behalf. That I consider to be hard,—and unjust. I cannot deny what he says. I did know of it while I was at Matching, for it was at Matching that you told me. But he implies that I knew it before. When you told me your story I did feel that it was my duty to see that the matter was not kept longer from him;—and I did my duty. Now your father takes upon himself to rebuke me,—and takes upon himself at the same time to forbid me to write to him again!'

'I will tell him all, Mrs Finn.'

'Let him understand this. I do not wish to write to him again. After what has passed I cannot say I wish to see him again. But I think he should acknowledge to me that he has been mistaken. He need not then fear that I shall trouble him with any reply. But I shall know that he has acquitted me of a fault of which I cannot bear to think I should be accused.' Then she took a somewhat formal though still an affectionate farewell of the girl.

'I want to see papa as soon as possible,' said Lady Mary when she was again with Lady Cantrip. The reason for her wish was soon given, and then the whole story told. 'You do not think that she should have gone to papa at once?' Lady Mary asked. It was a point of moral law on which the elder woman, who had had girls of her own, found it hard to give an immediate answer. It certainly is expedient that parents should know at once of any engagement by which their daughters may seek to contract themselves. It is expedient that they should be able to prevent any secret contracts. Lady Cantrip felt strongly that Mrs Finn having accepted the confidential charge of the daughter could not, without gross betrayal of trust, allow herself to be the depositary of such a secret. 'But she did not allow herself,' said Lady Mary, pleading for her friend.

'But she left the house without telling him, my dear.'

'But it was because of what she did that he was told.'

'That is true; but I doubt whether she should have left him an hour in ignorance.'

'But it was I who told her. She would have betrayed me.'

'She was not a fit recipient for your confidence, Mary. But I do not wish to accuse her. She seems to be a high-minded woman, and I think that your papa has been hard upon her.'

'And mamma knew it always,' said Mary. To this Lady Cantrip could give no answer. Whatever cause for anger the Duke might have against Mrs Finn, there had been cause for much more against his wife. But she had freed herself from all accusation by death.

Lady Mary wrote to her father, declaring that she was most particularly anxious to see him and talk to him about Mrs Finn.

## CHAPTER 13

### THE DUKE'S INJUSTICE

No advantage whatever was obtained by Lady Mary's interview with her father. He persisted that Mrs Finn had been untrue to him when she left Matching without telling him all that she knew of his daughter's engagement with Mr Tregear. No doubt by degrees that idea which he at first entertained was expelled from his head,—the idea that she had been cognisant of the whole thing before she came to Matching; but even this was done so slowly that there was no moment at which he became aware of any lessened feeling of indignation. To his thinking she had betrayed her trust, and he could not be got by his daughter to say that he would forgive her. He certainly could not be got to say that he would apologise for the accusation he had made. It was nothing less that his daughter asked; and he could hardly refrain himself from anger when she asked it. 'There should not have been a moment,' he said, 'before she came to me and told me all.' Poor Lady Mary's position was certainly uncomfortable enough. The great sin,*—the sin which was so great that to have known it for a day without revealing it was in itself a damning sin on the part of Mrs Finn,—was Lady Mary's sin. And she differed so entirely from her father as to think that this sin of her own was a virtue, and that to have spoken of it to him would have been, on the part of Mrs Finn, a treachery so deep that no woman ought to have forgiven it! When he spoke of a matter which deeply affected his honour,—she could hardly refrain from asserting that his honour was quite safe in his daughter's hands. And when in his heart he declared that it should have been Mrs Finn's first care to save him from disgrace, Lady Mary did break out. 'Papa, there could be no disgrace.' 'That for a moment shall be laid aside,' he said, with that manner by which even his peers in council had never been able not to be awed, 'but if you communicate with Mrs Finn at all you must make her understand that I regard her conduct as inexcusable.'

Nothing had been gained, and poor Lady Mary was compelled to write a few lines which were to her most painful in writing.

'MY DEAR MRS FINN,

'I have seen papa, and he thinks that you ought to have told him when I told you. It occurs to me that that would have been a cruel thing to do, and most unfair to Mr Tregear, who was quite willing to go to papa, and had only put off doing so because of poor mamma's death. As I had told mamma, of course it was right that he should tell papa. Then I told you, because you were so kind to me! I am so sorry that I have got you into this trouble; but what can I do?

'I told him I must write to you. I suppose it is better that I should, although what I have to say is so unpleasant. I hope it will all blow over in time, because I love you dearly. You may be quite sure of one thing,—that I shall never change.' In this assurance the writer was alluding not to her friendship for her friend but her love for her lover,— and so the friend understood her. 'I hope things will be settled some day, and then we may be able to meet.

'Your very affectionate friend,
'MARY PALLISER.'

Mrs Finn, when she received this, was alone in her house in Park Lane. Her husband was down in the North of England. On this subject she had not spoken to him, fearing that he would feel himself bound to take some steps to support his wife under the treatment she had received. Even though she must quarrel with the Duke, she was most anxious that her husband should not be compelled to do so. Their connection had been political rather than personal. There were many reasons why there should be no open cause of disruption between them. But her husband was hot-headed, and, were all this to be told him and that letter shown to him which the Duke had written, there would be words between him and the Duke which would probably make impossible any further connection between them.

It troubled her very much. She was by no means not alive to the honour of the Duke's friendship. Throughout her intimacy with the Duchess she had abstained from pressing herself on him, not because she had been indifferent about him, but that she had perceived that she might make her way with him better by standing aloof than by thrusting herself forward. And she had known that she had been successful. She could tell herself with pride that her conduct towards him had been always such as would become a lady of high spirit and fine feeling.

She knew that she had deserved well of him, that in all her intercourse
with him, with his uncle, and with his wife, she had given much and
had taken little. She was the last woman in the world to let a word on
such a matter pass her lips; but not the less was she conscious of her
merit towards him. And she had been led to act as she had done by
sincere admiration for the man. In all their political troubles, she had
understood him better than the Duchess had done. Looking on from a
distance she had understood the man's character as it had come to her
both from his wife and from her own husband.

That he was unjust to her,—cruelly unjust, she was quite sure. He
accused her of intentional privity* as to a secret which it behoved him
to know, and of being a party to that secrecy. Whereas from the moment
in which she had heard the secret she had determined that it must be
made known to him. She felt that she had deserved his good opinion in
all things, but in nothing more than in the way in which she had acted
in this matter. And yet he had treated her with an imperious harshness
which amounted to insolence. What a letter it was that he had written
to her! The very tips of her ears tingled with heat as she read it again to
herself. None of the ordinary courtesies of epistle-craft had been preserved either in the beginning or in the end. It was worse even than if
he had called her, Madam without an epithet. 'The Duke understands——' 'The Duke thinks——' 'The Duke feels——' feels that he
should not be troubled with either letters or conversation; the upshot of
it all being that the Duke declared her to have shown herself unworthy
of being treated like a lady! And this after all that she had done!

She would not bear it. That at present was all that she could say to
herself. She was not angry with Lady Mary. She did not doubt but that
the girl had done the best in her power to bring her father to reason.
But because Lady Mary had failed she, Mrs Finn, was not going to put
up with so grievous an injury. And she was forced to bear all this alone!
There was none with whom she could communicate;—no one from
whom she could ask advice. She would not bring her husband into a
quarrel which might be prejudicial to his position as a member of
his political party. There was no one else to whom she would tell the
secret of Lady Mary's love. And yet she could not bear this injustice
done to her.

Then she wrote as follows to the Duke:

'Mrs Finn presents her compliments to the Duke of Omnium.
Mrs Finn finds it to be essential to her that she should see the Duke in
reference to his letter to her. If his Grace will let her know on what day

and at what hour he will be kind enough to call on her, Mrs Finn will be at home to receive him.

'Park Lane. Thursday, 12th May, 18—.'*

## CHAPTER 14

### THE NEW MEMBER FOR SILVERBRIDGE

LORD SILVERBRIDGE was informed that it would be right that he should go down to Silverbridge a few days before the election, to make himself known to the electors. As the day for the election drew near it was understood that there would be no other candidate. The Conservative side was the popular side among the tradesmen of Silverbridge. Silverbridge had been proud to be honoured by the services of the heir of the house of Omnium, even while that heir had been a Liberal,—had regarded it as so much a matter of course that the borough should be at his disposal that no question as to politics had ever arisen while he retained the seat. And had the Duke chosen to continue to send them Liberals, one after another, when he went into the House of Lords, there would have been no question as to the fitness of the man or men so sent. Silverbridge had been supposed to be a Liberal as a matter of course,—because the Pallisers were Liberals. But when the matter was remitted to themselves,—when the Duke declared that he would not interfere any more, for it was thus that the borough had obtained its freedom;—then the borough began to feel Conservative predilections. 'If his Grace* really does mean us to do just what we please ourselves, which is a thing we never thought of asking from his Grace, then we find, having turned the matter over among ourselves, that we are upon the whole Conservative.' In this spirit the borough had elected a certain Mr Fletcher; but in doing so the borough had still a shade of fear that it would offend the Duke. The house of Palliser, Gatherum Castle, the Duke of Omnium, and this special Duke himself, were all so great in the eyes of the borough, that the first and only strong feeling in the borough was the one of duty. The borough did not altogether enjoy being enfranchised. But when the Duke had spoken once, twice, and thrice, then with a hesitating heart the borough returned Mr Fletcher. Now Mr Fletcher was wanted elsewhere, having been persuaded to stand for the county, and it was a comfort to the borough that it could resettle itself beneath the warmth of the wings of the Pallisers.

So the matter stood when Lord Silverbridge was told that his presence in the borough for a few hours would be taken as a compliment. Hitherto no one knew him at Silverbridge. During his boyhood he had not been much at Gatherum Castle, and had done his best to eschew the place since he had ceased to be a boy. All the Pallisers took a pride in Gatherum Castle, but they all disliked it. 'Oh yes; I'll go down,' he said to Mr Morton, who was up in town. 'I needn't go to the great barrack I suppose.' The great barrack was the Castle. 'I'll put up at the Inn.' Mr Morton begged the heir to come to his own house; but Silverbridge declared that he would prefer the Inn, and so the matter was settled. He was to meet sundry politicians,—Mr Sprugeon and Mr Sprout and Mr Du Boung,*—who would like to be thanked for what they had done. But who was to go with him? He would naturally have asked Tregear, but from Tregear he had for the last week or two been, not perhaps estranged, but separated. He had been much taken up with racing. He had gone down to Chester with Major Tifto, and under the Major's auspicious influences had won a little money;—and now he was very anxiously preparing himself for the Newmarket Second Spring Meeting. He had therefore passed much of his time with Major Tifto. And when this visit to Silverbridge was pressed on him he thoughtlessly asked Tifto to go with him. Tifto was delighted. Lord Silverbridge was to be met at Silverbridge by various well-known politicians from the neighbourhood, and Major Tifto was greatly elated by the prospect of such an introduction into the political world.

But no sooner had the offer been made by Lord Silverbridge than he saw his own indiscretion. Tifto was very well for Chester or Newmarket, very well perhaps for the Beargarden, but not very well for an electioneering expedition. An idea came to the young nobleman that if it should be his fate to represent Silverbridge in Parliament for the next twenty years, it would be well that Silverbridge should entertain respecting him some exalted estimation,—that Silverbridge should be taught to regard him as a fit son of his father and a worthy specimen of the British political nobility. Struck by serious reflections of this nature he did open his mind to Tregear. 'I am very fond of Tifto,' he said, 'but I don't know whether he's just the sort of fellow to take down to an election.'

'I should think not,' said Tregear very decidedly.

'He's a very good fellow, you know,' said Silverbridge. 'I don't know an honester man than Tifto anywhere.'

'I dare say. Or rather, I don't dare say. I know nothing about the Major's honesty, and I doubt whether you do. He rides very well.'

'What has that to do with it?'

'Nothing on earth. Therefore I advise you not to take him to Silverbridge.'

'You needn't preach.'

'You may call it what you like. Tifto would not hold his tongue, and there is nothing he could say there which would not be to your prejudice.'

'Will you go?'

'If you wish it,' said Tregear.

'What will the governor say?'

'That must be your look-out. In a political point of view I shall not disgrace you. I shall hold my tongue and look like a gentleman,— neither of which is in Tifto's power.'

And so it was settled, that on the day but one after this conversation Lord Silverbridge and Tregear should go together to Silverbridge. But the Major, when on the same night his noble friend's altered plans were explained to him, did not bear the disappointment with equanimity. 'Isn't that a little strange?' he said, becoming very red in the face.

'What do you call strange?' said the Lord.

'Well;—I'd made all my arrangements. When a man has been asked to do a thing like that, he doesn't like to be put off.'

'The truth is, Tifto, when I came to think of it, I saw that, going down to these fellows about Parliament and all that sort of thing, I ought to have a political atmosphere, and not a racing or a betting or a hunting atmosphere.'

'There isn't a man in London who cares more about politics than I do;—and not very many perhaps who understand them better. To tell you the truth, my Lord, I think you are throwing me over.'

'I'll make it up to you,' said Silverbridge, meaning to be kind. 'I'll go down to Newmarket with you and stick to you like wax.'

'No doubt you'll do that,' said Tifto, who, like a fool, failed to see where his advantage lay. 'I can be useful at Newmarket, and so you'll stick to me.'

'Look here, Major Tifto,' said Silverbridge; 'if you are dissatisfied, you and I can easily separate ourselves.'

'I am not dissatisfied,' said the little man, almost crying.

'Then don't talk as though you were. As to Silverbridge, I shall not want you there. When I asked you I was only thinking what would be pleasant to both of us; but since that I have remembered that business must be business.' Even this did not reconcile the angry little man, who as he turned away declared within his own little bosom that he would 'take it out of Silverbridge for that.'

Lord Silverbridge and Tregear went down to the borough together, and on the journey something was said about Lady Mary,—and something also about Lady Mabel. 'From the first, you know,' said Lady Mary's brother, 'I never thought it would answer.'

'Why not answer?'

'Because I knew the governor would not have it. Money and rank and those sort of things are not particularly charming to me. But still things should go together. It is all very well for you and me to be pals, but of course it will be expected that Mary should marry some——'

'Some swell?'*

'Some swell, if you will have it.'

'You mean to call yourself a swell?'

'Yes I do,' said Silverbridge, with considerable resolution. 'You ought not to make yourself disagreeable, because you understand all about it as well as anybody. Chance has made me the eldest son of a Duke and heir to an enormous fortune. Chance has made my sister the daughter of a Duke, and an heiress also. My intimacy with you ought to be proof at any rate to you that I don't on that account set myself up above other fellows. But when you come to talk of marriage, of course it is a serious thing.'

'But you have told me more than once that you have no objection on your own score.'

'Nor have I.'

'You are only saying what the Duke will think.'

'I am telling you that it is impossible, and I told you so before. You and she will be kept apart, and so——'

'And so she'll forget me.'

'Something of that kind.'

'Of course I have to trust to her for that. If she forgets me, well and good.'

'She needn't forget you. Lord bless me! you talk as though the thing were not done every day. You'll hear some morning that she is going to marry some fellow who has a lot of money and a good position; and what difference will it make then whether she has forgotten you or not?' It might almost have been supposed that the young man had been acquainted with his mother's history.

After this there was a pause, and there arose conversation about other things, and a cigar was smoked. Then Tregear returned once more to the subject. 'There is one thing I wish to say about it all.'

'What is that?'

'I want you to understand that nothing else will turn me away from my intention but such a marriage on her part as that of which you speak. Nothing that your father can do will turn me.'

'She can't marry without his leave.'

'Perhaps not.'

'That he'll never give,—and I don't suppose you look forward to waiting till his death.'

'If he sees that her happiness really depends on it he will give his leave. It all depends on that. If I judge your father rightly, he's just as soft-hearted as other people. The man who holds out is not the man of the firmest opinion, but the man of the hardest heart.'

'Somebody will talk Mary over.'

'If so, the thing is over. It all depends on her.' Then he went on to tell his friend that he had spoken of his engagement to Lady Mabel. 'I have mentioned it to no soul but to your father and to her.'

'Why to her?'

'Because we were friends together as children. I never had a sister, but she has been more like a sister to me than anyone else. Do you object to her knowing it?'

'Not particularly. It seems to me now that everybody knows everything. There are no longer any secrets.'

'But she is a special friend.'

'Of yours,' said Silverbridge.

'And of yours,' said Tregear.

'Well, yes;—in a sort of way. She is the jolliest girl I know.'

'Take her all round, for beauty, intellect, good sense, and fun at the same time, I don't know anyone equal to her.'

'It's a pity you didn't fall in love with her.'

'We knew each other too early for that. And then she has not a shilling. I should think myself dishonest if I did not tell you that I could not afford to love any girl who hadn't money. A man must live,—and a woman too.'

At the station they were met by Mr Sprugeon and Mr Sprout, who, with many apologies for the meanness of such entertainment, took them up to the George and Vulture,* which was supposed for the nonce to be the Conservative hotel in the town. Here they were met by other men of importance in the borough, and among them by Mr Du Boung. Now Mr Sprout and Mr Sprugeon were Conservatives, but Mr Du Boung was a strong Liberal.

'We are, all of us, particularly glad to see your Lordship among us,' said Mr Du Boung.

'I have told his Lordship how perfectly satisfied you are to see the borough in his Lordship's hands,' said Mr Sprugeon.

'I am sure it could not be in better,' said Mr Du Boung. 'For myself I am quite willing to postpone any peculiar shade of politics to the advantage of having your father's son as our representative.'

This Mr Du Boung said with much intention of imparting both grace and dignity to the occasion. He thought that he was doing a great thing for the house of Omnium, and that the house of Omnium ought to know it.

'That's very kind of you,' said Lord Silverbridge, who had not read as carefully as he should have done the letters which had been sent to him, and did not therefore quite understand the position.

'Mr Du Boung had intended to stand himself,' said Mr Sprout.

'But retired in your Lordship's favour,' said Mr Sprugeon.

'In doing which I considered that I studied the interest of the borough,' said Mr Du Boung.

'I thought you gave it up because there was hardly a footing for a Liberal,' said his Lordship, very imprudently.

'The borough was always Liberal till the last election,' said Mr Du Boung, drawing himself up.

'The borough wishes on this occasion to be magnanimous,' said Mr Sprout, probably having on his mind some confusion between magnanimity and unanimity.

'As your Lordship is coming among us, the borough is anxious to sink politics altogether for the moment,' said Mr Sprugeon. There had no doubt been a compact between the Sprugeon and Sprout party and the Du Boung party in accordance with which it had been arranged that Mr Du Boung should be entitled to a certain amount of glorification in the presence of Lord Silverbridge.

'And it was in compliance with that wish on the part of the borough, my Lord,' said Mr Du Boung,—'as to which my own feelings were quite as strong as that of any other gentleman in the borough,—that I conceived it to be my duty to give way.'

'His Lordship is quite aware how much he owes to Mr Du Boung,' said Tregear. Whereupon Lord Silverbridge bowed.

'And now what are we to do?' said Lord Silverbridge.

Then there was a little whispering between Mr Sprout and Mr Sprugeon. 'Perhaps, Mr Du Boung,' said Sprugeon, 'his Lordship had better call first on Dr Tempest.'*

'Perhaps,' said the injured brewer, 'as it is to be a party affair after all I had better retire from the scene.'

'I thought all that was to be given up,' said Tregear.

'Oh, certainly,' said Sprout. 'Suppose we go to Mr Walker* first?'

'I'm up to anything,' said Lord Silverbridge; 'but of course everybody understands that I am a Conservative.'

'Oh dear yes,' said Sprugeon.

'We are all aware of that,' said Sprout.

'And very glad we've all of us been to hear it,' said the landlord.

'Though there are some in the borough who could have wished, my Lord, that you had stuck to the old Palliser politics,' said Mr Du Boung.

'But I haven't stuck to the Palliser politics. Just at present I think that order and all that sort of thing should be maintained.'

'Hear, hear!' said the landlord.

'And now, as I have expressed my views generally, I am willing to go anywhere.'

'Then we'll go to Mr Walker first,' said Sprugeon. Now it was understood that in the borough, among those who really had opinions of their own, Mr Walker the old attorney stood first as a Liberal, and Dr Tempest the old rector first as a Conservative.

'I am glad to see your Lordship in the town which gives you its name,' said Mr Walker, who was a hale old gentleman with silvery-white hair, over seventy years of age. 'I proposed your father for this borough on, I think, six or seven different occasions. They used to go in and out then whenever they changed their offices.'

'We hope you'll propose Lord Silverbridge now,' said Mr Sprugeon.

'Oh; well;—yes. He's his father's son, and I never knew anything but good of the family. I wish you were going to sit on the same side, my Lord.'

'Times are changed a little perhaps,' said his Lordship.

'The matter is not to be discussed now,' said the old attorney. 'I understand that. Only I hope you'll excuse me if I say that a man ought to get up very early in the morning if he means to see further into politics than your father.'

'Very early indeed,' said Mr Du Boung, shaking his head.

'That's all right,' said Lord Silverbridge.

'I'll propose you, my Lord. I need not wish you success, because there is no one to stand against you.'

Then they went to Dr Tempest, who was also an old man. 'Yes, my Lord, I shall be proud to second you,' said the rector. 'I didn't think that I should ever do that to one of your name in Silverbridge.'

'I hope you think I've made a change for the better,' said the candidate.

'You've come over to my school of course, and I suppose I am bound to think that a change for the better. Nevertheless I have a kind of idea that certain people ought to be Tories and that other certain people ought to be Whigs. What does your father say about it?'

'My father wishes me to be in the House, and that he has not quarrelled with me you may know by the fact that had there been a contest he would have paid my expenses.'

'A father generally has to do that whether he approves of what his son is about or not,' said the caustic old gentleman.

There was nothing else to be done. They all went back to the hotel, and Mr Sprugeon with Mr Sprout and the landlord drank a glass of sherry at the candidate's expense, wishing him political long life and prosperity. There was no one else whom it was thought necessary that the candidate should visit, and the next day he returned to town with the understanding that on the day appointed in the next week he should come back again to be elected.

And on the day appointed the two young men again went to Silverbridge, and after he had been declared duly elected, the new Member of Parliament made his first speech. There was a meeting in the town-hall and many were assembled anxious to hear,—not the lad's opinions, for which probably nobody cared much,—but the tone of his voice and to see his manner. Of what sort was the eldest son of the man of whom the neighbourhood had been so proud? For the county was in truth proud of their Duke. Of this son whom they had now made a Member of Parliament they at present only knew that he had been sent away from Oxford,—not so very long ago,—for painting the Dean's house scarlet. The speech was not very brilliant. He told them that he was very much obliged to them for the honour they had done him. Though he could not follow exactly his father's political opinions,—he would always have before his eyes his father's political honesty and independence. He broke down two or three times and blushed, and repeated himself, and knocked his words a great deal too quickly one on the top of another. But it was taken very well, and was better than was expected. When it was over he wrote a line to the Duke.

'MY DEAR FATHER,

'I am Member of Parliament for Silverbridge,—as you used to be in the days which I can first remember. I hope you won't think that it does not make me unhappy to have differed from you. Indeed it does. I don't think that anybody has ever done so well in politics as you have.

But when a man does take up an opinion I don't see how he can help himself. Of course I could have kept myself quiet;—but then you wished me to be in the House. They were all very civil to me at Silverbridge, but there was very little said.

'Your affectionate Son,
'SILVERBRIDGE.'

## CHAPTER 15

### THE DUKE RECEIVES A LETTER,—AND WRITES ONE

THE DUKE, when he received Mrs Finn's note, demanding an interview, thought much upon the matter before he replied. She had made her demand as though the Duke had been no more than any other gentleman, almost as though she had a right to call upon him to wait upon her. He understood and admired the courage of this;—but nevertheless he would not go to her. He had trusted her with that which of all things was the most sacred to him, and she had deceived him! He wrote to her as follows:

'The Duke of Omnium presents his compliments to Mrs Finn. As the Duke thinks that no good could result either to Mrs Finn or to himself from an interview, he is obliged to say that he would rather not do as Mrs Finn has requested.

'But for the strength of this conviction the Duke would have waited upon Mrs Finn most willingly.'

Mrs Finn when she received this was not surprised. She had felt sure that such would be the nature of the Duke's answer; but she was also sure that if such an answer did come she would not let the matter rest. The accusation was so bitter to her that she would spare nothing in defending herself,—nothing in labour and nothing in time. She would make him know that she was in earnest. As she could not succeed in getting into his presence she must do this by letter,—and she wrote her letter, taking two days to think of her words.

'May 18, 18—.

'MY DEAR DUKE OF OMNIUM,

'As you will not come to me, I must trouble your Grace to read what I fear will be a long letter. For it is absolutely necessary that I should explain my conduct to you. That you have condemned me I am sure you will not deny;—nor that you have punished me as far as the power of punishment was in your hands. If I can succeed in making you see that you have judged me wrongly, I think you will admit your error and beg my pardon. You are not one who from your nature can be brought easily to do this; but you are one who will certainly do it if you can be made to feel that by not doing so you would be unjust. I am myself so clear as to my own rectitude of purpose and conduct, and am so well aware of your perspicuity, that I venture to believe that if you will read this letter I shall convince you.

'Before I go any further I will confess that the matter is one,—I was going to say almost of life and death to me. Circumstances, not of my own seeking, have for some years past thrown me so closely into inter-course with your family that now to be cast off, and to be put on one side as a disgraced person,—and that so quickly after the death of her who loved me so dearly and who was so dear to me,—is such an affront as I cannot bear and hold up my head afterwards. I have come to be known as her whom your uncle trusted and loved, as her whom your wife trusted and loved,—obscure as I was before;—and as her whom, may I not say, you yourself trusted? As there was much of honour and very much of pleasure in this, so also was there something of misfor-tune. Friendships are safest when the friends are of the same standing. I have always felt there was danger, and now the thing I feared has come home to me.

'Now I will plead my case. I fancy, that when first you heard that I had been cognisant of your daughter's engagement, you imagined that I was aware of it before I went to Matching. Had I been so, I should have been guilty of that treachery of which you accuse me. I did know nothing of it till Lady Mary told me on the day before I left Matching. That she should tell me was natural enough. Her mother had known it, and for the moment,—if I am not assuming too much in saying so,— I was filling her mother's place. But, in reference to you, I could not exercise the discretion which a mother might have used, and I told her at once, most decidedly, that you must be made acquainted with the fact.

'Then Lady Mary expressed to me her wish,—not that this matter should be kept any longer from you, for that it should be told she was as anxious as I was myself,—but that it should be told to you by Mr Tregear. It was not for me to raise any question as to Mr Tregear's fitness or unfitness,—as to which indeed I could know nothing. All I could do was to say that if Mr Tregear would make the communication at once, I should feel that I had done my duty. The upshot was that Mr Tregear came to me immediately on my return to London, and agreeing with me that it was imperative that you be informed, went to you and did inform you. In all of that, if I have told the story truly, where has been my offence? I suppose you will believe me, but your daughter can give evidence as to every word that I have written.

'I think that you have got it into your mind that I have befriended Mr Tregear's suit, and that, having received this impression, you hold it with the tenacity which is usual to you. There never was a greater mistake. I went to Matching as the friend of my dear friend;—but I stayed there at your request, as your friend. Had I been, when you asked me to do so, a participator in that secret I could not have honestly remained in the position you assigned to me. Had I done so, I should have deserved your ill opinion. As it is I have not deserved it, and your condemnation of me has been altogether unjust. Should I not now receive from you a full withdrawal of all charge against me, I shall be driven to think that after all the insight which circumstances have given me into your character, I have nevertheless been mistaken in the reading of it.

'I remain,
'Dear Duke of Omnium,
'Yours truly,
'M. FINN.

'I find on looking over my letter that I must add one word further. It might seem that I am asking for a return of your friendship. Such is not my purpose. Neither can you forget that you have accused me,—nor can I. What I expect is that you should tell me that you in your conduct to me have been wrong and that I in mine to you have been right. I must be enabled to feel that the separation between us has come from injury done to me, and not by me.'

He did read the letter more than once, and read it with tingling ears, and hot cheeks, and a knitted brow. As the letter went on, and as the woman's sense of wrong grew hot from her own telling of her own story, her words became stronger and still stronger, till at last they were almost insolent in their strength. Were it not that they came from one who did think herself to have been wronged, then certainly they would be insolent. A sense of injury, a burning conviction of wrong sustained, will justify language which otherwise would be unbearable. The Duke felt that, and though his ears were tingling and his brow knitted, he could have forgiven the language, if only he could have admitted the argument. He understood every word of it. When she spoke of tenacity she intended to charge him with obstinacy. Though she had dwelt but lightly on her own services she had made her thoughts on the matter clear enough. 'I, Mrs Finn, who am nobody, have done much to succour and assist you, the Duke of Omnium; and this is the return which I have received!' And then she told him to his face that unless he did something which it would be impossible that he should do, she would revoke her opinion of his honesty! He tried to persuade himself that her opinion about his honesty was nothing to him;—but he failed. Her opinion was very much to him. Though in his anger he had determined to throw her off from him, he knew her to be one whose good opinion was worth having.

Not a word of overt accusation had been made against his wife. Every allusion to her was full of love. But yet how heavy a charge was really made! That such a secret should be kept from him, the father, was acknowledged to be a heinous fault;—but the wife had known the secret and had kept it from him, the father! And then how wretched a thing it was for him that anyone should dare to write to him about the wife that had been taken away from him! In spite of all her faults her name was so holy to him that it had never once passed his lips since her death, except in low whispers to himself,—low whispers made in the perfect, double-guarded seclusion of his own chamber. 'Cora, Cora,' he had murmured, so that the sense of the sound and not the sound itself had come to him from his own lips. And now this woman wrote to him about her freely, as though there were nothing sacred, no religion in the memory of her.

'It was not for me to raise any question as to Mr Tregear's fitness.' Was it not palpable to all the world that he was unfit? Unfit! How could a man be more unfit? He was asking for the hand of one who was second only to royalty—who was possessed of everything, who was beautiful, well-born, rich, who was the daughter of the Duke of Omnium, and he had absolutely nothing of his own to offer.

But it was necessary that he should at last come to the consideration of the actual point as to which she had written to him so forcibly. He tried to set himself to the task in perfect honesty. He certainly had condemned her. He had condemned her and had no doubt punished her to the extent of his power. And if he could be brought to see that he had done this unjustly, then certainly must he beg her pardon. And when he considered it all, he had to own that her intimacy with his uncle and his wife had not been so much of her seeking as of theirs. It grieved him now that it should have been so, but so it was. And after all this,—after the affectionate surrender of herself to his wife's caprices which the woman had made,—he had turned upon her and driven her away with ignominy. That was all true. As he thought of it he became hot, and was conscious of a quivering feeling round his heart. These were bonds indeed; but they were bonds of such a nature as to be capable of being rescinded and cut away altogether by absolute bad conduct. If he could make it good to himself that in a matter of such magnitude as the charge of his daughter she had been untrue to him and had leagued herself against him, with an unworthy lover, then, then—all bonds would be rescinded! Then would his wrath be altogether justified! Then would it have been impossible that he should have done aught else than cast her out! As he thought of this he felt sure that she had betrayed him! How great would be the ignominy to him should he be driven to own to himself that she had not betrayed him! 'There should not have been a moment,' he said to himself over and over again,—'not a moment!' Yes;—she certainly had betrayed him.

There might still be safety for him in that confident assertion of 'not a moment'; but had there been anything of that conspiracy of which he had certainly at first judged her to be guilty? She had told her story, and had then appealed to Lady Mary for evidence. After five minutes of perfect stillness,—but five minutes of misery, five minutes during which great beads of perspiration broke out from him and stood upon his brow, he had to confess to himself that he did not want any evidence. He did believe her story. When he allowed himself to think she had been in league with Tregear he had wronged her. He wiped away the beads from his brow, and again repeated to himself those words which were now his only comfort, 'There should not have been a moment;—not a moment!'

It was thus and only thus that he was enabled to assure himself that there need be no acknowledgment of wrong done on his part. Having settled this in his own mind he forced himself to attend a meeting at which his assistance had been asked as to a complex question on Law Reform. The Duke endeavoured to give himself up entirely to the matter; but through it all there was the picture before him of Mrs Finn waiting for an answer to her letter. If he should confirm himself in his opinion that he had been right, then would any answer be necessary? He might just acknowledge the letter, after the fashion which has come up in official life, than which silence is an insult much more bearable. But he did not wish to insult, nor to punish her further. He would willingly have withdrawn the punishment under which she was groaning could he have done so without self-abasement. Or he might write as she had done,—advocating his own cause with all his strength, using that last one strong argument,—'there should not have been a moment.' But there would be something repulsive to his personal dignity in the continued correspondence which this would produce. 'The Duke of Omnium regrets to say, in answer to Mrs Finn's letter, that he thinks no good can be attained by a prolonged correspondence.' Such, or of such kind, he thought must be his answer. But, would this be a fair return for the solicitude shown by her to his uncle, for the love which had made her so patient a friend to his wife, for the nobility of her own conduct in many things? Then his mind reverted to certain jewels,— supposed to be of enormous value,—which were still in his possession though they were the property of this woman. They had been left to her by his uncle, and she had obstinately refused to take them. Now they were lying packed in the cellars of certain bankers,—but still they were in his custody. What should he now do in this matter? Hitherto, perhaps once in every six months, he had notified to her that he was keeping them as her curator, and she had always repeated that it was a charge from which she could not relieve him. It had become almost a joke between them. But how could he joke with a woman with whom he had quarrelled after this internecine fashion?

What if he were to consult Lady Cantrip? He could not do so without a pang that would be very bitter to him,—but any agony would be better than that arising from a fear that he had been unjust to one who had deserved well of him. No doubt Lady Cantrip would see it in the same light as he had done. And then he would be able to support himself by the assurance that that which he had judged to be right was approved of by one whom the world would acknowledge to be a good judge on such a matter.

When he got home he found his son's letter telling him of the election at Silverbridge. There was something in it which softened his heart to the young man,—or perhaps it was that in the midst of his many discomforts he wished to find something which at least was not painful to him. That his son and his heir should insist on entering political life in opposition to him was of course a source of pain; but, putting that aside, the thing had been done pleasantly enough, and the young member's letter had been written with some good feeling. So he answered the letter as pleasantly as he knew how.

'MY DEAR SILVERBRIDGE,

'I am glad that you are in Parliament and am glad also that you should have been returned by the old borough; though I would that you could have reconciled yourself to adhering to the politics of your family. But there is nothing disgraceful in such a change, and I am able to congratulate you as a father should a son and to wish you long life and success as a legislator.

'There are one or two things* I would ask you to remember;—and firstly this, that as you have voluntarily undertaken certain duties you are bound as an honest man to perform them as scrupulously as though you were paid for doing them.* There was no obligation in you to seek the post;—but having sought it and acquired it you cannot neglect the work attached to it without being untrue to the covenant you have made. It is necessary that a young member of Parliament should bear this in his mind, and especially a member who has not worked his way up to notoriety outside the House, because to him there will be great facility for idleness and neglect.

'And then I would have you always remember the purport for which there is a Parliament elected in this happy and free country. It is not that some men may shine there, that some may acquire power, or that all may plume themselves on being the elect of the nation. It often appears to me that some members of Parliament so regard their success in life,—as the fellows of our colleges do too often, thinking that their fellowships were awarded for their comfort and not for the furtherance of any object as education or religion. I have known gentlemen who have felt that in becoming members of Parliament they had achieved an object for themselves instead of thinking that they had put themselves in the way of achieving something for others. A member of Parliament should feel himself to be the servant of his country,—and like every other servant, he should serve. If this be distasteful to a man he need not go into Parliament. If the harness gall him he need not wear it. But if he takes the trappings, then he should draw the coach. You are there as the guardian of your fellow-countrymen,—that they may be safe, that they may be prosperous, that they may be well governed and lightly burdened,*—above all that they may be free. If you cannot feel this to be your duty, you should not be there at all.

'And I would have you remember also that the work of a member of Parliament can seldom be of that brilliant nature which is of itself charming; and that the young member should think of such brilliancy as being possible to him only at a distance. It should be your first care to sit and listen so that the forms and methods of the House may as it were soak into you gradually. And then you must bear in mind that speaking in the House is but a very small part of a member's work, perhaps that part which he may lay aside altogether with the least strain on his conscience. A good member of Parliament will be good upstairs in the Committee Rooms, good downstairs to make and to keep a House, good to vote, for his party if it may be nothing better, but for the measures also which he believes to be for the good of his country.

'Gradually, if you will give your thoughts to it, and above all your time, the theory of legislation will sink into your mind, and you will find that there will come upon you the ineffable delight of having served your country to the best of your ability.

'It is the only pleasure in life which has been enjoyed without alloy by your affectionate father,

'OMNIUM.'

The Duke in writing this letter was able for a few moments to forget Mrs Finn, and to enjoy the work which he had on hand.

## CHAPTER 16

### 'POOR BOY'

THE new member for Silverbridge, when he entered the House to take the oath, was supported on the right and left by two staunch old Tories. Mr Monk had seen him a few minutes previously,—Mr Monk who of all Liberals was the firmest and than whom no one had been more staunch to the Duke,*—and had congratulated him on his election, expressing at the same time some gentle regrets. 'I only wish you could have come among us on the other side,' he said.

'But I couldn't,' said the young Lord.

'I am sure nothing but a conscientious feeling would have separated you from your father's friends,' said the old Liberal. And then they were parted, and the member for Silverbridge was bustled up to the table between two staunch Tories.

Of what else was done on that occasion nothing shall be said here. No political work was required from him, except that of helping for an hour or two to crowd the Government benches. But we will follow him as he left the House. There were one or two others quite as anxious as to his political career as any staunch old Liberal. At any rate one other. He had promised that as soon as he could get away from the House he would go to Belgrave Square and tell Lady Mabel Grex all about it. When he reached the square it was past seven, but Lady Mabel and Miss Cassewary were still in the drawing-room.

'There seemed to be a great deal of bustle, and I didn't understand much about it,' said the member.

'But you heard the speeches?' These were the speeches made on the proposing and seconding of the address.

'Oh, yes;—Lupton did it very well. Lord George didn't seem to be quite so good. Then Sir Timothy Beeswax* made a speech, and then Mr Monk. After that I saw other fellows going away, so I bolted too.'

'If I were a member of Parliament I would never leave it while the House was sitting,' said Miss Cassewary.

'If all were like that there wouldn't be seats for them to sit upon,' said Silverbridge.

'A persistent member will always find a seat,' continued the positive old lady.

'I am sure that Lord Silverbridge means to do his duty,' said Lady Mabel.

'Oh yes;—I've thought a good deal about it, and I mean to try. As long as a man isn't called upon to speak I don't see why it shouldn't be easy enough.'

'I'm so glad to hear you say so! Of course after a little time you will speak. I should so like to hear you make your first speech.'

'If I thought you were there, I'm sure I should not make it at all.'

Just at this period Miss Cassewary, saying something as to the necessity of dressing, and cautioning her young friend that there was not much time to be lost, left the room.

'Dressing does not take me more than ten minutes,' said Lady Mabel.

Miss Cassewary declared this to be nonsense, but she nevertheless left the room. Whether she would have done so if Lord Silverbridge had not been Lord Silverbridge, but had been some young man with whom it would not have been expedient that Lady Mabel should fall in love, may perhaps be doubted. But then it may be taken as certain that under such circumstances Lady Mabel herself would not have remained. She had quite realised the duties of life, had had her little romance,—and had acknowledged that it was foolish.

'I do so hope that you will do well,' she said, going back to the parliamentary duties.

'I don't think I shall ever do much. I shall never be like my father.'

'I don't see why not.'

'There never was anybody like him. I am always amusing myself, but he never cared for amusement.'

'You are very young.'

'As far as I can learn he was just as he is now at my age. My mother has told me that long before she married him he used to spend all his time in the House. I wonder whether you would mind reading the letter he wrote me when he heard of my election.'

Then he took the epistle out of his pocket and handed it to Lady Mabel.

'He means all that he says.'

'He always does that.'

'And he really hopes that you will put your shoulder to the wheel;— even though you must do so in opposition to him.'

'That makes no difference. I think my father is a very fine fellow.'

'Shall you do all that he tells you?'

'Well;—I suppose not;—except that he advises me to hold my tongue. I think that I shall do that. I mean to go down there, you know, and I dare say I shall be much the same as others.'

'Has he talked to you much about it?'

'No;—he never talks much. Every now and then he will give me a downright lecture, or he will write me a letter like that; but he never talks to any of us.'

'How very odd.'

'Yes; he is odd. He seems to be fretful when we are with him. A good many things make him unhappy.'

'Your poor mother's death.'

'That first;—and then there are other things. I suppose he didn't like the way I came to an end at Oxford.'

'You were a boy then.'

'Of course I was very sorry for it,—though I hated Oxford. It was neither one thing nor another. You were your own master and yet you were not.'

'Now you must be your own master.'

'I suppose so.'

'You must marry, and become a lord of the Treasury. When I was a child I acted as a child. You know all about that.'

'Oh yes. And now I must throw off childish things.* You mean that I mustn't paint any man's house? Eh, Lady Mab.'

'That and the rest of it. You are a legislator now.'

'So is Popplecourt, who took his seat in the House of Lords two or three months ago. He's the biggest young fool I know out. He couldn't even paint a house.'

'He is not an elected legislator. It makes all the difference. I quite agree with what the Duke says. Lord Popplecourt can't help himself.

Whether he's an idle young scamp or not, he must be a legislator. But when a man goes in for it himself, as you have done, he should make up his mind to be useful.'

'I shall vote with my party of course.'

'More than that; much more than that. If you didn't care for politics you couldn't have taken a line of your own.' When she said this she knew that he had been talked into what he had done by Tregear,—by Tregear, who had ambition, and intelligence, and capacity for forming an opinion of his own. 'If you do not do it for your own sake, you will for the sake of those who,—who,—who are your friends,' she said at last, not feeling quite able to tell him that he must do it for the sake of those who loved him.

'There are not very many I suppose who care about it.'

'Your father.'

'Oh yes,—my father.'

'And Tregear.'

'Tregear has got his own fish to fry.'

'Are there none others? Do you think we care nothing about it here?'

'Miss Cassewary?'

'Well;—Miss Cassewary! A man might have a worse friend than Miss Cassewary;—and my father.'

'I don't suppose Lord Grex cares a straw about me.'

'Indeed he does,—a great many straws. And so do I. Do you think I don't care a straw about it?'

'I don't know why you should.'

'Because it is my nature to be earnest. A girl comes out into the world so young that she becomes serious, and steady as it were, so much sooner than a man does.'

'I always think that nobody is so full of chaff* as you are, Lady Mab.'

'I am not chaffing now in recommending you to go to work in the world like a man.'

As she said this they were sitting on the same sofa, but with some space between them. When Miss Cassewary had left the room Lord Silverbridge was standing, but after a little he had fallen into the seat, at the extreme corner, and had gradually come a little nearer to her. Now in her energy she put out her hand, meaning perhaps to touch lightly the sleeve of his coat, meaning perhaps not quite to touch him at all. But as she did so he put out his hand and took hold of hers.

She drew it away, not seeming to allow it to remain in his grasp for a moment; but she did so, not angrily, or hurriedly, or with any flurry.

She did it as though it were natural that he should take her hand and as natural that she should recover it.

'Indeed I have hardly more than ten minutes left for dressing,' she said, rising from her seat.

'If you will say that you care about it, you yourself, I will do my best.' As he made this declaration blushes covered his cheeks and forehead.

'I do care about it,—very much; I myself,' said Lady Mabel, not blushing at all. Then there was a knock at the door, and Lady Mabel's maid putting her head in, declared that my Lord had come in and had already been some time in his dressing-room. 'Good-bye, Lord Silverbridge,' she said quite gaily, and rather more aloud than would have been necessary, had she not intended that the maid also should hear her.

'Poor boy!' she said to herself as she was dressing. 'Poor boy!' Then, when the evening was over she spoke to herself again about him. 'Dear sweet boy!' And then she sat and thought. How was it that she was so old a woman, while he was so little more than a child? How fair he was, how far removed from conceit, how capable of being made into a man—in the process of time! What might not be expected from him if he could be kept in good hands for the next ten years! But in whose hands? What would she be in ten years, she who already seemed to know the town and all its belongings so well? And yet she was as young in years as he. He, as she knew, had passed his twenty-second birthday,—and so had she. That was all. It might be good for her that she should marry him. She was ambitious. And such a marriage would satisfy her ambition. Through her father's fault, and her brother's, she was likely to be poor. This man would certainly be rich. Many of those who were buzzing around her from day to day, were distasteful to her. From among them she knew that she could not take a husband, let their rank and wealth be what it might. She was too fastidious, too proud, too prone to think that things should be with her as she liked them! This last was in all things pleasant to her. Though he was but a boy, there was a certain boyish manliness about him. The very way in which he had grasped at her hand and had then blushed ruby-red at his own daring, had gone far with her. How gracious he was to look at! Dear sweet boy! Love him? No;—she did not know that she loved him. That dream was over. She was sure however that she liked him.

But how would it be with him? It might be well for her to become his wife, but could it be well for him that he should become her husband? Did she not feel that it would be better for him that he should become a man before he married at all? Perhaps so;—but then if she desisted would others desist? If she did not put out her bait would there not be other hooks,—others and worse? Would not such a one, so soft, so easy, so prone to be caught and so desirable for the catching, be sure to be made prey of by some snare?

But could she love him? That a woman should not marry a man without loving him, she partly knew. But she thought she knew also that there must be exceptions. She would do her very best to love him. That other man should be banished from her very thoughts. She would be such a wife to him that he should never know that he lacked anything. Poor boy! Sweet dear boy! He, as he went away to his dinner, had his thoughts also about her. Of all the girls he knew she was the jolliest,—and of all his friends she was the pleasantest. As she was anxious that he should go to work in the House of Commons he would go to work there. As for loving her! Well;—of course he must marry someone, and why not Lady Mab as well as anyone else?

## CHAPTER 17

### THE DERBY

AN attendance at the Newmarket Second Spring Meeting had unfortunately not been compatible with the Silverbridge election. Major Tifto had therefore been obliged to look after the affair alone. 'A very useful mare,' as Tifto had been in the habit of calling a leggy, thoroughbred, meagre-looking brute named Coalition, was on this occasion confided to the Major's sole care and judgment. But Coalition failed, as coalitions always do, and Tifto had to report to his noble patron that they had not pulled off the event. It had been a match for four hundred pounds, made indeed by Lord Silverbridge, but made at the suggestion of Tifto;—and now Tifto wrote in a very bad humour about it. It had been altogether his Lordship's fault in submitting to carry two pounds more* than Tifto had thought to be fair and equitable. The match had been lost. Would Lord Silverbridge be so good as to pay the money to Mr Green Griffin and debit him, Tifto, with the share of his loss?

We must acknowledge that the unpleasant tone of the Major's letter was due quite as much to the ill-usage he had received in reference to that journey to Silverbridge, as to the loss of the race. Within that little body there was a high-mounting heart, and that heart had been greatly wounded by his lordship's treatment. Tifto had felt himself to have been treated like a servant. Hardly an excuse had even been made. He had been simply told that he was not wanted. He was apt sometimes to tell himself that he knew on which side his bread was buttered. But perhaps he hardly knew how best to keep the butter going. There was a little pride about him which was antagonistic to the best interests of such a trade as his. Perhaps it was well that he should inwardly suffer when injured. But it could not be well that he should declare to such men as Nidderdale, and Dolly Longstaff, and Popplecourt that he didn't mean to put up with that sort of thing. He certainly should not have spoken in this strain before Tregear. Of all men living he hated and feared him the most. And he knew that no other man loved Silverbridge as did Tregear. Had he been thinking of his bread-and-butter, instead of giving way to the mighty anger of his little bosom, he would have hardly declared openly at the club that he would let Lord Silverbridge know that he did not mean to stand any man's airs. But these extravagances were due perhaps to whisky-and-water, and that kind of intoxication which comes to certain men from moment-ary triumphs. Tifto could always be got to make a fool of himself when surrounded by three or four men of rank who, for the occasion, would talk to him as an equal. He almost declared that Coalition had lost his match because he had not been taken down to Silverbridge.

'Tifto is in a deuce of a way with you,' said Dolly Longstaff to the young member.

'I know all about it,' said Silverbridge, who had had an interview with his partner since the race.

'If you don't take care he'll dismiss you.'

Silverbridge did not care much about this, knowing that words of wisdom did not ordinarily fall from the mouth of Dolly Longstaff. But he was more moved when his friend Tregear spoke to him. 'I wish you knew the kind of things that fellow Tifto says behind your back.'

'As if I cared!'

'But you ought to care.'

'Do you care what every fellow says about you?'

'I care very much what those say whom I choose to live with me. Whatever Tifto might say about me would be quite indifferent to me, because we have nothing in common. But you and he are bound together.'

'We have a horse or two in common; that's all.'

'But that is a great deal. The truth is he's a nasty, brawling, boasting, ill-conditioned little reptile.'

Silverbridge of course did not acknowledge that this was true. But he felt it, and almost repented of his trust in Tifto. But still Prime Minister* stood very well for the Derby. He was second favourite, the odds against him being only four to one. The glory of being part owner of a probable winner of the Derby was so much to him that he could not bring himself to be altogether angry with Tifto. There was no doubt that the horse's present condition was due entirely to Tifto's care. Tifto spent in these few days just before the race the greatest part of his time in the close vicinity of the horse, only running up to London now and then, as a fish comes up to the surface, for a breath of air. It was impossible that Lord Silverbridge should separate himself from the Major,—at any rate till after the Epsom meeting.

He had paid the money for the match without a word of reproach to his partner, but still with a feeling that things were not quite as they ought to be. In money matters his father had been liberal, but not very definite. He had been told that he ought not to spend above two thousand pounds a year, and had been reminded that there was a house for him to use both in town and in the country. But he had been given to understand also that any application made to Mr Morton, if not very unreasonable, would be attended with success. A solemn promise had been exacted from him that he would have no dealings with money-lenders;*—and then he had been set afloat. There had been a rather frequent correspondence with Mr Morton, who had once or twice submitted a total of the money paid on behalf of his correspondent. Lord Silverbridge, who imagined himself to be anything but extravagant, had wondered how the figures could mount up so rapidly. But the money needed was always forthcoming, and the raising of objections never seemed to be carried back beyond Mr Morton. His promise to his father about the money lenders had been scrupulously kept. As long as ready money can be made to be forthcoming without any charge for interest, a young man must be very foolish who will prefer to borrow it at twenty-five per cent.

Now had come the night before the Derby, and it must be acknowledged that the young Lord was much fluttered by the greatness of the coming struggle. Tifto, having seen his horse conveyed to Epsom,* had come up to London in order that he might dine with his partner and hear what was being said about the race at the Beargarden. The party dining there consisted of Silverbridge, Dolly Longstaff, Popplecourt, and Tifto. Nidderdale was to have joined them, but he told them on the day before, with a sigh, that domestic duties were too strong for him. Lady Nidderdale,—or if not Lady Nidderdale herself, then Lady Nidderdale's

mother,—was so far potent over the young nobleman as to induce him to
confine his Derby jovialities to the Derby Day. Another guest had also
been expected, the reason for whose non-appearance must be explained
somewhat at length. Lord Gerald Palliser, the Duke's second son, was at
this time at Cambridge,—being almost as popular at Trinity as his
brother had been at Christ Church. It was to him quite a matter of course
that he should see his brother's horse run for the Derby. But, unfortunately, in this very year a stand was being made by the University pundits* against a practice which they thought had become too general. For
the last year or two it had been considered almost as much a matter of
course that a Cambridge undergraduate should go to the Derby as that a
Member of Parliament should do so.* Against this three or four rigid
disciplinarians had raised their voices,—and as a result, no young man
up at Trinity could get leave to be away on the Derby pretext.

Lord Gerald raged against the restriction very loudly. He at first
proclaimed his intention of ignoring the college authorities altogether.
Of course he would be expelled. But the order itself was to his thinking
so absurd,—the idea that he should not see his brother's horse run was
so extravagant,—that he argued that his father could not be angry with
him for incurring dismissal in so excellent a cause. But his brother saw
things in a different light. He knew how his father had looked at him
when he had been sent away from Oxford, and he counselled moder-
ation. Gerald should see the Derby, but should not encounter that
heaviest wrath of all which comes from a man's not sleeping beneath
his college roof. There was a train which left Cambridge at an early
hour, and would bring him into London in time to accompany his
friends to the racecourse;—and another train, a special, which would
take him down after dinner, so that he and others should reach
Cambridge before the college gates were shut.

The dinner at the Beargarden was very joyous. Of course the state of
the betting in regard to Prime Minister was the subject generally popular for the night. Mr Lupton came in, a gentleman well known in all
fashionable circles, parliamentary, social, and racing, who was rather
older than his company on this occasion, but still not so much so as to
be found to be an incumbrance. Lord Glasslough too, and others joined
them, and a good deal was said about the horse. 'I never keep these
things dark,' said Tifto. 'Of course he's an uncertain horse.'

'Most horses are,' said Lupton.

'Just so, Mr Lupton. What I mean is, the Minister has got a bit of
temper. But if he likes to do his best I don't think any three-year-old*
in England can get his nose past him.'

'For half a mile he'd be nowhere with the Provence filly,' said Glasslough.

'I'm speaking of a Derby distance, my Lord.'

'That's a kind of thing nobody really knows,' said Lupton.

'I've seen him 'ave his gallops,' said the little man, who in his moments of excitement would sometimes fall away from that exact pronunciation which had been one of the studies of his life, 'and have measured his stride. I think I know what pace means. Of course I'm not going to answer for the 'orse. He's a temper, but if things go favourably, no animal that ever showed on the Downs* was more likely to do the trick. Is there any gentleman here who would like to bet me fifteen to one in hundreds against the two events,—the Derby and the Leger?'* The desired odds were at once offered by Mr Lupton, and the bet was booked.

This gave rise to other betting, and before the evening was over Lord Silverbridge had taken three-and-a-half to one against his horse to such an extent that he stood to lose twelve hundred pounds. The champagne which he had drunk, and the news that Quousque,* the first favourite, had so gone to pieces that now there was a question which was the first favourite, had so inflated him that, had he been left alone, he would almost have wagered even money on his horse. In the midst of his excitement there came to him a feeling that he was allowing himself to do just that which he had intended to avoid. But then the occasion was so peculiar! How often can it happen to a man in his life that he shall own a favourite for the Derby? The affair was one in which it was almost necessary that he should risk a little money.

Tifto, when he got into his bed, was altogether happy. He had added whisky-and-water to his champagne, and feared nothing. If Prime Minister should win the Derby he would be able to pay all that he owed, and to make a start with money in his pocket. And then there would be attached to him all the infinite glory of being the owner of a winner of the Derby. The horse was run in his name. Thoughts as to great successes crowded themselves upon his heated brain. What might not be open to him? Parliament! The Jockey Club!* The mastership of one of the crack shire packs!* Might it not come to pass that he should some day become the great authority in England upon races, race-horses, and hunters? If he could be the winner of a Derby and Leger he thought that Glasslough and Lupton would snub him no longer, that even Tregear would speak to him, and that his pal the Duke's son would never throw him aside again.

Lord Silverbridge had bought a drag* with all its appendages. There was a coach, the four bay horses, the harness, and the two regulation grooms. When making this purchase he had condescended to say a word to his father on the subject. 'Everybody belongs to the four-in-hand club now,' said the son.

'I never did,' said the Duke.

'Ah,—if I could be like you!'

The Duke had said that he would think about it, and then had told Mr Morton that he was to pay the bill for this new toy. He had thought about it, and had assured himself that driving a coach and four was at present regarded as a fitting amusement for young men of rank and wealth. He did not understand it himself. It seemed to him to be as unnatural as though a gentleman should turn blacksmith and make horseshoes for his amusement. Driving four horses was hard work. But the same might be said of rowing. There were men, he knew, who would spend their days standing at a lathe, making little boxes for their recreation. He did not sympathise with it. But the fact was so, and this driving of coaches was regarded with favour. He had been a little touched by that word his son had spoken. 'Ah,—if I could be like you!' So he had given the permission; the drag, horses, harness, and grooms had come into the possession of Lord Silverbridge; and now they were put into requisition to take their triumphant owner and his party down to Epsom. Dolly Longstaff's team was sent down to meet them half-way. Gerald Palliser, who had come up from Cambridge that morning, was allowed to drive the first stage out of town to compensate him for the cruelty done to him by the University pundits. Tifto, with a cigar in his mouth, with a white hat and a blue veil, and a new light-coloured coat, was by no means the least happy of the party.

How that race was run, and how both Prime Minister and Quousque were beaten by an outsider named Fishknife, Prime Minister, however, coming in a good second, the present writer having no aptitude in that way, cannot describe. Such, however, were the facts, and then Dolly Longstaff and Lord Silverbridge drove the coach back to London. The coming back was not so triumphant, though the young fellows bore their failure well. Dolly Longstaff had lost a 'pot of money', Silverbridge would have to draw upon that inexhaustible Mr Morton for something over two thousand pounds,—in regard to which he had no doubt as to the certainty with which the money would be forthcoming, but he feared that it would give rise to special notice from his father. Even the poor younger brother had lost a couple of hundred pounds, for which he would have to make his own special application to Mr Morton.

But Tifto felt it more than anyone. The horse ought to have won. Fishknife had been favoured by such a series of accidents that the whole affair had been a miracle. Tifto had these circumstances at his fingers' ends, and in the course of the afternoon and evening explained them accurately to all who would listen to him. He had this to say on his own behalf,—that before the party had left the course their horse stood first favourite for the Leger. But Tifto was unhappy as he came back to town, and in spite of the lunch, which had been very glorious, sat moody and sometimes even silent within his gay apparel.

'It was the unfairest start I ever saw,' said Tifto, almost getting up from his seat on the coach so as to address Dolly and Silverbridge on the box.

'What the —— is the good of that?' said Dolly from the coach-box. 'Take your licking and don't squeal.'

'That's all very well. I can take my licking as well as another man. But one has to look to the causes of these things. I never saw Peppermint ride so badly. Before he got round the Corner I wished I'd been on the horse myself.'

'I don't believe it was Peppermint's fault a bit,' said Silverbridge.

'Well;—perhaps not. Only I did think that I was a pretty good judge of riding.'

Then Tifto again settled down into silence.

But though much money had been lost, and a great deal of disappointment had to be endured by our party in reference to the Derby, the most injurious and most deplorable event in the day's history had not occurred yet. Dinner had been ordered at the Beargarden at seven,—an hour earlier than would have been named had it not been that Lord Gerald must be at the Eastern Counties Railway Station at nine p.m. An hour and a half for dinner and a cigar afterwards, and half an hour to get to the railway station would not be more than time enough.

But of all men alive Dolly Longstaff was the most unpunctual. He did not arrive till eight. The others were not there before half-past seven, and it was nearly eight before any of them sat down. At half-past eight Silverbridge began to be very anxious about his brother, and told him that he ought to start without further delay. A hansom cab* was waiting at the door, but Lord Gerald still delayed. He knew, he said, that the special would not start till half-past nine. There were a lot of fellows who were dining about everywhere, and they would never get to the station by the hour fixed. It became apparent to the elder brother that Gerald would stay altogether unless he were forced to go, and at last he did get up and pushed the young fellow out. 'Drive like the very devil,' he said to the cabman, explaining to him something of the circumstances. The cabman did do his best, but a cab cannot be made to travel from the Beargarden, which as all the world knows is close to St James's Street, to Liverpool Street* in the City in ten minutes. When Lord Gerald reached the station the train had started.

At twenty minutes to ten the young man reappeared at the club. 'Why on earth didn't you take a special for yourself?' exclaimed Silverbridge.

'They wouldn't give me one.' After that it was apparent to all of them that what had just happened had done more to ruffle our hero's temper than his failure and loss at the races.

'I wouldn't have had it happen for any money you could name,' said the elder brother to the younger, as he took him home to Carlton Terrace.

'If they do send me down, what's the odds?' said the younger brother, who was not quite as sober as he might have been.

'After what happened to me it will almost break the governor's heart,' said the heir.

## CHAPTER 18

### ONE OF THE RESULTS OF THE DERBY

ON the following morning at about eleven Silverbridge and his brother were at breakfast at an hotel in Jermyn Street. They had slept in Carlton Terrace, but Lord Gerald had done so without the knowledge of the Duke. Lord Silverbridge, as he was putting himself to bed, had made up his mind to tell the story to the Duke at once, but when the morning came his courage failed him. The two young men therefore slunk out of the house, and as there was no breakfasting at the Beargarden they went to this hotel. They were both rather gloomy, but the elder brother was the more sad of the two. 'I'd give anything I have in the world,' he said, 'that you hadn't come up at all.'

'Things have been so unfortunate!'

'Why the deuce wouldn't you go when I told you?'

'Who on earth would have thought that they'd have been so punctual? They never are punctual on the Great Eastern. It was an infernal shame. I think I shall go at once to Harnage and tell him all about it.' Mr Harnage was Lord Gerald's tutor.

'But you've been in ever so many rows before.'

'Well,—I've been gated,* and once when they'd gated me I came right upon Harnage on the bridge at King's.'

'What sort of a fellow is he?'

'He used to be good-natured. Now he has taken ever so many crotchets into his head. It was he who began all this about none of the men going to the Derby.'

'Did you ask him yourself for leave?'

'Yes. And when I told him about your owning Prime Minister he got savage and declared that was the very reason why I shouldn't go.'

'You didn't tell me that.'

'I was determined I would go. I wasn't going to be made a child of.'

At last it was decided that the two brothers should go down to Cambridge together. Silverbridge would be able to come back to London the same evening, so as to take his drag down to the Oaks* on the Friday,—a duty from which even his present misery would not deter him. They reached Cambridge at about three, and Lord Silverbridge at once called at the Master's lodge and sent in his card. The Master of Trinity* is so great that he cannot be supposed to see all comers, but on this occasion Lord Silverbridge was fortunate. With much trepidation he told his story. Such being the circumstances, could anything be done to moderate the vials of wrath which must doubtless be poured out over the head of his unfortunate brother?

'Why come to me?' said the Master. 'From what you say yourself, it is evident that you know that this must rest with the College tutor.'

'I thought, sir, if you would say a word.'

'Do you think it would be right that I should interfere for one special man, and that a man of special rank?'

'Nobody thinks that would count for anything. But——'

'But what?' asked the Master.

'If you knew my father, sir!'

'Everybody knows your father;—every Englishman I mean. Of course I know your father,—as a public man, and I know how much the country owes to him.'

'Yes, it does. But it is not that I mean. If you knew how this would,— would,—would break his heart.' Then there came a tear into the young man's eye,—and there was something almost like a tear in the eye of the old man too. 'Of course it was my fault. I got him to come. He hadn't the slightest intention of staying. I think you will believe what I say about that, sir.'

'I believe every word you say, my Lord.'

'I got into a row at Oxford. I dare say you heard. There never was anything so stupid. That was a great grief to my father,—a very great grief. It is so hard upon him because he never did anything foolish himself.'

'You should try to imitate him.' Silverbridge shook his head. 'Or at least not to grieve him.'

'That is it. He has got over the affair about me. As I'm the eldest son I've got into Parliament, and he thinks perhaps that all has been forgotten. An eldest son may, I fancy, be a greater ass than his younger brother.' The Master could not but smile as he thought of the selection which had been made of a legislator. 'But if Gerald is sent down,* I don't know how he'll get over it.' And now the tears absolutely rolled down the young man's face, so that he was forced to wipe them from his eyes.

The Master was much moved. That a young man should pray for himself would be nothing to him. The discipline of the college was not in his hands, and such prayers would avail nothing with him. Nor would a brother praying simply for a brother avail much. A father asking for his son might be resisted. But the brother asking pardon for the brother on behalf of the father was almost irresistible. But this man had long been in a position in which he knew that no such prayers should ever prevail at all. In the first place it was not his business. If he did anything, it would only be by asking a favour when he knew that no favour should be granted;—and a favour which he of all men should not ask, because to him of all men it could not be refused. And then the very altitude of the great statesman whom he was invited to befriend,— the position of this Duke who had been so powerful and might be powerful again, was against any such interference. Of himself he might be sure that he would certainly have done this as readily for any Mr Jones as for the Duke of Omnium; but were he to do it it would be said of him that it had been done because the man was Duke of Omnium. There are positions exalted beyond the reach of benevolence, because benevolence would seem to be self-seeking. 'Your father, if he were here,' said he, 'would know that I could not interfere.'

'And will he be sent down?'

'I do not know all the circumstances. From your own showing the case seems to be one of great insubordination. To tell the truth, Lord Silverbridge, I ought not to have spoken to you on the subject at all.'

'You mean that I should not have spoken to you.'

'Well; I did not say so. And if you have been indiscreet I can pardon that. I wish I could have served you; but I fear that it is not in my power.'

Then Lord Silverbridge took his leave, and going to his brother's rooms waited there till Lord Gerald had returned from his interview with the tutor.

'It's all up,' said he, chucking down his cap, striving to be at his ease. 'I may pack up and go—just where I please. He says that on no account will he have anything more to do with me. I asked him what I was to do, and he said that the Governor had better take my name off the books of the college. I did ask whether I couldn't go over to Maclean.'

'Who is Maclean?'

'One of the other tutors. But the brute only smiled.'

'He thought you meant it for chaff.'

'Well;—I suppose I did mean to show him that I was not going to be exterminated by him. He will write to the Governor to-day. And you will have to talk to the Governor.'

Yes! As Lord Silverbridge went back that afternoon to London he thought very much of that talking to the Governor! Never yet had he been able to say anything very pleasant to 'the Governor.' He had himself been always in disgrace at Eton, and had been sent away from Oxford. He had introduced Tregear into the family, which of all the troubles perhaps was the worst. He had changed his politics. He had spent more money than he ought to have done, and now at this very moment must ask for a large sum. And he had brought Gerald up to see the Derby, thereby causing him to be sent away from Cambridge! And through it all there was present to him a feeling that by no words which he could use would he be able to make his father understand how deeply he felt all this.

He could not bring himself to see the Duke that evening, and the next morning he was sent for before he was out of bed. He found his father at breakfast with the tutor's letter before him. 'Do you know anything about this?' asked the Duke very calmly.

'Gerald ran up to see the Derby, and in the evening missed the train.'

'Mr Harnage tells me that he had been expressly ordered not to go to these races.'

'I suppose he was, sir.'

Then there was silence between them for some minutes. 'You might as well sit down and eat your breakfast,' said the father. Then Lord Silverbridge did sit down and poured himself out a cup of tea. There was no servant in the room, and he dreaded to ring the bell. 'Is there anything you want?' asked the Duke. There was a small dish of fried bacon on the table, and some cold mutton on the sideboard. Silverbridge, declaring that he had everything that was necessary, got up and helped himself to the cold mutton. Then again there was silence, during which the Duke crunched his toast and made an attempt at reading the newspaper. But, soon pushing that aside, he again took up Mr Harnage's letter. Silverbridge watched every motion of his father as he slowly made his way through the slice of cold mutton. 'It seems that Gerald is to be sent away altogether.'

'I fear so, sir.'

'He has profited by your example at Oxford. Did you persuade him to come to these races?'

'I am afraid I did.'

'Though you knew the orders which had been given?'

'I thought it was meant that he should not be away the night.'

'He had asked permission to go to the Derby and had been positively refused. Did you know that?'

Silverbridge sat for some moments considering. He could not at first quite remember what he had known and what he had not known. Perhaps he entertained some faint hope that the question would be allowed to pass unanswered. He saw, however, from his father's eye that that was impossible. And then he did remember it all. 'I suppose I did know it.'

'And you were willing to imperil your brother's position in life, and my happiness, in order that he might see a horse, of which I believe you call yourself part owner, run a race?'

'I thought there would be no risk if he got back the same night. I don't suppose there is any good in my saying it, but I never was so sorry for anything in all my life. I feel as if I could go and hang myself.'

'That is absurd,—and unmanly,' said the Duke. The expression of sorrow, as it had been made, might be absurd and unmanly, but nevertheless it had touched him. He was severe because he did not know how far his severity wounded. 'It is a great blow,—another great blow! Races! A congregation of all the worst blackguards in the country mixed with the greatest fools.'

'Lord Cantrip was there,' said Silverbridge; 'and I saw Sir Timothy Beeswax.'

'If the presence of Sir Timothy be an allurement to you, I pity you indeed. I have nothing further to say about it. You have ruined your brother.' He had been driven to further anger by this reference to one man whom he respected, and to another whom he despised.

'Don't say that, sir.'

'What am I to say?'

'Let him be an attaché,* or something of that sort.'

'Do you believe it possible that he should pass any examination? I think that my children between them will bring me to the grave. You had better go now. I suppose you will want to be—at the races again.' Then the young man crept out of the room, and going to his own part of the house shut himself up alone for nearly an hour. What had he better do to give his father some comfort? Should he abandon racing altogether, sell his share of Prime Minister and Coalition, and go in hard and strong for committees, debates, and divisions? Should he get rid of his drag, and resolve to read up parliamentary literature? He was resolved upon one thing at any rate. He would not go to the Oaks that day. And then he was resolved on another thing. He would call on Lady Mab Grex and ask her advice. He felt so disconsolate and insufficient for himself that he wanted advice from someone whom he could trust.

He found Tifto, Dolly Longstaff, and one or two others at the stables, from whence it was intended that the drag should start. They were waiting, and rather angry because they had been kept waiting. But the news, when it came, was very sad indeed. 'You wouldn't mind taking the team down and back yourself; would you, Dolly?' he said to Longstaff.

'You aren't going!' said Dolly, assuming a look of much heroic horror.

'No;—I am not going to-day.'

'What's up?' asked Popplecourt.

'That's rather sudden; isn't it?' asked the Major.

'Well; yes; I suppose it is sudden.'

'It's throwing us over a little, isn't it?'

'Not that I see. You've got the trap and the horses.'

'Yes;—we've got the trap and the horses,' said Dolly, 'and I vote we make a start.'

'As you are not going yourself, perhaps I'd better drive your horses,' said Tifto.

'Dolly will take the team,' said his Lordship.

'Yes;—decidedly. I will take the team,' said Dolly. 'There isn't a deal of driving wanted on the road to Epsom, but a man should know how to hold his reins.' This of course gave rise to some angry words, but Silverbridge did not stop to hear them.

The poor Duke had no one to whom he could go for advice and consolation. When his son left him he turned to his newspaper, and

tried to read it—in vain. His mind was too ill at ease to admit of political matters. He was greatly grieved by this new misfortune as to
Gerald, and by Lord Silverbridge's propensity to racing.

But though these sorrows were heavy, there was a sorrow heavier
than these. Lady Cantrip had expressed an opinion almost in favour of
Tregear—and had certainly expressed an opinion in favour of
Mrs Finn. The whole affair in regard to Mrs Finn had been explained
to her, and she had told the Duke that, according to her thinking,
Mrs Finn had behaved well! When the Duke, with an energy which
was by no means customary with him, had asked that question, on the
answer to which so much depended, 'Should there have been a moment
lost?' Lady Cantrip had assured him that not a moment had been lost.
Mrs Finn had at once gone to work, and had arranged that the whole
affair should be told to him, the Duke, in the proper way. 'I think she
did,' said Lady Cantrip, 'what I myself should have done in similar
circumstances.'

If Lady Cantrip was right, then must his apology to Mrs Finn be
ample and abject. Perhaps it was this feeling which at the moment was
most vexatious to him.

# CHAPTER 19

### 'NO; MY LORD, I DO NOT'

BETWEEN two and three o'clock Lord Silverbridge, in spite of his
sorrow, found himself able to eat his lunch at his club. The place was
deserted, the Beargarden world having gone to the races. As he sat
eating cold lamb and drinking soda-and-brandy he did confirm himself
in certain modified resolutions, which might be more probably kept
than those sterner laws of absolute renunciation to which he had
thought of pledging himself in his half-starved morning condition. His
father had spoken in very strong language against racing,—saying that
those who went were either fools or rascals. He was sure that this was
exaggerated. Half the House of Lords and two-thirds of the House of
Commons were to be seen at the Derby; but no doubt there were
many rascals and fools, and he could not associate with the legislators
without finding himself among the fools and rascals. He would,—as
soon as he could,—separate himself from the Major. And he would
not bet. It was on that side of the sport that the rascals and the fools
showed themselves. Of what service could betting be to him whom

Providence had provided with all things wanted to make life pleasant? As to the drag, his father had in a certain measure approved of that, and he would keep the drag, as he must have some relaxation. But his great effort of all should be made in the House of Commons. He would endeavour to make his father perceive that he had appreciated that letter. He would always be in the House soon after four, and would remain there,—for, if possible, as long as the Speaker sat in the chair.* He had already begun to feel that there was a difficulty in keeping his seat upon those benches. The half-hours there would be so much longer than elsewhere! An irresistible desire of sauntering out would come upon him. There were men the very sound of whose voices was already odious to him. There had come upon him a feeling in regard to certain orators, that when once they had begun there was no reason why they should ever stop. Words of some sort were always forthcoming, like spiders' webs. He did not think that he could learn to take a pleasure in sitting in the House; but he hoped that he might be man enough to do it, though it was not pleasant. He would begin to-day, instead of going to the Oaks.

But before he went to the House he would see Lady Mabel Grex. And here it may be well to state that in making his resolutions as to a better life, he had considered much whether it would not be well for him to take a wife. His father had once told him that when he married, the house in Carlton Terrace should be his own. 'I will be a lodger if you will have me,' said the Duke; 'or if your wife should not like that, I will find a lodging elsewhere.' This had been in the sadness and tenderness which had immediately followed the death of the Duchess. Marriage would steady him. Were he a married man, Tifto would of course disappear. Upon the whole he thought it would be good that he should marry. And, if so, who could be so nice as Lady Mabel? That his father would be contented with Lady Mab, he was inclined to believe. There was no better blood in England. And Lady Mabel was known to be clever, beautiful, and, in her peculiar circumstances, very wise.

He was aware, however, of a certain drawback. Lady Mabel as his wife would be his superior, and in some degree his master. Though not older she was wiser than he,—and not only wiser but more powerful also. And he was not quite sure but that she regarded him as a boy. He thought that she did love him,—or would do so if he asked her,— but that her love would be bestowed upon him as on an inferior creature. He was already jealous of his own dignity, and fearful lest he should miss the glory of being loved by this lovely one for his own sake,—for his own manhood, and his own gifts and his own character.

And yet his attraction to her was so great that now in the day of his sorrow he could think of no solace but what was to be found in her company.

'Not at the Oaks!' she said as soon as he was shown into the drawing-room.

'No;—not at the Oaks. Lord Grex is there, I suppose?'

'Oh yes;—that is a matter of course. Why are you a recreant?'

'The House sits to-day.'

'How virtuous! Is it coming to that,—that when the House sits you will never be absent?'

'That's the kind of life I'm going to lead. You haven't heard about Gerald?'

'About your brother?'

'Yes—you haven't heard?'

'Not a word. I hope there is no misfortune.'

'But indeed there is,—a most terrible misfortune.' Then he told the whole story. How Gerald had been kept in London, and how he had gone down to Cambridge,—all in vain; how his father had taken the matter to heart, telling him that he had ruined his brother; and how he, in consequence, had determined not to go to the races. 'Then he said,' continued Silverbridge, 'that his children between them would bring him to his grave.'

'That was terrible.'

'Very terrible.'

'But what did he mean by that?' asked Lady Mabel, anxious to hear something about Lady Mary and Tregear.

'Well; of course what I did at Oxford made him unhappy; and now there is this affair of Gerald's.'

'He did not allude to your sister?'

'Yes he did. You have heard of all that. Tregear told you.'

'He told me something.'

'Of course my father does not like it.'

'Do you approve of it?'

'No,' said he—curtly and sturdily.

'Why not? You like Tregear.'

'Certainly I like Tregear. He is the friend, among men, whom I like the best. I have only two real friends.'

'Who are they?' she asked, sinking her voice very low.

'He is one;—and you are the other. You know that.'

'I hoped that I was one,' she said. 'But if you love Tregear so dearly, why do you not approve of him for your sister?'

'I always knew it would not do.'

'But why not?'

'Mary ought to marry a man of higher standing.'

'Of higher rank you mean. The daughters of Dukes have married commoners before.'

'It is not exactly that. I don't like to talk of it in that way. I knew it would make my father unhappy. In point of fact he can't marry her. What is the good of approving of a thing that is impossible?'

'I wish I knew your sister. Is she—firm?'

'Indeed she is.'

'I am not so sure that you are.'

'No,' said he, after considering awhile; 'nor am I. But she is not like Gerald or me. She is more obstinate.'

'Less fickle perhaps.'

'Yes, if you choose to call it fickle. I don't know that I am fickle. If I were in love with a girl I should be true to her.'

'Are you sure of that?'

'Quite sure. If I were really in love with her I certainly should not change. It is possible that I might be bullied out of it.'

'But she will not be bullied out of it?'

'Mary? No. That is just it. She will stick to it if he does.'

'I would if I were she. Where will you find any young man equal to Frank Tregear?'

'Perhaps you mean to cut poor Mary out.'

'That isn't a nice thing for you to say, Lord Silverbridge. Frank is my cousin,—as indeed you are also; but it so happens that I have seen a great deal of him all my life. And, though I don't want to cut your sister out, as you so prettily say, I love him well enough to understand that any girl whom he loves ought to be true to him.' So far what she said was very well, but she afterwards added a word which might have been wisely omitted. 'Frank and I are almost beggars.'

'What an accursed thing money is,' he exclaimed, jumping up from his chair.

'I don't agree with you at all. It is a very comfortable thing.'

'How is anybody who has got it to know if anybody cares for him?'

'You must find that out. There is such a thing I suppose as real sympathy.'

'You tell me to my face that you and Tregear would have been lovers only that you are both poor.'

'I never said anything of the kind.'

'And that he is to be passed on to my sister because it is supposed that she will have some money.'

'You are putting words into my mouth which I never spoke, and ideas into my mind which I never thought.'

'And of course I feel the same about myself. How can a fellow help it? I wish you had a lot of money, I know.'

'It is very kind of you;—but why?'

'Well;—I can't explain myself,' he said, blushing as was his wont. 'I dare say it wouldn't make any difference.'

'It would make a great difference to me. As it is, having none, and knowing as I do that papa and Percival are getting things into a worse mess every day, I am obliged to hope that I may some day marry a man who has got an income.'

'I suppose so,' said he, still blushing, but frowning at the same time.

'You see I can be very frank with a real friend. But I am sure of myself in this,—that I will never marry a man I do not love. A girl needn't love a man unless she likes it, I suppose. She doesn't tumble into love as she does into the fire. It would not suit me to marry a poor man, and so I don't mean to fall in love with a poor man.'

'But you do mean to fall in love with a rich one?'

'That remains to be seen, Lord Silverbridge. The rich man will at any rate have to fall in love with me first. If you know of any one you need not tell him to be too sure because he has a good income.'

'There's Popplecourt. He's his own master, and, fool as he is, he knows how to keep his money.'

'I don't want a fool. You must do better for me than Lord Popplecourt.'

'What do you say to Dolly Longstaff?'

'He would be just the man, only he never would take the trouble to come out and be married.'

'Or Glasslough?'

'I'm afraid he is cross, and wouldn't let me have my own way.'

'I can only think of one other;—but you would not take him.'

'Then you had better not mention him. It is no good crowding the list with impossibles.'

'I was thinking of——myself.'

'You are certainly one of the impossibles.'

'Why, Lady Mab?'

'For twenty reasons. You are too young, and you are bound to oblige your father, and you are to be wedded to Parliament,—at any rate for the next ten years. And altogether it wouldn't do,—for a great many reasons.'

'I suppose you don't like me well enough?'

'What a question to ask! No; my Lord, I do not. There; that's what you may call an answer. Don't you pretend to look offended, because if you do, I shall laugh at you. If you may have your joke surely I may have mine.'

'I don't see any joke in it.'

'But I do. Suppose I were to say the other thing. Oh, Lord Silverbridge, you do me so much honour! And now I come to think about it, there is no one in the world I am so fond of as you. Would that suit you?'

'Exactly.'

'But it wouldn't suit me. There's papa. Don't run away.'

'It's ever so much past five,' said the legislator, 'and I had intended to be in the House more than an hour ago. Good-bye. Give my love to Miss Cassewary.'

'Certainly. Miss Cassewary is your most devoted friend. Won't you bring your sister to see me some day?'

'When she is in town I will.'

'I should so like to know her. Good-bye.'

As he hurried down to the House in a hansom he thought over it all, and told himself that he feared it would not do. She might perhaps accept him, but if so, she would do it simply in order that she might become Duchess of Omnium. She might, he thought, have accepted him then, had she chosen. He had spoken plainly enough. But she had laughed at him. He felt that if she loved him, there ought to have been something of that feminine tremor, of that doubting, hesitating half-avowal of which he had perhaps read in novels, and which his own instincts taught him to desire. But there had been no tremor nor hesitating. 'No; my Lord, I do not,' she had said when he asked her to her face whether she liked him well enough to be his wife. 'No; my Lord, I do not.' It was not the refusal conveyed in these words which annoyed him. He did believe that if he were to press his suit with the usual forms she would accept him. But it was that there should be such a total absence of trepidation in her words and manner. Before her he blushed and hesitated and felt that he did not know how to express himself. If she would only have done the same, then there would have been an equality. Then he could have seized her in his arms and sworn that never, never, never would he care for any one but her.

In truth he saw everything as it was only too truly. Though she might choose to marry him if he pressed his request, she would never subject herself to him as he would have the girl do whom he loved. She was his superior, and in every word uttered between them showed that it was so. But yet how beautiful she was;—how much more beautiful than any other thing he had ever seen!

He sat on one of the high seats behind Sir Timothy Beeswax and Sir Orlando Drought,* listening, or pretending to listen, to the speeches of three or four gentlemen respecting sugar,* thinking of all this till half-past seven;—and then he went to dine with the proud consciousness of having done his duty. The forms and methods of the House were, he flattered himself, soaking into him gradually,—as his father had desired. The theory of legislation was sinking into his mind. The welfare of the nation depended chiefly on sugar. But he thought that, after all, his own welfare must depend on the possession of Mab Grex.

## CHAPTER 20

### 'THEN HE WILL COME AGAIN'

LADY MABEL, when her young lover left her, was for a time freed from the necessity of thinking about him by her father. He had returned from the Oaks in a very bad humour. Lord Grex had been very badly treated by his son, whom he hated worse than any one else in the world. On the Derby Day he had won a large sum of money, which had been to him at the time a matter of intense delight,—for he was in great want of money. But on this day he had discovered that his son and heir had lost more than he had won, and an arrangement had been suggested to him that his winnings should go to pay Percival's losings. This was a mode of settling affairs to which the Earl would not listen for a moment, had he possessed the power of putting a veto upon it. But there had been a transaction lately between him and his son with reference to the cutting off a certain entail* under which money was to be paid to Lord Percival. This money had not yet been forthcoming, and therefore the Earl was constrained to assent. This was very distasteful to the Earl, and he came home therefore in a bad humour, and said a great many disagreeable things to his daughter. 'You know, papa, if I could do anything I would.' This she said in answer to a threat, which he had made often before and now repeated, of getting rid altogether of the house in

Belgrave Square. Whenever he made this threat he did not scruple to tell her that the house had to be kept up solely for her welfare. 'I don't see why the deuce you don't get married. You'll have to do it sooner or later.' That was not a pleasant speech for a daughter to hear from her father. 'As to that,' she said, 'it must come or not as chance will have it. If you want me to sign anything I will sign it;'—for she had been asked to sign papers, or in other words to surrender rights;—'but for that other matter it must be left to myself.' Then he had been very disagreeable indeed.

They dined out together,—of course with all the luxury that wealth can give. There was a well-appointed carriage to take them backwards and forwards to the next square, such as an Earl should have. She was splendidly dressed, as became an Earl's daughter, and he was brilliant with some star which had been accorded to him by his sovereign's grateful minister in return for staunch parliamentary support.* No one looking at them could have imagined that such a father could have told such a daughter that she must marry herself out of the way because as an unmarried girl she was a burden.

During the dinner she was very gay. To be gay was the habit,—we may almost say the work,—of her life. It so chanced that she sat between Sir Timothy Beeswax, who in these days was a very great man indeed, and that very Dolly Longstaff, whom Silverbridge in his irony had proposed to her as a fitting suitor for her hand.

'Isn't Lord Silverbridge a cousin of yours?' asked Sir Timothy.

'A very distant one.'

'He has come over to us, you know. It is such a triumph.'

'I was so sorry to hear it.' This, however, as the reader knows, was a fib.

'Sorry!' said Sir Timothy. 'Surely Lord Grex's daughter must be a Conservative.'

'Oh yes;—I am a Conservative because I was born one. I think that people in politics should remain as they are born,—unless they are very wise indeed. When men come to be statesmen and all that kind of thing, of course they can change backwards and forwards.'

'I hope that is not intended for me, Lady Mabel.'

'Certainly not. I don't know enough about it to be personal.'

That, however, was again not quite true. 'But I have the greatest possible respect for the Duke, and I think it a pity that he should be made unhappy by his son. Don't you like the Duke?'

'Well;—yes;—in a way. He is a most respectable man; and has been a good public servant.'

'All our lot are ruined, you know,' said Dolly, talking of the races.

'Who are your lot, Mr Longstaff?'

'I'm one myself.'

'I suppose so.'

'I'm utterly smashed. Then there's Percival.'

'I hope he has not lost much. Of course you know he's my brother.'

'Oh laws;—so he is. I always put my foot in it. Well;—he has lost a lot. And so have Silverbridge and Tifto. Perhaps you don't know Tifto.'

'I have not the pleasure of knowing Mr Tifto.'

'He is a major. I think you'd like Major Tifto. He's a sort of racing coach to Silverbridge. You ought to know Tifto. And Tregear is pretty nearly cleared out.'

'Mr Tregear! Frank Tregear!'

'I'm told he has been hit very heavy. I hope he's not a friend of yours, Lady Mabel.'

'Indeed he is;—a very dear friend and a cousin.'

'That's what I hear. He's very much with Silverbridge you know.'

'I cannot think that Mr Tregear has lost money.'

'I hope he hasn't. I know I have. I wish someone would stick up for me, and say that it was impossible.'

'But that is not Mr Tregear's way of living. I can understand that Lord Silverbridge or Percival should lose money.'

'Or me?'

'Or you, if you like to say so.'

'Or Tifto?'

'I don't know anything about Mr Tifto.'

'Major Tifto.'

'Or Major Tifto;—what does it signify?'

'No;—of course. We inferior people may lose our money just as we please. But a man who can look as clever as Mr Tregear ought to win always.'

'I told you just now that he was a friend of mine.'

'But don't you think that he does look clever?' There could be no question but that Tregear, when he disliked his company, could show his dislike by his countenance; and it was not improbable that he had done so in the presence of Mr Adolphus Longstaff. 'Now tell the truth, Lady Mabel; does he not look conceited sometimes?'

'He generally looks as if he knew what he was talking about, which is more than some other people do.'

'Of course he is a great deal more clever than I am. I know that. But I don't think even he can be so clever as he looks. "Or you so stupid," that's what you ought to say now.'

'Sometimes, Mr Longstaff, I deny myself the pleasure of saying what I think.'

When all this was over she was very angry with herself for the anxiety she had expressed about Tregear. This Mr Longstaff was, she thought, exactly the man to report all she had said in the public room at the club. But she had been annoyed by what she had heard as to her friend. She knew that he of all men should keep himself free from such follies. Those others had, as it were, a right to make fools of themselves. It had seemed so natural that the young men of her own class should dissipate their fortunes and their reputations by every kind of extravagance! Her father had done so, and she had never even ventured to hope that her brother would not follow her father's example. But Tregear, if he gave way to such follies as these, would soon fall headlong into a pit from which there would be no escape. And if he did fall, she knew herself well enough to be aware that she could not stifle, nor even conceal, the misery which this would occasion her. As long as he stood well before the world she would be well able to assume indifference. But were he to be precipitated into some bottomless misfortunes then she could only throw herself after him. She could see him marry, and smile,—and perhaps even like his wife. And while he was doing so, she could also marry, and resolve that the husband whom she took should be made to think that he had a loving wife. But were Frank to die,—then must she fall upon his body as though he had been known by all the world to be her lover. Something of this feeling came upon her now, when she heard that he had been betting and had been unfortunate. She had been unable so to subdue herself as to seem to be perfectly careless about it. She had begun by saying that she had not believed it;—but she had believed it. It was so natural that Tregear should have done as the others did with whom he lived! But then the misfortune would be to him so terrible,—so irremediable! The reader, however, may as well know at once that there was not a word of truth in the assertion.*

After the dinner she went home alone. There were other festivities to be attended, had she pleased to attend them; and poor Miss Casseway was dressed ready to go with her as chaperone;—but Miss Casseway was quite satisfied to be allowed to go to bed in lieu of Mrs Montacute Jones's* great ball. And she had gone to her bedroom when Lady Mabel went to her. 'I am glad you are alone,' she said, 'because I want to speak to you.'

'Is anything wrong?'

'Everything is wrong. Papa says he must give up this house.'

'He says that almost always when he comes back from the races, and very often when he comes back from the club.'

'Percival has lost ever so much.'

'I don't think my Lord will hamper himself for your brother.'

'I can't explain it, but there is some horrible money complication. It is hard upon you and me.'

'Who am I?' said Miss Cassewary.

'About the dearest friend that ever a poor girl had. It is hard upon you,—and upon me. I have given up everything,—and what good have I done?'

'It is hard, my dear.'

'But after all I do not care much for all that. The thing has been going on so long that one is used to it.'

'What is it then?'

'Ah;—yes;—what is it? How am I to tell you?'

'Surely you can tell me,' said the old woman, putting out her hand so as to caress the arm of the younger one.

'I could tell no one else; I am sure of that. Frank Tregear has taken to gambling,—like the rest of them.'

'Who says so?'

'He has lost a lot of money at these races. A man who sat next me at dinner,—one of those stupid do-nothing fools that one meets everywhere,—told me so. He is one of the Beargarden set, and of course he knows all about it.'

'Did he say how much?'

'How is he to pay anything? Of all things that men do this is the worst. A man who would think himself disgraced for ever if he accepted a present of money will not scruple to use all his wits to rob his friend of everything that he has by studying the run of cards or by watching the paces of some brutes of horses! And they consider themselves to be fine gentlemen! A real gentleman should never want the money out of another man's pocket;—should never think of money at all.'

'I don't know how that is to be helped, my dear. You have got to think of money.'

'Yes; I have to think of it, and do think of it; and because I do so I am not what I call a gentleman.'

'No;—my dear; you're a lady.'

'Psha! you know what I mean. I might have had the feelings of a gentleman as well as the best man that ever was born. I haven't; but

I have never done anything so mean as gambling. Now I have got something else to tell you.'

'What is it? You do frighten me so when you look like that.'

'You may well be frightened,—for if this all comes round I shall very soon be able to dispense with you altogether. His Royal Highness Lord Silverbridge——'

'What do you mean, Mabel?'

'He's next door to a Royal Highness at any rate, and a much more topping man than most of them. Well then;—His Serene Highness* the heir of the Duke of Omnium has done me the inexpressible honour of asking me—to marry him.'

'No!'

'You may well say, No. And to tell the truth exactly, he didn't.'

'Then why do you say he did?'

'I don't think he did quite ask me, but he gave me to understand that he would do so if I gave him any encouragement.'

'Did he mean it?'

'Yes;—poor boy! He meant it. With a word;—with a look, he would have been down there kneeling. He asked me whether I liked him well enough. What do you think I did?'

'What did you do?'

'I spared him;—out of sheer downright Christian charity! I said to myself "Love your neighbours."* "Don't be selfish." "Do unto him as you would he should do unto you,"*—that is, think of his welfare. Though I had him in my net, I let him go. Shall I go to heaven for doing that?'

'I don't know,' said Miss Cassewary, who was so much perturbed by the news she had heard as to be unable to come to any opinion on the point just raised.

'Or mayn't I rather go to the other place? From how much embarrassment should I have relieved my father! What a friend I should have made for Percival! How much I might have been able to do for Frank! And then what a wife I should have made him!'

'I think you would.'

'He'll never get another half so good; and he'll be sure to get one before long. It is a sort of tenderness that is quite inefficacious. He will become a prey, as I should have made him a prey. But where is there another who will treat him so well?'

'I cannot bear to hear you speak of yourself in that way.'

'But it is true. I know the sort of girl he should marry. In the first place she should be two years younger, and four years fresher.

She should be able not only to like him and love him, but to worship him. How well I can see her! She should have fair hair, and bright green-gray eyes, with the sweetest complexion, and the prettiest little dimples;—two inches shorter than me, and the delight of her life should be to hang with two hands on his arm. She should have a feeling that her Silverbridge is an Apollo upon earth. To me he is a rather foolish, but very, very sweet-tempered young man;—anything rather than a god. If I thought that he would get the fresh young girl with the dimples then I ought to abstain.'

'If he was in earnest,' said Miss Cassewary, throwing aside all this badinage and thinking of the main point, 'if he was in earnest he will come again.'

'He was quite in earnest.'

'Then he will come again.'

'I don't think he will,' said Lady Mabel. 'I told him that I was too old for him, and I tried to laugh him out of it. He does not like being laughed at. He has been saved, and he will know it.'

'But if he should come again?'

'I shall not spare him again. No;—not twice. I felt it to be hard to do so once, because I so nearly love him! There are so many of them who are odious to me, as to whom the idea of marrying them seems to be mixed somehow with an idea of suicide.'

'Oh, Mabel!'

'But he is as sweet as a rose. If I were his sister, or his servant, or his dog, I could be devoted to him. I can fancy that his comfort and his success and his name should be everything to me.'

'That is what a wife ought to feel.'

'But I could never feel him to be my superior. That is what a wife ought in truth to feel. Think of those two young men and the difference between them! Well;—don't look like that at me. I don't often give way, and I dare say after all I shall live to be the Duchess of Omnium.' Then she kissed her friend and went away to her own room.

## CHAPTER 21

### SIR TIMOTHY BEESWAX

THERE had lately been a great Conservative reaction* in the country, brought about in part by the industry and good management of gentlemen who were strong on that side;—but due also in part to the blunders and quarrels of their opponents. That these opponents should have blundered and quarrelled, being men active and in earnest, was to have been expected. Such blunderings and quarrellings have been a matter of course since politics have been politics, and since religion has been religion. When men combine to do nothing, how should there be disagreement? When men combine to do much, how should there not be disagreement? Thirty men can sit still, each as like the other as peas. But put your thirty men up to run a race, and they will soon assume different forms. And in doing nothing, you can hardly do amiss. Let the doers of nothing have something of action forced upon them, and they, too, will blunder and quarrel.

The wonder is that there should ever be in a reforming party enough of consentaneous action to carry any reform. The reforming or Liberal party in British politics had thus stumbled,—and stumbled till it fell. And now there had been a great Conservative reaction! Many of the most Liberal constituencies in the country had been untrue to their old political convictions. And, as the result, Lord Drummond was Prime Minister in the House of Lords,—with Sir Timothy Beeswax acting as first man in the House of Commons.

It cannot be denied that Sir Timothy had his good points as a politician. He was industrious, patient, clear-sighted, intelligent, courageous, and determined. Long before he had had a seat in the House, when he was simply making his way up to the probability of a seat by making a reputation as an advocate, he had resolved that he would be more than an Attorney-General,* more than a judge,—more, as he thought it, than a Chief Justice;* but at any rate something different. This plan he had all but gained,—and it must be acknowledged that he had been moved by a grand and manly ambition. But there were drawbacks to the utility and beauty of Sir Timothy's character as a statesman. He had no idea as to the necessity or non-necessity of any measure whatever in reference to the well-being of the country. It may, indeed, be said that all such ideas were to him absurd, and the fact that they should be held by his friends and supporters was an inconvenience. He was not in accord with those who declare that a Parliament is a collection of windbags which puff, and blow, and crack to the annoyance of honest men. But to him Parliament was a debating place, by having a majority in which, and by no other means, he,—or another,—might become the great man of the day. By no other than parliamentary means could such a one as he come to be the chief man. And this use of Parliament, either on his own behalf or on behalf of others, had been for so many years present to his mind, that there seemed to be nothing absurd in an institution supported for such a purpose. Parliament was a club so eligible in its nature that all Englishmen wished to belong to it. They who succeeded were acknowledged to be the cream of the land.* They who dominated in it were the cream of the cream. Those two who were elected to be the chiefs of the two parties had more of cream in their composition than any others. But he who could be the chief of the strongest party, and who therefore, in accordance with the prevailing arrangements of the country, should have the power of making dukes, and bestowing garters* and appointing bishops, he who by attaining the first seat should achieve the right of snubbing all before him, whether friends or foes, he, according to the feelings of Sir Timothy, would have gained an Elysium of creaminess not to be found in any other position on the earth's surface. No man was more warmly attached to parliamentary government than Sir Timothy Beeswax; but I do not think that he ever cared much for legislation.

Parliamentary management was his forte. There have been various rocks on which men have shattered their barks in their attempts to sail successfully into the harbours of parliamentary management. There is the great Senator who declares to himself that personally he will have neither friend nor foe. There is his country before him and its welfare. Within his bosom is the fire of patriotism, and within his mind the examples of all past time. He knows that he can be just, he teaches himself to be eloquent, and he strives to be wise. But he will not bend;—and at last, in some great solitude, though closely surrounded by those whose love he had neglected to acquire,—he breaks his heart.

Then there is he who seeing the misfortune of that great one, tells himself that patriotism, judgment, industry, and eloquence will not suffice for him unless he himself can be loved. To do great things a man must have a great following, and to achieve that he must be popular. So he smiles and learns the necessary wiles. He is all for his country and his friends,—but for his friends first. He too must be eloquent and well instructed in the ways of Parliament, must be wise and diligent; but in all that he does and all that he says he must first study his party. It is well with him for a time;—but he has closed the door of his Elysium too rigidly. Those without gradually become stronger than his friends within, and so he falls.

But may not the door be occasionally opened to an outsider, so that the exterior force be diminished? We know how great is the pressure of water; and how the peril of an overwhelming weight of it may be removed by opening the way for a small current. There comes therefore the Statesman who acknowledges to himself that he will be pregnable. That, as a Statesman, he should have enemies is a matter of course. Against moderate enemies he will hold his own. But when there comes one immoderately forcible, violently inimical, then to that man he will open his bosom. He will tempt into his camp with an offer of high command any foe that may be worth his purchase. This too has answered well; but there is a Nemesis. The loyalty of officers so procured must be open to suspicion. The man who has said bitter things against you will never sit at your feet in contented submission, nor will your friend of old standing long endure to be superseded by such converts.

All these dangers Sir Timothy had seen and studied, and for each of them he had hoped to be able to provide an antidote. Love cannot do all. Fear may do more. Fear acknowledges a superior. Love desires an equal. Love is to be created by benefits done, and means gratitude, which we all know to be weak. But hope, which refers itself to benefits to come, is of all our feelings the strongest. And Sir Timothy had parliamentary doctrines concealed in the depths of his own bosom more important even than these. The Statesman who falls is he who does much, and thus injures many. The Statesman who stands the longest is he who does nothing and injures no one. He soon knew that the work which he had taken in hand required all the art of a great conjuror. He must be possessed of tricks so marvellous that not even they who sat nearest to him might know how they were performed.

For the executive or legislative business of the country he cared little. The one should be left in the hands of men who liked work;—of the other there should be little, or, if possible, none. But Parliament must be managed,—and his party. Of patriotism he did not know the meaning;—few, perhaps, do, beyond a feeling that they would like to lick the Russians,* or to get the better of the Americans in a matter of fisheries or frontiers.* But he invented a pseudo-patriotic conjuring phraseology which no one understood but which many admired. He was ambitious that it should be said of him that he was far-and-away the cleverest of his party. He knew himself to be clever. But he could only be far-and-away the cleverest by saying and doing that which no one could understand. If he could become master of some great hocus-pocus system which could be made to be graceful to the ears and eyes of many, which might for awhile seem to have within it some semi-divine attribute, which should have all but divine power of mastering the loaves and fishes, then would they who followed him believe in him more firmly than other followers who had believed in their leaders. When you see a young woman read a closed book placed on her dorsal vertebræ,*—if you do believe that she so reads it, you think that she is endowed with a wonderful faculty! And should you also be made to believe that the same young woman had direct communication with Abraham,* by means of some invisible wire, you would be apt to do a great many things as that young woman might tell you. Conjuring, when not known to be conjuring, is very effective.

Much, no doubt, of Sir Timothy's power had come from his praise-worthy industry. Though he cared nothing for the making of laws, though he knew nothing of finance, though he had abandoned his legal studies, still he worked hard. And because he had worked harder in a special direction than others around him, therefore he was enabled to lead them. The management of a party is a very great work in itself; and when to that is added the management of the House of Commons, a man has enough upon his hands even though he neglects altogether the ordinary pursuits of a Statesman. Those around Sir Timothy were fond of their party; but they were for the most part men who had not conde-scended to put their shoulders to the wheel as he had done. Had there been any very great light among them, had there been a Pitt or a Peel,* Sir Timothy would have probably become Attorney-General and have made his way to the bench;—but there had been no Pitt and no Peel, and he had seen his opening. He had studied the ways of Members. Parliamentary practice had become familiar to him. He had shown him-self to be ready at all hours to fight the battle of the party he had joined. And no man knew so well as did Sir Timothy how to elevate a simple legislative attempt into a good faction fight. He had so mastered his tricks of conjuring that no one could get to the bottom of them, and had assumed a look of preternatural gravity which made many young Members think that Sir Timothy was born to be a king of men.

There were no doubt some among his older supporters who felt their thraldom grievously. There were some lords in the Upper House and some sons of the lords in the Lower,—with pedigrees going back far enough for pride,—who found it irksome to recognise Sir Timothy as a master. No doubt he had worked very hard, and had worked for them. No doubt he knew how to do the work, and they did not. There was no other man among them to whom the lead could be conveniently transferred. But yet they were uncomfortable,—and perhaps a little ashamed.

It had arisen partly from this cause, that there had been something of a counter-reaction at the last general election. When the Houses met, the Ministers had indeed a majority, but a much lessened majority. The old Liberal constituencies had returned to an expression of their real feeling. This reassertion of the progress of the tide, this recovery from the partial ebb which checks the violence of every flow, is common enough in politics; but at the present moment there were many who said that all this had been accelerated by a feeling in the country that Sir Timothy was hardly all that the country required as the leader of the country party.

## CHAPTER 22

### THE DUKE IN HIS STUDY

It was natural that at such a time, when success greater than had been expected had attended the efforts of the Liberals, when some dozen unexpected votes had been acquired, the leading politicians of that party should have found themselves compelled to look about them and see how these good things might be utilised. In February they certainly had not expected to be called to power in the course of the existing session. Perhaps they did not expect it yet. There was still a Conservative majority,—though but a small majority. But the strength of the minority consisted, not in the fact that the majority against them was small, but that it was decreasing. How quickly does the snowball grow into hugeness as it is rolled on,—but when the change comes in the weather how quickly does it melt, and before it is gone become a thing ugly, weak, and formless! Where is the individual who does not assert to himself that he would be more loyal to a falling than to a rising friend? Such is perhaps the nature of each one of us. But when any large number of men act together, the falling friend is apt to be deserted. There was a general feeling among politicians that Lord Drummond's ministry,—or Sir Timothy's—was failing, and the Liberals, though they could not yet count the votes by which they might hope to be supported in power, nevertheless felt that they ought to be looking to their arms.

There had been a coalition. They who are well read in the political literature of their country will remember all about that.* It had perhaps succeeded in doing that for which it had been intended. The Queen's government had been carried on for two or three years. The Duke of Omnium had been the head of that Ministry; but during those years had suffered so much as to have become utterly ashamed of the coalition,—so much as to have said often to himself that under no circumstances would he again join any Ministry. At this time there was no idea of another coalition. That is a state of things which cannot come about frequently,—which can only be reproduced by men who have never hitherto felt the mean insipidity of such a condition. But they who had served on the Liberal side in that coalition must again put their shoulders to the wheel. Of course it was in every man's mouth that the Duke must be induced to forget his miseries and once more to take upon himself the duties of an active servant of the State.

But they who were most anxious on the subject, such men as Lord Cantrip, Mr Monk, our old friend Phineas Finn, and a few others, were almost afraid to approach him. At the moment when the coalition was broken up he had been very bitter in spirit, apparently almost arrogant, holding himself aloof from his late colleagues,—and since that, troubles had come to him, which had aggravated the soreness of his heart. His wife had died, and he had suffered much through his children. What Lord Silverbridge had done at Oxford was matter of general conversation, and also what he had not done.

That the heir of the family should have become a renegade in politics was supposed greatly to have affected the father. Now Lord Gerald had been expelled from Cambridge, and Silverbridge was on the turf in conjunction with Major Tifto! Something, too, had oozed out into general ears about Lady Mary,—something which should have been kept secret as the grave. It had therefore come to pass that it was difficult even to address the Duke.

There was one man, and but one, who could do this with ease to himself;—and that man was at last put into motion at the instance of the leaders of the party. The old Duke of St Bungay* wrote the following letter to the Duke of Omnium. The letter purported to be an excuse for the writer's own defalcation. But the chief object of the writer was to induce the younger Duke once more to submit to harness.

'Longroyston,* 3rd June, 187—.

'DEAR DUKE OF OMNIUM,

'How quickly the things come round! I had thought that I should never again have been called upon even to think of the formation of another Liberal Ministry; and now, though it was but yesterday that we were all telling ourselves that we were thoroughly manumitted from our labours by the altered opinions of the country, sundry of our old friends are again putting their heads together.

'Did they not do so they would neglect a manifest duty. Nothing is more essential to the political well-being of the country than that the leaders on both sides in politics should be prepared for their duties. But for myself, I am bound at last to put in the old plea with a determination that it shall be respected. "Solve senescentem."* It is now, if I calculate rightly, exactly fifty years since I first entered public life in obedience to the advice of Lord Grey.* I had then already sat five years in the House of Commons. I assisted humbly in the emancipation of the Roman Catholics,* and have learned by the legislative troubles of just half a century that those whom we then invited to sit with us in Parliament have been in all things our worst enemies. But what then? Had we benefited only those who love us, would not the sinners also,—or even the Tories,—have done as much as that?

'But such memories are of no avail now. I write to say that after so much of active political life, I will at last retire. My friends when they see me inspecting a pigsty or picking a peach are apt to remind me that I can still stand on my legs, and with more of compliment than of kindness will argue therefore that I ought still to undertake active duties in Parliament. I can select my own hours for pigs and peaches, and should I, through the dotage of age, make mistakes as to the breeding of the one or the flavour of the other, the harm done will not go far. In politics I have done my work. What you and others in the arena do will interest me more than all other things of this world, I think and hope, to my dying day. But I will not trouble the workers with the querulousness of old age.

'So much for myself. And now let me, as I go, say a parting word to him with whom in politics I have been for many years more in accord than with any other leading man. As nothing but age or infirmity would to my own mind have justified me in retiring, so do I think that you, who can plead neither age nor infirmity, will find yourself at last to want self-justification, if you permit yourself to be driven from the task either by pride or by indifference.

'I should express my feelings better were I to say by pride and diffidence. I look to our old friendship, to the authority given to me by my age, and to the thorough goodness of your heart for pardon in thus accusing you. That little men should have ventured to ill-use you, has hurt your pride. That these little men should have been able to do so has created your diffidence. Put you to a piece of work that a man may do, you have less false pride as to the way in which you may do it than any man I have known; and, let the way be open to you, as little diffidence as any. But in this political mill of ours in England, a man cannot always find the way open to do things. It does not often happen that an English statesman can go in and make a great score off his own bat. But not the less is he bound to play the game and to go to the wicket when he finds that his time has come.

'There are, I think, two things for you to consider in this matter, and two only. The first is your capacity, and the other is your duty. A man may have found by experience that he is unfitted for public life. You and I have known men in regard to whom we have thoroughly wished that such experience had been reached. But this is a matter in which a man who doubts himself is bound to take the evidence of those around him. The whole party is most anxious for your co-operation. If this be so,—and I make you the assurance from most conclusive evidence,—you are bound to accept the common consent of your political friends on that matter. You perhaps think that at a certain period of your life you failed. They all agree with me that you did not fail. It is a matter on which you should be bound by our opinion rather than by your own.

'As to that matter of duty I shall have less difficulty in carrying you with me. Though this renewed task may be personally disagreeable to you, even though your tastes should lead you to some other life,—which I think is not the case,—still if your country wants you, you should serve your country. It is a work as to which such a one as you has no option. Of most of those who choose public life,—it may be said that were they not there, there would be others as serviceable. But when a man such as you has shown himself to be necessary, as long as health and age permits he cannot recede without breach of manifest duty. The work to be done is so important, the numbers to be benefited are so great, that he cannot be justified in even remembering that he has a self.

'As I have said before, I trust that my own age and your goodness will induce you to pardon this great interference. But whether pardoned or not I shall always be

> 'Your most affectionate friend,
>                    'St Bungay.'

The Duke,—our Duke,—on reading this letter was by no means pleased by its contents. He could ill bear to be reminded either of his pride or of his diffidence. And yet the accusations which others made against him were as nothing to those with which he charged himself. He would do this till at last he was forced to defend himself against himself by asking himself whether he could be other than as God had made him. It is the last and the poorest makeshift of a defence to which a man can be brought in his own court! Was it his fault that he was so thin-skinned that all things hurt him? When some coarse man said to him that which ought not to have been said, was it his fault that at every word a penknife had stabbed him? Other men had borne these buffets without shrinking, and had shown themselves thereby to be more use-ful, much more efficacious; but he could no more imitate them than he could procure for himself the skin of a rhinoceros or the tusk of an elephant. And this shrinking was what men called pride,—was the pride of which his old friend wrote! 'Have I ever been haughty, unless in my own defence?' he asked himself, remembering certain passages of humility in his life,—and certain passages of haughtiness also.

And the Duke told him also that he was diffident. Of course he was diffident. Was it not one and the same thing? The very pride of which he was accused was no more than that shrinking which comes from the want of trust in oneself. He was a shy man. All his friends and all his enemies knew that;—it was thus that he still discoursed with himself;—a shy, self-conscious, timid, shrinking, thin-skinned man! Of course he was diffident. Then why urge him on to tasks for which he was by nature unfitted?

And yet there was much in his old friend's letter which moved him. There were certain words which he kept on repeating to himself. 'He cannot be justified in even remembering that he has a self.' It was a hard thing to say of any man, but yet a true thing of such a man as his correspondent had described. His correspondent had spoken of a man who should know himself to be capable of serving the State. If a man were capable, and was sure within his own bosom of his own capacity, it would be his duty. But what if he were not so satisfied? What if he felt that any labours of his would be vain, and all self-abnegation useless? His friend had told him that on that matter he was bound to take the opinion of others. Perhaps so. But if so, had not that opinion been given to him very plainly when he was told that he was both proud and diffident? That he was called upon to serve his country by good service, if such were within his power, he did acknowledge freely; but not that he should allow himself to be stuck up as a ninepin only to be knocked down! There are politicians for whom such occupation seems to be proper;—and who like it too. A little office, a little power, a little rank, a little pay, a little niche in the ephemeral history of the year will reward many men adequately for being knocked down.

And yet he loved power, and even when thinking of all this allowed his mind from time to time to run away into a dreamland of prosperous political labours. He thought what it would be to be an all-beneficent

Prime Minister, with a loyal majority, with a well-conditioned unanimous cabinet, with a grateful people, and an appreciative Sovereign. How well might a man spend himself night and day, even to death, in the midst of labours such as these.

Half an hour after receiving the Duke's letter he suddenly jumped up and sat himself down at his desk. He felt it to be necessary that he should at once write to his old friend;—and the more necessary that he should do so at once, because he had resolved that he would do so before he had made up his mind on the chief subject of that letter. It did not suit him to say either that he would or that he would not do as his friend advised him. The reply was made in a very few words. 'As to myself,' he said, after expressing his regret that the Duke should find it necessary to retire from public life—'as to myself, pray understand that whatever I may do I shall never cease to be grateful for your affectionate and high-spirited counsels.'

Then his mind recurred to a more immediate and, for the moment, a heavier trouble. He had as yet given no answer to that letter from Mrs Finn, which the reader will perhaps remember. It might indeed be passed over without an answer; but to him that was impossible. She had accused him in the very strongest language of injustice, and had made him understand that if he were unjust to her, then would he be most ungrateful. He, looking at the matter with his own lights, had thought that he had been right, but had resolved to submit the question to another person. As judge in the matter he had chosen Lady Cantrip, and Lady Cantrip had given judgment against him.

He had pressed Lady Cantrip for a decided opinion, and she had told him that she, in the same position, would have done just as Mrs Finn had done. He had constituted Lady Cantrip his judge, and had resolved that her judgment should be final. He declared to himself that he did not understand it. If a man's house be on fire, do you think of certain rules of etiquette before you bid him send for the engines? If a wild beast be loose, do you go through some ceremony before you caution the wanderers abroad? There should not have been a moment! But, nevertheless, it was now necessary that he should conform himself to the opinion of Lady Cantrip, and in doing so he must apologise for the bitter scorn with which he had allowed himself to treat his wife's most loyal and loving friend.

The few words to the Duke had not been difficult, but this letter seemed to be an Herculean task. It was made infinitely more difficult by the fact that Lady Cantrip had not seemed to think that this marriage was impossible. 'Young people when they have set their minds upon it do so generally prevail at last!' These had been her words, and they discomforted him greatly. She had thought the marriage to be possible. Had she not almost expressed an opinion that they ought to be allowed to marry? And if so, would it not be his duty to take his girl away from Lady Cantrip? As to the idea that young people, because they have declared themselves to be in love, were to have just what they wanted,— with that he did not agree at all. Lady Cantrip had told him that young people generally did prevail at last. He knew the story of one young person, whose position in her youth had been very much the same as that of his daughter now, and she had not prevailed. And in her case had not the opposition which had been made to her wishes been most fortunate? That young person had become his wife, his Glencora, his Duchess. Had she been allowed to have her own way when she was a child, what would have been her fate? Ah what! Then he had to think of it all. Might she not have been alive now, and perhaps happier than she had ever been with him? And had he remained always unmarried, devoted simply to politics, would not the troubles of the world have been lighter on him? But what had that to do with it? In these matters it was not the happiness of this or that individual which should be con-sidered. There is a propriety in things;—and only by an adherence to that propriety on the part of individuals can the general welfare be maintained. A King in this country, or the heir or the possible heir to the throne, is debarred from what might possibly be a happy marriage by regard to the good of his subjects. To the Duke's thinking the maintenance of the aristocracy of the country was second only in importance to the maintenance of the Crown. How should the aristoc-racy be maintained if its wealth were allowed to fall into the hands of an adventurer!

Such were the opinions with regard to his own order of one who was as truly Liberal in his ideas as any man in England, and who had argued out these ideas to their consequences. As by the spread of education and increase of general well-being every proletaire was brought nearer to a Duke, so by such action would the Duke be brought nearer to a proletaire. Such drawing-nearer of the classes was the object to which all this man's political action tended. And yet it was a dreadful thing to him that his own daughter should desire to marry a man so much beneath her own rank and fortune as Frank Tregear.

He would not allow himself to believe that the young people could ever prevail; but nevertheless, as the idea of the thing had not alarmed Lady Cantrip as it had him, it was necessary that he should make some apology to Mrs Finn. Each moment of procrastination was a prick to his conscience. He now therefore dragged out from the secrecy of some close drawer Mrs Finn's letter and read it through to himself once again. Yes—it was true that he had condemned her, and that he had punished her. Though he had done nothing to her, and said nothing, and written but very little, still he had punished her most severely.

She had written as though the matter was almost one of life and death to her. He could understand that too. His uncle's conduct to this woman, and his wife's, had created the intimacy which had existed. Through their efforts she had become almost as one of the family. And now to be dismissed, like a servant who had misbehaved herself! And then her arguments in her own defence were all so good,—if only that which Lady Cantrip had laid down as law was to be held as law. He was aware now that she had had no knowledge of the matter till his daughter had told her of the engagement at Matching. Then it was evident also that she had sent this Tregear to him immediately on her return to London. And at the end of the letter she accused him of what she had been pleased to call his usual tenacity in believing ill of her! He had been obstinate,—too obstinate in this respect, but he did not love her the better for having told him of it.

At last he did put his apology into words.

'MY DEAR MRS FINN,

'I believe I had better acknowledge to you at once that I have been wrong in my judgment as to your conduct in a certain matter. You tell me that I owe it to you to make this acknowledgment,—and I make it. The subject is, as you may imagine, so painful that I will spare myself, if possible, any further allusion to it. I believe I did you a wrong, and therefore I write to ask your pardon.

'I should perhaps apologise also for delay in my reply. I have had much to think of in this matter, and have many others also on my mind.

'Believe me to be,
'Yours faithfully,
'OMNIUM.'

It was very short, and as being short was infinitely less troublesome at the moment than a fuller epistle; but he was angry with himself, knowing that it was too short, feeling that it was ungracious. He should have expressed a hope that he might soon see her again,—only he had no such wish. There had been times at which he had liked her, but he knew that he did not like her now. And yet he was bound to be her friend! If he could only do some great thing for her, and thus satisfy his feeling of indebtedness towards her! But all the favours had been from her to him and his.

## CHAPTER 23

### FRANK TREGEAR WANTS A FRIEND

SIX or seven weeks had passed since Tregear had made his communication to the Duke, and during that time he had heard not a word about the girl he loved. He knew, indeed, that she was at The Horns, and probably had reason to suppose that she was being guarded there, as it were, out of his reach. This did not surprise him; nor did he regard it as a hardship. It was to be expected that she should be kept out of his sight. But this was a state of things to which, as he thought, there should not be more than a moderate amount of submission. Six weeks was not a very long period, but it was perhaps long enough for evincing that respect which he owed to the young lady's father. Something must be done some day. How could he expect her to be true to him unless he took some means of showing himself to be true to her?

In these days he did not live very much with her brother. He not only disliked, but distrusted Major Tifto, and had so expressed himself as to give rise to angry words. Silverbridge had said that he knew how to take care of himself. Tregear had replied that he had his doubts on that matter. Then the Member of Parliament had declared that at any rate he did not intend to be taken care of by Frank Tregear! In such a state of things it was not possible that there should be any close confidence as to Lady Mary. Nor does it often come to pass that the brother is the confidant of the sister's lover. Brothers hardly like their sisters to have lovers, though they are often well satisfied that their sisters should find husbands. Tregear's want of rank and wealth added something to this feeling in the mind of this brother; so that Silverbridge, though he felt himself to be deterred by friendship from any open opposition, still was almost inimical. 'It won't do, you know,' he had said to his brother Gerald, shaking his head.

Tregear, however, was determined to be active in the matter, to make some effort, to speak to somebody. But how to make an effort,— and to whom should he speak? Thinking of all this he remembered that Mrs Finn had sent for him and had told him to go with his love story to the Duke. She had been almost severe with him;—but after the interview was over, he had felt that she had acted well and wisely. He therefore determined that he would go to Mrs Finn.

She had as yet received no answer from the Duke, though nearly a fortnight had elapsed since she had written her letter. During that time she had become very angry. She felt that he was not treating her as a gentleman should treat a lady, and certainly not as the husband of her late friend should have treated the friend of his late wife. She had a proud consciousness of having behaved well to the Pallisers, and now this head of the Pallisers was rewarding her by evil treatment. She had been generous; he was ungenerous. She had been honest; he was deficient even in that honesty for which she had given him credit. And she had been unable to obtain any of that consolation which could have come to her from talking of her wrongs. She could not complain to her husband, because there were reasons that made it essential that her husband should not quarrel with the Duke. She was hot with indignation at the very moment in which Tregear was announced.

He began by apologising for his intrusion, and she of course assured him that he was welcome. 'After the liberty which I took with you, Mr Tregear, I am only too well pleased that you should come and see me.'

'I am afraid,' he said, 'that I was a little rough.'

'A little warm;—but that was to be expected. A gentleman never likes to be interfered with on such a matter.'

'The position was and is difficult, Mrs Finn.'

'And I am bound to acknowledge the very ready way in which you did what I asked you to do.'

'And now, Mrs Finn, what is to come next?'

'Ah!'

'Something must be done! You know of course that the Duke did not receive me with any great favour.'

'I did not suppose he would.'

'Nor did I. Of course he would object to such a marriage, But a man in these days cannot dictate to his daughter what husband she should marry.'

'Perhaps he can dictate to her what husband she shall not marry.'

'Hardly that. He may put impediments in the way; and the Duke will do so. But if I am happy enough to have won the affections of his daughter,—so as to make it essential to her happiness that she should become my wife,—he will give way.'

'What am I to say, Mr Tregear?'

'Just what you think.'

'Why should I be made to say what I think on so delicate a matter? Or of what use would be my thoughts? Remember how far I am removed from her.'

'You are his friend.'

'Not at all! No one less so!' As she said this she could not hinder the colour from coming into her face. 'I was her friend,—Lady Glencora's; but with the death of my friend there was an end of all that.'

'You were staying with him,—at his request. You told me so yourself.'

'I shall never stay with him again. But all that, Mr Tregear, is of no matter. I do not mean to say a word against him;—not a word. But if you wish to interest any one as being the Duke's friend, then I can assure you I am the last person in London to whom you should come. I know no one to whom the Duke is likely to entertain feelings so little kind as towards me.' This she said in a peculiarly solemn way that startled Tregear. But before he could answer her a servant entered the room with a letter. She recognised at once the Duke's handwriting. Here was the answer for which she had been so long waiting in silent expectation! She could not keep it unread till he was gone. 'Will you allow me a moment?' she whispered, and then she opened the envelope. As she read the few words her eyes became laden with tears. They quite sufficed to relieve the injured pride which had sat so heavy at her heart. 'I believe I did you a wrong, and therefore I ask your pardon!' It was so like what she had believed the man to be! She could not be longer angry with him. And yet the very last words she had spoken were words complaining of his conduct. 'This is from the Duke,' she said, putting the letter back into its envelope.

'Oh, indeed.'

'It is odd that it should have come while you were here.'

'Is it,—is it,—about Lady Mary?'

'No;—at least,—not directly. I perhaps spoke more harshly about him than I should have done. The truth is I had expected a line from him, and it had not come. Now it is here; but I do not suppose I shall ever see much of him. My intimacy was with her. But I would not wish you to remember what I said just now, if—if——'

'If what, Mrs Finn? You mean, perhaps, if I should ever be allowed to call myself his son-in-law. It may seem to you to be arrogant, but it is an honour which I expect to win.'

'Faint heart,*—you know, Mr Tregear.'

'Exactly. One has to tell oneself that very often. You will help me?'

'Certainly not,' she said, as though she were much startled. 'How can I help you?'

'By telling me what I should do. I suppose if I were to go down to Richmond I should not be admitted.'

'If you ask me, I think not;—not to see Lady Mary. Lady Cantrip would perhaps see you.'

'She is acting the part of—duenna.'\*

'As I should do also, if Lady Mary were staying with me. You don't suppose that if she were here I would let her see you in my house without her father's leave?'

'I suppose not.'

'Certainly not; and therefore I conceive that Lady Cantrip will not do so either.'

'I wish she were here.'

'It would be of no use. I should be a dragon in guarding her.'

'I wish you would let me feel that you were like a sister to me in this matter.'

'But I am not your sister, nor yet your aunt, nor yet your grandmother. What I mean is that I cannot be on your side.'

'Can you not?'

'No, Mr Tregear. Think how long I have known these other people.'

'But just now you said that he was your enemy.'

'I did say so; but as I have unsaid it since, you as a gentleman will not remember my words. At any rate I cannot help you in this.'

'I shall write to her.'

'It can be nothing to me. If you write she will show your letter either to her father or to Lady Cantrip.'

'But she will read it first.'

'I cannot tell how that may be. In fact I am the very last person in the world to whom you should come for assistance in this matter. If I gave any assistance to anybody I should be bound to give it to the Duke.'

'I cannot understand that, Mrs Finn.'

'Nor can I explain it, but it would be so. I shall always be very glad to see you, and I do feel that we ought to be friends,—because I took such a liberty with you. But in this matter I cannot help you.'

When she said this he had to take his leave. It was impossible that he should further press his case upon her, though he would have been very glad to extract from her some kindly word. It is such a help in a difficulty to have somebody who will express even a hope that the difficulty is perhaps not invincible! He had no one to comfort him in this matter. There was one dear friend,—as a friend dearer than any other,—to whom he might go, and who would after some fashion bid him prosper. Mabel would encourage him. She had said that she would do so. But in making that promise she had told him that Romeo would not have spoken of his love for Juliet to Rosalind, whom he had loved before he saw Juliet. No doubt she had gone on to tell him that he might come to her and talk freely of his love for Lady Mary,—but after what had been said before, he felt that he could not do so without leaving a sting behind. When a man's love goes well with him,—so well as to be in some degree oppressive to him even by its prosperity,—when the young lady has jumped into his arms and the father and mother have been quite willing, then he wants no confidant. He does not care to speak very much of the matter which among his friends is apt to become a subject for raillery. When you call a man Benedick he does not come to you with ecstatic descriptions of the beauty and the wit of his Beatrice.* But no one was likely to call him Benedick in reference to Lady Mary.

In spite of his manner, in spite of his apparent self-sufficiency, this man was very soft within. Less than two years back he had been willing to sacrifice all the world for his cousin Mabel, and his cousin Mabel had told him that he was wrong. 'It does not pay to sacrifice the world for love.' So cousin Mabel had said, and had added something as to its being necessary that she should marry a rich man, and expedient that he should marry a rich woman. He had thought much about it, and had declared to himself that on no account would he marry a woman for her money. Then he had encountered Lady Mary Palliser. There had been no doubt, no resolution after that, no thinking about it;—but downright love. There was nothing left of real regret for his cousin in his bosom. She had been right. That love had been impossible. But this would be possible,—ah, so deliciously possible,—if only her father and mother would assist! The mother, imprudent in this as in all things, had assented. The reader knows the rest.

It was in every way possible. 'She will have money enough,' the Duchess had said, 'if only her father can be brought to give it you.' So Tregear had set his heart upon it, and had said to himself that the thing was to be done. Then his friend the Duchess had died, and the real difficulties had commenced. From that day he had not seen his love, or heard from her. How was he to know whether she would be true to him? And where was he to seek for that sympathy which he felt to be so necessary to him? A wild idea had come into his head that Mrs Finn would be his friend;—but she had repudiated him.

He went straight home and at once wrote to the girl. The letter was a simple love-letter, and as such need not be given here. In what sweet-est language he could find he assured her that even though he should never be allowed to see her or to hear from her, that still he should cling to her. And then he added this passage: 'If your love for me be what I think it to be, no one can have a right to keep us apart. Pray be sure that I shall not change. If you change let me know it;—but I shall as soon expect the heavens to fall.'*

## CHAPTER 24

### 'SHE MUST BE MADE TO OBEY'

LADY MARY PALLISER down at The Horns had as much liberty allowed to her as is usually given to young ladies in these very free days. There was indeed no restriction placed upon her at all. Had Tregear gone down to Richmond and asked for the young lady, and had Lady Cantrip at the time been out and the young lady at home, it would have depended altogether upon the young lady whether she would have seen her lover or not. Nevertheless Lady Cantrip kept her eyes open, and when the letter came from Tregear she was aware that the letter had come. But the letter found its way into Lady Mary's hands and was read in the seclusion of her own bedroom. 'I wonder whether you would mind reading that,' she said very shortly afterwards to Lady Cantrip. 'What answer ought I to make?'

'Do you think any answer ought to be made, my dear?'

'Oh yes; I must answer him.'

'Would your papa wish it?'

'I told papa that I would not promise not to write to him. I think I told him that he should see any letters that there were. But if I show them to you, I suppose that will do as well.'

'You had better keep your word to him absolutely.'

'I am not afraid of doing so, if you mean that. I cannot bear to give him pain, but this is a matter in which I mean to have my own way.'

'Mean to have your own way!' said Lady Cantrip, much surprised by the determined tone of the young lady.

'Certainly I do. I want you to understand so much! I suppose papa can keep us from marrying for ever and ever if he pleases, but he never will make me say that I will give up Mr Tregear. And if he does not yield I shall think him cruel. Why should he wish to make me unhappy all my life?'

'He certainly does not wish that, my dear.'

'But he will do it.'

'I cannot go against your father, Mary.'

'No, I suppose not. I shall write to Mr Tregear, and then I will show you what I have written. Papa shall see it too if he pleases. I will do nothing secret, but I will never give up Mr Tregear.'

Lord Cantrip came down to Richmond that evening, and his wife told him that in her opinion it would be best that the Duke should allow the young people to marry, and should give them money enough to live upon. 'Is not that a strong order?' asked the Earl. The Countess acknowledged that it was a 'strong order,' but suggested that for the happiness of them all it might as well be done at first as at last.

The next morning Lady Mary showed her a copy of the reply which she had already sent to her lover.

'DEAR FRANK,

'You may be *quite sure* that I shall *never* give you up. I will not write more at present because papa does not wish me to do so. I shall show papa your letter and my answer.

                    'Your own most affectionate

                                        'MARY.'

'Has it gone?' asked the Countess.

'I put it myself into the pillar letter-box.'\* Then Lady Cantrip felt that she had to deal with a very self-willed young lady indeed.

That afternoon Lady Cantrip asked Lady Mary whether she might be allowed to take the two letters up to town with the express purpose of showing them to the Duke. 'Oh yes,' said Mary, 'I think it would be so much the best. Give papa my kindest love, and tell him from me that if he wants to make his poor little girl happy he will forgive her and be kind to her in all this.' Then the Countess made some attempt to argue the matter. There were proprieties! High rank might be a blessing or might be the reverse—as people thought of it;—but all men acknowledged that much was due to it. 'Noblesse oblige.'\* It was often the case in life that women were called upon by circumstances to sacrifice their inclinations! What right had a gentleman to talk of marriage who had no means? These things she said and very many more, but it was to no purpose. The young lady asserted that as the gentleman was a gentleman there need be no question as to rank, and that in regard to money there need be no difficulty if one of them had sufficient. 'But you have none but what your father may give you,' said Lady Cantrip. 'Papa can give it us without any trouble,' said Lady Mary. This child had a clear idea of what she thought to be her own rights. Being the child of rich parents she had the right to money. Being a woman she had a right to a husband. Having been born free she had a right to choose one for herself. Having had a man's love given to her she had a right to keep it. 'One doesn't know which she is most like, her father or her mother,' Lady Cantrip said afterwards to her husband. 'She has his cool determination, and her hot-headed obstinacy.'

She did show the letters to the Duke, and in answer to a word or two from him explained that she could not take upon herself to debar her guest from the use of the post. 'But she will write nothing without letting you know it.'

'She ought to write nothing at all.'

'What she feels is much worse than what she writes.'

'If there were no intercourse she would forget him.'

'Ah; I don't know,' said the Countess sorrowfully; 'I thought so once.'

'All children are determined as long as they are allowed to have their own way.'

'I mean to say that it is the nature of her character to be obstinate. Most girls are prone to yield. They have not character enough to stand against opposition. I am not speaking now only of affairs like this. It would be the same with her in any thing. Have you not always found it so?'

Then he had to acknowledge to himself that he had never found out anything in reference to his daughter's character. She had been properly educated;—at least he hoped so. He had seen her grow up, pretty, sweet, affectionate, always obedient to him;—the most charming plaything in the world on the few occasions in which he had allowed himself to play.* But as to her actual disposition, he had never taken any trouble to inform himself. She had been left to her mother,—as other girls are left. And his sons had been left to their tutors. And now he had no control over any of them. 'She must be made to obey like others,' he said at last, speaking through his teeth.

There was something in this which almost frightened Lady Cantrip. She could not bear to hear him say that the girl must be made to yield, with that spirit of despotic power under which women were restrained in years now passed. If she could have spoken her own mind it would have been to this effect: 'Let us do what we can to lead her away from this desire of hers; and in order that we may do so, let us tell her that her marriage with Mr Tregear is out of the question. But if we do not succeed,—say in the course of the next twelve months,—let us give way. Let us make it a matter of joy that the young man himself is so acceptable and well-behaved.' That was her idea, and with that she would have indoctrined the Duke had she been able. But his was different. 'She must be made to obey,' he said. And, as he said it, he seemed to be indifferent as to the sorrow which such enforced obedience might bring upon his child. In answer to this she could only shake her head. 'What do you mean?' he asked. 'Do you think we ought to yield?'

'Not at once, certainly.'

'But at last?'

'What can you do, Duke? If she be as firm as you, can you bear to see her pine away in her misery?'

'Girls do not do like that,' he said.

'Girls, like men, are very different. They generally will yield to external influences. English girls, though they become the most loving wives in the world, do not generally become so riven by an attachment as to become deep sufferers when it is disallowed. But here, I fear, we have to deal with one who will suffer after this fashion.'

'Why should she not be like others?'

'It may be so. We will try. But you see what she says in her letter to him. She writes as though your authority were to be nothing in that matter of giving up. In all that she says to me there is the same spirit. If she is firm, Duke, you must yield.'

'Never! She shall never marry him with my sanction.'

There was nothing more to be said, and Lady Cantrip went her way. But the Duke, though he could say nothing more, continued to think of it hour after hour. He went down to the House of Lords to listen to a debate in which it was intended to cover the ministers with heavy disgrace. But the Duke could not listen even to his own friends. He could listen to nothing as he thought of the condition of his children.

He had been asked whether he could bear to see his girl suffer, as though he were indifferent to the sufferings of his child. Did he not know of himself that there was no father who would do more for the welfare of his daughter? Was he not sure of the tenderness of his own heart? In all that he was doing was he governed by anything but a sense of duty? Was it personal pride or love of personal aggrandisement? He thought that he could assure himself that he was open to no such charge. Would he not die for her,—or for them,—if he could so serve

them? Surely this woman had accused him most wrongfully when she
had intimated that he could see his girl suffer without caring for it. In
his indignation he determined—for awhile,—that he would remove
her from the custody of Lady Cantrip. But then, where should he place
her? He was aware that his own house would be like a grave to a girl just
fit to come out into the world. In this coming autumn she must go
somewhere,—with someone. He himself, in his present frame of mind,
would be but a sorry travelling companion.

Lady Cantrip had said that the best hope of escape would lie in the
prospect of another lover. The prescription was disagreeable, but it
had availed in the case of his own wife. Before he had ever seen her as
Lady Glencora McCloskie she had been desirous of giving herself and
all her wealth to one Burgo Fitzgerald, who had been altogether
unworthy. The Duke could remember well how a certain old Lady
Midlothian had first hinted to him that Lady Glencora's property was
very large, and had then added that the young lady herself was very
beautiful. And he could remember how his uncle, the late Duke, who
had seldom taken much trouble in merely human affairs, had said a
word or two—'I have heard a whisper about you and Lady Glencora
McCloskie, nothing could be better.' The result had been undoubtedly
good. His Cora and all her money had been saved from a worthless
spendthrift. He had found a wife who he now thought had made him
happy. And she had found at any rate a respectable husband. The idea
when picked to pieces is not a nice idea. 'Let us look out for a husband
for this girl, so that we may get her married,—out of the way of her
lover.' It is not nice. But it had succeeded in one case, and why should
it not succeed in another?

But how was it to be done? Who should do it? Whom should he
select to play the part which he had undertaken in that other arrangement? No worse person could be found than himself for managing such
an affair. When the idea had first been raised he had thought that Lady
Cantrip would do it all; but now he was angry with Lady Cantrip.

How was it to be done? How should it be commenced? How had it
been commenced in his own case? He did not in the least know how he
had been chosen. Was it possible that his uncle, who was the proudest
man in England, should have condescended to make a bargain with an
old dowager whom everybody had despised? And in what way had he
been selected? No doubt he had been known to be the heir-apparent to
a dukedom and to ducal revenues. In his case old Lady Midlothian had
begun the matter with him. It occurred to him that in royal marriages
such beginnings are quite common.

But who should be the happy man? Then he began to count up the requisite attributes. He must be of high rank, and an eldest son, and the possessor of, or the heir to, a good estate. He did despise himself when he found that he put these things first,—as a matter of course. Nevertheless he did put them first. He was ejecting this other man because he possessed none of these attributes. He hurried himself on to add that the man must be of good character, and such as a young girl might learn to love. But yet he was aware that he added these things for his conscience's sake. Tregear's character was good, and certainly the girl loved him. But was it not clear to all who knew anything of such matters that Mr Francis Tregear should not have dared even to think of marrying the daughter of the Duke of Omnium?

Who should be the happy man? There were so many who evidently were unfit. Young Lord Percival was heir to a ruined estate and a beggared peerage. Lord Glasslough was odious to all men. There were three or four others of whom he thought that he knew some fatal objection. But when he remembered Lord Popplecourt there seemed to be no objection which need be fatal.

Lord Popplecourt was a young peer whose father had died two years since and whose estates were large and unembarrassed. The late lord, who had been a Whig of the old fashion, had been the Duke's friend. They had been at Oxford and in the House of Commons together, and Lord Popplecourt had always been true to his party. As to the son, the Duke remembered to have heard lately that he was not given to waste his money. He drove a coach about London a good deal, but had as yet not done anything very foolish. He had taken his degree at Oxford, thereby showing himself to be better than Silverbridge. He had also taken his seat in the House of Lords and had once opened his mouth. He had not indeed appeared often again; but at Lord Popplecourt's age much legislation is not to be expected from a young peer. Then he thought of the man's appearance. Popplecourt was not specially attractive, whereas Tregear was a very handsome man. But so also had been Burgo Fitzgerald,—almost abnormally beautiful, while he, Plantagenet Palliser, as he was then, had been quite as insignificant in appearance as Lord Popplecourt.

Lord Popplecourt might possibly do. But then how should the matter be spoken of to the young man? After all, would it not be best that he should trust Lady Cantrip?

## CHAPTER 25

### A FAMILY BREAKFAST-TABLE

LORD SILVERBRIDGE had paid all his Derby losses without any difficulty. They had not been very heavy for a man in his position, and the money had come without remonstrance. When asking for it he was half ashamed of himself, but could still find consolation by remembering how much worse had befallen many young men whom he knew. He had never 'plunged.'* In fact he had made the most prudent book* in the world; and had so managed affairs that even now the horse which had been beaten was worth more than all he had lost and paid. 'This is getting serious,' he had said to his partner when, on making out a rough account, he had brought the Major in a debtor to him of more than a thousand pounds. The Major had remarked that as he was half-owner of the horses his partner had good security for the money. Then something of an unwritten arrangement was made. The 'Prime Minister' was now one of the favourites for the Leger. If the horse won that race there would be money enough for everything. If that race were lost, then there should be a settlement by the transfer of the stud* to the younger partner. 'He's safe to pull it off,' said the Major.

At this time both his sons were living with the Duke in London. It had been found impracticable to send Lord Gerald back to Cambridge. The doors of Trinity were closed against him. But some interest had been made in his favour, and he was to be transferred to Oxford. All the truth had been told, and there had been a feeling that the lad should be allowed another chance. He could not however go to his new Alma Mater* till after the long vacation. In the meantime he was to be taken by a tutor down to a cottage on Dartmoor and there be made to read,*—with such amusement in the meantime as might be got from fishing, and playing cricket with the West Devon county club. 'It isn't a very bright look-out for the summer,' his brother had said to him, 'but it's better than breaking out on the loose altogether. You be a credit to the family and all that sort of thing. Then I'll give up the borough to you. But mind you stick to the Liberals. I've made an ass of myself.' However in these early days of June Lord Gerald had not yet got his tutor.

Though the father and the two young men were living together they did not see very much of each other. The Duke breakfasted at nine and the repast was a very simple one. When they failed to appear, he did not scold,—but would simply be disappointed. At dinner they never met.

It was supposed that Lord Gerald passed his mornings in reading, and some little attempts were made in that direction. It is to be feared they did not come to much. Silverbridge was very kind to Gerald, feeling an increased tenderness for him on account of that Cambridge mishap. Now they were much together, and occasionally, by a strong effort, would grace their father's breakfast-table with their company.

It was not often that he either reproached them or preached to them. Though he could not live with them on almost equal terms, as some fathers can live with their sons, though he could not laugh at their fun or make them laugh at his wit, he knew that it would have been better both for him and them if he had possessed this capacity. Though the life which they lived was distasteful to him,—though racehorses were an abomination to him, and the driving of coaches a folly, and club-life a manifest waste of time, still he recognised these things as being, if not necessary, yet unavoidable evils. To Gerald he would talk about Oxford, avoiding all allusions to past Cambridge misfortunes; but in the presence of Silverbridge, whose Oxford career had been so peculiarly unfortunate, he would make no allusion to either of the universities. To his eldest son he would talk of Parliament, which of all subjects would have been the most congenial had they agreed in politics. As it was he could speak more freely to him on that than any other matter.

One Thursday night as the two brothers went to bed on returning from the Beargarden, at a not very late hour, they agreed that they would 'give the governor a turn' the next morning,—by which they meant that they would drag themselves out of bed in time to breakfast with him. 'The worst of it is that he never will let them get anything to eat,' said Gerald. But Silverbridge explained that he had taken that matter into his own hands, and had specially ordered broiled salmon* and stewed kidneys. 'He won't like it, you know,' said Gerald. 'I'm sure he thinks it wicked to eat anything but toasted bacon before lunch.'

At a very little after nine Silverbridge was in the breakfast-room, and there found his father. 'I suppose Gerald is not up yet,' said the Duke almost crossly.

'Oh yes he is, sir. He'll be here directly.'

'Have you seen him this morning?'

'No; I haven't seen him. But I know he'll be here. He said he would, last night.'

'You speak of it as if it were an undertaking.'

'No, not that, sir. But we are not always quite up to time.'

'No; indeed you are not. Perhaps you sit late at the House.'

'Sometimes I do,' said the young member, with a feeling almost akin to shame as he remembered all the hours spent at the Beargarden. 'I have had Gerald there in the Gallery sometimes. It is just as well he should know what is being done.'

'Quite as well.'

'I shouldn't wonder if he gets a seat some day.'

'I don't know how that may be.'

'He won't change as I have done. He'll stick to your side. Indeed I think he'd do better in the House than I shall. He has more gift of the gab.'

'That is not the first thing requisite.'

'I know all that, sir. I've read your letter more than once, and I showed it to him.'

There was something sweet and pleasant in the young man's manner by which the father could hardly not be captivated. They had now sat down, and the servant had brought in the unusual accessories for a morning feast. 'What is all that?' asked the Duke.

'Gerald and I are so awfully hungry of a morning,' said the son apologising.

'Well;—it's a very good thing to be hungry;—that is if you can get plenty to eat. Salmon, is it? I don't think I'll have any myself. Kidneys! Not for me. I think I'll take a bit of fried bacon. I also am hungry, but not awfully hungry.'

'You never seem to me to eat anything, sir.'

'Eating is an occupation from which I think a man takes the more pleasure the less he considers it. A rural labourer who sits on the ditch-side with his bread and cheese and an onion has more enjoyment out of it than any Lucullus.'

'But he likes a good deal of it.'

'I do not think he ever over-eats himself,—which Lucullus does. I have envied a ploughman his power,—his dura ilia,*—but never an epicure the appreciative skill of his palate. If Gerald does not make haste he will have to exercise neither the one nor the other upon that fish.'

'I will leave a bit for him, sir,—and here he is. You are twenty minutes late, Gerald. My father says that bread and cheese and onions would be better for you than salmon and stewed kidneys.'

'No, Silverbridge;—I said no such thing; but that if he were a hedger and ditcher the bread and cheese and onions would be as good.'

'I should not mind trying them at all,' said Gerald. 'Only one never does have such things for breakfast. Last winter a lot of us skated to

Ely,* and we ate two or three loaves of bread and a whole cheese at a pot-house!* And as for beer, we drank the public* dry.'

'It was because for the time you had been a hedger and ditcher.'

'Proby was a ditcher I know, when he went right through into one of the dykes. Just push on that dish, Silverbridge. It's no good you having the trouble of helping me half-a-dozen times. I don't think things are a bit the nicer because they cost a lot of money. I suppose that is what you mean, sir.'

'Something of that kind, Gerald. Not to have money for your wants;—that must be troublesome.'

'Very bad indeed,' said Silverbridge, shaking his head wisely, as a Member of Parliament might do who felt that something should be done to put down such a lamentable state of things.

'I don't complain,' said Gerald. 'No fellow ever had less right to complain. But I never felt that I had quite enough. Of course it was my own fault.'

'I should say so, my boy. But then there are a great many like you. Let their means be what they may, they never have quite enough. To be in any difficulty with regard to money,—to owe what you cannot pay, or even to have to abstain from things which you have told yourself are necessary to yourself or to those who depend on you,—creates a feeling of meanness.'

'That is what I have always felt,' said Silverbridge. 'I cannot bear to think that I should like to have a thing and that I cannot afford it.'

'You do not quite understand me, I fear. The only case in which you can be justified in desiring that which you cannot afford is when the thing is necessary;—as bread may be, or clothes.'

'As when a fellow wants a lot of new breeches before he has paid his tailor's bill.'

'As when a poor man,' said the Duke impressively, 'may long to give his wife a new gown, or his children boots to keep their feet from the mud and snow.' Then he paused a moment, but the serious tone of his voice and the energy of his words had sent Gerald headlong among his kidneys. 'I say that in such cases money must be regarded as a blessing.'

'A ten-pound note will do so much,' said Silverbridge.

'But beyond that it ought to have no power of conferring happiness, and certainly cannot drive away sorrow. Not though you build palaces out into the deep,* can that help you. You read your Horace, I hope. "Scandunt eodum quo dominus minæ." '*

'I recollect that,' said Gerald. 'Black care sits behind the horseman.'

'Even though he have a groom riding after him beautiful with exquis-ite boots. As far as I have been able to look out into the world——'

'I suppose you know it as well as anybody,' said Silverbridge,—who was simply desirous of making himself pleasant to the 'dear old gover-nor.'

'As far as my experience goes, the happiest man is he who, being above the troubles which money brings, has his hands the fullest of work. If I were to name the class of men whose lives are spent with the most thorough enjoyment, I think I should name that of barristers who are in large practice and also in Parliament.'

'Isn't it a great grind, sir?' asked Silverbridge.

'A very great grind, as you call it. And there may be the grind and not the success. But——' He had now got up from his seat at the table and was standing with his back against the chimney-piece, and as he went on with his lecture,—as the word 'But' came from his lips—he struck the fingers of one hand lightly on the palm of the other as he had been known to do at some happy flight of oratory in the House of Commons. 'But it is the grind that makes the happiness. To feel that your hours are filled to overflowing, that you can barely steal minutes enough for sleep, that the welfare of many is entrusted to you, that the world looks on and approves, that some good is always being done to others,—above all things some good to your country;—that is happiness. For myself I can conceive none other.'

'Books,' suggested Gerald, as he put the last morsel of the last kidney into his mouth.

'Yes, books! Cicero and Ovid have told us that to literature only could they look for consolation in their banishment. But then they speak of a remedy for sorrow, not of a source of joy. No young man should dare to neglect literature. At some period of his life he will surely need consolation. And he may be certain that should he live to be an old man, there will be none other,—except religion. But for that feeling of self-contentment, which creates happiness—hard work, and hard work alone, can give it to you.'*

'Books are hard work themselves sometimes,' said Gerald.

'As for money,' continued the father, not caring to notice this inter-ruption, 'if it be regarded in any other light than as a shield against want, as a rampart under the protection of which you may carry on your battle, it will fail you. I was born a rich man.'

'Few people have cared so little about it as you,' said the elder son.

'And you, both of you, have been born to be rich.' This assertion did not take the elder brother by surprise. It was a matter of course.

But Lord Gerald, who had never as yet heard anything as to his future destiny from his father, was interested by the statement. 'When I think of all this,—of what constitutes happiness,—I am almost tempted to grieve that it should be so.'

'If a large fortune were really a bad thing,' said Gerald, 'a man could I suppose get rid of it.'

'No;—it is a thing of which a man cannot get rid,—unless by shameful means. It is a burden which he must carry to the end.'

'Does anybody wish to get rid of it, as Sindbad did of the Old Man?'* asked Gerald pertinaciously. 'At any rate I have enjoyed the kidneys.'

'You assured us just now that the bread and cheese at Ely were just as good.'* The Duke as he said this looked as though he knew that he had taken all the wind out of his adversary's sails. 'Though you add carriage to carriage, you will not be carried more comfortably.'

'A second horse out hunting is a comfort,' said Silverbridge.

'Then at any rate don't desire a third for show. But such comforts will cease to be joys when they become matters of course. That a boy who does not see a pudding once a year should enjoy a pudding when it comes I can understand; but the daily pudding, or the pudding twice a day, is soon no more than simple daily bread,—which will or will not be sweet as it shall or shall not have been earned.' Then he went slowly to the door, but, as he stood with the handle of it in his hand, he turned round and spoke another word. 'When, hereafter, Gerald, you may chance to think of that bread and cheese at Ely, always remember that you had skated from Cambridge.'

The two brothers then took themselves to some remote part of the house where arrangements had been made for smoking, and there they finished the conversation. 'I was very glad to hear what he said about you, old boy.' This of course came from Silverbridge.

'I didn't quite understand him.'

'He meant you to understand that you wouldn't be like other younger brothers.'

'Then what I have will be taken from you.'

'There is lots for three or four of us. I do agree that if a fellow has as much as he can spend he ought not to want anything more. Morton was telling me the other day something about the settled estates. I sat in that office with him all one morning. I could not understand it all, but I observed that he said nothing about the Scotch property.* You'll be a laird, and I wish you joy with all my heart. The governor will tell you all about it before long. He's going to have two eldest sons.'

'What an unnatural piece of cruelty to me;—and so unnecessary!'
'Why?'
'He says that a property is no better than a burden. But I'll try and bear it.'


## CHAPTER 26

### DINNER AT THE BEARGARDEN

THE Duke was in the gallery of the House of Commons which is devoted to the use of peers,* and Silverbridge, having heard that his father was there, had come up to him. It was then about half-past five, and the House had settled down to business. Prayers had been read, petitions had been presented, and Ministers had gone through their course of baiting with that equanimity and air of superiority which always belongs to a well-trained occupant of the Treasury bench.

The Duke was very anxious that his son should attend to his parliamentary duties, but he was too proud a man and too generous to come to the House as a spy. It was his present habit always to be in his own place when the Lords were sitting, and to remain there while the Lords sat. It was not, for many reasons, an altogether satisfactory occupation, but it was the best which his life afforded him. He would never, however, come across into the other House, without letting his son know of his coming, and Lord Silverbridge had on this occasion been on the look-out, and had come up to his father at once. 'Don't let me take you away,' said the Duke, 'if you are particularly interested in your Chief's defence,' for Sir Timothy Beeswax was defending some measure of legal reform in which he was said to have fallen into trouble.

'I can hear it up here, you know, sir.'
'Hardly if you are talking to me.'
'To tell the truth it's a matter I don't care much about. They've got into some mess as to the number of Judges and what they ought to do. Finn was saying that they had so arranged that there was one Judge who never could possibly do anything.'

'If Mr Finn said so it would probably be so, with some little allowance for Irish exaggeration.* He is a clever man, with less of his country's hyperbole than others;—but still not without his share.'

'You know him well, I suppose.'
'Yes;—as one man does know another in the political world.'

'But he is a friend of yours? I don't mean an "honourable friend," which is great bosh; but you know him at home.'

'Oh yes;—certainly. He has been staying with me at Matching. In public life such intimacies come from politics.'

'You don't care very much about him then.'

The Duke paused a moment before he answered. 'Yes I do;—and in what I said just now perhaps I wronged him. I have been under obligations to Mr Finn,*—in a matter as to which he behaved very well. I have found him to be a gentleman. If you come across him in the House I would wish you to be courteous to him. I have not seen him since we came from abroad. I have been able to see nobody. But if ever again I should entertain my friends at my table, Mr Finn would be one who would always be welcome there.' This he said with a sadly serious air as though wishing that his words should be noted. At the present moment he was remembering that he owed recompense to Mrs Finn, and was making an effort to pay the debt. 'But your leader is striking out into unwonted eloquence. Surely we ought to listen to him.'

Sir Timothy was a fluent speaker, and when there was nothing to be said was possessed of great plenty of words. And he was gifted with that peculiar power which enables a man to have the last word in every encounter,—a power which we are apt to call repartee, which is in truth the readiness which comes from continual practice. You shall meet two men of whom you shall know the one to be endowed with the brilliancy of true genius, and the other to be possessed of but moderate parts, and shall find the former never able to hold his own against the latter. In a debate, the man of moderate parts will seem to be greater than the man of genius. But this skill of tongue, this glibness of speech is hardly an affair of intellect at all. It is,—as is style to the writer,—not the wares which he has to take to market, but the vehicle in which they may be carried. Of what avail to you is it to have filled granaries with corn if you cannot get your corn to the consumer? Now Sir Timothy was a great vehicle, but he had not in truth much corn to send. He could turn a laugh against an adversary;—no man better. He could seize, at the moment, every advantage which the opportunity might give him.* The Treasury Bench on which he sat and the big box on the table before him were to him fortifications of which he knew how to use every stone. The cheers and the jeers of the House had been so measured by him that he knew the value and force of every sound. Politics had never been to him a study; but to parliamentary strategy he had devoted all his faculties. No one knew so well as Sir Timothy how to make arrangements for business, so that every detail should be troublesome to his opponents. He could foresee a month beforehand that on a certain day a Royal concert* would make the house empty, and would generously give that day to a less observant adversary. He knew how to blind the eyes of members to the truth. Those on the opposite side of the House would find themselves checkmated by his astuteness,—when, with all their pieces on the board, there should be none which they could move. And this to him was Government! It was to these purposes that he conceived that a great Statesman should devote himself! Parliamentary management! That, in his mind, was under this Constitution of ours the one act essential for Government.

In all this he was very great; but when it might fall to his duty either to suggest or to defend any real piece of proposed legislation he was less happy. On this occasion he had been driven to take the matter in hand because he had previously been concerned in it as a lawyer. He had allowed himself to wax angry as he endeavoured to answer certain personal criticisms. Now Sir Timothy was never stronger than when he simulated anger. His mock indignation was perhaps his most powerful weapon. But real anger is a passion which few men can use with judgment. And now Sir Timothy was really angry, and condescended to speak of our old friend Phineas who had made the onslaught as a bellicose Irishman. There was an over-true story as to our friend having once been seduced into fighting a duel,* and those who wished to decry him sometimes alluded to the adventure. Sir Timothy had been called to order, but the Speaker had ruled that 'bellicose Irishman' was not beyond the latitude of parliamentary animadversion. Then Sir Timothy had repeated the phrase with emphasis, and the Duke hearing it in the gallery had made his remark as to the unwonted eloquence of his son's parliamentary chief.

'Surely we ought to listen to him,' said the Duke. And for a short time they did listen. 'Sir Timothy is not a man I like, you know,' said the son, feeling himself obliged to apologise for his subjection to such a chief.

'I never particularly loved him myself.'

'They say that he is a sort of necessity.'

'A Conservative Fate,' said the Duke.

'Well, yes; he is so,—so awfully clever! We all feel that we could not get on without him. When you were in, he was one of your party.'

'Oh yes;—he was one of us. I have no right to complain of you for using him. But when you say you could not get on without him, does it not occur to you that should he,—let us say be taken up to heaven,— you would have to get on without him.'

'Then he would be,—out of the way, sir.'

'What you mean perhaps is that you do not know how to get rid of him.'

'Of course I don't pretend to understand much about it; but they all think that he does know how to keep the party together. I don't think we are proud of him.'

'Hardly that.'

'He is awfully useful. A man has to look out so sharp to be always ready for those other fellows! I beg your pardon, sir, but I mean your side.'

'I understand who the other fellows are.'

'And it isn't everybody who will go through such a grind. A man to do it must be always ready. He has so many little things to think of. As far as I can see we all feel that we could not get along very well without him.' Upon the whole the Duke was pleased with what he heard from his son. The young man's ideas about politics were boyish, but they were the ideas of a clear-headed boy. Silverbridge had picked up some of the ways of the place, though he had not yet formed any sound political opinions.

Then Sir Timothy finished a long speech with a flowery peroration, in which he declared that if Parliament were desirous of keeping the realms of Her Majesty free from the invasions of foreigners it must be done by maintaining the dignity of the Judicial bench. There were some clamours at this; and although it was now dinner-time Phineas Finn, who had been called a bellicose Irishman, was able to say a word or two. 'The Right Honourable gentleman no doubt means,' said Phineas, 'that we must carry ourselves with some increased external dignity. The world is bewigging* itself, and we must buy a bigger wig than any we have got, in order to confront the world with proper self-respect. Turveydrop and deportment* will suffice for us against any odds.'

About half-past seven the House became very empty. 'Where are you going to dine, sir?' asked Silverbridge. The Duke, with something like a sigh, said he supposed he should dine at home.

'You never were at the Beargarden;—were you, sir?' asked Silverbridge suddenly.

'Never,' said the Duke.

'Come and dine with me.'

'I am not a member of the club.'

'We don't care at all about that. Anybody can take in anybody.'

'Does not that make it promiscuous?'

'Well;—no; I don't know that it does. It seems to go on very well. I dare say there are some cads there sometimes. But I don't know where one doesn't meet cads. There are plenty in the House of Commons.'

'There is something in that, Silverbridge, which makes me think that you have not realised the difference between private and public life. In the former you choose your own associates and are responsible for your choice. In the latter you are concerned with others for the good of the State; and though, even for the State's sake, you would not willingly be closely allied with those whom you think dishonest, the outward manners and fashions of life need create no barriers. I should not turn up my nose at the House of Commons because some constituency might send them an illiterate shoemaker; but I might probably find the illiterate shoemaker an unprofitable companion for my private hours.'

'I don't think there will be any shoemakers at the Beargarden.'

'Even if there were I would go and dine with you. I shall be glad to see the place where you, I suppose, pass many hours.'

'I find it a very good shop to dine at. The place at the House is so stuffy and nasty. Besides, one likes to get away for a little time.'

'Certainly. I never was an advocate for living in the House. One should always change the atmosphere.' Then they got into a cab and went to the club. Silverbridge was a little afraid of what he was doing. The invitation had come from him on the spur of the moment, and he hardly ventured to think that his father would accept it. And now he did not quite know how the Duke would go through the ceremony. 'The other fellows' would all come and stare at a man whom they had all been taught to regard as the most un-Beargardenish of men. But he was especially anxious to make things pleasant for his father.

'What shall I order?' said the son as he took the Duke into a dressing-room to wash his hands. The Duke suggested that anything sufficient for his son would certainly be sufficient for him.

Nothing especial occurred during the dinner, which the Duke appeared to enjoy very much. 'Yes; I think it is very good soup,' he said. 'I don't think they ever give me any soup at home.' Then the son expressed his opinion that unless his father looked about rather more sharply, 'they' very soon would provide no dinner at all, remarking that experience had taught him that the less people demanded the more they were 'sat upon.' The Duke did like his dinner,—or rather he liked the feeling that he was dining with his son. A report that the Duke of Omnium was with Lord Silverbridge soon went round the room, and they who were justified by some previous acquaintance came up to greet him. To all who did so he was very gracious, and was specially so to Lord Popplecourt, who happened to pass close by the table.

'I think he is a fool,' whispered Silverbridge as soon as Popplecourt had passed.

'What makes you think so?'

'We thought him an ass at Eton.'

'He has done pretty well, however.'

'Oh yes, in a way.'

'Somebody has told me that he is a careful man about his property.'

'I believe he is all that,' said Silverbridge.

'Then I don't see why you should think him a fool.'

To this Silverbridge made no reply; partly perhaps because he had nothing to say,—but hindered also by the coming in of Tregear. This was an accident, the possibility of which had not crossed him. Unfortunately too the Duke's back was turned, so that Tregear, as he walked up the room, could not see who was sitting at his friend's table. Tregear coming up stood close to the Duke's elbow before he recognised the man, and spoke some word or two to Silverbridge. 'How do you do, Mr Tregear,' said the Duke, turning round.

'Oh, my Lord, I did not know that it was you.'

'You hardly would. I am quite a stranger here. Silverbridge and I came up from the House together, and he has been hospitable enough to give me a dinner. I will tell you an odd thing for a London man, Mr Tregear. I have not dined at a London club for fifteen years before this.'

'I hope you like it, sir,' said Silverbridge.

'Very much indeed. Good-evening, Mr Tregear. I suppose you have to go to your dinner now.'

Then they went into one of the rooms upstairs to have coffee, the son declining to go into the smoking-room, and assuring his father that he did not in the least care about a cigar after dinner. 'You would be smoth-ered, sir.' The Duke did as he was bidden and went upstairs. There was in truth a strong reason for avoiding the publicity of the smoking-room. When bringing his father to the club he had thought nothing about Tregear but he had thought about Tifto. As he entered he had seen Tifto at a table dining alone, and had bobbed his head at him. Then he had taken the Duke to the further end of the room, and had trusted that fear would keep the Major in his place. Fear had kept the Major in his place. When the Major learned who the stranger was, he had become silent and reserved. Before the father and son had finished their dinner, Tifto had gone to his cigar; and so that danger was over.

'By George, there's Silverbridge has got his governor to dinner,' said Tifto, standing in the middle of the room, and looking round as though he were announcing some confusion of the heavens and earth.

'Why shouldn't Lord Silverbridge have his father to dine with him?' asked Mr Lupton.

'I believe I know Silverbridge as well as any man, and by George it is the very last thing of the kind that I should have expected. There have been no end of quarrels.'

'There has been no quarrel at all,' said Tregear, who had then just entered the room. 'Nothing on earth would make Silverbridge quarrel with his father, and I think it would break the Duke's heart to quarrel with his son.' Tifto endeavoured to argue the matter out; but Tregear having made the assertion on behalf of his friend would not allow himself to be enticed into further speech. Nevertheless there was a good deal said by others, during which the Major drank two glasses of whisky-and-water. In the dining-room he had been struck with awe by the Duke's presence, and had certainly no idea of presenting himself personally to the great man. But Bacchus lent him aid, and when the discussion was over and the whisky had been swallowed, it occurred to him that he would go upstairs and ask to be introduced.

In the meantime the Duke and his son were seated in close conversation on one of the upstairs sofas. It was a rule at the Beargarden that men might smoke all over the house except in the dining-room;—but there was one small chamber called the library, in which the practice was not often followed. The room was generally deserted, and at this moment the father and son were the only occupants. 'A club,' said the Duke, as he sipped his coffee, 'is a comfortable and economical residence. A man gets what he wants well-served, and gets it cheap. But it has its drawbacks.'

'You always see the same fellows,' said Silverbridge.

'A man who lives much at a club is apt to fall into a selfish mode of life. He is taught to think that his own comfort should always be the first object. A man can never be happy unless his first objects are outside himself. Personal self-indulgence begets a sense of meanness which sticks to a man even when he has got beyond all hope of rescue. It is for that reason,—among others,—that marriage is so desirable.'

'A man should marry, I suppose.'

'Unless a man has on his shoulders the burden of a wife and children he should, I think, feel that he has shirked out of school. He is not doing his share of the work of the Commonwealth.'

'Pitt was not married, sir.'

'No;—and a great many other good men have remained unmarried. Do you mean to be another Pitt?'

'I don't intend to be a Prime Minister.'

'I would not recommend you to entertain that ambition. Pitt perhaps hardly had time for marriage. You may be more lucky.'

'I suppose I shall marry some day.'

'I should be glad to see you marry early,' said the Duke, speaking in a low voice, almost solemnly, but in his quietest, sweetest tone of voice. 'You are peculiarly situated. Though as yet you are only the heir to the property and honours of our family, still, were you married, almost everything would be at your disposal. There is so much which I should only be too ready to give up to you!'

'I can't bear to hear you talking of giving up anything,' said Silverbridge energetically.

Then the father looked round the room furtively, and seeing that the door was shut, and that they were assuredly alone, he put out his hand and gently stroked the young man's hair. It was almost a caress,—as though he would have said to himself, 'Were he my daughter, I would kiss him.' 'There is much I would fain give up,' he said. 'If you were a married man the house in Carlton Terrace would be fitter for you than for me. I have disqualified myself for taking that part in society which should be filled by the head of our family. You who have inherited so much from your mother would, if you married pleasantly, do all that right well.' He paused for a moment and then asked a straightforward question, very quickly—'You have never thought of anyone yet, I suppose?'

Silverbridge had thought very much of somebody. He was quite aware that he had almost made an offer to Lady Mabel. She certainly had not given him any encouragement; but the very fact that she had not done so allured him the more. He did believe that he was thoroughly in love with Lady Mabel. She had told him that he was too young,—but he was older than Lady Mab herself by a week. She was beautiful;—that was certain. It was acknowledged by all that she was clever. As for blood, of which he believed his father thought much, there was perhaps none better in England. He had heard it said of her,—as he now well remembered, in his father's presence,—that she had behaved remarkably well in trying circumstances. She had no fortune;—everybody knew that; but then he did not want fortune. Would not this be a good opportunity for breaking the matter to his father? 'You have never thought of any one?' said the Duke,—again very sweetly, very softly.

'But I have!' Lord Silverbridge as he made the announcement blushed up to the eyes.

Then there came over the father something almost of fear. If he was to be told, how would it be if he could not approve?

'Yes I have,' said Silverbridge, recovering himself. 'If you wish it, I will tell you who it is.'

'Nay, my boy;—as to that consult your own feelings. Are you sure of yourself?'

'Oh yes.'

'Have you spoken to her?'

'Well;—yes, in part. She has not accepted me, if you mean that. Rather the contrary.' Now the Duke would have been very unwilling to say that his son would certainly be accepted by any girl in England to whom he might choose to offer his hand. But when the idea of a doubt was suggested to him, it did seem odd that his son should ask in vain. What other young man was there who could offer so much, and who was at the same time so likely to be loved for his own sake? He smiled however and was silent. 'I suppose I may as well out with it,' continued Silverbridge. 'You know Lady Mabel Grex?'

'Lady Mabel Grex? Yes;—I know her.'

'Is there any objection?'

'Is she not your senior?'

'No, sir; no; she is younger than I am.'

'Her father is not a man I esteem.'

'But she has always been so good!' Then the Duke was again silent. 'Have you not heard that, sir?'

'I think I have.'

'Is not that a great deal?'

'A very great deal. To be good must of all qualities be the best. She is very beautiful.'

'I think so, sir. Of course she has no money.'

'It is not needed. It is not needed. I have no objection to make. If you are sure of your own mind——'

'I am quite sure of that, sir.'

'Then I will raise no objection. Lady Mabel Grex! Her father, I fear, is not a worthy man. I hear that he is a gambler.'

'He is so poor!'

'That makes it worse, Silverbridge. A man who gambles because he has money that he can afford to lose is, to my thinking, a fool. But he who gambles because he has none, is—well, let us hope the best of him. You may give her my love.'

'She has not accepted me.'

'But should she do so, you may.'

'She almost rejected me. But I am not sure that she was in earnest, and I mean to try again.' Just at that moment the door was opened and Major Tifto walked into the room.

# VOLUME II

## CHAPTER 27

### MAJOR TIFTO AND THE DUKE

'I BEG your pardon, Silverbridge,' said the Major, entering the room, 'but I was looking for Longstaff.'

'He isn't here,' said Silverbridge, who did not wish to be interrupted by his racing friend.

'Your father, I believe?' said Tifto. He was red in the face but was in other respects perhaps improved in appearance by his liquor. In his more sober moments he was not always able to assume that appearance of equality with his companions which it was the ambition of his soul to achieve. But a second glass of whisky-and-water would always enable him to cock his tail and bark before the company with all the courage of my lady's pug. 'Would you do me the great honour to introduce me to his Grace?'

Silverbridge was not prone to turn his back upon a friend because he was low in the world. He had begun to understand that he had made a mistake by connecting himself with the Major, but at the club he always defended his partner. Though he not unfrequently found himself obliged to snub the Major himself, he always countenanced the little Master of Hounds, and was true to his own idea of 'standing to a fellow.' Nevertheless he did not wish to introduce his friend to his father. The Duke saw it all at a glance, and felt that the introduction should be made. 'Perhaps,' said he, getting up from his chair, 'this is Major Tifto.'

'Yes;—my Lord Duke. I am Major Tifto.'

The Duke bowed graciously.

'My father and I were engaged about private matters,' said Silverbridge.

'I beg ten thousand pardons,' exclaimed the Major. 'I did not intend to intrude.'

'I think we had done,' said the Duke. 'Pray sit down, Major Tifto.' The Major sat down. 'Though now I bethink myself, I have to beg your pardon;—that I a stranger should ask you to sit down in your own club.'

'Don't mention it, my Lord Duke.'*

'I am so unused to clubs, that I forgot where I was.'

'Quite so, my Lord Duke. I hope you think that Silverbridge is looking well?'

'Yes;—yes. I think so.'

Silverbridge bit his lips and turned his face away to the door.

'We didn't make a very good thing of our Derby nag the other day. Perhaps your Grace has heard all that?'

'I did hear that the horse in which you are both interested had failed to win the race.'

'Yes, he did. The Prime Minister, we call him, your Grace,—out of compliment to a certain Ministry which I wish it was going on to-day instead of the seedy lot we've got in. I think, my Lord Duke, that any one you may ask will tell you that I know what running is. Well;—I can assure you,—your Grace, that is,—that since I've seen 'orses I've never seen a 'orse fitter than him. When he got his canter that morning, it was nearly even betting. Not that I or Silverbridge were fools enough to put on anything at that rate. But I never saw a 'orse so bad ridden. I don't mean to say anything, my Lord Duke, against the man. But if that fellow hadn't been squared,* or else wasn't drunk, or else wasn't off his head, that 'orse must have won,—my Lord Duke.'

'I do not know anything about racing, Major Tifto.'

'I suppose not, your Grace. But as I and Silverbridge are together in this matter I thought I'd just let your Grace know that we ought to have had a very good thing. I thought that perhaps your Grace might like to know that.'

'Tifto, you are making an ass of yourself,' said Silverbridge.

'Making an ass of myself!' exclaimed the Major.

'Yes;—considerably.'

'I think you are a little hard upon your friend,' said the Duke, with an attempt at a laugh. 'It is not to be supposed that he should know how utterly indifferent I am to everything connected with the turf.'

'I thought, my Lord Duke, you might care about learning how Silverbridge was going on.' This the poor little man said almost with a whine. His partner's roughness had knocked out of him nearly all the courage which Bacchus had given him.

'So I do; anything that interests him, interests me. But perhaps of all his pursuits racing is the one to which I am least able to lend an attentive ear. That every horse has a head, and that all did have tails till they were ill-used, is the extent of my stable knowledge.'

'Very good indeed, my Lord Duke; very good indeed! Ha, ha, ha!— all horses have heads, and all have tails! Heads and tails. Upon my word that is the best thing I have heard for a long time. I will do myself the honour of wishing your Grace good-night. By-bye, Silverbridge.' Then he left the room, having been made supremely happy by what he considered to have been the Duke's joke. Nevertheless he would remember the snubbing and would be even with Silverbridge some day. Did Lord Silverbridge think that he was going to look after his Lordship's 'orses, and do this always on the square,* and then be snubbed for doing it!

'I am very sorry that he should have come in to trouble you,' said the son.

'He has not troubled me much. I do not know whether he has troubled you. If you are coming down to the House again I will walk with you.' Silverbridge of course had to go down to the House again, and they started together. 'That man did not trouble me, Silverbridge; but the question is whether such an acquaintance must not be trouble-some to you.'

'I'm not very proud of him, sir.'

'But I think one ought to be proud of one's friends.'

'He isn't my friend in that way at all.'

'In what way then?'

'He understands racing.'

'He is the partner of your pleasure then;—the man in whose society you love to enjoy the recreation of the racecourse.'

'It is, sir, because he understands it.'

'I thought that a gentleman on the turf would have a trainer for that purpose;—not a companion. You mean to imply that you can save money by leaguing yourself with Major Tifto?'

'No, sir,—indeed.'

'If you associate with him, not for pleasure, then it surely must be for profit. That you should do the former would be to me so surprising that I must regard it as impossible. That you should do the latter—is, I think, a reproach.' This he said with no tone of anger in his voice,—so gently that Silverbridge at first hardly understood it. But gradually all that was meant came in upon him, and he felt himself to be ashamed of himself.

'He is bad,' he said at last.

'Whether he be bad I will not say; but I am sure that you can gain nothing by his companionship.'

'I will get rid of him,' said Silverbridge, after a considerable pause. 'I cannot do so at once, but I will do it.'

'It will be better, I think.'

'Tregear has been telling me the same thing.'

'Is he objectionable to Mr Tregear?' asked the Duke.

'Oh yes. Tregear cannot bear him. You treated him a great deal better than Tregear ever does.'

'I do not deny that he is entitled to be treated well;—but so also is your groom. Let us say no more about him. And so it is to be Mabel Grex?'

'I did not say so, sir. How can I answer for her? Only it was so pleasant for me to know that you would approve if it should come off.'

'Yes;—I will approve. When she has accepted you——'

'But I don't think she will.'

'If she should, tell her that I will go to her at once. It will be much to have a new daughter;—very much that you should have a wife. Where would she like to live?'

'Oh, sir, we haven't got as far as that yet.'

'I dare say not; I dare say not,' said the Duke. 'Gatherum is always thought to be dull.'

'She wouldn't like Gatherum, I'm sure.'

'Have you asked her?'

'No, sir. But nobody ever did like Gatherum.'

'I suppose not. And yet, Silverbridge, what a sum of money it cost!'

'I believe it did.'

'All vanity; and vexation of spirit!'*

The Duke no doubt was thinking of certain scenes* passed at the great house in question, which scenes had not been delightful to him. 'No, I don't suppose she would wish to live at Gatherum. The Horns was given expressly by my uncle to your dear mother, and I should like Mary to have the place.'

'Certainly.'

'You should live among your tenantry. I don't care so very much for Matching.'

'It is the one place you do like, sir.'

'However, we can manage all that. Carlton Terrace I do not particularly like; but it is a good house, and there you should hang up your hat when in London. When it is settled, let me know at once.'

'But if it should never be settled?'

'I will ask no questions; but if it be settled, tell me.' Then in Palace Yard he was turning to go, but before he did so, he said another word leaning on his son's shoulder. 'I do not think that Mabel Grex and Major Tifto would do well together at all.'

'There shall be an end to that, sir.'

'God bless you, my boy!' said the Duke.

Lord Silverbridge sat in the House—or, to speak more accurately, in the smoking-room of the House—for about an hour thinking over all that had passed between himself and his father. He certainly had not intended to say anything about Lady Mab, but on the spur of the moment it had all come out. Now at any rate it was decided for him that he must, in set terms, ask her to be his wife. The scene which had just occurred had made him thoroughly sick of Major Tifto. He must get rid of the Major, and there could be no way of doing this at once so easy and so little open to observation as marriage. If he were but once engaged to Mabel Grex the dismissal of Tifto would be quite a matter of course. He would see Lady Mabel again on the morrow and ask her in direct language to be his wife.

## CHAPTER 28

### MRS MONTACUTE JONES'S GARDEN-PARTY

IT was known to all the world that Mrs Montacute Jones's first great garden-party was to come off on Wednesday, 16th June, at Roehampton. Mrs Montacute Jones, who lived in Grosvenor Place and had a country house in Gloucestershire, and a place for young men to shoot at in Scotland, also kept a suburban elysium at Roehampton, in order that she might give two garden-parties every year. When it is said that all these costly luxuries appertained to Mrs Montacute Jones, it is to be understood that they did in truth belong to Mr Jones, of whom nobody heard much. But of Mrs Jones,—that is, Mrs Montacute Jones,— everybody heard a great deal. She was an old lady who devoted her life to the amusement of—not only her friends, but very many who were not her friends. No doubt she was fond of Lords and Countesses, and worked very hard to get round her all the rank and fashion of the day. It must be acknowledged that she was a worldly old woman. But no more good-natured old woman lived in London, and everybody liked to be asked to her garden-parties. On this occasion there was to be a considerable infusion of royal blood,—German, Belgian, French, Spanish, and of native growth. Everybody who was asked would go, and everybody had been asked,—who was anybody. Lord Silverbridge had been asked, and Lord Silverbridge intended to be there. Lady Mary, his sister, could not even be asked, because her mother was hardly more than three months dead; but it is understood in the world that women mourn longer than men.

Silverbridge had mounted a private hansom cab in which he could be taken about rapidly,—and, as he said himself, without being shut up in a coffin. In this vehicle he had himself taken to Roehampton, purporting to kill two birds with one stone. He had not as yet seen his sister since she had been with Lady Cantrip. He would on this day come back by The Horns.

He was well aware that Lady Mab would be at the garden-party. What place could be better for putting the question he had to ask? He was by no means so confident as the heir to so many good things might perhaps have been without overdue self-confidence.

Entering through the house into the lawn he encountered Mrs Montacute Jones, who, with a seat behind her on the terrace, surrounded by flowers, was going through the immense labour of receiving her guests.

'How very good of you to come all this way, Lord Silverbridge, to eat my strawberries.'

'How very good of you to ask me! I did not come to eat your strawberries but to see your friends.'

'You ought to have said you came to see me, you know. Have you met Miss Boncassen yet?'

'The American beauty? No. Is she here?'

'Yes; and she particularly wants to be introduced to you; you won't betray me, will you?'

'Certainly not; I am as true as steel.'

'She wanted, she said, to see if the eldest son of the Duke of Omnium really did look like any other man.'

'Then I don't want to see her,' said Silverbridge with a look of vexation.

'There you are wrong, for there was real downright fun in the way she said it. There they are, and I shall introduce you.' Then Mrs Montacute Jones absolutely left her post for a minute or two, and taking the young lord down the steps of the terrace did introduce him to Mr Boncassen, who was standing there amidst a crowd, and to Miss Boncassen the daughter.

Mr Boncassen was an American who had lately arrived in England with the object of carrying out certain literary pursuits in which he was engaged within the British Museum. He was an American who had nothing to do with politics and nothing to do with trade. He was a man of wealth and a man of letters. And he had a daughter who was said to be the prettiest young woman either in Europe or in America at the present time.

Isabel Boncassen was certainly a very pretty girl. I wish that my reader would believe my simple assurance. But no such simple assurance was ever believed, and I doubt even whether any description will procure for me from the reader that amount of faith which I desire to achieve. But I must make the attempt. General opinion generally considered Miss Boncassen to be small, but she was in truth something above the average height of English women. She was slight, without that look of slimness which is common to girls, and especially to American girls. That her figure was perfect the reader must believe on my word, as any detailed description of her arms, feet, bust, and waist, would be alto-gether ineffective. Her hair was dark brown and plentiful; but it added but little to her charms, which depended on other matters. Perhaps what struck the beholder first was the excessive brilliancy of her com-plexion. No pink was ever pinker, no alabaster whiteness was ever more like alabaster; but under and around and through it all there was a con-stantly changing hue which gave a vitality to her countenance which no fixed colours can produce. Her eyes, too, were full of life and brilliancy, and even when she was silent her mouth would speak. Nor was there a fault within the oval of her face upon which the hypercritics of mature age could set a finger. Her teeth were excellent both in form and colour, but were seen but seldom. Who does not know that look of ubiquitous ivory produced by teeth which are too perfect in a face which is other-wise poor? Her nose at the base spread a little,—so that it was not purely Grecian. But who has ever seen a nose to be eloquent and expressive, which did not so spread? It was, I think, the vitality of her countenance,— the way in which she could speak with every feature, the command which she had of pathos, of humour, of sympathy, of satire, the assur-ance which she gave by every glance of her eye, every elevation of her brow, every curl of her lip, that she was alive to all that was going on,—it was all this rather than those feminine charms which can be catalogued and labelled that made all acknowledge that she was beautiful.

'Lord Silverbridge,' said Mr Boncassen, speaking a little through his nose, 'I am proud to make your acquaintance, sir. Your father is a man for whom we in our country have a great respect. I think, sir, you must be proud of such a father.'

'Oh yes,—no doubt,' said Silverbridge awkwardly. Then Mr Boncassen continued his discourse with the gentlemen around him. Upon this our friend turned to the young lady. 'Have you been long in England, Miss Boncassen?'

'Long enough to have heard about you and your father,' she said, speaking with no slightest twang.

'I hope you have not heard any evil of me.'

'Well!'

'I'm sure you can't have heard much good.'

'I know you didn't win the Derby.'

'You've been long enough to hear that?'

'Do you suppose we don't interest ourselves about the Derby in New York? Why, when we arrived at Queenstown* I was leaning over the taffrail* so that I might ask the first man on board the tender* whether the Prime Minister had won.'

'And he said he hadn't.'

'I can't conceive why you of all men should call your horse by such a name. If my father had been President of the United States, I don't think I'd call a horse President.'

'I didn't name the horse.'

'I'd have changed it. But is it not very impudent in me to be finding fault with you the first time I have ever seen you? Shall you have a horse at Ascot?'*

'There will be something going, I suppose. Nothing that I care about.' Lord Silverbridge had made up his mind that he would go to no races with Tifto before the Leger. The Leger would be an affair of such moment as to demand his presence. After that should come the complete rupture between him and Tifto.

Then there was a movement among the elders, and Lord Silverbridge soon found himself walking alone with Miss Boncassen. It seemed to her to be quite natural to do so, and there certainly was no reason why he should decline anything so pleasant. It was thus that he had intended to walk with Mabel Grex;—only as yet he had not found her. 'Oh yes,' said Miss Boncassen, when they had been together about twenty minutes; 'we shall be here all the summer, and all the fall, and all the winter. Indeed father means to read every book in the British Museum before he goes back.'

'He'll have something to do.'

'He reads by steam, and he has two or three young men with him to take it all down and make other books out of it;—just as you'll see a lady take a lace shawl and turn it all about till she has trimmed a petticoat with it. It is the same lace all through,—and so I tell father it's the same knowledge.'

'But he puts it where more people will find it.'

'The lady endeavours to do the same with the lace. That depends on whether people look up or down. Father however is a very learned man. You mustn't suppose that I am laughing at him. He is going to write a very learned book. Only everybody will be dead before it can be half finished.' They still went on together, and then he gave her his arm and took her into the place where the strawberries and cream were prepared. As he was going in he saw Mabel Grex walking with Tregear, and she bowed to him pleasantly and playfully. 'Is that lady a great friend of yours?' asked Miss Boncassen.

'A very great friend indeed.'

'She is very beautiful.'

'And clever as well,—and good as gold.'

'Dear me! Do tell me who it is that owns all these qualities.'

'Lady Mabel Grex. She is daughter of Lord Grex. That man with her is my particular friend. His name is Frank Tregear, and they are cousins.'

'I am so glad they are cousins.'

'Why glad?'

'Because his being with her won't make you unhappy.'

'Supposing I was in love with her,—which I am not,—do you suppose it would make me jealous to see her with another man?'

'In our country it would not. A young lady may walk about with a young gentleman just as she might with another young lady; but I thought it was different here. Do you know, judging by English ways, I believe I am behaving very improperly in walking about with you so long. Ought I not to tell you to go away?'

'Pray do not.'

'As I am going to stay here so long I wish to behave well to English eyes.'

'People know who you are, and discount all that.'

'If the difference be very marked they do. For instance, I needn't wear a hideous long bit of cloth over my face in Constantinople because I am a woman. But when the discrepancies are small, then they have to be attended to. So I shan't walk about with you any more.'

'Oh yes, you will,' said Silverbridge, who began to think that he liked walking about with Miss Boncassen.

'Certainly not. There is Mr Sprottle. He is father's secretary. He will take me back.'

'Cannot I take you back as well as Mr Sprottle?'

'Indeed no;—I am not going to monopolise such a man as you. Do you think that I don't understand that everybody will be making remarks upon the American girl who won't leave the son of the Duke of Omnium alone? There is your particular friend Lady Mabel, and here is my particular friend Mr Sprottle.'

'May I come and call?'

'Certainly. Father will only be too proud,—and I shall be prouder. Mother will be the proudest of all. Mother very seldom goes out. Till we get a house we are at The Langham. Thank you, Mr Sprottle. I think we'll go and find father.'

Lord Silverbridge found himself close to Lady Mabel and Tregear, and also to Miss Cassewary, who had now joined Lady Mabel. He had been much struck with the American beauty, but was not on that account the less anxious to carry out his great plan. It was essentially necessary that he should do so at once, because the matter had been settled between him and his father. He was anxious to assure her that if she would consent, then the Duke would be ready to pour out all kinds of paternal blessings on their heads. 'Come and take a turn among the haycocks,' he said.

'Frank declares,' said Lady Mabel, 'that the hay is hired for the occasion. I wonder whether that is true.'

'Anybody can see,' said Tregear, 'that it has not been cut off the grass it stands upon.'

'If I could find Mrs Montacute Jones I'd ask her where she got it,' said Lady Mabel.

'Are you coming?' asked Silverbridge impatiently.

'I don't think I am. I have been walking round the haycocks till I am tired of them.'

'Anywhere else then?'

'There isn't anywhere else. What have you done with your American beauty? The truth is, Lord Silverbridge, you ask me for my company when she won't give you hers any longer. Doesn't it look like it, Miss Cassewary?'

'I don't think Lord Silverbridge is the man to forget an old friend for a new one.'

'Not though the new friend be as lovely as Miss Boncassen?'

'I don't know that I ever saw a prettier girl,' said Tregear.

'I quite admit it,' said Lady Mabel. 'But that is no salve for my injured feelings. I have heard so much about Miss Boncassen's beauty for the last week, that I mean to get up a company of British females, limited, for the express purpose of putting her down. Who is Miss Boncassen that we are all to be put on one side for her?'

Of course he knew that she was joking, but he hardly knew how to take her joke. There is a manner of joking which carries with it much serious intention. He did feel that Lady Mabel was not gracious to him because he had spent half an hour with this new beauty, and he was half inclined to be angry with her. Was it fitting that she should be cross with him, seeing that he was resolved to throw at her feet all the good things that he had in the world? 'Bother Miss Boncassen,' he said; 'you might as well come and take a turn with a fellow.'

'Come along, Miss Cassewary,' said she. 'We will go round the hay-cocks yet once again.' So they turned and the two ladies accompanied Lord Silverbridge.

But this was not what he wanted. He could not say what he had to say in the presence of Miss Cassewary,—nor could he ask her to take herself off in another direction. Nor could he take himself off. Now that he had joined himself to these two ladies he must make with them the tour of the gardens. All this made him cross. 'These kind of things are a great bore,' he said.

'I dare say you would rather be in the House of Commons;—or, better still, at the Beargarden.'

'You mean to be ill-natured when you say that, Lady Mab.'

'You ask us to come and walk with you, and then you tell us that we are bores!'

'I did nothing of the kind.'

'I should have thought that you would be particularly pleased with yourself for coming here to-day, seeing that you have made Miss Boncassen's acquaintance. To be allowed to walk half an hour alone with the acknowledged beauty of the two hemispheres ought to be enough even for Lord Silverbridge.'

'That is nonsense, Lady Mab.'

'Nothing gives so much zest to admiration as novelty. A republican charmer must be exciting after all the *blasées habituées** of the London drawing-rooms.'

'How can you talk such nonsense, Mabel?' said Miss Cassewary.

'But it is so. I feel that people must be sick of seeing me. I know I am very often sick of seeing them. Here is something fresh,—and not only unlike, but so much more lovely. I quite acknowledge that. I may be jealous, but no one can say that I am spiteful. I wish that some repub-lican Adonis or Apollo would crop up,—so that we might have our turn. But I don't think the republican gentlemen are equal to the republican ladies. Do you, Lord Silverbridge?'

'I haven't thought about it.'

'Mr Sprottle for instance.'

'I have not the pleasure of knowing Mr Sprottle.'

'Now we've been round the haycocks, and really, Lord Silverbridge, I don't think we have gained much by it. Those forced marches never do any good.' And so they parted.

He was thinking with a bitter spirit of the ill-result of his morning's work when he again found himself close to Miss Boncassen in the crowd of departing people on the terrace. 'Mind you keep your word,' she said. And then she turned to her father. 'Lord Silverbridge has promised to call.'

'Mrs Boncassen will be delighted to make his acquaintance.'

He got into his cab and was driven off towards Richmond. As he went he began to think of the two young women with whom he had passed his morning. Mabel had certainly behaved badly to him. Even if she suspected nothing of his object, did she not owe it to their friendship to be more courteous to him than she had been? And if she suspected that object, should she not at any rate have given him the opportunity?

Or could it be that she was really jealous of the American girl? No;—that idea he rejected instantly. It was not compatible with the innate modesty of his disposition. But no doubt the American girl was very lovely. Merely as a thing to be looked at she was superior to Mabel. He did feel that as to mere personal beauty she was in truth superior to anything he had ever seen before. And she was clever too;—and good-humoured;—whereas Mabel had been both ill-natured and unpleasant.

## CHAPTER 29

### THE LOVERS MEET

Lord Silverbridge found his sister alone. 'I particularly want you,' said he, 'to come and call on Mabel Grex. She wishes to know you, and I am sure you would like her.'

'But I haven't been out anywhere yet,' she said. 'I don't feel as though I wanted to go anywhere.'

Nevertheless she was very anxious to know Lady Mabel Grex, of whom she had heard much. A girl if she has had a former love passage says nothing of it to her new lover; but a man is not so reticent. Frank Tregear had perhaps not told her everything but he had told her something. 'I was very fond of her;—very fond of her,' he had said. 'And so

I am still,' he had added. 'As you are my love of loves, she is my friend of friends.' Lady Mary had been satisfied by the assurance, but had become anxious to see the friend of friends. She resisted at first her brother's entreaties. She felt that her father in delivering her over to the seclusion of The Horns had intended to preclude her from showing herself in London. She was conscious that she was being treated with cruelty, and had a certain pride in her martyrdom. She would obey her father to the letter; she would give him no right to call her conduct in question; but he and any other to whom he might entrust the care of her, should be made to know that she thought him cruel. He had his power to which she must submit. But she also had hers,—to which it was possible he might be made to submit. 'I do not know that papa would wish me to go,' she said.

'But it is just what he would wish. He thinks a good deal about Mabel.'

'Why should he think about her at all?'

'I can't exactly explain,' said Silverbridge, 'but he does.'

'If you mean to tell me that Mabel Grex is anything particular to you, and that papa approves of it, I will go all round the world to see her.' But he had not meant to tell her this. The request had been made at Lady Mabel's instance. When his sister had spoken of her father's possible objection, then he had become eager in explaining the Duke's feeling, not remembering that such anxiety might betray himself. At that moment Lady Cantrip came in, and the question was referred to her. She did not see any objection to such a visit, and expressed her opinion that it would be a good thing that Mary should be taken out. 'She should begin to go somewhere,' said Lady Cantrip. And so it was decided. On the next Friday he would come down early in his hansom and drive her up to Belgrave Square. Then he would take her to Carlton Terrace, and Lady Cantrip's carriage should pick her up there and bring her home. He would arrange it all.

'What did you think of the American beauty?' asked Lady Cantrip when that was settled.

'I thought she was a beauty.'

'So I perceived. You had eyes for nobody else,' said Lady Cantrip, who had been at the garden-party.

'Somebody introduced her to me, and then I had to walk about the grounds with her. That's the kind of thing one always does in those places.'

'Just so. That is what "those places" are meant for, I suppose. But it was not apparently a great infliction.' Lord Silverbridge had to explain

that it was not an infliction;—that it was a privilege, seeing that Miss
Boncassen was both clever and lovely; but that it did not mean anything in particular.

When he took his leave he asked his sister to go out into the grounds
with him for a moment. This she did almost unwillingly, fearing that
he was about to speak to her of Tregear. But he had no such purpose on
his mind. 'Of course you know,' he began, 'all that was nonsense you
were saying about Mabel.'

'I did not know.'

'I was afraid you might blurt out something before her.'

'I should not be so imprudent.'

'Girls do make such fools of themselves sometimes. They are always
thinking about people being in love. But it is the truth that my father
said to me the other day how very much he liked what he had heard of
her, and that he would like you to know her.'

On that same evening Silverbridge wrote from the Beargarden the
shortest possible note to Lady Mabel, telling her what he had arranged.
'I and Mary propose to call in B. Square on Friday at two. I must be
early because of the House. You will give us lunch. S.' There was
no word of endearment,—none even of those ordinary words which
people who hate each other use to one another. But he received the
next day at home a much more kindly-written note from her:

'DEAR LORD SILVERBRIDGE,

'You are so good! You always do just what you think people will like
best. Nothing could please me so much as seeing your sister, of whom
of course I have heard *very very* much. There shall be nobody here but
Miss Cass.

'Yours most sincerely,

'M. G.'

'How I do wish I were a man!' his sister said to him when they were
in the hansom together.

'You'd have a great deal more trouble.'

'But I'd have a hansom of my own, and go where I pleased. How
would you like to be shut up at a place like The Horns?'

'You can go out if you like it.'

'Not like you. Papa thinks it's the proper place for me to live in, and
so I must live there. I don't think a woman ever chooses how or where
she shall live herself.'

'You are not going to take up woman's rights,* I hope.'

'I think I shall if I stay at The Horns much longer. What would papa say if he heard that I was going to give a lecture at an Institute?'

'The governor has had so many things to bear that a trifle such as that would make but little difference.'

'Poor papa!'

'He was dreadfully cut up about Gerald. And then he is so good! He said more to me about Gerald than he ever did about my own little misfortune at Oxford; but to Gerald himself he said almost nothing. Now he has forgiven me because he thinks I am constant at the House.'

'And are you?'

'Not so much as he thinks. I do go there,—for his sake. He has been so good about my changing sides.'

'I think you were quite right there.'

'I am beginning to think I was quite wrong. What did it matter to me?'

'I suppose it did make papa unhappy.'

'Of course it did;—and then this affair of yours.' As soon as this was said Lady Mary at once hardened her heart against her father. Whether Silverbridge was or was not entitled to his own political opinions,— seeing that the Pallisers had for ages been known as staunch Whigs and Liberals,—might be a matter for question. But that she had a right to her own lover she thought that there could be no question. As they were sitting in the cab he could hardly see her face, but he was aware that she was in some fashion arming herself against opposition. 'I am sure that this makes him very unhappy,' continued Silverbridge.

'It cannot be altered,' she said.

'It will have to be altered.'

'Nothing can alter it. He might die, indeed;—or so might I.'

'Or he might see that it is no good,—and change his mind,' suggested Silverbridge.

'Of course that is possible,' said Lady Mary very curtly,—showing plainly by her manner that the subject was one which she did not choose to discuss any further.

'It is very good of you to come to me,' said Lady Mabel, kissing her new acquaintance. 'I have heard so much about you.'

'And I also of you.'

'I, you know, am one of your brother's stern Mentors. There are three or four of us determined to make him a pattern young legislator. Miss Cassewary is another. Only she is not quite so stern as I am.'

'He ought to be very much obliged.'

'But he is not;—not a bit. Are you, Lord Silverbridge?'

'Not so much as I ought to be, perhaps.'

'Of course there is an opposing force. There are the racehorses, and the drag, and Major Tifto. No doubt you have heard of Major Tifto. The Major is the Mr Worldly-Wiseman who won't let Christian go to the Strait Gate. I am afraid he hasn't read his Pilgrim's Progress.* But we shall prevail, Lady Mary, and he will get to the beautiful city at last.'

'What is the beautiful city?' he asked.

'A seat in the Cabinet, I suppose;—or that general respect which a young nobleman achieves when he has shown himself able to sit on a bench for six consecutive hours without appearing to go to sleep.'

Then they went to lunch, and Lady Mary did find herself to be happy with her new acquaintance. Her life since her mother's death had been so sad, that this short escape from it was a relief to her. Now for awhile she found herself almost gay. There was an easy liveliness about Lady Mabel,—a grain of humour and playfulness conjoined,— which made her feel at home at once. And it seemed to her as though her brother was at home. He called the girl Lady Mab, and Queen Mab, and once plain Mabel, and the old woman he called Miss Cass. It surely, she thought, must be the case that Lady Mabel and her brother were engaged.

'Come upstairs into my own room,—it is nicer than this,' said Lady Mabel, and they went from the dining-room into a pretty little sitting-room with which Silverbridge was very well acquainted. 'Have you heard of Miss Boncassen?' Mary said she had heard something of Miss Boncassen's great beauty. 'Everybody is talking about her. Your brother met her at Mrs Montacute Jones's garden-party, and was made a conquest of instantly.'

'I wasn't made a conquest of at all,' said Silverbridge.

'Then he ought to have been made a conquest of. I should be if I were a man. I think she is the loveliest person to look at and the nicest person to listen to that I ever came across. We all feel that, as far as this season is concerned, we are cut out. But we don't mind it so much because she is a foreigner.' Then just as she said this the door was opened and Frank Tregear was announced.

Everybody there present knew as well as does the reader, what was the connexion between Tregear and Lady Mary Palliser. And each knew that the other knew it. It was therefore impossible for them not to feel themselves guilty among themselves. The two lovers had not seen each other since they had been together in Italy. Now they were brought face to face in this unexpected manner! And nobody except Tregear was at first quite sure whether somebody had not done something to arrange the meeting. Mary might naturally suspect that Lady Mabel had done this in the interest of her friend Tregear, and Silverbridge could not but suspect that it was so. Lady Mabel, who had never before met the other girl, could hardly refrain from thinking that there had been some underhand communication,— and Miss Cassewary was clearly of opinion that there had been some understanding.

Silverbridge was the first to speak. 'Halloo, Tregear, I didn't know that we were to see you.'

'Nor I, that I should see you,' said he. Then of course there was a shaking of hands all round, in the course of which ceremony he came to Mary the last. She gave him her hand, but had not a word to say to him. 'If I had known that you were here,' he said, 'I should not have come; but I need hardly say how glad I am to see you,—even in this way.' Then the two girls were convinced that the meeting was accidental; but Miss Cass still had her doubts.

Conversation became at once very difficult. Tregear seated himself near, but not very near, to Lady Mary, and made some attempt to talk to both the girls at once. Lady Mabel plainly showed that she was not at her ease;—whereas Mary seemed to be stricken dumb by the presence of her lover. Silverbridge was so much annoyed by a feeling that this interview was a treason to his father, that he sat cudgelling his brain to think how he should bring it to an end. Miss Casseweary was dumbfounded by the occasion. She was the one elder in the company who ought to see that no wrong was committed. She was not directly responsible to the Duke of Omnium, but she was thoroughly permeated by a feeling that it was her duty to take care that there should be no clandestine love meetings in Lord Grex's house. At last Silverbridge jumped up from his chair. 'Upon my word, Tregear, I think you had better go,' said he.

'So do I,' said Miss Cassewary. 'If it is an accident——'

'Of course it is an accident,' said Tregear angrily,—looking round at Mary, who blushed up to her eyes.

'I did not mean to doubt it,' said the old lady. 'But as it has occurred, Mabel, don't you think that he had better go?'

'He won't bite anybody, Miss Cass.'

'She would not have come if she had expected it,' said Silverbridge.

'Certainly not,' said Mary, speaking for the first time. 'But now he is here——' Then she stopped herself, rose from the sofa, sat down, and then rising again, stepped up to her lover, who rose at the same moment,—and threw herself into his arms and put up her lips to be kissed.

'This won't do at all,' said Silverbridge. Miss Cassewary clasped her hands together and looked up to heaven. She probably had never seen such a thing done before. Lady Mabel's eyes were filled with tears, and though in all this there was much to cause her anguish, still in her heart of hearts she admired the brave girl who could thus show her truth to her lover.

'Now go,' said Mary through her sobs.

'My own one,' ejaculated Tregear.

'Yes, yes, yes; always your own. Go,—go; go.' She was weeping and sobbing as she said this, and hiding her face with her handkerchief. He stood for a moment irresolute, and then left the room without a word of adieu to any one.

'You have behaved very badly,' said the brother.

'She has behaved like an angel,' said Mabel, throwing her arms round Mary as she spoke, 'like an angel. If there had been a girl whom you loved and who loved you, would you not have wished it? Would you not have worshipped her for showing that she was not ashamed of her love?'

'I am not a bit ashamed,' said Mary.

'And I say that you have no cause. No one knows him as I do. How good he is, and how worthy!' Immediately after that Silverbridge took his sister away, and Lady Mabel, escaping from Miss Cass, was alone. 'She loves him almost as I have loved him,' she said to herself. 'I wonder whether he can love her as he did me?'

## CHAPTER 30

### WHAT CAME OF THE MEETING

NOT a word was said in the cab as Lord Silverbridge took his sister to Carlton Terrace, and he was leaving her without any reference to the scene which had taken place, when an idea struck him that this would be cruel. 'Mary,' he said, 'I was very sorry for all that.'

'It was not my doing.'

'I suppose it was nobody's doing. But I am very sorry that it occurred. I think that you should have controlled yourself.'

'No!' she almost shouted.

'I think so.'

'No;—if you mean by controlling myself, holding my tongue. He is the man I love,—whom I have promised to marry.'

'But, Mary,—do ladies generally embrace their lovers in public?'

'No;—nor should I. I never did such a thing in my life before. But as he was there I had to show that I was not ashamed of him! Do you think I should have done it if you all had not been there?' Then again she burst into tears.

He did not quite know what to make of it. Mabel Grex had declared that she had behaved like an angel. But yet, as he thought of what he had seen, he shuddered with vexation. 'I was thinking of the governor,' he said.

'He shall be told everything.'

'That you met Tregear?'

'Certainly; and that I—kissed him. I will do nothing that I am ashamed to tell everybody.'

'He will be very angry.'

'I cannot help it. He should not treat me as he is doing. Mr Tregear is a gentleman. Why did he let him come? Why did you bring him? But it is of no use. The thing is settled. Papa can break my heart, but he cannot make me say that I am not engaged to Mr Tregear.'

On that night Mary told the whole of her story to Lady Cantrip. There was nothing that she tried to conceal. 'I got up,' she said, 'and threw my arms round him. Is he not all the world to me?'

'Had it been planned?' asked Lady Cantrip.

'No;—no! Nothing had been planned. They are cousins and very intimate, and he goes there constantly. Now I want you to tell papa all about it.'

Lady Cantrip began to think that it had been an evil day for her when she had agreed to take charge of this very determined young lady; but she consented at once to write to the Duke. As the girl was in her hands she must take care not to lay herself open to reproaches. As this objectionable lover had either contrived a meeting, or had met her without contriving, it was necessary that the Duke should be informed. 'I would rather you wrote the letter,' said Lady Mary. 'But pray tell him that all along I have meant him to know all about it.'

Till Lady Cantrip seated herself at her writing-table she did not know how great the difficulty would be. It cannot in any circumstances be easy to write to a father as to his daughter's love for an objectionable lover; but the Duke's character added much to the severity of the task.

And then that embrace! She knew that the Duke would be struck with horror as he read of such a tale, and she found herself almost struck with horror as she attempted to write it. When she came to the point she found she could not write it. 'I fear there was a good deal of warmth shown on both sides,' she said, feeling that she was calumniating the man, as to whose warmth she had heard nothing. 'It is quite clear,' she added, 'that this is not a passing fancy on her part.'

It was impossible that the Duke should be made to understand exactly what had occurred. That Silverbridge had taken Mary he did understand, and that they had together gone to Lord Grex's house. He understood also that the meeting had taken place in the presence of Silverbridge and of Lady Mabel. 'No doubt it was all an accident,' Lady Cantrip wrote. How could it be an accident?

'You had Mary up in town on Friday,' he said to his son on the following Sunday morning.

'Yes, sir.'

'And that friend of yours came in?'

'Yes, sir.'

'Do you not know what my wishes are?'

'Certainly I do;—but I could not help his coming. You do not suppose that anybody had planned it?'

'I hope not.'

'It was simply an accident. Such an accident as must occur over and over again,—unless Mary is to be locked up.'

'Who talks of locking anybody up? What right have you to speak in that way?'

'I only meant that of course they will stumble across each other in London.'

'I think I will go abroad,' said the Duke. He was silent for awhile, and then repeated his words. 'I think I will go abroad.'

'Not for long, I hope, sir.'

'Yes;—to live there. Why should I stay here? What good can I do here? Everything I see and everything I hear is a pain to me.' The young man of course could not but go back in his mind to the last interview which he had had with his father, when the Duke had been so gracious and apparently so well pleased.

'Is there anything else wrong,—except about Mary?' Silverbridge asked.

'I am told that Gerald owes about fifteen hundred pounds at Cambridge.'

'So much as that! I knew he had a few horses there.'

'It is not the money, but the absence of principle,—that a young man should have no feeling that he ought to live within certain prescribed means! Do you know what you have had from Mr Morton?'

'Not exactly, sir.'

'It is different with you. But a man, let him be who he may, should live within certain means. As for your sister, I think she will break my heart.' Silverbridge found it to be quite impossible to say anything in answer to this. 'Are you going to church?' asked the Duke.

'I was not thinking of doing so particularly.'

'Do you not ever go?'

'Yes;—sometimes. I will go with you now, if you like it, sir.'

'I had thought of going, but my mind is too much harassed. I do not see why you should not go.'

But Silverbridge, though he had been willing to sacrifice his morning to his father,—for it was, I fear, in that way that he had looked at it,—did not see any reason for performing a duty which his father himself omitted. And there were various matters also which harassed him. On the previous evening, after dinner, he had allowed himself to back the Prime Minister for the Leger to a very serious amount. In fact he had plunged, and now stood to lose some twenty thousand pounds on the doings of the last night. And he had made these bets under the influence of Major Tifto. It was the remembrance of this, after the promise made to his father, that annoyed him the most. He was imbued with a feeling that it behoved him as a man to 'pull himself together', as he would have said himself, and to live in accordance with certain rules. He could make the rules easily enough, but he had never yet succeeded in keeping any one of them. He had determined to sever himself from Tifto; and, in doing that, had intended to sever himself from affairs of the turf generally. This resolution was not yet a week old. It was on that evening that he had resolved that Tifto should no longer be his companion; and now he had to confess to himself that because he had drunk three or four glasses of champagne he had been induced by Tifto to make those wretched bets.

And he had told his father that he intended to ask Mabel Grex to be his wife. He had so committed himself that the offer must now be made. He did not specially regret that, though he wished that he had been more reticent. 'What a fool a man is to blurt out everything!' he said to himself. A wife would be a good thing for him; and where could he possibly find a better wife than Mabel Grex? In beauty she was no doubt inferior to Miss Boncassen. There was something about Miss Boncassen which made it impossible to forget her. But Miss Boncassen was an American, and on many accounts out of the question. It did not occur to him that he would fall in love with Miss Boncassen; but still it seemed hard to him that this intention of marriage should stand in his way of having a good time with Miss Boncassen for a few weeks. No doubt there were objections to marriage. It clipped a fellow's wings. But then, if he were married, he might be sure that Tifto would be laid aside. It was such a great thing to have got his father's assured consent to a marriage. It meant complete independence in money matters.

Then his mind ran away to a review of his father's affairs. It was a genuine trouble to him that his father should be so unhappy. Of all the griefs which weighed upon the Duke's mind, that in reference to his sister was the heaviest. The money which Gerald owed at Cambridge would be nothing if that other sorrow could be conquered. Nor had Tifto and his own extravagance caused the Duke any incurable wounds. If Tregear could be got out of the way, his father, he thought, might be reconciled to other things. He felt very tender-hearted about his father; but he had no remorse in regard to his sister as he made up his mind that he would speak very seriously to Tregear.

He had wandered into St James's Park,* and had lighted by this time half-a-dozen cigarettes one after another, as he sat on one of the benches. He was a handsome youth, all but six feet high, with light hair, with round blue eyes, and with all that aristocratic look, which had belonged so peculiarly to the late Duke but which was less conspicuous in the present head of the family. He was a young man whom you would hardly pass in a crowd without observing,—but of whom you would say, after due observation, that he had not as yet put off all his childish ways. He now sat with his legs stretched out, with his cane in his hands, looking down upon the water. He was trying to think. He worked hard at thinking. But the bench was hard and, upon the whole, he was not satisfied with his position.* He had just made up his mind that he would look up Tregear, when Tregear himself appeared on the path before him.

'Tregear!' exclaimed Silverbridge.

'Silverbridge!' exclaimed Tregear.

'What on earth makes you walk about here on a Sunday morning?'

'What on earth makes you sit there? That I should walk here, which I often do, does not seem to me odd. But that I should find you is marvellous. Do you often come?'

'Never was here in my life before. I strolled in because I had things to think of.'

'Questions to be asked in Parliament? Notices of motions, Amendments in Committee, and that kind of thing?'

'Go on, old fellow.'

'Or perhaps Major Tifto has made important revelations.'

'D—— Major Tifto.'

'With all my heart,' said Tregear.

'Sit down here,' said Silverbridge. 'As it happened, at the moment when you came up I was thinking of you.'

'That was kind.'

'And I was determined to go to you. All this about my sister must be given up.'

'Must be given up?'

'It can never lead to any good. I mean that there never can be a marriage.' Then he paused, but Tregear was determined to hear him out. 'It is making my father so miserable that you would pity him if you could see him.'

'I dare say I should. When I see people unhappy I always pity them. What I would ask you to think of is this. If I were to commission you to tell your sister that everything between us should be given up, would not she be so unhappy that you would have to pity her?'

'She would get over it.'

'And so will your father.'

'He has a right to have his own opinion on such a matter.'

'And so have I. And so has she. His rights in this matter are very clear and very potential.* I am quite ready to admit that we cannot marry for many years to come, unless he will provide the money. You are quite at liberty to tell him that I say so. I have no right to ask your father for a penny, and I will never do so. The power is all in his hands. As far as I know my own purposes, I shall not make any immediate attempt even to see her. We did meet, as you saw, the other day, by the merest chance. After that, do you think that your sister wishes me to give her up?'

'As for supposing that girls are to have what they wish, that is nonsense.'

'For young men I suppose equally so. Life ought to be a life of self-denial, no doubt. Perhaps it might be my duty to retire from this affair, if by doing so I should sacrifice only myself. The one person of whom I am bound to think in this matter is the girl I love.'

'That is just what she would say about you.'

'I hope so.'

'In that way you support each other. If it were any other man circumstanced just like you are, and any other girl placed like Mary, you would be the first to say that the man was behaving badly. I don't like to use hard language to you, but in such a case you would be the first to say of another man—that he was looking after the girl's money.'

Silverbridge as he said this looked forward steadfastly on to the water, regretting much that cause for quarrel should have arisen, but thinking that Tregear would find himself obliged to quarrel. But Tregear, after a few moments' silence, having thought it out, determined that he would not quarrel. 'I think I probably might,' he said, laying his hand on Silverbridge's arm. 'I think I perhaps might express such an opinion.'

'Well then!'

'I have to examine myself, and find out whether I am guilty of the meanness which I might perhaps be too ready to impute to another. I have done so, and I am quite sure that I am not drawn to your sister by any desire for her money. I did not seek her because she was a rich man's daughter, nor,—because she is a rich man's daughter,—will I give her up. She shall be mistress of the occasion. Nothing but a word from her shall induce me to leave her;—but a word from her, if it comes from her own lips,—shall do so.' Then he took his friend's hand in his, and, having grasped it, walked away without saying another word.

## CHAPTER 31

### MISS BONCASSEN'S RIVER-PARTY. NO. I

THRICE within the next three weeks did Lord Silverbridge go forth to ask Mabel to be his wife, but thrice in vain. On one occasion she would talk on other things. On the second Miss Cassewary would not leave her. On the third the conversation turned in a very disagreeable way on Miss Boncassen, as to whom Lord Silverbridge could not but think that Lady Mabel said some very ill-natured things. It was no doubt true that he, during the last three weeks, had often been in Miss Boncassen's company, that he had danced with her, ridden with her, taken her to the House of Lords and to the House of Commons, and was now engaged to attend upon her at a river-party up above Maidenhead.* But Mabel had certainly no right to complain. Had he not thrice during the same period come there to lay his coronet at her feet;—and now, at this very moment, was it not her fault that he was not going through the ceremony?

'I suppose,' she said, laughing, 'that it is all settled.'

'What is all settled?'

'About you and the American beauty.'

'I am not aware that anything particular has been settled.'

'Then it ought to be,—oughtn't it? For her sake, I mean.'

'That is so like an English woman,' said Lord Silverbridge. 'Because you cannot understand a manner of life a little different from your own you will impute evil.'

'I have imputed no evil, Lord Silverbridge, and you have no right to say so.'

'If you mean to assert,' said Miss Cass, 'that the manners of American young ladies are freer than those of English young ladies, it is you that are taking away their characters.'

'I don't say it would be at all bad,' continued Lady Mabel. 'She is a beautiful girl, and very clever, and would make a charming Duchess. And then it would be such a delicious change to have an American Duchess.'

'She wouldn't be a Duchess.'

'Well, Countess, with Duchessship before her in the remote future. Wouldn't it be a change, Miss Cass?'

'Oh decidedly!' said Miss Cass.

'And very much for the better. Quite a case of new blood, you know. Pray don't suppose that I mean to object. Everybody who talks about it approves. I haven't heard a dissentient voice. Only as it has gone so far, and as English people are too stupid, you know, to understand all these new ways,—don't you think perhaps——?'

'No, I don't think. I don't think anything except that you are very ill-natured.' Then he got up and, after making formal adieux to both the ladies, left the house.

As soon as he was gone Lady Mabel began to laugh, but the least apprehensive* ears would have perceived that the laughter was affected. Miss Cassewary did not laugh at all, but sat bolt upright and looked very serious. 'Upon my honour,' said the younger lady, 'he is the most beautifully simple-minded human being I ever knew in my life.'

'Then I wouldn't laugh at him.'

'How can one help it? But of course I do it with a purpose.'

'What purpose?'

'I think he is making a fool of himself. If somebody does not interfere he will go so far that he will not be able to draw back without misbehaving.'

'I thought,' said Miss Cassewary, in a very low voice, almost whispering, 'I thought that he was looking for a wife elsewhere.'

'You need not think of that again,' said Lady Mab, jumping up from her seat. 'I had thought of it too. But as I told you before, I spared him. He did not really mean it with me;—nor does he mean it with this American girl. Such young men seldom mean. They drift into matrimony. But she will not spare him. It would be a national triumph. All the States would sing a pæan of glory. Fancy a New York belle having compassed a Duke!'

'I don't think it possible. It would be too horrid.'

'I think it quite possible. As for me, I could teach myself to think it best as it is, were I not so sure that I should be better for him than so many others. But I shouldn't love him.'

'Why not love him?'

'He is such a boy. I should always treat him like a boy,—spoiling him and petting him, but never respecting him. Don't run away with any idea that I should refuse him from conscientious motives, if he were really to ask me. I too should like to be a Duchess. I should like to bring all this misery at home to an end.'

'But you did refuse him.'

'Not exactly;—because he never asked me. For the moment I was weak, and so I let him have another chance. I shall not have been a good friend to him if it ends in his marrying this Yankee.'

Lord Silverbridge went out of the house in a very ill humour,— which however left him when in the course of the afternoon he found himself up at Maidenhead with Miss Boncassen. Miss Boncassen at any rate did not laugh at him. And then she was so pleasant, so full of common sense, and so completely intelligent! 'I like you,' she had said, 'because I feel that you will not think that you ought to make love to me. There is nothing I hate so much as the idea that a young man and a young woman can't be acquainted with each other without some such tomfoolery as that.' This had exactly expressed his own feeling. Nothing could be so pleasant as his intimacy with Isabel Boncassen.

Mrs Boncassen seemed to be a homely person, with no desire either to speak, or to be spoken to. She went out but seldom, and on those rare occasions did not in any way interfere with her daughter. Mr Boncassen filled a prouder situation. Everybody knew that Miss Boncassen was in England, because it suited Mr Boncassen to spend many hours in the British Museum. But still the daughter hardly seemed to be under control from the father. She went alone where she liked; talked to those she liked; and did what she liked. Some of the young ladies of the day thought that there was a good deal to be said in favour of the freedom which she enjoyed.

There is however a good deal to be said against it. All young ladies cannot be Miss Boncassens, with such an assurance of admirers as to be free from all fear of loneliness. There is a comfort for a young lady in having a pied-à-terre to which she may retreat in case of need. In American circles, where girls congregate without their mothers, there is a danger felt by young men that if a lady be once taken in hand, there will be no possibility of getting rid of her,—no mamma to whom she may be taken and under whose wings she may be dropped. 'My dear,' said an old gentleman the other day walking through an American ball-room, and addressing himself to a girl whom he knew well,— 'My dear——' But the girl bowed and passed on, still clinging to the arm of the young man who accompanied her. But the old gentleman was cruel, and possessed of a determined purpose. 'My dear,' said he again, catching the young man tight by the collar and holding him fast. 'Don't be afraid; I've got him; he shan't desert you; I'll hold him here till you have told me how your father does.' The young lady looked as if she didn't like it, and the sight of her misery gave rise to a feeling that, after all, mammas perhaps may be a comfort.

But in her present phase of life Miss Boncassen suffered no misfortune of this kind. It had become a privilege to be allowed to attend upon Miss Boncassen, and the feeling of this privilege had been enhanced by the manner in which Lord Silverbridge had devoted himself to her. Fashion of course makes fashion. Had not Lord Silverbridge been so very much struck by the charm of the young lady, Lords Glasslough and Popplecourt would not perhaps have found it necessary to run after her. As it was, even that most unenergetic of young men, Dolly Longstaff, was moved to profound admiration.

On this occasion they were all up the river at Maidenhead. Mr Boncassen had looked about for some means of returning the civilities offered to him, and had been instigated by Mrs Montacute Jones to do it after this fashion. There was a magnificent banquet spread in a summer-house on the river bank. There were boats, and there was a band, and there was a sward for dancing. There was lawn-tennis, and fishing-rods,—which nobody used,—and better still, long shady secluded walks in which gentlemen might stroll,—and ladies too, if they were kind enough. The whole thing had been arranged by Mrs Montacute Jones. As the day was fine, as many of the old people had abstained from coming, as there were plenty of young men of the best sort, and as nothing had been spared in reference to external comforts, the party promised to be a success. Every most lovely girl in London of course was there,—except Lady Mabel Grex. Lady Mabel was in the habit of going everywhere, but on this occasion she had refused Mrs Boncassen's invitation. 'I don't want to see her triumphs,' she had said to Miss Cass.

Everybody went down by railway of course, and innumerable flies* and carriages had been provided to take them to the scene of action. Some immediately got into boats and rowed themselves up from the bridge,—which, as the thermometer was standing at eighty* in the shade, was an inconsiderate proceeding. 'I don't think I am quite up to that,' said Dolly Longstaff, when it was proposed to him to take an oar. 'Miss Amazon will do it. She rows so well, and is so strong.' Whereupon Miss Amazon, not at all abashed, did take the oar; and as Lord Silverbridge was on the seat behind her with the other oar she probably enjoyed her task.

'What a very nice sort of person Lady Cantrip is.' This was said to Silverbridge by that generally silent young nobleman Lord Popplecourt. The remark was the more singular because Lady Cantrip was not at the party,—and the more so again because, as Silverbridge thought, there could be but little in common between the Countess who had his sister in charge and the young lord beside him, who was not fast only because he did not like to risk his money.

'Well,—yes; I dare say she is.'

'I thought so, peculiarly. I was at that place at Richmond yesterday.'

'The devil you were! What were you doing at The Horns?'

'Lady Cantrip's grandmother was,—I don't quite know what she was, but something to us. I know I've got a picture of her at Popplecourt. Lady Cantrip wanted to ask me something about it, and so I went down. I was so glad to make acquaintance with your sister.'

'You saw Mary, did you?'

'Oh yes; I lunched there. I'm to go down and meet the Duke some day.'

'Meet the Duke!'

'Why not?'

'No reason on earth,—only I can't imagine the governor going to Richmond for his dinner. Well! I am very glad to hear it. I hope you'll get on well with him.'

'I was so much struck with your sister.'

'Yes; I dare say,' said Silverbridge, turning away into the path where he saw Miss Boncassen standing with some other ladies. It certainly did not occur to him that Popplecourt was to be brought forward as a suitor for his sister's hand.

'I believe this is the most lovely place in the world,' Miss Boncassen said to him.

'We are so much the more obliged to you for bringing us here.'

'We don't bring you. You allow us to come with you and see all that is pretty and lovely.'

'Is it not your party?'

'Father will pay the bill, I suppose,—as far as that goes. And mother's name was put on the cards. But of course we know what that means. It is because you and a few others like you have been so kind to us, that we are able to be here at all.'

'Everybody, I should think, must be kind to you.'

'I do have a good time pretty much; but nowhere so good as here. I fear that when I get back I shall not like New York.'

'I have heard you say, Miss Boncassen, that Americans were more likeable than the English.'

'Have you? Well, yes; I think I have said so. And I think it is so. I'd sooner have to dance with a bank clerk in New York, than with a bank clerk here.'

'Do you ever dance with bank clerks?'

'Oh dear yes. At least I suppose so. I dance with whoever comes up. We haven't got lords in America, you know!'

'You have got gentlemen?'

'Plenty of them;—but they are not so easily defined as lords. I do like lords.'

'Do you?'

'Oh yes,—and ladies;—Countesses I mean and women of that sort. Your Lady Mabel Grex is not here. Why wouldn't she come?'

'Perhaps you didn't ask her.'

'Oh yes I did;—especially for your sake.'

'She is not my Lady Mabel Grex,' said Lord Silverbridge with unnecessary energy.

'But she will be.'

'What makes you think that?'

'You are devoted to her.'

'Much more to you, Miss Boncassen.'

'That is nonsense, Lord Silverbridge.'

'Not at all.'

'It is also—untrue.'

'Surely I must be the best judge of that myself?'

'Not a doubt; a judge not only whether it be true, but if true whether expedient,—or even possible. What did I say to you when we first began to know each other?'

'What did you say?'

'That I liked knowing you;—that was frank enough;—that I liked knowing you because I knew that there would be no tomfoolery of love-making.' Then she paused; but he did not quite know how to go on with the conversation at once, and she continued her speech. 'When you condescend to tell me that you are devoted to me, as though that were the kind of thing that I expect to have said when I take a walk with a young man in a wood, is not that the tomfoolery of love-making?' She stopped and looked at him, so that he was obliged to answer.

'Then why do you ask me if I am devoted to Lady Mabel? Would not that be tomfoolery too?'

'No. If I thought so, I would not have asked the question. I did specially invite her to come here because I thought you would like it. You have got to marry somebody.'

'Some day, perhaps.'

'And why not her?'

'If you come to that, why not you?' He felt himself to be getting into deep waters as he said this,—but he had a meaning to express if only he could find the words to express it. 'I don't say whether it is tomfoolery, as you call it, or not; but whatever it is, you began it.'

'Yes;—yes. I see. You punish me for my unpremeditated impertinence in suggesting that you are devoted to Lady Mabel by the premeditated impertinence of pretending to be devoted to me.'

'Stop a moment. I cannot follow that.' Then she laughed. 'I will swear that I did not intend to be impertinent.'

'I hope not.'

'I am devoted to you.'

'Lord Silverbridge!'

'I think you are——'

'Stop, stop. Do not say it.'

'Well I won't;—not now. But there has been no tomfoolery.'

'May I ask a question, Lord Silverbridge? You will not be angry? I would not have you angry with me.'

'I will not be angry,' he said.

'Are you not engaged to marry Lady Mabel Grex?'

'No.'

'Then I beg your pardon. I was told that you were engaged to her. And I thought your choice was so fortunate, so happy! I have seen no girl here that I admire half so much. She almost comes up to my idea of what a young woman should be.'

'Almost!'

'Now I am sure that if not engaged to her you must be in love with her, or my praise would have sufficed.'

'Though one knows a Lady Mabel Grex, one may become acquainted with a Miss Boncassen.'

There are moments in which stupid people say clever things, obtuse people say sharp things, and good-natured people say ill-natured things. 'Lord Silverbridge,' she said, 'I did not expect that from you.'

'Expect what? I meant it simply.'

'I have no doubt you meant it simply. We Americans think ourselves sharp, but I have long since found out that we may meet more than our matches over here. I think we will go back. Mother means to try to get up a quadrille.'

'You will dance with me?'

'I think not. I have been walking with you, and I had better dance with someone else.'

'You can let me have one dance.'

'I think not. There will not be many.'

'Are you angry with me?'

'Yes, I am; there.' But as she said this she smiled. 'The truth is, I thought I was getting the better of you, and you turned round and gave me a pat on the head to show me that you could be master when it pleased you. You have defended your intelligence at the expense of your good-nature.'

'I'll be shot if I know what it all means,' he said, just as he was parting with her.

## CHAPTER 32

### MISS BONCASSEN'S RIVER-PARTY. NO. 2

LORD SILVERBRIDGE made up his mind that as he could not dance with Miss Boncassen he would not dance at all. He was not angry at being rejected, and when he saw her stand up with Dolly Longstaff he felt no jealousy. She had refused to dance with him not because she did not like him, but because she did not wish to show that she liked him. He could understand that, though he had not quite followed all the ins and outs of her little accusations against him. She had flattered him—without any intention of flattery on her part. She had spoken of his intelligence and had complained that he had been too sharp to her.

Mabel Grex when most sweet to him, when most loving, always made him feel that he was her inferior. She took no trouble to hide her conviction of his youthfulness. This was anything but flattering. Miss Boncassen, on the other hand, professed herself to be almost afraid of him.

'There shall be no tomfoolery of love-making,' she had said. But what if it were not tomfoolery at all? What if it were good, genuine, earnest love-making? He certainly was not pledged to Lady Mabel. As regarded his father there would be a difficulty. In the first place he had been fool enough to tell his father that he was going to make an offer to Mabel Grex. And then his father would surely refuse his consent to a marriage with an American stranger. In such case there would be no unlimited income, no immediate pleasantness of magnificent life such as he knew would be poured out upon him if he were to marry Mabel Grex. As he thought of this, however, he told himself that he would not sell himself for money and magnificence. He could afford to be independent, and gratify his own taste. Just at this moment he was of opinion that Isabel Boncassen would be the sweeter companion of the two.

He had sauntered down to the place where they were dancing and stood by, saying a few words to Mrs Boncassen. 'Why are you not dancing, my Lord?' she asked.

'There are enough without me.'

'I guess you young aristocrats are never over-fond of doing much with your own arms and legs.'

'I don't know about that; polo, you know, for the legs, and lawn-tennis for the arms, is hard work enough.'

'But it must always be something new-fangled; and after all it isn't of much account. Our young men like to have quite a time at dancing.'

It all came through her nose! And she looked so common! What would the Duke say to her, or Mary, or even Gerald? The father was by no means so objectionable. He was a tall, straight, ungainly man, who always wore black clothes. He had dark, stiff, short hair, a long nose, and a forehead that was both high and broad. Ezekiel Boncassen was the very man,—from his appearance,—for a President of the United States; and there were men who talked of him for that high office. That he had never attended to politics was supposed to be in his favour. He had the reputation of being the most learned man in the States, and reputation itself often suffices to give a man dignity of manner. He, too, spoke through his nose, but the peculiar twang coming from a man would be supposed to be virile* and incisive. From a woman, Lord Silverbridge thought it to be unbearable. But as to Isabel, had she been born within the confines of some lordly park in Hertfordshire, she could not have been more completely free from the abomination.

'I am sorry that you should not be enjoying yourself,' said Mr Boncassen, coming to his wife's relief.

'Nothing could have been nicer. To tell the truth, I am standing idle by way of showing my anger against your daughter, who would not dance with me.'

'I am sure she would have felt herself honoured,' said Mr Boncassen.

'Who is the gentleman with her?' asked the mother.

'A particular friend of mine—Dolly Longstaff.'

'Dolly!' ejaculated Mrs Boncassen.

'Everybody calls him so. His real name I believe to be Adolphus.'

'Is he,—is he—just anybody?' asked the anxious mother.

'He is a very great deal,—as people go here. Everybody knows him. He is asked everywhere, but he goes nowhere. The greatest compliment paid to you here is his presence.'

'Nay, my Lord, there are the Countess Montague, and the Marchioness of Capulet, and Lord Tybalt,* and——'

'They go everywhere. They are nobodies. It is a charity to even invite them. But to have had Dolly Longstaff once is a triumph for life.'

'Laws!' said Mrs Boncassen, looking hard at the young man who was dancing. 'What has he done?'

'He never did anything in his life.'

'I suppose he's very rich.'

'I don't know. I should think not. I don't know anything about his riches, but I can assure you that having had him down here will quite give a character to the day.'

In the meantime Dolly Longstaff was in a state of great excitement. Some part of the character assigned to him by Lord Silverbridge was true. He very rarely did go anywhere, and yet was asked to a great many places. He was a young man,—though not a very young man,—with a fortune of his own and the expectation of a future fortune. Few men living could have done less for the world than Dolly Longstaff,—and yet he had a position of his own. Now he had taken it into his head to fall in love with Miss Boncassen. This was an accident which had probably never happened to him before, and which had disturbed him much. He had known Miss Boncassen a week or two before Lord Silverbridge had seen her, having by some chance dined out and sat next to her. From that moment he had become changed, and had gone hither and thither in pursuit of the American beauty. His passion having become suspected by his companions had excited their ridicule. Nevertheless he had persevered;—and now he was absolutely dancing with the lady out in the open air. 'If this goes on, your friends will have to look after you and put you somewhere,' Mr Lupton had said to him in one of the intervals of the dance. Dolly had turned round and scowled, and suggested that if Mr Lupton would mind his own affairs it would be as well for the world at large.

At the present crisis Dolly was very much excited. When the dance was over, as a matter of course, he offered the lady his arm, and as a matter of course she accepted it. 'You'll take a turn; won't you?' he said.

'It must be a very short turn,' she said,—'as I am expected to make myself busy.'

'Oh, bother that.'

'It bothers me; but it has to be done.'

'You have set everything going now. They'll begin dancing again without your telling them.'

'I hope so.'

'And I've got something I want to say.'

'Dear me; what is it?'

They were now on a path close to the riverside, in which there were many loungers. 'Would you mind coming up to the temple?' he said.

'What temple?'

'Oh such a beautiful place. The Temple of the Winds, I think they call it, or Venus;—or—or—Mrs Arthur de Bever.'

'Was she a goddess?'

'It is something built to her memory. Such a view of the river! I was here once before and they took me up there. Everybody who comes here goes and sees Mrs Arthur de Bever. They ought to have told you.'

'Let us go then,' said Miss Boncassen. 'Only it must not be long.'

'Five minutes will do it all.' Then he walked rather quickly up a flight of rural steps. 'Lovely spot; isn't it?'

'Yes, indeed.'

'That's Maidenhead Bridge;*—that's—somebody's place;—and now I've got something to say to you.'

'You're not going to murder me now you've got me up here alone?' said Miss Boncassen laughing.

'Murder you!' said Dolly, throwing himself into an attitude that was intended to express devoted affection. 'Oh no!'

'I am glad of that.'

'Miss Boncassen!'

'Mr Longstaff! If you sigh like that you'll burst yourself.'

'I'll—what?'

'Burst yourself!' and she nodded her head at him.

Then he clapped his hands together, and turned his head away from her towards the little temple. 'I wonder whether she knows what love is,' he said, as though he were addressing himself to Mrs Arthur de Bever.

'No, she don't,' said Miss Boncassen.

'But I do,' he shouted, turning back towards her. 'I do. If any man were ever absolutely, actually, really in love, I am the man.'

'Are you indeed, Mr Longstaff? Isn't it pleasant?'

'Pleasant;—pleasant? Oh, it could be so pleasant.'

'But who is the lady? Perhaps you don't mean to tell me that.'

'You mean to say you don't know?'

'Haven't the least idea in life.'

'Let me tell you then that it could only be one person. It never was but one person. It never could have been but one person. It is you.' Then he put his hand well on his heart.

'Me!' said Miss Boncassen, choosing to be ungrammatical* in order that he might be more absurd.

'Of course it is you. Do you think that I should have brought you all the way up here to tell you that I was in love with anybody else?'

'I thought I was brought to see Mrs de Somebody, and the view.'

'Not at all,' said Dolly emphatically.

'Then you have deceived me.'

'I will never deceive you. Only say that you will love me, and I will be as true to you as the North Pole.'

'Is that true to me?'

'You know what I mean.'

'But if I don't love you?'

'Yes, you do!'

'Do I?'

'I beg your pardon,' said Dolly. 'I didn't mean to say that. Of course a man shouldn't make sure of a thing.'

'Not in this case, Mr Longstaff; because really I entertain no such feeling.'

'But you can if you please. Just let me tell you who I am.'

'That will do no good whatever, Mr Longstaff.'

'Let me tell you at any rate. I have a very good income of my own as it is.'

'Money can have nothing to do with it.'

'But I want you to know that I can afford it. You might perhaps have thought that I wanted your money.'

'I will attribute nothing evil to you, Mr Longstaff. Only it is quite out of the question that I should—respond as I suppose you wish me to; and therefore, pray, do not say anything further.'

She went to the head of the little steps but he interrupted her. 'You ought to hear me,' he said.

'I have heard you.'

'I can give you as good a position as any man without a title in England.'

'Mr Longstaff, I rather fancy that wherever I may be I can make a position for myself. At any rate I shall not marry with the view of getting one. If my husband were an English Duke I should think myself nothing, unless I was something as Isabel Boncassen.'

When she said this she did not bethink herself that Lord Silverbridge would in the course of nature become an English Duke. But the allusion to an English Duke told intensely on Dolly, who had suspected that he had a noble rival. 'English Dukes aren't so easily got,' he said.

'Very likely not. I might have expressed my meaning better had I said an English Prince.'

'That's quite out of the question,' said Dolly. 'They can't do it,—by Act of Parliament,—except in a hugger-mugger* left-handed way, that wouldn't suit you at all.'

'Mr Longstaff,—you must forgive me—if I say—that of all the gentlemen—I have ever met in this country or in any other—you are the—most obtuse.' This she brought out in little disjointed sentences, not with any hesitation, but in a way to make every word she uttered more clear to an intelligence which she did not believe to be bright. But in this belief she did some injustice to Dolly. He was quite alive to the disgrace of being called obtuse, and quick enough to avenge himself at the moment.

'Am I?' said he. 'How humble-minded you must be when you think me a fool because I have fallen in love with such a one as yourself.'

'I like you for that,' she replied laughing, 'and withdraw the epithet as not being applicable. Now we are quits and can forget and forgive;—only let there be the forgetting.'

'Never!' said Dolly, with his hand again on his heart.

'Then let it be a little dream of your youth,—that you once met a pretty American girl who was foolish enough to refuse all that you would have given her.'

'So pretty! So awfully pretty!' Thereupon she curtsied. 'I have seen all the handsome women in England going for the last ten years, and there has not been one who has made me think that it would be worth my while to get off my perch for her.'

'And now you would desert your perch for me!'

'I have already.'

'But you can get up again. Let it be all a dream. I know men like to have had such dreams. And in order that the dream may be pleasant the last word between us shall be kind. Such admiration from such a one as you is an honour,—and I will reckon it among my honours. But it can be no more than a dream.' Then she gave him her hand. 'It shall be so;—shall it not?' Then she paused. 'It must be so, Mr Longstaff.'

'Must it?'

'That and no more. Now I wish to go down. Will you come with me? It will be better. Don't you think it is going to rain?'

Dolly looked up at the clouds. 'I wish it would with all my heart.'

'I know you are not so ill-natured. It would spoil all.'

'You have spoiled all.'

'No, no. I have spoiled nothing. It will only be a little dream about "that strange American girl, who really did make me feel queer for half an hour." Look at that. A great big drop—and the cloud has come over us as black as Erebus.* Do hurry down.' He was leading the way. 'What shall we do for carriages to get us to the inn?'

'There's the summer-house.'

'It will hold about half of us. And think what it will be to be in there waiting till the rain shall be over! Everybody has been so good-humoured and now they will be so cross!'

The rain was falling in big heavy drops, slow and far between, but almost black with their size. And the heaviness of the cloud which had garnered over them made everything black.

'Will you have my arm?' said Silverbridge, who saw Miss Boncassen scudding along, with Dolly Longstaff following as fast as he could.

'Oh dear no. I have got to mind my dress. There;—I have gone right into a puddle. Oh dear!' So she ran on, and Silverbridge followed close behind her, leaving Dolly Longstaff in the distance.

It was not only Miss Boncassen who got her feet into a puddle and splashed her stockings. Many did so who were not obliged by their position to maintain good-humour under their misfortunes. The storm had come on with such unexpected quickness that there had been a general stampede to the summer-house. As Isabel had said, there was comfortable room for not more than half of them. In a few minutes people were crushed who never ought to be crushed. A Countess for whom treble-piled sofas were hardly good enough was seated on the corner of a table till some younger and less gorgeous lady could be made to give way. And the Marchioness was declaring she was as wet through as though she had been dragged in a river. Mrs Boncassen was so absolutely quelled as to have retired into the kitchen attached to the summer-house. Mr Boncassen, with all his country's pluck and pride, was proving to a knot of gentlemen round him on the verandah, that such treachery in the weather was a thing unknown in his happier country. Miss Boncassen had to do her best to console the splashed ladies. 'Oh Mrs Jones, is it not a pity! What can I do for you?'

'We must bear it, my dear. It often does rain, but why on this special day should it come down out of buckets?'

'I never was so wet in all my life,' said Dolly Longstaff, poking in his head.

'There's somebody smoking,' said the Countess angrily. There was a crowd of men smoking out on the verandah. 'I never knew anything so nasty,' the Countess continued, leaving it in doubt whether she spoke of the rain, or the smoke, or the party generally.

Damp gauzes, splashed stockings, trampled muslins, and features which have perhaps known something of rouge and certainly encountered something of rain may be made, but can only, by supreme high breeding, be made compatible with good-humour. To be moist, muddy, rumpled and smeared, when by the very nature of your position it is your duty to be clear-starched up to the pellucidity of crystal, to be spotless as the lily, to be crisp as the ivy-leaf, and as clear in complexion as a rose,—is it not, O gentle readers, felt to be a disgrace? It came to pass, therefore, that many were now very cross. Carriages were ordered under the idea that some improvement might be made at the inn which was nearly a mile distant. Very few, however, had their own carriages, and there was jockeying for the vehicles. In the midst of all this Silverbridge remained as near to Miss Boncassen as circumstances would admit. 'You are not waiting for me,' she said.

'Yes, I am. We might as well go up to town together.'

'Leave me with father and mother. Like the captain of a ship, I must be the last to leave the wreck.'

'But I'll be the gallant sailor of the day who always at the risk of his life sticks to the skipper to the last moment.'

'Not at all;—just because there will be no gallantry. But come and see us to-morrow and find out whether we have got through it alive.'

## CHAPTER 33

### THE LANGHAM HOTEL

'WHAT an abominable climate,' Mrs Boncassen had said when they were quite alone at Maidenhead.

'My dear, you didn't think you were to bring New York along with you when you came here,' replied her husband.

'I wish I was going back to-morrow.'

'That's a foolish thing to say. People here are very kind, and you are seeing a great deal more of the world than you would ever see at home. I am having a very good time. What do you say, Bell?'

'I wish I could have kept my stockings clean.'

'But what about the young men?'

'Young men are pretty much the same everywhere, I guess. They never have their wits about them. They never mean what they say, because they don't understand the use of words. They are generally half impudent and half timid. When in love they do not at all understand what has befallen them. What they want they try to compass as a cow does when it stands stretching out its head towards a stack of hay which it cannot reach. Indeed there is no such thing as a young man, for a man is not really a man till he is middle-aged. But take them at their worst they are a deal too good for us, for they become men some day, whereas we must only be women to the end.'

'My word, Bella!' exclaimed the mother.

'You have managed to be tolerably heavy upon God's creatures, taking them in a lump,' said the father. 'Boys, girls, and cows! Something has gone wrong with you besides the rain.'

'Nothing on earth, sir,—except the boredom.'

'Some young man has been talking to you, Bella.'

'One or two, mother; and I got to be thinking* if any one of them should ask me to marry him, and if moved by some evil destiny I were to take him, whether I should murder him, or myself, or run away with one of the others.'

'Couldn't you bear with him till, according to your own theory, he would grow out of his folly?' said the father.

'Being a woman,—no. The present moment is always everything to me. When that horrid old harridan halloaed out that somebody was smoking, I thought I should have died. It was very bad just then.'

'Awful!' said Mrs Boncassen, shaking her head.

'I didn't seem to feel it much,' said the father. 'One doesn't look to have everything just what one wants always. If I did I should go nowhere;—but my total life would be less enjoyable. If ever you do get married, Bell, you should remember that.'

'I mean to get married some day, so that I shouldn't be made love to any longer.'

'I hope it will have that effect,' said the father.

'Mr Boncassen!' ejaculated the mother.

'What I say is true. I hope it will have that effect. It had with you, my dear.'

'I don't know that people didn't think of me as much as of anybody else, even though I was married.'

'Then, my dear, I never knew it.'

Miss Boncassen, though she had behaved serenely and with good temper during the process of Dolly's proposal, had not liked it. She had a very high opinion of herself, and was certainly entitled to have it by the undisguised admiration of all that came near her. She was not more indifferent to the admiration of young men than are other young ladies. But she was not proud of the admiration of Dolly Longstaff. She was here among strangers whose ways were unknown to her, whose rank and standing in the world were vague to her, and wonderful in their dimness. She knew that she was associating with men very different from those at home where young men were supposed to be under the necessity of earning their bread. At New York she would dance, as she had said, with bank clerks. She was not prepared to admit that a young London lord was better than a New York bank clerk. Judging the men on their own individual merits she might find the bank clerk to be the better of the two. But a certain sweetness of the aroma of rank was beginning to permeate her republican senses. The softness of a life in which no occupation was compulsory had its charms for her. Though she had complained of the insufficient intelligence of young men she was alive to the delight of having nothings said to her pleasantly. All this had affected her so strongly that she had almost felt that a life among these English luxuries would be a pleasant life. Like most Americans who do not as yet know the country, she had come with an inward feeling that as an American and a republican she might probably be despised.

There is not uncommonly a savageness of self-assertion about Americans which arises from a too great anxiety to be admitted to fellowship with Britons. She had felt this, and conscious of reputation already made by herself in the social life of New York, she had half

trusted that she would be well received in London, and had half convinced herself that she would be rejected. She had not been rejected.
She must have become quite aware of that. She had dropped very
quickly the idea that she would be scorned. Ignorant as she had been of
English life, she perceived that she had at once become popular. And
this had been so in spite of her mother's homeliness and her father's
awkwardness. By herself and by her own gifts she had done it. She had
found out concerning herself that she had that which would commend
her to other society than that of the Fifth Avenue.* Those lords of
whom she had heard were as plenty with her as blackberries. Young
Lord Silverbridge, of whom she was told that of all the young lords of
the day he stood first in rank and wealth, was peculiarly her friend. Her
brain was firmer than that of most girls, but even her brain was a little
turned. She never told herself that it would be well for her to become
the wife of such a one. In her more thoughtful moments she told herself that it would not be well. But still the allurement was strong upon
her. Park Lane was sweeter than the Fifth Avenue. Lord Silverbridge
was nicer than the bank clerk.

But Dolly Longstaff was not. She would certainly prefer the bank
clerk to Dolly Longstaff. And yet Dolly Longstaff was the one among
her English admirers who had come forward and spoken out. She did
not desire that any one should come forward and speak out. But it was
an annoyance to her that this special man should have done so.

The waiter at the Langham understood American ways perfectly,
and when a young man called between three and four o'clock, asking
for Mrs Boncassen, said that Miss Boncassen was at home. The young
man took off his hat, brushed up his hair, and followed the waiter up to
the sitting-room. The door was opened and the young man was
announced. 'Mr Longstaff.'

Miss Boncassen was rather disgusted. She had had enough of this
English lover. Why should he have come after what had occurred yesterday? He ought to have felt that he was absolved from the necessity
of making personal inquiries. 'I am glad to see that you got home safe,'
she said as she gave him her hand.

'And you too, I hope?'

'Well;—so, so; with my clothes a good deal damaged and my temper
rather worse.'

'I am so sorry.'

'It should not rain on such days. Mother has gone to church.'

'Oh;—indeed. I like going to church myself sometimes.'

'Do you now?'

'I know what would make me like to go to church.'

'And father is at the Athenæum.* He goes there to do a little light reading in the library on Sunday afternoon.'

'I shall never forget yesterday, Miss Boncassen.'

'You wouldn't if your clothes had been spoilt as mine were.'

'Money will repair that.'

'Well; yes; but when I've had a petticoat flounced particularly to order I don't like to see it ill-treated. There are emotions of the heart which money can't touch.'

'Just so;—emotions of the heart! That's the very phrase.'

She was determined if possible to prevent a repetition of the scene which had taken place up at Mrs de Bever's temple. 'All my emotions are about my dress.'

'All?'

'Well; yes; all. I guess I don't care much for eating and drinking.' In saying this she actually contrived to produce something of a nasal twang.

'Eating and drinking!' said Dolly. 'Of course they are necessities;— and so are clothes.'

'But new things are such ducks!'

'Trowsers may be,'* said Dolly.

Then she took a prolonged gaze at him, wondering whether he was or was not such a fool as he looked. 'How funny you are,' she said.

'A man does not generally feel funny after going through what I suffered yesterday, Miss Boncassen.'

'Would you mind ringing the bell?'

'Must it be done quite at once?'

'Quite,—quite,' she said. 'I can do it myself for the matter of that.' And she rang the bell somewhat violently. Dolly sank back again into his seat, remarking in his usual apathetic way that he had intended to obey her behest but had not understood that she was in so great a hurry. 'I am always in a hurry,' she said. 'I like things to be done— sharp.' And she hit the table a crack. 'Please bring me some iced water,' this of course was addressed to the waiter. 'And a glass for Mr Longstaff.'

'None for me, thank you.'

'Perhaps you'd like soda and brandy?'

'Oh dear no;—nothing of the kind. But I am so much obliged to you all the same.' As the water-bottle was in fact standing in the room, and as the waiter had only to hand the glass, all this created but little obstacle. Still it had its effect, and Dolly, when the man had retired, felt

that there was a difficulty in proceeding. 'I have called to-day——'
he began.

'That has been so kind of you. But mother has gone to church.'

'I am very glad that she has gone to church, because I wish to——'

'Oh laws! There's a horse has tumbled down in the street. I heard it.'

'He has got up again,' said Dolly, looking leisurely out of the window. 'But as I was saying——'

'I don't think that the water we Americans drink can be good.
It makes the women become ugly so young.'

'You will never become ugly.'

She got up and curtsied to him, and then, still standing, made him a
speech. 'Mr Longstaff, it would be absurd of me to pretend not to
understand what you mean. But I won't have any more of it. Whether
you are making fun of me, or whether you are in earnest, it is just the
same.'

'Making fun of you!'

'It does not signify. I don't care which it is. But I won't have it.
There!'

'A gentleman should be allowed to express his feelings and to explain
his position.'

'You have expressed and explained more than enough, and I won't
have any more. If you will sit down and talk about something else, or
else go away, there shall be an end of it;—but if you go on, I will ring
the bell again. What can a man gain by going on when a girl has spoken
as I have done?' They were both at this time standing up, and he was
now as angry as she was.

'I've paid you the greatest compliment a man can pay a woman,' he
began.

'Very well. If I remember rightly I thanked you for it yesterday. If
you wish it, I will thank you again to-day. But it is a compliment which
becomes very much the reverse if it be repeated too often. You are
sharp enough to understand that I have done everything in my power
to save us both from this trouble.'

'What makes you so fierce, Miss Boncassen?'

'What makes you so foolish?'

'I suppose it must be something peculiar to American ladies.'

'Just that;—something peculiar to American ladies. They don't
like—well; I don't want to say anything more that can be called fierce.'

At this moment the door was again opened and Lord Silverbridge
was announced. 'Halloa, Dolly, are you here?'

'It seems that I am.'

'And I am here too,' said Miss Boncassen, smiling her prettiest.

'None the worse for yesterday's troubles, I hope?'

'A good deal the worse. I have been explaining all that to Mr Longstaff, who has been quite sympathetic with me about my things.'

'A terrible pity that shower,' said Dolly.

'For you,' said Silverbridge, 'because, if I remember right, Miss Boncassen was walking with you;—but I was rather glad of it.'

'Lord Silverbridge!'

'I regarded it as a direct interposition of Providence, because you would not dance with me.'

'Any news to-day, Silverbridge?' asked Dolly.

'Nothing particular. They say that Coalheaver can't run for the Leger.'

'What's the matter?' asked Dolly vigorously.

'Broke down at Ascot. But I dare say it's a lie.'

'Sure to be a lie,' said Dolly. 'What do you think of Madame Scholzdam,* Miss Boncassen?'

'I am not a good judge.'

'Never heard anything equal to it yet in this world,' said Dolly. 'I wonder whether that's true about Coalheaver?'

'Tifto says so.'

'Which at the present moment,' asked Miss Boncassen, 'is the greater favourite with the public, Madame Scholzdam or Coalheaver?'

'Coalheaver is a horse, Miss Boncassen.'

'Oh,—a horse!'

'Perhaps I ought to say a colt.'

'Oh,—a colt.'

'Do you suppose, Dolly, that Miss Boncassen doesn't know all that?' asked Silverbridge.

'He supposes that my American ferocity has never been sufficiently softened for the reception of polite erudition.'

'You two have been quarrelling, I fear.'

'I never quarrel with a woman,' said Dolly.

'Nor with a man in my presence, I hope,' said Miss Boncassen.

'Somebody does seem to have got out of bed at the wrong side,' said Silverbridge.

'I did,' said Miss Boncassen. 'I got out of bed at the wrong side. I am cross. I can't get over the spoiling of my flounces. I think you had better both go away and leave me. If I could walk about the room for half an hour and stamp my feet, I should get better.' Silverbridge thought that as he had come last, he certainly ought to be left last. Miss Boncassen felt that, at any rate, Mr Longstaff should go. Dolly felt that his manhood required him to remain. After what had taken place he was not going to leave the field vacant for another. Therefore he made no effort to move.

'That seems rather hard upon me,' said Silverbridge. 'You told me to come.'

'I told you to come and ask after us all. You have come and asked after us, and have been informed that we are very bad. What more can I say? You accuse me of getting out of bed the wrong side, and I own that I did.'

'I meant to say that Dolly Longstaff had done so.'

'And I say it was Silverbridge,' said Dolly.

'We aren't very agreeable together, are we? Upon my word I think you'd better both go.' Silverbridge immediately got up from his chair; upon which Dolly also moved.

'What the mischief is up?' asked Silverbridge, when they were under the porch together.

'The truth is, you never can tell what you are to do with those American girls.'

'I suppose you have been making up to her.'

'Nothing in earnest. She seemed to me to like admiration; so I told her I admired her.'

'What did she say then?'

'Upon my word, you seem to be very great at cross-examining. Perhaps you had better go back and ask her.'

'I will, next time I see her.' Then he stepped into his cab, and in a loud voice ordered the man to drive him to the Zoo.* But when he had gone a little way up Portland Place, he stopped the driver and desired he might be taken back again to the hotel. As he left the vehicle he looked round for Dolly, but Dolly had certainly gone. Then he told the waiter to take his card to Miss Boncassen, and explain that he had something to say which he had forgotten.

'So you have come back again?' said Miss Boncassen, laughing.

'Of course I have. You didn't suppose I was going to let that fellow get the better of me. Why should I be turned out because he had made an ass of himself!'

'Who said he made an ass of himself?'

'But he had; hadn't he?'

'No;—by no means,' said she after a little pause.

'Tell me what he had been saying.'

'Indeed I shall do nothing of the kind. If I told you all he said, then I should have to tell the next man all that you may say. Would that be fair?'

'I should not mind,' said Silverbridge.

'I dare say not, because you have nothing particular to say. But the principle is the same. Lawyers and doctors and parsons talk of privileged communications. Why should not a young lady have her privileged communications?'

'But I have something particular to say.'

'I hope not.'

'Why should you hope not?'

'I hate having things said particularly. Nobody likes conversation so well as I do; but it should never be particular.'

'I was going to tell you that I came back to London yesterday in the same carriage with old Lady Clanfiddle, and that she swore that no consideration on earth would ever induce her to go to Maidenhead again.'

'That isn't particular.'

'She went on to say;—you won't tell of me; will you?'

'It shall all be privileged.'

'She went on to say that Americans couldn't be expected to understand English manners.'

'Perhaps they may be all the better for that.'

'Then I spoke up. I swore I was awfully in love with you.'

'You didn't.'

'I did;—that you were, out and away, the finest girl I ever saw in my life. Of course you understand that her two daughters were there. And that as for manners,—unless the rain could be attributed to American manners,—I did not think anything had gone wrong.'

'What about the smoking?'

'I told her they were all Englishmen, and that if she had been giving the party herself they would have smoked just as much. You must understand that she never does give any parties.'

'How could you be so ill-natured?'

'There was ever so much more of it. And it ended in her telling me that I was a schoolboy. I found out the cause of it all. A great spout of rain had come upon her daughter's hat, and that had produced a most melancholy catastrophe.'

'I would have given her mine willingly.'

'An American hat;—to be worn by Lady Violet Clanfiddle!'

'It came from Paris last week, sir.'

'But must have been contaminated by American contact.'

'Now, Lord Silverbridge,' said she, getting up, 'if I had a stick I'd whip you.'

'It was such fun.'

'And you come here and tell it all to me?'

'Of course I do. It was a deal too good to keep it to myself. "American manners!"' As he said this he almost succeeded in looking like Lady Clanfiddle.

At that moment Mr Boncassen entered the room, and was immediately appealed to by his daughter. 'Father, you must turn Lord Silverbridge out of the room.'

'Dear me! If I must,—of course I must. But why?'

'He is saying everything horrid he can about Americans.'

After this they settled down for a few minutes to general conversation, and then Lord Silverbridge again took his leave. When he was gone Isabel Boncassen almost regretted that the 'something particular' which he had threatened to say had not been less comic in its nature.

## CHAPTER 34

### LORD POPPLECOURT

WHEN the reader was told that Lord Popplecourt had found Lady Cantrip very agreeable it is to be hoped that the reader was disgusted. Lord Popplecourt would certainly not have given a second thought to Lady Cantrip unless he had been specially flattered. And why should such a man have been flattered by a woman who was in all respects his superior? The reader will understand. It had been settled by the wisdom of the elders that it would be a good thing that Lord Popplecourt should marry Lady Mary Palliser.

The mutual assent which leads to marriage should no doubt be spontaneous. Who does not feel that? Young love should speak from its first doubtful unconscious spark,—a spark which any breath of air may quench or cherish,—till it becomes a flame which nothing can satisfy but the union of the two lovers. No one should be told to love, or bidden to marry, this man or that woman. The theory of this is plain to us all, and till we have sons or daughters whom we feel imperatively obliged to control, the theory is unassailable. But the duty is so imperative! The Duke had taught himself to believe that as his wife would have been thrown away on the world had she been allowed to marry Burgo Fitzgerald, so would his daughter be thrown away were she allowed to marry Mr Tregear. Therefore the theory of spontaneous love* must in this case be set aside. Therefore the spark,—would that it had been no more!—must be quenched. Therefore there could be no union of two lovers;—but simply a prudent and perhaps splendid marriage.

Lord Popplecourt was a man in possession of a large estate which was unencumbered.* His rank in the peerage was not high; but his barony was of an old date,—and, if things went well with him, something higher in rank might be open to him. He had good looks of that sort which recommend themselves to pastors and masters, to elders and betters. He had regular features. He looked as though he were steady. He was not impatient nor rollicking. Silverbridge was also good-looking;—but his good looks were such as would give a pang to the hearts of anxious mothers of daughters. Tregear was the handsomest man of the three;—but then he looked us though he had no betters and did not care for his elders. Lord Popplecourt, though a very young man, had once stammered through half-a-dozen words in the House of Lords, and had been known to dine with the 'Benevolent Funds.' Lord Silverbridge had declared him to be a fool. No one thought him to be bright. But in the eyes of the Duke,—and of Lady Cantrip,—he had his good qualities.

But the work was very disagreeable. It was the more hard upon Lady Cantrip because she did not believe in it. If it could be done, it would be expedient. But she felt very strongly that it could not be done. No doubt that Lady Glencora had been turned from her evil destiny; but Lady Glencora had been younger than her daughter was now, and possessed of less character. Nor was Lady Cantrip blind to the difference between a poor man with a bad character, such as that Burgo had been, and a poor man with a good character, such as was Tregear. Nevertheless she undertook to aid the work, and condescended to pretend to be so interested in the portrait of some common ancestor as to persuade the young man to have it photographed, in order that the bringing down of the photograph might lead to something.

He took the photograph, and Lady Cantrip said very much to him about his grandmother, who was the old lady in question. 'She could,' she said, 'just remember the features of the dear old woman.' She was not habitually a hypocrite, and she hated herself for what she was doing, and yet her object was simply good,—to bring together two young people who might advantageously marry each other. The mere talking about the old woman would be of no service. She longed to bring out the offer plainly, and say, 'There is Lady Mary Palliser. Don't you think she'd make a good wife for you?' But she could not, as yet, bring herself to be so indelicately plain. 'You haven't seen the Duke since?' she asked.

'He spoke to me only yesterday in the House. I like the Duke.'

'If I may be allowed to say so, it would be for your advantage that he should like you;—that is, if you mean to take a part in politics.'

'I suppose I shall,' said Popplecourt. 'There isn't much else to do.'

'You don't go to races?' He shook his head. 'I am glad of that,' said Lady Cantrip. 'Nothing is so bad as the turf. I fear Lord Silverbridge is devoting himself to the turf.'

'I don't think it can be good for any man to have much to do with Major Tifto. I suppose Silverbridge knows what he's about.'

Here was an opportunity which might have been used. It would have been so easy for her to glide from the imperfections of the brother to the perfections of the sister. But she could not bring herself to do it quite at once. She approached the matter however as nearly as she could without making her grand proposition. She shook her head sadly in reference to Silverbridge, and then spoke of the Duke. 'His father is so anxious about him.'

'I dare say.'

'I don't know any man who is more painfully anxious about his children. He feels the responsibility so much since his wife's death. There is Lady Mary.'

'She's all right, I should say.'

'All right! oh yes. But when a girl is possessed of so many things,— rank, beauty, intelligence, large fortune,——'

'Will Lady Mary have much?'

'A large portion of her mother's money, I should say. When all these things are joined together, a father of course feels most anxious as to their disposal.'

'I suppose she is clever.'

'Very clever,' said Lady Cantrip.

'I think a girl may be too clever you know,' said Lord Popplecourt.

'Perhaps she may. But I know more who are too foolish. I am so much obliged to you for the photograph.'

'Don't mention it.'

'I really did not mean that you should send a man down.'

On that occasion the two young people did not see each other. Lady Mary did not come down, and Lady Cantrip lacked the courage to send for her. As it was, might it not be possible that the young man should be induced to make himself agreeable to the young lady without any further explanation? But love-making between young people cannot well take place unless they be brought together. There was a difficulty in bringing them together at Richmond. The Duke had indeed spoken of meeting Lord Popplecourt at dinner there;—but this was to have followed the proposition which Lady Cantrip should make to him. She could not yet make the proposition, and therefore she hardly knew how to arrange the dinner. She was obliged at last to let the wished-for lover go away without arranging anything. When the Duke should have settled his autumn plans, then an attempt must be made to induce Lord Popplecourt to travel in the same direction.

That evening Lady Cantrip said a few words to Mary respecting the proposed suitor. 'There is nothing I have such a horror of as gambling,' she said.

'It is dreadful.'

'I am very glad to think that Nidderdale does not do anything of that sort.' It was perhaps on the cards that Nidderdale should do things of which she knew nothing. 'I hope Silverbridge does not bet.'

'I don't think he does.'

'There's Lord Popplecourt,—quite a young man,—with everything at his own disposal, and a very large estate. Think of the evil he might do if he were given that way.'

'Does he gamble?'

'Not at all. It must be such a comfort to his mother!'

'He looks to me as though he never would do anything,' said Lady Mary. Then the subject was dropped.

It was a week after this, towards the end of July, that the Duke wrote a line to Lady Cantrip, apologizing for what he had done, but explaining that he had asked Lord Popplecourt to dine at The Horns on a certain Sunday. He had, he said, been assured by Lord Cantrip that such an arrangement would be quite convenient. It was clear from his letter that he was much in earnest. Of course there was no reason why the dinner should not be eaten. Only the speciality of the invitation to Lord Popplecourt must not be so glaring that he himself should be struck by the strangeness of it. There must be a little party made up. Lord Nidderdale and his wife were therefore bidden to come down, and Silverbridge, who at first consented rather unwillingly,—and Lady Mabel Grex, as to whom the Duke made a special request that she might be asked. This last invitation was sent express from Lady Mary, and included Miss Cass. So the party was made up. The careful reader will perceive that there were to be ten of them.

'Isn't it odd papa wanting to have Lady Mabel?' Mary said to Lady Cantrip.

'Does he not know her, my dear?'

'He hardly ever spoke to her. I'll tell you what; I expect Silverbridge is going to marry her.'

'Why shouldn't he?'

'I don't know why he shouldn't. She is very beautiful, and very clever. But if so, papa must know all about it. It does seem so odd that papa of all people should turn match-maker, or even that he should think of it.'

'So much is thrown upon him now,' said Lady Cantrip

'Poor papa!' Then she remembered herself, and spoke with a little start. 'Of course I am not thinking of myself. Arranging a marriage is very different from preventing any one from marrying.'

'Whatever he may think to be his duty he will be sure to do it,' said the elder lady very solemnly.

Lady Mabel was surprised by the invitation, but she was not slow to accept it. 'Papa will be here and will be so glad to meet you,' Lady Mary had said. Why should the Duke of Omnium wish to meet her? 'Silverbridge will be here too,' Mary had gone on to say. 'It is just a family party. Papa, you know, is not going anywhere; nor am I.' By all this Lady Mabel's thoughts were much stirred, and her bosom somewhat moved. And Silverbridge also was moved by it. Of course he could not but remember that he had pledged himself to his father to ask Lady Mabel to be his wife. He had faltered since. She had been, he thought, unkind to him, or at any rate indifferent. He had surely said enough to her to make her know what he meant; and yet she had taken no trouble to meet him half way. And then Isabel Boncassen had intervened. Now he was asked to dinner in a most unusual manner!

Of all the guests invited Lord Popplecourt was perhaps the least disturbed. He was quite alive to the honour of being noticed by the Duke of Omnium, and alive also to the flattering courtesy shown to him by Lady Cantrip. But justice would not be done him unless it were acknowledged that he had as yet flattered himself with no hopes in regard to Lady Mary Palliser. He, when he prepared himself for his journey down to Richmond, thought much more of the Duke than of the Duke's daughter.

'Oh yes, I can drive you down if you like that kind of thing,' Silverbridge said to him on the Saturday evening.

'And bring me back?'

'If you will come when I am coming. I hate waiting for a fellow.'

'Suppose we leave at half-past ten.'

'I won't fix any time; but if we can't make it suit there'll be the governor's carriage.'

'Will the Duke go down in his carriage?'

'I suppose so. It's quicker and less trouble than the railway.' Then Lord Popplecourt reflected that he would certainly come back with the Duke if he could so manage it, and there floated before his eyes visions of under-secretaryships, all of which might owe their origin to this proposed drive up from Richmond.

At six o'clock on the Sunday evening Silverbridge called for Lord Popplecourt. 'Upon my word,' said he, 'I didn't ever expect to see you in my cab.'

'Why not me especially?'

'Because you're not one of our lot.'

'You'd sooner have Tifto, I dare say.'

'No, I wouldn't. Tifto is not at all a pleasant companion, though he understands horses. You're going in for heavy politics, I suppose.'

'Not particularly heavy.'

'If not, why on earth does my governor take you up? You won't mind my smoking, I dare say.' After this there was no conversation between them.

## CHAPTER 35

### 'DON'T YOU THINK——?'

I T was pretty to see the Duke's reception of Lady Mabel. 'I knew your mother many years ago,' he said, 'when I was young myself. Her mother and my mother were first cousins and dear friends.' He held her hand as he spoke and looked at her as though he meant to love her. Lady Mabel saw that it was so. Could it be possible that the Duke had heard anything;—that he should wish to receive her? She had told herself and had told Miss Cassewary that though she had spared Silverbridge, yet she knew that she would make him a good wife. If the Duke thought so also, then surely she need not doubt.

'I knew we were cousins,' she said, 'and have been so proud of the connection! Lord Silverbridge does come and see us sometimes.'

Soon after that Silverbridge and Popplecourt came in. If the story of the old woman in the portrait may be taken as evidence of a family connexion between Lady Cantrip and Lord Popplecourt, everybody there was more or less connected with everybody else. Nidderdale had been a first cousin of Lady Glencora, and he had married a daughter of Lady Cantrip. They were manifestly a family party,—thanks to the old woman in the picture.

It is a point of conscience among the—perhaps not ten thousand,* but say one thousand of bluest blood,—that everybody should know who everybody is. Our Duke, though he had not given his mind much to the pursuit, had nevertheless learned his lesson. It is a knowledge which the possession of the blue blood itself produces. There are countries with bluer blood than our own in which to be without such knowledge is a crime.

When the old lady in the portrait had been discussed, Popplecourt was close to Lady Mary. They two had no idea why such vicinity had been planned. The Duke knew, of course, and Lady Cantrip. Lady Cantrip had whispered to her daughter that such a marriage would be suitable, and the daughter had hinted it to her husband. Lord Cantrip of course was not in the dark. Lady Mabel had expressed a hint on the matter to Miss Cass, who had not repudiated it. Even Silverbridge had suggested to himself that something of the kind might be in the wind, thinking that, if so, none of them knew much about his sister Mary. But Popplecourt himself was divinely innocent. His ideas of marriage had as yet gone no farther than a conviction that girls generally were things which would be pressed on him, and against which he must arm himself with some shield. Marriage would have to come, no doubt; but not the less was it his duty to live as though it were a pit towards which he would be tempted by female allurements. But that a net should be spread over him here he was much too humble-minded to imagine.

'Very hot,' he said to Lady Mary.

'We found it warm in church to-day.'

'I dare say. I came down here with your brother in his hansom cab. What a very odd thing to have a hansom cab!'

'I should like one.'

'Should you indeed?'

'Particularly if I could drive it myself. Silverbridge does, at night, when he thinks people won't see him.'

'Drive the cab in the streets! What does he do with his man?'

'Puts him inside. He was out once without the man and took up a fare,—an old woman, he said. And when she was going to pay him he touched his hat and said he never took money from ladies.'

'Do you believe that?'

'Oh yes. I call that good fun, because it did no harm. He had his lark. The lady was taken where she wanted to go, and she saved her money.'

'Suppose he had upset her,' said Lord Popplecourt, looking as an old philosopher might have looked when he had found some clenching answer to another philosopher's argument.

'The real cabman might have upset her worse,' said Lady Mary.

'Don't you feel it odd that we should meet here?' said Lord Silverbridge to his neighbour, Lady Mabel.

'Anything unexpected is odd,' said Lady Mabel. It seemed to her to be very odd,—unless certain people had made up their minds as to the expediency of a certain event.

'That is what you call logic;—isn't it? Anything unexpected is odd!'

'Lord Silverbridge, I won't be laughed at. You have been at Oxford and ought to know what logic is.'

'That at any rate is ill-natured,' he replied, turning very red in the face.

'You don't think I meant it. Oh, Lord Silverbridge, say that you don't think I meant it. You cannot think I would willingly wound you. Indeed, indeed, I was not thinking.' It had in truth been an accident. She could not speak aloud because they were closely surrounded by others, but she looked up in his face to see whether he were angry with her. 'Say that you do not think I meant it.'

'I do not think you meant it.'

'I would not say a word to hurt you,—oh, for more than I can tell you.'

'It is all bosh, of course,' he said laughing; 'but I do not like to hear the old place named. I have always made a fool of myself. Some men do it and don't care about it. But I do it, and yet it makes me miserable.'

'If that be so you will soon give over making—what you call a fool of yourself. For myself I like the idea of wild oats. I look upon them like measles. Only you should have a doctor ready when the disease shows itself.'

'What sort of a doctor ought I to have?'

'Ah;—you must find out that yourself. That sort of feeling which makes you feel miserable;—that is a doctor itself.'

'Or a wife?'

'Or a wife,—if you can find a good one. There are wives, you know, who aggravate the disease. If I had a fast* husband I should make him faster by being fast myself. There is nothing I envy so much as the power of doing half-mad things.'

'Women can do that too.'

'But they go to the dogs. We are dreadfully restricted. If you like champagne you can have a bucketful. I am obliged to pretend that I only want a very little. You can bet thousands. I must confine myself to gloves. You can flirt with any woman you please. I must wait till some-body comes,—and put up with it if nobody does come.'

'Plenty come, no doubt.'

'But I want to pick and choose. A man turns the girls over one after another as one does the papers when one is fitting up a room, or rolls them out as one rolls out the carpets. A very careful young man like Lord Popplecourt might reject a young woman because her hair didn't suit the colour of his furniture.'

'I don't think that I shall choose my wife as I would papers and carpets.'

The Duke, who sat between Lady Cantrip and her daughter, did his best to make himself agreeable. The conversation had been semi-political,—political to the usual feminine extent, and had consisted chiefly of sarcasms from Lady Cantrip against Sir Timothy Beeswax. 'That England should put up with such a man,' Lady Cantrip had said, 'is to me shocking! There used to be a feeling in favour of gentlemen.' To this the Duke had responded by asserting that Sir Timothy had displayed great aptitude for parliamentary life, and knew the House of Commons better than most men. He said nothing against his foe, and very much in his foe's praise. But Lady Cantrip perceived that she had succeeded in pleasing him.

When the ladies were gone the politics became more serious. 'That unfortunate quarrel* is to go on the same as ever, I suppose,' said the Duke, addressing himself to the two young men who had seats in the House of Commons. They were both on the Conservative side in politics. The three peers present were all Liberals.

'Till next session, I think, sir,' said Silverbridge.

'Sir Timothy, though he did lose his temper, has managed it well,' said Lord Cantrip.

'Phineas Finn lost his temper worse than Sir Timothy,' said Lord Nidderdale.

'But yet I think he had the feeling of the House with him,' said the Duke. 'I happened to be present in the gallery at the time.'

'Yes,' said Nidderdale, 'because he "owned up." The fact is if you "own up" in a genial sort of way the House will forgive anything.

If I were to murder my grandmother, and when questioned about it were to acknowledge that I had done it——' Then Lord Nidderdale stood up and made his speech as he might have made it in the House of Commons. ' "I regret to say, sir, that the old woman did get in my way when I was in a passion. Unfortunately I had a heavy stick in my hand and I did strike her over the head. Nobody can regret it so much as I do! Nobody can feel so acutely the position in which I am placed! I have sat in this House for many years, and many gentlemen know me well. I think, Sir, that they will acknowledge that I am a man not deficient in filial piety or general humanity. Sir, I am sorry for what I did in a moment of heat. I have now spoken the truth, and I shall leave myself in the hands of the House." My belief is I should get such a round of applause as I certainly shall never achieve in any other way. It is not only that a popular man may do it,—like Phineas Finn,—but the most unpopular man in the House may make himself liked by owning freely that he has done something that he ought to be ashamed of.' Nidderdale's unwonted eloquence was received in good part by the assembled legislators.

'Taking it altogether,' said the Duke, 'I know of no assembly in any country in which good-humour prevails so generally, in which the members behave to each other so well, in which rules are so universally followed, or in which the president is so thoroughly sustained by the feeling of the members.'

'I hear men say that it isn't quite what it used to be,'* said Silverbridge.

'Nothing will ever be quite what it used to be.'

'Changes for the worse, I mean. Men are doing all kinds of things, just because the rules of the House allow them.'

'If they be within rule,' said the Duke, 'I don't know who is to blame them. In my time, if any man stretched a rule too far the House would not put up with it.'

'That's just it,' said Nidderdale. 'The House puts up with anything now. There is a great deal of good feeling no doubt, but there's no earnestness about anything. I think you are more earnest than we; but then you are such horrid bores. And each earnest man is in earnest about something that nobody else cares for.'

When they were again in the drawing-room, Lord Popplecourt was seated next to Lady Mary. 'Where are you going this autumn?' he asked.

'I don't know in the least. Papa said something about going abroad.'

'You won't be at Custins?' Custins was Lord Cantrip's country seat in Dorsetshire.

'I know nothing about myself as yet. But I don't think I shall go anywhere unless papa goes too.'

'Lady Cantrip has asked me to be at Custins in the middle of October. They say it is about the best pheasant-shooting in England.'

'Do you shoot much?'

'A great deal. I shall be in Scotland on the Twelfth.* I and Reginald Dobbs have a place together. I shall get to my own partridges on the 1st of September. I always manage that. Popplecourt is in Suffolk, and I don't think any man in England can beat me for partridges.'

'What do you do with all you slay?'

'Leadenhall Market.* I make it pay,—or very nearly. Then I shall run back to Scotland for the end of the stalking, and I can easily manage to be at Custins by the middle of October. I never touch my own pheasants till November.'

'Why are you so abstemious?'

'The birds are heavier and it answers better. But if I thought you would be at Custins it would be much nicer.' Lady Mary again told him that as yet she knew nothing of her father's autumn movements.

But at the same time the Duke was arranging his autumn movements, or at any rate those of his daughter. Lady Cantrip had told him that the desirable son-in-law had promised to go to Custins, and suggested that he and Mary should also be there. In his daughter's name he promised, but he would not bind himself. Would it not be better that he should be absent? Now that the doing of this thing was brought nearer to him so that he could see and feel its details, he was disgusted by it. And yet it had answered so well with his wife!

'Is Lord Popplecourt intimate here?' Lady Mabel asked her friend, Lord Silverbridge.

'I don't know. I am not.'

'Lady Cantrip seems to think a great deal about him.'

'I dare say. I don't.'

'Your father seems to like him.'

'That's possible too. They're going back to London together in the governor's carriage. My father will talk high politics all the way, and Popplecourt will agree with everything.'

'He isn't intended to—to——? You know what I mean.'

'I can't say that I do.'

'To cut out poor Frank.'

'It's quite possible.'

'Poor Frank!'

'You had a great deal better say poor Popplecourt!—or poor governor, or poor Lady Cantrip.'

'But a hundred countesses can't make your sister marry a man she doesn't like.'

'Just that. They don't go the right way about it.'

'What would you do?'

'Leave her alone. Let her find out gradually that what she wants can't be done.'

'And so linger on for years,' said Lady Mabel reproachfully.

'I say nothing about that. The man is my friend.'

'And you ought to be proud of him.'

'I never knew anybody yet that was proud of his friends. I like him well enough, but I can quite understand that the governor should object.'

'Yes, we all know that,' said she sadly.

'What would your father say if you wanted to marry someone who hadn't a shilling?'

'I should object myself,—without waiting for my father. But then,—neither have I a shilling. If I had money, do you think I wouldn't like to give it to the man I loved?'

'But this is a case of giving somebody else's money. They won't make her give it up by bringing such a young ass as that down here. If my father has persistency enough to let her cry her eyes out, he'll succeed.'

'And break her heart. Could you do that?'

'Certainly not. But then I'm soft. I can't refuse.'

'Can't you?'

'Not if the person who asks me is in my good books. You try me.'

'What shall I ask for?'

'Anything.'

'Give me that ring off your finger,' she said. He at once took it off his hand. 'Of course you know I am in joke. You don't imagine that I would take it from you?' He still held it towards her. 'Lord Silverbridge, I expect that with you I may say a foolish word without being brought to sorrow by it. I know that that ring belonged to your great-uncle,—and to fifty Pallisers before.'

'What would it matter?'

'And it would be wholly useless to me, as I could not wear it.'

'Of course it would be too big,' said he, replacing the ring on his own finger. 'But when I talk of anyone being in my good books, I don't

mean a thing like that. Don't you know there is nobody on earth I———'
there he paused and blushed, and she sat motionless, looking at
him expecting, with her colour too somewhat raised,—'whom I like so
well as I do you?' It was a lame conclusion. She felt it to be lame. But
as regarded him, the lameness at the moment had come from a timidity
which forbade him to say the word 'love' even though he had meant to
say it.

She recovered herself instantly. 'I do believe it,' she said. 'I do think
that we are real friends.'

'Would you not take a ring from a—real friend?'

'Not that ring;—nor a ring at all after I had asked for it in joke. You
understand it all. But to go back to what we were talking about,—if you
can do anything for Frank, pray do. You know it will break her heart.
A man of course bears it better, but he does not perhaps suffer the
less. It is all his life to him. He can do nothing while this is going on.
Are you not true enough to your friendship to exert yourself for him?'
Silverbridge put his hand up and rubbed his head as though he were
vexed. 'Your aid would turn everything in his favour.'

'You do not know my father.'

'Is he so inexorable?'

'It is not that, Mabel. But he is so unhappy. I cannot add to his
unhappiness by taking part against him.'

In another part of the room Lady Cantrip was busy with Lord
Popplecourt. She had talked about pheasants, and had talked about
grouse, had talked about moving the address in the House of Lords in
some coming Session, and the great value of political alliances early in
life, till the young peer began to think that Lady Cantrip was the nicest
of women. Then after a short pause she changed the subject.

'Don't you think Lady Mary very beautiful?'

'Uncommon,' said his Lordship.

'And her manners so perfect. She has all her mother's ease without
any of that—— You know what I mean.'

'Quite so,' said his Lordship.

'And then she has got so much in her.'

'Has she though?'

'I don't know any girl of her age so thoroughly well educated. The
Duke seems to take to you.'

'Well, yes;—the Duke is very kind.'

'Don't you think——?'

'Eh!'

'You have heard of her mother's fortune?'

'Tremendous!'

'She will have, I take it, quite a third of it. Whatever I say I'm sure you will take in confidence; but she is a dear dear girl; and I am anxious for her happiness almost as though she belonged to me.'

Lord Popplecourt went back to town in the Duke's carriage, but was unable to say a word about politics. His mind was altogether filled with the wonderful words that had been spoken to him. Could it be that Lady Mary had fallen violently in love with him? He would not at once give himself up to the pleasing idea, having so thoroughly grounded himself in the belief that female nets were to be avoided. But when he got home he did think favourably of it. The daughter of a Duke,—and such a Duke! So lovely a girl, and with such gifts! And then a fortune which would make a material addition to his own large property!

## CHAPTER 36

### TALLY-HO LODGE

We all know that very clever distich\* concerning the great fleas and the little fleas which tells us that no animal is too humble to have its parasite. Even Major Tifto had his inferior friend. This was a certain Captain Green,—for the friend also affected military honours. He was a man somewhat older than Tifto, of whose antecedents no one was supposed to know anything. It was presumed of him that he lived by betting, and it was boasted by those who wished to defend his character that when he lost he paid his money like a gentleman. Tifto during the last year or two had been anxious to support Captain Green, and had always made use of this argument: 'Where the d—— he gets his money I don't know;—but when he loses, there it is.'

Major Tifto had a little 'box' of his own in the neighbourhood of Egham, at which he had a set of stables a little bigger than his house, and a set of kennels a little bigger than his stables. It was here he kept his horses and hounds, and himself too when business connected with his sporting life did not take him to town. It was now the middle of August and he had come to Tally-ho Lodge, there to look after his establishments, to make arrangements for cub-hunting, and to prepare for the autumn racing campaign. On this occasion Captain Green was enjoying his hospitality and assisting him by sage counsels. Behind the little box was a little garden,—a garden that was very little; but, still, thus close to the parlour window, there was room for a small table to be put on the grass-plat,* and for a couple of armchairs. Here the Major and the Captain were seated about eight o'clock one evening, with convivial good things within their reach. The good things were gin-and-water and pipes. The two gentlemen had not dressed strictly for dinner. They had spent a great part of the day handling the hounds and the horses, dressing wounds, curing sores, and ministering to canine ailments, and had been detained over their work too long to think of their toilet. As it was they had an eye to business. The stables at one corner and the kennels at the other were close to the little garden, and the doings of a man and a boy who were still at work among the animals could be directed from the armchairs on which the two sportsmen were sitting.

It must be explained that ever since the Silverbridge election there had been a growing feeling in Tifto's mind that he had been ill-treated by his partner. The feeling was strengthened by the admirable condition of Prime Minister. Surely more consideration had been due to a man who had produced such a state of things!

'I wouldn't quarrel with him, but I'd make him pay his way,' said the prudent Captain.

'As for that, of course he does pay—his share.'

'Who does all the work?'

'That's true.'

'The fact is, Tifto, you don't make enough out of it. When a small man like you has to deal with a big man like that, he may take it out of him in one of two ways. But he must be deuced clever if he can get it both ways.'

'What are you driving at?' asked Tifto, who did not like being called a small man, feeling himself to be every inch a master of foxhounds.

'Why, this!—Look at that d—— fellow fretting that 'orse with a switch. If you can't strap a 'orse* without a stick in your hand, don't you strap him at all, you——.' Then there came a volley of abuse out of the Captain's mouth, in the middle of which the man threw down the rubber he was using and walked away.

'You come back,' hallooed Tifto, jumping up from his seat with his pipe in his mouth. Then there was a general quarrel between the man and his two masters, in which the man at last was victorious. And the horse was taken into the stable in an unfinished condition. 'It's all very well to say "Get rid of him," but where am I to get anybody better? It has come to such a pass that now if you speak to a fellow he walks out of the yard.'

They then returned to the state of affairs, as it was between Tifto and Lord Silverbridge. 'What I was saying is this,' continued the Captain. 'If you choose to put yourself up to live with a fellow like that on equal terms——'

'One gentleman with another, you mean?'

'Put it so. It don't quite hit it off, but put it so. Why then you get your wages when you take his arm and call him Silverbridge.'

'I don't want wages from any man,' said the indignant Major.

'That comes from not knowing what wages is. I do want wages. If I do a thing I like to be paid for it. You are paid for it after one fashion, I prefer the other.'

'Do you mean he should give me——a salary?'

'I'd have it out of him some way. What's the good of young chaps of that sort if they aren't made to pay? You've got this young swell in tow. He's going to be about the richest man in England;—and what the deuce better are you for it?' Tifto sat meditating, thinking of the wisdom which was being spoken. The same ideas had occurred to him. The happy chance which had made him intimate with Lord Silverbridge had not yet enriched him. 'What is the good of chaps of that sort if they are not made to pay?' The words were wise words. But yet how glorious he had been when he was elected at the Beargarden, and had entered the club as the special friend of the heir of the Duke of Omnium.

After a short pause, Captain Green pursued his discourse. 'You said salary.'

'I did mention the word.'

'Salary and wages is one. A salary is a nice thing if it's paid regular. I had a salary once myself for looking after a stud of 'orses at Newmarket, only the gentleman broke up and it never went very far.'

'Was that Marley Bullock?'

'Yes; that was Marley Bullock. He's abroad somewhere now with nothing a year paid quarterly to live on. I think he does a little at cards. He'd had a good bit of money once, but most of it was gone when he came my way.'

'You didn't make by him?'

'I didn't lose nothing. I didn't have a lot of 'orses under me without getting something out of it.'

'What am I to do?' asked Tifto. 'I can sell him a horse now and again. But if I give him anything good there isn't much to come out of that.'

'Very little I should say. Don't he put his money on his 'orses?'

'Not very free. I think he's coming out freer now.'

'What did he stand to win on the Derby?'

'A thousand or two perhaps.'

'There may be something got handsome out of that,' said the Captain, not venturing to allow his voice to rise above a whisper. Major Tifto looked hard at him but said nothing. 'Of course you must see your way.'

'I don't quite understand.'

'Race 'orses are expensive animals,—and races generally is expensive.'

'That's true.'

'When so much is dropped, somebody has to pick it up. That's what I've always said to myself. I'm as honest as another man.'

'That's of course,' said the Major civilly.

'But if I don't keep my mouth shut, somebody'll have my teeth out of my head. Every one for himself and God for us all. I suppose there's a deal of money flying about. He'll put a lot of money on this 'orse of yours for the Leger if he's managed right. There's more to be got out of that than calling him Silverbridge and walking arm-in-arm. Business is business. I don't know whether I make myself understood.'

The gentleman did not quite make himself understood; but Tifto endeavoured to read the riddle. He must in some way make money out of his friend Lord Silverbridge. Hitherto he had contented himself with the brilliancy of the connection; but now his brilliant friend had taken to snubbing him, and had on more than one occasion made himself disagreeable. It seemed to him that Captain Green counselled him to put up with that, but counselled him at the same time to—pick up some of his friend's money. He didn't think that he could ask Lord Silverbridge for a salary—he who was a Master of Foxhounds, and a member of the Beargarden. Then his friend had suggested something about the young lord's bets. He was endeavouring to unriddle all this with a brain that was already somewhat muddled with alcohol, when Captain Green got up from his chair and standing over the Major spoke his last words for that night as from an oracle. 'Square is all very well, as long as others are square to you;—but when they aren't, then I say square be d——. Square! what comes of it? Work your heart out, and then it's no good.'

The Major thought about it much that night, and was thinking about it still when he awoke on the next morning. He would like to make Lord Silverbridge pay for his late insolence. It would answer his purpose to make a little money,—as he told himself,—in any honest way. At the present moment he was in want of money, and on looking into his affairs declared to himself that he had certainly impoverished himself by his devotion to Lord Silverbridge's interests. At breakfast on the following morning he endeavoured to bring his friend back to the subject. But the Captain was cross, rather than oracular. 'Everybody,' he said, 'ought to know his own business. He wasn't going to meddle or make. What he had said had been taken amiss.' This was hard upon Tifto, who had taken nothing amiss.

'Square be d——!' There was a great deal in the lesson there enunciated which demanded consideration. Hitherto the Major had fought his battles with a certain adherence to squareness. If his angles had not all been perfect angles, still there had always been an attempt at geometrical accuracy. He might now and again have told a lie about a horse—but who that deals in horses has not done that? He had been alive to the value of underhand information from racing-stables, but who won't use a tip if he can get it? He had lied about the expense of his hounds, in order to enhance the subscription of his members. Those were things which everybody did in his line. But Green had meant something beyond this.

As far as he could see out in the world at large, nobody was square. You had to keep your mouth shut, or your teeth would be stolen out of it. He didn't look into a paper without seeing that on all sides of him men had abandoned the idea of squareness. Chairmen, directors, members of Parliament, ambassadors,—all the world, as he told himself,—were trying to get on by their wits. He didn't see why he should be more square than anybody else. Why hadn't Silverbridge taken him down to Scotland for the grouse?

## CHAPTER 37

### GREX

FAR away from all known places, in the northern limit of the Craven district, on the borders of Westmorland but in Yorkshire, there stands a large, rambling, most picturesque old house called Grex. The people around call it the Castle, but it is not a castle. It is an old brick building supposed to have been erected in the days of James the First, having oriel windows, twisted chimneys, long galleries, gable ends, a quadrangle of which the house surrounds three sides, terraces, sun-dials, and fishponds. But it is so sadly out of repair as to be altogether unfit for the residence of a gentleman and his family. It stands not in a park, for the land about it is divided into paddocks by low stone walls, but in the midst of lovely scenery, the ground rising all round it in low irregular hills or fells, and close to it, a quarter of a mile from the back of the house, there is a small dark lake, not serenely lovely as are some of the lakes in Westmorland, but attractive by the darkness of its waters and the gloom of the woods around it.

This is the country seat of Earl Grex,—which however he had not visited for some years. Gradually the place had got into such a condition that his absence is not surprising. An owner of Grex, with large means at his disposal and with a taste for the picturesque to gratify,—one who could afford to pay for memories and who was willing to pay dearly for such luxuries, might no doubt restore Grex. But the Earl had neither the money nor the taste.

Lord Grex had latterly never gone near the place, nor was his son Lord Percival fond of looking upon the ruin of his property. But Lady Mabel loved it with a fond love. With all her lightness of spirit she was prone to memories, prone to melancholy, prone at times almost to seek the gratification of sorrow. Year after year when the London season was over she would come down to Grex and spend a week or two amidst its desolation. She was now going on to a seat in Scotland belonging to Mrs Montacute Jones called Killancodlem; but she was in the meanwhile passing a desolate fortnight at Grex in company with Miss Cassewary. The gardens were let,—and being let of course were not kept in further order than as profit might require. The man who rented them lived in the big house with his wife, and they on such occasions as this would cook and wait upon Lady Mabel.

Lady Mabel was at the home of her ancestors, and the faithful Miss Cass was with her. But at the moment and at the spot at which the reader shall see her, Miss Cass was not with her. She was sitting on a rock about twelve feet above the lake looking upon the black water; and on another rock a few feet from her was seated Frank Tregear. 'No,' she said, 'you should not have come. Nothing can justify it. Of course as you are here I could not refuse to come out with you. To make a fuss about it would be the worst of all. But you should not have come.'

'Why not? Whom does it hurt? It is a pleasure to me. If it be the reverse to you, I will go.'

'Men are so unmanly. They take such mean advantages. You know it is a pleasure to me to see you.'

'I had hoped so.'

'But it is a pleasure I ought not to have,—at least not here.'

'That is what I do not understand,' said he. 'In London, where the Earl could bark at me if he happened to find me, I could see the inconvenience of it. But here, where there is nobody but Miss Cass——'

'There are a great many others. There are the rooks, and stones, and old women;—all of which have ears.'

'But of what is there to be ashamed? There is nothing in the world to me so pleasant as the companionship of my friends.'

'Then go after Silverbridge.'

'I mean to do so;—but I am taking you by the way.'

'It is all unmanly,' she said, rising from her stone; 'you know that it is so. Friends! Do you mean to say that it would make no difference whether you were here with me or with Miss Cass?'

'The greatest difference in the world.'

'Because she is an old woman and I am a young one, and because in intercourse between young men and young women there is something dangerous to the women and therefore pleasant to the men.'

'I never heard anything more unjust. You cannot think I desire anything injurious to you.'

'I do think so.' She was still standing and spoke now with great vehemence. 'I do think so. You force me to throw aside the reticence I ought to keep. Would it help me in my prospects if your friend Lord Silverbridge knew that I was here?'

'How should he know?'

'But if he did? Do you suppose that I want to have visits paid to me of which I am afraid to speak? Would you dare to tell Lady Mary that you had been sitting alone with me on the rocks at Grex?'

'Certainly I would.'

'Then it would be because you have not dared to tell her certain other things which have gone before. You have sworn to her no doubt that you love her better than all the world.'

'I have.'

'And you have taken the trouble to come here to tell me that,—to wound me to the core by saying so; to show me that, though I may still be sick, you have recovered,—that is if you ever suffered! Go your way and let me go mine. I do not want you.'

'Mabel!'

'I do not want you. I know you will not help me, but you need not destroy me.'

'You know that you are wronging me.'

'No! You understand it all though you look so calm. I hate your

Lady Mary Palliser. There! But if by anything I could do I could secure her to you I would do it,—because you want it.'

'She will be your sister-in-law,—probably.'

'Never. It will never be so.'

'Why do you hate her?'

'There again! You are so little of a man that you can ask me why!' Then she turned away as though she intended to go down to the marge* of the lake.

But he rose up and stopped her. 'Let us have this out, Mabel, before we go,' he said. 'Unmanly is a heavy word to hear from you, and you have used it a dozen times.'

'It is because I have thought it a thousand times. Go and get her if you can;—but why tell me about it?'

'You said you would help me.'

'So I would, as I would help you do anything you might want; but you can hardly think that after what has passed I can wish to hear about her.'

'It was you spoke of her.'

'I told you you should not be here,—because of her and because of me. And I tell you again, I hate her. Do you think I can hear you speak of her as though she were the only woman you had ever seen without feeling it? Did you ever swear that you loved any one else?'

'Certainly, I have so sworn.'

'Have you ever said that nothing could alter that love?'

'Indeed I have.'

'But it is altered. It has all gone. It has been transferred to one who has more advantages of beauty, youth, wealth, and position.'

'Oh Mabel, Mabel!'

'But it is so.'

'When you say this do you not think of yourself?'

'Yes. But I have never been false to any one. You are false to me.'

'Have I not offered to face all the world with you?'

'You would not offer it now?'

'No,' he said, after a pause,—'not now. Were I to do so, I should be false. You bade me take my love elsewhere, and I did so.'

'With the greatest ease.'

'We agreed it should be so; and you have done the same.'

'That is false. Look me in the face and tell me whether you do not know it to be false!'

'And yet I am told that I am injuring you with Silverbridge.'

'Oh,—so unmanly again! Of course I have to marry. Who does

not know it? Do you want to see me begging my bread about the streets? You have bread; or if not, you might earn it. If you marry for money——'

'The accusation is altogether unjustifiable.'

'Allow me to finish what I have to say. If you marry for money you will do that which is in itself bad, and which is also unnecessary. What other course would you recommend me to take? No one goes into the gutter while there is a clean path open. If there be no escape but through the gutter, one has to take it.'

'You mean that my duty to you should have kept me from marrying all my life.'

'Not that;—but a little while, Frank; just a little while. Your bloom is not fading; your charms are not running from you. Have you not a strength which I cannot have? Do you not feel that you are a tree, standing firm in the ground, while I am a bit of ivy that will be trodden in the dirt unless it can be made to cling to something? You should not liken yourself to me, Frank.'

'If I could do you any good!'

'Good! What is the meaning of good? If you love, it is good to be loved again. It is good not to have your heart torn in pieces. You know that I love you.' He was standing close to her, and put out his hand as though he would twine his arm round her waist. 'Not for worlds,' she said. 'It belongs to that Palliser girl. And as I have taught myself to think that what there is left of me may perhaps belong to some other one, worthless as it is, I will keep it for him. I love you,—but there can be none of that softness of love between us.' Then there was a pause, but as he did not speak she went on. 'But remember, Frank,—our position is not equal. You have got over your little complaint. It probably did not go deep with you, and you have found a cure. Perhaps there is a satisfaction in finding that two young women love you.'

'You are trying to be cruel to me.'

'Why else should you be here? You know I love you,—with all my heart, with all my strength, and that I would give the world to cure myself. Knowing this, you come and talk to me of your passion for this other girl.'

'I had hoped we might both talk rationally as friends.'

'Friends! Frank Tregear, I have been bold enough to tell you I love you; but you are not my friend, and cannot be my friend. If I have before asked you to help me in this mean catastrophe of mine, in my attack upon that poor boy, I withdraw my request. I think I will go back to the house now.'

'I will walk back to Ledburgh if you wish it without going to the house again.'

'No; I will have nothing that looks like being ashamed. You ought not to have come, but you need not run away.' Then they walked back to the house together and found Miss Cassewary on the terrace. 'We have been to the lake,' said Mabel, 'and have been talking of old days. I have but one ambition now in the world.' Of course Miss Cassewary asked what the remaining ambition was. 'To get money enough to purchase this place from the ruins of the Grex property. If I could own the house and the lake, and the paddocks about, and had enough income to keep one servant and bread for us to eat—of course including you, Miss Cass——'

'Thank'ee, my dear; but I am not sure I should like it.'

'Yes; you would. Frank would come and see us perhaps once a year. I don't suppose anybody else cares about the place, but to me it is the dearest spot in the world.' So she went on in almost high spirits, though alluding to the general decadence of the Grex family, till Tregear took his leave.

'I wish he had not come,' said Miss Cassewary when he was gone.

'Why should you wish that? There is not so much here to amuse me that you should begrudge me a stray visitor.'

'I don't think that I grudge you anything in the way of pleasure, my dear; but still he should not have come. My lord, if he knew it, would be angry.'

'Then let him be angry. Papa does not do so much for me that I am bound to think of him at every turn.'

'But I am,—or rather I am bound to think of myself, if I take his bread.'

'Bread!'

'Well;—I do take his bread, and I take it on the understanding that I will be to you what a mother might be,—or an aunt.'

'Well,—and if so! Had I a mother living would not Frank Tregear have come to visit her, and in visiting her, would he not have seen me,—and should we not have walked out together?'

'Not after all that has come and gone.'

'But you are not a mother nor yet an aunt, and you have to do just what I tell you. And don't I know that you trust me in all things? And am I not trustworthy?'

'I think you are trustworthy.'

'I know what my duty is and I mean to do it. No one shall ever have to say of me that I have given way to self-indulgence. I couldn't help his coming, you know.'

That same night, after Miss Cassewary had gone to bed, when the moon was high in the heavens and the world around her was all asleep, Lady Mabel again wandered out to the lake, and again seated herself on the same rock, and there she sat thinking of her past life and trying to think of that before her. It is so much easier to think of the past than of the future—to remember what has been than to resolve what shall be! She had reminded him of the offer which he had made and repeated to her more than once,—to share with her all his chances in life. There would have been almost no income for them. All the world would have been against her. She would have caused his ruin. Her light on the matter had been so clear that it had not taken her very long to decide that such a thing must not be thought of. She had at last been quite stern in her decision.

Now she was broken-hearted because she found that he had left her in very truth. Oh yes;—she would marry the boy, if she could so arrange. Since that meeting at Richmond he had sent her the ring reset. She was to meet him down in Scotland within a week or two from the present time. Mrs Montacute Jones had managed that. He had all but offered to her a second time at Richmond. But all that would not serve to make her happy. She declared to herself that she did not wish to see Frank Tregear again; but still it was a misery to her that his heart should in truth be given to another woman.

## CHAPTER 38

### CRUMMIE-TODDIE

ALMOST at the last moment Silverbridge and his brother Gerald were induced to join Lord Popplecourt's shooting-party in Scotland. The party perhaps might more properly be called the party of Reginald Dobbes, who was a man knowing in such matters. It was he who made the party up. Popplecourt and Silverbridge were to share the expense between them, each bringing three guns. Silverbridge brought his brother and Frank Tregear,—having refused a most piteous petition on the subject from Major Tifto. With Popplecourt of course came Reginald Dobbes, who was, in truth, to manage everything, and Lord Nidderdale, whose wife had generously permitted him this recreation. The shooting was in the west of Perthshire, known as Crummie-Toddie, and comprised an enormous acreage of so-called forest and moor. Mr Dobbes declared that nothing like it had as yet been produced in Scotland. Everything had been made to give way to deer and grouse. The thing had been managed so well that the tourist nuisance had been considerably abated. There was hardly a potato patch left in the district, nor a head of cattle to be seen. There were no inhabitants remaining, or so few that they could be absorbed in game-preserving or cognate duties. Reginald Dobbes, who was very great at grouse, and supposed to be capable of outwitting a deer by venatical* wiles more perfectly than any other sportsman in Great Britain, regarded Crummie-Toddie as the nearest thing there was to a Paradise on earth. Could he have been allowed to pass one or two special laws for his own protection, there might still have been improvement. He would like the right to have all intruders thrashed by the gillies* within an inch of their lives; and he would have had a clause in his lease against the making of any new roads, opening of footpaths, or building of bridges. He had seen somewhere in print a plan for running a railway from Callender to Fort Augustus right through Crummie-Toddie! If this were done in his time the beauty of the world would be over. Reginald Dobbes was a man of about forty, strong, active, well-made, about five feet ten in height, with broad shoulders and greatly-developed legs. He was not a handsome man, having a protrusive nose, high cheek-bones, and long upper lip; but there was a manliness about his face which redeemed it. Sport was the business of his life, and he thoroughly despised all who were not sportsmen. He fished and shot and hunted during nine or ten months of the year, filling up his time as best he might with coaching, polo, and pigeon-shooting. He regarded it as a great duty to keep his body in the firmest possible condition. All his eating and all his drinking was done upon a system, and he would consider himself to be guilty of weak self-indulgence were he to allow himself to break through sanitary rules. But it never occurred to him that his whole life was one of self-indulgence.* He could walk his thirty miles with his gun on his shoulder as well now as he could ten years ago; and being sure of this, was thoroughly contented with himself. He had a patrimony amounting to perhaps £1000 a year, which he husbanded so as to enjoy all his amusements to perfection. No one had ever heard of his sponging on his friends. Of money he rarely spoke, sport being in his estimation the only subject worthy of a man's words. Such was Reginald Dobbes, who was now to be the master of the shooting at Crummie-Toddie.

Crummie-Toddie was but twelve miles from Killancodlem, Mrs Montacute Jones's highland seat; and it was this vicinity which first induced Lord Silverbridge to join the party. Mabel Grex was to be at Killancodlem, and, determined as he still was to ask her to be his wife, he would make this his opportunity. Of real opportunity there had been none at Richmond. Since he had had his ring altered and had sent it to her there had come but a word or two of answer. 'What am I to say? You unkindest of men! To keep it or to send it back would make me equally miserable. I shall keep it till you are married, and then give it to your wife.' This affair of the ring had made him more intent than ever. After that he heard that Isabel Boncassen would also be at Killancodlem, having been induced to join Mrs Montacute Jones's swarm of visitors. Though he was dangerously devoid of experience, still he felt that this was unfortunate. He intended to marry Mabel Grex. And he could assure himself that he thoroughly loved her. Nevertheless he liked making love to Isabel Boncassen. He was quite willing to marry and settle down, and looked forward with satisfaction to having Mabel Grex for his wife. But it would be pleasant to have a six-months run of flirting and love-making before this settlement, and he had certainly never seen anyone with whom this would be so delightful as with Miss Boncassen. But that the two ladies should be at the same house was unfortunate.

He and Gerald reached Crummie-Toddie late on the evening of August 11th, and found Reginald Dobbes alone. That was on Wednesday. Popplecourt and Nidderdale ought to have made their appearance on that morning, but had telegraphed to say that they would be detained two days on their route. Tregear, whom hitherto Dobbes had never seen, had left his arrival uncertain. This carelessness on such matters was very offensive to Mr Dobbes, who loved discipline and exactitude. He ought to have received the two young men with open arms because they were punctual; but he had been somewhat angered by what he considered the extreme youth of Lord Gerald. Boys who could not shoot were, he thought, putting themselves forward before their time. And Silverbridge himself was by no means a first-rate shot. Such a one as Silverbridge had to be endured because from his position and wealth he could facilitate such arrangements as these. It was much to have to do with a man who would not complain if an extra fifty pounds were wanted. But he ought to have understood that he was bound in honour to bring down competent friends. Of Tregear's shooting Dobbes had been able to learn nothing. Lord Gerald was a lad from the Universities; and Dobbes hated University lads. Popplecourt and Nidderdale were known to be efficient. They were men who could work hard and do their part of the required slaughter. Dobbes proudly knew that he could make up for some deficiency by his own prowess; but he could not struggle against three bad guns. What was the use of so perfecting Crummie-Toddie as to make it the best bit of ground for grouse and deer in Scotland, if the men who came there failed by their own incapacity to bring up the grand total of killed to a figure which would render Dobbes and Crummie-Toddie famous through the whole shooting world? He had been hard at work on other matters. Dogs had gone amiss,—or guns, and he had been made angry by the champagne which Popplecourt caused to be sent down. He knew what champagne meant. Whisky-and-water, and not much of it, was the liquor which Reginald Dobbes loved in the mountains.

'Don't you call this a very ugly country?' Silverbridge asked as soon as he arrived. Now it is the case that the traveller who travels into Argyllshire, Perthshire, and Inverness, expects to find lovely scenery; and it was also true that the country through which they had passed for the last twenty miles had been not only bleak and barren, but uninteresting and ugly. It was all rough open moorland, never rising into mountains, and graced by no running streams, by no forest scenery, almost by no foliage. The lodge itself did indeed stand close upon a little river, and was reached by a bridge that crossed it; but there was nothing pretty either in the river or the bridge. It was a placid black little streamlet, which in that portion of its course was hurried by no steepness, had no broken rocks in its bed, no trees on its low banks, and played none of those gambols which make running water beautiful. The bridge was a simple low construction with a low parapet, carrying an ordinary roadway up to the hall door. The lodge itself was as ugly as a house could be, white, of two stories, with the door in the middle and windows on each side, with a slate roof, and without a tree near it. It was in the middle of the shooting, and did not create a town around itself as do sumptuous mansions, to the great detriment of that seclusion which is favourable to game. 'Look at Killancodlem,' Dobbes had been heard to say—'a very fine house for ladies to flirt in; but if you find a deer within six miles of it I will eat him first and shoot him afterwards.' There was a Spartan simplicity about Crummie-Toddie which pleased the Spartan mind of Reginald Dobbes.

'Ugly, do you call it?'

'Infernally ugly,' said Lord Gerald.

'What did you expect to find? A big hotel, and a lot of cockneys? If you come after grouse, you must come to what the grouse thinks pretty.'

'Nevertheless, it is ugly,' said Silverbridge, who did not choose to be 'sat upon.' 'I have been at shootings in Scotland before, and sometimes they are not ugly. This I call beastly.' Whereupon Reginald Dobbes turned upon his heel and walked away.

'Can you shoot?' he said afterwards to Lord Gerald.

'I can fire off a gun, if you mean that,' said Gerald.

'You have never shot much?'

'Not what you call very much. I'm not so old as you are, you know. Everything must have a beginning.' Mr Dobbes wished 'the beginning' might have taken place elsewhere; but there had been some truth in the remark.

'What on earth made you tell him crammers* like that?' asked Silverbridge, as the brothers sat together afterwards smoking on the wall of the bridge.

'Because he made an ass of himself; asking me whether I could shoot.'

On the next morning they started at seven. Dobbes had determined to be cross, because, as he thought, the young men would certainly keep him waiting; and was cross because by their punctuality they robbed him of any just cause for offence. During the morning on the moor they were hardly ever near enough each other for much conversation, and very little was said. According to arrangement made they returned to the house for lunch, it being their purpose not to go far from home till their numbers were complete. As they came over the bridge and put down their guns near the door, Mr Dobbes spoke the first good-humoured word they had heard from his lips. 'Why did you tell me such an infernal ——, I would say lie, only perhaps you mightn't like it?'

'I told you no lie,' said Gerald.

'You've only missed two birds all the morning, and you have shot forty-two. That's uncommonly good sport.'

'What have you done?'

'Only forty,' and Mr Dobbes seemed for the moment to be gratified by his own inferiority. 'You are a deuced sight better than your brother.'

'Gerald's about the best shot I know,' said Silverbridge.

'Why didn't he tell?'

'Because you were angry when we said the place was ugly.'

'I see all about it,' said Dobbes. 'Nevertheless when a fellow comes to shoot he shouldn't complain because a place isn't pretty. What you want is a decent house as near as you can have it to your ground. If there is anything in Scotland to beat Crummie-Toddie I don't know where to find it. Shooting is shooting you know, and touring is touring.'

Upon that he took very kindly to Lord Gerald, who, even after the arrival of the other men, was second only in skill to Dobbes himself. With Nidderdale, who was an old companion, he got on very well. Nidderdale ate and drank too much, and refused to be driven beyond a certain amount of labour, but was in other respects obedient and knew what he was about. Popplecourt was disagreeable, but he was a fairly good shot and understood what was expected of him. Silverbridge was so good-humoured, that even his manifest faults,—shooting carelessly, lying in bed and wanting his dinner,—were, if not forgiven, at least endured. But Tregear was an abomination. He could shoot well enough and was active, and when he was at the work seemed to like it;—but he would stay away whole days by himself, and when spoken to would answer in a manner which seemed to Dobbes to be flat mutiny. 'We are not doing it for our bread,' said Tregear.

'I don't know what you mean.'

'There's no duty in killing a certain number of these animals.' They had been driving deer on the day before and were to continue the work on the day in question. 'I'm not paid fifteen shillings a week for doing it.'

'I suppose if you undertake to do a thing you mean to do it. Of course you're not wanted. We can make the double party without you.'

'Then why the mischief should you growl at me?'

'Because I think a man should do what he undertakes to do. A man who gets tired after three days' work of this kind would become tired if he were earning his bread.'

'Who says I am tired? I came here to amuse myself.'

'Amuse yourself!'

'And as long as it amuses me I shall shoot, and when it does not I shall give it up.'

This vexed the governor of Crummie-Toddie much. He had learned to regard himself as the arbiter of the fate of men while they were sojourning under the same autumnal roof as himself. But a defalcation which occurred immediately afterwards was worse. Silverbridge declared his intention of going over one morning to Killancodlem. Reginald Dobbes muttered a curse between his teeth, which was visible by the anger on his brow to all the party. 'I shall be back to-night, you know,' said Silverbridge.

'A lot of men and women who pretend to come there for shooting,' said Dobbes angrily, 'but do all the mischief they can.'

'One must go and see one's friends, you know.'

'Some girl!' said Dobbes.

But worse happened than the evil so lightly mentioned. Silverbridge did go over to Killancodlem; and presently there came back a man with a cart, who was to return with a certain not small proportion of his luggage.

'It's hardly honest, you know,' said Reginald Dobbes.

## CHAPTER 39

### KILLANCODLEM

MR DOBBES was probably right in his opinion that hotels, tourists, and congregations of men are detrimental to shooting. Crummie-Toddie was in all respects suited for sport. Killancodlem, though it had the name of a shooting-place, certainly was not so. Men going there took their guns. Gamekeepers were provided and gillies,—and, in a moderate quantity, game. On certain grand days a deer or two might be shot,—and would be very much talked about afterwards. But a glance at the place would suffice to show that Killancodlem was not intended for sport. It was a fine castellated mansion, with beautiful though narrow grounds, standing in the valley of the Archay River, with a mountain behind and the river in front. Between the gates and the river there was a public road on which a stage-coach ran, with loud-blown horns and the noise of many tourists. A mile beyond the Castle was the famous Killancodlem hotel which made up a hundred and twenty beds, and at which half as many more guests would sleep on occasions under the tables. And there was the Killancodlem post-office halfway between the two. At Crummie-Toddie they had to send nine miles for their letters and newspapers. At Killancodlem there was lawn-tennis* and a billiard-room and dancing every night. The costumes of the ladies were lovely, and those of the gentlemen, who were wonderful in knickerbockers, picturesque hats and variegated stockings, hardly less so. And then there were carriages and saddle-horses, and paths had been made hither and thither through the rocks and hills for the sake of the scenery. Scenery! To hear Mr Dobbes utter the single word was as good as a play. Was it for such cockney purposes as those that Scotland had been created, fit mother for grouse and deer?

Silverbridge arrived just before lunch, and was soon made to understand that it was impossible that he should go back that day. Mrs Jones was very great on that occasion. 'You are afraid of Reginald Dobbes,' she said severely.

'I think I am rather.'

'Of course you are. How came it to pass that you of all men should submit yourself to such a tyrant?'

'Good shooting, you know,' said Silverbridge.

'But you dare not call an hour your own—or your soul. Mr Dobbes and I are sworn enemies. We both like Scotland, and unfortunately we have fallen into the same neighbourhood. He looks upon me as the genius of sloth. I regard him as the incarnation of tyranny. He once said there should be no women in Scotland,—just an old one here and there, who would know how to cook grouse. I offered to go and cook his grouse!'

'Any friend of mine,' continued Mrs Jones, 'who comes down to Crummie-Toddie without staying a day or two with me,—will never be my friend any more. I do not hesitate to tell you, Lord Silverbridge, that I call for your surrender, in order that I may show my power over Reginald Dobbes. Are you a Dobbite?'

'Not thorough-going,' said Silverbridge.

'Then be a Montacute Jones-ite; or a Boncassenite, if, as is possible, you prefer a young woman to an old one.' At this moment Isabel Boncassen was standing close to them.

'Killancodlem against Crummie-Toddie for ever!' said Miss Boncassen, waving her handkerchief. As a matter of course a messenger was sent back to Crummie-Toddie for the young lord's wearing apparel.

The whole of that afternoon he spent playing lawn-tennis with Miss Boncassen. Lady Mabel was asked to join the party, but she refused, having promised to take a walk to a distant waterfall where the Codlem falls into the Archay. A gentleman in knickerbockers was to have gone with her, and two other young ladies; but when the time came she was weary, she said,—and she sat almost the entire afternoon looking at the game from a distance. Silverbridge played well, but not so well as the pretty American. With them were joined two others somewhat inferior, so that Silverbridge and Miss Boncassen were on different sides. They played game after game, and Miss Boncassen's side always won.

Very little was said between Silverbridge and Miss Boncassen which did not refer to the game. But Lady Mabel, looking on, told herself that they were making love to each other before her eyes. And why shouldn't they? She asked herself that question in perfect good faith. Why should they not be lovers? Was ever anything prettier than the girl in her country dress, active as a fawn and as graceful? Or could anything be more handsome, more attractive to a girl, more good-humoured, or better bred in his playful emulation than Silverbridge?

'When youth and pleasure meet, To chase the glowing hours with flying feet!'* she said to herself over and over again.

But why had he sent her the ring? She would certainly give him back the ring and bid him bestow it at once upon Miss Boncassen. Inconstant boy! Then she would get up and wander away for a time and rebuke herself. What right had she even to think of inconstancy? Could she be so irrational, so unjust, as to be sick for his love, as to be angry with him because he seemed to prefer another? Was she not well aware that she herself did not love him;—but that she did love another man? She had made up her mind to marry him in order that she might be a duchess, and because she could give herself to him without any of that horror which would be her fate in submitting to matrimony with one or another of the young men around her. There might be disappointment. If he escaped her there would be bitter disappointment. But seeing how it was, had she any further ground for hope? She certainly had no ground for anger!

It was thus, within her own bosom, she put questions to herself. And yet all this before her was simply a game of play in which the girl and the young man were as eager for victory as though they were children. They were thinking neither of love nor love-making. That the girl should be so lovely was no doubt a pleasure to him;—and perhaps to her also that he should be joyous to look at and sweet of voice. But he, could he have been made to tell all the truth within him, would have still owned that it was his purpose to make Mabel his wife.

When the game was over and the propositions made for further matches and the like,—Miss Boncassen said that she would betake herself to her own room. 'I never worked so hard in my life before,' she said. 'And I feel like a navvie.* I could drink beer out of a jug and eat bread and cheese. I won't play with you any more, Lord Silverbridge, because I am beginning to think it is unladylike to exert myself.'

'Are you not glad you came over?' said Lady Mabel to him as he was going off the ground almost without seeing her.

'Pretty well,' he said.

'Is not that better than stalking?'

'Lawn-tennis?'

'Yes;—lawn-tennis,—with Miss Boncassen.'

'She plays uncommonly well.'

'And so do you.'

'Ah, she has such an eye for distances.'

'And you,—what have you an eye for? Will you answer me a question?'

'Well;—yes; I think so.'

'Truly.'

'Certainly; if I do answer it.'

'Do you not think her the most beautiful creature you ever saw in your life?' He pushed back his cap and looked at her without making any immediate answer. 'I do. Now tell me what you think.'

'I think that perhaps she is.'

'I knew you would say so. You are so honest that you could not bring yourself to tell a fib,—even to me about that. Come here and sit down for a moment.' Of course he sat down by her. 'You know that Frank came to see me at Grex?'

'He never mentioned it.'

'Dear me;—how odd!'

'It was odd,' said he in a voice which showed that he was angry. She could hardly explain to herself why she told him this at the present moment. It came partly from jealousy, as though she had said to herself, 'Though he may neglect me, he shall know that there is some-one who does not;'—and partly from an eager half-angry feeling that she would have nothing concealed. There were moments with her in which she thought that she could arrange her future life in accordance with certain wise rules over which her heart should have no influence. There were others, many others, in which her feelings completely got the better of her. And now she told herself that she would be afraid of nothing. There should be no deceit, no lies!

'He went to see you at Grex!' said Silverbridge.

'Why should he not have come to me at Grex?'

'Only it is so odd that he did not mention it. It seems to me that he is always having secrets with you of some kind.'

'Poor Frank! There is no one else who would come to see me at that tumbledown old place. But I have another thing to say to you. You have behaved badly to me.'

'Have I?'

'Yes, sir. After my folly about that ring you should have known better than to send it to me. You must take it back again.'

'You shall do exactly what you said you would. You shall give it to my wife,—when I have one.'

'That did very well for me to say in a note. I did not want to send my anger to you over a distance of two or three hundred miles by the post-man. But now that we are together you must take it back.'

'I will do no such thing,' said he sturdily.

'You speak as though this were a matter in which you can have your own way.'

'I mean to have mine about that.'

'Any lady then must be forced to take any present that a gentleman may send her! Allow me to assure you that the usages of society do not run in that direction. Here is the ring. I knew that you would come over to see—well, to see someone here, and I have kept it ready in my pocket.'

'I came over to see you.'

'Lord Silverbridge! But we know that in certain employments all things are fair.' He looked at her not knowing what were the employments to which she alluded.* 'At any rate you will oblige me by—by—by not being troublesome, and putting this little trinket into your pocket.'

'Never! Nothing on earth shall make me do it.'

At Killancodlem they did not dine till half-past eight. Twilight was now stealing on these two, who were still out in the garden, all the others having gone in to dress. She looked round to see that no other eyes were watching them as she still held the ring. 'It is there,' she said, putting it on the bench between them. Then she prepared to rise from the seat so that she might leave it with him.

But he was too quick for her, and was away at a distance before she had collected her dress. And from a distance he spoke again, 'If you choose that it shall be lost, so be it.'

'You had better take it,' said she, following him slowly. But he would not turn back;—nor would she. They met again in the hall for a moment. 'I should be sorry it should be lost,' said he, 'because it belonged to my great-uncle. And I had hoped that I might live to see it very often.'

'You can fetch it,' she said, as she went to her room. He however would not fetch it. She had accepted it, and he would not take it back again, let the fate of the gem be what it might.

But to the feminine and more cautious mind the very value of the trinket made its position out there on the bench, within the grasp of any dishonest gardener, a burden to her. She could not reconcile it to her conscience that it should be so left. The diamond was a large one, and she had heard it spoken of as a stone of great value,—so much so, that Silverbridge had been blamed for wearing it ordinarily. She had asked for it in joke, regarding it as a thing which could not be given away. She could not go down herself and take it up again; but neither could she allow it to remain. As she went to her room she met Mrs Jones already coming from hers. 'You will keep us all waiting,' said the hostess.

'Oh no;—nobody ever dressed so quickly. But, Mrs Jones, will you do me a favour?'

'Certainly.'

'And will you let me explain something?'

'Anything you like,—from a hopeless engagement down to a broken garter.'

'I am suffering neither from one or the other. But there is a most valuable ring lying out in the garden. Will you send for it?' Then of course the story had to be told. 'You will, I hope, understand how I came to ask for it foolishly. It was because it was the one thing which I was sure he would not give away.'

'Why not take it?'

'Can't you understand? I wouldn't for the world. But you will be good enough,—won't you, to see that there is nothing else in it?'

'Nothing of love?'

'Nothing in the least. He and I are excellent friends. We are cousins, and intimate, and all that. I thought I might have had my joke, and now I am punished for it. As for love, don't you see he is over head and ears in love with Miss Boncassen?'

This was very imprudent on the part of Lady Mabel, who, had she been capable of clinging fast to her policy, would not now in a moment of strong feeling have done so much to raise obstacles in her own way. 'But you will send for it, won't you, and have it put on his dressing-table to-night?' When he went to bed Lord Silverbridge found it on his table.

But before that time came he had twice danced with Miss Boncassen, Lady Mabel having refused to dance with him. 'No,' she said, 'I am angry with you. You ought to have felt that it did not become you as a gentleman to subject me to inconvenience by throwing upon me the charge of that diamond. You may be foolish enough to be indifferent about its value, but as you have mixed me up with it I cannot afford to have it lost.'

'It is yours.'

'No, sir; it is not mine, nor will it ever be mine. But I wish you to understand that you have offended me.'

This made him so unhappy for the time that he almost told the story to Miss Boncassen. 'If I were to give you a ring,' he said, 'would not you accept it?'

'What a question!'

'What I mean is, don't you think all those conventional rules about men and women are absurd?'

'As a progressive American, of course I am bound to think all conventional rules are an abomination.'

'If you had a brother and I gave him a stick he'd take it.'

'Not across his back, I hope.'

'Or if I gave your father a book?'

'He'd take books to any extent, I should say.'

'And why not you a ring?'

'Who said I wouldn't? But after all this you mustn't try me.'

'I was not thinking of it.'

'I'm so glad of that! Well;—if you'll promise that you'll never offer me one, I'll promise that I'll take it when it comes. But what does all this mean?'

'It is not worth talking about.'

'You have offered somebody a ring, and somebody hasn't taken it. May I guess?'

'I had rather you did not.'

'I could, you know.'

'Never mind about that. Now come and have a turn. I am bound not to give you a ring; but you are bound to accept anything else I may offer.'

'No, Lord Silverbridge;—not at all. Nevertheless we'll have a turn.'

That night before he went up to his room he had told Isabel Boncassen that he loved her. And when he spoke he was telling her the truth. It had seemed to him that Mabel had become hard to him, and had over and over again rejected the approaches to tenderness which he had attempted to make in his intercourse with her. Even though she were to accept him, what would that be worth to him if she did not love him? So many things had been added together! Why had Tregear gone to Grex, and having gone there why had he kept his journey a secret? Tregear he knew was engaged to his sister;—but for all that, there was a closer intimacy between Mabel and Tregear than between Mabel and himself. And surely she might have taken his ring!

And then Isabel Boncassen was so perfect! Since he had first met her he had heard her loveliness talked of on all sides. It seemed to be admitted everywhere that so beautiful a creature had never before been seen in London. There is even a certain dignity attached to that which is praised by all lips. Miss Boncassen as an American girl, had she been judged to be beautiful only by his own eyes, might perhaps have seemed to him to be beneath his serious notice. In such a case he might have felt himself unable to justify so extraordinary a choice. But there was an acclamation of assent as to this girl! Then came the dancing,—the one dance after another; the pressure of the hand, the entreaty that she would not, just on this occasion, dance with any other man, the attendance on her when she took her glass of wine, the whispered encouragement of Mrs Montacute Jones, the half-resisting and yet half-yielding conduct of the girl. 'I shall not dance at all again,' she said when he asked her to stand up for another. 'Think of all that lawn-tennis this morning.'

'But you will play to-morrow?'

'I thought you were going.'

'Of course I shall stay now,' he said, and as he said it he put his hand on her hand, which was on his arm. She drew it away at once. 'I love you so dearly,' he whispered to her; 'so dearly.'

'Lord Silverbridge!'

'I do. I do. Can you say that you will love me in return?'

'I cannot,' she said slowly. 'I have never dreamed of such a thing. I hardly know now whether you are in earnest.'

'Indeed, indeed I am.'

'Then I will say good-night, and think about it. Everybody is going. We will have our game to-morrow at any rate.'

When he went to his room he found the ring on his dressing-table.


## CHAPTER 40

### 'AND THEN!'


ON the next morning Miss Boncassen did not appear at breakfast. Word came that she had been so fatigued by the lawn-tennis as not to be able to leave her bed. 'I have been to her,' said Mrs Montacute Jones, whispering to Lord Silverbridge, as though he were particularly interested. 'There's nothing really the matter. She will be down to lunch.'

'I was afraid she might be ill,' said Silverbridge, who was now hardly anxious to hide his admiration.

'Oh no;—nothing of that sort; but she will not be able to play again to-day. It was your fault. You should not have made her dance last night.' After that Mrs Jones said a word about it all to Lady Mabel. 'I hope the Duke will not be angry with me.'

'Why should he be angry with you?'

'I don't suppose he will approve of it, and perhaps he'll say I brought them together on purpose.'

Soon afterwards Mabel asked Silverbridge to walk with her to the waterfall. She had worked herself into such a state of mind that she hardly knew what to do, what to wish, or how to act. At one moment she would tell herself that it was better in every respect that she should cease to think of being Duchess of Omnium. It was not fit that she should think of it. She herself cared but little for the young man, and he—she would tell herself—now appeared to care as little for her. And yet to be Duchess of Omnium! But was it not clear that he was absolutely in love with this other girl? She had played her cards so badly that the game was now beyond her powers. Then other thoughts would come. Was it beyond her powers? Had he not told her in London that he loved her? Had he not given her the ring which she well knew he valued? Ah;—if she could but have been aware of all that had passed between Silverbridge and the Duke, how different would have been her feelings! And then would it not be so much better for him that he should marry her, one of his own class, than this American girl, of whom nobody knew anything? And then,—to be the daughter of the Duke of Omnium, to be the future Duchess, to escape from all the cares which her father's vices and follies had brought upon her, to have come to an end of all her troubles! Would it not be sweet?

She had made her mind up to nothing when she asked him to walk up to the waterfall. There was present to her only the glimmer of an idea that she ought to caution him not to play with the American girl's feelings. She knew herself to be aware that, when the time for her own action came, her feminine feelings would get the better of her purpose. She could not craftily bring him to the necessity of bestowing himself upon her. Had that been within the compass of her powers, opportunities had not been lacking to her. On such occasions she had always 'spared him.' And should the opportunity come again, again she would spare him. But she might perhaps do some good,—not to herself, that was now out of the question,—but to him, by showing him how wrong he was in trifling with this girl's feelings.

And so they started for their walk. He of course would have avoided it had it been possible. When men in such matters have two strings to their bow, much inconvenience is felt when the two become entangled. Silverbridge no doubt had come over to Killancodlem for the sake of making love to Mabel Grex, and instead of doing so he had made love to Isabel Boncassen. And during the watches of the night, and as he had dressed himself in the morning, and while Mrs Jones had been whispering to him her little bulletin as to the state of the young lady's health, he had not repented himself of the change. Mabel had been, he thought, so little gracious to him that he would have given up that notion earlier, but for his indiscreet declaration to his father. On the other hand, making love to Isabel Boncassen seemed to him to possess some divine afflatus of joy which made it of all imaginable occupations the sweetest and most charming. She had admitted of no embrace. Indeed he had attempted none, unless that touch of the hand might be so called, from which she had immediately withdrawn. Her conduct had been such that he had felt it to be incumbent on him, at the very moment, to justify the touch by a declaration of love. Then she had told him that she would not promise to love him in return. And yet it had been so sweet, so heavenly sweet!

During the morning he had almost forgotten Mabel. When Mrs Jones told him that Isabel would keep her room, he longed to ask for leave to go and make some inquiry at the door. She would not play lawn-tennis with him. Well;—he did not now care much for that. After what he had said to her she must at any rate give him some answer. She had been so gracious to him that his hopes ran very high. It never occurred to him to fancy that she might be gracious to him because he was heir to the Dukedom of Omnium. She herself was so infinitely superior to all wealth, to all rank, to all sublunary arrangements, conventions, and considerations, that there was no room for confidence of that nature. But he was confident because her smile had been sweet, and her eyes bright,—and because he was conscious, though unconsciously conscious, of something of the sympathy of love.

But he had to go to the waterfall with Mabel. Lady Mabel was always dressed perfectly,—having great gifts of her own in that direction. There was a freshness about her which made her morning costume more charming than that of the evening, and never did she look so well as when arrayed for a walk. On this occasion she had certainly done her best. But he, poor blind idiot, saw nothing of this. The white gauzy fabric which had covered Isabel's satin petticoat on the previous evening still filled his eyes. Those perfect boots, the little glimpses of party-coloured* stockings above them, the looped-up skirt, the jacket fitting but never binding that lovely body and waist, the jaunty hat with its small fresh feathers, all were nothing to him. Nor was the bright honest face beneath the hat anything to him now;—for it was an honest face, though misfortunes which had come had somewhat marred the honesty of the heart.

At first the conversation was about indifferent things,—Killancodlem and Mrs Jones, Crummie-Toddie and Reginald Dobbes. They had gone along the high-road as far as the post-office, and had turned up through the wood and reached a seat whence there was a beautiful view down upon the Archay, before a word was said affecting either Miss Boncassen or the ring. 'You got the ring safe?' she said.

'Oh yes.'

'How could you be so foolish as to risk it?'

'I did not regard it as mine. You had accepted it,—I thought.'

'But if I had, and then repented of my fault in doing so, should you not have been willing to help me in setting myself right with myself? Of course, after what had passed, it was a trouble to me when it came. What was I to do? For a day or two I thought I would take it, not as liking to take it, but as getting rid of the trouble in that way. Then I remembered its value, its history, the fact that all who knew you would want to know what had become of it,—and I felt that it should be given back. There is only one person to whom you must give it.'

'Who is that?' he said quickly.

'Your wife;—or to her who is to become your wife. No other woman can be justified in accepting such a present.'

'There has been a great deal more said about it than it's worth,' said he, not anxious at the present moment to discuss any matrimonial projects with her. 'Shall we go on to the Fall?' Then she got up and led the way till they came to the little bridge from which they could see the Falls of the Codlem below them. 'I call that very pretty,' he said.

'I thought you would like it.'

'I never saw anything of that kind more jolly. Do you care for scenery, Mabel?'

'Very much. I know no pleasure equal to it. You have never seen Grex?'

'Is it like this?'

'Not in the least. It is wilder than this, and there are not so many trees; but to my eyes it is very beautiful. I wish you had seen it.'

'Perhaps I may some day.'

'That is not likely now,' she said. 'The house is in ruins. If I had just money enough to keep it for myself, I think I could live alone there and be happy.'

'You;—alone! Of course you mean to marry?'

'Mean to marry! Do persons marry because they mean it? With nineteen men out of twenty the idea of marrying them would convey the idea of hating them. You can mean to marry. No doubt you do mean it.'

'I suppose I shall,—some day. How very well the house looks from here.' It was incumbent upon him at the present moment to turn the conversation.

But when she had a project in her head it was not so easy to turn her away. 'Yes, indeed,' she said, 'very well. But as I was saying,—you can mean to marry.'

'Anybody can mean it.'

'But you can carry out a purpose. What are you thinking of doing now?'

'Upon my honour, Mabel, that is unfair.'

'Are we not friends?'

'I think so.'

'Dear friends?'

'I hope so.'

'Then may I not tell you what I think? If you do not mean to marry that American young lady you should not raise false hopes.'

'False—hopes!' He had hopes, but he had never thought that Isabel could have any.

'False hopes;—certainly. Do you not know that everyone was looking at you last night?'

'Certainly not.'

'And that old woman is going about talking of it as her doing, pretending to be afraid of your father, whereas nothing would please her better than to humble a family so high as yours.'

'Humble!' exclaimed Lord Silverbridge.

'Do you think your father would like it? Would you think that another man would be doing well for himself by marrying Miss Boncassen?'

'I do,' said he energetically.

'Then you must be very much in love with her.'

'I say nothing about that.'

'If you are so much in love with her that you mean to face the displeasure of all your friends——'

'I do not say what I mean. I could talk more freely to you than to anyone else, but I won't talk about that even to you. As regards Miss Boncassen, I think that any man might marry her, without discredit. I won't have it said that she can be inferior to me,—or to anybody.'

There was a steady manliness in this which took Lady Mabel by surprise. She was convinced that he intended to offer his hand to the girl, and now was actuated chiefly by a feeling that his doing so would be an outrage to all English propriety. If a word might have an effect it would be her duty to speak that word. 'I think you are wrong there, Lord Silverbridge.'

'I am sure I am right.'

'What have you yourself felt about your sister and Mr Tregear?'

'It is altogether different;—altogether. Frank's wife will be simply his wife. Mine, should I outlive my father, will be Duchess of Omnium.'

'But your father? I have heard you speak with bitter regret of this affair of Lady Mary's, because it vexes him. Would your marriage with an American lady vex him less?'

'Why should it vex him at all? Is she vulgar, or ill to look at, or stupid?'

'Think of her mother.'

'I am not going to marry her mother. Nor for the matter of that am I going to marry her. You are taking all that for granted in a most unfair way.'

'How can I help it after what I saw yesterday?'

'I will not talk any more about it. We had better go down or we shall get no lunch.' Lady Mabel, as she followed him, tried to make herself believe that all her sorrow came from regret that so fine a scion of the British nobility should throw himself away upon an American adventuress.

The guests were still at lunch when they entered the dining-room, and Isabel was seated close to Mrs Jones. Silverbridge at once went up to her,—and place was made for him as though he had almost a right to be next to her. Miss Boncassen herself bore her honours well, seeming to regard the little change at table as though it was of no moment. 'I became so eager about that game,' she said, 'that I went on too long.'

'I hope you are now none the worse.'

'At six o'clock this morning I thought I should never use my legs again.'

'Were you awake at six?' said Silverbridge, with pitying voice.

'That was it. I could not sleep. Now I begin to hope that sooner or later I shall unstiffen.'

During every moment, at every word that he uttered, he was thinking of the declaration of love which he had made to her. But it seemed to him as though the matter had not dwelt on her mind. When they drew their chairs away from the table he thought that not a moment was to be lost before some further explanation of their feelings for each other should be made. Was not the matter which had been so far discussed of vital importance for both of them? And, glorious as she was above all other women, the offer which he had made must have some weight with her. He did not think that he proposed to give more than she deserved, but still, that which he was so willing to give was not a little. Or was it possible that she had not understood his meaning? If so, he would not willingly lose a moment before he made it plain to her. But she seemed content to hang about with the other women, and when she sauntered about the grounds seated herself on a garden-chair with Lady Mabel, and discussed with great eloquence the general beauty of Scotch scenery. An hour went on in this way. Could it be that she knew that he had offered to make her his wife? During this time he went and returned more than once, but still she was there, on the same garden-seat, talking to those who came in her way.

Then on a sudden she got up and put her hand on his arm. 'Come and take a turn with me,' she said. 'Lord Silverbridge, do you remember anything of last night?'

'Remember!'

'I thought for a while this morning that I would let it pass as though it had been mere trifling.'

'It would have wanted two to let it pass in that way,' he said, almost indignantly.

On hearing this she looked up at him, and there came over her face that brilliant smile, which to him was perhaps the most potent of her spells. 'What do you mean by—wanting two?'

'I must have a voice in that as well as you.'

'And what is your voice?'

'My voice is this. I told you last night that I loved you. This morning I ask you to be my wife.'

'It is a very clear voice,' she said,—almost in a whisper; but in a tone so serious that it startled him.

'It ought to be clear,' he said doggedly.

'Do you think I don't know that? Do you think that if I liked you well last night I don't like you better now?'

'But do you—like me?'

'That is just the thing I am going to say nothing about.'

'Isabel!'

'Just the one thing I will not allude to. Now you must listen to me.'

'Certainly.'

'I know a great deal about you. We Americans are an inquiring people, and I have found out pretty much everything.' His mind misgave him as he felt she had ascertained his former purpose respecting Mabel. 'You,' she said, 'among young men in England are about the foremost, and therefore,—as I think,—about the foremost in the world. And you have all personal gifts;—youth and spirits—— Well, I will not go on and name the others. You are, no doubt, supposed to be entitled to the best and sweetest of God's feminine creatures.'

'You are she.'

'Whether you be entitled to me or not I cannot yet say. Now I will tell you something of myself. My father's father came to New York as a labourer from Holland, and worked upon the quays in that city. Then he built houses, and became rich, and was almost a miser;—with the good sense, however, to educate his only son. What my father is you see. To me he is sterling gold, but he is not like your people. My dear mother is not at all like your ladies. She is not a lady in your sense,— though with her unselfish devotion to others she is something infinitely better. For myself I am,—well, meaning to speak honestly, I will call myself pretty and smart. I think I know how to be true.'

'I am sure you do.'

'But what right have you to suppose I shall know how to be a Duchess?'

'I am sure you will.'

'Now listen to me. Go to your friends and ask them. Ask that Lady Mabel;—ask your father;—ask that Lady Cantrip. And above all, ask yourself. And allow me to require you to take three months to do this. Do not come to see me for three months.'

'And then?'

'What may happen then I cannot tell, for I want three months also to think of it myself. Till then, good-bye.' She gave him her hand and left it in his for a few seconds. He tried to draw her to him; but she resisted him, still smiling. Then she left him.

# CHAPTER 41

## ISCHL

It was a custom with Mrs Finn almost every autumn to go off to Vienna, where she possessed considerable property, and there to inspect the circumstances of her estate. Sometimes her husband would accompany her, and he did so in this year of which we are now speaking. One morning in September they were together at an hotel at Ischl,* whither they had come from Vienna, when as they went through the hall into the courtyard, they came, in the very doorway, upon the Duke of

Omnium and his daughter. The Duke and Lady Mary had just arrived, having passed through the mountains from the salt-mine district, and were about to take up their residence in the hotel for a few days. They had travelled very slowly, for Lady Mary had been ill, and the Duke had expressed his determination to see a doctor at Ischl.

There is no greater mistake than in supposing that only the young blush. But the blushes of middle life are luckily not seen through the tan which has come from the sun and the gas and the work and the wiles of the world. Both the Duke and Phineas blushed; and though their blushes were hidden, that peculiar glance of the eye which always accompanies a blush was visible enough from one to the other. The elder lady kept her countenance admirably, and the younger one had no occasion for blushing. She at once ran forward and kissed her friend. The Duke stood with his hat off waiting to give his hand to the lady, and then took that of his late colleague. 'How odd that we should meet here,' he said, turning to Mrs Finn.

'Odd enough to us that your Grace should be here,' she said, 'because we had heard nothing of your intended coming.'

'It is so nice to find you,' said Lady Mary. 'We are this moment come. Don't say that you are this moment going.'

'At this moment we are only going as far as Halstadt.'*

'And are coming back to dinner? Of course they will dine with us. Will they not, papa?' The Duke said that he hoped they would. To declare that you are engaged at an hotel, unless there be some real engagement, is almost an impossibility. There was no escape, and before they were allowed to get into their carriage they had promised they would dine with the Duke and his daughter.

'I don't know that it is especially a bore,' Mrs Finn said to her husband in the carriage. 'You may be quite sure that of whatever trouble there may be in it, he has much more than his share.'

'His share should be the whole,' said her husband. 'No one else has done anything wrong.'

When the Duke's apology had reached her, so that there was no longer any ground for absolute hostility, then she had told the whole story to her husband. He at first was very indignant. What right had the Duke to expect that any ordinary friend should act duenna over his daughter in accordance with his caprices? This was said and much more of the kind. But any humour towards quarrelling which Phineas Finn might have felt for a day or two was quieted by his wife's prudence. 'A man,' she said, 'can do no more than apologise. After that there is no room for reproach.'

At dinner the conversation turned at first on British politics, in which Mrs Finn was quite able to take her part. Phineas was decidedly of opinion that Sir Timothy Beeswax and Lord Drummond could not live another session. And on this subject a good deal was said. Later in the evening the Duke found himself sitting with Mrs Finn in the broad verandah over the hotel garden, while Lady Mary was playing to Phineas within. 'How do you think she is looking?' asked the father.

'Of course I see that she has been ill. She tells me that she was far from well at Salzburg.'

'Yes;—indeed for three or four days she frightened me much. She suffered terribly from headaches.'

'Nervous headaches?'*

'So they said there. I feel quite angry with myself because I did not bring a doctor with us. The trouble and ceremony of such an accompaniment is no doubt disagreeable.'

'And I suppose seemed when you started to be unnecessary?'

'Quite unnecessary.'

'Does she complain again now?'

'She did to-day—a little.'

The next day Lady Mary could not leave her bed; and the Duke in his sorrow was obliged to apply to Mrs Finn. After what had passed on the previous day Mrs Finn of course called, and was shown at once up to her young friend's room. There she found the girl in great pain, lying with her two thin hands up to her head, and hardly able to utter more than a word. Shortly after that Mrs Finn was alone with the Duke, and then there took place a conversation between them which the lady thought to be very remarkable.

'Had I better send for a doctor from England?' he asked. In answer to this Mrs Finn expressed her opinion that such a measure was hardly necessary, that the gentleman from the town who had been called in seemed to know what he was about, and that the illness, lamentable as it was, did not seem to be in any way dangerous. 'One cannot tell what it comes from,' said the Duke dubiously.

'Young people, I fancy, are often subject to such maladies.'

'It must come from something wrong.'

'That may be said of all sickness.'

'And therefore one tries to find out the cause. She says that she is unhappy.' These last words he spoke slowly and in a low voice. To this Mrs Finn could make no reply. She did not doubt but that the girl was unhappy, and she knew well why; but the source of Lady Mary's

misery was one to which she could not very well allude. 'You know all
the misery about that young man.'

'That is a trouble that requires time to cure it,' she said,—not meaning to imply that time would cure it by enabling the girl to forget her
lover; but because in truth she had not known what else to say.

'If time will cure it.'

'Time, they say, cures all sorrows.'

'But what should I do to help time? There is no sacrifice I would not
make,—no sacrifice! Of myself I mean. I would devote myself to her,—
leave everything else on one side. We purpose being back in England in
October; but I would remain here if I thought it better for her comfort.'

'I cannot tell, Duke.'

'Neither can I. But you are a woman and might know better than
I do. It is so hard that a man should be left with a charge of which from
its very nature he cannot understand the duties.' Then he paused, but
she could find no words which would suit at the moment. It was almost
incredible to her that after what had passed he should speak to her at
all as to the condition of his daughter. 'I cannot, you know,' he said
very seriously, 'encourage a hope that she should be allowed to marry
that man.'

'I do not know.'

'You yourself, Mrs Finn, felt that when she told you about it at
Matching.'

'I felt that you would disapprove of it.'

'Disapprove of it! How could it be otherwise? Of course you felt
that. There are ranks in life in which the first comer that suits a maid-
en's eye may be accepted as a fitting lover. I will not say but that they
who are born to such a life may be the happier. They are, I am sure,
free from troubles to which they are incident whom fate has called to a
different sphere. But duty is—duty;—and whatever pang it may cost,
duty should be performed.'

'Certainly.'

'Certainly;—certainly; certainly,' he said, re-echoing her word.

'But then, Duke, one has to be so sure what duty requires. In many
matters this is easy enough, and the only difficulty comes from
temptation. There are cases in which it is so hard to know.'

'Is this one of them?'

'I think so.'

'Then the maiden should—in any class of life—be allowed to take
the man—that just suits her eye?' As he said this his mind was intent
on his Glencora and on Burgo Fitzgerald.

'I have not said so. A man may be bad, vicious, a spendthrift,—eaten up by bad habits.' Then he frowned, thinking that she also had her mind intent on his Glencora and on that Burgo Fitzgerald, and being most unwilling to have the difference between Burgo and Frank Tregear pointed out to him. 'Nor have I said,' she continued, 'that even were none of these faults apparent in the character of a suitor, the lady should in all cases be advised to accept a young man because he has made himself agreeable to her. There may be discrepancies.'

'There are,' said he, still with a low voice but with infinite energy,— 'insurmountable discrepancies.'

'I only said that this was a case in which it might be difficult for you to see your duty plainly.'

'Why should it be?'

'You would not have her—break her heart?' Then he was silent for awhile, turning over in his mind the proposition which now seemed to have been made to him. If the question came to that,—should she be allowed to break her heart and die, or should he save her from that fate by sanctioning her marriage with Tregear? If the choice could be put to him plainly by some supernal power, what then would he choose? If duty required him to prevent this marriage, his duty could not be altered by the fact that his girl would avenge herself upon him by dying! If such a marriage were in itself wrong, that wrong could not be made right by the fear of such a catastrophe. Was it not often the case that duty required that someone should die? And yet as he thought of it,— thought that the someone whom his mind had suggested was the one female creature now left belonging to him,—he put his hand up to his brow and trembled with agony. If he knew, if in truth he believed that such would be the result of firmness on his part,—then he would be infirm, then he must yield. Sooner than that, he must welcome this Tregear to his house. But why should he think that she would die? This woman had now asked him whether he would be willing to break his girl's heart. It was a frightful question; but he could see that it had come naturally in the sequence of the conversation which he had forced upon her. Did girls break their hearts in such emergencies? Was it not all romance? 'Men have died and worms have eaten them,—but not for love.'* He remembered it all and carried on the argument in his mind, though the pause was but for a minute. There might be suffering, no doubt. The higher the duties the keener the pangs! But would it become him to be deterred from doing right because she for a time might find that she had made the world bitter to herself? And were there not feminine wiles,—tricks by which women learn to have their way in opposition to the judgment of their lords and masters? He did not think that his Mary was wilfully guilty of any scheme. The suffering he knew was true suffering. But not the less did it become him to be on his guard against attacks of this nature.

'No,' he said at last; 'I would not have her break her heart,—if I understand what such words mean. They are generally, I think, used fantastically.'

'You would not wish to see her overwhelmed by sorrow?'

'Wish it! What a question to ask a father!'

'I must be more plain in my language, Duke. Though such a marriage be distasteful to you, it might perhaps be preferable to seeing her sorrowing always.'

'Why should it? I have to sorrow always. We are told that man is born to sorrow as surely as the sparks fly upwards.'*

'Then I can say nothing further.'

'You think I am cruel.'

'If I am to say what I really think I shall offend you.'

'No;—not unless you mean offence.'

'I shall never do that to you, Duke. When you talk as you do now you hardly know yourself. You think you could see her suffering, and not be moved by it. But were it to be continued long you would give way. Though we know that there is an infinity of grief in this life, still we struggle to save those we love from grieving. If she be steadfast enough to cling to her affection for this man, then at last you will have to yield.' He looked at her frowning, but did not say a word. 'Then it will perhaps be a comfort for you to know that the man himself is trustworthy and honest.'

There was a terrible rebuke in this; but still, as he had called it down upon himself, he would not resent it, even in his heart. 'Thank you,' he said, rising from his chair. 'Perhaps you will see her again this afternoon.' Of course she assented, and, as the interview had taken place in his rooms, she took her leave.

This which Mrs Finn had said to him was all to the same effect as that which had come from Lady Cantrip; only it was said with a higher spirit. Both the women saw the matter in the same light. There must be a fight between him and his girl; but she, if she could hold out for a certain time, would be the conqueror. He might take her away and try what absence would do, or he might have recourse to that specific which had answered so well in reference to his own wife; but if she continued to sorrow during absence, and if she would have nothing to do with the other lover,—then he must at last give way! He had declared that he was willing to sacrifice himself,—meaning thereby that if a lengthened visit to the cities of China, or a prolonged sojourn in the Western States of America would wean her from her love, he would go to China or to the Western States. At present his self-banishment had been carried no farther than Vienna. During their travels hitherto Tregear's name had not once been mentioned. The Duke had come away from home resolved not to mention it,—and she was minded to keep it in reserve till some seeming catastrophe should justify a declaration of her purpose. But from first to last she had been sad, and latterly she had been ill. When asked as to her complaint she would simply say that she was not happy. To go on with this through the Chinese cities could hardly be good for either of them. She would not wake herself to any enthusiasm in regard to scenery, costume, pictures, or even discomforts. Wherever she was taken it was all barren to her.

As their plans stood at present, they were to return to England so as to enable her to be at Custins by the middle of October. Had he taught himself to hope that any good could be done by prolonged travelling he would readily have thrown over Custins and Lord Popplecourt. He could not bring himself to trust much to the Popplecourt scheme. But the same contrivance had answered on that former occasion. When he spoke to her about their plans, she expressed herself quite ready to go back to England. When he suggested those Chinese cities, her face became very long and she was immediately attacked by paroxysms of headaches.

'I think I should take her to some place on the seashore in England,' said Mrs Finn.

'Custins is close to the sea,' he replied. 'It is Lord Cantrip's place in Dorsetshire. It was partly settled that she was to go there.'

'I suppose she likes Lady Cantrip.'

'Why should she not?'

'She has not said a word to me to the contrary. I only fear she would feel that she was being sent there,—as to a convent.'

'What ought I to do then?'

'How can I venture to answer that? What she would like best, I think, would be to return to Matching with you, and to settle down in a quiet way for the winter.' The Duke shook his head. That would be worse than travelling. She would still have headaches and still tell him that she was unhappy. 'Of course I do not know what your plans are, and pray believe me that I should not obtrude my advice if you did not ask me.'

'I know it,' he said. 'I know how good you are and how reasonable. I know how much you have to forgive.'

'Oh, no.'

'And, if I have not said so as I should have done, it has not been from want of feeling. I do believe you did what you thought best when Mary told you that story at Matching.'

'Why should your Grace go back to that?'

'Only that I may acknowledge my indebtedness to you, and say to you somewhat fuller than I could do in my letter that I am sorry for the pain which I gave you.'

'All that is over now,—and shall be forgotten.'

Then he spoke of his immediate plans. He would at once go back to England by slow stages,—by very slow stages,—staying a day or two at Salzburg, at Ratisbon, at Nuremberg, at Frankfort, and so on. In this way he would reach England about the 10th of October, and Mary would then be ready to go to Custins by the time appointed.

In a day or two Lady Mary was better. 'It is terrible while it lasts,' she said, speaking to Mrs Finn of her headache, 'but when it has gone then I am quite well. Only'—she added after a pause—'only I can never be happy again while papa thinks as he does now.' Then there was a party made up before they separated for an excursion to the Hintersee and the Obersee.* On this occasion Lady Mary seemed to enjoy herself, as she liked the companionship of Mrs Finn. Against Lady Cantrip she never said a word. But Lady Cantrip was always a duenna to her, whereas Mrs Finn was a friend. While the Duke and Phineas were discussing politics together—thoroughly enjoying the weakness of Lord Drummond and the iniquity of Sir Timothy—which they did with augmented vehemence from their ponies' backs, the two women in lower voices talked over their own affairs. 'I dare say you will be happy at Custins', said Mrs Finn.

'No; I shall not. There will be people there whom I don't know, and I don't want to know. Have you heard anything about him, Mrs Finn?'

Mrs Finn turned round and looked at her,—for a moment almost angrily. Then her heart relented. 'Do you mean—Mr Tregear?'

'Yes, Mr Tregear.'

'I think I heard that he was shooting with Lord Silverbridge.'

'I am glad of that,' said Mary.

'It will be pleasant for both of them.'

'I am very glad they should be together. While I know that, I feel that we are not altogether separated. I will never give it up,

Mrs Finn,—never; never. It is no use taking me to China.' In that Mrs Finn quite agreed with her.

## CHAPTER 42

### AGAIN AT KILLANCODLEM

SILVERBRIDGE remained at Crummie-Toddie under the dominion of Reginald Dobbes till the second week in September. Popplecourt, Nidderdale, and Gerald Palliser were there also, very obedient, and upon the whole efficient. Tregear was intractable, occasional, and untrustworthy. He was the cause of much trouble to Mr Dobbes. He would entertain a most heterodox and injurious idea that, as he had come to Crummie-Toddie for amusement, he was not bound to do anything that did not amuse him. He would not understand that in sport as in other matters there was an ambition, driving a man on to excel always and be ahead of others. In spite of this Mr Dobbes had cause for much triumph. It was going to be the greatest thing ever done by six guns in Scotland. As for Gerald, whom he had regarded as a boy, and who had offended him by saying that Crummie-Toddie was ugly,—he was ready to go round the world for him. He had indoctrinated Gerald with all his ideas of a sportsman,—even to a contempt for champagne and a conviction that tobacco should be moderated. The three lords too had proved themselves efficient, and the thing was going to be a success. But just when a day was of vital importance, when it was essential that there should be a strong party for a drive, Silverbridge found it absolutely necessary that he should go over to Killancodlem.

'She has gone,' said Nidderdale.

'Who the —— is she?' asked Silverbridge, almost angrily.

'Everybody knows who she is,' said Popplecourt.

'It will be a good thing when some She has got hold of you, my boy, so as to keep you in your proper place.'

'If you cannot withstand that sort of attraction you ought not to go in for shooting at all,' said Dobbes.

'I shouldn't wonder at his going,' continued Nidderdale, 'if we didn't all know that the American is no longer there. She has gone to—Bath I think they say.'

'I suppose it's Mrs Jones herself,' said Popplecourt.

'My dear boys,' said Silverbridge, 'you may be quite sure that when I say that I am going to Killancodlem I mean to go to Killancodlem, and that no chaff about young ladies,—which I think very disgusting,— will stop me. I shall be sorry if Dobbes's roll of the killed should be lessened by a single hand, seeing that his ambition sets that way. Considering the amount of slaughter we have perpetrated, I really think that we need not be over anxious.' After this nothing further was said. Tregear, who knew that Mabel Grex was still at Killancodlem, had not spoken.

In truth Mabel had sent for Lord Silverbridge, and this had been her letter:

'DEAR LORD SILVERBRIDGE,

'Mrs Montacute Jones is cut to the heart because you have not been over to see her again, and she says that it is lamentable to think that such a man as Reginald Dobbes should have so much power over you. "Only twelve miles," she says, "and he knows that we are here!" I told her that you knew Miss Boncassen was gone.

'But though Miss Boncassen has left us we are a very pleasant party, and surely you must be tired of such a place as Crummie-Toddie. If only for the sake of getting a good dinner once in a way do come over again. I shall be here yet for ten days. As they will not let me go back to Grex I don't know where I could be more happy. I have been asked to go to Custins, and suppose I shall turn up there some time in the autumn.

'And now shall I tell you what I expect? I do expect that you will come over to—see me. "I did see her the other day," you will say, "and she did not make herself pleasant." I know that. How was I to make myself pleasant when I found myself so completely snuffed out by your American beauty? Now she is away, and Richard will be himself.* Do come, because in truth I want to see you.

'Yours always sincerely,
'MABEL GREX.'

On receiving this he at once made up his mind to go to Killancodlem, but he could not make up his mind why it was that she had asked him. He was sure of two things; sure in the first place that she had intended to let him know that she did not care about him; and then sure that she was aware of his intention in regard to Miss Boncassen. Everybody at Killancodlem had seen it,—to his disgust; but still that it was so had been manifest. And he had consoled himself, feeling that it would matter nothing should he be accepted. She had made an attempt to talk him out of his purpose. Could it be that she thought it possible a second attempt might be successful? If so, she did not know him.

She had in truth thought not only that this, but that something further than this, might be possible. Of course the prize loomed larger before her eyes as the prospects of obtaining it became less. She could not doubt that he had intended to offer her his hand when he had spoken to her of his love in London. Then she had stopped him;—had 'spared him,' as she had told her friend. Certainly she had then been swayed by some feeling that it would be ungenerous in her to seize greedily the first opportunity he had given her. But he had again made an effort. He surely would not have sent her the ring had he not intended her to regard him as her lover. When she received the ring her heart had beat very high. Then she had sent that little note, saying that she would keep it till she could give it to his wife. When she wrote that she had intended the ring should be her own. And other things pressed upon her mind. Why had she been asked to the dinner at Richmond? Why was she invited to Custins? Little hints had reached her of the Duke's goodwill towards her. If on that side the marriage were approved, why should she destroy her own hopes?

Then she had seen him with Miss Boncassen, and in her pique had forced the ring back upon him. During that long game on the lawn her feelings had been very bitter. Of course the girl was the lovelier of the two. All the world was raving of her beauty. And there was no doubt as to the charm of her wit and manner. And then she had no touch of that blasé used-up way of life of which Lady Mabel was conscious herself. It was natural that it should be so. And was she, Mabel Grex, the girl to stand in his way and to force herself upon him, if he loved another? Certainly not,—though there might be a triple ducal coronet to be had.

But were there not other considerations? Could it be well that the heir of the house of Omnium should marry an American girl, as to whose humble birth whispers were already afloat? As his friend, would it not be right that she should tell him what the world would say? As his friend, therefore, she had given him her counsel.

When he was gone the whole thing weighed heavily upon her mind. Why should she lose the prize if it might still be her own? To be Duchess of Omnium! She had read of many of the other sex, and of one or two of her own, who by settled resolution had achieved greatness* in opposition to all obstacles. Was this thing beyond her reach? To hunt him, and catch him, and marry him to his own injury,—that would be impossible to her. She was sure of herself there. But how infinitely better would this be for him! Would she not have all his family with her,—and all the world of England? In how short a time would he not repent his marriage with Miss Boncassen! Whereas, were she his wife, she would so stir herself for his joys, for his good, for his honour, that there should be no possibility of repentance. And he certainly had loved her. Why else had he followed her, and spoken such words to her? Of course he had loved her! But then there had come this blaze of beauty and had carried off,—not his heart but his imagination. Because he had yielded to such fascination, was she to desert him, and also to desert herself? From day to day she thought of it, and then she wrote that letter. She hardly knew what she would do, what she might say; but she would trust to the opportunity to do and say something.

'If you have no room for me,' he said to Mrs Jones, 'you must scold Lady Mab. She has told me that you told her to invite me.'

'Of course I did. Do you think I would not sleep in the stables, and give you up my own bed if there were no other? It is so good of you to come!'

'So good of you, Mrs Jones, to ask me.'

'So very kind to come when all the attraction has gone!' Then he blushed and stammered, and was just able to say that his only object in life was to pour out his adoration at the feet of Mrs Montacute Jones herself.

There was a certain Lady Fawn,*—a pretty mincing married woman of about twenty-five, with a husband much older, who liked mild flirtations with mild young men. 'I am afraid we've lost your great attraction,' she whispered to him.

'Certainly not as long as Lady Fawn is here,' he said, seating himself close to her on a garden bench, and seizing suddenly hold of her hand. She gave a little scream and a jerk, and so relieved herself from him. 'You see,' said he, 'people do make such mistakes about a man's feelings.'

'Lord Silverbridge!'

'It's quite true, but I'll tell you all about it another time,' and so he left her. All these little troubles, his experience in the 'House,' the necessity of snubbing Tifto, the choice of a wife, and his battle with Reginald Dobbes, were giving him by degrees age and flavour.

Lady Mabel had fluttered about him on his first coming, and had been very gracious, doing the part of an old friend. 'There is to be a big shooting to-morrow,' she said, in presence of Mrs Jones.

'If it is to come to that,' he said, 'I might as well go back to Dobbydom.'

'You may shoot if you like,' said Lady Mabel.

'I haven't even brought a gun with me.'

'Then we'll have a walk,—a whole lot of us,' she said.

In the evening, about an hour before dinner, Silverbridge and Lady Mabel were seated together on the bank of a little stream which ran on the other side of the road, but on a spot not more than a furlong from the hall-door. She had brought him there, but she had done so without any definite scheme. She had made no plan of campaign for the evening, having felt relieved when she found herself able to postpone the project of her attack till the morrow. Of course there must be an attack, but how it should be made she had never had the courage to tell herself. The great women of the world,* the Semiramises, the Pocahontas, the Ida Pfeiffers, and the Charlotte Cordays, had never been wanting to themselves when the moment for action came. Now she was pleased to have this opportunity added to her; this pleasant minute in which some soft preparatory word might be spoken; but the great effort should be made on the morrow.

'Is not this nicer than shooting with Mr Dobbes?' she asked.

'A great deal nicer. Of course I am bound to say so.'

'But in truth. I want to find out what you really like. Men are so different. You need not pay me any compliment; you know that well enough.'

'I like you better than Dobbes,—if you mean that.'

'Even so much is something.'

'But I am fond of shooting.'

'Only a man may have enough of it.'

'Too much, if he is subject to Dobbes, as Dobbes likes them to be. Gerald likes it.'

'Did you think it odd,' she said after a pause, 'that I should ask you to come over again?'

'Was it odd?' he replied.

'That is as you may take it. There is certainly no other man in the world to whom I would have done it.'

'Not to Tregear?'

'Yes,' she said; 'yes,—to Tregear, could I have been as sure of a welcome for him as I am for you. Frank is in all respects the same as a brother to me. That would not have seemed odd;—I mean to myself.'

'And has this been—odd,—to yourself?'

'Yes. Not that anybody else has felt it so. Only I,—and perhaps you. You felt it so?'

'Not especially. I thought you were a very good fellow. I have always thought that;—except when you made me take back the ring.'

'Does that still fret you?'

'No man likes to take back a thing. It makes him seem to have been awkward and stupid in giving it.'

'It was the value——'

'You should have left me to judge of that.'

'If I have offended you I will beg your pardon. Give me anything else, anything but that, and I will take it.'

'But why not that?' said he.

'Now that you have fitted it for a lady's finger it should go to your wife. No one else should have it.'

Upon this he brought the ring once more out of his pocket and again offered it to her. 'No; anything but that. That your wife must have.' Then he put the ring back again. 'It would have been nicer for you had Miss Boncassen been here.' In saying this she followed no plan. It came rather from pique. It was almost as though she had asked him whether Miss Boncassen was to have the ring.

'What makes you say that?'

'But it would.'

'Yes, it would,' he replied stoutly, turning round as he lay on the ground and facing her.

'Has it come to that?'

'Come to what? You ask me a question and I answer you truly.'

'You cannot be happy without her?'

'I did not say so. You ask me whether I should like to have her here,—and I say Yes. What would you think of me if I said No?'

'My being here is not enough?' This should not have been said, of course, but the little speech came from the exquisite pain of the moment. She had meant to have said hardly anything. She had intended to be happy with him, just touching lightly on things which might lead to that attack which must be made on the morrow. But words will often lead whither the speaker has not intended. So it was now, and in the soreness of her heart she spoke. 'My being here is not enough?'

'It would be enough,' he said, jumping on his feet, 'if you understood all, and would be kind to me.'

'I will at any rate be kind to you,' she replied, as she sat upon the bank looking at the running water.

'I have asked Miss Boncassen to be my wife.'

'And she has accepted?'

'No; not as yet. She is to take three months to think of it. Of course I love her best of all. If you will sympathise with me in that, then I will be as happy with you as the day is long.'

'No,' said she, 'I cannot. I will not.'

'Very well.'

'There should be no such marriage. If you have told me in confidence——'

'Of course I have told you in confidence.'

'It will go no farther; but there can be no sympathy between us. It—it—it is not,—is not——' Then she burst into tears.

'Mabel!'

'No, sir, no; no! What did you mean? But never mind. I have no questions to ask, not a word to say. Why should I? Only this,—that such a marriage will disgrace your family. To me it is no more than to anybody else. But it will disgrace your family.'

How she got back to the house she hardly knew; nor did he. That evening they did not again speak to each other, and on the following morning there was no walk to the mountains. Before dinner he drove himself back to Crummie-Toddie, and when he was taking his leave she shook hands with him with her usual pleasant smile.

## CHAPTER 43

### WHAT HAPPENED AT DONCASTER

THE Leger this year was to be run on the 14th September, and while Lord Silverbridge was amusing himself with the deer at Crummie-Toddie and at Killancodlem with the more easily pursued young ladies, the indefatigable Major was hard at work in the stables. This came a little hard on him. There was the cub-hunting to be looked after, which made his presence at Runnymede necessary, and then that 'pig-headed fellow, Silverbridge' would not have the horses trained anywhere but at Newmarket. How was he to be in two places at once? Yet he was in two places almost at once: cub-hunting in the morning at Egham and Bagshot, and sitting on the same evening at the stable-door at Newmarket, with his eyes fixed upon Prime Minister.

Gradually had he and Captain Green come to understand each other, and though they did at last understand each other, Tifto would talk as though there were no such correct intelligence;—when for instance he would abuse Lord Silverbridge for being pig-headed. On such occasions the Captain's remark would generally be short. 'That be blowed!' he would say, implying that that state of things between the two partners, in which such complaints might be natural, had now been brought to an end. But on one occasion, about a week before the race, he spoke out a little plainer. 'What's the use of your going on with all that before me? It's settled what you've got to do.'

'I don't know that anything is settled,' said the Major.

'Ain't it? I thought it was. If it ain't you'll find yourself in the wrong box. You've as straight a tip as a man need wish for, but if you back out you'll come to grief. Your money's all on the other way already.'

On the Friday before the race Silverbridge dined with Tifto at the Beargarden. On the next morning they went down to Newmarket to see the horse get a gallop, and came back the same evening. During all this time, Tifto was more than ordinarily pleasant to his patron. The horse and the certainty of the horse's success were the only subjects mooted. 'It isn't what I say,' repeated Tifto, 'but look at the betting. You can't get five to four against him. They tell me that if you want to do anything on the Sunday the pull* will be the other way.'

'I stand to lose over £20,000 already,' said Silverbridge, almost frightened by the amount.

'But how much are you on to win?' said Tifto. 'I suppose you could sell your bets for £5,000 down.'

'I wish I knew how to do it,' said Silverbridge. But this was an arrangement, which, if made just now, would not suit the Major's views.

They went to Newmarket, and there they met Captain Green. 'Tifto,' said the young Lord, 'I won't have that fellow with us when the horse is galloping.'

'There isn't an honester man, or a man who understands a horse's paces better in all England,' said Tifto.

'I won't have him standing alongside of me on the Heath,' said his Lordship.

'I don't know how I'm to help it.'

'If he's there I'll send the horse in;—that's all.' Then Tifto found it best to say a few words to Captain Green. But the Captain also said a few words to himself. 'D—— young fool; he don't know what he's dropping into.' Which assertion, if you lay aside the unnecessary expletive, was true to the letter. Lord Silverbridge was a young fool, and did not at all know into what a mess he was being dropped by the united experience, perspicuity, and energy of the man whose company on the Heath he had declined.

The horse was quite a 'picture to look at.' Mr Pook the trainer assured his Lordship that for health and condition he had never seen anything better. 'Stout all over,' said Mr Pook, 'and not an ounce of what you may call flesh. And bright! just feel his coat, my Lord! That's 'ealth,—that is; not dressing, nor yet macassar!'*

And then there were various evidences produced of his pace,—how he had beaten that horse, giving him two pounds; how he had been beaten by that, but only on a mile course; the Leger distance* was just the thing for Prime Minister; how by a lucky chance that marvellous quick rat of a thing that had won the Derby had not been entered for the autumn race; how Coalheaver was known to have had bad feet. 'He's a stout 'orse, no doubt,—is the 'Eaver,' said Mr Pook, 'and that's why the betting-men have stuck to him. But he'll be nowhere on Wednesday. They're beginning to see it now, my Lord. I wish they wasn't so sharp-sighted.'

In the course of the day, however, they met a gentleman who was of a different opinion. He said loudly that he looked on the Heaver as the best three-year-old in England. Of course as matters stood he wasn't going to back the Heaver at even money;—but he'd take twenty-five to thirty in hundreds between the two. All this ended in the bet being accepted and duly booked* by Lord Silverbridge. And in this way Silverbridge added two thousand four hundred pounds to his responsibilities.

But there was worse than this coming. On the Sunday afternoon he went down to Doncaster, of course in company with the Major. He was alive to the necessity of ridding himself of the Major; but it had been acknowledged that that duty could not be performed till after this race had been run. As he sat opposite to his friend on their journey to Doncaster, he thought of this in the train. It should be done immediately on their return to London after the race. But the horse, his Prime Minister, was by this time so dear to him that he intended if possible to keep possession of the animal.

When they reached Doncaster the racing-men were all occupied with Prime Minister. The horse and Mr Pook had arrived that day from Newmarket, viâ Cambridge and Peterborough. Tifto, Silverbridge, and Mr Pook visited him together three times that afternoon and evening;—and the Captain also visited the horse, though not in company with Lord Silverbridge. To do Mr Pook justice, no one could be more careful. When the Captain came round with the Major, Mr Pook was there. But Captain Green did not enter the box,—had no wish to do so, was of opinion that on such occasions no one whose business did not carry him there should go near a horse. His only object seemed to be to compliment Mr Pook as to his care, skill, and good fortune.

It was on the Tuesday evening that the chief mischief was done. There was a club at which many of the racing-men dined, and there Lord Silverbridge spent his evening. He was the hero of the hour, and everybody flattered him. It must be acknowledged that his head was turned. They dined at eight and much wine was drunk. No one was tipsy, but many were elated; and much confidence in their favourite animals was imparted to men who had been sufficiently cautious before dinner. Then cigars and soda-and-brandy became common and our young friend was not more abstemious than others. Large sums were named, and at last in three successive bets Lord Silverbridge backed his horse for more than forty thousand pounds. As he was making the second bet Mr Lupton came across to him and begged him to hold his hand. 'It will be a nasty sum for you to lose, and winning it will be nothing to you,' he said. Silverbridge took it good-humouredly, but said that he knew what he was about. 'These men will pay,' whispered Lupton; 'but you can't be quite sure what they're at.' The young man's brow was covered with perspiration. He was smoking quick and had already smoked more than was good for him. 'All right,' he said. 'I'll mind what I'm about.' Mr Lupton could do no more, and retired. Before the night was over bets had been booked to the amount stated, and the Duke's son, who had promised that he would never plunge, stood to lose about seventy thousand pounds* upon the race.

While this was going on Tifto sat not far from his patron, but completely silent. During the day and early in the evening a few sparks of the glory which scintillated from the favourite horse flew in his direction. But he was on this occasion unlike himself, and though the horse was to be run in his name had very little to say in the matter. Not a boast came out of his mouth during dinner or after dinner. He was so moody that his partner, who was generally anxious to keep him quiet, more than once endeavoured to encourage him. But he was unable to rouse himself. It was still within his power to run straight; to be on the square, if not with Captain Green, at any rate with Lord Silverbridge. But to do so he must make a clean breast with his Lordship and confess the intended sin. As he heard all that was being done, his conscience troubled him sorely. With pitch* of this sort he had never soiled himself before. He was to have three thousand pounds from Green, and then there would be the bets he himself had laid* against the horse,—by

Green's assistance! It would be the making of him. Of what use had been all his 'square' work to him? And then Silverbridge had behaved so badly to him! But still, as he sat there during the evening, he would have given a hand to have been free from the attempt. He had had no conception before that he could become subject to such misery from such a cause. He would make it straight with Silverbridge this very night,—but that Silverbridge was ever lighting fresh cigars and ever having his glass refilled. It was clear to him that on this night Silverbridge could not be made to understand anything about it. And the deed in which he himself was to be the chief actor was to be done very early in the following morning. At last he slunk away to bed.

On the following morning, the morning of the day on which the race was to be run, the Major tapped at his patron's door about seven o'clock. Of course there was no answer, though the knock was repeated. When young men overnight drink as much brandy-and-water as Silverbridge had done, and smoke as many cigars, they are apt not to hear knocks at their door made at seven o'clock. Nor was his Lordship's servant up,—so that Tifto had no means of getting at him except by personal invasion of the sanctity of his bedroom. But there was no time, not a minute, to be lost. Now, within this minute that was pressing on him, Tifto must choose his course. He opened the door and was standing at the young man's head.

'What the d—— does this mean?' said his Lordship angrily, as soon as his visitor had succeeded in waking him. Tifto muttered something about the horse which Silverbridge failed to understand. The young man's condition was by no means pleasant. His mouth was furred by the fumes of tobacco. His head was aching. He was heavy with sleep, and this intrusion seemed to him to be a final indignity offered to him by the man whom he now hated. 'What business have you to come in here?' he said, leaning on his elbow. 'I don't care a straw for the horse. If you have anything to say send my servant. Get out!'

'Oh;—very well,' said Tifto;—and Tifto got out.

It was about an hour afterwards that Tifto returned, and on this occasion a groom from the stables, and the young Lord's own servant, and two or three other men were with him. Tifto had been made to understand that the news now to be communicated, must be communicated by himself, whether his Lordship were angry or not. Indeed, after what had been done his Lordship's anger was not of much moment. In his present visit he was only carrying out the pleasant little plan which had been arranged for him by Captain Green. 'What the mischief is up?' said Silverbridge, rising in his bed.

Then Tifto told his story, sullenly, doggedly, but still in a perspicuous* manner, and with words which admitted of no doubt. But before he told the story he had excluded all but himself and the groom. He and the groom had taken the horse out of the stable, it being the animal's nature to eat his corn better after slight exercise, and while doing so a nail had been picked up.

'Is it much?' asked Silverbridge, jumping still higher in his bed. Then he was told that it was very much,—that the iron had driven itself into the horse's frog,* and that there was actually no possibility that the horse should run on that day.

'He can't walk, my Lord,' said the groom, in that authoritative voice which grooms use when they desire to have their own way, and to make their masters understand that they at any rate are not to have theirs.

'Where is Pook?' asked Silverbridge. But Mr Pook was also still in bed.

It was soon known to Lord Silverbridge as a fact that in very truth the horse could not run. Then sick with headache, with a stomach suffering unutterable things, he had, as he dressed himself, to think of his seventy thousand pounds. Of course the money would be forthcoming. But how would his father look at him? How would it be between him and his father now? After such a misfortune how would he be able to break that other matter to the Duke, and say that he had changed his mind about his marriage,—that he was going to abandon Lady Mabel Grex, and give his hand and a future Duchess's coronet to an American girl whose grandfather had been a porter?

A nail in his foot! Well! He had heard of such things before. He knew that such accidents had happened. What an ass must he have been to risk such a sum on the well-being and safety of an animal who might any day pick up a nail in his foot? Then he thought of the caution which Lupton had given him. What good would the money have done him had he won it? What more could he have than he now enjoyed? But to lose such a sum of money! With all his advantages of wealth he felt himself to be as forlorn and wretched as though he had nothing left in the world before him.

## CHAPTER 44

### HOW IT WAS DONE

THE story was soon about the town, and was the one matter for discussion in all racing quarters. About the town! It was about England, about all Europe. It had travelled to America and the Indies, to Australia and the Chinese cities before two hours were over. Before the race was run the accident was discussed and something like the truth surmised in Cairo, Calcutta, Melbourne, and San Francisco. But at Doncaster it was so all-pervading a matter that down to the tradesmen's daughters and the boys at the free-school* the town was divided into two parties, one party believing it to have been a 'plant,' and the other holding that the cause had been natural. It is hardly necessary to say that the ring,* as a rule, belonged to the former party. The ring always suspects. It did not behove even those who would win by the transaction to stand up for its honesty.

The intention had been to take the horse round a portion of the outside of the course near to which his stable stood. A boy rode him and the groom and Tifto went with him. At a certain spot on their return Tifto had exclaimed that the horse was going lame in his off fore-foot. As to this exclamation the boy and the two men were agreed. The boy was then made to dismount and run for Mr Pook; and as he started Tifto commenced to examine the horse's foot. The boy saw him raise the off fore-leg. He himself had not found the horse lame under him, but had been so hustled and hurried out of the saddle by Tifto and the groom that he had not thought on that matter till he was questioned. So far the story told by Tifto and the groom was corroborated by the boy,—except as to the horse's actual lameness. So far the story was believed by all men,—except in regard to the actual lameness. And so far it was true. Then, according to Tifto and the groom, the other foot was looked at, but nothing was seen. This other foot, the near fore-foot, was examined by the groom, who declared himself to be so flurried by the lameness of such a horse at such a time, that he hardly knew what he saw or what he did not see. At any rate then in his confusion he found no cause of lameness, but the horse was led into the stable as lame as a tree. Here Tifto found the nail inserted into the very cleft of the frog of the near fore-foot, and so inserted that he could not extract it till the farrier came. That the farrier had extracted the nail from the part of the foot indicated was certainly a fact.

Then there was the nail. Only those who were most peculiarly privileged were allowed to see the nail. But it was buzzed about the racing quarters that the head of the nail,—an old rusty, straight, and well-pointed nail,—bore on it the mark of a recent hammer. In answer to this it was alleged that the blacksmith in extracting the nail with his pincers, had of course operated on its head, had removed certain particles of rust, and might easily have given it the appearance of having been struck. But in answer to this the farrier, who was a sharp fellow, and quite beyond suspicion in the matter, declared that he had very particularly looked at the nail before he extracted it,—had looked at it with the feeling on his mind that something base might too probably have been done,—and that he was ready to swear that the clear mark on the head of the nail was there before he touched it. And then not in the stable, but lying under the little dungheap away from the stable-door, there was found a small piece of broken iron bar, about a foot long, which might have answered for a hammer,—a rusty bit of iron; and amidst the rust of this was found such traces as might have been left had it been used in striking such a nail. There were some who declared that neither on the nail nor on the iron could they see anything. And among these was the Major. But Mr Lupton brought a strong magnifying-glass to bear, and the world of examiners was satisfied that the marks were there.

It seemed however to be agreed that nothing could be done. Silverbridge would not lend himself at all to those who suspected mischief. He was miserable enough, but in this great trouble he would not separate himself from Tifto. 'I don't believe a word of all that,' he said to Mr Lupton.

'It ought to be investigated at any rate,' said Lupton.

'Mr Pook may do as he likes, but I will have nothing to do with it.'

Then Tifto came to him swaggering. Tifto had to go through a considerable amount of acting, for which he was not very well adapted. The Captain would have done it better. He would have endeavoured to put himself altogether into the same boat with his partner, and would have imagined neither suspicion or enmity on his partner's part till suspicion or enmity had been shown. But Tifto, who had not expected that the matter would be allowed to pass over without some inquiry, began by assuming that Silverbridge would think evil of him. Tifto, who at this moment would have given all that he had in the world not to have done the deed, who now hated the instigator of the deed, and felt something almost akin to love for Silverbridge, found himself to be forced by circumstances to defend himself by swaggering. 'I don't understand all this that's going on, my Lord,' he said.

'Neither do I,' replied Silverbridge.

'Any horse is subject to an accident. I am, I suppose, as great a sufferer as you are, and a deuced sight less able to bear it.'

'Who has said anything to the contrary? As for bearing it, we must take it as it comes,—both of us. You may as well know now as later that I have done with racing—for ever.'

'What do you tell me that for? You can do as you like and I can do as I like about that. If I had had my way about the horse this never would have happened. Taking a horse out at that time in the morning,—before a race!'

'Why, you went with him yourself.'

'Yes;—by Pook's orders. You allowed Pook to do just as he pleased. I should like to know what money Pook has got on it, and which way he laid it.' This disgusted Silverbridge so much that he turned away and would have no more to say to Tifto.

Before one o'clock, at which hour it was stated nominally that the races would commence, general opinion had formed itself,—and general opinion had nearly hit the truth. General opinion declared that the nail had been driven in wilfully,—that it had been done by Tifto himself, and that Tifto had been instigated by Captain Green. Captain Green perhaps overacted his part a little. His intimacy with the Major was well known, and yet, in all this turmoil, he kept himself apart as though he had no interest in the matter. 'I have got my little money on, and what little I have I lose,' he said in answer to inquiries. But everyone knew that he could not but have a great interest in a race, as to which the half owner of the favourite was a peculiarly intimate friend of his own. Had he come down to the stables and been seen about the place with Tifto it might have been better. As it was, though he was very quiet, his name was soon mixed up in the matter. There was one man who asserted it as a fact known to himself that Green and Villiers,—one Gilbert Villiers,—were in partnership together. It was very well known that Gilbert Villiers would win two thousand five hundred pounds* from Lord Silverbridge.

Then minute investigation was made into the betting of certain individuals. Of course there would be great plunder, and where would the plunder go? Who would get the money which poor Silverbridge would lose? It was said that one at least of the large bets made on that Tuesday evening could be traced to the same Villiers though not actually made by him. More would be learned when the settling-day should come. But there was quite enough already to show that there were many men determined to get to the bottom of it all if possible.

There came upon Silverbridge in his trouble a keen sense of his position and a feeling of the dignity which he ought to support. He clung during great part of the morning to Mr Lupton. Mr Lupton was much his senior and they had never been intimate; but now there was comfort in his society. 'I am afraid you are hit heavily,' said Mr Lupton.

'Something over seventy thousand pounds!'

'Looking at what will be your property it is of course nothing. But if——'

'If what?'

'If you go to the Jews* for it then it will become a great deal.'

'I shall certainly not do that.'

'Then you may regard it as a trifle,' said Lupton.

'No, I can't. It is not a trifle. I must tell my father. He'll find the money.'

'There is no doubt about that.'

'He will. But I feel at present that I would rather change places with the poorest gentleman I know than have to tell him. I have done with races, Lupton.'

'If so, this will have been a happy day for you. A man in your position can hardly make money by it, but he may lose so much! If a man really likes the amusement,—as I do,—and risks no more than what he has in his pocket, that may be very well.'

'At any rate I have done with it.'

Nevertheless he went to see the race run, and everybody seemed to be touched with pity for him. He carried himself well, saying as little as he could of his own horse, and taking, or affecting to take, great interest in the race. After the race he managed to see all those to whom he had lost heavy stakes,—having to own to himself, as he did so, that not one of them was a gentleman to whom he should like to give his hand. To them he explained that his father was abroad,—that probably his liabilities could not be settled till after his father's return. He however would consult his father's agent and would then appear on settling-day. They were all full of the blandest courtesies. There was not one of them who had any doubt as to getting his money,—unless the whole thing might be disputed on the score of Tifto's villany. Even then payment could not be disputed, unless it was proved that he who demanded the money had been one of the actual conspirators. After having seen his creditors he went away up alone to London.

When in London he went to Carlton Terrace and spent the night in absolute solitude. It had been his plan to join Gerald for some partridge-shooting at Matching, and then to go yachting till such time as he should be enabled to renew his suit to Miss Boncassen. Early in November he would again ask her to be his wife. These had been his plans. But now it seemed that everything was changed. Partridge-shooting and yachting must be out of the question till this terrible load was taken off his shoulders. Soon after his arrival at the house two telegrams followed him from Doncaster. One was from Gerald. 'What is all this about Prime Minister? Is it a sell? I am so unhappy.' The other was from Lady Mabel,—for among other luxuries Mrs Montacute Jones had her own telegraph-wire* at Killancodlem. 'Can this be true? We are all so miserable. I do hope it is not much.' From which he learned that his misfortune was already known to all his friends.

And now what was he to do? He ate his supper, and then without hesitating for a moment,—feeling that if he did hesitate the task would not be done on that night,—he sat down and wrote the following letter:

'Carlton Terrace, Sept. 14, 18—.

'MY DEAR MR MORETON,

'I have just come up from Doncaster. You have probably heard what has been Prime Minister's fate. I don't know whether any horse has ever been such a favourite for the Leger. Early in the morning he was taken out and picked up a nail. The consequence was he could not run.

'Now I must come to the bad part of my story. I have lost seventy thousand pounds! It is no use beating about the bush. The sum is something over that. What am I to do? If I tell you that I shall give up racing altogether I dare say you will not believe me. It is a sort of thing a man always says when he wants money; but I feel now I cannot help saying it.

'But what shall I do? Perhaps, if it be not too much trouble, you will come up to town and see me. You can send me a word by the wires.

'You may be sure of this, I shall make no attempt to raise the money elsewhere, unless I find that my father will not help me. You will understand that of course it must be paid. You will understand also what I must feel about telling my father, but I shall do so at once. I only wait till I can hear from you.

'Yours faithfully,
'SILVERBRIDGE.'

During the next day two despatches reached Lord Silverbridge, both of them coming as he sat down to his solitary dinner. The first consisted of a short but very civil note.

'Messrs Comfort and Criball present their compliments to the Earl of Silverbridge.

'Messrs C. and C. beg to offer their apologies for interfering, but desire to inform his Lordship that should cash be wanting to any amount in consequence of the late races, they will be happy to accommodate his Lordship on most reasonable terms at a moment's notice, upon his Lordship's single bond.

'Lord Silverbridge may be sure of absolute secrecy.

'Crasham Court, Crutched Friars, Sept. 15, 18—.'

The other despatch was a telegram from Mr Moreton saying that he would be in Carlton Terrace by noon on the following day.

## CHAPTER 45

### 'THERE SHALL NOT BE ANOTHER WORD ABOUT IT'

EARLY in October the Duke was at Matching with his daughter, and Phineas Finn and his wife were both with them. On the day after they parted at Ischl the first news respecting Prime Minister had reached him,—namely, that his son's horse had lost the race. This would not have annoyed him at all, but that the papers which he read contained some vague charge of swindling against somebody, and hinted that Lord Silverbridge had been a victim. Even this would not have troubled him,—might in some sort have comforted him,—were it not made evident to him that his son had been closely associated with swindlers in these transactions. If it were a mere question of money, that might be settled without difficulty. Even though the sum lost might have grown out of what he might have expected into some few thousands, still he would bear it without a word, if only he could separate his boy from bad companions. Then came Mr Moreton's letter telling the whole.

At the meeting which took place between Silverbridge and his father's agent at Carlton Terrace it was settled that Mr Moreton should write the letter. Silverbridge tried and found that he could not do it. He did not know how to humiliate himself sufficiently, and yet could not keep himself from making attempts to prove that according to all recognised chances his bets had been good bets.

Mr Moreton was better able to accomplish the task. He knew the Duke's mind. A very large discretion had been left in Mr Moreton's hands in regard to moneys which might be needed on behalf of that dangerous heir!—so large that he had been able to tell Lord Silverbridge that if the money was in truth lost according to Jockey Club rules, it should all be forthcoming on the settling-day,—certainly without assistance from Messrs Comfort and Criball. The Duke had been nervously afraid of such men of business as Comfort and Criball, and from the earliest days of his son's semi-manhood had been on his guard against them. Let any sacrifice be made so that his son might be kept clear from Comforts and Criballs. To Mr Moreton he had been very explicit. His own pecuniary resources were so great that they could bear some ravaging without serious detriment. It was for his son's character and standing in the world, for his future respectability and dignity, that his fears were so keen, and not for his own money. By one so excitable, so fond of pleasure as Lord Silverbridge, some ravaging would probably be made. Let it be met by ready money. Such had been the Duke's instructions to his own trusted man of business, and, acting on these instructions, Mr Moreton was able to tell the heir that the money should be forthcoming.

Mr Moreton, after detailing the extent and the nature of the loss, and the steps which he had decided upon taking, went on to explain the circumstances as best he could. He had made some inquiry, and felt no doubt that a gigantic swindle had been perpetrated by Major Tifto and others. The swindle had been successful. Mr Moreton had consulted certain gentlemen of high character versed in affairs of the turf. He mentioned Mr Lupton among others,—and had been assured that though the swindle was undoubted, the money had better be paid. It was thought to be impossible to connect the men who had made the bets with the perpetrators of the fraud;—and if Lord Silverbridge were to abstain from paying his bets because his own partner had ruined the animal which belonged to them jointly, the feeling would be against him rather than in his favour. In fact the Jockey Club could not sustain him in such refusal. Therefore the money would be paid. Mr Moreton, with some expressions of doubt, trusted that he might be thought to have exercised a wise discretion. Then he went on to express his own opinion in regard to the lasting effect which the matter would have upon the young man. 'I think,' said he, 'that his Lordship is heartily sickened of racing, and that he will never return to it.'

The Duke was of course very wretched when these tidings first reached him. Though he was a rich man, and of all men the least careful of his riches, still he felt that seventy thousand pounds was a large sum of money to throw away among a nest of swindlers. And then it was excessively grievous to him that his son should have been mixed up with such men. Wishing to screen his son, even from his own anger, he was careful to remember that the promise made that Tifto should be dismissed, was not to take effect till after this race had been run. There had been no deceit in that. But then Silverbridge had promised that he would not 'plunge.' There are, however, promises which from their very nature may be broken without falsehood. Plunging is a doubtful word, and the path down to it, like all doubtful paths,—is slippery and easy! If that assurance with which Mr Moreton ended his letter could only be made true, he could bring himself to forgive even this offence. The boy must be made to settle himself in life. The Duke resolved that his only revenge should be to press on that marriage with Mabel Grex.

At Coblenz,* on their way home, the Duke and his daughter were caught up by Mr and Mrs Finn, and the matter of the young man's losses was discussed. Phineas had heard all about it, and was loud in denunciations against Tifto, Captain Green, Gilbert Villiers, and others whose names had reached him. The money, he thought, should never have been paid. The Duke however declared that the money would not cause a moment's regret, if only the whole thing could be got rid of at that cost. It had reached Finn's ears that Tifto was already at loggerheads with his associates. There was some hope that the whole thing might be brought to light by this means. For all that the Duke cared nothing. If only Silverbridge and Tifto could for the future be kept apart, as far as he and his were concerned, good would have been done rather than harm. While they were in this way together on the Rhine it was decided that very soon after their return to England Phineas and Mrs Finn should go down to Matching.

When the Duke arrived in London his sons were not there. Gerald had gone back to Oxford, and Silverbridge had merely left an address. Then his sister wrote him a very short letter. 'Papa will be so glad if you will come to Matching. Do come.' Of course he came, and presented himself some few days after the Duke's arrival.

But he dreaded this meeting with his father which, however, let it be postponed for ever so long, must come at last. In reference to this he made a great resolution,—that he would go instantly as soon as he might be sent for. When the summons came he started; but, though he was by courtesy an Earl, and by fact was not only a man but a Member of Parliament, though he was half engaged to marry one young lady and ought to have been engaged to marry another, though he had come to an age at which Pitt was a great minister and Pope a great poet, still his heart was in his boots, as a schoolboy's might be, when he was driven up to the house at Matching.

In two minutes, before he had washed the dust from his face and hands, he was with his father. 'I am glad to see you, Silverbridge,' said the Duke, putting out his hand.

'I hope I see you well, sir.'

'Fairly well. Thank you. Travelling I think agrees with me. I miss, not my comforts, but a certain knowledge of how things are going on, which comes to us I think through our skins when we are at home. A feeling of absence pervades me. Otherwise I like it. And you;—what have you been doing?'

'Shooting a little,' said Silverbridge, in a mooncalf* tone.

'Shooting a great deal, if what I see in the newspapers be true about Mr Reginald Dobbes and his party. I presume it is a religion to offer up hecatombs* to the autumnal gods,—who must surely take a keener delight in blood and slaughter than those bloodthirsty gods of old.'

'You should talk to Gerald about that, sir.'

'Has Gerald been so great at his sacrifices? How will that suit with Plato? What does Mr Simcox say?'

'Of course they were all to have a holiday just at that time. But Gerald is reading. I fancy that Gerald is clever.'

'And he is a great Nimrod?'*

'As to hunting.'

'Nimrod I fancy got his game in any way that he could compass it. I do not doubt but that he trapped foxes.'

'With a rifle at deer, say for four hundred yards, I would back Gerald against any man of his age in England or Scotland.'

'As for backing, Silverbridge, do not you think that we had better have done with that?' This was said hardly in a tone of reproach, with something even of banter in it; and as the question was asked the Duke was smiling. But in a moment all that sense of joyousness which the young man had felt in singing his brother's praises was expelled. His face fell, and he stood before his father almost like a culprit. 'We might as well have it out about this racing,' continued the Duke. 'Something has to be said about it. You have lost an enormous sum of money.' The Duke's tone in saying this became terribly severe. Such at least was its sound in his son's ears. He did not mean to be severe.

But when he did speak of that which displeased him his voice naturally assumed that tone of indignation with which in days of yore he had been wont to denounce the public extravagance of his opponents in the House of Commons. The father paused, but the son could not speak at the moment.

'And worse than that,' continued the Duke; 'you have lost it in as bad company as you could have found had you picked all England through.'

'Mr Lupton, and Sir Henry Playfair, and Lord Stirling were in the room when the bets were made.'

'Were the gentlemen you name concerned with Major Tifto?'

'No, sir.'

'Who can tell with whom he may be in a room? Though rooms of that kind are, I think, best avoided.' Then the Duke paused again, but Silverbridge was now sobbing so that he could hardly speak. 'I am sorry that you should be so grieved,' continued the father, 'but such delights cannot, I think, lead to much real joy.'

'It is for you, sir,' said the son, rubbing his eyes with the hand which supported his head.

'My grief in the matter might soon be cured.'

'How shall I cure it? I will do anything to cure it.'

'Let Major Tifto and the horses go.'

'They are gone,' said Silverbridge energetically, jumping from his chair as he spoke. 'I will never own a horse again, or a part of a horse. I will have nothing more to do with races. You will believe me?'

'I will believe anything that you tell me.'

'I won't say I will not go to another race, because——'

'No; no. I would not have you hamper yourself. Nor shall you bind yourself by any further promises. You have done with racing.'

'Indeed, indeed I have, sir.'

Then the father came up to the son and put his arms round the young man's shoulders and embraced him. 'Of course it made me unhappy.'

'I knew it would.'

'But if you are cured of this evil, the money is nothing. What is it all for but for you and your brother and sister? It was a large sum, but that shall not grieve me. The thing itself is so dangerous that, if with that much of loss we can escape, I will think that we have made not a bad market. Who owns the horse now?'

'The horses shall be sold.'

'For anything they may fetch so that we may get clear of this dirt. And the Major?'

'I know nothing of him. I have not seen him since that day.'

'Has he claims on you?'

'Not a shilling. It is all the other way.'

'Let it go then. Be quit of him, however it may be. Send a messenger so that he may understand that you have abandoned racing altogether. Mr Moreton might perhaps see him.'

That his father should forgive so readily and yet himself suffer so deeply, affected the son's feelings so strongly that for a time he could hardly repress his sobs. 'And now there shall not be a word more said about it,' said the Duke suddenly.

Silverbridge in his confusion could make no answer.

'There shall not be another word said about it,' said the Duke again. 'And now what do you mean to do with yourself immediately?'

'I'll stay here, sir, as long as you do. Finn, and Warburton, and I have still a few coverts to shoot.'

'That's a good reason for staying anywhere.'

'I meant that I would remain while you remained, sir.'

'That at any rate is a good reason, as far as I am concerned. But we go to Custins next week.'

'There's a deal of shooting to be done at Gatherum,' said the heir.

'You speak of it as if it were the business of your life,—on which your bread depended.'

'One can't expect game to be kept up if nobody goes to shoot it.'

'Can't one? I didn't know.* I should have thought that the less was shot the more there would be to shoot; but I am ignorant in such matters.' Silverbridge then broke forth into a long explanation as to coverts, gamekeepers, poachers, breeding, and the expectations of the neighbourhood at large, in the middle of which he was interrupted by the Duke. 'I am afraid, my dear boy, that I am too old to learn. But as it is so manifestly a duty, go and perform it like a man. Who will go with you?'

'I will ask Mr Finn to be one.'

'He will be very hard upon you in the way of politics.'

'I can answer him better than I can you, sir. Mr Lupton said he would come for a day or two. He'll stand to me.'

After that his father stopped him as he was about to leave the room. 'One more word, Silverbridge. Do you remember what you were saying when you walked down to the House with me from your club that night?' Silverbridge remembered very well what he had said. He had undertaken to ask Mabel Grex to be his wife, and had received his father's ready approval to the proposition. But at this moment he was unwilling to refer to that matter. 'I have thought about it very much since that,' said the Duke. 'I may say that I have been thinking of it every day. If there were anything to tell me, you would let me know;—would you not?'

'Yes, sir.'

'Then there is nothing to be told? I hope you have not changed your mind.'

Silverbridge paused a moment, trusting that he might be able to escape the making of any answer;—but the Duke evidently intended to have an answer. 'It appeared to me, sir, that it did not seem to suit her,' said the hardly-driven young man. He could not now say that Mabel had shown a disposition to reject his offer, because as they had been sitting by the brookside at Killancodlem, even he, with all his self-diffidence, had been forced to see what were her wishes. Her confusion, and too evident despair when she heard of the offer to the American girl, had plainly told her tale. He could not now plead to his father that Mabel Grex would refuse his offer. But his self-defence, when first he found that he had lost himself in love for the American, had been based on that idea. He had done his best to make Mabel understand him. If he had not actually offered to her, he had done the next thing to it. And he had run after her, till he was ashamed of such running. She had given him no encouragement;—and therefore he had been justified. No doubt he must have been mistaken; that he now perceived; but still he felt himself to be justified. It was impossible that he should explain all this to his father. One thing he certainly could not say,—just at present. After his folly in regard to those heavy debts he could not at once risk his father's renewed anger by proposing to him an American daughter-in-law. That must stand over, at any rate till the girl had accepted him positively. 'I am afraid it won't come off, sir,' he said at last.

'Then I am to presume that you have changed your mind?'

'I told you when we were speaking of it that I was not confident.'

'She has not——'

'I can't explain it all, sir,—but I fear it won't come off.'

Then the Duke, who had been sitting, got up from his chair and with his back to the fire made a final little speech. 'We decided just now, Silverbridge, that nothing more should be said about that unpleasant racing business, and nothing more shall be said by me. But you must not be surprised if I am anxious to see you settled in life. No young man could be more bound by duty to marry early than you are. In the first place you have to repair the injury done by my inaptitude for society. You have explained to me that it is your duty to have the Barsetshire coverts properly shot, and I have acceded to your views. Surely it must be equally your duty to see your Barsetshire neighbours. And you are a young man every feature of whose character would be improved by matrimony. As far as means are concerned you are almost as free to make arrangements as though you were already the head of the family.'

'No, sir.'

'I could never bring myself to dictate to a son in regard to his choice of a wife. But I will own that when you told me that you had chosen I was much gratified. Try and think again when you are pausing amidst your sacrifices at Gatherum, whether that be possible. If it be not, still I would wish you to bear in mind what is my idea as to your duty.' Silverbridge said that he would bear this in mind, and then escaped from the room.

## CHAPTER 46

### LADY MARY'S DREAM

WHEN the Duke and his daughter reached Custins they found a large party assembled, and were somewhat surprised at the crowd. Lord and Lady Nidderdale were there, which might have been expected as they were part of the family. With Lord Popplecourt had come his recent friend Adolphus Longstaff. That too might have been natural. Mr and Miss Boncassen were there also, who at this moment were quite strangers to the Duke; and Mr Lupton. The Duke also found Lady Chiltern,* whose father-in-law had more than once sat in the same Cabinet with himself, and Mr Monk, who was generally spoken of as the head of the coming Liberal Government, and the Ladies Adelaide and Flora FitzHoward, the still unmarried but not very juvenile daughters of the Duke of St Bungay. These with a few others made a large party, and rather confused the Duke, who had hardly reflected that discreet and profitable love-making was more likely to go on among numbers, than if the two young people were thrown together with no other companions.

Lord Popplecourt had been made to understand what was expected of him, and after some hesitation had submitted himself to the conspiracy. There would not be less at any rate than two hundred thousand pounds;—and the connexion would be made with one of the highest families in Great Britain. Though Lady Cantrip had said very few words, those words had been expressive; and the young bachelor peer had given in his adhesion. Some vague half-defined tale had been told him,—not about Tregear, as Tregear's name had not been mentioned,—but respecting some dream of a young man who had flitted across the girl's path during her mother's lifetime. 'All girls have such dreams,' Lady Cantrip had suggested. Whereupon Lord Popplecourt said that he supposed it was so. 'But a softer, purer, more unsullied flower never waited on its stalk till the proper fingers should come to pluck it,' said Lady Cantrip, rising to unaccustomed poetry on behalf of her friend the Duke. Lord Popplecourt accepted the poetry and was ready to do his best to pluck the flower.

Soon after the Duke's arrival Lord Popplecourt found himself in one of the drawing-rooms with Lady Cantrip and his proposed father-in-law. A hint had been given him that he might as well be home early from shooting, so as to be in the way. As the hour in which he was to make himself specially agreeable, both to the father and to the daughter, had drawn nigh, he became somewhat nervous, and now, at this moment, was not altogether comfortable. Though he had been concerned in no such matter before, he had an idea that love was a soft kind of thing which ought to steal on one unawares and come and go without trouble. In his case it came upon him with a rough demand for immediate hard work. He had not previously thought that he was to be subjected to such labours, and at this moment almost resented the interference with his ease. He was already a little angry with Lady Cantrip, but at the same time felt himself to be so much in subjection to her that he could not rebel.

The Duke himself when he saw the young man was hardly more comfortable. He had brought his daughter to Custins, feeling that it was his duty to be with her; but he would have preferred to leave the whole operation to the care of Lady Cantrip. He hardly liked to look at the fish whom he wished to catch for his daughter. Whenever this aspect of affairs presented itself to him, he would endeavour to console himself by remembering the past success of a similar transaction. He thought of his own first interview with his wife. 'You have heard,' he had said, 'what our friends wish.' She had pouted her lips, and when gently pressed had at last muttered, with her shoulder turned to him, that she supposed it was to be so. Very much more coercion had been used to her then than either himself or Lady Cantrip had dared to apply to his daughter. He did not think that his girl in her present condition of mind would signify to Lord Popplecourt that 'she supposed it was to be so.' Now that the time for the transaction was present he felt almost sure it would never be transacted. But still he must go on with it. Were he now to abandon his scheme, would it not be tantamount to abandoning everything? So he wreathed his face in smiles,—or made some attempt at it,—as he greeted the young man.

'I hope you and Lady Mary had a pleasant journey abroad,' said Lord Popplecourt. Lord Popplecourt, being aware that he had been chosen as a son-in-law, felt himself called upon to be familiar as well as pleasant. 'I often thought of you and Lady Mary, and wondered what you were about.'

'We were visiting lakes and mountains, churches and picture galleries, cities and salt-mines,'* said the Duke.

'Does Lady Mary like that sort of thing?'

'I think she was pleased with what she saw.'

'She has been abroad a great deal before, I believe. It depends so much on whom you meet when abroad.'

This was unfortunate, because it recalled Tregear to the Duke's mind. 'We saw very few people whom we knew,' he said.

'I've been shooting in Scotland with Silverbridge, and Gerald, and Reginald Dobbes, and Nidderdale,—and that fellow Tregear, who is so thick with Silverbridge.'

'Indeed!'

'I'm told that Lord Gerald is going to be the great shot of his day,' said Lady Cantrip.

'It is a distinction,' said the Duke bitterly.

'He did not beat me by so much,' continued Popplecourt. 'I think Tregear did the best with his rifle. One morning he potted three. Dobbes was disgusted. He hated Tregear.'

'Isn't it stupid,—half-a-dozen men getting together in that way?' asked Lady Cantrip.

'Nidderdale is always jolly.'

'I am glad to hear that,' said the mother-in-law.

'And Gerald is a regular brick.' The Duke bowed. 'Silverbridge used always to be going off to Killancodlem, where there were a lot of ladies. He is very sweet, you know, on this American girl whom you have here.' Again the Duke winced.* 'Dobbes is awfully good as to making out the shooting, but then he is a tyrant. Nevertheless I agree with him, if you mean to do a thing you should do it.'

'Certainly,' said the Duke. 'But you should make up your mind first whether the thing is worth doing.'

'Just so,' said Popplecourt. 'And as grouse and deer together are about the best things out, most of us made up our minds that it was worth doing. But that fellow Tregear would argue it out. He said a gentleman oughtn't to play billiards as well as a marker.'*

'I think he was right,' said the Duke.

'Do you know Mr Tregear, Duke?'

'I have met him—with my son.'

'Do you like him?'

'I have seen very little of him.'

'I cannot say I do. He thinks so much of himself. Of course he is very intimate with Silverbridge, and that is all that any one knows of him.' The Duke bowed almost haughtily, though why he bowed he could hardly have explained to himself. Lady Cantrip bit her lips in disgust. 'He's just the fellow,' continued Popplecourt, 'to think that some princess has fallen in love with him.' Then the Duke left the room.

'You had better not talk to him about Mr Tregear,' said Lady Cantrip.

'Why not?'

'I don't know whether he approves of the intimacy between him and Lord Silverbridge.'

'I should think not;—a man without any position or a shilling in the world.'

'The Duke is peculiar. If a subject is distasteful to him he does not like it to be mentioned. You had better not mention Mr Tregear.' Lady Cantrip, as she said this, blushed inwardly at her own hypocrisy.

It was of course contrived at dinner that Lord Popplecourt should take out Lady Mary. It is impossible to discover how such things get wind, but there was already an idea prevalent at Custins that Lord Popplecourt had matrimonial views, and that these views were looked upon favourably. 'You may be quite sure of it, Mr Lupton,' Lady Adelaide FitzHoward had said. 'I'll make a bet they're married before this time next year.'

'It will be a terrible case of Beauty and the Beast,' said Lupton.

Lady Chiltern had whispered a suspicion of the same kind, and had expressed a hope that the lover would be worthy of the girl. And Dolly Longstaff had chaffed his friend Popplecourt on the subject, Popplecourt having laid himself open by indiscreet allusions to Dolly's love for Miss Boncassen. 'Everybody can't have it as easily arranged for him as you,—a Duke's daughter and a pot of money without so much as the trouble of asking for it!'

'What do you know about the Duke's children?'

'That's what it is to be a lord and not to have a father.' Popplecourt tried to show that he was disgusted; but he felt himself all the more strongly bound to go on with his project.

It was therefore a matter of course that these should-be lovers would be sent out of the room together. 'You'll give your arm to Mary,' Lady Cantrip said, dropping the ceremonial prefix. Lady Mary of course went out as she was bidden. Though everybody else knew it, no idea of what was intended had yet come across her mind.

The should-be lover immediately reverted to the Austrian tour, expressing a hope that his neighbour had enjoyed herself. 'There's nothing I like so much myself,' said he, remembering some of the Duke's words, 'as mountains, cities, salt-mines, and all that kind of thing. There's such a lot of interest about it.'

'Did you ever see a salt-mine?'

'Well,—not exactly a salt-mine; but I have coalmines on my property in Staffordshire. I'm very fond of coal. I hope you like coal.'

'I like salt a great deal better—to look at.'

'But which do you think pays best? I don't mind telling you,— though it's a kind of thing I never talk about to strangers,—the royal-ties* from the Blogownie and Toodlem mines go up regularly two thousand pounds every year.'

'I thought we were talking about what was pretty to look at.'

'So we were. I'm as fond of pretty things as anybody. Do you know Reginald Dobbes?'

'No, I don't. Is he pretty?'

'He used to be so angry with Silverbridge, because Silverbridge would say Crummie-Toddie was ugly.'

'Was Crummie-Toddie ugly?'

'Just a plain house on a moor.'

'That sounds ugly.'

'I suppose your family like pretty things?'

'I hope so.'

'I do, I know.' Lord Popplecourt endeavoured to look as though he intended her to understand that she was the pretty thing which he most particularly liked. She partly conceived his meaning, and was disgusted accordingly. On the other side of her sat Mr Boncassen, to whom she had been introduced in the drawing-room,—and who had said a few words to her about some Norwegian poet. She turned round to him, and asked him some questions about the Skald,* and so, getting into conversation with him, managed to turn her shoulder to her suitor. On the other side of him sat Lady Rosina de Courcy,* to whom, as being an old woman and an old maid, he felt very little inclined to be courteous. She said a word, asking him whether he did not think the weather was treacherous. He answered her very curtly, and sat bolt upright, looking forward on the table, and taking his dinner as it came to him. He had been put there in order that Lady Mary Palliser might talk to him, and he regarded interference on the part of that old American as being ungentlemanlike. But the old American disregarded him, and went on with his quotations from the Scandinavian bard.

But Mr Boncassen sat next to Lady Cantrip, and when at last he was called upon to give his ear to the Countess, Lady Mary was again vacant for Popplecourt's attentions.

'Are you very fond of poetry?' he asked.

'Very fond.'

'So am I. Which do you like best, Tennyson or Shakespeare?'

'They are very unlike.'

'Yes;—they are unlike. Or Moore's Melodies.* I am very fond of "When in death I shall calm recline." I think this equal to anything. Reginald Dobbes would have it that poetry is all bosh.'

'Then I think that Mr Reginald Dobbes must be all bosh himself.'

'There was a man there named Tregear who had brought some books.' Then there was a pause. Lady Mary had not a word to say. 'Dobbes used to declare that he was always pretending to read poetry.'

'Mr Tregear never pretends anything.'

'Do you know him?' asked the rival.

'He is my brother's most particular friend.'

'Ah! yes. I dare say Silverbridge has talked to you about him. I think he's a stuck-up sort of fellow.' To this there was not a word of reply. 'Where did your brother pick him up?'

'They were at Oxford together.'

'I must say I think he gives himself airs;—because, you know, he's nobody.'

'I don't know anything of the kind,' said Lady Mary, becoming very red. 'And as he is my brother's most particular friend,—his very friend of friends,—I think you had better not abuse him to me.'

'I don't think the Duke is very fond of him.'

'I don't care who is fond of him. I am very fond of Silverbridge, and I won't hear his friend ill-spoken of. I dare say he had some books with him. He is not at all the sort of a man to go to a place and satisfy himself with doing nothing but killing animals.'

'Do you know him, Lady Mary?'

'I have seen him, and of course I have heard a great deal of him from Silverbridge. I would rather not talk any more about him.'

'You seem to be very fond of Mr Tregear,' he said angrily.

'It is no business of yours, Lord Popplecourt, whether I am fond of anybody or not. I have told you that Mr Tregear is my brother's friend, and that ought to be enough.'

Lord Popplecourt was a young man possessed of a certain amount of ingenuity. It was said of him that he knew on which side his bread was buttered, and that if you wished to take him in you must get up early. After dinner and during the night he pondered a good deal on what he had heard. Lady Cantrip had told him there had been a—dream. What was he to believe about that dream? Had he not better avoid the error of putting too fine a point upon it, and tell himself at once that a dream in this instance meant a—lover? Lady Mary had already been troubled by a lover! He was disposed to believe that young ladies often do have objectionable lovers, and that things get themselves right afterwards. Young ladies can be made to understand the beauty of coal-mines almost as readily as young gentlemen. There would be the two hundred thousand pounds; and there was the girl, beautiful, well-born, and thoroughly well-mannered. But what if this Tregear and the dream were one and the same? If so, had he not received plenty of evidence that the dream had not yet passed away? A remnant of affection for the dream would not have been a fatal barrier, had not the girl been so fierce with him in defence of her dream. He remembered, too, what the Duke had said about Tregear, and Lady Cantrip's advice to him to be silent in respect to this man. And then do girls generally defend their brothers' friends as she had defended Tregear? He thought not. Putting all these things together on the following morning he came to an uncomfortable belief that Tregear was the dream.

Soon after that he found himself near to Dolly Longstaff as they were shooting. 'You know that fellow Tregear, don't you?'

'Oh Lord, yes. He is Silverbridge's pal.'

'Did you ever hear anything about him?'

'What sort of thing?'

'Was he ever—ever in love with anyone?'

'I fancy he used to be awfully spooney on Mab Grex. I remember hearing that they were to have been married, only that neither of them had sixpence.'

'Oh—Lady Mabel Grex! That's a horse of another colour.'*

'And which is the horse of your colour?'

'I haven't got a horse,' said Lord Popplecourt, going away to his own corner.


## CHAPTER 47

### MISS BONCASSEN'S IDEA OF HEAVEN

IT was generally known that Dolly Longstaff had been heavily smitten by the charms of Miss Boncassen; but the world hardly gave him credit for the earnestness of his affection. Dolly had never been known to be in earnest in anything;—but now he was in very truth in love. He had agreed to be Popplecourt's companion at Custins because he had heard that Miss Boncassen would be there. He had thought over the matter with more consideration than he had ever before given to any subject. He had gone so far as to see his own man of business, with a view of ascertaining what settlements* he could make and what income he might be able to spend. He had told himself over and over again that he was not the 'sort of fellow' that ought to marry; but it was all of no avail. He confessed to himself that he was completely 'bowled over,'— 'knocked off his pins!'

'Is a fellow to have no chance?' he said to Miss Boncassen at Custins.

'If I understand what a fellow means, I am afraid not.'

'No man alive was ever more in earnest than I am.'

'Well, Mr Longstaff, I do not suppose that you have been trying to take me in all this time.'

'I hope you do not think ill of me.'

'I may think well of a great many gentlemen without wishing to marry them.'

'But does love go for nothing?' said Dolly, putting his hand upon his heart. 'Perhaps there are so many that love you.'

'Not above half-a-dozen or so.'

'You can make a joke of it, when I——. But I don't think, Miss Boncassen, you at all realise what I feel. As to settlements and all that, your father could do what he likes with me.'

'My father has nothing to do with it, and I don't know what settlements mean. We never think anything of settlements in our country.* If two young people love each other they go and get married.'

'Let us do the same here.'

'But the two young people don't love each other. Look here, Mr Longstaff; it's my opinion that a young woman ought not to be pestered.'

'Pestered!'

'You force me to speak in that way. I've given you an answer ever so many times. I will not be made to do it over and over again.'

'It's that d—— fellow, Silverbridge,' he exclaimed almost angrily. On hearing this Miss Boncassen left the room without speaking another word, and Dolly Longstaff found himself alone. He saw what he had done as soon as she was gone. After that he could hardly venture to persevere again—here at Custins. He weighed it over in his mind for a long time, almost coming to a resolution in favour of hard drink. He had never felt anything like this before. He was so uncomfortable that he couldn't eat his luncheon, though in accordance with his usual habit he had breakfasted off soda-and-brandy and a morsel of devilled toast. He did not know himself in his changed character. 'I wonder whether she understands that I have four thousand pounds a year of my own, and shall have twelve thousand pounds more when my governor goes! She was so headstrong that it was impossible to explain anything to her.'

'I'm off to London,' he said to Popplecourt that afternoon.

'Nonsense! you said you'd stay for ten days.'

'All the same, I'm going at once. I've sent to Bridport for a trap,* and I shall sleep to-night at Dorchester.'

'What's the meaning of it all?'

'I've had some words with somebody. Don't mind asking any more.'

'Not with the Duke?'

'The Duke! No; I haven't spoken to him.'

'Or Lord Cantrip?'

'I wish you wouldn't ask questions.'

'If you've quarrelled with anybody you ought to consult a friend.'

'It's nothing of that kind.'

'Then it's a lady. It's the American girl!'

'Don't I tell you I don't want to talk about it? I'm going. I've told Lady Cantrip that my mother wasn't well and wants to see me. You'll stop your time out, I suppose?'

'I don't know.'

'You've got it all square, no doubt. I wish I'd a handle to my name. I never cared for it before.'

'I'm sorry you're so down in the mouth. Why don't you try again? The thing is to stick to 'em like wax. If ten times of asking won't do, go in twenty times.'

Dolly shook his head despondently. 'What can you do when a girl walks out of the room and slams the door in your face? She'll get it hot and heavy before she has done. I know what she's after. She might as well cry for the moon.' And so Dolly got into the trap and went to Bridport, and slept that night at the hotel at Dorchester.

Lord Popplecourt, though he could give such excellent advice to his friend, had been able as yet to do very little in his own case. He had been a week at Custins, and had said not a word to denote his passion. Day after day he had prepared himself for the encounter, but the lady had never given him the opportunity. When he sat next to her at dinner she would be very silent. If he stayed at home on a morning she was not visible. During the short evenings he could never get her attention. And he made no progress with the Duke. The Duke had been very courteous to him at Richmond, but here he was monosyllabic and almost sullen.

Once or twice Lord Popplecourt had a little conversation with Lady Cantrip. 'Dear girl!' said her ladyship. 'She is so little given to seeking admiration.'

'I dare say.'

'Girls are so different, Lord Popplecourt. With some of them it seems that a gentleman need have no trouble in explaining what it is that he wishes.'

'I don't think Lady Mary is like that at all.'

'Not in the least. Any one who addresses her must be prepared to explain himself fully. Nor ought he to hope to get much encouragement at first. I do not think that Lady Mary will bestow her heart till she is sure she can give it with safety.' There was an amount of falsehood in this which was proof at any rate of very strong friendship on the part of Lady Cantrip.

After a few days Lady Mary became more intimate with the American and his daughter than with any others of the party. Perhaps she liked to talk about the Scandinavian poets, of whom Mr Boncassen was so fond. Perhaps she felt sure that her transatlantic friend would not make love to her. Perhaps it was that she yielded to the various allurements of Miss Boncassen. Miss Boncassen saw the Duke of Omnium for the first time at Custins, and there had the first opportunity of asking herself how such a man as that would receive from his son and heir such an announcement as Lord Silverbridge would have to make him should she at the end of three months accept his offer. She was quite aware that Lord Silverbridge need not repeat the offer unless he were so pleased. But she thought that he would come again. He had so spoken that she was sure of his love; and had so spoken as to obtain hers. Yes;—she was sure that she loved him. She had never seen anything like him before;—so glorious in his beauty, so gentle in his manhood, so powerful and yet so little imperious, so great in condition, and yet so little confident in his own greatness, so bolstered up with external advantages, and so little apt to trust anything but his own heart and his own voice. In asking for her love he had put forward no claim but his own love. She was glad he was what he was. She counted at their full value all his natural advantages. To be an English Duchess! Oh—yes; her ambition understood it all! But she loved him, because in the expression of his love no hint had fallen from him of the greatness of the benefits which he could confer upon her. Yes, she would like to be a Duchess; but not to be a Duchess would she become the wife of a man who should begin his courtship by assuming a superiority.

Now the chances of society had brought her into the company of his nearest friends. She was in the house with his father and with his sister. Now and again the Duke spoke a few words to her, and always did so with a peculiar courtesy. But she was sure that the Duke had heard nothing of his son's courtship. And she was equally sure that the matter had not reached Lady Mary's ears. She perceived that the Duke and her father would often converse together. Mr Boncassen would discuss republicanism generally, and the Duke would explain that theory of monarchy as it prevails in England, which but very few Americans have ever been made to understand. All this Miss Boncassen watched with pleasure. She was still of opinion that it would not become her to force her way into a family which would endeavour to repudiate her. She would not become this young man's wife if all connected with the young man were resolved to reject the contact. But if she could conquer them,—then,—then she thought that she could put her little hand into that young man's grasp with a happy heart.

It was in this frame of mind that she laid herself out not unsuccessfully to win the esteem of Lady Mary Palliser. 'I do not know whether you approve it,' Lady Cantrip said to the Duke; 'but Mary has become very intimate with our new American friend.' At this time Lady Cantrip had become very nervous,—so as almost to wish that Lady Mary's difficulties might be unravelled elsewhere than at Custins.

'They seem to be sensible people,' said the Duke. 'I don't know when I have met a man with higher ideas on politics than Mr Boncassen.'

'His daughter is popular with everybody.'

'A nice ladylike girl,' said the Duke, 'and appears to have been well educated.'

It was now near the end of October, and the weather was peculiarly fine. Perhaps in our climate, October would of all months be the most delightful if something of its charms were not detracted from by the feeling that with it will depart the last relics of the delights of summer. The leaves are still there with their gorgeous colouring, but they are going. The last rose still lingers on the bush, but it is the last. The woodland walks are still pleasant to the feet, but caution is heard on every side as to the coming winter.

The park at Custins, which was spacious, had many woodland walks attached to it, from which, through vistas of the timber, distant glimpses of the sea were caught. Within half a mile of the house the woods were reached, and within a mile the open sea was in sight,—and yet the wanderers might walk for miles without going over the same ground. Here, without other companions, Lady Mary and Miss Boncassen found themselves one afternoon, and here the latter told her story to her lover's sister. 'I so long to tell you something,' she said.

'Is it a secret?' asked Lady Mary.

'Well; yes; it is,—if you will keep it so. I would rather you should keep it a secret. But I will tell you.' Then she stood still, looking into the other's face. 'I wonder how you will take it.'

'What can it be?'

'Your brother has asked me to be his wife.'

'Silverbridge!'

'Yes;—Lord Silverbridge. You are astonished.'

Lady Mary was very much astonished,—so much astonished that words escaped from her, which she regretted afterwards. 'I thought there was someone else.'

'Who else?'

'Lady Mabel Grex. But I know nothing.'

'I think not,' said Miss Boncassen slowly. 'I have seen them together and I think not. There might be somebody, though I think not her. But why do I say that? Why do I malign him, and make so little of myself? There is no one else, Lady Mary. Is he not true?'

'I think he is true.'

'I am sure he is true. And he has asked me to be his wife.'

'What did you say?'

'Well;—what do you think? What is it probable that such a girl as I would say when such a man as your brother asks her to be his wife? Is he not such a man as a girl would love?'

'Oh yes.'

'Is he not handsome as a god?' Mary stared at her with all her eyes. 'And sweeter than any god those pagan races knew? And is he not good-tempered, and loving; and has he not that perfection of manly dash without which I do not think I could give my heart to any man?'

'Then you have accepted him?'

'And his rank and his wealth! The highest position in all the world in my eyes.'

'I do not think you should take him for that.'

'Does it not all help? Can you put yourself in my place? Why should I refuse him? No, not for that. I would not take him for that. But if I love him,—because he is all that my imagination tells me that a man ought to be;—if to be his wife seems to me to be the greatest bliss that could happen to a woman; if I feel that I could die to serve him, that I could live to worship him, that his touch would be sweet to me, his voice music, his strength the only support in the world on which I would care to lean,—what then?'

'Is it so?'

'Yes, it is so. It is after that fashion that I love him. He is my hero;— and not the less so because there is none higher than he among the nobles of the greatest land under the sun. Would you have me for a sister?' Lady Mary could not answer all at once. She had to think of her father;—and then she thought of her own lover. Why should not Silverbridge be as well entitled to his choice as she considered herself to be? And yet how would it be with her father? Silverbridge would in process of time be the head of the family. Would it be proper that he should marry an American?

'You would not like me for a sister?'

'I was thinking of my father. For myself I like you.'

'Shall I tell you what I said to him?'

'If you will.'

'I told him that he must ask his friends;—that I would not be his wife to be rejected by them all. Nor will I. Though it be heaven I will not creep there through a hole. If I cannot go in with my head upright, I will not go even there.' Then she turned round as though she were prepared in her emotion to walk back to the house alone. But Lady Mary ran after her, and having caught her, put her arm round her waist and kissed her.

'I at any rate will love you,' said Lady Mary.

'I will do as I have said,' continued Miss Boncassen. 'I will do as I have said. Though I love your brother down to the ground he shall not marry me without his father's consent.' Then they returned arm-in-arm close together; but very little more was said between them.

When Lady Mary entered the house she was told that Lady Cantrip wished to see her in her own room.

## CHAPTER 48

### THE PARTY AT CUSTINS IS BROKEN UP

THE message was given to Lady Mary after so solemn a fashion that she was sure some important communication was to be made to her. Her mind at that moment had been filled with her new friend's story. She felt that she required some time to meditate before she could determine what she herself would wish; but when she was going to her own room, in order that she might think it over, she was summoned to Lady Cantrip. 'My dear,' said the Countess, 'I wish you to do something to oblige me.'

'Of course I will.'

'Lord Popplecourt wants to speak to you.'

'Who?'

'Lord Popplecourt.'

'What can Lord Popplecourt have to say to me?'

'Can you not guess? Lord Popplecourt is a young nobleman, standing very high in the world, possessed of ample means, just in that position in which it behoves such a man to look about for a wife.' Lady Mary pressed her lips together, and clenched her two hands. 'Can you not imagine what such a gentleman may have to say?' Then there was a pause, but she made no immediate answer. 'I am to tell you, my dear, that your father would approve of it.'

'Approve of what?'

'He approves of Lord Popplecourt as a suitor for your hand.'

'How can he?'

'Why not, Mary? Of course he has made it his business to ascertain all particulars as to Lord Popplecourt's character and property.'

'Papa knows that I love somebody else.'

'My dear Mary, that is all vanity.'

'I don't think that papa can want to see me married to a man when he knows that with all my heart and soul——'

'Oh Mary!'

'When he knows,' continued Mary, who would not be put down, 'that I love another man with all my heart. What will Lord Popplecourt say if I tell him that? If he says anything to me, I shall tell him. Lord Popplecourt! He cares for nothing but his coal-mines. Of course, if you bid me see him I will; but it can do no good. I despise him, and if he troubles me I shall hate him. As for marrying him,—I would sooner die this minute.'

After this Lady Cantrip did not insist on the interview. She expressed her regret that things should be as they were,—explained in sweetly innocent phrases that in a certain rank of life young ladies could not always marry the gentlemen to whom their fancies might attach them, but must, not unfrequently, postpone their youthful inclinations to the will of their elders,—or in less delicate language, that though they might love in one direction they must marry in another; and then expressed a hope that her dear Mary would think over these things and try to please her father. 'Why does he not try to please me?' said Mary. Then Lady Cantrip was obliged to see Lord Popplecourt, a necessity which was a great nuisance to her. 'Yes;—she understands what you mean. But she is not prepared for it yet. You must wait awhile.'

'I don't see why I am to wait.'

'She is very young,—and so are you, indeed. There is plenty of time.'

'There is somebody else I suppose.'

'I told you,' said Lady Cantrip, in her softest voice, 'that there has been a dream across her path.'

'It's that Tregear!'

'I am not prepared to mention names,' said Lady Cantrip, astonished that he should know so much. 'But indeed you must wait.'

'I don't see it, Lady Cantrip.'

'What can I say more? If you think that such a girl as Lady Mary Palliser, the daughter of the Duke of Omnium, possessed of fortune, beauty, and every good gift, is to come like a bird to your call, you will find yourself mistaken. All that her friends can do for you will be done. The rest must remain with yourself.' During that evening Lord Popplecourt endeavoured to make himself pleasant to one of the FitzHoward young ladies, and on the next morning he took his leave of Custins.

'I will never interfere again in reference to anybody else's child as long as I live,' Lady Cantrip said to her husband that night.

Lady Mary was very much tempted to open her heart to Miss Boncassen. It would be delightful to her to have a friend; but were she to engage Miss Boncassen's sympathies on her behalf, she must of course sympathise with Miss Boncassen in return. And what if, after all, Silverbridge were not devoted to the American beauty! What if it should turn out that he was going to marry Lady Mabel Grex! 'I wish you would call me Isabel,' her friend said to her. 'It is so odd,—since I have left New York I have never heard my name from any lips except father's and mother's.'

'Has not Silverbridge ever called you by your Christian name?'

'I think not. I am sure he never has.' But he had, though it had passed by her at the moment without attention. 'It all came from him so suddenly. And yet I expected it. But it was too sudden for Christian names and pretty talk. I do not even know what his name is.'

'Plantagenet,*—but we always call him Silverbridge.'

'Plantagenet is very much prettier. I shall always call him Plantagenet. But I recall that. You will not remember that against me?'

'I will remember nothing that you do not wish.'

'I mean that if,—if all the grandeurs of all the Pallisers could consent to put up with poor me, if heaven were opened to me with a straight gate, so that I could walk out of our republic into your aristocracy with my head erect, with the stars and stripes waving proudly round me till I had been accepted into the shelter of the Omnium griffins*,—then I would call him——'

'There's one Palliser would welcome you.'

'Would you, dear? Then I will love you so dearly. May I call you Mary?'

'Of course you may.'

'Mary is the prettiest name under the sun. But Plantagenet is so grand! Which of the kings did you branch off from?'

'I know nothing about it. From none of them, I should think. There is some story about a Sir Guy* who was a king's friend. I never trouble myself about it. I hate aristocracy.'

'Do you, dear?'

'Yes,' said Mary, full of her own grievances. 'It is an abominable bondage, and I do not see that it does any good at all.'

'I think it is so glorious,' said the American. 'There is no such mischievous nonsense in all the world as equality. That is what father says. What men ought to want is liberty.'

'It is terrible to be tied up in a small circle,' said the Duke's daughter.

'What do you mean, Lady Mary?'

'I thought you were to call me Mary. What I mean is this. Suppose that Silverbridge loves you better than all the world.'

'I hope he does. I think he does.'

'And suppose he cannot marry you, because of his—aristocracy?'

'But he can.'

'I thought you were saying yourself——'

'Saying what? That he could not marry me! No, indeed! But that under certain circumstances I would not marry him. You don't suppose that I think he would be disgraced? If so I would go away at once, and he should never again see my face or hear my voice. I think myself good enough for the best man God ever made. But if others think differently, and those others are so closely concerned with him, and would be so closely concerned with me, as to trouble our joint lives,—then will I neither subject him to such sorrow nor will I encounter it myself.'

'It all comes from what you call aristocracy.'

'No, dear;—but from the prejudices of an aristocracy. To tell the truth, Mary, the more difficult a place is to get into, the more the right of going in is valued. If everybody could be a Duchess and a Palliser, I should not perhaps think so much about it.'

'I thought it was because you loved him.'

'So I do. I love him entirely. I have said not a word of that to him;—but I do, if I know at all what love is. But if you love a star, the pride you have in your star will enhance your love. Though you know that you must die of your love, still you must love your star.'

And yet Mary could not tell her tale in return. She could not show the reverse picture;—that she being a star was anxious to dispose of herself after the fashion of poor human rushlights.* It was not that she was ashamed of her love, but that she could not bring herself to yield altogether in reference to the great descent which Silverbridge would have to make.

On the day after this,—the last day of the Duke's sojourn at Custins, the last also of the Boncassens' visit,—it came to pass that the Duke and Mr Boncassen, with Lady Mary and Isabel, were all walking in the woods together. And it so happened when they were at a little distance from the house, each of the girls was walking with the other girl's father. Isabel had calculated what she would say to the Duke should a time for speaking come to her. She could not tell him of his son's love. She could not ask his permission. She could not explain to him all her feelings, or tell him what she thought of her proper way of getting into heaven. That must come afterwards if it should ever come at all. But there was something that she could tell. 'We are so different from you,' she said, speaking of her own country.

'And yet so like,' said the Duke smiling;—'your language, your laws, your habits!'

'But still there is such a difference! I do not think there is a man in the whole Union more respected than father.'

'I dare say not.'

'Many people think that if he would only allow himself to be put in nomination, he might be the next president.'

'The choice, I am sure, would do your country honour.'

'And yet his father was a poor labourer who earned his bread among the shipping at New York. That kind of thing would be impossible here.'

'My dear young lady, there you wrong us.'

'Do I?'

'Certainly! A Prime Minister with us might as easily come from the same class.'

'Here you think so much of rank. You are—a Duke.'

'But a Prime Minister can make a Duke; and if a man can raise himself by his own intellect to that position, no one will think of his father or his grandfather. The sons of merchants have with us been Prime Ministers more than once, and no Englishmen ever were more honoured among their countrymen. Our peerage is being continually recruited from the ranks of the people, and hence it gets its strength.'

'Is it so?'

'There is no greater mistake than to suppose that inferiority of birth is a barrier to success in this country.'

She listened to this and to much more on the same subject with attentive ears,—not shaken in her ideas as to the English aristocracy in general, but thinking that she was perhaps learning something of his own individual opinions. If he were more liberal than others, on that liberality might perhaps be based her own happiness and fortune.

He, in all this, was quite unconscious of the working of her mind. Nor in discussing such matters generally did he ever mingle his own private feelings, his own pride of race and name, his own ideas of what was due to his ancient rank with the political creed by which his conduct in public life was governed. The peer who sat next to him in the House of Lords, whose grandmother had been a washerwoman and whose father an innkeeper, was to him every whit as good a peer as himself. And he would as soon sit in counsel with Mr Monk, whose father had risen from a mechanic to be a merchant, as with any nobleman who could count ancestors against himself. But there was an inner feeling in his bosom as to his own family, his own name, his own children, and his own personal self, which was kept altogether apart from his grand political theories. It was a subject on which he never spoke; but the feeling had come to him as a part of his birthright. And he conceived that it would pass through him to his children after the same fashion. It was this which made the idea of a marriage between his daughter and Tregear intolerable to him, and which would operate as strongly in regard to any marriage which his son might contemplate. Lord Grex was not a man with whom he would wish to form any intimacy. He was, we may say, a wretched unprincipled old man, bad all round; and such the Duke knew him to be. But the blue blood and the rank were there; and as the girl was good herself, he would have been quite contented that his son should marry the daughter of Lord Grex. That one and the same man should have been in one part of himself so unlike the other part,—that he should have one set of opinions so contrary to another set,—poor Isabel Boncassen did not understand.

# CHAPTER 49

## THE MAJOR'S FATE

THE affair of Prime Minister and the nail was not allowed to fade away into obscurity. Through September and October it was made matter for pungent inquiry. The Jockey Club was alive. Mr Pook was very instant,—with many Pookites anxious to free themselves from suspicion. Sporting men declared that the honour of the turf required that every detail of the case should be laid open. But by the end of October, though every detail had been surmised, nothing had in truth been discovered. Nobody doubted but that Tifto had driven the nail into the horse's foot, and that Green and Gilbert Villiers had shared the bulk of the plunder. They had gone off on their travels together, and the fact that each of them had been in possession of about twenty thousand pounds was proved. But then there is no law against two gentlemen having such a sum of money. It was notorious that Captain Green and Mr Gilbert Villiers had enriched themselves to this extent by the failure of Prime Minister. But yet nothing was proved!

That the Major had either himself driven in the nail or seen it done, all racing men were agreed. He had been out with the horse in the morning and had been the first to declare that the animal was lame. And he had been with the horse till the farrier had come. But he had concocted a story for himself. He did not dispute that the horse had been lamed by the machinations of Green and Villiers,—with the assistance of the groom. No doubt, he said, these men, who had been afraid to face an inquiry, had contrived and had carried out the iniquity. How the lameness had been caused he could not pretend to say. The groom who was at the horse's head, and who evidently knew how these things were done, might have struck a nerve in the horse's foot with his boot. But when the horse was got into the stable he, Tifto,—so he declared,—at once ran out to send for the farrier. During the minutes so occupied the operation must have been made with the nail. That was Tifto's story,—and as he kept his ground, there were some few who believed it.

But though the story was so far good, he had at moments been imprudent, and had talked when he should have been silent. The whole matter had been a torment to him. In the first place his conscience made him miserable. As long as it had been possible to prevent the evil he had hoped to make a clean breast of it to Lord Silverbridge. Up to this period of his life everything had been 'square' with him. He had betted 'square,' and had ridden 'square,' and had run horses 'square.' He had taken a pride in this, as though it had been a great virtue. It was not without great inward grief that he had deprived himself of the consolations of these reflections! But when he had approached his noble partner, his noble partner snubbed him at every turn,—and he did the deed.

His reward was to be three thousand pounds,—and he got his money. The money was very much to him,—would perhaps have been almost enough to comfort him in his misery, had not those other rascals got so much more. When he heard that the groom's fee was higher than his own, it almost broke his heart. Green and Villiers, men of infinitely lower standing,—men at whom the Beargarden would not have looked,—had absolutely netted fortunes on which they could live in comfort. No doubt they had run away while Tifto still stood his ground;—but he soon began to doubt whether to have run away with twenty thousand pounds was not better than to remain with such small plunder as had fallen to his lot, among such faces as those which now looked upon him! Then when he had drunk a few glasses of whisky-and-water, he said something very foolish as to his power of punishing that swindler Green.

An attempt had been made to induce Silverbridge to delay the payment of his bets;—but he had been very eager that they should be paid. Under the joint auspices of Mr Lupton and Mr Moreton the horses were sold, and the establishment was annihilated,—with considerable loss, but with great despatch. The Duke had been urgent. The Jockey Club, and the racing world, and the horsey fraternity generally, might do what seemed to them good,—so that Silverbridge was extricated from the matter. Silverbridge was extricated,—and the Duke cared nothing for the rest.

But Silverbridge could not get out of the mess quite so easily as his father wished. Two questions arose about Major Tifto, outside the racing world, but within the domain of the world of sport and pleasure generally, as to one of which it was impossible that Silverbridge should not express an opinion. The first question had reference to the Mastership of the Runnymede hounds. In this our young friend was not bound to concern himself. The other affected the Beargarden Club; and, as Lord Silverbridge had introduced the Major, he could hardly forbear from the expression of an opinion.

There was a meeting of the subscribers to the hunt in the last week of October. At that meeting Major Tifto told his story. There he was, to answer any charge which might be brought against him. If he had made money by losing the race,—where was it and whence had it come? Was it not clear that a conspiracy might have been made without his knowledge;—and clear also that the real conspirators had levanted?* He had not levanted! The hounds were his own. He had undertaken to hunt the country for this season, and they had undertaken to pay him a certain sum of money. He should expect and demand that sum of money. If they chose to make any other arrangement for the year following they could do so. Then he sat down and the meeting was adjourned,—the secretary having declared that he would not act in that capacity any longer, nor collect the funds. A farmer had also asserted that he and his friends had resolved that Major Tifto should not ride over their fields. On the next day the Major had his hounds out, and some of the London men, with a few of the neighbours, joined him. Gates were locked; but the hounds ran, and those who chose to ride managed to follow them. There are men who will stick to their sport though Apollyon* himself should carry the horn. Who cares whether the lady who fills a theatre be or be not a moral young woman, or whether the bandmaster who keeps such excellent time in a ball has or has not paid his debts? There were men of this sort who supported Major Tifto;—but then there was a general opinion that the Runnymede hunt would come to an end unless a new master could be found.

Then in the first week in November a special meeting was called at the Beargarden, at which Lord Silverbridge was asked to attend. 'It is impossible that he should be allowed to remain in the club.' This was said to Lord Silverbridge by Mr Lupton. 'Either he must go or the club must be broken up.'

Silverbridge was very unhappy on the occasion. He had at last been reasoned into believing that the horse had been made the victim of foul play; but he persisted in saying that there was no conclusive evidence against Tifto. The matter was argued with him. Tifto had laid bets against the horse; Tifto had been hand-and-glove with Green; Tifto could not have been absent from the horse above two minutes; the thing could not have been arranged without Tifto. As he had brought Tifto into the club, and had been his partner on the turf, it was his business to look into the matter. 'But for all that,' said he, 'I'm not going to jump on a man when he's down, unless I feel sure that he's guilty.'

Then the meeting was held, and Tifto himself appeared. When the accusation was made by Mr Lupton, who proposed that he should be expelled, he burst into tears. The whole story was repeated,—the nail, and the hammer, and the lameness; and the moments were counted up, and poor Tifto's bets and friendship with Green were made apparent,— and the case was submitted to the club. An old gentleman who had been connected with the turf all his life, and who would not have scrupled, by square betting, to rob his dearest friend of his last shilling, seconded the proposition,—telling all the story over again. Then Major Tifto was asked whether he wished to say anything.

'I've got to say that I'm here,' said Tifto, still crying, 'and if I'd done anything of that kind, of course I'd have gone with the rest of 'em. I put it to Lord Silverbridge to say whether I'm that sort of fellow.' Then he sat down.

Upon this there was a pause, and the club was manifestly of opinion that Lord Silverbridge ought to say something. 'I think that Major Tifto should not have betted against the horse,' said Silverbridge.

'I can explain that,' said the Major. 'Let me explain that. Everybody knows that I'm a man of small means. I wanted to 'edge,* I only wanted to 'edge.'

Mr Lupton shook his head. 'Why have you not shown me your book?'

'I told you before that it was stolen. Green got hold of it. I did win a little. I never said I didn't. But what has that to do with hammering a nail into a horse's foot? I have always been true to you, Lord Silverbridge, and you ought to stick up for me now.'

'I will have nothing further to do with the matter,' said Silverbridge, 'one way or the other,' and he walked out of the room,—and out of the club. The affair was ended by a magnanimous declaration on the part of Major Tifto that he would not remain in a club in which he was suspected, and by a consent on the part of the meeting to receive the Major's instant resignation.

## CHAPTER 50

### THE DUKE'S ARGUMENTS

THE Duke before he left Custins had an interview with Lady Cantrip, at which that lady found herself called upon to speak her mind freely. 'I don't think she cares about Lord Popplecourt,' Lady Cantrip said.

'I am sure I don't know why she should,' said the Duke, who was often very aggravating even to his friend.

'But as we had thought——'

'She ought to do as she is told,' said the Duke, remembering how obedient his Glencora had been. 'Has he spoken to her?'

'I think not.'

'Then how can we tell?'

'I asked her to see him, but she expressed so much dislike that I could not press it. I am afraid, Duke, that you will find it difficult to deal with her.'

'I have found it very difficult!'

'As you have trusted me so much——'

'Yes;—I have trusted you, and do trust you. I hope you understand that I appreciate your kindness.'

'Perhaps then you will let me say what I think.'

'Certainly, Lady Cantrip.'

'Mary is a very peculiar girl,—with great gifts,—but——'

'But what?'

'She is obstinate. Perhaps it would be fairer to say that she has great firmness of character. It is within your power to separate her from Mr Tregear. It would be foreign to her character to—to—leave you, except with your approbation.'

'You mean, she will not run away.'

'She will do nothing without your permission. But she will remain unmarried unless she be allowed to marry Mr Tregear.'

'What do you advise then?'

'That you should yield. As regards money, you could give them what they want. Let him go into public life. You could manage that for him.'

'He is Conservative!'

'What does that matter when the question is one of your daughter's happiness? Everybody tells me that he is clever and well conducted.'

He betrayed nothing by his face as this was said to him. But as he got into the carriage he was a miserable man. It is very well to tell a man that he should yield, but there is nothing so wretched to a man as yielding. Young people and women have to yield,—but for such a man as this, to yield is in itself a misery. In this matter the Duke was quite certain of the propriety of his judgment. To yield would be not only to mortify himself, but to do wrong at the same time. He had convinced himself that the Popplecourt arrangement would come to nothing. Nor had he and Lady Cantrip combined been able to exercise over her the sort of power to which Lady Glencora had been subjected. If he persevered,—and he still was sure, almost sure, that he would persevere,—his object must be achieved after a different fashion. There must be infinite suffering,—suffering both to him and to her. Could she have been made to consent to marry someone else, terrible as the rupture might have been, she would have reconciled herself at last to her new life. So it had been with his Glencora, after a time. Now the misery must go on from day to day beneath his eyes, with the knowledge on his part that he was crushing all joy out of her young life, and the conviction on her part that she was being treated with continued cruelty by her father! It was a terrible prospect! But if it was manifestly his duty to act after this fashion, must he not do his duty?

If he were to find that by persevering in this course he would doom her to death, or perchance to madness,—what then? If it were right, he must still do it. He must still do it, if the weakness incident to his human nature did not rob him of the necessary firmness. If every foolish girl were indulged, all restraint would be lost, and there would be an end to those rules as to birth and position by which he thought his world was kept straight. And then, mixed with all this, was his feeling of the young man's arrogance in looking for such a match. Here was a man without a shilling, whose manifest duty it was to go to work so that he might earn his bread, who instead of doing so, had hoped to raise himself to wealth and position by entrapping the heart of an unwary girl! There was something to the Duke's thinking base in this, and much more base because the unwary girl was his own daughter. That such a man as Tregear should make an attack upon him and select his rank, his wealth, and his child as the stepping-stones by which he intended to rise! What could be so mean as that a man should seek to live by looking out for a wife with money? But what so impudent, so .

arrogant, so unblushingly disregardful of propriety, as that he should endeavour to select his victim from such a family as that of the Pallisers, and that he should lay his impious hand on the very daughter of the Duke of Omnium?

But together with all this there came upon him moments of ineffable tenderness. He felt as though he longed to take her in his arms and tell her, that if she were unhappy, so would he be unhappy too,—to make her understand that a hard necessity had made this sorrow common to them both. He thought that, if she would only allow it, he could speak of her love as a calamity which had befallen them, as from the hand of fate, and not as a fault. If he could make a partnership in misery with her, so that each might believe that each was acting for the best, then he could endure all that might come. But, as he was well aware, she regarded him as being simply cruel to her. She did not understand that he was performing an imperative duty. She had set her heart upon a certain object, and having taught herself that in that way happiness might be reached, had no conception that there should be something in the world, some idea of personal dignity, more valuable to her than the fruition of her own desires! And yet every word he spoke to her was affectionate. He knew that she was bruised, and if it might be possible he would pour oil into her wounds,—even though she would not recognise the hand which relieved her.

They slept one night in town,—where they encountered Silverbridge soon after his retreat from the Beargarden. 'I cannot quite make up my mind, sir, about that fellow Tifto,' he said to his father.

'I hope you have made up your mind that he is no fit companion for yourself.'

'That's over. Everybody understands that, sir.'

'Is anything more necessary?'

'I don't like feeling that he has been ill-used. They have made him resign the club, and I fancy they won't have him at the hunt.'

'He has lost no money by you?'

'Oh no.'

'Then I think you may be indifferent. From all that I hear I think he must have won money,—which will probably be a consolation to him.'

'I think they have been hard upon him,' continued Silverbridge. 'Of course he is not a good man, nor a gentleman, nor possessed of very high feelings. But a man is not to be sacrificed altogether for that. There are so many men who are not gentlemen, and so many gentlemen who are bad fellows.'

'I have no doubt Mr Lupton knew what he was about,' replied the Duke.

On the next morning the Duke and Lady Mary went down to Matching, and as they sat together in the carriage after leaving the railway the father endeavoured to make himself pleasant to his daughter. 'I suppose we shall stay at Matching now till Christmas,' he said.

'I hope so.'

'Whom would you like to have here?'

'I don't want any one, papa.'

'You will be very sad without somebody. Would you like the Finns?'

'If you please, papa. I like her. He never talks anything but politics.'

'He is none the worse for that, Mary. I wonder whether Lady Mabel Grex would come.'

'Lady Mabel Grex!'

'Do you not like her?'

'Oh yes, I like her;—but what made you think of her, papa?'

'Perhaps Silverbridge would come to us then.'

Lady Mary thought that she knew a great deal more about that than her father did. 'Is he fond of Lady Mabel, papa?'

'Well,—I don't know. There are secrets which should not be told. I think they are very good friends. I would not have her asked unless it would please you.'

'I like her very much, papa.'

'And perhaps we might get the Boncassens to come to us. I did say a word to him about it.' Now, as Mary felt, difficulty was heaping itself upon difficulty. 'I have seldom met a man in whose company I could take more pleasure than in that of Mr Boncassen; and the young lady seems to be worthy of her father.' Mary was silent, feeling the complication of the difficulties. 'Do you not like her?' asked the Duke.

'Very much indeed,' said Mary.

'Then let us fix a day and ask them. If you will come to me after dinner with an almanac we will arrange it. Of course you will invite that Miss Cassewary too?'

The complication seemed to be very bad indeed. In the first place was it not clear that she, Lady Mary, ought not to be a party to asking Miss Boncassen to meet her brother at Matching? Would it not be imperative on her part to tell her father the whole story? And yet how could she do that? It had been told her in confidence, and she remembered what her own feelings had been when Mrs Finn had suggested the propriety of telling the story which had been told to her! And how would it be possible to ask Lady Mabel to come to Matching to meet Miss Boncassen in the presence of Silverbridge? If the party could be made up without Silverbridge things might run smoothly.

As she was thinking of this in her own room, thinking also how happy she could be if one other name might be added to the list of guests, the Duke had gone alone into his library. There a pile of letters reached him, among which he found one marked 'Private,' and addressed in a hand which he did not recognise. This he opened suddenly,—with a conviction that it would contain a thorn,—and, turning over the page, found the signature to it was 'Francis Tregear.' The man's name was wormwood* to him. He at once felt that he would wish to have his dinner, his fragment of a dinner, brought to him in that solitary room, and that he might remain secluded for the rest of the evening. But still he must read the letter;—and he read it.

'MY DEAR LORD DUKE,

   'If my mode of addressing your Grace be too familiar I hope you will excuse it. It seems to me that if I were to use one more distant, I should myself be detracting something from my right to make the claim which I intend to put forward. You know what my feelings are in reference to your daughter. I do not pretend to suppose that they should have the least weight with you. But you know also what her feelings are for me. A man seems to be vain when he expresses his conviction of a woman's love for himself. But this matter is so important to her as well as to me that I am compelled to lay aside all pretence. If she do not love me as I love her, then the whole thing drops to the ground. Then it will be for me to take myself off from out of your notice,—and from hers, and to keep to myself whatever heart-breaking I may have to undergo. But if she be as steadfast in this matter as I am,—if her happiness be fixed on marrying me as mine is on marrying her,—then, I think, I am entitled to ask you whether you are justified in keeping us apart.

   'I know well what are the discrepancies. Speaking from my own feeling I regard very little those of rank. I believe myself to be as good a gentleman as though my father's forefathers had sat for centuries past in the House of Lords. I believe that you would have thought so also, had you and I been brought in contact on any other subject. The discrepancy in regard to money is, I own, a great trouble to me. Having no wealth of my own I wish that your daughter were so circumstanced that I could go out into the world and earn bread for her. I know myself so well that I dare say positively that her money,—if it be that she will have money,—had no attractions for me when I first became acquainted with her, and adds nothing now to the persistency with which I claim her hand.

'But I venture to ask whether you can dare to keep us apart if her happiness depends on her love for me? It is now more than six months since I called upon you in London and explained my wishes. You will understand me when I say that I cannot be contented to sit idle, trusting simply to the assurance which I have of her affection. Did I doubt it, my way would be more clear. I should feel in that case that she would yield to your wishes, and I should then, as I have said before, just take myself out of the way. But if it be not so, then I am bound to do something,—on her behalf as well as my own. What am I to do? Any endeavour to meet her clandestinely is against my instincts, and would certainly be rejected by her. A secret correspondence would be equally distasteful to both of us. Whatever I do in this matter, I wish you to know that I do it.

'Yours always,
'Most faithfully, and with the greatest respect,
'FRANCIS TREGEAR.'

He read the letter very carefully, and at first was simply astonished by what he considered to be the unparalleled arrogance of the young man. In regard to rank this young gentleman thought himself to be as good as anybody else! In regard to money he did acknowledge some inferiority. But that was a misfortune, and could not be helped! Not only was the letter arrogant;—but the fact that he should dare to write any letter on such a subject was proof of most unpardonable arrogance. The Duke walked about the room thinking of it till he was almost in a passion. Then he read the letter again and was gradually pervaded by a feeling of its manliness. Its arrogance remained, but with its arrogance there was a certain boldness which induced respect. Whether I am such a son-in-law as you would like or not, it is your duty to accept me, if by refusing to do so you will render your daughter miserable. That was Mr Tregear's argument. He himself might be prepared to argue in answer that it was his duty to reject such a son-in-law, even though by rejecting him he might make his daughter miserable. He was not shaken; but with his condemnation of the young man there was mingled something of respect.

He continued to digest the letter before the hour of dinner, and when the almanac was brought to him he fixed on certain days. The Boncassens he knew would be free from engagements in ten days' time. As to Lady

Mabel, he seemed to think it almost certain that she would come. 'I believe she is always going about from one house to another at this time of the year,' said Mary.

'I think she will come to us if it be possible,' said the Duke. 'And you must write to Silverbridge.'

'And what about Mr and Mrs Finn?'

'She promised she would come again, you know. They are at their own place in Surrey. They will come unless they have friends with them. They have no shooting, and nothing brings people together now except shooting. I suppose there are things here to be shot. And be sure you write to Silverbridge.'

## CHAPTER 51

### THE DUKE'S GUESTS

'THE DUKE OF OMNIUM presents his compliments to Mr Francis Tregear, and begs to acknowledge the receipt of Mr Tregear's letter of ——. The Duke has no other communication to make to Mr Tregear, and must beg to decline any further correspondence.' This was the reply which the Duke wrote to the applicant for his daughter's hand. And he wrote it at once. He had acknowledged to himself that Tregear had shown a certain manliness in his appeal; but not on that account was such a man to have all that he demanded! It seemed to the Duke that there was no alternative between such a note as that given above and a total surrender.

But the post did not go out during the night, and the note lay hidden in the Duke's private drawer till the morning. There was still that 'locus pœnitentiæ'* which should be accorded to all letters written in anger. During the day he thought over it all constantly, not in any spirit of yielding, not descending a single step from that altitude of conviction which made him feel that it might be his duty absolutely to sacrifice his daughter,—but asking himself whether it might not be well that he should explain the whole matter at length to the young man. He thought he could put the matter strongly. It was not by his own doing that he belonged to an aristocracy which, if all exclusiveness were banished from it, must cease to exist. But being what he was, having been born to such privileges and such limitations, was he not bound in duty to maintain a certain exclusiveness? He would appeal to the young man himself to say whether marriage ought to be free between all classes of the community. And if not between all, who was to maintain the limits but they to whom authority in such matters is given? So much in regard to rank! And then he would ask this young man whether he thought it fitting that a young man whose duty, according to all known principles, it must be to earn his bread, should avoid that manifest duty by taking a wife who could maintain him. As he roamed about his park alone he felt that he could write such a letter as would make an impression even upon a lover. But when he had come back to his study, other reflections came to his aid. Though he might write the most appropriate letter in the world, would there not certainly be a reply? As to conviction, had he ever known an instance of a man who had been convinced by an adversary? Of course there would be a reply,—and replies. And to such a correspondence there would be no visible end. Words when once written remain, or may remain, in testimony for ever. So at last when the moment came he sent off those three lines, with his uncourteous compliments and his demand that there should be no further correspondence.

At dinner he endeavoured to make up for this harshness by increased tenderness to his daughter, who was altogether ignorant of the correspondence. 'Have you written your letters, dear?' She said she had written them.

'I hope the people will come.'

'If it will make you comfortable, papa!'

'It is for your sake I wish them to be here. I think that Lady Mabel and Miss Boncassen are just such girls as you would like.'

'I do like them; only——'

'Only what?'

'Miss Boncassen is an American.'

'Is that an objection? According to my ideas it is desirable to become acquainted with persons of various nations. I have heard, no doubt, many stories of the awkward manners displayed by American ladies. If you look for them you may probably find American women who are not polished. I do not think I shall calumniate my own country if I say the same of English women. It should be our object to select for our own acquaintances the best we can find of all countries. It seems to me that Miss Boncassen is a young lady with whom any other young lady might be glad to form an acquaintance.'

This was a little sermon which Mary was quite contented to endure in silence. She was, in truth, fond of the young American beauty, and had felt a pleasure in the intimacy which the girl had proposed to her. But she thought it inexpedient that Miss Boncassen, Lady Mabel, and

Silverbridge should be at Matching together. Therefore she made a reply to her father's sermon which hardly seemed to go to the point at issue. 'She is so beautiful!' she said.

'Very beautiful,' said the Duke. 'But what has that to do with it? My girl need not be jealous of any girl's beauty.' Mary laughed and shook her head. 'What is it, then?'

'Perhaps Silverbridge might admire her.'

'I have no doubt he would,—or does, for I am aware that they have met. But why should he not admire her?'

'I don't know,' said Lady Mary sheepishly.

'I fancy that there is no danger in that direction. I think Silverbridge understands what is expected from him.' Had not Silverbridge plainly shown that he understood what was expected from him when he selected Lady Mabel? Nothing could have been more proper, and the Duke had been altogether satisfied. That in such a matter there should have been a change in so short a time did not occur to him. Poor Mary was now completely silenced. She had been told that Silverbridge understood what was expected from him; and of course could not fail to carry home to herself an accusation that she failed to understand what was expected from her.

She had written her letters, but had not as yet sent them. Those to Mrs Finn and to the two young ladies had been easy enough. Could Mr and Mrs Finn come to Matching on the 20th of November? 'Papa says that you promised to return, and thinks this time will perhaps suit you.' And then to Lady Mabel: 'Do come if you can; and papa particularly says that he hopes Miss Cassewary will come also.' To Miss Boncassen she had written a long letter, but that too had been written very easily. 'I write to you instead of your mamma, because I know you. You must tell her that, and then she will not be angry. I am only papa's messenger, and I am to say how much he hopes that you will come on the 20th. Mr Boncassen is to bring the whole British Museum if he wishes.' Then there was a little postscript which showed that there was already considerable intimacy between the two young ladies. 'We won't have either Mr L. or Lord P.' Not a word was said about Lord Silverbridge. There was not even an initial to indicate his name.

But the letter to her brother was more difficult. In her epistles to those others she had so framed her words as if possible to bring them to Matching. But in writing to her brother, she was anxious so to write as to deter him from coming. She was bound to obey her father's commands. He had desired that Silverbridge should be asked to come,—and he was asked to come. But she craftily endeavoured so to word the invitation that he should be induced to remain away. 'It is all papa's doing,' she said; 'and I am glad that he should like to have people here. I have asked the Finns, with whom papa seems to have made up everything. Mr Warburton* will be here of course, and I think Mr Moreton is coming. He seems to think that a certain amount of shooting ought to be done. Then I have invited Lady Mabel Grex and Miss Cassewary,—all of papa's choosing, and the Boncassens. Now you will know whether the set will suit you. Papa has particularly begged that you will come,—apparently because of Lady Mabel. I don't at all know what that means. Perhaps you do. As I like Lady Mabel, I hope she will come.' Surely Silverbridge would not run himself into the jaws of the lion. When he heard that he was specially expected by his father to come to Matching in order that he might make himself agreeable to one young lady, he would hardly venture to come, seeing that he would be bound to make love to another young lady!

To Mary's great horror, all the invitations were accepted. Mr and Mrs Finn quite at the Duke's disposal. That she had expected. The Boncassens would all come. This was signified in a note from Isabel, which covered four sides of the paper and was full of fun. But under her signature had been written a few words,—not in fun,— words which Lady Mary perfectly understood. 'I wonder, I wonder, I wonder!' Did the Duke when inviting her know of anything of his son's inclinations? Would he be made to know them now, during this visit? And what would he say when he did know them?

That the Boncassens would come was a matter of course; but Mary had thought that Lady Mabel would refuse. She had told Lady Mabel that the Boncassens had been asked, and to her thinking it had not been improbable that the young lady would be unwilling to meet her rival at Matching. But the invitation was accepted.

But it was her brother's ready acquiescence which troubled Mary chiefly. He wrote as though there were no doubt about the matter. 'Of course there is a deal of shooting to be done,' he said, 'and I consider myself bound to look after it. There ought not to be less than four guns,—particularly if Warburton is to be one of them. I like Warburton very much, and I think he shoots badly to ingratiate himself with the governor. I wonder whether the governor would get leave for Gerald for a week. He has been sticking to his work like a brick. If not, would he mind my bringing someone? You ask the governor and let me know. I'll be there on the 20th. I wonder whether they'll let me hear what goes on among them about politics. I'm sure there is not one of them hates

Sir Timothy worse than I do. Lady Mab is a brick, and I'm glad you have asked her. I don't think she'll come, as she likes shutting herself up at Grex. Miss Boncassen is another brick. And if you can manage about Gerald I will say that you are a third.'

This would have been all very well had she not known that secret. Could it be that Miss Boncassen had been mistaken? She was forced to write again to say that her father did not think it right that Gerald should be brought away from his studies for the sake of shooting, and that the necessary fourth gun would be there in the person of one Barrington Erle.* Then she added: 'Lady Mabel Grex is coming, and so is Miss Boncassen.' But to this she received no reply.

Though Silverbridge had written to his sister in his usual careless style, he had considered the matter much. The three months were over. He had no idea of any hesitation on his part. He had asked her to be his wife, and he was determined to go on with his suit. Had he ever been enabled to make the same request to Mabel Grex, or had she answered him when he did half make it in a serious manner, he would have been true to her. He had not told his father, or his sister, or his friends, as Isabel had suggested. He would not do so till he should have received some more certain answer from her. But in respect to his love he was prepared to be quite as obstinate as his sister. It was a matter for his own consideration, and he would choose for himself. The three months were over, and it was now his business to present himself to the lady again.

That Lady Mabel should also be at Matching, would certainly be a misfortune. He thought it probable that she, knowing that Isabel Boncassen and he would be there together, would refuse the invitation. Surely she ought to do so. That was his opinion when he wrote to his sister. When he heard afterwards that she intended to be there, he could only suppose that she was prepared to accept the circumstances as they stood.

## CHAPTER 52

### MISS BONCASSEN TELLS THE TRUTH

ON the 20th of the month all the guests came rattling in at Matching one after another. The Boncassens were the first, but Lady Mabel with Miss Cassewary followed them quickly. Then came the Finns, and with them Barrington Erle. Lord Silverbridge was the last. He arrived by a train which reached the station at 7 p.m., and only entered the house as his father was taking Mrs Boncassen into the dining-room. He dressed himself in ten minutes, and joined the party as they had finished their fish. 'I am awfully sorry,' he said, rushing up to his father, 'but I thought that I should just hit it.'

'There is no occasion for awe,' said the Duke, 'as a sufficiency of dinner is left. But how you should have hit it, as you say,—seeing that the train is not due at Bridstock till 7.5, I do not know.'

'I've done it often, sir,' said Silverbridge, taking the seat left vacant for him next to Lady Mabel. 'We've had a political caucus of the party,—all the members who could be got together in London,—at Sir Timothy's, and I was bound to attend.'

'We've all heard of that,' said Phineas Finn.

'And we pretty well know all the points of Sir Timothy's eloquence,' said Barrington Erle.

'I am not going to tell any of the secrets. I have no doubt that there were reporters present, and you will see the whole of it in the papers to-morrow.' Then Silverbridge turned to his neighbour. 'Well, Lady Mab, and how are you this long time?'

'But how are you? Think what you have gone through since we were at Killancodlem!'

'Don't talk of it.'

'I suppose it is not to be talked of.'

'Though upon the whole it has happened very luckily. I have got rid of the accursed horses, and my governor has shown what a brick he can be. I don't think there is another man in England who would have done as he did.'

'There are not many who could.'

'There are fewer who would. When they came into my bedroom that morning and told me that the horse could not run, I thought I should have broken my heart. Seventy thousand pounds gone!'

'Seventy thousand pounds!'

'And the honour and glory of winning the race! And then the feeling that one had been so awfully swindled! Of course I had to look as though I did not care a straw about it, and to go and see the race, with a jaunty air and a cigar in my mouth. That is what I call hard work.'

'But you did it!'

'I tried. I wish I could explain to you my state of mind that day. In the first place the money had to be got. Though it was to go into the hands of swindlers, still it had to be paid. I don't know how your father and Percival get on together;—but I felt very like the prodigal son.'

'It is very different with papa.'

'I suppose so. I felt very like hanging myself when I was alone that evening. And now everything is right again.'

'I am glad that everything is right,' she said, with a strong emphasis on the 'everything'.

'I have done with racing, at any rate. The feeling of being in the power of a lot of low blackguards is so terrible! I did love the poor brute so dearly. And now what have you been doing?'

'Just nothing;—and have seen nobody. I went back to Grex after leaving Killancodlem, and shut myself up in my misery.'

'Why misery?'

'Why misery! What a question for you to ask! Though I love Grex, I am not altogether fond of living alone; and though Grex has its charms, they are of a melancholy kind. And when I think of the state of our family affairs, that is not reassuring. Your father has just paid seventy thousand pounds for you. My father has been good enough to take something less than a quarter of that sum from me;—but still it was all that I was ever to have.'

'Girls don't want money.'

'Don't they? When I look forward it seems to me that a time will come when I shall want it very much.'

'You will marry,' he said. She turned round for a moment and looked at him, full in the face, after such a fashion that he did not dare to promise her further comfort in that direction. 'Things always do come right, somehow.'

'Let us hope so. Only nothing has ever come right with me yet. What is Frank doing?'

'I haven't seen him since he left Crummie-Toddie.'

'And your sister?' she whispered.

'I know nothing about it at all.'

'And you? I have told you everything about myself.'

'As for me, I think of nothing but politics now. I have told you about my racing experiences. Just at present shooting is up. Before Christmas I shall go into Chiltern's country for a little hunting.'

'You can hunt here?'

'I shan't stay long enough to make it worth while to have my horses down. If Tregear will go with me to the Brake,* I can mount him for a day or two. But I dare say you know more of his plans than I do. He went to see you at Grex.'

'And you did not.'

'I was not asked.'

'Nor was he.'

'Then all I can say is,' replied Silverbridge, speaking in a low voice, but with considerable energy, 'that he can use a freedom with Lady Mabel Grex upon which I cannot venture.'

'I believe you begrudge me his friendship. If you had no one else belonging to you with whom you could have any sympathy, would not you find comfort in a relation who could be almost as near to you as a brother?'

'I do not grudge him to you.'

'Yes; you do. And what business have you to interfere?'

'None at all;—certainly. I will never do it again.'

'Don't say that, Lord Silverbridge. You ought to have more mercy on me. You ought to put up with anything from me,—knowing how much I suffer.'

'I will put up with anything,' said he.

'Do, do. And now I will try to talk to Mr Erle.'

Miss Boncassen was sitting on the other side of the table, between Mr Monk and Phineas Finn, and throughout the dinner talked mock politics with the greatest liveliness. Silverbridge when he entered the room had gone round the table and had shaken hands with everyone. But there had been no other greeting between him and Isabel, nor had any sign passed from one to the other. No such greeting or sign had been possible. Nothing had been left undone which she had expected, or hoped. But, though she was lively, nevertheless she kept her eye upon her lover and Lady Mabel. Lady Mary had said that she thought her brother was in love with Lady Mabel. Could it be possible? In her own land she had heard absurd stories—stories which seemed to her to be absurd, of the treachery of lords and countesses, of the baseness of aristocrats, of the iniquities of high life in London. But her father had told her that, go where she might, she would find people in the main to be very like each other. It had seemed to her that nothing could be more ingenuous than this young man had been in the declaration of his love. No simplest republican could have spoken more plainly. But now, at this moment, she could not doubt but that her lover was very intimate with this other girl. Of course he was free. When she had refused to say a word to him of her own love or want of love, she had necessarily left him his liberty. When she had put him off for three months, of course he was to be his own master. But what must she think of him if it were so? And how could he have the courage to face her in his father's house if he intended to treat her in such a fashion? But of all this she showed nothing, nor was there a tone in her voice which betrayed her.

She said her last word to Mr Monk with so sweet a smile that that old bachelor wished he were younger for her sake.

In the evening after dinner there was music. It was discovered that Miss Boncassen sang divinely, and both Lady Mabel and Lady Mary accompanied her. Mr Erle, and Mr Warburton, and Mr Monk, all of whom were unmarried, stood by enraptured. But Lord Silverbridge kept himself apart, and interested himself in a description which Mrs Boncassen gave him of their young men and their young ladies in the States. He had hardly spoken to Miss Boncassen,—till he offered her sherry or soda-water before she retired for the night. She refused his courtesy with her usual smile, but showed no more emotion than though they two had now met for the first time in their lives.

He had quite made up his mind as to what he would do. When the opportunity should come in his way he would simply remind her that the three months were passed. But he was shy of talking to her in the presence of Lady Mabel and his father. He was quite determined that the thing should be done at once, but he certainly wished that Lady Mabel had not been there. In what she had said to him at the dinner-table she had made him understand that she would be a trouble to him. He remembered her look when he told her she would marry. It was as though she had declared to him that it was he who ought to be her husband. It referred back to that proffer of love which he had once made to her. Of course all this was disagreeable. Of course it made things difficult for him. But not the less was it a thing quite assured that he would press his suit to Miss Boncassen. When he was talking to Mrs Boncassen he was thinking of nothing else. When he was offering Isabel the glass of sherry he was telling himself that he would find his opportunity on the morrow,—though now, at that moment, it was impossible that he should make a sign. She, as she went to bed, asked herself whether it were possible that there should be such treachery;— whether it were possible that he should pass it all by as though he had never said a word to her!

During the whole of the next day, which was Sunday, he was equally silent. Immediately after breakfast, on the Monday, shooting commenced, and he could not find a moment in which to speak. It seemed to him that she purposely kept out of his way. With Mabel he did find himself for a few minutes alone, and was then interrupted by his sister and Isabel. 'I hope you have killed a lot of things,' said Miss Boncassen.

'Pretty well, among us all.'

'What an odd amusement it seems, going out to commit wholesale slaughter. However it is the proper thing, no doubt.'

'Quite the proper thing,' said Lord Silverbridge, and that was all.

On the next morning he dressed himself for shooting,—and men sent out the party without him. He had heard, he said, of a young horse for sale in the neighbourhood, and had sent to desire that it might be brought to him. And now he found his occasion.

'Come and play a game of billiards,' he said to Isabel, as the three girls with the other ladies were together in the drawing-room. She got up very slowly from her seat, and very slowly crept away to the door. Then she looked round as though expecting the others to follow her. None of them did follow her. Mary felt that she ought to do so; but, knowing all that she knew, did not dare. And what good could she have done by one such interruption? Lady Mabel would fain have gone too;—but neither did she quite dare. Had there been no special reason why she should or should not have gone with them, the thing would have been easy enough. When two people go to play billiards, a third may surely accompany them. But now, Lady Mabel found that she could not stir. Mrs Finn, Mrs Boncassen, and Miss Cassewary were all in the room, but none of them moved. Silverbridge led the way quickly across the hall, and Isabel Boncassen followed him very slowly. When she entered the room she found him standing with a cue in his hand. He at once shut the door, and walking up to her dropped the butt of the cue on the floor and spoke one word. 'Well!' he said.

'What does "well" mean?'

'The three months are over.'

'Certainly they are "over." '

'And I have been a model of patience.'

'Perhaps your patience is more remarkable than your constancy. Is not Lady Mabel Grex in the ascendant just now?'

'What do you mean by that? Why do you ask that? You told me to wait for three months. I have waited, and here I am.'

'How very—very—downright you are.'

'Is not that the proper thing?'

'I thought I was downright,—but you beat me hollow. Yes, the three months are over. And now what have you got to say?' He put down his cue, and stretched out his arms as though he were going to take her and hold her to his heart. 'No;—no; not that,' she said laughing. 'But if you will speak, I will hear you.'

'You know what I said before. Will you love me, Isabel?'

'And you know what I said before. Do they know that you love me? Does your father know it, and your sister? Why did they ask me to come here?'

'Nobody knows it. But say that you love me, and everyone shall know it at once. Yes; one person knows it. Why did you mention Lady Mabel's name? She knows it.'

'Did you tell her?'

'Yes. I went again to Killancodlem after you were gone, and then I told her.'

'But why her? Come, Lord Silverbridge. You are straightforward with me, and I will be the same with you. You have told Lady Mabel; I have told Lady Mary.'

'My sister!'

'Yes;—your sister. And I am sure she disapproves it. She did not say so; but I am sure it is so. And then she told me something.'

'What did she tell you?'

'Has there never been reason to think that you intended to offer your hand to Lady Mabel Grex?'

'Did she tell you so?'

'You should answer my question, Lord Silverbridge. It is surely one which I have a right to ask.' Then she stood waiting for his reply, keeping herself at some little distance from him as though she were afraid that he would fly upon her. And indeed there seemed to be cause for such fear from the frequent gestures of his hands. 'Why do you not answer me? Has there been reason for such expectations?'

'Yes;—there has.'

'There has!'

'I thought of it,—not knowing myself; before I had seen you. You shall know it all if you will only say that you love me.'

'I should like to know it all first.'

'You do know it all;—almost. I have told you that she knows what I said to you at Killancodlem. Is not that enough?'

'And she approves!'

'What has that to do with it? Lady Mabel is my friend, but not my guardian.'

'Has she a right to expect that she should be your wife?'

'No;—certainly not. Why should you ask all this? Do you love me? Come, Isabel; say that you love me. Will you call me vain if I say that I almost think you do? You cannot doubt about my love;—not now.'

'No;—not now.'

'You needn't. Why won't you be as honest to me? If you hate me, say so;—but if you love me——!'

'I do not hate you, Lord Silverbridge.'

'And is that all?'

'You asked me the question.'

'But you do love me? By George, I thought you would be more honest and straightforward.'

Then she dropped her badinage and answered him seriously. 'I thought I had been honest and straightforward. When I found that you were in earnest at Killancodlem——'

'Why did you ever doubt me?'

'When I felt that you were in earnest, then I had to be in earnest too. And I thought so much about it that I lay awake nearly all that night. Shall I tell you what I thought?'

'Tell me something that I should like to hear.'

'I will tell you the truth. "Is it possible," I said to myself, "that such a man as that can want me to be his wife; he an Englishman, of the highest rank and the greatest wealth, and one that any girl in the world would love?"'

'Psha!' he exclaimed.

'That is what I said to myself.' Then she paused, and looking into her face he saw that there was a glimmer of a tear in each eye. 'One that any girl must love when asked for her love;—because he is so sweet, so good, and so pleasant.'

'I know that you are chaffing.'

'Then I went on asking myself questions. And is it possible that I, who by all his friends will be regarded as a nobody, who am an American,—with merely human workaday blood in my veins,—that such a one as I should become his wife? Then I told myself that it was not possible. It was not in accordance with the fitness of things. All the dukes in England would rise up against it, and especially that duke whose good-will would be imperative.'

'Why should he rise up against it?'

'You know he will. But I will go on with my story of myself. When I had settled that in my mind, I just cried myself to sleep. It had been a dream. I had come across one who in his own self seemed to combine all that I had ever thought of as being lovable in man——'

'Isabel!'

'And in his outward circumstances soared as much above my thoughts as the heaven is above the earth. And he had whispered to me soft, loving, heavenly words. No;—no, you shall not touch me. But you shall listen to me. In my sleep I could be happy again and not see the barriers. But when I woke I made up my mind. "If he comes to me again," I said—"if it should be that he should come to me again, I will tell him that he shall be my heaven on earth,—if,—if,—if the ill-will of his friends would not make that heaven a hell to both of us." I did not tell you quite all that.'

'You told me nothing but that I was to come again in three months.'

'I said more than that. I bade you ask your father. Now you have come again. You cannot understand a girl's fears and doubts. How should you? I thought perhaps you would not come. When I saw you whispering to that highly-born well-bred beauty, and remembered what I was myself, I thought that—you would not come.'

'Then you must love me.'

'Love you! Oh, my darling!—No, no, no,' she said, as she retreated from him round the corner of the billiard-table, and stood guarding herself from him with her little hands. 'You ask if I love you. You are entitled to know the truth. From the sole of your foot to the crown of your head I love you as I think a man would wish to be loved by the girl he loves. You have come across my life, and have swallowed me up, and made me all your own. But I will not marry you to be rejected by your people. No; nor shall there be a kiss between us till I know that it will not be so.'

'May I speak to your father?'

'For what good? I have not spoken to father or mother because I have known that it must depend upon your father. Lord Silverbridge, if he will tell me that I shall be his daughter I will become your wife,—oh, with such perfect joy, with such perfect truth! If it can never be so, then let us be torn apart,—with whatever struggle, still at once. In that case I will get myself back to my own country as best I may, and will pray to God that all this may be forgotten.' Then she made her way round to the door, leaving him fixed to the spot in which she had been standing. But as she went she made a little prayer to him. 'Do not delay my fate. It is all in all to me.' And so he was left alone in the billiard-room.

# CHAPTER 53

### 'THEN I AM AS PROUD AS A QUEEN'

DURING the next day or two the shooting went on without much interruption from love-making. The love-making was not prosperous all round. Poor Lady Mary had nothing to comfort her. Could she have been allowed to see the letter which her lover had written to her father, the comfort would have been, if not ample, still very great. Mary told herself again and again that she was quite sure of Tregear;—but it was hard upon her that she could not be made certain that her certainty was well grounded. Had she known that Tregear had written, though she had not seen a word of his letter, it would have comforted her. But she had heard nothing of the letter. In June last she had seen him, by chance, for a few minutes, in Lady Mabel's drawing-room. Since that she had not heard from him or of him. That was now more than five months since. How could her love serve her,—how could her very life serve her, if things were to go on like that? How was she to bear it? Thinking of this she resolved—she almost resolved—that she would go boldly to her father and desire that she might be given up to her lover.

Her brother, though more triumphant,—for how could he fail to triumph after such words as Isabel had spoken to him?—still felt his difficulties very seriously. She had imbued him with a strong sense of her own firmness, and she had declared that she would go away and leave him altogether if the Duke should be unwilling to receive her. He knew that the Duke would be unwilling. The Duke, who certainly was not handy in those duties of match-making which seemed to have fallen upon him at the death of his wife, showed by a hundred little signs his anxiety that his son and heir should arrange his affairs with Lady Mabel. These signs were manifest to Mary,—were disagreeably manifest to Silverbridge,—were unfortunately manifest to Lady Mabel herself. They were manifest to Mrs Finn, who was clever enough to perceive that the inclinations of the young heir were turned in another direction. And gradually they became manifest to Isabel Boncassen. The host himself, as host, was courteous to all his guests. They had been of his own selection, and he did his best to make himself pleasant to them all. But he selected two for his peculiar notice,—and those two were Miss Boncassen and Lady Mabel. While he would himself walk, and talk, and argue after his own peculiar fashion with the American beauty,—explaining to her matters political and social, till he persuaded her to promise to read his pamphlet upon decimal coinage,—* he was always making awkward efforts to throw Silverbridge and Lady Mabel together. The two girls saw it all and knew well how the matter was,—knew that they were rivals, and knew each the ground on which she herself and on which the other stood. But neither was satisfied with her advantage, or nearly satisfied. Isabel would not take the prize without the Duke's consent;—and Mabel could not have it without that other consent. 'If you want to marry an English Duke,' she once said to

Isabel in that anger which she was unable to restrain, 'there is the Duke himself. I never saw a man more absolutely in love.' 'But I do not want to marry an English Duke,' said Isabel, 'and I pity any girl who has any idea of marriage except that which comes from a wish to give back love for love.'

Through it all the father never suspected the real state of his son's mind. He was too simple to think it possible that the purpose which Silverbridge had declared to him as they walked together from the Beargarden had already been thrown to the winds. He did not like to ask why the thing was not settled. Young men, he thought, were sometimes shy, and young ladies not always ready to give immediate encouragement. But, when he saw them together, he concluded that matters were going in the right direction. It was, however, an opinion which he had all to himself.

During the three or four days which followed the scene in the billiard-room Isabel kept herself out of her lover's way. She had explained to him that which she wished him to do, and she left him to do it. Day by day she watched the circumstances of the life around her, and knew that it had not been done. She was sure that it could not have been done while the Duke was explaining to her the beauty of quints,* and expatiating on the horrors of twelve pennies, and twelve inches, and twelve ounces,—variegated in some matters by sixteen and fourteen!* He could not know that she was ambitious of becoming his daughter-in-law, while he was opening out to her the mysteries of the House of Lords, and explaining how it came to pass that while he was a member of one House of Parliament, his son should be sitting as a member of another;—how it was that a nobleman could be a commoner, and how a peer of one part of the Empire could sit as the representative of a borough in another part. She was an apt scholar. Had there been a question of any other young man marrying her, he would probably have thought that no other young man could have done better.

Silverbridge was discontented with himself. The greatest misfortune was that Lady Mabel should be there. While she was present to his father's eyes he did not know how to declare his altered wishes. Every now and then she would say to him some little word indicating her feelings of the absurdity of his passion. 'I declare I don't know whether it is you or your father that Miss Boncassen most affects,' she said. But to this and to other similar speeches he would make no answer. She had extracted his secret from him at Killancodlem, and might use it against him if she pleased. In his present frame of mind he was not disposed to joke with her upon the subject.

On that second Sunday,—the Boncassens were to return to London on the following Tuesday,—he found himself alone with Isabel's father. The American had been brought out at his own request to see the stables, and had been accompanied round the premises by Silverbridge and by Mr Warburton, by Isabel and by Lady Mary. As they got out into the park the party were divided, and Silverbridge found himself with Mr Boncassen. Then it occurred to him that the proper thing for a young man in love was to go, not to his own father, but to the lady's father. Why should not he do as others always did? Isabel no doubt had suggested a different course. But that which Isabel had suggested was at the present moment impossible to him. Now, at this instant, without a moment's forethought, he determined to tell his story to Isabel's father,—as any other lover might tell it to any other father.

'I am very glad to find ourselves alone, Mr Boncassen,' he said. Mr Boncassen bowed and showed himself prepared to listen. Though so many at Matching had seen the whole play, Mr Boncassen had seen nothing of it.

'I don't know whether you are aware of what I have got to say.'

'I cannot quite say that I am, my lord. But whatever it is, I am sure I shall be delighted to hear it.'

'I want to marry your daughter,' said Silverbridge. Isabel had told him that he was downright, and in such a matter he had hardly as yet learned how to express himself with those paraphrases in which the world delights. Mr Boncassen stood stock still, and in the excitement of the moment pulled off his hat. 'The proper thing is to ask your permission to go on with it.'

'You want to marry my daughter!'

'Yes. That is what I have got to say.'

'Is she aware of your——intention?'

'Quite aware. I believe I may say that if other things go straight, she will consent.'

'And your father—the Duke?'

'He knows nothing about it,—as yet.'

'Really this takes me quite by surprise. I am afraid you have not given enough thought to the matter.'

'I have been thinking about it for the last three months,' said Lord Silverbridge.

'Marriage is a very serious thing.'

'Of course it is.'

'And men generally like to marry their equals.'

'I don't know about that. I don't think that counts for much. People don't always know who are their equals.'

'That is quite true. If I were speaking to you or to your father theoretically I should perhaps be unwilling to admit superiority on your side because of your rank and wealth. I could make an argument in favour of any equality with the best Briton that ever lived,—as would become a true-born Republican.'

'That is just what I mean.'

'But when the question becomes one of practising,—a question for our lives, for our happiness, for our own conduct, then, knowing what must be the feelings of an aristocracy in such a country as this, I am prepared to admit that your father would be as well justified in objecting to a marriage between a child of his and a child of mine, as I should be in objecting to one between my child and the son of some mechanic in our native city.'

'He wouldn't be a gentleman,' said Silverbridge.

'That is a word of which I don't quite know the meaning.'

'I do,' said Silverbridge confidently.

'But you could not define it. If a man be well educated, and can keep a good house over his head, perhaps you may call him a gentleman. But there are many such with whom your father would not wish to be so closely connected as you propose.'

'But I may have your sanction?' Mr Boncassen again took off his hat and walked along thoughtfully. 'I hope you don't object to me personally.'

'My dear young lord, your father has gone out of his way to be civil to me. Am I to return his courtesy by bringing a great trouble upon him?'

'He seems to be very fond of Miss Boncassen.'

'Will he continue to be fond of her when he has heard this? What does Isabel say?'

'She says the same as you, of course.'

'Why of course;—except that it is evident to you as it is to me that she could not with propriety say anything else?'

'I think she would,—would like it, you know.'

'She would like to be your wife!'

'Well;—yes. If it were all serene, I think she would consent.'

'I dare say she would consent,—if it were all serene. Why should she not? Do not try her too hard, Lord Silverbridge. You say you love her.'

'I do, indeed.'

'Then think of the position in which you are placing her. You are struggling to win her heart.' Silverbridge as he heard this assured himself that there was no need for any further struggling in that direction. 'Perhaps you have won it. Yet she may feel that she cannot become your wife. She may well say to herself that this which is offered to her is so great, that she does not know how to refuse it; and may yet have to say, at the same time, that she cannot accept it without disgrace. You would not put one that you love into such a position?'

'As for disgrace,—that is nonsense. I beg your pardon, Mr Boncassen.'

'Would it be no disgrace that she should be known here, in England, to be your wife, and that none of those of your rank,—of what would then be her own rank,—should welcome her into her new world?'

'That would be out of the question.'

'If your own father refused to welcome her, would not others follow suit?'

'You don't know my father.'

'You seem to know him well enough to fear that he would object.'

'Yes;—that is true.'

'What more do I want to know?'

'If she were once my wife he would not reject her. Of all human beings he is in truth the kindest and most affectionate.'

'And therefore you would try him after this fashion? No, my lord; I cannot see my way through these difficulties. You can say what you please to him as to your own wishes. But you must not tell him that you have any sanction from me.'

That evening the story was told to Mrs Boncassen, and the matter was discussed among the family. Isabel in talking to them made no scruple of declaring her own feelings; and though in speaking to Lord Silverbridge she had spoken very much as her father had done afterwards, yet in this family conclave she took her lover's part. 'That is all very well, father,' she said; 'I told him the same thing myself. But if he is man enough to be firm I shall not throw him over,—not for all the dukes in Europe. I shall not stay here to be pointed at. I will go back home. If he follows me then I shall choose to forget all about his rank. If he loves me well enough to show that he is in earnest, I shall not disappoint him for the sake of pleasing his father.' To this neither Mr nor Mrs Boncassen was able to make any efficient answer. Mrs Boncassen, dear good woman, could see no reason why two young people who loved each other should not be married at once. Dukes and duchesses were nothing to her. If they couldn't be happy in England, then let them come and live in New York. She didn't understand that anybody could be too good for her daughter. Was there not an idea that Mr Boncassen would be the next President? And was not the President of the United States as good as the Queen of England?

Lord Silverbridge, when he left Mr Boncassen, wandered about the park by himself. King Cophetua married the beggar's daughter.* He was sure of that. King Cophetua probably had not a father; and the beggar, probably, was not high-minded. But the discrepancy in that case was much greater. He intended to persevere, trusting much to a belief that when once he was married his father would 'come round.' His father always did come round. But the more he thought of it the more impossible it seemed to him that he should ask his father's consent at the present moment. Lady Mabel's presence in the house was an insuperable obstacle. He thought that he could do it if he and his father were alone together, or comparatively alone. He must be prepared for an opposition, at any rate of some days, which opposition would make his father quite unable to entertain his guests while it lasted.

But as he could not declare his wishes to his father, and was thus disobeying Isabel's behests, he must explain the difficulty to her. He felt already that she would despise him for his cowardice,—that she would not perceive the difficulties in his way, or understand that he might injure his cause by precipitation. Then he considered whether he might not possibly make some bargain with his father. How would it be if he should consent to go back to the Liberal party on being allowed to marry the girl he loved? As far as his political feelings were concerned he did not think that he would much object to make the change. There was only one thing certain,—that he must explain his condition to Miss Boncassen before she went.

He found no difficulty now in getting the opportunity. She was equally anxious, and as well disposed to acknowledge her anxiety. After what had passed between them she was not desirous of pretending that the matter was one of small moment to herself. She had told him that it was all the world to her, and had begged him to let her know her fate as quickly as possible. On that last Monday morning they were in the grounds together, and Lady Mabel, who was walking with Mrs Finn, saw them pass through a little gate which led from the gardens into the Priory ruins. 'It all means nothing,' Mabel said with a little laugh to her companion.

'If so, I am sorry for the young lady,' said Mrs Finn.

'Don't you think that one always has to be sorry for the young ladies? Young ladies generally have a bad time of it. Did you ever hear of a gentleman who had always to roll a stone* to the top of a hill, but it would always come back upon him?'

'That gentleman I believe never succeeded,' said Mrs Finn. 'The young ladies I suppose do sometimes.'

In the meantime Isabel and Silverbridge were among the ruins together. 'This is where the old Pallisers used to be buried,' he said.

'Oh, indeed. And married, I suppose.'

'I dare say. They had a priest of their own, no doubt, which must have been convenient. This block of a fellow without any legs left is supposed to represent Sir Guy.* He ran away with half-a-dozen heiresses, they say. I wish things were as easily done now.'

'Nobody should have run away with me. I have no idea of going on such a journey except on terms of equality,—just step and step alike.' Then she took hold of his arm and put out one foot. 'Are you ready?'

'I am very willing.'

'But are you ready,—for a straightforward walk off to church before all the world? None of your private chaplains, such as Sir Guy had at his command. Just the registrar, if there is nothing better,—so that it be public, before all the world.'

'I wish we could start this instant.'

'But we can't,—can we?'

'No, dear. So many things have to be settled.'

'And what have you settled on since you last spoke to me?'

'I have told your father everything.'

'Yes;—I know that. What good does that do? Father is not a Duke of Omnium. No one supposed that he would object.'

'But he did,' said Silverbridge.

'Yes;—as I do,—for the same reason; because he would not have his daughter creep in at a hole. But to your own father you have not ventured to speak.' Then he told his story, as best he knew how. It was not that he feared his father, but that he felt that the present moment was not fit. 'He wishes you to marry that Lady Mabel Grex,' she said. He nodded his head. 'And you will marry her?'

'Never! I might have done so, had I not seen you. I should have done so, if she had been willing. But now I never can,—never, never.' Her hand had dropped from his arm, but now she put it up again for a moment, so that he might feel the pressure of her fingers. 'Say that you believe me.'

'I think I do.'

'You know I love you.'

'I think you do. I am sure I hope you do. If you don't, then I am—a miserable wretch.'

'With all my heart I do.'

'Then I am as proud as a queen. You will tell him soon?'

'As soon as you are gone. As soon as we are alone together. I will;—and then I will follow you to London. Now shall we not say, Good-bye?'

'Good-bye, my own,' she whispered.

'You will let me have one kiss?'

Her hand was in his, and she looked about as though to see that no eyes were watching them. But then, as the thoughts came rushing to her mind, she changed her purpose. 'No,' she said. 'What is it but a trifle! It is nothing in itself. But I have bound myself to myself by certain promises, and you must not ask me to break them. You are as sweet to me as I can be to you, but there shall be no kissing till I know that I shall be your wife. Now take me back.'

# VOLUME III

## CHAPTER 54

### 'I DON'T THINK SHE IS A SNAKE'

On the following day, Tuesday, the Boncassens went, and then there were none of the guests left but Mrs Finn and Lady Mabel Grex,—with of course Miss Casseway. The Duke had especially asked both Mrs Finn and Lady Mabel to remain, the former, through his anxiety to show his repentance for the injustice he had formerly done her, and the latter in the hope that something might be settled as soon as the crowd of visitors should have gone. He had never spoken quite distinctly to Mabel. He had felt that the manner in which he had learned his son's purpose,—that which once had been his son's purpose,—forbade him to do so. But he had so spoken as to make Lady Mabel quite aware of his wish. He would not have told her how sure he was that Silverbridge would keep no more racehorses, how he trusted that Silverbridge had done with betting, how he believed that the young member would take a real interest in the House of Commons, had he not intended that she should take a special interest in the young man. And then he had spoken about the house in London. It was to be made over to Silverbridge as soon as Silverbridge should marry. And there was Gatherum Castle. Gatherum was rather a trouble than otherwise. He had ever felt it to be so, but had nevertheless always kept it open perhaps for a month in the year. His uncle had always resided there for a fortnight at Christmas. When Silverbridge was married it would become the young man's duty to do something of the same kind. Gatherum was the White Elephant of the family, and Silverbridge must enter in upon his share of the trouble. He did not know that in saying all this he was offering his son as a husband to Lady Mabel, but she understood it as thoroughly as though he had spoken the words.

But she knew the son's mind also. He had indeed himself told her all his mind. 'Of course I love her best of all,' he had said. When he told her of it she had been so overcome that she had wept in her despair;—had wept in his presence. She had declared to him her secret,—that it had been her intention to become his wife, and then he had rejected her! It had all been shame, and sorrow, and disappointment to her. And she could not but remember that there had been a moment when she might have secured him by a word. A look would have done it; a touch of her finger on that morning. She had known then that he had intended to be in earnest,—that he only waited for encouragement. She had not given it because she had not wished to grasp too eagerly at the prize,—and now the prize was gone! She had said that she had spared him;—but then she could afford to joke, thinking that he would surely come back to her.

She had begun her world with so fatal a mistake! When she was quite young, when she was little more than a child but still not a child, she had given all her love to a man whom she soon found that it would be impossible she should ever marry. He had offered to face the world with her, promising to do the best to smooth the rough places, and to soften the stones for her feet. But she, young as she was, had felt that both he and she belonged to a class which could hardly endure poverty with contentment. The grinding need for money, the absolute necessity of luxurious living, had been pressed upon her from her childhood. She had seen it and acknowledged it, and had told him, with precocious wisdom, that that which he offered to do for her sake would be a folly for them both. She had not stinted the assurance of her love, but had told him that they must both turn aside and learn to love elsewhere. He had done so, with too complete readiness! She had dreamed of a second love, which should obliterate the first,—which might still leave to her the memory of the romance of her early passion. Then this boy had come in her way! With him all her ambition might have been satisfied. She desired high rank and great wealth. With him she might have had it all. And then, too, though there would always be the memory of that early passion, yet she could in another fashion love this youth. He was pleasant to her, and gracious;—and she had told herself that if it should be so that this great fortune might be hers, she would atone to him fully for that past romance by the wife-like devotion of her life. The cup had come within the reach of her fingers, but she had not grasped it. Her happiness, her triumphs, her great success had been there, present to her, and she had dallied with her fortune. There had been a day on which he had been all but at her feet, and on the next he had been prostrate at the feet of another. He had even dared to tell her so,—saying of that American that 'of course he loved her the best!'

Over and over again since that, she had asked herself whether there was no chance. Though he had loved that other one best she would take him if it were possible. When the invitation came from the Duke she would not lose a chance. She had told him that it was impossible that he, the heir to the Duke of Omnium, should marry an American. All his family, all his friends, all his world would be against him. And then he was so young,—and, as she thought, so easily led. He was lovable and prone to love;—but surely his love could not be very strong, or he would not have changed so easily.

She did not hesitate to own to herself that this American was very lovely. She too, herself, was beautiful. She too had a reputation for grace, loveliness, and feminine high-bred charm. She knew all that, but she knew also that her attractions were not so bright as those of her rival. She could not smile or laugh and throw sparks of brilliance around her as did the American girl. Miss Boncassen could be graceful as a nymph in doing the awkwardest thing! When she had pretended to walk stiffly along, to some imaginary marriage ceremony, with her foot stuck out before her, with her chin in the air, and one arm akimbo, Silverbridge had been all afire with admiration. Lady Mabel understood it all. The American girl must be taken away,—from out of the reach of the young man's senses,—and then the struggle must be made.

Lady Mabel had not been long at Matching before she learned that she had much in her favour. She perceived that the Duke himself had no suspicion of what was going on, and that he was strongly disposed in her favour. She unravelled it all in her own mind. There must have been some agreement, between the father and the son, when the son had all but made his offer to her. More than once she was half-minded to speak openly to the Duke, to tell him all that Silverbridge had said to her and all that he had not said, and to ask the father's help in scheming against that rival. But she could not find the words with which to begin. And then, might he not despise her, and, despising her, reject her, were she to declare her desire to marry a man who had given his heart to another woman? And so, when the Duke asked her to remain after the departure of the other guests, she decided that it would be best to bide her time. The Duke, as she assented, kissed her hand, and she knew that this sign of grace was given to his intended daughter-in-law.

In all this she half confided her thoughts and her prospects to her old friend, Miss Cassewary. 'That girl has gone at last,' she said to Miss Cass.

'I fear she has left her spells behind her, my dear.'

'Of course she has. The venom out of the snake's tooth will poison all the blood; but still the poor bitten wretch does not always die.'

'I don't think she is a snake.'

'Don't be moral, Cass. She is a snake in my sense. She has got her weapons, and of course it is natural enough that she should use them. If I want to be Duchess of Omnium, why shouldn't she?'

'I hate to hear you talk of yourself in that way.'

'Because you have enough of the old school about you to like conventional falsehood. This young man did in fact ask me to be his wife. Of course I meant to accept him,—but I didn't. Then comes this convict's granddaughter.'*

'Not a convict's!'

'You know what I mean. Had he been a convict it would have been all the same. I take upon myself to say that, had the world been informed that an alliance had been arranged between the eldest son of the Duke of Omnium and the daughter of Earl Grex,—the world would have been satisfied. Every unmarried daughter of every peer in England would have envied me,—but it would have been comme il faut.'*

'Certainly, my dear.'

'But what would be the feeling as to the convict's granddaughter?'

'You don't suppose that I would approve it;—but it seems to me that in these days young men do just what they please.'

'He shall do what he pleases, but he must be made to be pleased with me.' So much she said to Miss Casseweary; but she did not divulge any plan. The Boncassens had just gone off to the station, and Silverbridge was out shooting. If anything could be done here at Matching, it must be done quickly, as Silverbridge would soon take his departure. She did not know it, but, in truth, he was remaining in order that he might, as he said, 'have all this out with the governor.'

She tried to realise for herself some plan, but when the evening came nothing was fixed. For a quarter of an hour, just as the sun was setting, the Duke joined her in the gardens,—and spoke to her more plainly than he had ever spoken before. 'Has Silverbridge come home?' he asked.

'I have not seen him.'

'I hope you and Mary get on well together.'

'I think so, Duke. I am sure we should if we saw more of each other.'

'I sincerely hope you may. There is nothing I wish for Mary so much as that she should have a sister. And there is no one whom I would be so glad to hear her call by that name as yourself.' How could he have spoken plainer?

The ladies were all together in the drawing-room when Silverbridge came bursting in rather late. 'Where's the governor?' he asked, turning to his sister.

'Dressing, I should think; but what is the matter?'

'I want to see him. I must be off to Cornwall to-morrow morning.'

'To Cornwall!' said Miss Cassewary. 'Why to Cornwall?' asked Lady Mabel. But Mary, connecting Cornwall with Frank Tregear, held her peace.

'I can't explain it all now, but I must start very early to-morrow.' Then he went off to his father's study, and finding the Duke still there explained the cause of his intended journey. The member for Polpenno had died, and Frank Tregear had been invited to stand for the borough. He had written to his friend to ask him to come and assist in the struggle. 'Years ago there used to be always a Tregear in for Polpenno,' said Silverbridge.

'But he is a younger son.'*

'I don't know anything about it,' said Silverbridge, 'but as he has asked me to go I think I ought to do it.' The Duke, who was by no means the man to make light of the political obligations of friendship, raised no objection.

'I wish,' said he, 'that something could have been arranged between you and Mabel before you went.' The young man stood in the gloom of the dark room aghast. This was certainly not the moment for explaining everything to his father. 'I have set my heart very much upon it, and you ought to be gratified by knowing that I quite approve your choice.'

All that had been years ago,—in last June;—before Mrs Montacute Jones's garden-party, before that day in the rain at Maidenhead, before the brightness of Killancodlem, before the glories of Miss Boncassen had been revealed to him. 'There is no time for that kind of thing now,' he said weakly.

'I thought that when you were here together——'

'I must dress now, sir; but I will tell you all about it when I get back from Cornwall. I will come back direct to Matching, and will explain everything.' So he escaped.

It was clear to Lady Mabel that there was no opportunity now for any scheme. Whatever might be possible must be postponed till after this Cornish business had been completed. Perhaps it might be better so. She had thought that she would appeal to himself, that she would tell him of his father's wishes, of her love for him,—of the authority which he had once given her for loving him,—and of the absolute impossibility of his marriage with the American. She thought that she could do it, if not efficiently at any rate effectively. But it could not be done on the very day on which the American had gone.

It came out in the course of the evening that he was going to assist Frank Tregear in his canvass. The matter was not spoken of openly, as Tregear's name could hardly be mentioned. But everybody knew it, and it gave occasion to Mabel for a few words apart with Silverbridge. 'I am so glad you are going to him,' she said in a little whisper.

'Of course I go when he wishes me. I don't know that I can do him any good.'

'The greatest good in the world. Your name will go so far! It will be everything to him to be in Parliament. And when are we to meet again?' she said.

'I shall turn up somewhere,' he replied as he gave her his hand to wish her good-bye.

On the following morning the Duke proposed to Lady Mabel that she should stay at Matching for yet another fortnight,—or even for a month if it might be possible. Lady Mabel, whose father was still abroad, was not sorry to accept the invitation.

## CHAPTER 55

### POLPENNO*

POLWENNING, the seat of Mr Tregear, Frank's father, was close to the borough of Polpenno,—so close that the gates of the grounds opened into the town. As Silverbridge had told his father, many of the Tregear family had sat for the borough. Then there had come changes, and strangers had made themselves welcome by their money. When the vacancy now occurred a deputation waited upon Squire Tregear and asked him to stand. The deputation would guarantee that the expense should not exceed—a certain limited sum. Mr Tregear for himself had no such ambition. His eldest son was abroad and was not at all such a man as one would choose to make into a Member of Parliament. After much consideration in the family, Frank was invited to present himself to the constituency. Frank's aspirations in regard to Lady Mary Palliser were known at Polwenning, and it was thought that they would have a better chance of success if he could write the letters M.P. after his name. Frank acceded, and as he was starting wrote to ask the assistance of his friend Lord Silverbridge. At that time there were only nine days more before the election, and Mr Carbottle, the Liberal candidate, was already living in great style at the Camborne Arms.

Mr and Mrs Tregear and an elder sister of Frank's,* who quite acknowledged herself to be an old maid, were very glad to welcome Frank's friend. On the first morning of course they discussed the candidates' prospects. 'My best chance of success,' said Frank, 'arises from the fact that Mr Carbottle is fatter than the people here seem to approve.'

'If his purse be fat,' said old Mr Tregear, 'that will carry off any personal defect.' Lord Silverbridge asked whether the candidate was not too fat to make speeches. Miss Tregear declared that he had made three speeches daily for the last week, and that Mr Williams the rector, who had heard him, declared him to be a godless dissenter. Mrs Tregear thought that it would be much better that the place should be disfranchised altogether than that such a horrid man should be brought into the neighbourhood. 'A godless dissenter!' she said, holding up her hands in dismay. Frank thought that they had better abstain from allusion to their opponent's religion. Then Mr Tregear made a little speech. 'We used,' he said, 'to endeavour to get someone to represent us in Parliament, who would agree with us on vital subjects, such as the Church of England and the necessity of religion. Now it seems to be considered ill-mannered to make any allusion to such subjects!' From which it may be seen that this old Tregear was very conservative indeed.*

When the old people were gone to bed the two young men discussed the matter. 'I hope you'll get in,' said Silverbridge. 'And if I can do anything for you of course I will.'

'It is always good to have a real member along with one,' said Tregear.

'But I begin to think I am a very shaky Conservative myself.'

'I am sorry for that.'

'Sir Timothy is such a beast,' said Silverbridge.

'Is that your notion of a political opinion? Are you to be this or that in accordance with your own liking or disliking for some particular man? One is supposed to have opinions of one's own.'

'Your father would be down on a man because he is a dissenter.'

'Of course my father is old-fashioned.'

'It does seem so hard to me,' said Silverbridge, 'to find any difference between the two sets. You who are a true Conservative are much more like to my father, who is a Liberal, than to your own, who is on the same side as yourself.'

'It may be so, and still I may be a good Conservative.'

'It seems to me in the House to mean nothing more than choosing one set of companions or choosing another. There are some awful cads who sit along with Mr Monk;—fellows that make you sick to hear them, and whom I couldn't be civil to. But I don't think there is anybody I hate so much as old Beeswax. He has a contemptuous way with his nose which makes me long to pull it.'

'And you mean to go over in order that you may be justified in doing so. I think I soar a little higher,' said Tregear.

'Oh, of course. You're a clever fellow,' said Silverbridge, not without a touch of sarcasm.

'A man may soar higher than that without being very clever. If the party that calls itself Liberal were to have all its own way who is there that doesn't believe that the church would go at once, then all distinction between boroughs, the House of Lords immediately afterwards, and after that the Crown?'

'Those are not my governor's ideas.'*

'Your governor couldn't help himself. A Liberal party, with plenipotentiary power, must go on right away to the logical conclusion of its arguments. It is only the conservative feeling of the country which saves such men as your father from being carried headlong to ruin by their own machinery. You have read Carlyle's French Revolution.'

'Yes, I have read that.'

'Wasn't it so there? There were a lot of honest men who thought they could do a deal of good by making everybody equal. A good many were made equal by having their heads cut off. That's why I mean to be member for Polpenno and to send Mr Carbottle back to London. Carbottle probably doesn't want to cut anybody's head off.'

'I dare say he's as conservative as anybody.'

'But he wants to be a member of Parliament; and, as he hasn't thought much about anything, he is quite willing to lend a hand to communism, radicalism, socialism, chopping people's heads off, or anything else.'

'That's all very well,' said Silverbridge, 'but where should we have been if there had been no Liberals? Robespierre and his pals cut off a lot of heads, but Louis XIV and Louis XV locked up more in prison.' And so he had the last word in the argument.

The whole of the next morning was spent in canvassing, and the whole of the afternoon. In the evening there was a great meeting at the Polwenning Assembly Room, which at the present moment was in the hands of the Conservative party. Here Frank Tregear made an oration, in which he declared his political convictions. The whole speech was said at the time to be very good; but the portion of it which was apparently esteemed the most, had direct reference to Mr Carbottle.

Who was Mr Carbottle? Why had he come to Polpenno? Who had sent for him? Why Mr Carbottle rather than anybody else? Did not the people of Polpenno think that it might be as well to send Mr Carbottle back to the place from whence he had come? These questions, which seemed to Silverbridge to be as easy as they were attractive, almost made him desirous of making a speech himself.

Then Mr Williams, the rector, followed, a gentleman who had many staunch friends and many bitter enemies in the town. He addressed himself chiefly to that bane of the whole country,—as he conceived them,—the godless dissenters; and was felt by Tregear to be injuring the cause by every word he spoke. It was necessary that Mr Williams should liberate his own mind, and therefore he persevered with the godless dissenters at great length,—not explaining, however, how a man who thought enough about his religion to be a dissenter could be godless, or how a godless man should care enough about religion to be a dissenter.

Mr Williams was heard with impatience, and then there was a clamour for the young lord. He was the son of an ex-Prime Minister, and therefore of course he could speak. He was himself a member of Parliament, and therefore could speak. He had boldly severed himself from the faulty political tenets of his family, and therefore on such an occasion as this was peculiarly entitled to speak. When a man goes electioneering, he must speak. At a dinner-table to refuse is possible:—or in any assembly convened for a semi-private purpose, a gentleman may declare that he is not prepared for the occasion. But in such an emergency as this, a man,—and a member of Parliament,—cannot plead that he is not prepared. A son of a former Prime Minister who had already taken so strong a part in politics as to have severed himself from his father, not prepared to address the voters of a borough whom he had come to canvass! The plea was so absurd, that he was thrust on to his feet before he knew what he was about.

It was in truth his first public speech. At Silverbridge he had attempted to repeat a few words, and in his failure had been covered by the Sprugeons and the Sprouts. But now he was on his legs in a great room, in an unknown town, with all the aristocracy of the place before him! His eyes at first swam a little, and there was a moment in which he thought he would run away. But, on that morning, as he was dressing, there had come to his mind the idea of the possibility of such a moment as this, and a few words had occurred to him. 'My friend Frank Tregear,' he began, rushing at once at his subject, 'is a very good fellow, and I hope you'll elect him.' Then he paused, not remembering what was to come next; but the sentiment which he had uttered appeared to his auditors to be so good in itself and so well-delivered, that they filled up a long pause with continued clappings and exclamations. 'Yes,' continued the young member of Parliament, encouraged by the kindness of the crowd, 'I have known Frank Tregear ever so long, and I don't think you could find a better member of Parliament anywhere.' There were many ladies present and they thought that the Duke's son was just the person who ought to come electioneering among them. His voice was much pleasanter to their ears than that of old Mr Williams. The women waved their handkerchiefs and the men stamped their feet. Here was an orator come among them! 'You all know all about it just as well as I do,' continued the orator, 'and I am sure you feel that he ought to be member for Polpenno.' There could be no doubt about that as far as the opinion of the audience went. 'There can't be a better fellow than Frank Tregear, and I ask you all to give three cheers for the new member.' Ten times three cheers were given, and the Carbottleites outside the door who had come to report what was going on at the Tregear meeting were quite of opinion that this eldest son of the former Prime Minister was a tower of strength. 'I don't know anything about Mr Carbottle,' continued Silverbridge, who was almost growing to like the sound of his own voice. 'Perhaps he's a good fellow too.' 'No; no, no. A very bad fellow indeed,' was heard from different parts of the room. 'I don't know anything about him. I wasn't at school with Carbottle.' This was taken as a stroke of the keenest wit, and was received with infinite cheering. Silverbridge was in the pride of his youth, and Carbottle was sixty at the least. Nothing could have been funnier. 'He seems to be a stout old party, but I don't think he's the man for Polpenno. I think you'll return Frank Tregear. I was at school with him;—and I tell you, that you can't find a better fellow anywhere than Frank Tregear.' Then he sat down, and I am afraid he felt that he had made the speech of the evening. 'We are so much obliged to you, Lord Silverbridge,' Miss Tregear said as they were walking home together. 'That's just the sort of thing that the people like. So reassuring, you know. What Mr Williams says about the dissenters is of course true; but it isn't reassuring.'

'I hope I didn't make a fool of myself to-night,' Silverbridge said when he was alone with Tregear,—probably with some little pride in his heart.

'I ought to say that you did, seeing that you praised me so violently. But, whatever it was, it was well taken. I don't know whether they will elect me; but had you come down as a candidate, I am quite sure they would have elected you.' Silverbridge was hardly satisfied with this.

He wished to have been told that he had spoken well. He did not, however, resent his friend's coldness. 'Perhaps, after all, I did make a fool of myself,' he said to himself as he went to bed.

On the next day, after breakfast, it was found to be raining heavily. Canvassing was of course the business of the hour, and canvassing is a business which cannot be done indoors. It was soon decided that the rain should go for nothing. Could an agreement have been come to with the Carbottleites it might have been decided that both parties should abstain, but as that was impossible the Tregear party could not afford to lose the day. As Mr Carbottle, by reason of his fatness and natural slowness, would perhaps be specially averse to walking about in the slush and mud, it might be that they would gain something; so after breakfast they started with umbrellas,—Tregear, Silverbridge, Mr Newcomb the curate, Mr Pinebott the conservative attorney, with four or five followers who were armed with books and pencils, and who ticked off on the list of the voters the names of the friendly, the doubtful, and the inimical.

Parliamentary canvassing* is not a pleasant occupation. Perhaps nothing more disagreeable, more squalid, more revolting to the senses, more opposed to personal dignity, can be conceived. The same words have to be repeated over and over again in the cottages, hovels, and lodgings of poor men and women who only understand that the time has come round in which they are to be flattered instead of being the flatterers. 'I think I am right in supposing that your husband's principles are Conservative, Mrs Bubbs.' 'I don't know nothing about it. You'd better call again and see Bubbs hissel.' 'Certainly I will do so. I shouldn't at all like to leave the borough without seeing Mr Bubbs. I hope we shall have your influence, Mrs Bubbs.' 'I don't know nothing about it. My folk at home allays vote buff;* and I think Bubbs ought to go buff too. Only mind this; Bubbs don't never come home to his dinner. You must come arter six, and I hope he's to have some'at for his trouble. He won't have my word to vote unless he have some'at. 'Such is the conversation in which the candidate takes a part, while his cortège at the door is criticising his very imperfect mode of securing Mrs Bubbs' good wishes. Then he goes on to the next house, and the same thing with some variation is endured again. Some guide, philosopher, and friend, who accompanies him, and who is the chief of the cortège, has calculated on his behalf that he ought to make twenty such visitations an hour, and to call on two hundred constituents in the course of the day. As he is always falling behind in his number, he is always being driven on by his philosopher, till he comes to hate the poor creatures to whom he is forced to address himself, with a most cordial hatred.

It is a nuisance to which no man should subject himself in any weather. But when it rains there is superadded a squalor and an ill humour to all the party which makes it almost impossible for them not to quarrel before the day is over. To talk politics to Mrs Bubbs under any circumstances is bad, but to do so with the conviction that the moisture is penetrating from your greatcoat through your shirt to your bones, and that while so employed you are breathing the steam from those seven other wet men at the door, is abominable. To have to go through this is enough to take away all the pride which a man might otherwise take from becoming a member of Parliament. But to go through it and then not to become a member is base indeed! To go through it and to feel that you are probably paying at the rate of a hundred pounds a day for the privilege is most disheartening. Silverbridge, as he backed up Tregear in the uncomfortable work, congratulated himself on the comfort of having a Mr Sprugeon and a Mr Sprout who could manage his borough for him without a contest.

They worked on that day all the morning till one, when they took luncheon, all reeking with wet, at the King's Head,—so that a little money might be legitimately spent in the cause. Then, at two, they sallied out again, vainly endeavouring to make their twenty calls within the hour; About four, when it was beginning to be dusk, they were very tired, and Silverbridge had ventured to suggest that as they were all wet through, and as there was to be another meeting in the Assembly Room that night, and as nobody in that part of the town seemed to be at home, they might perhaps be allowed to adjourn for the present. He was thinking how nice it would be to have a glass of hot brandy-and-water and then lounge till dinner-time. But the philosophers received the proposition with stern disdain. Was his Lordship aware that Mr Carbottle had been out all day from eight in the morning, and was still at work; that the Carbottleites had already sent for lanterns and were determined to go on till eight o'clock among the artisans who would then have returned from their work? When a man had put his hand to the plough, the philosophers thought that that man should complete the furrow!

The philosophers' view had just carried the day, the discussion having been held under seven or eight wet umbrellas at the corner of a dirty little lane leading into the High Street; when suddenly, on the other side of the way, Mr Carbottle's cortège made its appearance. The philosophers at once informed them that on such occasions it was customary that the rival candidates should be introduced. 'It will take ten minutes,' said the philosophers; 'but then it will take them ten minutes too.' Upon this Tregear, as being the younger of the two, crossed over the road, and the introduction was made.

There was something comfortable in it to the Tregear party, as no imagination could conceive anything more wretched than the appearance of Mr Carbottle. He was a very stout man of sixty, and seemed to be almost carried along by his companions. He had pulled his coat-collar up and his hat down till very little of his face was visible, and in attempting to look at Tregear and Silverbridge he had to lift up his chin till the rain ran off his hat on to his nose. He had an umbrella in one hand and a stick in the other, and was wet through to his very skin. What were his own feelings cannot be told, but his philosophers, guides, and friends would allow him no rest. 'Very hard work, Mr Tregear,' he said, shaking his head.

'Very hard indeed, Mr Carbottle.' Then the two parties went on, each their own way, without another word.

## CHAPTER 56

### THE NEWS IS SENT TO MATCHING

THERE were nine days of this work, during which Lord Silverbridge became very popular and made many speeches. Tregear did not win half so many hearts, or recommend himself so thoroughly to the political predilections of the borough;—but nevertheless he was returned. It would probably be unjust to attribute this success chiefly to the young Lord's eloquence. It certainly was not due to the strong religious feelings of the rector. It is to be feared that even the thoughtful political convictions of the candidate did not altogether produce the result. It was that chief man among the candidate's guides and friends, that leading philosopher who would not allow anybody to go home from the rain, and who kept his eyes so sharply open to the pecuniary doings of the Carbottleites, that Mr Carbottle's guides and friends had hardly dared to spend a shilling;—it was he who had in truth been efficacious. In every attempt they had made to spend their money they had been looked into and circumvented. As Mr Carbottle had been brought down to Polpenno on purpose that he might spend money,—as he had nothing but his money to recommend him, and as he had not spent it,—the free and independent electors of the borough had not seen their way to vote for him. Therefore the Conservatives were very elate with their triumph. There was a great Conservative reaction. But the electioneering guide, philosopher, and friend, in the humble retirement of his own home,—he was a tailor in the town, whose assistance at such periods had long been in requisition,—he knew very well how the seat had been secured. Ten shillings a head would have sent three hundred true Liberals to the ballot-boxes!* The mode of distributing the money had been arranged; but the Conservative tailor had been too acute, and not half-a-sovereign could be passed. The tailor got twenty-five pounds for his work, and that was smuggled in among the bills for printing.

Mr Williams, however, was sure that he had so opened out the iniquities of the dissenters as to have convinced the borough. Yes; every Salem and Zion and Ebenezer* in his large parish would be closed. 'It is a great thing for the country,' said Mr Williams.

'He'll make a capital member,' said Silverbridge, clapping his friend on the back.

'I hope he'll never forget,' said Mr Williams, 'that he owes his seat to the Protestant and Church-of-England principles which have sunk so deeply into the minds of the thoughtful portion of the inhabitants of this borough.'

'Whom should they elect but a Tregear?' said the mother, feeling that her rector took too much of the praise to himself.

'I think you have done more for us than any one else,' whispered Miss Tregear to the young Lord. 'What you said was so reassuring!' The father before he went to bed expressed to his son, with some trepidation, a hope that all this would lead to no great permanent increase of expenditure.

That evening before he went to bed Lord Silverbridge wrote to his father an account of what had taken place at Polpenno.

'Polwenning, 15th December.
'MY DEAR FATHER,

'Among us all we have managed to return Tregear. I am afraid you will not be quite pleased because it will be a vote lost to your party. But I really think that he is just the fellow to be in Parliament. If he were on your side I'm sure he's the kind of man you'd like to bring into office. He is always thinking about those sort of things. He says that, if there were no Conservatives, such Liberals as you and Mr Monk would be destroyed by the Jacobins.* There is something in that. Whether a man is a Conservative or not himself, I suppose there

ought to be Conservatives.' The Duke as he read this made a memorandum in his own mind that he would explain to his son that every
carriage should have a drag to its wheels, but that an ambitious soul
would choose to be the coachman rather than the drag.

'It was beastly work!' The Duke made another memorandum to
instruct his son that no gentleman above the age of a schoolboy should
allow himself so use such a word in such a sense. 'We had to go about
in the rain up to our knees in mud for eight or nine days, always saying
the same thing. And of course all that we said was bosh.' Another
memorandum—or rather two, one as to the slang, and another as to the
expediency of teaching something to the poor voters on such occasions.
'Our only comfort was that the Carbottle people were quite as badly off
as us.' Another memorandum as to the grammar. The absence of
Christian charity did not at the moment affect the Duke. 'I made ever
so many speeches, till at last it seemed to be quite easy.' Here there was
a very grave memorandum. Speeches easy to young speakers are generally very difficult to old listeners. 'But of course it was all bosh.' This
required no separate memorandum.

'I have promised to go up to town with Tregear for a day or two.
After that I will stick to my purpose of going to Matching again. I will
be there about the 22nd, and will then stay over Christmas. After that
I am going into the Brake country for some hunting. It is such a shame
to have a lot of horses and never to ride them!

> 'Your most affectionate Son,
> 'SILVERBRIDGE.'

The last sentence gave rise in the Duke's mind to the necessity of a
very elaborate memorandum on the subject of amusements generally.

By the same post another letter went from Polpenno to Matching
which also gave rise to some mental memoranda. It was as follows:

'MY DEAR MABEL,

'I am a Member of the British House of Commons! I have sometimes regarded myself as being one of the most peculiarly unfortunate
men in the world, and yet now I have achieved that which all commoners in England think to be the greatest honour within their reach, and
have done so at an age at which very few achieve it but the sons of the
wealthy and the powerful.

'I now come to my misfortunes. I know that as a poor man I ought
not to be a member of Parliament. I ought to be earning my bread as a
lawyer or a doctor. I have no business to be what I am, and when I am

forty I shall find that I have eaten up all my good things instead of having them to eat.

'I have one chance before me. You know very well what that is. Tell her that my pride in being a member of Parliament is much more on her behalf than on my own. The man who dares to love her ought at any rate to be something in the world. If it might be,—if ever it may be,—I should wish to be something for her sake. I am sure you will be glad of my success yourself, for my own sake.

'Your affectionate Friend and Cousin,

'FRANCIS TREGEAR.'

The first mental memorandum in regard to this came from the writer's assertion that he at forty would have eaten up all his good things. No! He being a man might make his way to good things though he was not born to them. He surely would win his good things for himself. But what good things were in store for her? What chance of success was there for her? But the reflection which was the most bitter to her of all came from her assurance that his love for that other girl was so genuine. Even when he was writing to her there was no spark left of the old romance! Some hint of a recollection of past feelings, some half-concealed reference to the former passion might have been allowed to him! She as a woman,—as a woman all whose fortune must depend on marriage,—could indulge in no such allusions; but surely he need not have been so hard!

But still there was another memorandum. At the present moment she would do all that he desired as far as it was in her power. She was anxious that he should marry Lady Mary Palliser, though so anxious also that something of his love should remain with herself! She was quite willing to convey that message,—if it might be done without offence to the Duke. She was there with the object of ingratiating herself with the Duke. She must not impede her favour with the Duke by making herself the medium of any secret communications between Mary and her lover.

But how should she serve Tregear without risk of offending the Duke? She read the letter again and again, and thinking it to be a good letter she determined to show it to the Duke.

'Mr Tregear has got in at Polpenno,' she said on the day on which she and the Duke had received their letters.

'So I hear from Silverbridge.'

'It will be a good thing for him, I suppose.'

'I do not know,' said the Duke coldly.

'He is my cousin, and I have always been interested in his welfare.'

'That is natural.'

'And a seat in Parliament will give him something to do.'

'Certainly it ought,' said the Duke.

'I do not think that he is an idle man.' To this the Duke made no answer. He did not wish to be made to talk about Tregear. 'May I tell you why I say all this?' she asked softly, pressing her hand on the Duke's arm ever so gently. To this the Duke assented, but still coldly. 'Because I want to know what I ought to do. Would you mind reading that letter? Of course you will remember that Frank and I have been brought up almost as brother and sister.'

The Duke took the letter in his hand and did read it, very slowly. 'What he says about young men without means going into Parliament is true enough.' This was not encouraging, but as the Duke went on reading, Mabel did not think it necessary to argue the matter. He had to read the last paragraph twice before he understood it. He did read it twice, and then folding the letter very slowly gave it back to his companion.

'What ought I to do?' asked Lady Mabel.

'As you and I, my dear, are friends, I think that any carrying of a message to Mary would be breaking confidence. I think that you should not speak to Mary about Mr Tregear.' Then he changed the subject. Lady Mabel of course understood that after that she could not say a word to Mary about the election at Polpenno.

## CHAPTER 57

### THE MEETING AT 'THE BOBTAILED FOX'

It was now the middle of December, and matters were not comfortable in the Runnymede country. The Major with much pluck had carried on his operations in opposition to the wishes of the resident members of the hunt. The owners of coverts had protested, and farmers had sworn that he should not ride over their lands. There had even been some talk among the younger men of thrashing him if he persevered. But he did persevere, and had managed to have one or two good runs. Now it was the fortune of the Runnymede hunt that many of those who rode with the hounds were strangers to the country,—men who came down by train from London, gentlemen of perhaps no great distinction, who could ride hard, but as to whom it was thought that as they did not provide the land to ride over, or the fences to be destroyed, or the coverts for the foxes, or the greater part of the subscription, they ought not to oppose those by whom all these things were supplied. But the Major, knowing where his strength lay, had managed to get a party to support him. The contract to hunt the country had been made with him in last March, and was good for one year. Having the kennels and the hounds under his command he did hunt the country; but he did so amidst a storm of contumely and ill will.

At last it was decided that a general meeting of the members of the hunt should be called together with the express object of getting rid of the Major. The gentlemen of the neighbourhood felt that the Major was not to be borne, and the farmers were very much stronger against him than the gentlemen. It had now become a settled belief among sporting men in England that the Major had with his own hands driven the nail into the horse's foot. Was it to be endured that the Runnymede farmers should ride to hounds under a master who had been guilty of such an iniquity as that? 'The Staines and Egham Gazette,' which had always supported the Runnymede hunt, declared in very plain terms that all who rode with the Major were enjoying their sport out of the plunder which had been extracted from Lord Silverbridge. Then a meeting was called for Saturday, the 18th December, to be held at that well-known sporting little inn The Bobtailed Fox. The members of the hunt were earnestly called upon to attend. It was,—so said the printed document which was issued,—the only means by which the hunt could be preserved. If gentlemen who were interested did not put their shoulders to the wheel, the Runnymede hunt must be regarded as a thing of the past. One of the documents was sent to the Major with an intimation that if he wished to attend no objection would be made to his presence. The chair would be taken at half-past twelve punctually by that popular and well-known old sportsman Mr Mahogany Topps.

Was ever the master of a hunt treated in such a way! His presence not objected to! As a rule the master of a hunt does not attend hunt meetings, because the matter to be discussed is generally that of the money to be subscribed for him, as to which it is as well he should not hear the pros and cons. But it is presumed that he is to be the hero of the hour, and that he is to be treated to his face, and spoken of behind his back, with love, admiration, and respect. But now this master was told his presence would be allowed! And then this fox-hunting meeting was summoned for half-past twelve on a hunting-day;—when, as all the world knew, the hounds were to meet at eleven, twelve miles off!

Was ever anything so base? said the Major to himself. But he resolved that he would be equal to the occasion. He immediately issued cards to all the members, stating that on that day the meet had been changed from Croppingham Bushes, which was ever so much on the other side of Bagshot, to The Bobtailed Fox,—for the benefit of the hunt at large, said the card,—and that the hounds would be there at half-past one.

Whatever might happen, he must show a spirit. In all this there were one or two of the London brigade who stood fast to him. 'Cock your tail, Tifto,' said one hard-riding supporter, 'and show 'em you aren't afraid of nothing.' So Tifto cocked his tail and went to the meeting in his best new scarlet coat, with his whitest breeches, his pinkest boots, and his neatest little bows at his knees. He entered the room with his horn in his hand, as a symbol of authority, and took off his hunting-cap to salute the assembly with a jaunty air. He had taken two glasses of cherry brandy,* and as long as the stimulant lasted would no doubt be able to support himself with audacity.

Old Mr Topps, in rising from his chair, did not say very much. He had been hunting in the Runnymede country for nearly fifty years, and had never seen anything so sad as this before. It made him, he knew, very unhappy. As for foxes, there were always plenty of foxes in his coverts. His friend Mr Jawstock, on the right, would explain what all this was about. All he wanted was to see the Runnymede hunt properly kept up. Then he sat down, and Mr Jawstock rose to his legs.

Mr Jawstock was a gentleman well known in the Runnymede country, who had himself been instrumental in bringing Major Tifto into these parts. There is often someone in a hunting country who never becomes a master of hounds himself, but who has almost as much to say about the business as the master himself. Sometimes at hunt meetings he is rather unpopular, as he is always inclined to talk. But there are occasions on which his services are felt to be valuable,—as were Mr Jawstock's at present. He was about forty-five years of age, was not much given to riding, owned no coverts himself, and was not a man of wealth; but he understood the nature of hunting, knew all its laws, and was a judge of horses, of hounds,—and of men; and could say a thing when he had to say it.

Mr Jawstock sat on the right hand of Mr Topps, and a place was left for the master opposite. The task to be performed was neither easy nor pleasant. It was necessary that the orator should accuse the gentleman opposite to him,—a man with whom he himself had been very intimate,—of iniquity so gross and so mean, that nothing worse can be conceived. 'You are a swindler, a cheat, a rascal of the very deepest dye;—a rogue so mean that it is revolting to be in the same room with you!' That was what Mr Jawstock had to say. And he said it. Looking round the room, occasionally appealing to Mr Topps, who on these occasions would lift up his hands in horror, but never letting his eye fall for a moment on the Major, Mr Jawstock told his story. 'I did not see it done,' said he. 'I know nothing about it. I never was at Doncaster in my life. But you have evidence of what the Jockey Club thinks. The Master of our Hunt has been banished from racecourses.' Here there was considerable opposition, and a few short but excited little dialogues were maintained;—throughout all which Tifto restrained himself like a Spartan. 'At any rate he has been thoroughly disgraced,' continued Mr Jawstock, 'as a sporting man. He has been driven out of the Beargarden Club.' 'He resigned in disgust at their treatment,' said a friend of the Major's. 'Then let him resign in disgust at ours,' said Mr Jawstock, 'for we won't have him here. Cæsar wouldn't keep a wife who was suspected of infidelity, nor will the Runnymede country endure a Master of Hounds who is supposed to have driven a nail into a horse's foot.'

Two or three other gentlemen had something to say before the Major was allowed to speak,—the upshot of the discourse of all of them being the same. The Major must go.

Then the Major got up, and certainly as far as attention went he had full justice done him. However clamorous they might intend to be afterwards that amount of fair play they were all determined to afford him. The Major was not excellent at speaking, but he did perhaps better than might have been expected. 'This is a very disagreeable position,' he said, 'very disagreeable indeed. As for the nail in the horse's foot I know no more about it than the babe unborn. But I've got two things to say, and I'll say what aren't the most consequence first. These hounds belong to me.' Here he paused, and a loud contradiction came from many parts of the room. Mr Jawstock, however, proposed that the Major should be heard to the end. 'I say they belong to me,' repeated the Major. 'If anybody tries his hand at anything else the law will soon set that to rights. But that aren't of much consequence. What I've got to say is this. Let the matter be referred. If that 'orse had a nail run into his foot,—and I don't say he hadn't,—who was the man most injured? Why, Lord Silverbridge. Everybody knows that. I suppose he dropped well on to eighty thousand pounds! I propose to leave it to him. Let him say. He ought to know more about it than any one. He and I were partners in the horse. His Lordship aren't very sweet upon me just at present. Nobody need fear that he'll do me a good turn. I say leave it to him.'

In this matter the Major had certainly been well advised. A rumour had become prevalent among sporting circles that Silverbridge had refused to condemn the Major. It was known that he had paid his bets without delay, and that he had, to some extent, declined to take advice from the leaders of the Jockey Club. The Major's friends were informed that the young lord had refused to vote against him at the club. Was it not more than probable that if this matter were referred to him he would refuse to give a verdict against his late partner?

The Major sat down, put on his cap, and folded his arms akimbo, with his horn sticking out from his left hand. For a time there was general silence, broken, however, by murmurs in different parts of the room. Then Mr Jawstock whispered something into the ear of the Chairman, and Mr Topps, rising from his seat, suggested to Tifto that he should retire. 'I think so,' said Mr Jawstock. 'The proposition you have made can be discussed only in your absence.' Then the Major held a consultation with one of his friends, and after that did retire.

When he was gone the real hubbub of the meeting commenced. There were some there who understood the nature of Lord Silverbridge's feelings in the matter. 'He would be the last man in England to declare him guilty,' said Mr Jawstock. 'Whatever my lord says, he shan't ride across my land,' said a farmer in the background. 'I don't think any gentleman ever made a fairer proposition,—since anything was anything,' said a friend of the Major's, a gentleman who kept livery stables in Long Acre. 'We won't have him here,' said another farmer,—whereupon Mr Topps shook his head sadly. 'I don't think any gentleman ought to be condemned without a 'earing,' said one of Tifto's admirers, 'and where you're to get anyone to hunt the country like him, I don't know as any body is prepared to say.' 'We'll manage that,' said a young gentleman from the neighbourhood of Bagshot, who thought that he could hunt the country himself quite as well as Major Tifto. 'He must go from here; that's the long and the short of it,' said Mr Jawstock. 'Put it to the vote, Mr Jawstock,' said the livery-stable keeper. Mr Topps, who had had great experience in public meetings, hereupon expressed an opinion that they might as well go to a vote. No doubt he was right if the matter was one which must sooner or later be decided in that manner.

Mr Jawstock looked round the room trying to calculate what might be the effect of a show of hands. The majority was with him; but he was well aware that of this majority some few would be drawn away by the apparent justice of Tifto's proposition. And what was the use of voting? Let them vote as they might, it was out of the question that Tifto should remain master of the hunt. But the chairman had acceded, and on such occasions it is difficult to go against the chairman.

Then there came a show of hands,—first for those who desired to refer the matter to Lord Silverbridge, and afterwards for Tifto's direct enemies,—for those who were anxious to banish Tifto out of hand, without reference to any one. At last the matter was settled. To the great annoyance of Mr Jawstock and the farmers, the meeting voted that Lord Silverbridge should be invited to give his opinion as to the innocence or guilt of his late partner.

The Major's friends carried the discussion out to him as he sat on horseback, as though he had altogether gained the battle and was secure in his position as Master of the Runnymede Hunt for the next dozen years. But at the same time there came a message from Mr Mahogany Topps. It was now half-past two, and Mr Topps expressed a hope that Major Tifto would not draw the country on the present occasion. The Major, thinking that it might, be as well to conciliate his enemies, rode solemnly and slowly home to Tallyho Lodge in the middle of his hounds.

## CHAPTER 58

### THE MAJOR IS DEPOSED

WHEN Silverbridge undertook to return with Tregear to London instead of going off direct to Matching, it is to be feared that he was simply actuated by a desire to postpone his further visit to his father's house. He had thought that Lady Mabel would surely be gone before his task at Polpenno was completed. As soon as he should again find himself in his father's presence he would at once declare his intention of marrying Isabel Boncassen. But he could not see his way to doing it while Lady Mabel should be in the house.

'I think you will find Mabel still at Matching,' said Tregear on their way up. 'She will wait for you, I fancy.'

'I don't know why she should wait for me,' said Silverbridge almost angrily.

'I thought that you and she were fast friends.'

'I suppose we are—after a fashion. She might wait for you perhaps.'

'I think she would,—if I could go there.'

'You are much thicker with her than I ever was. You went to see her at Grex,—when nobody else was there.'

'Is Miss Cassewary nobody?'

'Next door to it,' said Silverbridge, half jealous of the favours shown to Tregear.

'I thought,' said Tregear, 'that there would be a closer intimacy between you and her.'

'I don't know why you should think so.'

'Had you never any such idea yourself?'

'I haven't any now,—so there may be an end of it. I don't think a fellow ought to be cross-questioned on such a subject.'

'Then I am very sorry for Mabel,' said Tregear. This was uttered solemnly, so that Silverbridge found himself debarred from making any flippant answer. He could not altogether defend himself. He had been quite justified, he thought, in changing his mind, but he did not like to own that he had changed it so quickly.

'I think we had better not talk any more about it,' he said, after pausing for a few moments. After that nothing more was said between them on the subject.

Up in town Silverbridge spent two or three days pleasantly enough, while a thunderbolt was being prepared for him, or rather, in truth, two thunderbolts. During these days he was much with Tregear; and though he could not speak freely of his own matrimonial projects, still he was brought round to give some sort of assent to the engagement between Tregear and his sister. This new position which his friend had won for himself did in some degree operate on his judgment. It was not perhaps that he himself imagined that Tregear as a member of Parliament would be worthier, but that he fancied that such would be the Duke's feelings. The Duke had declared that Tregear was nobody. That could hardly be said of a man who had a seat in the House of Commons;—certainly could not be said by so staunch a politician as the Duke.

But had he known of those two thunderbolts he would not have enjoyed his time at the Beargarden. The thunderbolts fell upon him in the shape of two letters which reached his hands at the same time, and were as follows:

'The Bobtailed Fox. Egham. 18th December.

'MY LORD,

'At a meeting held in this house to-day in reference to the hunting of the Runnymede country, it was proposed that the management of the hounds should be taken out of the hands of Major Tifto, in consequence of certain conduct of which it is alleged that he was guilty at the last Doncaster races.

'Major Tifto was present, and requested that your Lordship's opinion should be asked as to his guilt. I do not know myself that we are
warranted in troubling your Lordship on the subject. I am, however,
commissioned by the majority of the gentlemen who were present to
ask you whether you think that Major Tifto's conduct on that occasion
was of such a nature as to make him unfit to be the depositary of that
influence, authority, and intimacy which ought to be at the command
of a Master of Hounds.

'I feel myself bound to inform your Lordship that the hunt generally
will be inclined to place great weight upon your opinion; but that it
does not undertake to reinstate Major Tifto, even should your opinion
be in his favour.

> 'I have the honour to be,
> 'My Lord,
> 'Your Lordship's most obedient Servant,
> 'JEREMIAH JAWSTOCK.

'Juniper Lodge, Staines.'

Mr Jawstock, when he had written this letter, was proud of his
own language, but still felt that the application was a very lame one.
Why ask any man for an opinion, and tell him at the same time that his
opinion might probably not be taken? And yet no other alternative
had been left to him. The meeting had decided that the application
should be made; but Mr Jawstock was well aware that let the young
Lord's answer be what it might, the Major would not be endured as
master in the Runnymede country. Mr Jawstock felt that the passage in
which he explained that a Master of Hounds should be a depositary of
influence and intimacy, was good;—but yet the application was lame,
very lame.

Lord Silverbridge as he read it thought that it was very unfair. It was
a most disagreeable thunderbolt. Then he opened the second letter, of
which he well knew the handwriting. It was from the Major. Tifto's
letters were very legible, but the writing was cramped, showing that
the operation had been performed with difficulty. Silverbridge had
hoped that he might never receive another epistle from his late partner.
The letter, as follows, had been drawn out for Tifto in rough by the
livery-stable keeper in Long Acre.

'MY DEAR LORD SILVERBRIDGE,

'I venture respectfully to appeal to your Lordship for an act of justice. Nobody has more of a true-born Englishman's feeling of fair play

between man and man than your Lordship; and as you and me have been a good deal together, and your Lordship ought to know me pretty well, I venture to appeal to your Lordship for a good word.

'All that story from Doncaster has got down into the country where I am M.F.H. Nobody could have been more sorry than me that your Lordship dropped your money. Would not I have been prouder than anything to have a horse in my name win the race! Was it likely I should lame him? Anyways I didn't, and I don't think your Lordship thinks it was me. Of course your Lordship and me is two now;—but that don't alter the facts.

'What I want is your Lordship to send me a line, just stating your Lordship's opinion that I didn't do it, and didn't have nothing to do with it;—which I didn't. There was a meeting at The Bobtailed Fox yesterday, and the gentlemen was all of one mind to go by what your Lordship would say. I couldn't desire nothing fairer. So I hope your Lordship will stand to me now, and write something that will pull me through.

'With all respects I beg to remain,
'Your Lordship's most dutiful Servant,
'T. TIFTO.'

There was something in this letter which the Major himself did not quite approve. There was an absence of familiarity about it which annoyed him. He would have liked to call upon his late partner to declare that a more honourable man than Major Tifto had never been known on the turf. But he felt himself to be so far down in the world that it was not safe for him to hold an opinion of his own, even against the livery-stable keeper!

Silverbridge was for a time in doubt whether he should answer the letters at all, and if so how he should answer them. In regard to Mr Jawstock and the meeting at large, he regarded the application as an impertinence. But as to Tifto himself he vacillated much between pity, contempt, and absolute condemnation. Everybody had assured him that the man had certainly been guilty. The fact that he had made bets against their joint horse,—bets as to which he had said nothing till after the race was over,—had been admitted by himself. And yet it was possible that the man might not be such a rascal as to be unfit to manage the Runnymede hounds. Having himself got rid of Tifto, he would have been glad that the poor wretch should have been left with his hunting honours. But he did not think that he could write to his late partner any letter that would preserve those honours to him.

At Tregear's advice he referred the matter to Mr Lupton. Mr
Lupton was of opinion that both the letters should be answered, but
that the answer to each should be very short. 'There is a prejudice
about the world just at present,' said Mr Lupton, 'in favour of answer-
ing letters. I don't see why I am to be subjected to an annoyance because
another man has taken a liberty. But it is better to submit to public
opinion. Public opinion thinks that letters should be answered.' Then
Mr Lupton dictated the answers.

'Lord Silverbridge presents his compliments to Mr Jawstock, and
begs to say that he does not feel himself called upon to express any
opinion as to Major Tifto's conduct at Doncaster.' That was the first.
The second was rather less simple, but not much longer.

'SIR,
    'I do not feel myself called upon to express any opinion either to you
or to others as to your conduct at Doncaster. Having received a letter
on the subject from Mr Jawstock I have written to him to this effect.
                            'Your obedient Servant,
                                        'SILVERBRIDGE.
'To T. Tifto, Esq.,
    'Tallyho Lodge.'

Poor Tifto, when he got this very curt epistle, was broken-hearted.
He did not dare to show it. Day after day he told the livery-stable
keeper that he had received no reply, and at last asserted that his appeal
had remained altogether unanswered. Even this he thought was better
than acknowledging the rebuff which had reached him. As regarded
the meeting which had been held,—and any further meetings which
might be held,—at The Bobtailed Fox, he did not see the necessity, as
he explained to the livery-stable keeper, of acknowledging that he had
written any letter to Lord Silverbridge.

The letter to Mr Jawstock was of course brought forward. Another
meeting at The Bobtailed Fox was convened. But in the meantime
hunting had been discontinued in the Runnymede country. The Major
with all his pluck, with infinite cherry brandy, could not do it. Men
who had a few weeks since been on very friendly terms, and who had
called each other Dick and Harry when the squabble first began, were
now talking of 'punching' each other's heads. Special whips had been
procured by men who intended to ride, and special bludgeons by the
young farmers who intended that nobody should ride as long as Major

Tifto kept the hounds. It was said that the police would interfere. It was whispered that the hounds would be shot,—though Mr Topps, Mr Jawstock, and others declared that no crime so heinous as that had ever been contemplated in the Runnymede country.

The difficulties were too many for poor Tifto, and the hounds were not brought out again under his influence.

A second meeting was summoned, and an invitation was sent to the Major similar to that which he had before received;—but on this occasion he did not appear. Nor were there many of the gentlemen down from London. This second meeting might almost have been called select. Mr Mahogany Topps was there of course, in the chair, and Mr Jawstock took the place of honour and of difficulty on his right hand. There was the young gentleman from Bagshot, who considered himself quite fit to take Tifto's place if somebody else would pay the bills and settle the money, and there was the sporting old parson from Croppingham. Three or four other members of the hunt were present, and perhaps half-a-dozen farmers, ready to declare that Major Tifto should never be allowed to cross their fields again.

But there was no opposition. Mr Jawstock read the young lord's note, and declared that it was quite as much as he expected. He considered that the note, short as it was, must be decisive. Major Tifto, in appealing to Lord Silverbridge, had agreed to abide by his Lordship's answer, and that answer was now before them. Mr Jawstock ventured to propose that Major Tifto should be declared to be no longer Master of the Runnymede Hounds. The parson from Croppingham seconded the proposition, and Major Tifto was formally deposed.

## CHAPTER 59

### NO ONE CAN TELL WHAT MAY COME TO PASS

Then Lord Silverbridge necessarily went down to Matching, knowing that he must meet Mabel Grex. Why should she have prolonged her visit? No doubt it might be very pleasant for her to be his father's guest at Matching, but she had been there above a month! He could understand that his father should ask her to remain. His father was still brooding over that foolish communication which had been made to him on the night of the dinner at the Beargarden. His father was still intending to take Mabel to his arms as a daughter-in-law. But Lady Mabel herself knew that it could not be so! The whole truth had been told to her. Why should she remain at Matching for the sake of being mixed up in a scene the acting of which could not fail to be disagreeable to her?

He found the house very quiet and nearly empty. Mrs Finn was there with the two girls, and Mr Warburton had come back. Miss Cassewary had gone to a brother's house. Other guests to make Christmas merry there were none. As he looked round at the large rooms he reflected that he himself was there only for a special purpose. It was his duty to break the news of his intended marriage to his father. As he stood before the fire, thinking how best he might do this, it occurred to him that a letter from a distance would have been the ready and simple way. But then it had occurred to him also, when at a distance, that a declaration of his purpose face to face was the simplest and readiest way. If you have to go headlong into the water you should take your plunge without hesitating. So he told himself, making up his mind that he would have it all out that evening.

At dinner Lady Mabel sat next to his father, and he could watch the special courtesy with which the Duke treated the girl whom he was so desirous of introducing to his house. Silverbridge could not talk about the election at Polpenno because all conversation about Tregear was interdicted in the presence of his sister. He could say nothing as to the Runnymede hunt and the two thunderbolts which had fallen on him, as Major Tifto was not a subject on which he could expatiate in the presence of his father. He asked a few questions about the shooting, and referred with great regret to his absence from the Brake country.

'I am sure Mr Cassewary could spare you for another fortnight,' the Duke said to his neighbour, alluding to a visit which she now intended to make.

'If so he would have to spare me altogether,' said Mabel, 'for I must meet my father in London in the middle of January.'

'Could you not put it off to another year?'

'You would think I had taken root and was growing at Matching.'

'Of all our products you would be the most delightful, and the most charming,—and we would hope the most permanent,' said the courteous Duke.

'After being here so long I need hardly say that I like Matching better than any place in the world. I suppose it is the contrast to Grex.'

'Grex was a palace,' said the Duke, 'before a wall of this house had been built.'

'Grex is very old, and very wild,—and very uncomfortable. But I love it dearly. Matching is the very reverse of Grex.'

'Not I hope in your affections.'

'I did not mean that. I think one likes a contrast. But I must go, say on the first of January, to pick up Miss Cassewary.'

It was certain, therefore, that she was going on the first of January. How would it be if he put off the telling of his story for yet another week, till she should be gone? Then he looked around and bethought himself that the time would hang very heavy with him. And his father would daily expect from him a declaration exactly opposed to that which he had to make. He had no horses to ride. As he went on listening he almost convinced himself that the proper thing to do would be to go back to London and thence write to his father. He made no confession to his father on that night.

On the next morning there was a heavy fall of snow, but nevertheless everybody managed to go to church. The Duke, as he looked at Lady Mabel tripping along over the swept paths in her furs and short petticoats and well-made boots, thought that his son was a lucky fellow to have the chance of winning the love of such a girl. No remembrance of Miss Boncassen came across his mind as he saw them close together. It was so important that Silverbridge should marry and thus be kept from further follies! And it was so momentous to the fortunes of the Palliser family generally that he should marry well! In thinking so it did not occur to him that the granddaughter of an American labourer might be offered to him. A young lady fit to be Duchess of Omnium was not to be found everywhere. But this girl, he thought as he saw her walking briskly and strongly through the snow, with every mark of health about her, with every sign of high breeding, very beautiful, exquisite in manner, gracious as a goddess, was fit to be a Duchess! Silverbridge at this moment was walking close to her side,—in good looks, in gracious manner, in high breeding her equal,—in worldly gifts infinitely her superior. Surely she would not despise him! Silverbridge at the moment was expressing a hope that the sermon would not be very long.

After lunch Mabel came suddenly behind the chair on which Silverbridge was sitting and asked him to take a walk with her. Was she not afraid of the snow? 'Perhaps you are,' she said laughing. 'I do not mind it in the least.' When they were but a few yards from the front door, she put her hand upon his arm, and spoke to him as though she had arranged the walk with reference to that special question, 'And now tell me all about Frank.'

She had arranged everything. She had a plan before her now, and had determined in accordance with that plan that she would say nothing to disturb him on this occasion. If she could succeed in bringing

him into good humour with herself, that should be sufficient for
to-day. 'Now tell me everything about Frank.'

'Frank is member of Parliament for Polpenno. That is all.'

'That is so like a man and so unlike a woman. What did he say? What
did he do? How did he look? What did you say? What did you do? How
did you look?'

'We looked very miserable, when we got wet through, walking about
all day in the rain.'

'Was that necessary?'

'Quite necessary. We looked so mean and draggled that nobody
would have voted for us, only that poor Mr Carbottle looked meaner
and more draggled.'

'The Duke says you made ever so many speeches.'

'I should think I did. It is very easy to make speeches down at a place
like that. Tregear spoke like a book.'

'He spoke well?'

'Awfully well. He told them that all the good things that had ever
been done in Parliament had been carried by the Tories. He went back
to Pitt's time,* and had it all at his fingers' ends.'

'And quite true.'

'That's just what it was not. It was all a crammer. But it did as well.'

'I am glad he is a member. Don't you think the Duke will come
round a little now?'

When Tregear and the election had been sufficiently discussed, they
came by degrees to Major Tifto and the two thunderbolts. Silverbridge,
when he perceived that nothing was to be said about Isabel Boncassen,
or his own freedom in the matter of love-making, was not sorry to have
a friend from whom he could find sympathy for himself in his own
troubles. With some encouragement from Mabel the whole story was
told. 'Was it not a great impertinence?' she asked.

'It was an awful bore. What could I say? I was not going to pro-
nounce judgment against the poor devil. I dare say he was good enough
for Mr Jawstock.'

'But I suppose he did cheat horribly?'

'I dare say he did. A great many of them do cheat. But what of that?
I was not bound to give him a character, bad or good.'

'Certainly not.'

'He had not been my servant. It was such a letter. I'll show it you
when we get in!—asking whether Tifto was fit to be the depositary of
the intimacy of the Runnymede hunt! And then Tif's letter;—I almost
wept over that.'

'How could he have had the audacity to write at all?'

'He said that "him and me had been a good deal together." Unfortunately that was true. Even now I am not quite sure that he lamed the horse himself.'

'Everybody thinks he did. Percival says there is no doubt about it.'

'Percival knows nothing about it. Three of the gang ran away, and he stood his ground. That's about all we do know.'

'What did you say to him?'

'I had to address him as Sir, and beg him not to write to me any more. Of course they mean to get rid of him, and I couldn't do him any good. Poor Tifto! Upon the whole I think I hate Jawstock worse than Tifto.'

Lady Mabel was content with her afternoon's work. When they had been at Matching before the Polpenno election, there had apparently been no friendship between them,—at any rate no confidential friendship. Miss Boncassen had been there, and he had had neither ears nor eyes for any one else. But now something like the feeling of old days had been restored. She had not done much towards her great object;— but then she had known that nothing could be done till he should again be in a good humour with her.

On the Sunday, the Monday, and the Tuesday they were again together. In some of these interviews Silverbridge described the Polpenno people, and told her how Miss Tregear had been reassured by his eloquence. He also read to her the Jawstock and Tifto correspondence, and was complimented by her as to his prudence and foresight. 'To tell the truth I consulted Mr Lupton,' he said, not liking to take credit for wisdom which had not been his own. Then they talked about Grex, and Killancodlem, about Gerald and the shooting, about Mary's love for Tregear, and about the work of the coming Session. On all these subjects they were comfortable and confidential,—Miss Boncassen's name never having been as yet so much as mentioned.

But still the real work was before her. She had not hoped to bring him round to kneel once more at her feet by such gentle measures as these. She had not dared to dream that he could in this way be taught to forget the past autumn and all its charms. She knew well that there was something very difficult before her. But, if that difficult thing might be done at all, these were the preparations which must be made for the doing of it.

It was arranged that she should leave Matching on Saturday, the first day of the new year. Things had gone on in the manner described till the Thursday had come. The Duke had been impatient but had restrained himself. He had seen that they were much together and that they were apparently friends. He too told himself that there were two more days, and that before the end of those days everything might be pleasantly settled!

It had become a matter of course that Silverbridge and Mabel should walk together in the afternoon. He himself had felt that there was danger in this,—not danger that he should be untrue to Isabel, but that he should make others think that he was true to Mabel. But he excused himself on the plea that he and Mabel had been intimate friends,— were still intimate friends, and that she was going away in a day or two. Mary, who watched it all, was sure that misery was being prepared for someone. She was aware that by this time her father was anxious to welcome Mabel as his daughter-in-law. She strongly suspected that something had been said between her father and her brother on the subject. But then she had Isabel Boncassen's direct assurance that Silverbridge was engaged to her! Now when Isabel's back was turned, Silverbridge and Mabel were always together.

On the Thursday after lunch they were again out together. It had become so much a habit that the walk repeated itself without an effort. It had been part of Mabel's scheme that it should be so. During all this morning she had been thinking of her scheme. It was all but hopeless. So much she had declared to herself. But forlorn hopes do sometimes end in splendid triumphs. That which she might gain was so much! And what could she lose? The sweet bloom of her maiden shame? That, she told herself, with bitterest inward tears, was already gone from her. Frank Tregear at any rate knew where her heart had been given. Frank Tregear knew that having lost her heart to one man she was anxious to marry another. He knew that she was willing to accept the coronet of a duchess as her consolation. That bloom of her maiden shame, of which she quite understood the sweetness, the charm, the value—was gone when she had brought herself to such a state that any human being should know that, loving one man, she should be willing to marry another. The sweet treasure was gone from her. Its aroma was fled. It behoved her now to be ambitious, cautious,—and if possible successful.

When first she had so resolved, success seemed to be easily within her reach. Of all the golden youths that crossed her path no one was so pleasant to her eye, to her ear, to her feelings generally as this Duke's young heir. There was a coming manliness about him which she liked,—and she liked even the slight want of present manliness. Putting aside Frank Tregear she could go nearer to loving him than any other man she had ever seen. With him she would not be turned from her duties by disgust, by dislike, or dismay. She could even think that the time would come when she might really love him. Then she had all but succeeded, and she might have succeeded altogether had she been but a little more prudent. But she had allowed her great prize to escape from her fingers.

But the prize was not yet utterly beyond her grasp. To recover it,—to recover even the smallest chance of recovering it, there would be need of great exertion. She must be bold, sudden, unwomanlike,—and yet with such display of woman's charm that he at least should discover no want. She must be false, but false with such perfect deceit, that he must regard her as a pearl of truth. If anything could lure him back it must be his conviction of her passionate love. And she must be strong;—so strong as to overcome not only his weakness, but all that was strong in him. She knew that he did love that other girl,—and she must overcome even that. And to do this she must prostrate herself at his feet,—as, since the world began, it has been man's province to prostrate himself at the feet of the woman he loves.

To do this she must indeed bid adieu to the sweet bloom of her maiden shame! But had she not done so already when, by the side of the brook at Killancodlem, she had declared to him plainly enough her despair at hearing that he loved that other girl? Though she were to grovel at his feet she could not speak more plainly than she had spoken then. She could not tell her story now more plainly than she had done then; but,—though the chances were small,—perchance she might tell it more effectually.

'Perhaps this will be our last walk,' she said. 'Come down to the seat over the river.'

'Why should it be the last? You'll be here to-morrow.'

'There are so many slips in such things,' she said laughing. 'You may get a letter from your constituents that will want all the day to answer. Or your father may have a political communication to make to me. But at any rate come.' So they went to the seat.

It was a spot in the park from whence there was a distant view over many lands, and low beneath the bench, which stood on the edge of a steep bank, ran a stream which made a sweeping bend in this place, so that a reach of the little river might be seen both to the right and to the left. Though the sun was shining, the snow under their feet was hard with frost. It was an air such as one sometimes finds in England, and often in America. Though the cold was very perceptible, though water in the shade was freezing at this moment, there was no feeling of damp, no sense of bitter wind. It was a sweet and jocund air, such as would make young people prone to run and skip. 'You are not going to sit down with all the snow on the bench,' said Silverbridge.

On their way thither she had not said a word that would disturb him. She had spoken to him of the coming Session, and had managed to display to him the interest which she took in his parliamentary career. In doing this she had flattered him to the top of his bent.* If he would return to his father's politics, then would she too become a renegade. Would he speak in the next Session? She hoped he would speak. And if he did, might she be there to hear him? She was cautious not to say a word of Frank Tregear, understanding something of that strange jealousy which could exist even when he who was jealous did not love the woman who caused it.

'No,' she said, 'I do not think we can sit. But still I like to be here with you. All that some day will be your own.' Then she stretched her hands out to the far view.

'Some of it, I suppose. I don't think it is all ours. As for that, if we cared for extent of acres, one ought to go to Barsetshire.'

'Is that larger?'

'Twice as large, I believe, and yet none of the family like being there. The rental* is very well.'

'And the borough,' she said, leaning on his arm and looking up into his face. 'What a happy fellow you ought to be.'

'Bar Tifto,—and Mr Jawstock.'

'You have got rid of Tifto and all those troubles very easily.'

'Thanks to the governor.'

'Yes, indeed. I do love your father so dearly.'

'So do I—rather.'

'May I tell you something about him?' As she asked the question she was standing very close to him, leaning upon his arm, with her left hand crossed upon her right. Had others been there, of course she would not have stood in such a guise. She knew that,—and he knew it too. Of course there was something in it of declared affection,—of that kind of love which most of us have been happy enough to give and receive, without intending to show more than true friendship will allow at special moments.

'Don't tell me anything about him I shan't like to hear.'

'Ah;—that is so hard to know. I wish you would like to hear it.'

'What can it be?'

'I cannot tell you now.'

'Why not? And why did you offer?'

'Because—— Oh, Silverbridge.'

He certainly as yet did not understand it. It had never occurred to him that she would know what were his father's wishes. Perhaps he was slow of comprehension as he urged her to tell him what this was about his father. 'What can you tell me about him, that I should not like to hear?'

'You do not know? Oh, Silverbridge, I think you know.' Then there came upon him a glimmering of the truth. 'You do know.' And she stood apart looking him full in the face.

'I do not know what you can have to tell me.'

'No;—no. It is not I that should tell you. But yet it is so. Silverbridge, what did you say to me when you came to me that morning in the Square?'

'What did I say?'

'Was I not entitled to think that you—loved me?' To this he had nothing to reply, but stood before her silent and frowning. 'Think of it, Silverbridge. Was it not so? And because I did not at once tell you all the truth, because I did not there say that my heart was all yours, were you right to leave me?'

'You only laughed at me.'

'No;—no; no; I never laughed at you. How could I laugh when you were all the world to me? Ask Frank;—he knew. Ask Miss Cass;—she knew. And can you say you did not know; you, you, you yourself? Can any girl suppose that such words as these are to mean nothing when they have been spoken? You knew I loved you.'

'No;—no.'

'You must have known it. I will never believe but that you knew it. Why should your father be so sure of it?'

'He never was sure of it.'

'Yes, Silverbridge; yes. There is not one in the house who does not see that he treats me as though he expected me to be his son's wife. Do you not know that he wishes it?' He fain would not have answered this; but she paused for his answer and then repeated her question. 'Do you not know that he wishes it?'

'I think he does,' said Silverbridge; 'but it can never be so.'

'Oh, Silverbridge;—oh, my loved one! Do not say that to me! Do not kill me at once!' Now she placed her hands one on each arm as she stood opposite to him and looked up into his face. 'You said you loved me once. Why do you desert me now? Have you a right to treat me like that;—when I tell you that you have all my heart?' The tears were now streaming down her face, and they were not counterfeit tears.

'You know,' he said, submitting to her hands, but not lifting his arm to embrace her.

'What do I know?'

'That I have given all I have to give to another.' As he said this he looked away sternly, over her shoulder, to the distance.

'That American girl!' she exclaimed, starting back, with some show of sternness also on her brow.

'Yes;—that American girl,' said Silverbridge.

Then she recovered herself immediately. Indignation, natural indignation, would not serve her turn in the present emergency. 'You know that cannot be. You ought to know it. What will your father say? You have not dared to tell him. That is so natural,' she added, trying to appease his frown. 'How possibly can it be told to him? I will not say a word against her.'

'No; do not do that.'

'But there are fitnesses of things which such a one as you cannot disregard without preparing for yourself a whole life of repentance.'

'Look here, Mabel.'

'Well?'

'I will tell you the truth.'

'Well?'

'I would sooner lose all;—the rank I have; the rank that I am to have; all these lands that you have been looking on; my father's wealth, my seat in Parliament,—everything that fortune has done for me,—I would give them all up, sooner than lose her.' Now at any rate he was a man. She was sure of that now. This was more, very much more, not only than she had expected from him, but more than she had thought it possible that his character should have produced.

His strength reduced her to weakness. 'And I am nothing,' she said.

'Yes, indeed; you are Lady Mabel Grex,—whom all women envy, and whom all men honour.'

'The poorest wretch this day under the sun.'

'Do not say that. You should take shame to say that.'

'I do take shame;—and I do say it. Sir, do you not feel what you owe me? Do you not know that you have made me the wretch I am? How did you dare to talk to me as you did talk when you were in London? You tell me that I am Lady Mabel Grex;—and yet you come to me with a lie on your lips,—with such a lie as that! You must have taken me for some nursemaid on whom you had condescended to cast your eye! It cannot be that even you should have dared to treat Lady Mabel

Grex after such a fashion as that! And now you have cast your eye on this other girl. You can never marry her!'

'I shall endeavour to do so.'

'You can never marry her,' she said, stamping her foot. She had now lost all the caution which she had taught herself for the prosecution of her scheme,—all the care with which she had burdened herself. Now she was natural enough. 'No,—you can never marry her. You could not show yourself after it in your clubs, or in Parliament, or in the world. Come home, do you say? No, I will not go to your home. It is not my home. Cold;—of course I am cold;—cold through to the heart.'

'I cannot leave you alone here,' he said, for she had now turned from him, and was walking with hurried steps and short turns on the edge of the bank, which at this place was almost a precipice.

'You have left me,—utterly in the cold—more desolate than I am here even though I should spend the night among the trees. But I will go back, and will tell your father everything. If my father were other than he is,—if my brother were better to me, you would not have done this.'

'If you had a legion of brothers it would have been the same,' he said, turning sharp upon her.

They walked on together, but without a word till the house was in sight. Then she looked round at him, and stopped him on the path as she caught his eye. 'Silverbridge!' she said.

'Lady Mabel.'

'Call me Mabel. At any rate call me Mabel. If I have said anything to offend you—I beg your pardon.'

'I am not offended—but unhappy.'

'If you are unhappy, what must I be? What have I to look forward to? Give me your hand, and say that we are friends.'

'Certainly we are friends,' he said, as he gave her his hand.

'Who can tell what may come to pass?' To this he would make no answer, as it seemed to imply that some division between himself and Isabel Boncassen might possibly come to pass. 'You will not tell any one that I love you?'

'I tell such a thing as that!'

'But never forget it yourself. No one can tell what may come to pass.'

Lady Mabel at once went up to her room. She had played her scene, but was well aware that she had played it altogether unsuccessfully.

## CHAPTER 60

### LORD GERALD IN FURTHER TROUBLE

WHEN Silverbridge got back to the house he was by no means well pleased with himself. In the first place he was unhappy to think that Mabel was unhappy, and that he had made her so. And then she had told him that he would not have dared to have acted as he had done, but that her father and her brother were careless to defend her. He had replied fiercely that a legion of brothers, ready to act on her behalf, would not have altered his conduct; but not the less did he feel that he had behaved badly to her. It could not now be altered. He could not now be untrue to Isabel. But certainly he had said a word or two to Mabel which he could not remember without regret. He had not thought that a word from him could have been so powerful. Now, when that word was recalled to his memory by the girl to whom it had been spoken, he could not quite acquit himself.

And Mabel had declared to him that she would at once appeal to his father. There was an absurdity in this at which he could not but smile,—that the girl should complain to his father because he would not marry her! But even in doing this she might cause him great vexation. He could not bring himself to ask her not to tell her story to the Duke. He must take all that as it might come.

While he was thinking of all this in his own room a servant brought him two letters. From the first which he opened he soon perceived that it contained an account of more troubles. It was from his brother Gerald, and was written from Auld Reikie, the name of a house in Scotland belonging to Lord Nidderdale's people.

'DEAR SILVER,
    'I have got into a most awful scrape. That fellow Percival is here, and Dolly Longstaff, and Nidderdale, and Popplecourt, and Jack Hindes, and Perry who is in the Coldstreams,* and one or two more, and there has been a lot of cards, and I have lost ever so much money. I wouldn't mind it so much but Percival has won it all,—a fellow I hate; and now I owe him—three thousand four hundred pounds! He has just told me he is hard up and that he wants the money before the week is over. He can't be hard up because he has won from everybody;—but of course I had to tell him that I would pay him.

    'Can you help me? Of course I know that I have been a fool. Percival knows what he is about and plays regularly for money. When I began

I didn't think that I could lose above twenty or thirty pounds. But it got on from one thing to another, and when I woke this morning I felt I didn't know what to do with myself. You can't think how the luck went against me. Everybody says that they never saw such cards.

'And now do tell me how I am to get out of it. Could you manage it with Mr Moreton?* Of course I will make it all right with you some day. Moreton always lets you have whatever you want. But perhaps you couldn't do this without letting the governor know. I would rather anything than that. There is some money owing at Oxford also, which of course he must know.

'I was thinking that perhaps I might get it from some of those fellows in London. There are people called Comfort and Criball, who let men have money constantly. I know two or three up at Oxford who have had it from them. Of course I couldn't go to them as you could do, for, in spite of what the governor said to us up in London one day, there is nothing that must come to me. But you could do anything in that way, and of course I would stand to it.

'I know you won't throw me over, because you always have been such a brick. But above all things don't tell the governor. Percival is such a nasty fellow, otherwise I shouldn't mind it. He spoke this morning as though I was treating him badly,—though the money was only lost last night; and he looked at me in a way that made me long to kick him. I told him not to flurry himself, and that he should have his money. If he speaks to me like that again I will kick him.

'I will be at Matching as soon as possible, but I cannot go till this is settled. Nid'—meaning Lord Nidderdale,—'is a brick.

'Your affectionate Brother,
'GERALD.'

The other was from Nidderdale, and referred to the same subject.

'DEAR SILVERBRIDGE,

'Here has been a terrible nuisance. Last night some of the men got to playing cards, and Gerald lost a terribly large sum to Percival. I did all that I could to stop it, because I saw that Percival was going in for a big thing. I fancy that he got as much from Dolly Longstaff as he did from Gerald;—but it won't matter much to Dolly; or if it does, nobody cares. Gerald told me he was writing to you about it, so I am not betraying him.

'What is to be done? Of course Percival is behaving badly. He always does. I can't turn him out of the house, and he seems to intend to stick to Gerald till he has got the money. He has taken a cheque from Dolly dated two months hence. I am in an awful funk for fear Gerald should pitch into him. He will, in a minute, if anything rough is said to him. I suppose the straightest thing would be to go to the Duke at once, but Gerald won't hear of it. I hope you won't think me wrong to tell you. If I could help him I would. You know what a bad doctor I am for that sort of complaint.

'Yours always,
'NIDDERDALE.'

The dinner-bell had rung before Silverbridge had come to an end of thinking of this new vexation, and he had not as yet made up his mind what he had better do for his brother. There was one thing as to which he was determined,—that it should not be done by him, nor, if he could prevent it, by Gerald. There should be no dealings with Comfort and Criball. The Duke had succeeded, at any rate, in filling his son's mind with a horror of aid of that sort. Nidderdale had suggested that the 'straightest' thing would be to go direct to the Duke. That no doubt would be straight,—and efficacious. The Duke would not have allowed a boy of his to be a debtor to Lord Percival for a day, let the debt have been contracted how it might. But Gerald had declared against this course,—and Silverbridge himself would have been most unwilling to adopt it. How could he have told that story to the Duke, while there was that other infinitely more important story of his own, which must be told at once?

In the midst of all these troubles he went down to dinner. 'Lady Mabel,' said the Duke, 'tells me that you two have been to see Sir Guy's look-out.'

She was standing close to the Duke and whispered a word into his ear. 'You said you would call me Mabel.'

'Yes, sir,' said Silverbridge, 'and I have made up my mind that Sir Guy never stayed there very long in winter. It was awfully cold.'

'I had furs on,' said Mabel. 'What a lovely spot it is, even in this weather.' Then dinner was announced. She had not been cold. She could still feel the tingling heat of her blood as she had implored him to love her.

Silverbridge felt that he must write to his brother by the first post. The communication was of a nature that would bear no delay. If his hands had been free he would himself have gone off to Auld Reikie. At last he made up his mind. The first letter he wrote was neither to Nidderdale nor to Gerald, but to Lord Percival himself.

'DEAR PERCIVAL,

'Gerald writes me word that he has lost to you at cards £3,400, and he wants me to get him the money. It is a terrible nuisance, and he has been an ass. But of course I shall stand to him for anything he wants. I haven't got £3,400 in my pocket, and I don't know any one who has;—that is among our set. But I send you my I. O. U. for the amount, and will promise to get you the money in two months. I suppose that will be sufficient, and that you will not bother Gerald any more about it.

'Yours truly,

'SILVERBRIDGE.'

Then he copied this letter and enclosed the copy in another which he wrote to his brother.

'DEAR GERALD,

'What an ass you have been! But I don't suppose you are worse than I was at Doncaster. I will have nothing to do with such people as Comfort and Criball. That is the sure way to the D——! As for telling Moreton, that is only a polite and roundabout way of telling the governor. He would immediately ask the governor what was to be done. You will see what I have done. Of course I must tell the governor before the end of February, as I cannot get the money in any other way. But that I will do. It does seem hard upon him. Not that the money will hurt him much; but that he would so like to have a steady-going son.

'I suppose Percival won't make any bother about the I. O. U. He'll be a fool if he does. I wouldn't kick him if I were you,—unless he says anything very bad. You would be sure to come to grief somehow. He is a beast.

'Your affectionate Brother,

'SILVERBRIDGE.'

With these letters that special grief was removed from his mind for awhile. Looking over the dark river of possible trouble which seemed to run between the present moment and the time at which the money must be procured, he thought that he had driven off this calamity of Gerald's to infinite distance. But into that dark river he must now plunge almost at once. On the next day, he managed so that there should be no walk with Mabel. In the evening he could see that the Duke was uneasy;—but not a word was said to him. On the following morning Lady Mabel took her departure. When she went from the door, both the Duke and Silverbridge were there to bid her farewell.

She smiled and was as gracious as though everything had gone according to her heart's delight. 'Dear Duke, I am so obliged to you for your kindness,' she said, as she put up her cheek for him to kiss. Then she gave her hand to Silverbridge. 'Of course you will come and see me in town.' And she smiled upon them all;—having courage enough to keep down all her sufferings.

'Come in here a moment, Silverbridge,' said the father as they returned into the house together. 'How is it now between you and her?'

# CHAPTER 61

## 'BONE OF MY BONE'

How is it now between you and her?' That was the question which the Duke put to his son as soon as he had closed the door of the study. Lady Mabel had just been dismissed from the front door on her journey, and there could be no doubt as to the 'her' intended. No such question would have been asked had not Silverbridge himself declared to his father his purpose of making Lady Mabel his wife. On that subject the Duke, without such authority, would not have interfered. But he had been consulted, had acceded, and had encouraged the idea by excessive liberality on his part. He had never dropped it out of his mind for a moment. But when he found that the girl was leaving his house without any explanation, then he became restless and inquisitive.

They say that perfect love casteth out fear.* If it be so the love of children to their parents is seldom altogether perfect,—and perhaps had better not be quite perfect. With this young man it was not that he feared anything which his father could do to him, that he believed that in consequence of the declaration which he had to make his comforts and pleasures would be curtailed, or his independence diminished. He knew his father too well to dread such punishment. But he feared that he would make his father unhappy, and he was conscious that he had so often sinned in that way. He had stumbled so frequently! Though in action he would so often be thoughtless,—yet he understood perfectly the effect which had been produced on his father's mind by his conduct. He had it at heart 'to be good to the governor,' to gratify that most loving of all possible friends, who, as he knew well, was always thinking of his welfare. And yet he never had been 'good to the governor';—nor had Gerald;—and to all this was added his sister's determined perversity. It was thus he feared his father.

He paused for a moment, while the Duke stood with his back to the fire looking at him. 'I'm afraid that it is all over, sir,' he said.

'All over!'

'I am afraid so.'

'Why is it all over? Has she refused you?'

'Well, sir;—it isn't quite that.' Then he paused again. It was so difficult to begin about Isabel Boncassen.

'I am sorry for that,' said the Duke, almost hesitating; 'very sorry. You will understand, I hope, that I should make no inquiry in such a matter, unless I had felt myself warranted in doing so by what you had yourself told me in London.'

'I understand all that.'

'I have been very anxious about it, and have even gone so far as to make some preparations for what I had hoped would be your early marriage.'

'Preparations!' exclaimed Silverbridge, thinking of church bells, bride cake, and wedding presents.

'As to the property. I am so anxious that you should enjoy all the settled independence which can belong to an English gentleman. I never plough or sow. I know no more of sheep and bulls than of the extinct animals of earlier ages. I would not have it so with you. I would fain see you surrounded by those things which ought to interest a nobleman in this country. Why is it all over with Lady Mabel Grex?'

The young man looked imploringly at his father, as though earnestly begging that nothing more might be said about Mabel. 'I had changed my mind before I found out that she was really in love with me!' He could not say that. He could not hint that he might still have Mabel if he would. The only thing for him was to tell everything about Isabel Boncassen. He felt that in doing this he must begin with himself. 'I have rather changed my mind, sir,' he said, 'since we were walking together in London that night.'

'Have you quarrelled with Lady Mabel?'

'Oh dear no. I am very fond of Mabel;—only not just like that.'

'Not just like what?'

'I had better tell the whole truth at once.'

'Certainly tell the truth, Silverbridge. I cannot say that you are bound in duty to tell the whole truth even to your father in such a matter.'

'But I mean to tell you everything. Mabel did not seem to care for me much—in London. And then I saw someone,—someone I liked better.'

Then he stopped, but as the Duke did not ask any questions he plunged on. 'It was Miss Boncassen.'

'Miss Boncassen!'

'Yes, sir,' said Silverbridge, with a little access of decision.

'The American young lady?'

'Yes, sir.'

'Do you know anything of her family?'

'I think I know all about her family. It is not much in the way of—family.'

'You have not spoken to her about it?'

'Yes, sir;—I have settled it all with her, on condition——'

'Settled it with her that she is to be your wife!'

'Yes, sir,—on condition that you will approve.'

'Did you go to her, Silverbridge, with such a stipulation as that?'

'It was not like that.'

'How was it then?'

'She stipulated. She will marry me if you will consent.'

'It was she then who thought of my wishes and my feeling;—not you?'

'I knew that I loved her. What is a man to do when he feels like that? Of course I meant to tell you.' The Duke was now looking very black. 'I thought you liked her, sir.'

'Liked her! I did like her. I do like her. What has that to do with it? Do you think I like none but those with whom I should think it fitting to ally myself in marriage? Is there to be no duty in such matters, no restraint, no feeling of what is due to your own name, and to others who bear it? The lad out there who is sweeping the walks can marry the first girl that pleases his eye if she will take him. Perhaps his lot is the happier because he owns such liberty. Have you the same freedom?'

'I suppose I have,—by law.'

'Do you recognise no duty but what the laws impose upon you? Should you be disposed to eat and drink in bestial excess, because the laws would not hinder you? Should you lie and sleep all the day, the law would say nothing! Should you neglect every duty which your position imposes on you, the law could not interfere! To such a one as you the law can be no guide. You should so live as not to come near the law,—or to have the law to come near to you. From all evil against which the law bars you, you should be barred, at an infinite distance, by honour, by conscience, and nobility. Does the law require patriotism, philanthropy, self-abnegation, public service, purity of purpose, devotion to the needs of others who have been placed in the world below you? The law is a great thing,—because men are poor and weak, and bad. And it is great, because where it exists in its strength, no tyrant can be above it. But between you and me there should be no mention of law as the guide of conduct. Speak to me of honour, of duty, and of nobility; and tell me what they require of you.'

Silverbridge listened in silence and with something of true admiration in his heart. But he felt the strong necessity of declaring his own convictions on one special point here, at once, in this new crisis of the conversation. That accident in regard to the colour of the Dean's lodge had stood in the way of his logical studies,—so that he was unable to put his argument into proper shape; but there belonged to him a certain natural astuteness which told him that he must put in his rejoinder at this particular point. 'I think I am bound in honour and in duty to marry Miss Boncassen,' he said. 'And, if I understand what you mean, by nobility just as much.'

'Because you have promised.'

'Not only for that. I have promised and therefore I am bound. She has—well, she has said that she loves me, and therefore of course I am bound. But it is not only that.'

'What do you mean?'

'I suppose a man ought to marry the woman he loves,—if he can get her.'

'No; no; not so; not always so. Do you think that love is a passion that cannot be withstood?'

'But here we are both of one mind, sir. When I saw how you seemed to take to her——'

'Take to her! Can I not interest myself in human beings without wishing to make them flesh of my flesh, bone of my bone?* What am I to think of you? It was but the other day that all that you are now telling me of Miss Boncassen, you were telling me of Lady Mabel Grex.' Here poor Silverbridge bit his lips and shook his head, and looked down upon the ground. This was the weak part of his case. He could not tell his father the whole story about Mabel,—that she had coyed his love, so that he had been justified in thinking himself free from any claim in that direction when he had encountered the infinitely sweeter charms of Isabel Boncassen. 'You are weak as water,' said the unhappy father.

'I am not weak in this.'

'Did you not say exactly the same about Lady Mabel?'

There was a pause, so that he was driven to reply. 'I found her as I thought indifferent, and then—I changed my mind.'

'Indifferent! What does she think about it now? Does she know of this? How does it stand between you two at the present moment?'

'She knows that I am engaged to—Miss Boncassen.'

'Does she approve of it?'

'Why should I ask her, sir? I have not asked her.'

'Then why did you tell her? She could not but have spoken her mind when you told her. There must have been much between you when this was talked of.'

The unfortunate young man was obliged to take some time before he could answer this appeal. He had to own that his father had some justice on his side, but at the same time he could reveal nothing of Mabel's secret. 'I told her because we were friends. I did not ask her approval; but she did disapprove. She thought that your son should not marry an American girl without family.'

'Of course she would feel that.'

'Now I have told you what she said, and I hope you will ask me no further questions about her. I cannot make Lady Mabel my wife;— though, for the matter of that, I ought not to presume that she would take me if I wished it. I had intended to ask you to-day to consent to my marriage with Miss Boncassen.'

'I cannot give you my consent.'

'Then I am very unhappy.'

'How can I believe as to your unhappiness when you would have said the same about Lady Mabel Grex a few weeks ago?'

'Nearly eight months,' said Silverbridge.

'What is the difference? It is not the time, but the disposition of the man! I cannot give you my consent. The young lady sees it in the right light, and that will make your escape easy.'

'I do not want to escape.'

'She has indicated the cause which will separate you.'

'I will not be separated from her,' said Silverbridge, who was beginning to feel that he was subjugated to tyranny. If he chose to marry Isabel, no one could have a right to hinder him.

'I can only hope that you will think better of it, and that when next you speak to me on that or any other subject you will answer me with less arrogance.'

This rebuke was terrible to the son, whose mind at the present moment was filled with two ideas, that of constancy to Isabel Boncassen, and then of respect and affection for his father. 'Indeed, sir,' he said, 'I am not arrogant, and if I have answered improperly I beg your pardon. But my mind is made up about this, and I thought you had better know how it is.'

'I do not see that I can say anything else to you now.'

'I think of going to Harrington this afternoon.' Then the Duke, with further very visible annoyance, asked where Harrington was. It was explained that Harrington was Lord Chiltern's seat, Lord Chiltern being the Master of the Brake hounds;—that it was his son's purpose to remain six weeks among the Brake hounds, but that he should stay only a day or two with Lord Chiltern. Then it appeared that Silverbridge intended to put himself up at a hunting inn in the neighbourhood, and the Duke did not at all like the plan. That his son should choose to live at an inn, when the comforts of an English country house were open to him, was distasteful and almost offensive to the Duke. And the matter was not improved when he was made to understand that all this was to be done for the sake of hunting. There had been the shooting in Scotland; then the racing,—ah, alas! yes,—the racing, and the betting at Doncaster! Then the shooting at Matching had been made to appear to be the chief reason why he himself had been living in his own house! And now his son was going away to live at an inn in order that more time might be devoted to hunting! 'Why can't you hunt here at home, if you must hunt?'

'It is all woodland,' said Silverbridge.

'I thought you wanted woods. Lord Chiltern is always troubling me about Trumpington Wood.'*

This breeze about the hunting enabled the son to escape without any further allusion to Miss Boncassen. He did escape, and proceeded to turn over in his mind all that had been said. His tale had been told. A great burden was thus taken off his shoulders. He could tell Isabel so much, and thus free himself from the suspicion of having been afraid to declare his purpose. She should know what he had done, and should be made to understand that he had been firm. He had, he thought, been very firm and gave himself some credit on that head. His father, no doubt, had been firm too, but that he had expected. His father had said much. All that about honour and duty had been very good; but this was certain,—that when a young man had promised a young woman he ought to keep his word. And he thought that there were certain changes going on in the management of the world which his father did not quite understand. Fathers never do quite understand the changes which are manifest to their sons. Some years ago it might have been improper that an American girl should be elevated to the rank of an English Duchess; but now all that was altered.

The Duke spent the rest of the day alone, and was not happy in his solitude. All that Silverbridge had told him was sad to him. He had taught himself to think that he could love Lady Mabel as an affection-ate father wishes to love his son's wife. He had set himself to wish to like her, and had been successful. Being most anxious that his son should marry he had prepared himself to be more than ordinarily liberal,—to be in every way gracious. His children were now every-thing to him, and among his children his son and heir was the chief. From the moment in which he had heard from Silverbridge that Lady Mabel was chosen he had given himself up to considering how he might best promote their interests,—how he might best enable them to live, with that dignity and splendour which he himself had unwisely despised. That the son who was to come after him should be worthy of the place assigned to his name had been, of personal objects, the near-est to his heart. There had been failures, but still there had been left room for hope. The boy had been unfortunate at Eton;—but how many unfortunate boys had become great men! He had disgraced himself by his folly at college,—but, though some lads will be men at twenty, others are then little more than children. The fruit that ripens the soonest is seldom the best. Then had come Tifto and the racing mania. Nothing could be worse than Tifto and race-horses. But from that evil Silverbridge had seemed to be made free by the very disgust which the vileness of the circumstance had produced. Perhaps Tifto driving a nail into his horse's foot had on the whole been serviceable. That apos-tacy from the political creed of the Pallisers had been a blow,—much more felt than the loss of the seventy thousand pounds;—but even under that blow he had consoled himself by thinking that a Conservative patriotic nobleman may serve his country,—even as a Conservative. In the midst of this he had felt that the surest resource for his son against evil would be in an early marriage. If he would marry becomingly, then might everything still be made pleasant. If his son would marry becomingly nothing which a father could do should be wanting to add splendour and dignity to his son's life.

In thinking of all this he had by no means regarded his own mode of life with favour. He knew how jejune* his life had been,—how devoid of other interests than that of the public service to which he had devoted himself. He was thinking of this when he told his son that he had neither ploughed and sowed or been the owner of sheep or oxen. He often thought of this, when he heard those around him talking of the sports, which, though he condemned them as the employments of a life, he now regarded wistfully, hopelessly as far as he himself was concerned, as proper recreations for a man of wealth. Silverbridge should have it all, if he could arrange it. The one thing necessary was a fitting wife;—and the fitting wife had been absolutely chosen by Silverbridge himself.

It may be conceived, therefore, that he was again unhappy. He had already been driven to acknowledge that these children of his,—thoughtless, restless, though they seemed to be,—still had a will of their own. In all which how like they were to their mother! With her, however, his word, though it might be resisted, had never lost its authority. When he had declared that a thing should not be done, she had never persisted in saying that she would do it. But with his children it was otherwise. What power had he over Silverbridge,—or for the matter of that, even over his daughter? They had only to be firm and he knew that he must be conquered.

'I thought that you liked her,' Silverbridge had said to him. How utterly unconscious, thought the Duke, must the young man have been of all that his position required of him when he used such an argument! Liked her! He did like her. She was clever, accomplished, beautiful, well-mannered,—as far as he knew endowed with all good qualities! Would not many an old Roman have said as much for some favourite Greek slave,—for some freedman whom he would admit to his very heart? But what old Roman ever dreamed of giving his daughter to the son of a Greek bondsman! Had he done so, what would have become of the name of a Roman citizen? And was it not his duty to fortify and maintain that higher, smaller, more precious pinnacle of rank on which Fortune had placed him and his children?

Like her! Yes! he liked her certainly. He had by no means always found that he best liked the companionship of his own order. He had liked to feel around him the free battle of the House of Commons. He liked the power of attack and defence in carrying on which an English politician cares nothing for rank. He liked to remember that the son of any tradesman might, by his own merits, become a peer of Parliament. He would have liked to think that his son should share all these tastes with him. Yes,—he liked Isabel Boncassen. But how different was that liking from a desire that she should be bone of his bone, and flesh of his flesh!

## CHAPTER 62

### THE BRAKE COUNTRY*

'WHAT does your father mean to do about Trumpington Wood?' That was the first word from Lord Chiltern after he had shaken hands with his guest.

'Isn't it all right yet?'

'All right? No! How can a wood like that be all right without a man about the place who knows anything of the nature of a fox? In your grandfather's time——'

'My great-uncle you mean.'

'Well;—your great-uncle!—they used to trap the foxes there. There was a fellow named Fothergill who used to come there for shooting. Now it is worse than ever. Nobody shoots there because there is nothing to shoot. There isn't a keeper. Every scamp is allowed to go where he pleases, and of course there isn't a fox in the whole place. My huntsman laughs at me when I ask him to draw it.' As the indignant Master of the Brake Hounds said this the very fire flashed from his eyes.

'My dear,' said Lady Chiltern expostulating, 'Lord Silverbridge hasn't been in the house above half an hour.'

'What does that matter? When a thing has to be said it had better be said at once.'

Phineas Finn was staying at Harrington with his intimate friends* the Chilterns, as were also a certain Mr and Mrs Maule, both of whom were addicted to hunting,—the lady, whose maiden name had been Palliser, being a cousin to Lord Silverbridge. On that day also a certain Mr and Mrs Spooner dined at Harrington. Mr and Mrs Spooner were both very much given to hunting, as seemed to be necessarily the case with everybody admitted to that house. Mr Spooner was a gentleman who might be on the wrong side of fifty, with a red nose, very vigorous, and submissive in regard to all things but port-wine. His wife was perhaps something more than half his age, a stout, hard-riding, handsome woman. She had been the penniless daughter of a retired officer,—but yet had managed to ride on whatever animal any one would lend her. Then Mr Spooner, who had for many years been part and parcel of the Brake hunt, and who was much in want of a wife, had, luckily for her, cast his eyes upon Miss Leatherside. It was thought that upon the whole she made him a good wife. She hunted four days a week, and he could afford to keep horses for her. She never flirted, and wanted no one to open gates. Tom Spooner himself was not always so forward as he used to be; but his wife was always there and would tell him all that he did not see himself. And she was a good housewife, taking care that nothing should be spent lavishly, except upon the stable. Of him, too, and of his health, she was careful, never scrupling to say a word in season when he was likely to hurt himself, either among the fences or among the decanters. 'You ain't so young as you were, Tom. Don't think of doing it.' This she would say to him with a loud voice when she would find him pausing at a fence. Then she would hop over herself and he would go round. She was 'quite a providence to him,' as her mother, old Mrs Leatherside, would say.

She was hardly the woman that one would have expected to meet as a friend in the drawing-room of Lady Chiltern. Lord Chiltern was perhaps a little rough, but Lady Chiltern was all that a mother, a wife, and a lady ought to be. She probably felt that some little apology ought to be made for Mrs Spooner. 'I hope you like hunting,' she said to Silverbridge.

'Best of all things,' said he enthusiastically.

'Because you know this is Castle Nimrod,* in which nothing is allowed to interfere with the one great business of life.'

'It's like that; is it?'

'Quite like that. Lord Chiltern has taken up hunting as his duty in life, and he does it with his might and main. Not to have a good day is a misery to him;—not for himself but because he feels that he is responsible. We had one blank day last year, and I thought that he never would recover it. It was that unfortunate Trumpington Wood.'

'How he will hate me.'

'Not if you will praise the hounds judiciously. And then there is a Mr Spooner coming here to-night. He is the first-lieutenant. He understands all about the foxes, and all about the farmers. He has got a wife.'

'Does she understand anything?'

'She understands him. She is coming too. They have not been married long, and he never goes anywhere without her.'

'Does she ride?'

'Well; yes. I never go out myself now because I have so much of it all at home.* But I fancy she does ride a good deal. She will talk hunting too. If Chiltern were to leave the country I think they ought to make her master. Perhaps you'll think her rather odd; but really she is a very good woman.'

'I am sure I shall like her.'

'I hope you will. You know Mr Finn. He is here. He and my husband are very old friends. And Adelaide Maule is your cousin. She hunts too. And so does Mr Maule,—only not quite so energetically. I think that is all we shall have.'

Immediately after that all the guests came in at once, and a discussion was heard as they were passing through the hall. 'No;—that wasn't it,' said Mrs Spooner loudly. 'I don't care what Dick said.' Dick Rabbit was the first whip, and seemed to have been much exercised with the matter now under dispute. 'The fox never went into Grobby Gorse at all. I was there and saw Sappho give him a line down the bank.'

'I think he must have gone into the gorse, my dear,' said her husband. 'The earth was open, you know.'

'I tell you she didn't. You weren't there, and you can't know. I'm sure it was a vixen by her running. We ought to have killed that fox, my Lord.' Then Mrs Spooner made her obeisance to her hostess. Perhaps she was rather slow in doing this, but the greatness of the subject had been the cause. These are matters so important, that the ordinary civilities of the world should not stand in their way.

'What do you say, Chiltern?' asked the husband.

'I say that Mrs Spooner isn't very often wrong, and that Dick Rabbit isn't very often right about a fox.'

'It was a pretty run,' said Phineas.

'Just thirty-four minutes,' said Mr Spooner.

'Thirty-two up to Grobby Gorse,' asserted Mrs Spooner. 'The hounds never hunted a yard after that. Dick hurried them into the gorse, and the old hound wouldn't stick to his line when she found that no one believed her.'

This was on a Monday evening, and the Brake hounds went out generally five days a week. 'You'll hunt to-morrow, I suppose?' Lady Chiltern said to Silverbridge.

'I hope so.'

'You must hunt to-morrow. Indeed there is nothing else to do. Chiltern has taken such a dislike to shooting-men, that he won't shoot pheasants himself. We don't hunt on Wednesdays or Sundays, and then everybody lies in bed. Here is Mr Maule, he lies in bed on other mornings as well, and spends the rest of his day riding about the country looking for the hounds.'

'Does he ever find them?'

'What did become of you all to-day?' said Mr Maule, as he took his place at the dinner-table. 'You can't have drawn any of the coverts regularly.'

'Then we found our foxes without drawing them,' said the master.

'We chopped one* at Bromleys,' said Mr Spooner.

'I went there.'

'Then you ought to have known better,' said Mrs Spooner. 'When a man loses the hounds in that country, he ought to go direct to Brackett's Wood. If you had come on to Brackett's, you'd have seen as good a thirty-two minutes as ever you wished to ride.' When the ladies went out of the room Mrs Spooner gave a parting word of advice to her husband, and to the host. 'Now, Tom, don't you drink port-wine. Lord Chiltern, look after him, and don't let him have port-wine.'

Then there began an altogether different phase of hunting conversation. As long as the ladies were there it was all very well to talk of hunting as an amusement, good sport, a thirty minutes or so, the delight of having a friend in a ditch, or the glory of a stiff-built rail were fitting subjects for a lighter hour. But now the business of the night was to begin. The difficulties, the enmities, the precautions, the resolutions, the resources of the Brake hunt were to be discussed. And from thence the conversation of these devotees strayed away to the perils at large to which hunting in these modern days is subjected;—not the perils of broken necks and crushed ribs, which can be reduced to an average, and so an end made of that small matter; but the perils from outsiders, the perils from new-fangled prejudices,* the perils from more modern sports, the perils from over-cultivation, the perils from extended population, the perils from increasing railroads, the perils from literary ignorances, the perils from intruding cads, the perils from indifferent magnates,—the Duke of Omnium, for instance;—and that peril of perils, the peril of decrease of funds and increase of expenditure! The jaunty gentleman who puts on his dainty breeches, and his pair of boots, and on his single horse rides out on a pleasant morning to some neighbouring meet, thinking himself a sportsman, has but a faint idea of the troubles which a few staunch workmen endure in order that he may not be made to think that his boots, and his breeches, and his horse, have been in vain.

A word or two further was at first said about that unfortunate wood for which Silverbridge at the present felt himself responsible. Finn said that he was sure the Duke would look to it, if Silverbridge would mention it. Chiltern simply groaned. Silverbridge said nothing, remembering how many troubles he had on hand at this moment. Then by degrees their solicitude worked itself round to the cares of a neighbouring hunt. The A. R. U. had lost their master. One Captain Glomax* was going, and the county had been driven to the necessity of advertising for a successor. 'When hunting comes to that,' said Lord Chiltern, 'one begins to think that it is in a bad way.' It may always be observed that when hunting-men speak seriously of their sport, they speak despondingly. Everything is going wrong. Perhaps the same thing may be remarked in other pursuits. Farmers are generally on the verge of ruin. Trade is always bad. The Church is in danger. The House of Lords isn't worth a dozen years' purchase. The throne totters.

'An itinerant master with a carpet-bag* never can carry on a country,' said Mr Spooner.

'You ought really to have a gentleman of property in the county,' said Lord Chiltern, in a self-deprecating tone. His father's acres lay elsewhere.

'It should be someone who has a real stake in the country,' replied Mr Spooner,—'whom the farmers can respect. Glomax understood hunting no doubt, but the farmers didn't care for him. If you don't have the farmers with you you can't have hunting.' Then he filled a glass of port.

'If you don't approve of Glomax, what do you think of a man like Major Tifto?' asked Mr Maule.

'That was in the Runnymede,' said Spooner contemptuously.

'Who is Major Tifto?' asked Lord Chiltern.

'He is the man,' said Silverbridge boldly, 'who owned Prime Minister with me, when he didn't win the Leger last September.'

'There was a deuce of a row,' said Maule. Then Mr Spooner, who read his 'Bell's Life' and 'Field' very religiously, and who never missed an article in 'Bayley's,'* proceeded to give them an account of everything that had taken place in the Runnymede Hunt. It mattered but little that he was wrong in all his details. Narrations always are. The result to which he came was nearly right when he declared that the Major had been turned off, that a committee had been appointed, and that Messrs Topps and Jawstock had been threatened with a lawsuit.

'That comes,' said Lord Chiltern solemnly, 'of employing men like Major Tifto in places for which they are radically unfit. I dare say Major Tifto knew how to handle a pack of hounds,—perhaps almost as well as my huntsman, Fowler. But I don't think a county would get on very well which appointed Fowler Master of Hounds. He is an honest man, and therefore would be better than Tifto. But—it would not do. It is a position in which a man should at any rate be a gentleman. If he be not, all those who should be concerned in maintaining the hunt will turn their backs upon him. When I take my hounds over this man's ground, and that man's ground, certainly without doing him any good, I have to think of a great many things. I have to understand that those whom I cannot compensate by money, I have to compensate by courtesy. When I shake hands with a farmer and express my obligation to him because he does not lock his gates, he is gratified. I don't think any decent farmer would care much for shaking hands with Major Tifto. If we fall into that kind of thing there must soon be an end of hunting. Major Tiftos are cheap no doubt; but in hunting, as in most other things, cheap and nasty go together. If men don't choose to put their hands in their pockets they had better say so, and give the thing up altogether. If you won't take any more wine, we'll go to the ladies. Silverbridge, the trap will start from the door to-morrow morning precisely at 9.30 a.m. Grantingham Cross is fourteen miles.' Then they all left their chairs,—but as they did so Mr Spooner finished the bottle of port-wine.

'I never heard Chiltern speak so much like a book before,' said Spooner to his wife, as she drove him home that night.

The next morning everybody was ready for a start at half-past nine, except Mr Maule,—as to whom his wife declared that she had left him in bed when she came down to breakfast. 'He can never get there if we don't take him,' said Lord Chiltern, who was in truth the most good-natured man in the world. Five minutes were allowed him, and then he came down with a large sandwich in one hand and a button-hook in the other, with which he was prepared to complete his toilet. 'What the deuce makes you always in such a hurry?' were the first words he spoke as Lord Chiltern got on the box. The Master knew him too well to argue the point. 'Well;—he always is in a hurry,' said the sinner, when his wife accused him of ingratitude.

'Where's Spooner?' asked the Master when he saw Mrs Spooner without her husband at the meet.

'I knew how it would be when I saw the port-wine,' she said in a whisper that could be heard all round. 'He has got it this time sharp,— in his great toe.* We shan't find at Grantingham. They were cutting wood there last week. If I were you, my Lord, I'd go away to the Spinnies at once.'

'I must draw the country regularly,' muttered the Master.

The country was drawn regularly, but in vain till about two o'clock. Not only was there no fox at Grantingham Wood, but none even at the Spinnies. And at two, Fowler, with an anxious face, held a consultation with his more anxious master. Trumpington Wood lay on their right, and that no doubt would have been the proper draw. 'I suppose we must try it,' said Lord Chiltern.

Old Fowler looked very sour. 'You might as well look for a fox under my wife's bed, my Lord.'

'I dare say we should find one there,' said one of the wags of the hunt. Fowler shook his head, feeling that this was no time for joking.

'It ought to be drawn,' said Chiltern.

'Of course you know best, my Lord. I wouldn't touch it,—never no more. Let 'em all know what the Duke's Wood is.'

'This is Lord Silverbridge, the Duke's son,' said Chiltern laughing.

'I beg your Lordship's pardon,' said Fowler, taking off his cap. 'We shall have a good time coming, some day. Let me trot 'em off to Michaelmas Daisies, my Lord. I'll be there in thirty minutes.' In the neighbouring parish of St Michael de Dezier there was a favourite little gorse which among hunting-men had acquired this unreasonable name. After a little consideration the Master yielded, and away they trotted.

'You'll cross the ford, Fowler?' asked Mrs Spooner.

'Oh yes, ma'am; we couldn't draw the Daisies this afternoon if we didn't.'

'It'll be up to the horses' bellies.'

'Those who don't like it can go round.'

'They'd never be there in time, Fowler.'

'There's a many, ma'am, as don't mind that. You won't be one to stay behind.' The water was up to the horses' bellies, but, nevertheless, Mrs Spooner was at the gorse side when the Daisies were drawn.

They found and were away in a minute. It was all done so quickly that Fowler, who had alone gone into the gorse, had hardly time to get out with his hounds. The fox ran right back, as though he were making for the Duke's pernicious wood. In the first field or two there was a succession of gates, and there was not much to do in the way of jumping. Then the fox, keeping straight ahead, deviated from the line by which they had come, making for the brook by a more direct course. The ruck of the horsemen, understanding the matter very well, left the hounds, and went to the right, riding for the ford. The ford was of such a nature that but one horse could pass it at a time, and that one had to scramble through deep mud. 'There'll be the devil to pay there,' said Lord Chiltern, going straight with his hounds. Phineas Finn and Dick Rabbit were close after him. Old Fowler had craftily gone to the ford; but Mrs Spooner, who did not intend to be shaken off, followed the Master, and close with her was Lord Silverbridge. 'Lord Chiltern hasn't got it right,' she said. 'He can't do it among these bushes.' As she spoke the Master put his horse at the bushes and then—disappeared. The lady had been right. There was no ground at that spot to take off from, and the bushes had impeded him. Lord Chiltern got over, but his horse was in the water. Dick Rabbit and poor Phineas Finn were stopped in their course by the necessity of helping the Master in his trouble.

But Mrs Spooner, the judicious Mrs Spooner, rode at the stream where it was, indeed, a little wider, but at a place in which the horse could see what he was about, and where he could jump from and to firm ground. Lord Silverbridge followed her gallantly. They both jumped the brook well, and then were together. 'You'll beat me in pace,' said the lady as he rode alongside of her. 'Take the fence ahead straight, and then turn sharp to your right.' With all her faults Mrs Spooner was a thorough sportsman.

He did take the fence ahead,—or rather tried to do so. It was a bank and a double ditch,—not very great in itself, but requiring a horse to land on the top and go off with a second spring. Our young friend's nag, not quite understanding the nature of the impediment, endeavoured to 'swallow it whole,' as hard-riding men say, and came down in the further ditch. Silverbridge came down on his head, but the horse pursued his course,—across a heavily-ploughed field.

This was very disagreeable. He was not in the least hurt, but it became his duty to run after his horse. A very few furrows of that work suffice to make a man think that hunting altogether is a 'beastly sort of thing.' Mrs Spooner's horse, who had shown himself to be a little less quick of foot than his own, had known all about the bank and the double ditch, and had, apparently of his own accord, turned down to the right, either seeing or hearing the hounds, and knowing that the ploughed ground was to be avoided. But his rider soon changed his course. She went straight after the riderless horse, and when Silverbridge had reduced himself to utter speechlessness by his exertions, brought him back his steed.

'I am,—I am, I am—so sorry,' he struggled to say,—and then as she held his horse for him he struggled up into the saddle.

'Keep down this furrow,' said Mrs Spooner, 'and we shall be with them in the second field. There's nobody near them yet.'

## CHAPTER 63

### 'I'VE SEEN 'EM LIKE THAT BEFORE'

ON this occasion Silverbridge stayed only a few days at Harrington, having promised Tregear to entertain him at The Baldfaced Stag. It was here that his horses were standing, and he now intended, by limiting himself to one horse a day, to mount his friend for a couple of weeks. It was settled at last that Tregear should ride his friend's horse one day, hire the next, and so on. 'I wonder what you'll think of Mrs Spooner?' he said.

'Why should I think anything of her?'

'Because I doubt whether you ever saw such a woman before. She does nothing but hunt.'

'Then I certainly shan't want to see her again.'

'And she talks as I never heard a lady talk before.'

'Then I don't care if I never see her at all.'

'But she is the most plucky and most good-natured human being I ever saw in my life. After all, hunting is very good fun.'

'Very; if you don't do it so often as to be sick of it.'

'Long as I have known you I don't think I ever saw you ride yet.'

'We used to have hunting down in Cornwall, and thought we did it pretty well. And I have ridden in South Wales, which I can assure you isn't an easy thing to do. But you mustn't expect much from me.'

They were both out the Monday and Tuesday in that week, and then again on the Thursday without anything special in the way of sport. Lord Chiltern, who had found Silverbridge to be a young man after his own heart, was anxious that he should come back to Harrington and bring Tregear with him. But to this Tregear would not assent, alleging that he should feel himself to be a burden both to Lord and Lady Chiltern. On the Friday Tregear did not go out, saying that he would avoid the expense, and on that day there was a good run. 'It is always the way,' said Silverbridge. 'If you miss a day, it is sure to be the best thing of the season. An hour and a quarter with hardly anything you could call a check! It is the only very good thing I have seen since I have been here. Mrs Spooner was with them all through.'

'And I suppose you were with Mrs Spooner.'

'I wasn't far off. I wish you had been there.'

On the next day the meet was at the kennels, close to Harrington, and Silverbridge drove his friend over in a gig. The Master and Lady Chiltern, Spooner and Mrs Spooner, Maule and Mrs Maule, Phineas

Finn, and a host of others condoled with the unfortunate young man because he had not seen the good thing yesterday. 'We've had it a little faster once or twice,' said Mrs Spooner with deliberation, 'but never for so long. Then it was straight as a line, and a real open kill. No changing, you know. We did go through the Daisies, but I'll swear to its being the same fox.' All of which set Tregear wondering. How could she swear to her fox? And if they had changed, what did it matter? And if it had been a little crooked, why would it have been less enjoyable? And was she really so exact a judge of pace as she pretended to be? 'I'm afraid we shan't have anything like that to-day,' she continued. 'The wind's in the west, and I never do like a westerly wind.'

'A little to the north,' said her husband, looking round the compass.

'My dear,' said the lady, 'you never know where the wind comes from. Now don't you think of taking off your comforter. I won't have it.'

Tregear was riding his friend's favourite hunter, a thoroughbred bay horse, very much more than up to his rider's weight, and supposed to be peculiarly good at timber, water, or any well-defined kind of fence, however high or however broad. They found at a covert near the kennels, and killed their fox after a burst of a few minutes. They found again, and having lost their fox, all declared that there was not a yard of scent. 'I always know what a west wind means,' said Mrs Spooner.

Then they lunched, and smoked, and trotted about with an apparent acknowledgement that there wasn't much to be done. It was not right that they should expect much after so good a thing as they had had yesterday. At half-past two Mr Spooner had been sent home by his Providence, and Mrs Spooner was calculating that she would be able to ride her horse again on the Tuesday, when on a sudden the hounds were on a fox. It turned out afterwards that Dick Rabbit had absolutely ridden him up among the stubble, and that the hounds had nearly killed him before he had gone a yard. But the astute animal, making the best use of his legs till he could get the advantage of the first ditch, ran, and crept, and jumped absolutely through the pack. Then there was shouting, and yelling, and riding. The men who were idly smoking threw away their cigars. Those who were loitering at a distance lost their chance. But the real sportsmen, always on the alert, always thinking of the business in hand, always mindful that there may be at any moment a fox just before the hounds, had a glorious opportunity of getting 'well away.' Among these no one was more intent, or, when the moment came, 'better away', than Mrs Spooner.

Silverbridge had been talking to her and had the full advantage of her care. Tregear was riding behind with Lord Chiltern, who had been pressing him to come with his friend to Harrington. As soon as the shouting was heard Chiltern was off like a rocket. It was not only that he was anxious to 'get well away,' but that a sense of duty compelled him to see how the thing was being done. Old Fowler certainly was a little slow, and Dick Rabbit, with the true bloody-minded instinct of a whip,* was a little apt to bustle a fox back into covert. And then, when a run commences with a fast rush, riders are apt to over-ride the hounds, and then the hounds will over-run the fox. All of which has to be seen to by a Master who knows his business.

Tregear followed, and being mounted on a fast horse was soon as forward as a judicious rider would desire. 'Now, Runks, don't you press on and spoil it all,' said Mrs Spooner to the hard-riding objectionable son of old Runks the vet from Rufford. But young Runks did press on till the Master spoke a word. The word shall not be repeated, but it was efficacious.

At that moment there had been a check,—as there is generally after a short spurt, when fox, hounds, and horsemen get off together, and not always in the order in which they have been placed here. There is too much bustle, and the pack becomes disconcerted. But it enabled Fowler to get up, and by dint of growling at the men and conciliating his hounds, he soon picked up the scent. 'If they'd all stand still for two minutes and be —— to them,' he muttered aloud to himself, 'they'd 'ave some'at to ride arter. They might go then, and there's some of 'em 'd soon be nowhere.'

But in spite of Fowler's denunciations there was, of course, another rush. Runks had slunk away, but by making a little distance was now again ahead of the hounds. And unfortunately there was half-a-dozen with him. Lord Chiltern was very wrath. 'When he's like that,' said Mrs Spooner to Tregear, 'it's always well to give him a wide berth.' But as the hounds were now running fast it was necessary that even in taking this precaution due regard should be had to the fox's line. 'He's back for Harrington bushes,' said Mrs Spooner. And as she said so, she rode at a bank, with a rail at the top of it perhaps a foot-and-a-half high, with a deep drop into the field beyond. It was not a very nice place, but it was apparently the only available spot in the fence. She seemed to know it well, for as she got close to it she brought her horse almost to a stand and so took it. The horse cleared the rail, seemed just to touch the bank on the other side, while she threw herself back almost on to his crupper, and so came down with perfect ease. But she, knowing that it would not be easy to all horses, paused a moment to see what would happen.

Tregear was next to her and was intending to 'fly' the fence. But when he saw Mrs Spooner pull her horse and pause, he also had to pull his horse. This he did so as to enable her to take her leap without danger or encumbrance from him, but hardly so as to bring his horse to the bank in the same way. It may be doubted whether the animal he was riding would have known enough and been quiet enough to have performed the acrobatic manœuvre which had carried Mrs Spooner so pleasantly over the peril. He had some idea of this, for the thought occurred to him that he would turn and ride fast at the jump. But before he could turn he saw that Silverbridge was pressing on him. It was thus his only resource to do as Mrs Spooner had done. He was too close to the rail, but still he tried it. The horse attempted to jump, caught his foot against the bar, and of course went over headforemost. This probably would have been nothing, had not Silverbridge with his rushing beast been immediately after them. When the young lord saw that his friend was down it was too late for him to stop his course. His horse was determined to have the fence,—and did have it. He touched nothing, and would have skimmed in glory over the next field had he not come right down on Tregear and Tregear's steed. There they were, four of them, two men and two horses in one confused heap.

The first person with them was Mrs Spooner, who was off her horse in a minute. And Silverbridge too was very soon on his legs. He at any rate was unhurt, and the two horses were up before Mrs Spooner was out of her saddle. But Tregear did not move. 'What are we to do?' said Lord Silverbridge, kneeling down over his friend. 'Oh, Mrs Spooner, what are we to do?'

The hunt had passed on and no one else was immediately with them. But at this moment Dick Rabbit, who had been left behind to bring up his hounds, appeared above the bank. 'Leave your horse and come down,' said Mrs Spooner. 'Here is a gentleman who has hurt himself.' Dick wouldn't leave his horse, but was soon on the scene, having found his way through another part of the fence.

'No; he ain't dead,' said Dick—'I've seen 'em like that before, and they wurn't dead. But he's had a hawful squeege.' Then he passed his hand over the man's neck and chest. 'There's a lot of 'em is broke,' said he. 'We must get him into farmer Tooby's.'

After awhile he was got into farmer Tooby's, when that surgeon came who is always in attendance on a hunting-field. The surgeon declared that he had broken his collar-bone, two of his ribs, and his

left arm. And then one of the animals had struck him on the chest as he
raised himself. A little brandy was poured down his throat, but even
under that operation he gave no sign of life. 'No, missis, he aren't dead,'
said Dick to Mrs Tooby; 'no more he won't die this bout; but he's got
it very nasty.'

That night Silverbridge was sitting by his friend's bedside at ten
o'clock in Lord Chiltern's house. Tregear had spoken a few words, and
the bones had been set. But the doctor had not felt himself justified in
speaking with that assurance which Dick had expressed. The man's
whole body had been bruised by the horse which had fallen on him.
The agony of Silverbridge was extreme, for he knew that it had been
his doing. 'You were a little too close,' Mrs Spooner had said to him,
'but nobody saw it and we'll hold our tongues.' Silverbridge however
would not hold his tongue. He told everybody how it had happened,
how he had been unable to stop his horse, how he had jumped upon
his friend, and perhaps killed him. 'I don't know what I am to do. I am
so miserable,' he said to Lady Chiltern with the tears running down
his face.

The two remained at Harrington and their luggage was brought over
from The Baldfaced Stag. The accident had happened on a Saturday.
On the Sunday there was no comfort. On the Monday the patient's
recollection and mind were re-established, and the doctor thought that
perhaps, with great care, his constitution would pull him through. On
that day the consternation at Harrington was so great that Mrs Spooner
would not go to the meet. She came over from Spoon Hall, and spent a
considerable part of the day in the sick man's room. 'It's sure to come
right if it's above the vitals,' she said, expressing an opinion which had
come from much experience. 'That is,' she added, 'unless the neck's
broke. When poor old Jack Stubbs drove his head into his cap and dislocated his wertebury, of course it was all up with him.' The patient
heard this and was seen to smile.

On the Tuesday there arose the question of family communication.
As the accident would make its way into the papers a message had been
sent to Polwenning to say that various bones had been broken, but that
the patient was upon the whole doing well. Then there had been different messages backwards and forwards, in all of which there had been an
attempt to comfort old Mrs Tregear. But on the Tuesday letters were
written. Silverbridge, sitting in his friend's room, sent a long account
of the accident to Mrs Tregear, giving a list of the injuries done.

'Your sister,' whispered the poor fellow from his pillow.

'Yes,—yes;—yes, I will.'

'And Mabel Grex.' Silverbridge nodded assent and again went to the writing-table. He did write to his sister, and in plain words told her everything. 'The doctor says he is not now in danger.' Then he added a postscript. 'As long as I am here I will let you know how he is.'

# CHAPTER 64

## 'I BELIEVE HIM TO BE A WORTHY YOUNG MAN'

LADY MARY and Mrs Finn were alone when the tidings came from Silverbridge. The Duke had been absent, having gone to spend an unpleasant week in Barsetshire. Mary had taken the opportunity of his absence to discuss her own prospects at full length. 'My dear,' said Mrs Finn, 'I will not express an opinion. How can I after all that has passed? I have told the Duke the same. I cannot be heart and hand with either without being false to the other.' But still Lady Mary continued to talk about Tregear.

'I don't think papa has a right to treat me in this way,' she said. 'He wouldn't be allowed to kill me, and this is killing me.'

'While there is life there is hope,' said Mrs Finn.

'Yes; while there is life there is hope. But one doesn't want to grow old first.'

'There is no danger of that yet, Mary.'

'I feel very old. What is the use of life without something to make it sweet? I am not even allowed to hear anything that he is doing. If he were to ask me, I think I would go away with him to-morrow.'

'He would not be foolish enough for that.'

'Because he does not suffer as I do. He has his borough, and his public life, and a hundred things to think of. I have got nothing but him. I know he is true;—quite as true as I am. But it is I that have the suffering in all this. A man can never be like a girl. Papa ought not to make me suffer like this.'

That took place on the Monday. On the Tuesday Mrs Finn received a letter from her husband giving his account of the accident. 'As far as I can learn,' he said, 'Silverbridge will write about it to-morrow.' Then he went on to give a by no means good account of the state of the patient. The doctor had declared him to be out of immediate danger, and had set the broken bones. As tidings would be sent on the next day she had better say nothing about the accident to Lady Mary. This letter reached Matching on Tuesday and made the position of Mrs Finn very disagreeable. She was bound to carry herself as though nothing was amiss, knowing, as she did so, the condition of Mary's lover.

On the evening of that day Lady Mary was more lively than usual, though her liveliness was hardly of a happy nature. 'I don't know what papa can expect. I've heard him say a hundred times that to be in Parliament is the highest place a gentleman can fill, and now Frank is in Parliament.' Mrs Finn looked at her with beseeching eyes, as though begging her not to speak of Tregear. 'And then to think of their having that Lord Popplecourt there! I shall always hate Lady Cantrip, for it was her place. That she should have thought it possible! Lord Popplecourt! Such a creature! Hyperion to a satyr.* Isn't it true? Oh, that papa should have thought it possible!' Then she got up, and walked about the room, beating her hands together. All this time Mrs Finn knew that Tregear was lying at Harrington with half his bones broken, and in danger of his life!

On the next morning Lady Mary received her letters. There were two lying before her plate when she came into breakfast, one from her father and the other from Silverbridge. She read that from the Duke first while Mrs Finn was watching her. 'Papa will be home on Saturday,' she said. 'He declares that the people in the borough are quite delighted with Silverbridge for a member. And he is quite jocose. "They used to be delighted with me once," he says, "but I suppose everybody changes."' Then she began to pour out the tea before she opened her brother's letter. Mrs Finn's eyes were still on her anxiously. 'I wonder what Silverbridge has got to say about the Brake Hunt.' Then she opened her letter.

'Oh;—oh!' she exclaimed,—'Frank has killed himself.'

'Killed himself! Not that. It is not so bad as that.'

'You had heard it before?'

'How is he, Mary?'

'Oh, heavens! I cannot read it. Do you read it. Tell me all. Tell me the truth. What am I to do? Where shall I go?' Then she threw up her hands, and with a loud scream fell on her knees with her head upon the chair. In the next moment Mrs Finn was down beside her on the floor. 'Read it; why do you not read it? If you will not read it, give it to me.'

Mrs Finn did read the letter, which was very short, but still giving by no means an unfavourable account of the patient. 'I am sorry to say he has broken ever so many bones, and we were very much frightened about him.' Then the writer went into details, from which a reader who did not read the words carefully might well imagine that the man's life was still in danger.

Mrs Finn did read it all, and did her best to comfort her friend. 'It has been a bad accident,' she said, 'but it is clear that he is getting better. Men do so often break their bones, and then seem to think nothing of it afterwards.'

'Silverbridge says it was his fault. What does he mean?'

'I suppose he was riding too close to Mr Tregear, and that they came down together. Of course it is distressing, but I do not think you need make yourself positively unhappy about it.'

'Would you not be unhappy if it were Mr Finn?' said Mary, jumping up from her knees. 'I shall go to him. I should go mad if I were to remain here and know nothing about it but what Silverbridge will tell me.'

'I will telegraph to Mr Finn.'

'Mr Finn won't care. Men are so heartless. They write about each other just as though it did not signify in the least whether anybody were dead or alive. I shall go to him.'

'You cannot do that.'

'I don't care now what anybody may think. I choose to be considered as belonging to him, and if papa were here I would say the same.' It was of course not difficult to make her understand that she could not go to Harrington, but it was by no means easy to keep her tranquil. She would send a telegram herself. This was debated for a long time, till at last Lady Mary insisted that she was not subject to Mrs Finn's authority. 'If papa were here, even then I would send it.' And she did send it, in her own name, regardless of the fact pointed out to her by Mrs Finn, that the people at the post-office would thus know her secret. 'It is no secret,' she said. 'I don't want it to be a secret.' The telegram went in the following words: 'I have heard it. I am so wretched. Send me one word to say how you are.' She got an answer back, with Tregear's own name to it, on that afternoon. 'Do not be unhappy. I am doing well. Silverbridge is with me.'

On the Thursday Gerald came home from Scotland. He had arranged his little affair with Lord Percival, not however without some difficulty. Lord Percival had declared he did not understand I.O.U.'s in an affair of that kind. He had always thought that gentlemen did not play for stakes which they could not pay at once. This was not said to Gerald himself;—or the result would have been calamitous. Nidderdale was the go-between, and at last arranged it,—not however till he had pointed out that Percival, having won so large a sum of money from a lad under twenty-one years of age, was very lucky in receiving substantial security for its payment.

Gerald had chosen the period of his father's absence for his return. It was necessary that the story of the gambling debt should be told the Duke in February. Silverbridge had explained that to him, and he had quite understood it. He, indeed, would be up at Oxford in February, and, in that case, the first horror of the thing would be left to poor Silverbridge! Thinking of this, Gerald felt that he was bound to tell his father himself. He resolved that he would do so, but was anxious to postpone the evil day. He lingered therefore in Scotland till he knew that his father was in Barsetshire.

On his arrival he was told of Tregear's accident. 'Oh, Gerald; have you heard?' said his sister. He had not as yet heard, and then the history was repeated to him. Mary did not attempt to conceal her own feelings. She was as open with her brother as she had been with Mrs Finn.

'I suppose he'll get over it,' said Gerald.

'Is that all you say?' she asked.

'What can I say better? I suppose he will. Fellows always do get over that kind of thing. Herbert de Burgh smashed both his thighs, and now he can move about again,—of course with crutches.'

'Gerald! How can you be so unfeeling!'

'I don't know what you mean. I always liked Tregear, and I am very sorry for him. If you would take it a little quieter, I think it would be better.'

'I could not take it quietly. How can I take it quietly when he is more than all the world to me?'

'You should keep that to yourself.'

'Yes,—and so let people think that I didn't care, till I broke my heart! I shall say just the same to papa when he comes home.' After that the brother and sister were not on very good terms with each other for the remainder of the day.

On the Saturday there was a letter from Silverbridge to Mrs Finn. Tregear was better; but was unhappy because it had been decided that he could not be moved for the next month. This entailed two misfortunes on him;—first that of being the enforced guest of persons who were not,—or, hitherto had not been, his own friends,—and then his absence from the first meeting of Parliament. When a gentleman has been in Parliament some years he may be able to reconcile himself to an obligatory vacation with a calm mind. But when the honours and glory are new, and the tedium of the benches has not yet been experienced, then such an accident is felt to be a grievance. But the young member was out of danger, and was, as Silverbridge declared, in the very best quarters which could be provided for a man in such a position.

Phineas Finn told him all the politics; Mrs Spooner related to him, on Sundays and Wednesdays, all the hunting details; while Lady Chiltern read to him light literature, because he was not allowed to hold a book in his hand. 'I wish it were me,' said Gerald. 'I wish I were there to read to him,' said Mary.

Then the Duke came home. 'Mary,' said he, 'I have been distressed to hear of this accident.' This seemed to her to be the kindest word she had heard from him for a long time. 'I believe him to be a worthy young man. I am sorry that he should be the cause of so much sorrow to you—and to me.'

'Of course I was sorry for his accident,' she replied, after pausing awhile; 'but now that he is better I will not call him a cause of sorrow—to me.' Then the Duke said nothing further about Tregear; nor did she.

'So you have come at last,' he said to Gerald. That was the first greeting,—to which the son responded by an awkward smile. But in the course of the evening he walked straight up to his father—'I have something to tell you, sir,' said he.

'Something to tell me?'

'Something that will make you very angry.'

# CHAPTER 65

## 'DO YOU EVER THINK WHAT MONEY IS?'

GERALD told his story, standing bolt upright, and looking his father full in the face as he told it. 'You lost three thousand four hundred pounds at one sitting to Lord Percival—at cards!'

'Yes, sir.'

'In Lord Nidderdale's house?'

'Yes, sir. Nidderdale wasn't playing. It wasn't his fault.'

'Who were playing?'

'Percival, and Dolly Longstaff, and Jack Hinde,—and I. Popplecourt was playing at first.'

'Lord Popplecourt!'

'Yes, sir. But he went away when he began to lose.'

'Three thousand four hundred pounds! How old are you?'

'I am just twenty-one.'

'You are beginning the world well, Gerald! What is the engagement which Silverbridge has made with Lord Percival?'

'To pay him the money at the end of next month.'

'What had Silverbridge to do with it?'

'Nothing, sir. I wrote to Silverbridge because I didn't know what to do. I knew he would stand to me.'

'Who is to stand to either of you if you go on thus I do not know.' To this Gerald of course made no reply, but an idea came across his mind that he knew who would stand both to himself and his brother. 'How did Silverbridge mean to get the money?'

'He said he would ask you. But I thought that I ought to tell you.'

'Is that all?'

'All what, sir?'

'Are there other debts?' To this Gerald made no reply. 'Other gambling debts.'

'No, sir;—not a shilling of that kind. I have never played before.'

'Does it ever occur to you that going on at that rate you may very soon lose all the fortune that will ever come to you? You were not yet of age and you lost three thousand four hundred pounds at cards to a man whom you probably knew to be a professed gambler!' The Duke seemed to wait for a reply, but poor Gerald had not a word to say. 'Can you explain to me what benefit you proposed to yourself when you played for such stakes as that?'

'I hoped to win back what I had lost.'

'Facilis descensus Averni!' said the Duke, shaking his head. 'Noctes atque dies patet atri janua Ditis.'* No doubt, he thought, that as his son was at Oxford, admonitions in Latin would serve him better than in his native tongue. But Gerald, when he heard the grand hexameter rolled out in his father's grandest tone, entertained a comfortable feeling that the worst of the interview was over. 'Win back what you had lost! Do you think that that is the common fortune of young gamblers when they fall among those who are more experienced than themselves?'

'One goes on, sir, without reflecting.'

'Go on without reflecting! Yes; and where to? where to? Oh Gerald, where to? Whither will such progress without reflection take you?' 'He means—to the devil,' the lad said inwardly to himself, without moving his lips. 'There is but one goal for such going on as that. I can pay three thousand four hundred pounds for you certainly. I think it hard that I should have to do so; but I can do it,—and I will do it.'

'Thank you, sir,' murmured Gerald.

'But how can I wash your young mind clean from the foul stain which has already defiled it? Why did you sit down to play? Was it to win the money which these men had in their pockets?'

'Not particularly.'

'It cannot be that a rational being should consent to risk the money he has himself,—to risk even the money which he has not himself,— without a desire to win that which as yet belongs to his opponents. You desired to win.'

'I suppose I did hope to win.'

'And why? Why did you want to extract their property from their pockets, and to put it into your own? That the footpad on the road should have such desire when, with his pistol, he stops the traveller on his journey we all understand. And we know what we think of the footpad,—and what we do to him. He is a poor creature, who from his youth upwards has had no good thing done for him, uneducated, an outcast, whom we should pity more than we despise him. We take him as a pest which we cannot endure, and lock him up where he can harm us no more. On my word, Gerald, I think that the so-called gentleman who sits down with the deliberate intention of extracting money from the pockets of his antagonists, who lays out for himself that way of repairing the shortcomings of fortune, who looks to that resource as an aid to his means,—is worse, much worse, than the public robber! He is meaner, more cowardly, and has I think in his bosom less of the feelings of an honest man. And he probably has been educated,—as you have been. He calls himself a gentleman. He should know black from white. It is considered terrible to cheat at cards.'

'There was nothing of that, sir.'

'The man who plays and cheats has fallen low indeed.'

'I understand that, sir.'

'He who plays that he may make an income, but does not cheat, has fallen nearly as low. Do you ever think what money is?'

The Duke paused so long, collecting his own thoughts and thinking of his own words, that Gerald found himself obliged to answer. 'Cheques, and sovereigns, and bank-notes,' he replied with much hesitation.

'Money is the reward of labour,' said the Duke, 'or rather, in the shape it reaches you, it is your representation of that reward. You may earn it yourself, or, as is, I am afraid, more likely to be the case with you, you may possess it honestly as prepared for you by the labour of others who have stored it up for you. But it is a commodity of which you are bound to see that the source is not only clean but noble. You would not let Lord Percival give you money.'

'He wouldn't do that, sir, I am sure.'

'Nor would you take it. There is nothing so comfortable as money,— but nothing so defiling if it be come by unworthily; nothing so comfortable, but nothing so noxious if the mind be allowed to dwell upon it constantly. If a man have enough, let him spend it freely. If he wants it, let him earn it honestly. Let him do something for it, so that the man who pays it to him may get its value. But to think that it may be got by gambling, to hope to live after that fashion, to sit down with your fingers almost in your neighbour's pockets, with your eye on his purse, trusting that you may know better than he some studied calculations as to the pips* concealed in your hands, praying to the only god you worship that some special card may be vouchsafed to you,—that I say is to have left far, far behind you, all nobility, all gentleness, all manhood! Write me down Lord Percival's address and I will send him the money.'

Then the Duke wrote a cheque for the money claimed and sent it with a note, as follows:—'The Duke of Omnium presents his compliments to Lord Percival. The Duke has been informed by Lord Gerald Palliser that Lord Percival has won at cards from him the sum of three thousand four hundred pounds. The Duke now encloses a cheque for that amount, and requests that the document which Lord Percival holds from Lord Silverbridge as security for the amount, may be returned to Lord Gerald.' Let the noble gambler have his prey. He was little solicitous about that. If he could only so operate on the mind of this son,—so operate on the minds of both his sons, as to make them see the foolishness of folly, the ugliness of what is mean, the squalor and dirt of ignoble pursuits, then he could easily pardon past faults. If it were half his wealth, what would it signify if he could teach his children to accept those lessons without which no man can live as a gentleman, let his rank be the highest known, let his wealth be as the sands, his fashion unrivalled?

The word or two which his daughter had said to him, declaring that she still took pride in her lover's love, and then this new misfortune on Gerald's part, upset him greatly. He almost sickened of politics when he thought of his domestic bereavement and his domestic misfortunes. How completely had he failed to indoctrinate his children with the ideas by which his own mind was fortified and controlled! Nothing was so base to him as a gambler, and they had both commenced their career by gambling. From their young boyhood nothing had seemed so desirable to him as that they should be accustomed by early training to devote themselves to the service of their country. He saw other young noblemen around him who at eighteen were known as debaters at their colleges, or at twenty-five were already deep in politics, social science, and educational projects. What good would all his wealth or all his position do for his children if their minds could rise to nothing beyond the shooting of deer and the hunting of foxes? There was young Lord Buttercup, the son of the Earl of Woolantallow, only a few months older than Silverbridge,—who was already a junior lord, and as constant at his office, or during the Session on the Treasury Bench, as though there were not a pack of hounds or a card-table in Great Britain! Lord Buttercup, too, had already written an article in 'The Fortnightly'* on the subject of Turkish finance. How long would it be before Silverbridge would write an article, or Gerald sign his name in the service of the public?

And then those proposed marriages,—as to which he was beginning to know that his children would be too strong for him! Anxious as he was that both his sons should be permeated by Liberal politics, studious as he had ever been to teach them that the highest duty of those high in rank was to use their authority to elevate those beneath them, still he was hardly less anxious to make them understand that their second duty required them to maintain their own position. It was by feeling this second duty,—by feeling it and performing it,—that they would be enabled to perform the rest. And now both Silverbridge and his girl were bent upon marriages by which they would depart out of their own order! Let Silverbridge marry whom he might, he could not be other than heir to the honours of his family. But by his marriage he might either support or derogate from these honours. And now, having at first made a choice that was good, he had altered his mind from simple freak, captivated by a pair of bright eyes and an arch smile; and without a feeling in regard to his family, was anxious to take to his bosom the granddaughter of an American day-labourer!

And then his girl,—of whose beauty he was so proud, from whose manners, and tastes, and modes of life he had expected to reap those good things, in a feminine degree, which his sons as young men seemed so little fitted to give him! By slow degrees he had been brought round to acknowledge that the young man was worthy. Tregear's conduct had been felt by the Duke to be manly. The letter he had written was a good letter. And then he had won for himself a seat in the House of Commons. When forced to speak of him to this girl he had been driven by justice to call him worthy. But how could he serve to support and strengthen that nobility, the endurance and perpetuation of which should be the peculiar care of every Palliser?

And yet as the Duke walked about his room he felt that his opposition either to the one marriage or to the other was vain. Of course they would marry according to their wills.

That same night Gerald wrote to his brother before he went to bed, as follows:

'DEAR SILVER,—I was awfully obliged to you for sending me the I.O.U. for that brute Percival. He only sneered when he took it, and would have said something disagreeable, but that he saw that I was in earnest. I know he did say something to Nid, only I can't find out what. Nid is an easy-going fellow, and, as I saw, didn't want to have a rumpus.

'But now what do you think I've done? Directly I got home I told the governor all about it! As I was in the train I made up my mind that I would. I went slap at it. If there is anything that never does any good, it's craning.* I did it all at one rush, just as though I was swallowing a dose of physic. I wish I could tell you all that the governor said, because it was really tip-top. What is a fellow to get by playing high,—a fellow like you and me? I didn't want any of that beast's money. I don't suppose he had any. But one's dander gets up, and one doesn't like to be done, and so it goes on. I shall cut that kind of thing altogether. You should have heard the governor spouting Latin! And then the way he sat upon Percival, without mentioning the fellow's name! I do think it mean to set yourself to work to win money at cards,—and it is awfully mean to lose more than you have got to pay.

'Then at the end the governor said he'd send the beast a cheque for the amount. You know his way of finishing up, just like two fellows fighting;—when one has awfully punished the other he goes up and shakes hands with him. He did pitch into me,—not abusing me, nor even saying a word about the money, which he at once promised to pay, but laying it on to gambling with a regular cat-o'-nine-tails. And then there was an end of it. He just asked the fellow's address and said that he would send him the money. I will say this;—I don't think there's a greater brick than the governor out anywhere.

'I am awfully sorry about Tregear. I can't quite make out how it happened. I suppose you were too near him, and Melrose always does rush at his fences. One fellow shouldn't be too near another fellow,—only it so often happens that it can't be helped. It's just like anything else, if nothing comes of it then it's all right. But if anybody comes to grief then he has got to be pitched into. Do you remember when I nearly cut over old Sir Simon Slobody? Didn't I hear about it!

'I am awfully glad you didn't smash up Tregear altogether, because of Mary. I am quite sure it is no good anybody setting up his back against that. It's one of the things that have got to be. You always have said that he is a good fellow. If so, what's the harm? At any rate it has got to be.

'Your affectionate Brother,<br>'GERALD.

'I go up in about a week.'

## CHAPTER 66

### THE THREE ATTACKS

DURING the following week the communications between Harrington and Matching were very frequent. There were no further direct messages between Tregear and Lady Mary, but she heard daily of his progress. The Duke was conscious of the special interest which existed in his house as to the condition of the young man, but, after his arrival, not a word was spoken for some days between him and his daughter on the subject. Then Gerald went back to his college, and the Duke made his preparations for going up to town and making some attempt at parliamentary activity.

It was by no concert that an attack was made upon him from three quarters at once as he was preparing to leave Matching. On the Sunday morning during church time,—for on that day Lady Mary went to her devotions alone,—Mrs Finn was closeted for an hour with the Duke in his study. 'I think you ought to be aware,' she said to the Duke, 'that though I trust Mary implicitly and know her to be thoroughly high principled, I cannot be responsible for her, if I remain with her here.'

'I do not quite follow your meaning.'

'Of course there is but one matter on which there can, probably, be any difference between us. If she should choose to write to Mr Tregear, or to send him a message, or even to go to him, I could not prevent it.'

'Go to him!' exclaimed the horrified Duke.

'I merely suggest such a thing in order to make you understand that I have absolutely no control over her.'

'What control have I?'

'Nay; I cannot define that. You are her father, and she acknowledges your authority. She regards me as a friend—and as such treats me with the sweetest affection. Nothing can be more gratifying than her manner to me personally.'

'It ought to be so.'

'She has thoroughly won my heart. But still I know that if there were a difference between us she would not obey me. Why should she?'

'Because you hold my deputed authority.'

'Oh, Duke, that goes for very little anywhere. No one can depute authority. It comes too much from personal accidents, and too little from reason or law to be handed over to others. Besides, I fear, that on one matter concerning her you and I are not agreed.'

'I shall be sorry if it be so.'

'I feel that I am bound to tell you my opinion.'

'Oh yes.'

'You think that in the end Lady Mary will allow herself to be separated from Tregear. I think that in the end they will become man and wife.'

This seemed to the Duke to be not quite so bad as it might have been. Any speculation as to results were very different from an expressed opinion as to propriety. Were he to tell the truth as to his own mind, he might perhaps have said the same thing. But one is not to relax in one's endeavours to prevent that which is wrong, because one fears that the wrong may be ultimately perpetrated. 'Let that be as it may,' he said, 'it cannot alter my duty.'

'Nor mine, Duke, if I may presume to think that I have a duty in this matter.'

'That you should encounter the burden of the duty binds me to you for ever.'

'If it be that they will certainly be married one day——'

'Who has said that? Who has admitted that?'

'If it be so; if it seems to me that it must be so,—then how can I be anxious to prolong her sufferings? She does suffer terribly.' Upon this the Duke frowned, but there was more of tenderness in his frown than in the hard smile which he had hitherto worn. 'I do not know whether you see it all.' He well remembered all that he had seen when he and Mary were travelling together. 'I see it; and I do not pass half an hour with her without sorrowing for her.' On hearing this he sighed and turned his face away. 'Girls are so different! There are many who though they be genuinely in love, though their natures are sweet and affectionate, are not strong enough to support their own feelings in resistance to the will of those who have authority over them.' Had it been so with his wife? At this moment all the former history passed through his mind. 'They yield to that which seems to be inevitable, and allow themselves to be fashioned by the purposes of others. It is well for them often that they are so plastic. Whether it would be better for her that she should be so I will not say.'

'It would be better,' said the Duke doggedly.

'But such is not her nature. She is as determined as ever.'

'I may be determined too.'

'But if at last it will be of no use,—if it be her fate either to be married to this man or die of a broken heart——'

'What justifies you in saying that? How can you torture me by such a threat?'

'If I think so, Duke, I am justified. Of late I have been with her daily,—almost hourly. I do not say that this will kill her now,—in her youth. It is not often, I fancy, that women die after that fashion. But a broken heart may bring the sufferer to the grave after a lapse of many years. How will it be with you if she should live like a ghost beside you for the next twenty years, and you should then see her die, faded and withered before her time,—all her life gone without a joy,—because she had loved a man whose position in life was displeasing to you? Would the ground on which the sacrifice had been made then justify itself to you? In thus performing your duty to your order would you feel satisfied that you had performed that to your child?'

She had come there determined to say it all,—to liberate her own soul as it were,—but had much doubted the spirit in which the Duke would listen to her. That he would listen to her she was sure,—and then if he chose to cast her out, she would endure his wrath. It would not be to her now as it had been when he accused her of treachery. But, nevertheless, bold as she was and independent, he had imbued her, as he did all those around him, with so strong a sense of his personal dignity, that when she had finished she almost trembled as she looked in his face. Since he had asked her how she could justify to herself the threats which she was using he had sat still with his eyes fixed upon her. Now, when she had done, he was in no hurry to speak. He rose slowly and walking towards the fireplace stood with his back towards her, looking down upon the fire. She was the first to speak again. 'Shall I leave you now?' she said in a low voice.

'Perhaps it will be better,' he answered. His voice, too, was very low. In truth he was so moved that he hardly knew how to speak at all. Then she rose and was already on her way to the door when he followed her.

'One moment, if you please,' he said almost sternly. 'I am under a debt of gratitude to you of which I cannot express my sense in words. How far I may agree with you, and where I may disagree, I will not attempt to point out to you now.'

'Oh no.'

'But all that you have troubled yourself to think and to feel in this matter, and all that true friendship has compelled you to say to me, shall be written down in the tablets of my memory.'

'Duke!'

'My child has at any rate been fortunate in securing the friendship of such a friend.' Then he turned back to the fireplace, and she was constrained to leave the room without another word.

She had determined to make the best plea in her power for Mary; and while she was making the plea had been almost surprised by her own vehemence; but the greater had been her vehemence, the stronger, she thought, would have been the Duke's anger. And as she had watched the workings of his face she had felt for a moment that the vials of his wrath were about to be poured out upon her. Even when she left the room she almost believed that had he not taken those moments for consideration at the fireplace his parting words would have been different. But, as it was, there could be no question now of her departure. No power was left to her of separating herself from Lady Mary. Though the Duke had not as yet acknowledged himself to be conquered, there was no doubt to her now but that he would be conquered. And she, either here or in London, must be the girl's nearest friend up to the day when she should be given over to Mr Tregear.

That was one of the three attacks which were made upon the Duke before he went up to his parliamentary duties.

The second was as follows: Among the letters on the following morning one was brought to him from Tregear. It is hoped that the reader will remember the lover's former letter and the very unsatisfactory answer which had been sent to it. Nothing could have been colder, less propitious, or more inveterately hostile than the reply. As he lay in bed with his broken bones at Harrington he had ample time for thinking over all this. He knew every word of the Duke's distressing note by heart, and had often lashed himself to rage as he had repeated it. But he could effect nothing by showing his anger. He must go on and still do something. Since the writing of that letter he had done something. He had got his seat in Parliament. And he had secured the interest of his friend Silverbridge. This had been partially done at Polwenning; but the accident in the Brake country had completed the work. The brother had at last declared himself in his friend's favour. 'Of course I should be glad to see it,' he had said while sitting by Tregear's bedside. 'The worst is that everything does seem to go against the poor governor.'

Then Tregear made up his mind that he would write another letter. Personally he was not in the best condition for doing this as he was lying in bed with his left arm tied up, and with straps and bandages all round his body. But he could sit up in bed, and his right hand and arm were free. So he declared to Lady Chiltern his purpose of writing a letter. She tried to dissuade him gently and offered to be his secretary. But when he assured her that no secretary could write this letter for him she understood pretty well what would be the subject of the letter. With considerable difficulty Tregear wrote his letter.

'MY LORD DUKE,'—On this occasion he left out the epithet which he had before used—

'Your Grace's reply to my last letter was not encouraging, but in spite of your prohibition I venture to write to you again. If I had the slightest reason for thinking that your daughter was estranged from me, I would not persecute either you or her. But if it be true that she is as devoted to me as I am to her, can I be wrong in pleading my cause? Is it not evident to you that she is made of such stuff that she will not be controlled in her choice,—even by your will?

'I have had an accident in the hunting-field and am now writing from Lord Chiltern's house, where I am confined to bed. But I think you will understand me when I say that even in this helpless condition I feel myself constrained to do something. Of course I ask for nothing from you on my own behalf,—but on her behalf may I not add my prayers to hers?

'I have the honour to be,
'Your Grace's very faithful Servant,
'FRANCIS TREGEAR.'

This coming alone would perhaps have had no effect. The Duke had desired the young man not to address him again; and the young man had disobeyed him. No mere courtesy would now have constrained him to send any reply to this further letter. But coming as it did while his heart was still throbbing with the effects of Mrs Finn's words, it was allowed to have a certain force. The argument used was a true argument. His girl was devoted to the man who sought her hand. Mrs Finn had told him that sooner or later he must yield,—unless he was prepared to see his child wither and fade at his side. He had once thought that he would be prepared even for that. He had endeavoured to strengthen his own will by arguing with himself that when he saw a duty plainly before him, he should cleave to that let the results be what they might. But that picture of her face withered and wan after twenty years of sorrowing had had its effect upon his heart. He even made excuses within his own breast in the young man's favour. He was in Parliament now, and what may not be done for a young man in Parliament? Altogether the young man appeared to him in a light different from that through which he had viewed the presumptuous, arrogant, utterly unjustifiable suitor who had come to him, now nearly a year since, in Carlton Terrace.

He went to breakfast with Tregear's letter in his pocket, and was then gracious to Mrs Finn, and tender to his daughter. 'When do you go, papa?' Mary asked.

'I shall take the 11.45 train. I have ordered the carriage at a quarter before eleven.'

'May I go to the train with you, papa?'

'Certainly; I shall be delighted.'

'Papa!' Mary said as soon as she found herself seated beside her father in the carriage.

'My dear.'

'Oh, papa!' and she threw herself on to his breast. He put his arm round her and kissed her,—as he would have had so much delight in doing, as he would have done so often before, had there not been this ground of discord. She was very sweet to him. It had never seemed to him that she had disgraced herself by loving Tregear—but that a great misfortune had fallen upon her. Silverbridge when he had gone into a racing partnership with Tifto, and Gerald when he had played for money which he did not possess, had—degraded themselves in his estimation. He would not have used such a word; but it was his feeling. They were less noble, less pure than they might have been, had they kept themselves free from such stain. But this girl,—whether she should live and fade by his side, or whether she should give her hand to some fitting noble suitor,—or even though she might at last become the wife of this man who loved her, would always have been pure. It was sweet to him to have something to caress. Now in the solitude of his life, as years were coming on him, he felt how necessary it was that he should have someone who would love him. Since his wife had left him he had been debarred from these caresses by the necessity of showing his antagonism to her dearest wishes. It had been his duty to be stern. In all his words to his daughter he had been governed by a conviction that he never ought to allow the duty of separating her from her lover to be absent from his mind. He was not prepared to acknowledge that that duty had ceased;—but yet there had crept over him a feeling that as he was half conquered, why should he not seek some recompense in his daughter's love? 'Papa,' she said, 'you do not hate me?'

'Hate you, my darling?'

'Because I am disobedient. Oh, papa, I cannot help it. He should not have come. He should not have been let to come.' He had not a word to say to her. He could not as yet bring himself to tell her,—that it should be as she desired. Much less could he now argue with her as to the impossibility of such a marriage as he had done on former occasions when the matter had been discussed. He could only press his arm tightly round her waist, and be silent. 'It cannot be altered now, papa. Look at me. Tell me that you love me.'

'Have you doubted my love?'

'No, papa,—but I would do anything to make you happy; anything that I could do. Papa, you do not want me to marry Lord Popplecourt?'

'I would not have you marry any man without loving him.'

'I never can love anybody else. That is what I wanted you to know, papa.'

To this he made no reply, nor was there anything else said upon the subject before the carriage drove up to the railway station. 'Do not get out, dear,' he said, seeing that her eyes had been filled with tears. 'It is not worth while. God bless you, my child! You will be up in London I hope in a fortnight, and we must try to make the house a little less dull for you.'

And so he had encountered the third attack.

Lady Mary, as she was driven home, recovered her spirits wonderfully. Not a word had fallen from her father which she could use hereafter as a refuge from her embarrassments. He had made her no promise. He had assented to nothing. But there had been something in his manner, in his gait, in his eye, in the pressure of his arm, which made her feel that her troubles would soon be at an end.

'I do love you so much,' she said to Mrs Finn late on that afternoon.

'I am glad of that, dear.'

'I shall always love you,—because you have been on my side all through.'

'No, Mary;—that is not so.'

'I know it is so. Of course you have to be wise because you are older. And papa would not have you here with me if you were not wise. But I know you are on my side,—and papa knows it too. And someone else shall know it some day.'

## CHAPTER 67

### 'HE IS SUCH A BEAST'

LORD SILVERBRIDGE remained hunting in the Brake country till a few days before the meeting of Parliament, and had he been left to himself he would have had another week in the country and might probably have overstayed the opening day; but he had not been left to himself. In the last week in January an important despatch reached his hands, from no less important a person than Sir Timothy Beeswax, suggesting to him that he should undertake the duty of seconding the address in the House of Commons. When the proposition first reached him it made his hair stand on end. He had never yet risen to his feet in the House. He had spoken at those election meetings in Cornwall, and had found it easy enough. After the first or second time he had thought it good fun. But he knew that standing up in the House of Commons would be different from that. Then there would be the dress! 'I should so hate to fig* myself out and look like a guy,' he said to Tregear, to whom of course he confided the offer that was made to him. Tregear was very anxious that he should accept it. 'A man should never refuse anything of that kind which comes in his way,' Tregear said.

'It is only because I am the governor's son,' Silverbridge pleaded.

'Partly so perhaps. But if it be altogether so, what of that? Take the goods the gods provide you. Of course all these things which our ambition covets are easier to Duke's sons than to others. But not on that account should a Duke's son refuse them. A man when he sees a rung vacant on the ladder should always put his feet there.'

'I'll tell you what,' said Silverbridge. 'If I thought this was all fair sailing I'd do it. I should feel certain that I should come a cropper, but still I'd try it. As you say, a fellow should try. But it's all meant as a blow at the governor. Old Beeswax thinks that if he can get me up to swear that he and his crew are real first-chop hands,* that will hit the governor hard. It's as much as saying to the governor,—"This chap belongs to me, not to you." That's a thing I won't go in for.'

Then Tregear counselled him to write to his father for advice, and at the same time to ask Sir Timothy to allow him a day or two for consideration. This counsel he took. His letter reached his father two days before he left Matching. In answer to it there came first a telegram begging Silverbridge to be in London on the Monday, and then a letter, in which the Duke expressed himself as being anxious to see his son before giving a final answer to the question. Thus it was that Silverbridge had been taken away from his hunting.

Isabel Boncassen, however, was now in London, and from her it was possible that he might find consolation. He had written to her soon after reaching Harrington, telling her that he had had it all out with the governor. 'There is a good deal that I can only tell you when I see you,' he said. Then he assured her with many lover's protestations that he was and always would be till death altogether her own most loving S. To this he had received an answer by return of post. She would be delighted to see him up in town,—as would her father and mother. They had now got a comfortable house in Brook Street. And then she signed herself his sincere friend, Isabel. Silverbridge thought that it was cold, and remembered certain scraps in another feminine handwriting in which more passion was expressed. Perhaps this was the way with American young ladies when they were in love.

'Yes,' said the Duke, 'I am glad that you have come up at once, as Sir Timothy should have his answer without further delay.'

'But what shall I say?'

The Duke, though he had already considered the matter very seriously, nevertheless took a few minutes to consider it again. 'The offer,' said he, 'must be acknowledged as very flattering.'

'But the circumstances are not usual.'

'It cannot often be the case that a minister should ask the son of his keenest political opponent to render him such a service. But, however, we will put that aside.'

'Not quite, sir.'

'For the present we will put that on one side. Not looking at the party which you may be called upon to support, having for the moment no regard to this or that line in politics, there is no opening to the real duties of parliamentary life which I would sooner see accorded to you than this.'

'But if I were to break down?' Talking to his father he could not quite venture to ask what might happen if he were to 'come a cropper.'*

'None but the brave deserve the fair,'* said the Duke slapping his hands upon the table. 'Why, if we fail, "We fail! But screw your courage to the sticking place, And we'll not fail."* What high point would ever be reached if caution such as that were allowed to prevail? What young men have done before cannot you do? I have no doubt of your capacity. None.'

'Haven't you, sir?' said Silverbridge, considerably gratified,—and also surprised.

'None in the least. But, perhaps, some of your diligence.'

'I could learn it by heart, sir,—if you mean that.'

'But I don't mean that; or rather I mean much more than that. You have first to realise in your mind the thing to be said, and then the words in which you should say it, before you come to learning by heart.'

'Some of them I suppose would tell me what to say.'

'No doubt with your inexperience it would be unfit that you should be left entirely to yourself. But I would wish you to know,—perhaps I should say to feel,—that the sentiments to be expressed by you were just.'

'I should have to praise Sir Timothy.'

'Not that necessarily. But you would have to advocate that course in Parliament which Sir Timothy and his friends have taken and propose to take.'

'But I hate him like poison.'

'There need be no personal feeling in the matter. I remember that when I moved the address in your house Mr Mildmay was Prime Minister,—a man for whom my regard and esteem were unbounded,—who had been in political matters the preceptor of my youth, whom as a patriotic statesman I almost worshipped, whom I now remember as a man whose departure from the arena of politics left the country very destitute. No one has sprung up since like to him,—or hardly second to him. But in speaking on so large a subject as the policy of a party, I thought it beneath me to eulogise a man. The same policy reversed may keep you silent respecting Sir Timothy.'

'I needn't of course say what I think about him.'

'I suppose you do agree with Sir Timothy as to his general policy? On no other condition can you undertake such a duty.'

'Of course I have voted with him.'

'So I have observed,—not so regularly perhaps as Mr Roby would have desired.' Mr Roby* was the Conservative whip.

'And I suppose the people at Silverbridge expect me to support him.'

'I hardly know how that may be. They used to be contented with my poor services. No doubt they feel they have changed for the better.'

'You shouldn't say that, sir.'

'I am bound to suppose that they think so, because when the matter was left in their own hands they at once elected a Conservative. You need not fear that you will offend them by seconding the address. They will probably feel proud to see their young member brought forward on such an occasion; as I shall be proud to see my son.'

'You would if it were on the other side, sir.'

'Yes, Silverbridge, yes; I should be very proud if it were on the other side. But there is a useful old adage which bids us not cry for spilt milk. You have a right to your opinions, though perhaps I may think that in adopting what I must call new opinions you were a little precipitate. We cannot act together in politics. But not the less on that account do I wish to see you take an active and useful part on that side to which you have attached yourself.' As he said this he rose from his seat and spoke with emphasis, as though he were addressing some imaginary Speaker or a house of legislators around. 'I shall be proud to hear you second the address. If you do it as gracefully and as fitly as I am sure you may if you will give yourself the trouble, I shall hear you do it with infinite satisfaction, even though I shall feel at the same time anxious to answer all your arguments and to disprove all your assertions. I should be listening no doubt to my opponent;—but I should be proud to feel that I was listening to my son. My advice to you is to do as Sir Timothy has asked you.'

'He is such a beast, sir,' said Silverbridge.

'Pray do not speak in that way on matters so serious.'

'I do not think you quite understand it, sir.'

'Perhaps not. Can you enlighten me?'

'I believe he has done this only to annoy you.'

The Duke, who had again seated himself, and was leaning back in his chair, raised himself up, placed his hands on the table before him, and looked his son hard in the face. The idea which Silverbridge had just expressed had certainly occurred to himself. He remembered well all the circumstances of the time when he and Sir Timothy Beeswax had been members of the same government;—and he remembered how animosities had grown, and how treacherous he had thought the man. From the moment in which he had read the minister's letter to the young member, he had felt that the offer had too probably come from a desire to make the political separation between himself and his son complete. But he had thought that in counselling his son he was bound to ignore such a feeling; and it certainly had not occurred to him that Silverbridge would be astute enough to perceive the same thing.

'What makes you fancy that?' said the Duke, striving to conceal by his manner, but not altogether successful in concealing, the gratification which he certainly felt.

'Well, sir, I am not sure that I can explain it. Of course it is putting you in a different boat from me.'

'You have already chosen your boat.'

'Perhaps he thinks I may get out again. I dislike the skipper so much, that I am not sure that I shall not.'

'Oh, Silverbridge,—that is such a fault! So much is included in that which is unstatesmanlike, unpatriotic, almost dishonest! Do you mean to say that you would be this or that in politics according to your personal liking for an individual?'

'When you don't trust the leader, you can't believe very firmly in the followers,' said Silverbridge doggedly. 'I won't say, sir, what I may do. Though I dare say that what I think is not of much account, I do think a good deal about it.'

'I am glad of that.'

'And as I think it not at all improbable that I may go back again, if you don't mind it, I will refuse.' Of course after that the Duke had no further arguments to use in favour of Sir Timothy's proposition.

## CHAPTER 68

### BROOK STREET

SILVERBRIDGE had now a week on his hands which he felt he might devote to the lady of his love. It was a comfort to him that he need have nothing to do with the address. To have to go, day after day, to the Treasury in order that he might learn his lesson, would have been disagreeable to him. He did not quite know how the lesson would have been communicated, but fancied it would have come from 'Old Roby,' whom he did not love much better than Sir Timothy. Then the speech must have been composed, and afterwards submitted to someone,— probably to old Roby again, by whom no doubt it would be cut and slashed, and made quite a different speech than he had intended. If he had not praised Sir Timothy himself, Roby,—or whatever other tutor might have been assigned to him,—would have put the praise in. And then how many hours it would have taken to learn 'the horrid thing' by heart. He proudly felt that he had not been prompted by idleness to decline the task; but not the less was he glad to have shuffled the burden from off his shoulders.

Early the next morning he was in Brook Street, having sent a note to say he would call, and having even named the hour. And yet when he knocked at the door, he was told with the utmost indifference by a London footman, that Miss Boncassen was not at home,—also that Mrs Boncassen was not at home;—also that Mr Boncassen was not at home. When he asked at what hour Miss Boncassen was expected home, the man answered him, just as though he had been anybody else, that he knew nothing about it. He turned away in disgust, and had himself driven to the Beargarden. In his misery he had recourse to game-pie and a pint of champagne* for his lunch. 'Halloa, old fellow, what is this I hear about you?' said Nidderdale, coming in and sitting opposite to him.

'I don't know what you have heard.'

'You are going to second the address. What made them pick you out from the lot of us?'

'It is just what I am not going to do.'

'I saw it all in the papers.'

'I dare say;—and yet it isn't true. I shouldn't wonder if they ask you.' At this moment a waiter handed a large official letter to Lord Nidderdale, saying that the messenger who had brought it was waiting for an answer in the hall. The letter bore the important signature of T. Beeswax on the corner of the envelope, and so disturbed Lord Nidderdale that he called at once for a glass of soda-and-brandy. When opened it was found to be very nearly a counterpart of that which Silverbridge had received down in the country. There was, however, added a little prayer that Lord Nidderdale would at once come down to the Treasury Chambers.

'They must be very hard up,' said Lord Nidderdale. 'But I shall do it. Cantrip is always at me to do something, and you see if I don't butter them up properly.' Then having fortified himself with game-pie and a glass of brown sherry he went away at once to the Treasury Chambers.

Silverbridge felt himself a little better after his lunch,—better still when he had smoked a couple of cigarettes walking about the empty smoking-room. And as he walked he collected his thoughts. She could hardly have meant to slight him. No doubt her letter down to him at Harrington had been very cold. No doubt he had been ill-treated in being sent away so unceremoniously from the door. But yet she could hardly intend that everything between them should be over. Even an American girl could not be so unreasonable as that. He remembered the passionate way in which she had assured him of her love. All that could not have been forgotten! He had done nothing by which he could have forfeited her esteem. She had desired him to tell the whole affair to her father, and he had done so. Mr Boncassen might perhaps have objected. It might be that this American was so prejudiced against English aristocrats as to desire no commerce with them. There were not many Englishmen who would not have welcomed him as son-in-law, but Americans might be different. Still,—still Isabel would hardly have shown her obedience to her father in this way. She was too independent to obey her father in a matter concerning her own heart. And if he had not been the possessor of her heart at that last interview, then she must have been false indeed! So he got once more into his hansom and had himself taken back to Brook Street.

Mrs Boncassen was in the drawing-room alone.

'I am so sorry,' said the lady, 'but Mr Boncassen has, I think, just gone out.'

'Indeed! and where is Isabel?'

'Isabel is downstairs,—that is if she hasn't gone out too. She did talk of going with her father to the Museum. She is getting quite bookish. She has got a ticket, and goes there, and has all the things brought to her just like the other learned folks.'

'I am anxious to see her, Mrs Boncassen.'

'My! If she has gone out it will be a pity. She was only saying yesterday she wouldn't wonder if you shouldn't turn up.'

'Of course I've turned up, Mrs Boncassen. I was here an hour ago.'

'Was it you who called and asked all them questions? My! We couldn't make out who it was. The man said it was a flurried young gentleman who wouldn't leave a card,—but who wanted to see Mr Boncassen most especial.'

'It was Isabel I wanted to see. Didn't I leave a card? No; I don't think I did. I felt so—almost at home, that I didn't think of a card.'

'That's very kind of you, Lord Silverbridge.'

'I hope you are going to be my friend, Mrs Boncassen.'

'I am sure I don't know, Lord Silverbridge. Isabel is most used to having her own way, I guess. I think when hearts are joined almost nothing ought to stand between them. But Mr Boncassen does have doubts. He don't wish as Isabel should force herself anywhere. But here she is, and now she can speak for herself.' Whereupon not only did Isabel enter the room, but at the same time Mrs Boncassen most discreetly left it. It must be confessed that American mothers are not afraid of their daughters.

Silverbridge, when the door was closed, stood looking at the girl for a moment and thought that she was more lovely than ever. She was dressed for walking. She still had on her fur jacket, but had taken off her hat. 'I was in the parlour downstairs,' she said, 'when you came in, with papa; and we were going out together; but when I heard who was here, I made him go alone. Was I not good?'

He had not thought of a word to say, or a thing to do;—but he felt as he looked at her that the only thing in the world worth living for, was to have her for his own. For a moment he was half abashed. Then in the next she was close in his arms with his lips pressed to hers. He had been so sudden that she had been unable, at any rate thought that she had been unable, to repress him. 'Lord Silverbridge,' she said, 'I told you I would not have it. You have offended me.'

'Isabel!'

'Yes; Isabel! Isabel is offended with you. Why did you do it?'

Why did he do it? It seemed to him to be the most unnecessary question. 'I want you to know how I love you.'

'Will that tell me? That only tells me how little you think of me.'

'Then it tells you a falsehood;—for I am thinking of you always. And I always think of you as being the best and dearest and sweetest thing in the world. And now I think you dearer and sweeter than ever.' Upon this she tried to frown; but her frown at once broke out into a smile. 'When I wrote to say that I was coming why did you not stay at home for me this morning?'

'I got no letter, Lord Silverbridge.'

'Why didn't you get it?'

'That I cannot say, Lord Silverbridge.'

'Isabel, if you are so formal, you will kill me.'

'Lord Silverbridge, if you are so forward, you will offend me.' Then it turned out that no letter from him had reached the house; and as the letter had been addressed to Bruton Street instead of Brook Street, the failure on the part of the post-office was not surprising.*

Whether or no she were offended or he killed he remained with her the whole of that afternoon. 'Of course I love you,' she said. 'Do you suppose I should be here with you if I did not, or that you could have remained in the house after what you did just now? I am not given to run into rhapsodies quite so much as you are,—and being a woman perhaps it is as well that I don't. But I think I can be quite as true to you as you are to me.'

'I am so much obliged to you for that,' he said, grasping at her hand.

'But I am sure that rhapsodies won't do any good. Now I'll tell you my mind.'

'You know mine,' said Silverbridge.

'I will take it for granted that I do. Your mind is to marry me will ye nill ye, as the people say.' He answered this by merely nodding his head and getting a little nearer to her. 'That is all very well in its way, and I am not going to say but what I am gratified.' Then he did grasp her hand. 'If it pleases you to hear me say so, Lord Silverbridge——'

'Not Lord!'

'Then I shall call you Plantagenet;—only it sounds so horribly historical. Why are you not Thomas or Abraham?* But if it will please you to hear me say so, I am ready to acknowledge that nothing in all my life ever came near to the delight I have in your love.' Hereupon he almost succeeded in getting his arm round her waist. But she was strong, and seized his hand and held it. 'And I speak no rhapsodies. I tell you a truth which I want you to know and to keep in your heart,—so that you may be always, always sure of it.'

'I never will doubt it.'

'But that marrying will ye nill ye, will not suit me. There is so much wanted for happiness in life.'

'I will do all that I can.'

'Yes. Even though it be hazardous, I am willing to trust you. If you were as other men are, if you could do as you please as lower men may do, I would leave father and mother and my own country,— that I might be your wife. I would do that because I love you. But what will my life be here, if they who are your friends turn their backs upon me? What will your life be, if, through all that, you continue to love me?'

'That will all come right.'

'And what will your life be, or mine,' she said, going on with her own thoughts without seeming to have heard his last words, 'if in such a condition as that you did not continue to love me?'

'I should always love you.'

'It might be very hard:—and if once felt to be hard, then impossible. You have not looked at it as I have done. Why should you? Even with a wife that was a trouble to you——'

'Oh, Isabel!'

His arm was now round her waist, but she continued speaking as though she were not aware of the embrace. 'Yes, a trouble! I shall not be always just what I am now. Now I can be bright and pretty and hold my own with others because I am so. But are you sure,—I am not,—that I am such stuff as an English lady should be made of? If in ten years' time you found that others did not think so,—that, worse again, you did not think so yourself, would you be true to me then?'

'I will always be true to you.'

She gently extricated herself, as though she had done so that she might better turn round and look into his face. 'Oh, my own one, who can say of himself that it would be so? How could it be so, when you would have all the world against you? You would still be what you are,—with a clog round your leg while at home. In Parliament, among your friends, at your clubs, you would be just what you are. You would be that Lord Silverbridge who had all good things at his disposal,— except that he had been unfortunate in his marriage! But what should I be?' Though she paused he could not answer her,—not yet. There was a solemnity in her speech which made it necessary that he should hear her to the end. 'I, too, have my friends in my own country. It is no disgrace to me there that my grandfather worked on the quays. No one holds her head higher than I do, or is more sure of being able to hold it. I have there that assurance of esteem and honour which you have here. I would lose it all to do you a good. But I will not lose it to do you an injury.'

'I don't know about injuries,' he said, getting up and walking about the room. 'But I am sure of this. You will have to be my wife.'

'If your father will take me by the hand and say that I shall be his daughter, I will risk all the rest. Even then it might not be wise; but we love each other too well not to run some peril. Do you think that I want anything better than to preside in your home, to soften your cares, to welcome your joys, to be the mother perhaps of your children, and to know that you are proud that I should be so? No, my darling. I can see a Paradise;—only, only, I may not be fit to enter it. I must use some judgment better than my own, sounder, dear, than yours. Tell the Duke what I say;—tell him with what language a son may use to his father. And remember that all you ask for yourself you will ask doubly for me.'

'I will ask him so that he cannot refuse me.'

'If you do I shall be contented. And now go. I have said ever so much, and I am tired.'

'Isabel! Oh, my love!'

'Yes; Isabel;—your love! I am that at any rate for the present,—and proud to be so as a queen. Well, if it must be, this once,—as I have been so hard to you.' Then she gave him her cheek to kiss, but of course he took more than she gave.

When he got out into the street it was dark and there was still standing the faithful cab. But he felt that at the present moment it would be impossible to sit still, and he dismissed the equipage. He walked rapidly along Brook Street into Park Lane, and from thence to the park, hardly knowing whither he went in the enthusiasm of the moment. He walked back to the Marble Arch, and thence round by the drive to the Guard House and the bridge over the Serpentine, by the Knightsbridge Barracks to Hyde Park Corner. Though he should give up everything and go and live in her own country with her, he would marry her. His politics, his hunting, his address to the Queen, his horses, his guns, his father's wealth, and his own rank,—what were they all to Isabel Boncassen? In meeting her he had met the one human being in all the world who could really be anything to him either in friendship or in love. When she had told him what she would do for him to make his home happy, it had seemed to him that all other delights must fade away from him for ever. How odious were Tifto and his racehorses, how unmeaning the noise of his club, how terrible the tedium of those parliamentary benches! He could not tell his love as she had told hers! He acknowledged to himself that his words could not be as her words,— nor his intellect as hers. But his heart could be as true. She had spoken to him of his name, his rank, and all his outside world around him. He would make her understand at last that they were nothing to him in comparison with her. When he had got round to Hyde Park Corner, he felt that he was almost compelled to go back again to Brook Street. In no other place could there be anything to interest him;—nowhere else could there be light, or warmth, or joy! But what would she think of him? To go back hot, and soiled with mud, in order that he might say one more adieu,—that possibly he might ravish one more kiss,— would hardly be manly. He must postpone all that for the morrow. On the morrow of course he would be there.

But his work was all before him! That prayer had to be made to his father; or rather some wonderful effort of eloquence must be made by which his father might be convinced that this girl was so infinitely superior to anything of feminine creation that had ever hitherto been seen or heard of, that all ideas as to birth, country, rank, or name ought in this instance to count for nothing. He did believe himself that he had found such a pearl, that no question of setting need be taken into consideration. If the Duke would not see it the fault would be in the Duke's eyes, or perhaps in his own words,—but certainly not in the pearl.

Then he compared her to poor Lady Mabel, and in doing so did arrive at something near the truth in his inward delineation of the two characters. Lady Mabel with all her grace, with all her beauty, with all her talent, was a creature of efforts, or, as it might be called, a manufactured article. She strove to be graceful, to be lovely, to be agreeable and clever. Isabel was all this and infinitely more without any struggle. When he was most fond of Mabel, most anxious to make her his wife, there had always been present to him a feeling that she was old. Though he knew her age to a day,—and knew her to be younger than himself, yet she was old. Something had gone of her native bloom, something had been scratched and chipped from the first fair surface, and this had been repaired by varnish and veneering. Though he had loved her he had never been altogether satisfied with her. But Isabel was as young as Hebe.* He knew nothing of her actual years, but he did know that to have seemed younger, or to have seemed older,—to have seemed in any way different from what she was,—would have been to be less perfect.

## CHAPTER 69

### 'PERT POPPET!'

ON a Sunday morning,—while Lord Silverbridge was alone in a certain apartment in the house in Carlton Terrace which was called his own sitting-room, the name was brought him of a gentleman who was anxious to see him. He had seen his father and had used all the eloquence of which he was master,—but not quite with the effect which he had desired. His father had been very kind, but he, too, had been eloquent;—and had, as is often the case with orators, been apparently more moved by his own words than by those of his adversary. If he had not absolutely declared himself as irrevocably hostile to Miss Boncassen he had not said a word that might be supposed to give token of assent.

Silverbridge, therefore, was moody, contemplative, and desirous of solitude. Nothing that the Duke had said had shaken him. He was still sure of his pearl, and quite determined that he would wear it. Various thoughts were running through his brain. What if he were to abdicate the title and become a republican? He was inclined to think that he could not abdicate, but he was quite sure that no one could prevent him from going to America and calling himself Mr Palliser. That his father would forgive him and accept the daughter-in-law brought to him, were he in the first place to marry without sanction, he felt quite sure.

What was there that his father would not forgive? But then Isabel would not assent to this. He was turning it all in his head and ever and anon trying to relieve his mind by 'Clarissa,'* which he was reading in conformity with his father's advice, when the gentleman's card was put into his hand. 'Whatever does he want here?' he said to himself; and then he ordered that the gentleman might be shown up. The gentleman in question was our old friend Dolly Longstaff. Dolly Longstaff and Silverbridge had been intimate as young men are. But they were not friends, nor, as far as Silverbridge knew, had Dolly ever set his foot in that house before. 'Well, Dolly,' said he, 'what's the matter now?'

'I suppose you are surprised to see me?'

'I didn't think that you were ever up so early.' It was at this time almost noon.

'Oh, come now, that's nonsense. I can get up as early as anybody else. I have changed all that for the last four months. I was at breakfast this morning very soon after ten.'

'What a miracle! Is there anything I can do for you?'

'Well yes,—there is. Of course you are surprised to see me?'

'You never were here before; and therefore it is odd.'

'It is odd; I felt that myself. And when I tell you what I have come about you will think it more odd. I know I can trust you with a secret.'

'That depends, Dolly.'

'What I mean is, I know you are good-natured. There are ever so many fellows that are one's most intimate friends, that would say anything on earth they could that was ill-natured.'

'I hope they are not my friends.'

'Oh yes, they are. Think of Glasslough, or Popplecourt, or Hindes! If they knew anything about you that you didn't want to have known,— about a young lady or anything of that kind,—don't you think they'd tell everybody?'

'A man can't tell anything he doesn't know.'

'That's true. I had thought of that myself. But then there's a particular reason for my telling you this. It is about a young lady! You won't tell; will you?'

'No, I won't. But I can't see why on earth you should come to me. You are ever so many years older than I am.'

'I had thought of that too. But you are just the person I must tell. I want you to help me.'

These last words were said in a whisper, and Dolly as he said them had drawn nearer to his friend. Silverbridge remained in suspense, saying nothing by way of encouragement. Dolly, either in love with his own mystery or doubtful of his own purpose, sat still, looking eagerly at his companion. 'What the mischief is it?' asked Silverbridge impatiently.

'I have quite made up my own mind.'

'That's a good thing at any rate.'

'I am not what you would have called a marrying sort of man.'

'I should have said,—no. But I suppose most men do marry sooner or later.'

'That's just what I said to myself. It has to be done, you know. There are three different properties coming to me. At least one has come already.'

'You're a lucky fellow.'

'I've made up my mind; and when I say a thing I mean to do it.'

'But what can I do?'

'That's just what I'm coming to. If a man does marry I think he ought to be attached to her.' To this, as a broad proposition, Silverbridge was ready to accede. But, regarding Dolly as a middle-aged sort of fellow, one of those men who marry because it is convenient to have a house kept for them, he simply nodded his head. 'I am awfully attached to her,' Dolly went on to say.

'That's all right.'

'Of course there are fellows who marry girls for their money. I've known men who have married their grandmothers.'

'Not really!'

'That kind of thing. When a woman is old it does not much matter who she is. But my one! She's not old!'

'Nor rich?'

'Well; I don't know about that. But I'm not after her money. Pray understand that. It's because I'm downright fond of her. She's an American.'

'A what!' said Silverbridge, startled.

'You know her. That's the reason I've come to you. It's Miss Boncassen.' A dark frown came across the young man's face. That all this should be said to him was disgusting. That an owl like that should dare to talk of loving Miss Boncassen was offensive to him.

'It's because you know her that I've come to you. She thinks that you're after her.' Dolly as he said this lifted himself quickly up in his seat, and nodded his head mysteriously as he looked into his companion's face. It was as much as though he should say, 'I see you are surprised, but so it is.' Then he went on. 'She does, the pert poppet!' This was almost too much for Silverbridge; but still he contained himself. 'She won't look at me because she has got it into her head that perhaps some day she may be Duchess of Omnium! That of course is out of the question.'

'Upon my word all this seems to me to be so very—very,—distasteful that I think you had better say nothing more about it.'

'It is distasteful,' said Dolly; 'but the truth is I am so downright,—what you may call enamoured——'

'Don't talk such stuff as that here,' said Silverbridge, jumping up. 'I won't have it.'

'But I am. There is nothing I wouldn't do to get her. Of course it's a good match for her. I've got three separate properties; and when the governor goes off I shall have a clear fifteen thousand a year.'

'Oh, bother!'

'Of course that's nothing to you, but it is a very tidy income for a commoner. And how is she to do better?'

'I don't know how she could do much worse,' said Silverbridge in a transport of rage. Then he pulled his moustache in vexation, angry with himself that he should have allowed himself to say even a word on so preposterous a supposition. Isabel Boncassen and Dolly Longstaff! It was Titania and Bottom over again. It was absolutely necessary that he should get rid of this intruder, and he began to be afraid that he could not do this without using language which would be uncivil. 'Upon my word,' he said, 'I think you had better not talk about it any more. The young lady is one for whom I have a very great respect.'

'I mean to marry her,' said Dolly, thinking thus to vindicate himself.

'You might as well think of marrying one of the stars.'

'One of the stars!'

'Or a royal princess!'

'Well! Perhaps that is your opinion, but I can't say that I agree with you. I don't see why she shouldn't take me. I can give her a position which you may call A1 out of the Peerage. I can bring her into society. I can make an English lady of her.'

'You can't make anything of her,—except to insult her,—and me too by talking of her.'

'I don't quite understand this,' said the unfortunate lover, getting up from his seat. 'Very likely she won't have me. Perhaps she has told you so.'

'She never mentioned your name to me in her life. I don't suppose she remembers your existence.'

'But I say that there can be no insult in such a one as me asking such a one as her to be my wife. To say that she doesn't remember my existence is absurd.'

'Why should I be troubled with all this?'

'Because I think you're making a fool of her, and because I'm honest. That's why,' said Dolly with much energy. There was something in this which partly reconciled Silverbridge to his despised rival. There was a touch of truth about the man, though he was so utterly mistaken in his ideas. 'I want you to give over in order that I may try again. I don't think you ought to keep a girl from her promotion, merely for the fun of a flirtation. Perhaps you're fond of her;—but you won't marry her. I am fond of her, and I shall.'

After a minute's pause Silverbridge resolved that he would be magnanimous. 'Miss Boncassen is going to be my wife,' he said.

'Your wife!'

'Yes;—my wife. And now I think you will see that nothing further can be said about this matter.'

'Duchess of Omnium!'

'She will be Lady Silverbridge.'

'Oh; of course she'll be that first. Then I've got nothing further to say. I'm not going to enter myself to run against you.* Only I shouldn't have believed it if anybody else had told me.'

'Such is my good fortune.'

'Oh ah,—yes; of course. That is one way of looking at it. Well; Silverbridge, I'll tell you what I shall do; I shall hook it.'*

'No; no, not you.'

'Yes, I shall. I dare say you won't believe me, but I've got such a feeling about me here'—as he said this he laid his hand upon his heart,— 'that if I stayed I should go in for hard drinking. I shall take the great Asiatic tour.* I know a fellow that wants to go, but he hasn't got any money. I dare say I shall be off before the end of next month. You don't know any fellow that would buy half-a-dozen hunters; do you?' Silverbridge shook his head. 'Good-bye,' said Dolly in a melancholy tone; 'I am sure I am very much obliged to you for telling me. If I'd known you'd meant it, I shouldn't have meddled, of course. Duchess of Omnium!'

'Look here, Dolly, I have told you what I should not have told any one, but I wanted to screen the young lady's name.'

'It was so kind of you.'

'Do not repeat it. It is a kind of thing that ladies are particular about. They choose their own time for letting everybody know.' Then Dolly promised to be as mute as a fish, and took his departure.

Silverbridge had felt, towards the end of the interview, that he had been arrogant to the unfortunate man,—particularly in saying that the young lady would not remember the existence of such a suitor,—and had also recognised a certain honesty in the man's purpose, which had not been the less honest because it was so absurd. Actuated by the consciousness of this, he had swallowed his anger, and had told the whole truth. Nevertheless things had been said which were horrible to him. This buffoon of a man had called his Isabel a—pert poppet! How was he to get over the remembrance of such an offence? And then the wretch had declared that he was—enamoured! There was sacrilege in the term when applied by such a man to Isabel Boncassen. He had thoughts of days to come, when everything would be settled, when he might sit close to her, and call her pretty names,—when he might in sweet familiarity tell her that she was a little Yankee and a fierce republican, and 'chaff' her about the stars and stripes; and then, as he pictured the scene to himself in his imagination, she would lean upon him and would give him back his chaff, and would call him an aristocrat and would laugh at his titles. As he thought of all this he would be proud with the feeling that such privileges would be his own. And now this wretched man had called her a pert poppet!

There was a sanctity about her,—a divinity which made it almost a profanity to have talked about her at all to such a one as Dolly Longstaff. She was his Holy of Holies, at which vulgar eyes should not even be allowed to gaze. It had been a most unfortunate interview. But this was clear; that, as he had announced his engagement to such a one as Dolly Longstaff, the matter now would admit of no delay. He would explain to his father that as tidings of the engagement had got abroad, honour to the young lady would compel him to come forward openly as her suitor at once. If this argument might serve him, then perhaps this intrusion would not have been altogether a misfortune.

## CHAPTER 70

### 'LOVE MAY BE A GREAT MISFORTUNE'

SILVERBRIDGE when he reached Brook Street that day was surprised to find that a large party was going to lunch there. Isabel had asked him to come, and he had thought her the dearest girl in the world for doing so. But now his gratitude for that favour was considerably abated. He did not care just now for the honour of eating his lunch in the presence of Mr Gotobed,* the American minister, whom he found there already in the drawing-room with Mrs Gotobed, nor with Ezekiel Sevenkings,* the great American poet from the far West, who sat silent and stared at him in an unpleasant way. When Sir Timothy Beeswax was announced, with Lady Beeswax and her daughter, his gratification certainly was not increased. And the last comer,—who did not arrive indeed till they were all seated at the table,—almost made him start from his chair and take his departure suddenly. That last comer was no other than Mr Adolphus Longstaff. As it happened he was seated next to Dolly, with Lady Beeswax on the other side of him. Whereas his Holy of Holies was on the other side of Dolly! The arrangement made seemed to him to have been monstrous. He had endeavoured to get next to Isabel; but she had so manœuvred that there should be a vacant chair between them. He had not much regarded this because a vacant chair may be pushed on one side. But before he had made all his calculations Dolly Longstaff was sitting there! He almost thought that Dolly winked at him in triumph,—that very Dolly who an hour ago had promised to take himself off upon his Asiatic travels!

Sir Timothy and the minister kept up the conversation very much between them, Sir Timothy flattering everything that was American, and the minister finding fault with very many things that were English. Now and then Mr Boncassen would put in a word to soften the severe honesty of his countryman, or to correct the euphemistic falsehoods of Sir Timothy. The poet seemed always to be biding his time. Dolly ventured to whisper a word to his neighbour. It was but to say that the frost had broken up. But Silverbridge heard it and looked daggers at everyone. Then Lady Beeswax expressed to him a hope that he was going to do great things in Parliament this session. 'I don't mean to go near the place,' he said, not at all conveying any purpose to which he had really come, but driven by the stress of the moment to say something that should express his general hatred of everybody. Mr Lupton was there, on the other side of Isabel, and was soon engaged with her in a pleasant familiar conversation. Then Silverbridge remembered that he had always thought Lupton to be a most conceited prig. Nobody gave himself so many airs, or was so careful as to the dyeing of his whiskers. It was astonishing that Isabel should allow herself to be amused by such an antiquated coxcomb. When they had finished eating they moved about and changed their places, Mr Boncassen being rather anxious to stop the flood of American eloquence which came from his friend Mr Gotobed. British viands had become subject to his criticism, and Mr Gotobed had declared to Mr Lupton that he didn't believe that London could produce a dish of squash or tomatoes. He was quite sure you couldn't have sweet corn. Then there had been a moving of seats in which the minister was shuffled off to Lady Beeswax, and the poet found himself by the side of Isabel. 'Do you not regret our mountains and our prairies,' said the poet; 'our great waters and our green savannahs?' 'I think more perhaps of Fifth Avenue,' said Miss Boncassen. Silverbridge, who at this moment was being interrogated by Sir Timothy, heard every word of it.

'I was so sorry, Lord Silverbridge,' said Sir Timothy, 'that you could not accede to our little request.'

'I did not quite see my way,' said Silverbridge, with his eye upon Isabel.

'So I understood, but I hope that things will make themselves clearer to you shortly. There is nothing that I desire so much as the support of young men such as yourself,—the very cream, I may say, of the whole country. It is to the young conservative thoughtfulness and the truly British spirit of our springing aristocracy that I look for that reaction which I am sure will at last carry us safely over the rocks and shoals of communistic propensities.'

'I shouldn't wonder if it did,' said Silverbridge. They didn't think that he was going to remain down there talking politics to an old humbug like Sir Timothy when the sun, and moon, and all the stars had gone up into the drawing-room! For at that moment Isabel was making her way to the door.

But Sir Timothy had buttonholed him. 'Of course it is late now to say anything further about the address. We have arranged that. Not quite as I would have wished, for I had set my heart upon initiating you into the rapturous pleasure of parliamentary debate. But I hope that a good time is coming. And pray remember this, Lord Silverbridge;—there is no member sitting on our side of the House, and I need hardly say on the other, whom I would go farther to oblige than your father's son.'

'I'm sure that's very kind,' said Silverbridge, absolutely using a little force as he disengaged himself. Then he at once followed the ladies upstairs, passing the poet on the stairs. 'You have hardly spoken to me,' he whispered to Isabel. He knew that to whisper to her now, with the eyes of many upon him, with the ears of many open, was an absurdity; but he could not refrain himself.

'There are so many to be,—entertained, as people say! I don't think I ought to have to entertain you,' she answered, laughing. No one heard her but Silverbridge, yet she did not seem to whisper. She left him, however, at once, and was soon engaged in conversation with Sir Timothy.

A convivial lunch I hold to be altogether bad, but the worst of its many evils is that vacillating mind which does not know when to take its owner off. Silverbridge was on this occasion quite determined not to take himself off at all. As it was only a lunch the people must go, and then he would be left with Isabel. But the vacillation of the others was distressing to him. Mr Lupton went, and poor Dolly got away apparently without a word. But the Beeswaxes and the Gotobeds would not go, and the poet sat staring immovably. In the meanwhile Silverbridge endeavoured to make the time pass lightly by talking to Mrs Boncassen. He had been so determined to accept Isabel with all her adjuncts that he had come almost to like Mrs Boncassen, and would certainly have taken her part violently had any one spoken ill of her in his presence.

Then suddenly he found that the room was nearly empty. The Beeswaxes and the Gotobeds were gone; and at last the poet himself, with a final glare of admiration at Isabel, had taken his departure. When Silverbridge looked round, Isabel also was gone. Then too Mrs Boncassen had left the room suddenly. At the same instant Mr Boncassen entered by another door, and the two men were alone together. 'My dear Lord Silverbridge,' said the father, 'I want to have a few words with you.' Of course there was nothing for him but to submit. 'You remember what you said to me down at Matching?'

'Oh yes; I remember that.'

'You did me the great honour of expressing a wish to make my child your wife.'

'I was asking for a very great favour.'

'That also;—for there is no greater favour I could do to any man than to give him my daughter. Nevertheless, you were doing me a great honour,—and you did it, as you do everything, with an honest grace that went far to win my heart. I am not at all surprised, sir, that you should have won hers.' The young man as he heard this could only blush and look foolish. 'If I know my girl, neither your money nor your title would go for anything.'

'I think much more of her love, Mr Boncassen, than I do of anything else in the world.'

'But love, my Lord, may be a great misfortune.' As he said this the tone of his voice was altered, and there was a melancholy solemnity not only in his words but in his countenance. 'I take it that young people when they love rarely think of more than the present moment. If they did so the bloom would be gone from their romance. But others have to do this for them. If Isabel had come to me saying that she loved a poor man, there would not have been much to disquiet me. A poor man may earn bread for himself and his wife, and if he failed I could have found them bread. Nor, had she loved somewhat below her own degree, should I have opposed her. So long as her husband had been an educated man, there might have been no future punishment to fear.'

'I don't think she could have done that,' said Silverbridge.

'At any rate she has not done so. But how am I to look upon this that she has done?'

'I'll do my best for her, Mr Boncassen.'

'I believe you would. But even your love can't make her an Englishwoman. You can make her a Duchess.'

'Not that, sir.'

'But you can't give her a parentage fit for a Duchess ;—not fit at least in the opinion of those with whom you will pass your life, with whom,—or perhaps without whom,—she will be destined to pass her life, if she becomes your wife! Unfortunately it does not suffice that you should think it fit. Though you loved each other as well as any man and woman that ever were brought into each other's arms by the benefi-cence of God, you cannot make her happy.—unless you can assure her the respect of those around her.'

'All the world will respect her.'

'Her conduct,—yes. I think the world, your world, would learn to do that. I do not think it could help itself. But that would not suffice. I may respect the man who cleans my boots. But he would be a wretched man if he were thrown on me for society. I would not give him my society. Will your Duchesses and your Countesses give her theirs?'

'Certainly they will.'

'I do not ask for it as thinking it to be of more value than that of others; but were she to become your wife she would be so abnormally placed as to require it for her comfort. She would have become a lady of high rank,—not because she loves rank, but because she loves you.'

'Yes, yes, yes,' said Silverbridge, hardly himself knowing why he became impetuous.

'But having removed herself into that position, being as she would be, a Countess, or a Duchess, or what not, how could she be happy if she were excluded from the community of Countesses and Duchesses?'

'They are not like that,' said Silverbridge.

'I will not say that they are, but I do not know. Having Anglican* tendencies, I have been wont to contradict my countrymen when they have told me of the narrow exclusiveness of your nobles. Having found your nobles and your commoners all alike in their courtesy,—which is a cold word; in their hospitable friendships,—I would now not only contradict, but would laugh to scorn any such charge,'—so far he spoke somewhat loudly, and then dropped his voice as he concluded,—'were it anything less than the happiness of my child that is in question.'

'What am I to say, sir? I only know this; I am not going to lose her.'

'You are a fine fellow. I was going to say that I wished you were an American, so that Isabel need not lose you. But, my boy, I have told you that I do not know how it might be. Of all whom you know, who could best tell me the truth on such a subject? Who is there whose age will have given him experience, whose rank will have made him famil-iar with this matter, who from friendship to you would be least likely to decide against your wishes, who from his own native honesty would be most sure to tell the truth?'

'You mean my father,' said Silverbridge.

'I do mean your father. Happily he has taken no dislike to the girl herself. I have seen enough of him to feel sure that he is devoted to his own children.'

'Indeed he is.'

'A just and a liberal man;—one I should say not carried away by prejudices! Well,—my girl and I have just put our heads together, and we have come to a conclusion. If the Duke of Omnium will tell us that she would be safe as your wife,—safe from the contempt of those around her,—you shall have her. And I shall rejoice to give her to you,—not because you are Lord Silverbridge, not because of your rank and wealth; but because you are—that individual human being whom I now hold by the hand.'

When the American had come to an end, Silverbridge was too much moved to make any immediate answer. He had an idea in his own mind that the appeal was not altogether fair. His father was a just man,—just, affectionate, and liberal. But then it will so often happen that fathers do not want their sons to marry those very girls on whom the sons have set their hearts. He could only say that he would speak to his father again on the subject. 'Let him tell me that he is contented,' said Mr Boncassen, 'and I will tell him that I am contented. Now, my friend, good-bye.' Silverbridge begged that he might be allowed to see Isabel before he was turned out; but Isabel had left the house in company with her mother.

## CHAPTER 71

### 'WHAT AM I TO SAY, SIR?'

WHEN Silverbridge left Mr Boncassen's house he was resolved to go to his father without an hour's delay, and represent to the Duke exactly how the case stood. He would be urgent, piteous, submissive, and eloquent. In any other matter he would promise to make whatever arrangements his father might desire. He would make his father understand that all his happiness depended on this marriage. When once married he would settle down, even at Gatherum Castle if the Duke should wish it. He would not think of race-horses, he would desert the Beargarden, he would learn blue-books by heart, and only do as much shooting and hunting as would become a young nobleman in his position. All this he would say as eagerly and as pleasantly as it might be said. But he would add to all this an assurance of his unchangeable intention. It was his purpose to marry Isabel Boncassen. If he could do this with his father's good will,—so best. But at any rate he would marry her!

The world at this time was altogether busy with political rumours; and it was supposed that Sir Timothy Beeswax would do something very clever. It was supposed also that he would sever himself from some of his present companions. On that point everybody was agreed,— and on that point only everybody was right. Lord Drummond, who was the titular Prime Minister, and Sir Timothy, had, during a considerable part of the last session, and through the whole vacation, so belarded each other with praise in all their public expressions that it was quite manifest that they had quarrelled. When any body of statesmen make public asseverations by one or various voices, that there is no discord among them, not a dissentient voice on any subject, people are apt to suppose that they cannot hang together much longer. It is the man who has no peace at home that declares abroad that his wife is an angel. He who lives on comfortable terms with the partner of his troubles can afford to acknowledge the ordinary rubs of life. Old Mr Mildmay,* who was Prime Minister for so many years, and whom his party worshipped, used to say that he had never found a gentleman who had quite agreed with him all round; but Sir Timothy has always been in exact accord with all his colleagues,—till he has left them, or they him. Never had there been such concord as of late,—and men, clubs, and newspapers now protested that as a natural consequence there would soon be a break-up.

But not on that account would it perhaps be necessary that Sir Timothy should resign,—or not necessary that his resignation should be permanent. The Conservative majority had dwindled,—but still there was a majority. It certainly was the case that Lord Drummond could not get on without Sir Timothy. But might it not be possible that Sir Timothy should get on without Lord Drummond? If so he must begin his action in this direction by resigning. He would have to place his resignation, no doubt with infinite regret, in the hands of Lord Drummond. But if such a step were to be taken now, just as Parliament was about to assemble, what would become of the Queen's speech, of the address, and of the noble peers and noble and other commoners who were to propose and second it in the two Houses of Parliament? There were those who said that such a trick played at the last moment would be very shabby. But then again there were those who foresaw that the shabbiness would be made to rest anywhere rather than on the shoulders of Sir Timothy. If it should turn out that he had striven manfully to make things run smoothly;—that the Premier's incompetence, or the Chancellor's obstinacy, or this or that Secretary's peculiarity of temper had done it all;—might not Sir Timothy then be able to emerge from the confused flood, and swim along pleasantly with his head higher than ever above the waters?

In these great matters parliamentary management goes for so much! If a man be really clever and handy at his trade, if he can work hard and knows what he is about, if he can give and take and be not thin-skinned or sore-bored, if he can ask pardon for a peccadillo and seem to be sorry with a good grace, if above all things he be able to surround himself with the prestige of success, then so much will be forgiven him! Great gifts of eloquence are hardly wanted, or a deep-seated patriotism which is capable of strong indignation. A party has to be managed, and he who can manage it best, will probably be its best leader. The subordinate task of legislation and of executive government may well fall into the inferior hands of less astute practitioners. It was admitted on both sides that there was no man like Sir Timothy for managing the House or coercing a party, and there was therefore a general feeling that it would be a pity that Sir Timothy should be squeezed out. He knew all the little secrets of the business;—could arrange, let the cause be what it might, to get a full House for himself and his friends, and empty benches for his opponents,—could foresee a thousand little things to which even a Walpole would have been blind, which a Pitt would not have condescended to regard, but with which his familiarity made him a very comfortable leader of the House of Commons. There were various ideas prevalent as to the politics of the coming session; but the prevailing idea was in favour of Sir Timothy.

The Duke was at Longroyston, the seat of his old political ally the Duke of St Bungay, and had been absent from Sunday the 6th till the morning of Friday the 11th, on which day Parliament was to meet. On that morning at about noon a letter came to the son saying that his father had returned and would be glad to see him. Silverbridge was going to the House on that day and was not without his own political anxieties. If Lord Drummond remained in, he thought that he must, for the present, stand by the party which he had adopted. If, however, Sir Timothy should become Prime Minister there would be a loophole for escape. There were some three or four besides himself who detested Sir Timothy, and in such case he might perhaps have company in his desertion. All this was on his mind; but through all this he was aware that there was a matter of much deeper moment which required his energies. When his father's message was brought to him he told himself at once that now was the time for his eloquence.

'Well, Silverbridge,' said the Duke, 'how are matters going on with you?' There seemed to be something in his father's manner more than ordinarily jocund and good-humoured.

'With me, sir?'

'I don't mean to ask any party secrets. If you and Sir Timothy understand each other, of course you will be discreet.'

'I can't be discreet, sir, because I don't know anything about him.'

'When I heard,' said the Duke smiling, 'of your being in close conference with Sir Timothy——'

'I, sir?'

'Yes, you. Mr Boncassen told me that you and he were so deeply taken up with each other at his house, that nobody could get a word with either of you.'

'Have you seen Mr Boncassen?' asked the son, whose attention was immediately diverted from his father's political badinage.

'Yes;—I have seen him. I happened to meet him where I was dining last Sunday, and he walked home with me. He was so intent upon what he was saying that I fear he allowed me to take him out of his way.'

'What was he talking about?' said Silverbridge. All his preparations, all his eloquence, all his method, now seemed to have departed from him.

'He was talking about you,' said the Duke.

'He had told me that he wanted to see you. What did he say, sir?'

'I suppose you can guess what he said. He wished to know what I thought of the offer you have made to his daughter.' The great subject had come up so easily, so readily, that he was almost aghast when he found himself in the middle of it. And yet he must speak of the matter, and that at once.

'I hope you raised no objection, sir,' he said.

'The objection came mainly from him; and I am bound to say that every word that fell from him was spoken with wisdom.'

'But still he asked you to consent.'

'By no means. He told me his opinion,—and then he asked me a question.'

'I am sure he did not say that we ought not to be married.'

'He did say that he thought you ought not to be married, if——'

'If what, sir?'

'If there were probability that his daughter would not be well received as your wife. Then he asked me what would be my reception of her.' Silverbridge looked up into his father's face with beseeching imploring eyes as though everything now depended on the next few words that he might utter. 'I shall think it an unwise marriage,' continued the Duke. Silverbridge when he heard this at once knew that he had gained his cause. His father had spoken of the marriage as a thing that was to happen. A joyous light dawned in his eyes, and the look of pain went from his brow, all which the Duke was not slow to perceive. 'I shall think it an unwise marriage,' he continued, repeating his words; 'but I was bound to tell him that were Miss Boncassen to become your wife she would also become my daughter.'

'Oh, sir.'

'I told him why the marriage would be distasteful to me. Whether I may be wrong or right I think it to be for the good of our country, for the good of our order, for the good of our individual families, that we should support each other by marriage. It is not as though we were a narrow class, already too closely bound together by family alliances. The room for choice might be wide enough for you without going across the Atlantic to look for her who is to be the mother of your children. To this Mr Boncassen replied that he was to look solely to his daughter's happiness. He meant me to understand that he cared nothing for my feelings. Why should he? That which to me is deep wisdom is to him an empty prejudice. He asked me then how others would receive her.'

'I am sure that everybody would like her,' said Silverbridge.

'I like her. I like her very much.'

'I am so glad.'

'But still all this is a sorrow to me. When however he put that question to me about the world around her,—as to those among whom her lot would be cast, I could not say that I thought she would be rejected.'

'Oh no!' The idea of rejecting Isabel!

'She has a brightness and a grace all her own,' continued the Duke, 'which will ensure her acceptance in all societies.'

'Yes, yes;—it is just that, sir.'

'You will be a nine days' wonder,—the foolish young nobleman who chose to marry an American.'

'I think it will be just the other way up, sir,—among the men.'

'But her place will I think be secure to her. That is what I told Mr Boncassen.'

'It is all right with him then,—now?'

'If you call it all right. You will understand of course that you are acting in opposition to my advice,—and my wishes.'

'What am I to say, sir?' exclaimed Silverbridge, almost in despair. 'When I love the girl better than my life, and when you tell me that she can be mine if I choose to take her; when I have asked her to be my wife, and have got her to say that she likes me; when her father has given way, and all the rest of it, would it be possible that I should say now that I will give her up?'

'My opinion is to go for nothing,—in anything!' The Duke as he said this knew that he was expressing aloud a feeling which should have been restrained within his own bosom. It was natural that there should have been such plaints. The same suffering must be encountered in regard to Tregear and his daughter. In every way he had been thwarted. In every direction he was driven to yield. And yet now he had to undergo rebuke from his own son, because one of those inward plaints would force itself from his lips! Of course this girl was to be taken in among the Pallisers and treated with an idolatrous love,—as perfect as though 'all the blood of all the Howards'* were running in her veins. What further inch of ground was there for a fight? And if the fight were over, why should he rob his boy of one sparkle from off the joy of his triumph? Silverbridge was now standing before him abashed by that plaint, inwardly sustained no doubt by the conviction of his great success, but subdued by his father's wailing. 'However,—perhaps we had better let that pass,' said the Duke, with a long sigh. Then Silverbridge took his father's hand, and looked up in his face. 'I most sincerely hope that she may make you a good and loving wife,' said the Duke, 'and that she may do her duty by you in that not easy sphere of life to which she will be called.'

'I am quite sure she will,' said Silverbridge, whose ideas as to Isabel's duties were confined at present to a feeling that she would now have to give him kisses without stint.

'What I have seen of her personally recommends her to me,' said the Duke. 'Some girls are fools——'

'That's quite true, sir.'

'Who think that the world is to be nothing but dancing, and going to parties.'

'Many have been doing it for so many years,' said Silverbridge, 'that they can't understand that there should be an end of it.'

'A wife ought to feel the great responsibility of her position. I hope she will.'

'And the sooner she begins the better,' said Silverbridge stoutly.

'And now,' said the Duke, looking at his watch, 'we might as well have lunch and go down to the House. I will walk with you if you please. It will be about time for each of us.' Then the son was forced to go down and witness the somewhat faded ceremony of seeing Parliament opened by three Lords sitting in commission before the throne. Whereas but for such stress as his father had laid upon him, he would have disregarded his parliamentary duties and have rushed at once up to Brook Street. As it was he was so handed over from one political pundit to another, was so buttonholed by Sir Timothy, so chaffed as to the address by Phineas Finn, and at last so occupied with the whole matter that he was compelled to sit in his place till he had heard Nidderdale make his speech. This the young Scotch Lord did so well, and received so much praise for the doing of it, and looked so well in his uniform, that Silverbridge almost regretted the opportunity he had lost. At seven the sitting was over, the speeches, though full of interest, having been shorter than usual. They had been full of interest, but nobody understood in the least what was going to happen. 'I don't know anything about the Prime Minister,' said Mr Lupton as he left the House with our hero and another not very staunch supporter of the Government, 'but I'll back Sir Timothy to be the Leader of the House on the last day of the session, against all comers. I don't think it much matters who is Prime Minister nowadays.'

At half-past seven Silverbridge was at the door in Brook Street. Yes; Miss Boncassen was at home. The servant thought that she was upstairs dressing. Then Silverbridge made his way without further invitation into the drawing-room. There he remained alone for ten minutes.

At last the door opened, and Mrs Boncassen entered. 'Dear! Lord Silverbridge, who ever dreamed of seeing you? I thought all you Parliament gentlemen were going through your ceremonies. Isabel had a ticket and went down, and saw your father.'

'Where is Isabel?'

'She's gone.'

'Gone! Where on earth has she gone to?' asked Silverbridge, as though fearing lest she had been carried off to the other side of the Atlantic. Then Mrs Boncassen explained. Within the last three minutes Mrs Montacute Jones had called and carried Isabel off to the play. Mrs Jones was up in town for a week, and this had been a very old engagement. 'I hope you did not want her very particularly,' said Mrs Boncassen.

'But I did,—most particularly,' said Lord Silverbridge. The door was opened and Mr Boncassen entered the room. 'I beg your pardon for coming at such a time,' said the lover, 'but I did so want to see Isabel.'

'I rather think she wants to see you,' said the father.

'I shall go to the theatre after her.'

'That might be awkward,—particularly as I doubt whether anybody knows what theatre they are gone to. Can I receive a message for her, my lord?' This was certainly not what Lord Silverbridge had intended. 'You know, perhaps, that I have seen the Duke.'

'Oh yes;—and I have seen him. Everything is settled.'

'That is the only message she will want to hear when she comes home. She is a happy girl and I am proud to think that I should live to call such a grand young Briton as you my son-in-law.' Then the American took the young man's two hands and shook them cordially, while Mrs Boncassen bursting into tears insisted on kissing him.

'Indeed she is a happy girl,' said she; 'but I hope Isabel won't be carried away too high and mighty.'

## CHAPTER 72

### CARLTON TERRACE

THREE days after this it was arranged that Isabel should be taken to Carlton Terrace to be accepted there into the full good graces of her future father-in-law, and to go through the pleasant ceremony of seeing the house in which it was to be her destiny to live as mistress. What can be more interesting to a girl than this first visit to her future home? And now Isabel Boncassen was to make her first visit to the house in Carlton Terrace, which the Duke had already declared his purpose of surrendering to the young couple. She was going among very grand things,— so grand that those whose affairs in life are less magnificent may think that her mind should have soared altogether above chairs and tables, and reposed itself among diamonds, gold and silver ornaments, rich necklaces, the old masters, and alabaster statuary. But Dukes and Duchesses must sit upon chairs,—or at any rate on sofas,—as well as their poorer brethren, and probably have the same regard for their comfort. Isabel was not above her future furniture, or the rooms that were to be her rooms, or the stairs which she would have to tread, or the pillow on which her head must rest. She had never yet seen even the outside of the house in which she was to live, and was now prepared to make her visit with as much enthusiasm as though her future abode was to be prepared for her in a small house in a small street beyond Islington.*

But the Duke was no doubt more than the house, the father-in-law more than the tables. Isabel, in the ordinary way of society, he had already known almost with intimacy. She, the while, had been well aware that if all things could possibly be made to run smoothly with her, this lordly host, who was so pleasantly courteous to her, would become her father-in-law. But she had known also that he, in his courtesy, had been altogether unaware of any such intention on her part, and that she would now present herself to him in an aspect very different from that in which she had hitherto been regarded. She was well aware that the Duke had not wished to take her into his family,—would not himself have chosen her for his son's wife. She had seen enough to make her sure that he had even chosen another bride for his heir. She had been too clever not to perceive that Lady Mabel Grex had been not only selected,—but almost accepted as though the thing had been certain. She had learned nearly the whole truth from Silverbridge, who was not good at keeping a secret from one to whom his heart was open. That story had been all but read by her with exactness. 'I cannot lose you now,' she had said to him, leaning on his arm;—'I cannot afford to lose you now. But I fear that someone else is losing you.' To this he answered nothing, but simply pressed her closer to his side. 'Someone else,' she continued, 'who perhaps may have reason to think that you have injured her.' 'No,' he said boldly; 'no; there is no such person.' For he had never ceased to assure himself that in all that matter with Mabel Grex he had been guilty of no treachery. There had been a moment, indeed, in which she might have taken him; but she had chosen to let it pass from her. All of which, or nearly all of which,—Isabel now saw, and had seen also that the Duke had been a consenting party to that other arrangement. She had reason therefore to doubt the manner of her acceptance.

But she had been accepted. She had made such acceptance by him a stipulation in her acceptance of his son. She was sure of the ground on which she trod and was determined to carry herself, if not with pride, yet with dignity. There might be difficulties before her, but it should not be her fault if she were not as good a Countess, and,—when time would have it so,—as good a Duchess as another.

The visit was made not quite in the fashion in which Silverbridge himself had wished. His idea had been to call for Isabel in his cab and take her down to Carlton Terrace. 'Mother must go with me,' she had said. Then he looked blank,—as he could look when he was disappointed, as he had looked when she would not talk to him at the lunch, when she told him that it was not her business to entertain him. 'Don't be selfish,' she added, laughing. 'Do you think that mother will not want to have seen the house that I am to live in?'

'She shall come afterwards as often as she likes.'

'What,—paying me morning visits from New York! She must come now, if you please. Love me, love my mother.'

'I am awfully fond of her,' said Silverbridge, who felt that he really had behaved well to the old lady.

'So am I,—and therefore she shall go and see the house now. You are as good as gold,—and do everything just as I tell you. But a good time is coming, when I shall have to do everything that you tell me.' Then it was arranged that Mrs and Miss Boncassen were to be taken down to the house in their own carriage, and were to be received at the door by Lord Silverbridge.

Another arrangement had also been made. Isabel was to be taken to the Duke immediately upon her arrival and to be left for awhile with him, alone, so that he might express himself as he might find fit to do to this newly-adopted child. It was a matter to him of such importance that nothing remaining to him in his life could equal it. It was not simply that she was to be the wife of his son,—though that in itself was a consideration very sacred. Had it been Gerald who was bringing to him a bride, the occasion would have had less of awe. But this girl, this American girl, was to be the mother and grandmother of future Dukes of Omnium,—the ancestress, it was to be hoped, of all future Dukes of Omnium! By what she might be, by what she might have in her of mental fibre, of high or low quality, of true or untrue womanliness, were to be fashioned those who in days to come might be amongst the strongest and most faithful bulwarks of the constitution. An England without a Duke of Omnium,—or at any rate without any Duke,— what would it be? And yet he knew that with bad Dukes his country would be in worse stress than though she had none at all. An aristocracy;—yes; but an aristocracy that shall be of the very best! He believed himself thoroughly in his order; but if his order, or many of his order, should become as was now Lord Grex, then, he thought, that his order not only must go to the wall but that, in the cause of humanity, it had better do so. With all this daily, hourly, always in his mind, this matter of the choice of a wife for his heir was to him of solemn importance.

When they arrived Silverbridge was there and led them first of all into the dining-room. 'My!' said Mrs Boncassen, as she looked around her. 'I thought that our Fifth Avenue parlours whipped everything in the way of city houses.'

'What a nice little room for Darby and Joan* to sit down to eat a mutton-chop in,' said Isabel.

'It's a beastly great barrack,' said Silverbridge;—'but the best of it is that we never use it. We'll have a cosy little place for Darby and Joan;— you'll see. Now come to the governor. I've got to leave you with him.'

'Oh me! I am in such a fright.'

'He can't eat you,' said Mrs Boncassen.

'And he won't even bite,' said Silverbridge.

'I should not mind that because I could bite again. But if he looks as though he thought I shouldn't do, I shall drop.'

'My belief is that he's almost as much in love with you as I am,' said Silverbridge, as he took her to the door of the Duke's room. 'Here we are, sir.'

'My dear,' said the Duke, rising up and coming to her, 'I am very glad to see you. It is good of you to come to me.' Then he took her in both his hands and kissed her forehead and her lips. She, as she put her face up to him, stood quite still in his embrace, but her eyes were bright with pleasure.

'Shall I leave her?' said Silverbridge.

'For a few minutes.'

'Don't keep her too long, for I want to take her all over the house.'

'A few minutes,—and then I will bring her up to the drawing-room.' Upon this the door was closed, and Isabel was alone with her new father. 'And so, my dear, you are to be my child.'

'If you will have me.'

'Come here and sit down by me. Your father has already told you that;—has he not?'

'He has told me that you had consented.'

'And Silverbridge has said as much?'

'I would sooner hear it from you than from either of them.'

'Then hear it from me. You shall be my child. And if you will love me you shall be very dear to me. You shall be my own child,—as dear as my own. I must either love his wife very dearly, or else I must be an unhappy man. And she must love me dearly, or I must be unhappy.'

'I will love you,' she said, pressing his hand.

'And now let me say some few words to you, only let there be no bitterness in them to your young heart. When I say that I take you to my heart, you may be sure that I do so thoroughly. You shall be as dear to me and as near as though you had been all English.'

'Shall I?'

'There shall no difference be made. My boy's wife shall be my daughter in very deed. But I had not wished it to be so.'

'I knew that;—but could I have given him up?'

'He at any rate could not give you up. There were little prejudices;— you can understand that.'

'Oh yes.'

'We who wear black coats could not bring ourselves readily to put on scarlet garments; nor should we sit comfortably with our legs crossed like Turks.'

'I am your scarlet coat and your cross-legged Turk,' she said, with feigned self-reproach in her voice, but with a sparkle of mirth in her eye.

'But when I have once got into my scarlet coat I can be very proud of it, and when I am once seated in my divan I shall find it of all postures the easiest. Do you understand me?'

'I think so.'

'Not a shade of any prejudice shall be left to darken my mind. There shall be no feeling but that you are in truth his chosen wife. After all neither can country, nor race, nor rank, nor wealth, make a good woman. Education can do much. But nature must have done much also.'

'Do not expect too much of me.'

'I will so expect that all shall be taken for the best. You know, I think, that I have liked you since I first saw you.'

'I know that you have always been good to me.'

'I have liked you from the first. That you are lovely perhaps is no merit; though, to speak the truth, I am well pleased that Silverbridge should have found so much beauty.'

'That is all a matter of taste, I suppose,' she said, laughing.

'But there is much that a young woman may do for herself which I think you have done. A silly girl, though she had been a second Helen, would hardly have satisfied me.'

'Or perhaps him,' said Isabel.

'Or him; and it is in that feeling that I find my chief satisfaction,— that he should have had the sense to have liked such a one as you better than others. Now I have said it. As not being one of us I did at first object to his choice. As being what you are yourself, I am altogether reconciled to it. Do not keep him long waiting.'

'I do not think he likes to be kept waiting for anything.'

'I dare say not. I dare say not. And now there is one thing else.' Then the Duke unlocked a little drawer that was close to his hand, and taking out a ring put it on her finger. It was a bar of diamonds, perhaps a dozen of them, fixed in a little circlet of gold. 'This must never leave you,' he said.

'It never shall,—having come from you.'

'It was the first present that I gave to my wife, and it is the first that I give to you. You may imagine how sacred it is to me. On no other hand could it be worn without something which to me would be akin to sacrilege. Now I must not keep you longer or Silverbridge will be storming about the house. He of course will tell me when it is to be; but do not you keep him long waiting.' Then he kissed her and led her up into the drawing-room. When he had spoken a word of greeting to Mrs Boncassen, he left them to their own devices.

After that they spent the best part of an hour in going over the house; but even that was done in a manner unsatisfactory to Silverbridge. Wherever Isabel went, there Mrs Boncassen went also. There might have been some fun in showing even the back kitchens to his bride-elect, by herself;—but there was none in wandering about those vast underground regions with a stout lady who was really interested with the cooking apparatus and the wash-houses. The bedrooms one after another became tedious to him when Mrs Boncassen would make communications respecting each of them to her daughter. 'That is Gerald's room,' said Silverbridge. 'You have never seen Gerald. He is such a brick.' Mrs Boncassen was charmed with the whips and sticks and boxing-gloves in Gerald's room, and expressed an opinion that young men in the States mostly carried their knick-knacks about with them to the Universities. When she was told that he had another collection of 'knick-knacks' at Matching, and another at Oxford, she thought that he was a very extravagant young man. Isabel, who had heard all about the gambling in Scotland, looked round at her lover and smiled.

'Well, my dear,' said Mrs Boncassen, as they took their leave, 'it is a very grand house, and I hope with all my heart you may have your health there and be happy. But I don't know that you'll be any happier because it's so big.'

'Wait till you see Gatherum,' said Silverbridge. 'That, I own, does make me unhappy. It has been calculated that three months at Gatherum Castle would drive a philosopher mad.'

In all this there had been a certain amount of disappointment for Silverbridge; but on that evening, before dinner in Brook Street, he received compensation. As the day was one somewhat peculiar in its nature he decided that it should be kept altogether as a holiday, and he did not therefore go down to the House. And not going to the House of course he spent the time with the Boncassens. 'You know you ought to go,' Isabel said to him when they found themselves alone together in the back drawing-room.

'Of course I ought.'

'Then go. Do you think I would keep a Briton from his duties?'

'Not though the constitution should fall in ruins. Do you suppose that a man wants no rest after inspecting all the pots and pans in that establishment? A woman, I believe, could go on doing that kind of thing all day long.'

'You should remember at least that the—woman was interesting herself about your pots and pans.'

'And now, Bella, tell me what the governor said to you.' Then she showed him the ring. 'Did he give you that?' She nodded her head in assent. 'I did not think he would ever have parted with that.'

'It was your mother's.'

'She wore it always. I almost think that I never saw her hand without it. He would not have given you that unless he had meant to be very good to you.'

'He was very good to me. Silverbridge, I have a great deal to do, to learn to be your wife.'

'I'll teach you.'

'Yes; you'll teach me. But will you teach me right? There is something almost awful in your father's serious dignity and solemn appreciation of the responsibilities of his position. Will you ever come to that?'

'I shall never be a great man as he is.'

'It seems to me that life to him is a load;—which he does not object to carry, but which he knows must be carried with a great struggle.'

'I suppose it ought to be so with everyone.'

'Yes,' she said, 'but the higher you put your foot on the ladder the more constant should be your thought that your stepping requires care. I fear that I am climbing too high.'

'You can't come down now, my young woman.'

'I have to go on now,—and do it as best I can. I will try to do my best. I will try to do my best. I told him so, and now I tell you so. I will try to do my best.'

'Perhaps after all I am only a "pert poppet",' she said half an hour afterwards, for Silverbridge had told her of that terrible mistake made by poor Dolly Longstaff.

'Brute!' he exclaimed.

'Not at all. And when we are settled down in the real Darby-and-Joan way I shall hope to see Mr Longstaff very often. I dare say he won't call me a pert poppet, and I shall not remind him of the word. But I shall always think of it; and remembering the way in which my character struck an educated Englishman,—who was not altogether ill-disposed towards me,—I may hope to improve myself.'

## CHAPTER 73

### 'I HAVE NEVER LOVED YOU'

SILVERBRIDGE had now been in town three or four weeks, and Lady Mabel Grex had also been in London all that time, and yet he had not seen her. She had told him that she loved him and had asked him plainly to make her his wife. He had told her that he could not do so,—that he was altogether resolved to make another woman his wife. Then she had rebuked him, and had demanded from him how he had dared to treat her as he had done. His conscience was clear. He had his own code of morals as to such matters, and had, as he regarded it, kept within the law. But she thought that she was badly treated, and had declared that she was now left out in the cold for ever through his treachery. Then her last word had been almost the worst of all, 'Who can tell what may come to pass?'—showing too plainly that she would not even now give up her hope. Before the month was up she wrote to him as follows:

'DEAR LORD SILVERBRIDGE,

'Why do you not come and see me? Are friends so plentiful with you that one so staunch as I may be thrown over? But of course I know why you do not come. Put all that aside,—and come. I cannot hurt you. I have learned to feel that certain things which the world regards as too awful to be talked of,—except in the way of scandal, may be discussed and then laid aside just like other subjects. What though I wear a wig or a wooden leg, I may still be fairly comfortable among my companions unless I crucify myself by trying to hide my misfortune. It is not the presence of the skeleton that crushes us. Not even that will hurt us much if we let him go about the house as he lists. It is the everlasting effort which the horror makes to peep out of his cupboard that robs us of our ease. At any rate come and see me.

'Of course I know that you are to be married to Miss Boncassen. Who does not know it? The trumpeters have been at work for the last week.

'Your very sincere friend,
'MABEL.'

He wished that she had not written. Of course he must go to her. And though there was a word or two in her letter which angered him, his feelings towards her were kindly. Had not that American angel flown across the Atlantic to his arms he could have been well content to make her his wife. But the interview at the present moment could hardly be other than painful. She could, she said, talk of her own misfortunes, but the subject would be very painful to him. It was not to him a skeleton, to be locked out of sight; but it had been a misfortune, and the sooner that such misfortunes could be forgotten the better.

He knew what she meant about trumpeters. She had intended to signify that Isabel in her pride had boasted of her matrimonial prospects. Of course there had been trumpets. Are there not always trumpets when a marriage is contemplated, magnificent enough to be called an alliance? As for that he himself had blown the trumpets. He had told everybody that he was going to be married to Miss Boncassen. Isabel had blown no trumpets. In her own straightforward way she had told the truth to whom it concerned. Of course he would go and see Lady Mabel, but he trusted that for her own sake nothing would be said about trumpets.

'So you have come at last,' Mabel said when he entered the room. 'No;—Miss Cassewary is not here. As I wanted to see you alone I got her to go out this morning. Why did you not come before?'

'You said in your letter that you knew why.'

'But in saying so I was accusing you of cowardice;—was I not?'

'It was not cowardice.'

'Why then did you not come?'

'I thought you would hardly wish to see me so soon,—after what passed.'

'That is honest at any rate. You felt that I must be too much ashamed of what I said to be able to look you in the face.'

'Not that exactly.'

'Any other man would have felt the same, but no other man would be honest enough to tell me so. I do not think that ever in your life you have constrained yourself to the civility of a lie.'

'I hope not.'

'To be civil and false is often better than to be harsh and true. I may be soothed by the courtesy and yet not deceived by the lie. But what I told you in my letter,—which I hope you have destroyed——'

'I will destroy it.'

'Do. It was not intended for the partner of your future joys. As I told you then, I can talk freely. Why not? We know it,—both of us. How your conscience may be I cannot tell; but mine is clear from that soil with which you think it should be smirched.'

'I think nothing of the sort.'

'Yes, Silverbridge, you do. You have said to yourself this;—That girl has determined to get me, and she has not scrupled as to how she would do it.'

'No such idea has ever crossed my mind.'

'But you have never told yourself of the encouragement which you gave me. Such condemnation as I have spoken of would have been just if my efforts had been sanctioned by no words, no looks, no deeds from you. Did you give me warrant for thinking that you were my lover?'

That theory by which he had justified himself to himself seemed to fall away from him under her questioning. He could not now remember his words to her in those old days before Miss Boncassen had crossed his path; but he did know that he had once intended to make her understand that he loved her. She had not understood him;—or, understanding, had not accepted his words; and therefore he had thought himself free. But it now seemed that he had not been entitled so to regard himself. There she sat, looking at him, waiting for his answer; and he who had been so sure that he had committed no sin against her, had not a word to say to her.

'I want your answer to that, Lord Silverbridge. I have told you that I would have no skeleton in the cupboard. Down at Matching, and before that at Killancodlem, I appealed to you, asking you to take me as your wife.'

'Hardly that.'

'Altogether that! I will have nothing denied that I have done,—nor will I be ashamed of anything. I did do so,—even after this infatuation. I thought then that one so volatile might perhaps fly back again.'

'I shall not do that,' said he, frowning at her.

'You need trouble yourself with no assurance, my friend. Let us understand each other now. I am not now supposing that you can fly back again. You have found your perch, and you must settle on it like a good domestic barn-door fowl.' Again he scowled. If she were too hard upon him he would certainly turn upon her. 'No; you will not fly back again now;—but was I, or was I not, justified when you came to Killancodlem in thinking that my lover had come there?'

'How can I tell? It is my own justification I am thinking of.'

'I see all that. But we cannot both be justified. Did you mean me to suppose that you were speaking to me words in earnest when there,— sitting in that very spot,—you spoke to me of your love.'

'Did I speak of my love?'

'Did you speak of your love! And now, Silverbridge,—for if there be an English gentleman on earth I think that you are one,—as a gentleman tell me this. Did you not even tell your father that I should be your wife? I know you did.'

'Did he tell you?'

'Men such as you and he, who cannot even lie with your eyelids, who will not condescend to cover up a secret by a moment of feigned inanimation, have many voices. He did tell me; but he broke no confidence. He told me, but did not mean to tell me. Now you also have told me.'

'I did. I told him so. And then I changed my mind.'

'I know you changed your mind. Men often do. A pinker pink, a whiter white,—a finger that will press you just half an ounce the closer,—a cheek that will consent to let itself come just a little nearer——!'

'No; no; no!' It was because Isabel had not easily consented to such approaches!

'Trifles such as these will do it;—and some such trifles have done it with you. It would be beneath me to make comparisons where I might seem to be the gainer. I grant her beauty. She is very lovely. She has succeeded.'

'I have succeeded.'

'But—I am justified, and you are condemned. Is it not so? Tell me like a man.'

'You are justified.'

'And you are condemned? When you told me that I should be your wife, and then told your father the same story, was I to think it all meant nothing! Have you deceived me?'

'I did not mean it.'

'Have you deceived me? What; you cannot deny it, and yet have not the manliness to own it to a poor woman who can only save herself from humiliation by extorting the truth from you!'

'Oh, Mabel, I am so sorry it should be so.'

'I believe you are,—with a sorrow that will last till she is again sitting close to you. Nor, Silverbridge, do I wish it to be longer. No;—no;—no. Your fault after all has not been great. You deceived, but did not mean to deceive me?'

'Never; never.'

'And I fancy you have never known how much you bore about with you. Your modesty has been so perfect that you have not thought of yourself as more than other men. You have forgotten that you have had in your hand the disposal to some one woman of a throne in Paradise.'

'I don't suppose you thought of that.'

'But I did. Why should I tell falsehoods now? I have determined that you should know everything,—but I could better confess to you my own sins when I had shown that you too have not been innocent. Not think of it! Do not men think of high titles and great wealth and power and place? And if men, why should not women? Do not men try to get them;—and are they not even applauded for their energy? A woman has but one way to try. I tried.'

'I do not think it was all for that.'

'How shall I answer that without a confession which even I am not hardened enough to make? In truth, Silverbridge, I have never loved you.'

He drew himself up slowly before he answered her, and gradually assumed a look very different from that easy boyish smile which was customary to him. 'I am glad of that,' he said.

'Why are you glad?'

'Now I can have no regrets.'

'You need have none. It was necessary to me that I should have my little triumph;—that I should show you that I knew how far you had wronged me! But now I wish that you should know everything. I have never loved you.'

'There is an end of it then.'

'But I have liked you so well,—so much better than all others! A dozen men have asked me to marry them. And though they might be nothing till they made that request, then they became—things of horror to me. But you were not a thing of horror. I could have become your wife, and I think that I could have learned to love you.'

'It is best as it is.'

'I ought to say so too; but I have a doubt I should have liked to be Duchess of Omnium, and perhaps I might have fitted the place better than one who can as yet know but little of its duties or its privileges. I may, perhaps, think that that other arrangement would have been better even for you.'

'I can take care of myself in that.'

'I should have married you without loving you, but I should have done so determined to serve you with a devotion which a woman who does love hardly thinks necessary. I would have so done my duty that you should never have guessed that my heart had been in the keeping of another man.'

'Another man!'

'Yes; of course. If there had been no other man, why not you? Am I so hard, do you think that I can love no one? Are you not such a one that a girl would naturally love,—were she not preoccupied? That a woman should love seems as necessary as that a man should not.'

'A man can love too.'

'No;—hardly. He can admire, and he can like, and he can fondle and be fond. He can admire, and approve, and perhaps worship. He can know of a woman that she is part of himself, the most sacred part, and therefore will protect her from the very winds. But all that will not make love. It does not come to a man that to be separated from a woman is to be dislocated from his very self. A man has but one centre, and that is himself. A woman has two. Though the second may never be seen by her, may live in the arms of another, may do all for that other that man can do for woman,—still, still, though he be half the globe asunder from her, still he is to her the half of her existence. If she really love, there is, I fancy, no end of it. To the end of time I shall love Frank Tregear.'

'Tregear!'

'Who else?'

'He is engaged to Mary.'

'Of course he is. Why not;—to her or whomsoever else he might like best? He is as true I doubt not to your sister as you are to your American beauty,—or as you would have been to me had fancy held. He used to love me.'

'You were always friends.'

'Always;—dear friends. And he would have loved me if a man were capable of loving. But he could sever himself from me easily, just when he was told to do so. I thought that I could do the same. But I cannot. A jackal is born a jackal, and not a lion, and cannot help himself. So is a woman born—a woman. They are clinging, parasite things, which cannot but adhere; though they destroy themselves by adhering. Do not suppose that I take a pride in it. I would give one of my eyes to be able to disregard him.'

'Time will do it.'

'Yes; time,—that brings wrinkles and rouge-pots and rheumatism. Though I have so hated those men as to be unable to endure them, still I want some man's house, and his name,—some man's bread and wine,—some man's jewels and titles and woods and parks and gardens,—if I can get them. Time can help a man in his sorrow. If he begins at forty to make speeches, or to win races, or to breed oxen, he can yet live a prosperous life. Time is but a poor consoler for a young woman who has to be married.'

'Oh, Mabel.'

'And now let there be not a word more about it. I know—that I can trust you.'

'Indeed you may.'

'Though you will tell her everything else you will not tell her this.'

'No;—not this.'

'And surely you will not tell your sister!'

'I shall tell no one.'

'It is because you are so true that I have dared to trust you. I had to justify myself,—and then to confess. Had I at that one moment taken you at your word, you would never have known anything of all this. "There is a tide in the affairs of men——!"* But I let the flood go by! I shall not see you again now before you are married; but come to me afterwards.'

# CHAPTER 74

### 'LET US DRINK A GLASS OF WINE TOGETHER'

SILVERBRIDGE pondered it all much as he went home. What a terrible story was that he had heard! The horror to him was chiefly in this,— that she should yet be driven to marry some man without even fancying that she could love him! And this was Lady Mabel Grex, who, on his own first entrance into London life, now not much more than twelve months ago, had seemed to him to stand above all other girls in beauty, charm, and popularity!

As he opened the door of the house with his latch-key, who should be coming out but Frank Tregear,—Frank Tregear with his arm in a sling, but still with an unmistakable look of general satisfaction. 'When on earth did you come up?' asked Silverbridge. Tregear told him that he had arrived on the previous evening from Harrington. 'And why? The doctor would not have let you come if he could have helped it.'

'When he found he could not help it, he did let me come. I am nearly all right. If I had been nearly all wrong I should have had to come.'

'And what are you doing here?'

'Well; if you'll allow me I'll go back with you for a moment. What do you think I have been doing?'

'Have you seen my sister?'

'Yes, I have seen your sister. And I have done better than that. I have seen your father. Lord Silverbridge,—behold your brother-in-law.'

'You don't mean to say that it is arranged?'

'I do.'

'What did he say?'

'He made me understand by most unanswerable arguments, that I had no business to think of such a thing. I did not fight the point with him,—but simply stood there, as conclusive evidence of my business. He told me that we should have nothing to live on unless he gave us an income. I assured him that I would never ask him for a shilling. "But I cannot allow her to marry a man without an income," he said.'

'I know his way so well.'

'I had just two facts to go upon,—that I would not give her up, and that she would not give me up. When I pointed that out he tore his hair,—in a mild way, and said that he did not understand that kind of thing at all.'

'And yet he gave way.'

'Of course he did. They say that when a king of old would consent to see a petitioner for his life, he was bound by his royalty to mercy. So it was with the Duke. Then, very early in the argument, he forgot himself, and called her—Mary. I knew he had thrown up the sponge then.'

'How did he give way at last?'

'He asked me what were my ideas about life in general. I said that I thought Parliament was a good sort of thing, that I was lucky enough to have a seat, and that I should take lodgings somewhere in Westminster till——. "Till what?" he asked. "Till something is settled," I replied. Then he turned away from me and remained silent. "May I see Lady Mary?" I asked. "Yes; you may see her," he replied, as he rang the bell. Then when the servant was gone he stopped me. "I love her too dearly to see her grieve," he said. "I hope you will show that you can be worthy of her." Then I made some sort of protestation and went upstairs. While I was with Mary there came a message to me, telling me to come to dinner.'

'The Boncassens are all dining here.'

'Then we shall be a family party. So far I suppose I may say it is settled. When he will let us marry heaven only knows. Mary declares that she will not press him. I certainly cannot do so. It is all a matter of money.'

'He won't care about that.'

'But he may perhaps think that a little patience will do us good. You will have to soften him.' Then Silverbridge told all that he knew about himself. He was to be married in May, was to go to Matching for a week or two after his wedding, was then to see the Session to an end, and after that to travel with his wife in the United States. 'I don't suppose we shall be allowed to run about the world together so soon as that,' said Tregear, 'but I am too well satisfied with my day's work to complain.'

'Did he say what he meant to give her?'

'Oh dear no;—nor even that he meant to give her anything. I should not dream of asking a question about it. Nor when he makes any proposition shall I think of having any opinion of my own.'

'He'll make it all right;—for her sake, you know.'

'My chief object as regards him, is that he should not think that I have been looking after her money. Well; good-bye. I suppose we shall all meet at dinner?'

When Tregear left him, Silverbridge went to his father's room. He was anxious that they should understand each other as to Mary's engagement.

'I thought you were at the House,' said the Duke.

'I was going there, but I met Tregear at the door. He tells me you have accepted him for Mary.'

'I wish that he had never seen her. Do you think that a man can be thwarted in everything and not feel it?'

'I thought—you had reconciled yourself—to Isabel.'

'If it were that alone I could do so the more easily, because person-ally she wins upon me. And this man, too;—it is not that I find fault with himself.'

'He is in all respects a high-minded gentleman.'

'I hope so. But yet, had he a right to set his heart there, where he could make his fortune,—having none of his own?'

'He did not think of that.'

'He should have thought of it. A man does not allow himself to love without any consideration or purpose. You say that he is a gentleman. A gentleman should not look to live on means brought to him by a wife. You say that he did not.'

'He did not think of it.'

'A gentleman should do more than not think of it. He should think that it shall not be so. A man should own his means or should earn them.'

'How many men, sir, do neither?'

'Yes; I know,' said the Duke. 'Such a doctrine nowadays is caviare to the general.* One must live as others live around one, I suppose. I could not see her suffer. It was too much for me. When I became convinced that this was no temporary passion, no romantic love which time might banish, that she was of such a temperament that she could not change,—then I had to give way. Gerald, I suppose, will bring me some kitchen-maid for his wife.'

'Oh, sir, you should not say that to me.'

'No;—I should not have said it to you. I beg your pardon, Silverbridge.' Then he paused a moment, turning over certain thoughts within his own bosom. 'Perhaps, after all, it is well that a pride of which I am conscious should be rebuked. And it may be that the rebuke has come in such a form that I should be thankful. I know that I can love Isabel.'

'That to me will be everything.'

'And this young man has nothing that should revolt me. I think he has been wrong. But now that I have said it I will let all that pass from me. He will dine with us to-day.'

Silverbridge then went up to see his sister. 'So you have settled your little business, Mary?'

'Oh, Silverbridge, you will wish me joy?'

'Certainly. Why not?'

'Papa is so stern with me. Of course he has given way, and of course I am grateful. But he looks at me as though I had done something to be forgiven.'

'Take the good the gods provide you, Mary. That will all come right.'

'But I have not done anything wrong. Have I?'

'That is a matter of opinion. How can I answer about you when I don't quite know whether I have done anything wrong or not myself? I am going to marry the girl I have chosen. That's enough for me.'

'But you did change.'

'We need not say anything about that.'

'But I have never changed. Papa just told me that he would consent, and that I might write to him. So I did write, and he came. But papa looks at me as though I had broken his heart.'

'I tell you what it is, Mary. You expect too much from him. He has not had his own way with either of us, and of course he feels it.'

As Tregear had said, there was quite a family party in Carlton Terrace, though as yet the family was not bound together by family ties. All the Boncassens were there, the father, the mother, and the promised bride. Mr Boncassen bore himself with more ease than any one in the company, having at his command a gift of manliness which enabled him to regard this marriage exactly as he would have done any other. America was not so far distant but what he would be able to see his girl occasionally. He liked the young man and he believed in the comfort of wealth. Therefore he was satisfied. But when the marriage was spoken of, or written of, as 'an alliance,' then he would say a hard word or two about dukes and lords in general. On such an occasion as this he was happy and at his ease.

So much could not be said for his wife, with whom the Duke attempted to place himself on terms of family equality. But in doing this he failed to hide the attempt even from her, and she broke down under it. Had he simply walked into the room with her as he would have done on any other occasion, and then remarked that the frost was keen or the thaw disagreeable, it would have been better for her. But when he told her that he hoped she would often make herself at home in that house, and looked, as he said it, as though he were asking her to take a place among the goddesses of Olympus, she was troubled as to her answer. 'Oh, my Lord Duke,' she said, 'when I think of Isabel living here and being called by such a name, it almost upsets me.'

Isabel had all her father's courage, but she was more sensitive; and though she would have borne her honours well, was oppressed by the feeling that the weight was too much for her mother. She could not keep her ear from listening to her mother's words, or her eye from watching her mother's motions. She was prepared to carry her mother everywhere. 'As other girls have to be taken with their belongings, so must I, if I be taken at all.' This she had said plainly enough. There should be no division between her and her mother. But still, knowing that her mother was not quite at ease, she was hardly at ease herself.

Silverbridge came in at the last moment, and of course occupied a chair next to Isabel. As the House was sitting, it was natural that he should come up in a flurry. 'I left Phineas,' he said, 'pounding away in his old style at Sir Timothy. By-the-bye, Isabel, you must come down some day and hear Sir Timothy badgered. I must be back again about ten. Well, Gerald, how are they all at Lazarus?'* He made an effort to be free and easy, but even he soon found that it was an effort.

Gerald had come up from Oxford for the occasion that he might make acquaintance with the Boncassens. He had taken Isabel in to dinner, but had been turned out of his place when his brother came in. He had been a little confused by the first impression made upon him by Mrs Boncassen, and had involuntarily watched his father. 'Silver is going to have an odd sort of a mother-in-law,' he said afterwards to Mary, who remarked in reply that this would not signify, as the mother-in-law would be in New York.

Tregear's part was very difficult to play. He could not but feel that though he had succeeded, still he was as yet looked upon askance. Silverbridge had told him that by degrees the Duke would be won round, but that it was not to be expected that he should swallow at once all his regrets. The truth of this could not but be accepted. The immediate inconvenience, however, was not the less felt. Each and everyone there knew the position of each and everyone;—but Tregear felt it difficult to act up to his. He could not play the well-pleased lover openly, as did Silverbridge. Mary herself was disposed to be very silent. The heart-breaking tedium of her dull life had been removed. Her determination had been rewarded. All that she had wanted had been granted to her, and she was happy. But she was not prepared to show off her happiness before others. And she was aware that she was thought to have done evil by introducing her lover into her august family.

But it was the Duke who made the greatest efforts, and with the least success. He had told himself again and again that he was bound by every sense of duty to swallow all regrets. He had taken himself to task on this matter. He had done so even out loud to his son. He had declared that he would 'let it all pass from him.' But who does not know how hard it is for a man in such matters to keep his word to himself? Who has not said to himself at the very moment of his own delinquency, 'Now,—it is now,—at this very instant of time, that I should crush, and quench, and kill the evil spirit within me; it is now that I should abate my greed, or smother my ill-humour, or abandon my hatred. It is now, and here, that I should drive out the fiend, as I have sworn to myself that I would do,'—and yet has failed?

That it would be done, would be done at last, by this man was very certain. When Silverbridge assured his sister that 'it would come all right very soon,' he had understood his father's character. But it could not be completed quite at once. Had he been required to take Isabel only to his heart, it would have been comparatively easy. There are men, who do not seem at first sight very susceptible to feminine attractions, who nevertheless are dominated by the grace of flounces, who succumb to petticoats unconsciously, and who are half in love with every woman merely for her womanhood. So it was with the Duke. He had given way in regard to Isabel with less than half the effort that Frank Tregear was likely to cost him.

'You were not at the House, sir,' said Silverbridge when he felt that there was a pause.

'No, not to-day.' Then there was a pause again.

'I think that we shall beat Cambridge this year to a moral,' said Gerald, who was sitting at the round table opposite to his father. Mr Boncassen, who was next to him, asked, in irony probably rather than in ignorance, whether the victory was to be achieved by mathematical or classical proficiency. Gerald turned and looked at him. 'Do you mean to say that you have never heard of the University boat-races?'

'Papa, you have disgraced yourself for ever,' said Isabel.

'Have I, my dear? Yes, I have heard of them. But I thought Lord Gerald's protestation was too great for a mere aquatic triumph.'

'Now you are poking your fun at me,' said Gerald.

'Well he may,' said the Duke sententiously. 'We have laid ourselves very open to having fun poked at us in this matter.'

'I think, sir,' said Tregear, 'that they are learning to do the same sort of thing at the American Universities.'

'Oh, indeed,' said the Duke in a solemn, dry, funereal tone. And then all the little life which Gerald's remark about the boat-race had produced, was quenched at once. The Duke was not angry with

Tregear for his little word of defence,—but he was not able to bring himself into harmony with this one guest, and was almost savage to him without meaning it. He was continually asking himself why Destiny had been so hard upon him as to force him to receive there at his table as his son-in-law a man who was distasteful to him. And he was endeavouring to answer the question, taking himself to task and telling himself that his destiny had done him no injury, and that the pride which had been wounded was a false pride. He was making a brave fight; but during the fight he was hardly fit to be the genial father and father-in-law of young people who were going to be married to one another. But before the dinner was over he made a great effort. 'Tregear,' he said,—and even that was an effort, for he had never hitherto mentioned the man's name without the formal Mister,—'Tregear, as this is the first time you have sat at my table, let me be old-fashioned, and ask you to drink a glass of wine with me.'

The glass of wine was drunk and the ceremony afforded infinite satisfaction at least to one person there. Mary could not keep herself from some expression of joy by pressing her finger for a moment against her lover's arm. He, though not usually given to such manifestations, blushed up to his eyes. But the feeling produced on the company was solemn rather than jovial. Everyone there understood it all. Mr Boncassen could read the Duke's mind down to the last line. Even Mrs Boncassen was aware that an act of reconciliation had been intended. 'When the governor drank that glass of wine it seemed as though half the marriage ceremony had been performed,' Gerald said to his brother that evening. When the Duke's glass was replaced on the table, he himself was conscious of the solemnity of what he had done, and was half ashamed of it.

When the ladies had gone upstairs the conversation became political and lively. The Duke could talk freely about the state of things to Mr Boncassen, and was able gradually to include Tregear in the badinage with which he attacked the Conservatism of his son. And so the half-hour passed well. Upstairs the two girls immediately came together, leaving Mrs Boncassen to chew the cud of the grandeur around her in the sleepy comfort of an arm-chair. 'And so everything is settled for both of us,' said Isabel.

'Of course I knew it was to be settled for you. You told me so at Custins.'

'I did not know it myself then. I only told you that he had asked me. And you hardly believed me.'

'I certainly believed you.'

'But you knew about—Lady Mabel Grex.'

'I only suspected something, and now I know it was a mistake. It has never been more than a suspicion.'

'And why, when we were at Custins, did you not tell me about yourself?'

'I had nothing to tell.'

'I can understand that. But is it not joyful that it should all be settled? Only poor Lady Mabel! You have got no Lady Mabel to trouble your conscience.' From which it was evident that Silverbridge had not told all.

## CHAPTER 75

### THE MAJOR'S STORY

BY the end of March Isabel was in Paris, whither she had forbidden her lover to follow her. Silverbridge was therefore reduced to the shifts of a bachelor's life, in which his friends seemed to think that he ought now to take special delight. Perhaps he did not take much delight in them. He was no doubt impatient to commence that steady married life for which he had prepared himself. But nevertheless, just at present, he lived a good deal at the Beargarden. Where was he to live? The Boncassens were in Paris, his sister was at Matching with a houseful of other Pallisers, and his father was again deep in politics.

Of course he was much in the House of Commons, but that also was stupid. Indeed everything would be stupid till Isabel came back. Perhaps dinner was more comfortable at the club than at the House. And then, as everybody knew, it was a good thing to change the scene. Therefore he dined at the club, and though he would keep his hansom and go down to the House again in the course of the evening, he spent many long hours at the Beargarden. 'There'll very soon be an end of this as far as you are concerned,' said Mr Lupton to him one evening as they were sitting in the smoking-room after dinner.

'The sooner the better as far as this place is concerned.'

'This place is as good as any other. For the matter of that I like the Beargarden since we got rid of two or three not very charming characters.'

'You mean my poor friend Tifto,' said Silverbridge.

'No;—I was not thinking of Tifto. There were one or two here who were quite as bad as Tifto. I wonder what has become of that poor devil?'

'I don't know in the least. You heard of that row about the hounds?'

'And his letter to you.'

'He wrote to me,—and I answered him, as you know. But whither he vanished, or what he is doing, or how he is living, I have not the least idea.'

'Gone to join those other fellows abroad, I should say. Among them they got a lot of money,—as the Duke ought to remember.'

'He is not with them,' said Silverbridge, as though he were in some degree mourning over the fate of his unfortunate friend.

'I suppose Captain Green was the leader in all that?'

'Now it is all done and gone I own to a certain regard for the Major. He was true to me till he thought I snubbed him. I would not let him go down to Silverbridge with me. I always thought that I drove the poor Major to his malpractices.'

At this moment Dolly Longstaff sauntered into the room and came up to them. It may be remembered that Dolly had declared his purpose of emigrating. As soon as he heard that the Duke's heir had serious thoughts of marrying the lady whom he loved he withdrew at once from the contest, but, as he did so, he acknowledged that there could be no longer a home for him in the country which Isabel was to inhabit as the wife of another man. Gradually, however, better thoughts returned to him. After all, what was she but a 'pert poppet'? He determined that marriage 'clips a fellow's wings confoundedly,' and so he set himself to enjoy life after his old fashion. There was perhaps a little swagger as he threw himself into a chair and addressed the happy lover. 'I'll be shot if I didn't meet Tifto at the corner of the street.'

'Tifto!'

'Yes, Tifto. He looked awfully seedy, with a greatcoat buttoned up to his chin, a shabby hat and old gloves.'

'Did he speak to you?' asked Silverbridge.

'No;—nor I to him. He hadn't time to think whether he would speak or not, and you may be sure I didn't.'

Nothing further was said about the man, but Silverbridge was uneasy and silent. When his cigar was finished he got up saying that he should go back to the House. As he left the club he looked about him as though expecting to see his old friend, and when he had passed through the first street and had got into the Haymarket there he was! The Major came up to him, touched his hat, asked to be allowed to say a few words. 'I don't think it can do any good,' said Silverbridge. The man had not attempted to shake hands with him, or affected familiarity; but seemed to be thoroughly humiliated. 'I don't think I can be of any service to you, and therefore I had rather decline.'

'I don't want you to be of any service, my Lord.'

'Then what's the good?'

'I have something to say. May I come to you to-morrow?'

Then Silverbridge allowed himself to make an appointment, and an hour was named at which Tifto might call in Carlton Terrace. He felt that he almost owed some reparation to the wretched man,—whom he had unfortunately admitted among his friends, whom he had used, and to whom he had been uncourteous. Exactly at the hour named the Major was shown into his room.

Dolly had said that he was shabby,—but the man was altered rather than shabby. He still had rings on his fingers and studs in his shirt, and a jewelled pin in his cravat;—but he had shaven off his moustache and the tuft from his chin, and his hair had been cut short, and in spite of his jewellery there was a hang-dog look about him. 'I've got something that I particularly want to say to you, my Lord.' Silverbridge would not shake hands with him, but could not refrain from offering him a chair.

'Well;—you can say it now.'

'Yes;—but it isn't so very easy to be said. There are some things, though you want to say them ever so, you don't quite know how to do it.'

'You have your choice, Major Tifto. You can speak or hold your tongue.'

Then there was a pause, during which Silverbridge sat with his hands in his pockets trying to look unconcerned. 'But if you've got it here, and feel it as I do,'—the poor man as he said this put his hand upon his heart,—'you can't sleep in your bed till it's out. I did that thing that they said I did.'

'What thing?'

'Why, the nail! It was I lamed the horse.'

'I am sorry for it. I can say nothing else.'

'You ain't so sorry for it as I am. Oh no; you can never be that, my Lord. After all, what does it matter to you?'

'Very little. I meant that I was sorry for your sake.'

'I believe you are, my Lord. For though you could be rough you was always kind. Now I will tell you everything, and then you can do as you please.'

'I wish to do nothing. As far as I am concerned the matter is over. It made me sick of horses, and I do not wish to have to think of it again.'

'Nevertheless, my Lord, I've got to tell it. It was Green who put me up to it. He did it just for the plunder. As God is my judge it was not for the money I did it.'

'Then it was revenge.'

'It was the devil got hold of me, my Lord. Up to that I had always been square,—square as a die! I got to think that your Lordship was upsetting. I don't know whether your Lordship remembers, but you did put me down once or twice rather uncommon.'

'I hope I was not unjust.'

'I don't say you was, my Lord. But I got a feeling on me that you wanted to get rid of me, and I all the time doing the best I could for the 'orses. I did do the best I could up to that very morning at Doncaster. Well;—it was Green put me up to it. I don't say I was to get nothing; but it wasn't so much more than I could have got by the 'orse winning. And I've lost pretty nearly all that I did get. Do you remember, my Lord,'—and now the Major sank his voice to a whisper,—'when I come up to your bedroom that morning?'

'I remember it.'

'The first time?'

'Yes; I remember it.'

'Because I came twice, my Lord. When I came first it hadn't been done. You turned me out.'

'That is true, Major Tifto.'

'You was very rough then. Wasn't you rough?'

'A man's bedroom is generally supposed to be private.'

'Yes, my Lord,—that's true. I ought to have sent your man in first. I came then to confess it all, before it was done.'

'Then why couldn't you let the horse alone?'

'I was in their hands. And then you was so rough with me! So I said to myself I might as well do it;—and I did it.'

'What do you want me to say? As far as my forgiveness goes, you have it!'

'That's saying a great deal, my Lord,—a great deal,' said Tifto, now in tears. 'But I ain't said it all yet. He's here; in London!'

'Who's here?'

'Green. He's here. He doesn't think that I know, but I could lay my hand on him to-morrow.'

'There is no human being alive, Major Tifto, whose presence or absence could be a matter of more indifference to me.'

'I'll tell you what I'll do, my Lord. I'll go before any judge, or magistrate, or police-officer in the country, and tell the truth. I won't ask even for a pardon. They shall punish me and him too. I'm in that state of mind that any change would be for the better. But he,—he ought to have it heavy.'

'It won't be done by me, Major Tifto. Look here, Major Tifto; you have come here to confess that you have done me a great injury?'

'Yes, I have.'

'And you say you are sorry for it.'

'Indeed I am.'

'And I have forgiven you. There is only one way in which you can show your gratitude. Hold your tongue about it. Let it be as a thing done and gone. The money has been paid. The horse has been sold. The whole thing has gone out of my mind, and I don't want to have it brought back again.'

'And nothing is to be done to Green!'

'I should say nothing,—on that score.'

'And he has got they say five-and-twenty thousand pounds clear money.'

'It is a pity, but it cannot be helped. I will have nothing further to do with it. Of course I cannot bind you, but I have told you my wishes.' The poor wretch was silent, but still it seemed as though he did not wish to go quite yet. 'If you have said what you have got to say, Major Tifto, I may as well tell you that my time is engaged.'

'And must that be all?'

'What else?'

'I am in such a state of mind, Lord Silverbridge, that it would be a satisfaction to tell it all, even against myself.'

'I can't prevent you.'

Then Tifto got up from his chair, as though he were going. 'I wish I knew what I was going to do with myself.'

'I don't know that I can help you, Major Tifto.'

'I suppose not, my Lord. I haven't twenty pounds left in all the world. It's the only thing that wasn't square that ever I did in all my life. Your Lordship couldn't do anything for me? We was very much together at one time, my Lord.'

'Yes, Major Tifto, we were.'

'Of course I was a villain. But it was only once; and your Lordship was so rough to me! I am not saying but what I was a villain. Think of what I did for myself by that one piece of wickedness! Master of hounds! member of the club! And the horse would have run in my name and won the Leger! And everybody knew as your Lordship and me was together in him!' Then he burst out into a paroxysm of tears and sobbing.

The young Lord certainly could not take the man into partnership again, nor could he restore to him either the hounds or his club,—or his clean hands. Nor did he know in what way he could serve the man, except by putting his hand into his pocket,—which he did. Tifto accepted the gratuity, and ultimately became an annual pensioner on his former noble partner, living on the allowance made him in some obscure corner of South Wales.

## CHAPTER 76

### ON DEPORTMENT

FRANK TREGEAR had come up to town at the end of February. He remained in London, with an understanding that he was not to see Lady Mary again till the Easter holidays. He was then to pay a visit to Matching, and to enter in, it may be presumed, on the full fruition of his advantages as accepted suitor. All this had been arranged with a good deal of precision,—as though there had still been a hope left that Lady Mary might change her mind. Of course there was no such hope. When the Duke asked the young man to dine with him, when he invited him to drink that memorable glass of wine, when the young man was allowed, in the presence of the Boncassens, to sit next Lady Mary, it was of course settled. But the father probably found some relief in yielding by slow degrees. 'I would rather that there should be no correspondence till then,' he had said both to Tregear and to his daughter. And they had promised there should be no correspondence. At Easter they would meet. After Easter Mary was to come up to London to be present at her brother's wedding, to which also Tregear had been formally invited; and it was hoped that then something might be settled as to their own marriage. Tregear, with the surgeon's permission, took his seat in Parliament. He was introduced by two leading Members on the Conservative side, but immediately afterwards found himself seated next to his friend Silverbridge on the top bench behind the ministers. The House was very full, as there was a feverish report abroad that Sir Timothy Beeswax intended to make a statement. No one quite knew what the statement was to be; but every politician in the House and out of it thought that he knew that the statement would be a bid for higher power on the part of Sir Timothy himself. If there had been dissensions in the Cabinet, the secret of them had been well kept. To Tregear who was not as yet familiar with the House there was no special appearance of activity; but Silverbridge could see that there was more than wonted animation. That the Treasury bench should be full at this time was a thing of custom. A whole broadside of questions would be fired off, one after another, like a rattle of musketry down the ranks, when as nearly as possible the report of each gun is made to follow close upon that of the gun before,—with this exception, that in such case each little sound is intended to be as like as possible to the preceding; whereas with the rattle of the questions and answers, each question and each answer becomes a little more authoritative and less courteous than the last. The Treasury bench was ready for its usual responsive firing, as the questioners were of course in their places. The opposition front bench was also crowded, and those behind were nearly equally full. There were many Peers in the gallery, and a general feeling of sensation prevailed. All this Silverbridge had been long enough in the House to appreciate;—but to Tregear the House was simply the House.

'It's odd enough we should have a row the very first day you come,' said Silverbridge.

'You think there will be a row?'

'Beeswax has something special to say. He's not here yet, you see. They've left about six inches for him there between Roper and Sir Orlando. You'll have the privilege of looking just down on the top of his head when he does come. I shan't stay much longer after that.'

'Where are you going?'

'I don't mean to-day. But I should not have been here now,—in this very place I mean,—but I want to stick to you just at first. I shall move down below the gangway; and not improbably creep over to the other side before long.'

'You don't mean it?'

'I think I shall. I begin to feel I've made a mistake.'

'In coming to this side at all?'

'I think I have. After all it is not very important.'

'What is not important? I think it very important.'

'Perhaps it may be to you, and perhaps you may be able to keep it up. But the more I think of it the less excuse I seem to have for deserting the old ways of the family. What is there in those fellows down there to make a fellow feel that he ought to bind himself to them neck and heels?'

'Their principles.'

'Yes, their principles! I believe I have some vague idea as to support-
ing property and land and all that kind of thing. I don't know that
anybody wants to attack anything.'

'Somebody soon would want to attack it if there were no defenders.'

'I suppose there is an outside power,—the people, or public opinion,
or whatever they choose to call it. And the country will have to go very
much as that outside power chooses. Here, in Parliament, everybody
will be as Conservative as the outside will let them. I don't think it matters on which side you sit;—but it does matter that you shouldn't have
to act with those who go against the grain with you.'

'I never heard a worse political argument in my life.'

'I dare say not. However, here's Sir Timothy. When he looks in that
way, all buckram,* deportment, and solemnity, I know he's going to
pitch into somebody.'

At this moment the Leader of the House came in from behind the
Speaker's chair and took his place between Mr Roper and Sir Orlando
Drought. Silverbridge had been right in saying that Sir Timothy's air
was solemn. When a man has to declare a solemn purpose on a solemn
occasion in a solemn place, it is needful that he should be solemn himself. And though the solemnity which befits a man best will be that
which the importance of the moment may produce, without thought
given by himself to his own outward person, still, who is there can
refrain himself from some attempt? Who can boast, who that has been
versed in the ways and duties of high places, that he has kept himself
free from all study of grace, of feature, of attitude, of gait—or even of
dress? For most of our bishops, for most of our judges, of our statesmen, our orators, our generals, for many even of our doctors and our
parsons, even our attorneys, our tax-gatherers, and certainly our but-
lers and our coachmen, Mr Turveydrop the great professor of deportment, has done much. But there should always be the art to underlie
and protect the art;—the art that can hide the art. The really clever
archbishop,—the really potent chief justice, the man who, as a politician, will succeed in becoming a king of men, should know how to
carry his buckram without showing it. It was in this that Sir Timothy
perhaps failed a little. There are men who look as though they were
born to wear blue ribbons. It has come, probably, from study, but it
seems to be natural. Sir Timothy did not impose on those who looked
at him as do these men. You could see a little of the paint, you could
hear the crumple of the starch and the padding; you could trace something of uneasiness in the would-be composed grandeur of the brow.
'Turveydrop!' the spectator would say to himself. But after all it may

be a question whether a man be open to reproach for not doing that well which the greatest among us,—if we could find one great enough,—would not do at all.

For I think we must hold that true personal dignity should be achieved,—must, if it be quite true, have been achieved,—without any personal effort. Though it be evinced, in part, by the carriage of the body, that carriage should be the fruit of the operation of the mind. Even when it be assisted by external garniture such as special clothes, and wigs, and ornaments, such garniture should have been prescribed by the sovereign or by custom, and should not have been selected by the wearer. In regard to speech a man may study all that which may make him suasive,* but if he go beyond that he will trench on those histrionic efforts which he will know to be wrong because he will be ashamed to acknowledge them. It is good to be beautiful, but it should come of God and not of the hairdresser. And personal dignity is a great possession; but a man should struggle for it no more than he would for beauty. Many, however, do struggle for it, and with such success that, though they do not achieve quite the real thing, still they get something on which they can bolster themselves up and be mighty.

Others, older men than Silverbridge, saw as much as did our young friend, but they were more complaisant and more reasonable. They, too, heard the crackle of the buckram, and were aware that the last touch of awe had come upon that brow just as its owner was emerging from the shadow of the Speaker's chair;—but to them it was a thing of course. A real Cæsar is not to be found every day, nor can we always have a Pitt to control our debates. That kind of thing, that last touch has its effect. Of course it is all paint,—but how would the poor girl look before the gaslights if there were no paint? The House of Commons likes a little deportment on occasions. If a special man looks bigger than you, you can console yourself by reflecting that he also looks bigger than your fellows. Sir Timothy probably knew what he was about, and did himself on the whole more good than harm by his little tricks.

As soon as Sir Timothy had taken his seat, Mr Rattler got up from the opposition bench to ask him some question on a matter of finance. The brewers were anxious about publican licences.* Could the Chancellor of the Exchequer say a word on the matter? Notice had of course been given, and the questioner had stated a quarter of an hour previously that he would postpone his query till the Chancellor of the Exchequer was in the House.

Sir Timothy rose from his seat, and in his blandest manner began by apologising for his late appearance. He was sorry that he had been prevented by public business from being in his place to answer the honourable gentleman's question in its proper turn. And even now, he feared that he must decline to give any answer which could be supposed to be satisfactory. It would probably be his duty to make a statement to the House on the following day,—a statement which he was not quite prepared to make at the present moment. But in the existing state of things he was unwilling to make any reply to any question by which he might seem to bind the government to any opinion. Then he sat down. And rising again not long afterwards, when the House had gone through certain formal duties, he moved that it should be adjourned till the next day. Then all the members trooped out, and with the others Tregear and Lord Silverbridge. 'So that is the end of your first day of Parliament,' said Silverbridge.

'What does it all mean?'

'Let us go to the Carlton and hear what the fellows are saying.'

On that evening both the young men dined at Mr Boncassen's house. Though Tregear had been cautioned not to write to Lady Mary, and though he was not to see her before Easter, still it was so completely understood that he was about to become her husband, that he was entertained in that capacity by all those who were concerned in the family. 'And so they will all go out,' said Mr Boncassen.

'That seems to be the general idea,' said the expectant son-in-law. 'When two men want to be first and neither will give way, they can't very well get on in the same boat together.' Then he expatiated angrily on the treachery of Sir Timothy, and Tregear in a more moderate way joined in the same opinion.

'Upon my word, young men, I doubt whether you are right,' said Mr Boncassen. 'Whether it can be possible that a man should have risen to such a position with so little patriotism as you attribute to our friend, I will not pretend to say. I should think that in England it was impossible. But of this I am sure, that the facility which exists here for a minister or ministers to go out of office without disturbance of the Crown, is a great blessing. You say the other party will come in.'

'That is most probable,' said Silverbridge.

'With us the other party never comes in,—never has a chance of coming in,—except once in four years, when the President is elected. That one event binds us all for four years.'

'But you do change your ministers,' said Tregear.

'A secretary may quarrel with the President, or he may have the gout, or be convicted of peculation.'*

'And yet you think yourselves more nearly free than we are.'

'I am not so sure of that. We have had a pretty difficult task, that of carrying on a government in a new country, which is nevertheless more populous than almost any old country. The influxions are so rapid, that every ten years the nature of the people is changed. It isn't easy; and though I think on the whole we've done pretty well, I am not going to boast that Washington is as yet the seat of a political Paradise.'

## CHAPTER 77

### 'MABEL, GOOD-BYE'

WHEN Tregear first came to town with his arm in a sling, and bandages all round him,—in order that he might be formally accepted by the Duke,—he had himself taken to one other house besides the house in Carlton Terrace. He went to Belgrave Square, to announce his fate to Lady Mabel Grex;—but Lady Mabel Grex was not there. The Earl was ill at Brighton, and Lady Mabel had gone down to nurse him. The old woman who came to him in the hall told him that the Earl was very ill;—he had been attacked by the gout, but in spite of the gout, and in spite of the doctors, he had insisted on being taken to his club. Then he had been removed to Brighton, under the doctor's advice, chiefly in order that he might be kept out of the way of temptation. Now he was supposed to be very ill indeed. 'My Lord is so imprudent!' said the old woman, shaking her old head in real unhappiness. For though the Earl had been a tyrant to everyone near him, yet when a poor woman becomes old it is something to have a tyrant to protect her. 'My Lord' always had been imprudent. Tregear knew that it had been the theory of my Lord's life that to eat and drink and die was better than to abstain and live. Then Tregear wrote to his friend as follows:

'MY DEAR MABEL,

'I am up in town again as you will perceive, although I am still in a helpless condition and hardly able to write even this letter. I called to-day and was very sorry to hear so bad an account of your father. Had I been able to travel I should have come down to you. When I am able I will do so if you would wish to see me. In the meantime pray tell me how he is, and how you are.

'My news is this. The Duke has accepted me. It is great news to me, and I hope will be acceptable to you. I do believe that if ever a friend has been anxious for a friend's welfare you have been anxious for mine,—as I have been and ever shall be for yours.

'Of course this thing will be very much to me. I will not speak now of my love for the girl who is to become my wife. You might again call me Romeo. Nor do I like to say much of what may now be pecuniary prospects. I did not ask Mary to become my wife because I supposed she would be rich. But I could not have married her or any one else who had not money. What are the Duke's intentions I have not the slightest idea, nor shall I ask him. I am to go down to Matching at Easter, and shall endeavour to have some time fixed. I suppose the Duke will say something about money. If he does not, I shall not.

'Pray write to me at once, and tell me when I shall see you.

'Your affectionate Cousin,

'F. O. TREGEAR.'

In answer to this there came a note in a very few words. She congratulated him,—not very warmly,—but expressed a hope that she might see him soon. But she told him not to come to Brighton. The Earl was better but very cross, and she would be up in town before long.

Towards the end of the month it became suddenly known in London that Lord Grex had died at Brighton. There was a Garter to be given away, and everybody was filled with regret that such an ornament to the Peerage should have departed from them. The Conservative papers remembered how excellent a politician he had been in his younger days, and the world was informed that the family of Grex of Grex was about the oldest in Great Britain of which authentic records were in existence. Then there came another note from Lady Mabel to Tregear. 'I shall be in town on the 31st in the old house, with Miss Cassewary, and will see you if you can come on the 1st. Come early, at eleven, if you can.'

On the day named and at the hour fixed he was in Belgrave Square. He had known this house since he was a boy, and could well remember how, when he first entered it, he had thought with some awe of the grandeur of the Earl. The Earl had then not paid much attention to him, but he had become very much taken by the grace and good-nature of the girl who had owned him as a cousin. 'You are my cousin Frank,' she had said; 'I am so glad to have a cousin.' He could remember the words now as though they had been spoken only yesterday. Then there had quickly grown to be friendship between him and this, as he thought, sweetest of all girls. At that time he had just gone to Eton; but before he left Eton they had sworn to love each other. And so it had been and the thing had grown, till at last, just when he had taken his degree, two matters had been settled between them; the first was that each loved the other irretrievably, irrevocably, passionately; the second, that it was altogether out of the question that they should ever marry each other.

It is but fair to Tregear to say that this last decision originated with the lady. He had told her that he certainly would hold himself engaged to marry her at some future time; but she had thrown this aside at once. How was it possible, she said, that two such beings, brought up in luxury, and taught to enjoy all the good things of the world, should expect to live and be happy together without an income? He offered to go to the bar;—but she asked him whether he thought it well that such a one as she should wait say a dozen years for such a process. 'When the time comes, I should be an old woman and you would be a wretched man.' She released him,—declared her own purpose of marrying well; and then, though there had been a moment in which her own assurance of her own love had been passionate enough, she went so far as to tell him that she was heart-whole. 'We have been two foolish children but we cannot be children any longer,' she said. 'There must be an end of it.'

What had hitherto been the result of this the reader knows,—and Tregear knew also. He had taken the privilege given to him, and had made so complete a use of it that he had in truth transferred his heart as well as his allegiance. Where is the young man who cannot do so;— how few are there who do not do so when their first fit of passion has come on them at one-and-twenty? And he had thought that she would do the same. But gradually he found that she had not done so, did not do so, could not do so! When she first heard of Lady Mary she had not reprimanded him,—but she could not keep herself from showing the bitterness of her disappointment. Though she would still boast of her own strength and of her own purpose, yet it was too clear to him that she was wounded and very sore. She would have liked him to remain single at any rate till she herself were married. But the permission had been hardly given before he availed himself of it. And then he talked to her not only of the brilliancy of his prospects,—which she could have forgiven,—but of his love—his love!

Then she had refused one offer after another, and he had known it all. There was nothing in which she was concerned that she did not tell him. Then young Silverbridge had come across her, and she had determined that he should be her husband. She had been nearly successful,—so nearly that at moments she had felt sure of success.

But the prize had slipped from her through her own fault. She knew well enough that it was her own fault. When a girl submits to play such a game as that, she should not stand on too nice scruples. She had told herself this many a time since;—but the prize was gone.

All this Tregear knew, and knowing it almost dreaded the coming interview. He could not without actual cruelty have avoided her. Had he done so before he could not have continued to do so now, when she was left alone in the world. Her father had not been much to her, but still his presence had enabled her to put herself before the world as being somebody. Now she would be almost nobody. And she had lost her rich prize, while he,—out of the same treasury as it were,—had won his!

The door was opened to him by the same old woman, and he was shown, at a funereal pace, up into the drawing-room which he had known so well. He was told that Lady Mabel would be down to him directly. As he looked about him he could see that already had been commenced that work of division of spoil which is sure to follow the death of most of us. Things were already gone which used to be familiar to his eyes, and the room, though not dismantled, had been deprived of many of its little prettinesses and was ugly.

In about ten minutes she came down to him,—with so soft a step that he would not have been aware of her entrance had he not seen her form in the mirror. Then, when he turned round to greet her, he was astonished by the blackness of her appearance. She looked as though she had become ten years older since he had last seen her. As she came up to him she was grave and almost solemn in her gait, but there was no sign of any tears. Why should there have been a tear? Women weep, and men too, not from grief, but from emotion. Indeed, grave and slow as was her step, and serious, almost solemn, as was her gait, there was something of a smile on her mouth as she gave him her hand. And yet her face was very sad, declaring to him too plainly something of the hopelessness of her heart. 'And so the Duke has consented,' she said. He had told her that in his letter, but, since that, her father had died, and she had been left, he did not as yet know how far impoverished, but, he feared, with no pleasant worldly prospects before her.

'Yes, Mabel;—that I suppose will be settled. I have been so shocked to hear all this.'

'It has been very sad;—has it not? Sit down, Frank. You and I have a good deal to say to each other now that we have met. It was no good your going down to Brighton. He would not have seen you, and at last I never left him.'

'Was Percival there?' She only shook her head. 'That was dreadful.'

'It was not Percival's fault. He would not see him; nor till the last hour or two would he believe in his own danger. Nor was he ever frightened for a moment,—not even then.'

'Was he good to you?'

'Good to me! Well;—he liked my being there. Poor papa! It had gone so far with him that he could not be good to any one. I think that he felt that it would be unmanly not to be the same to the end.'

'He would not see Percival.'

'When it was suggested he would only ask what good Percival could do him. I did send for him at last, in my terror, but he did not see his father alive. When he did come he only told me how badly his father had treated him! It was very dreadful!'

'I did so feel for you.'

'I am sure you did, and will. After all, Frank, I think that the pious godly people have the best of it in this world. Let them be ever so covetous, ever so false, ever so hard-hearted, the mere fact that they must keep up appearances, makes them comfortable to those around them. Poor papa was not comfortable to me. A little hypocrisy, a little sacrifice to the feelings of the world, may be such a blessing.'

'I am sorry that you should feel it so.'

'Yes; it is sad. But you;—everything is smiling with you! Let us talk about your plans.'

'Another time will do for that. I had come to hear about your own affairs.'

'There they are,' she said, pointing round the room. 'I have no other affairs. You see that I am going from here.'

'And where are you going?' She shook her head. 'With whom will you live?'

'With Miss Cass,—two old maids together! I know nothing further.'

'But about money? That is if I am justified in asking.'

'What would you not be justified in asking? Do you not know that I would tell you every secret of my heart,—if my heart had a secret? It seems that I have given up what was to have been my fortune. There was a claim of £12,000 on Grex. But I have abandoned it.'

'And there is nothing.'

'There will be scrapings they tell me,—unless Percival refuses to agree. This house is mortgaged, but not for its value. And there are some jewels. But all that is detestable,—a mere grovelling among mean hundreds; whereas you,—you will soar among——'

'Oh Mabel! do not say hard things to me.'

'No, indeed! why should I,—I who have been preaching that comfortable doctrine of hypocrisy? I will say nothing hard. But I would sooner talk of your good things than of my evil ones.'

'I would not.'

'Then you must talk about them for my sake. How was it that the Duke came round at last?'

'I hardly know. She sent for me.'

'A fine high-spirited girl. These Pallisers have more courage about them than *one* expects from their outward manner. Silverbridge has plenty of it.'

'I remember telling you he could be obstinate.'

'And I remember that I did not believe you. Now I know it. He has the sort of pluck which enables a man to break a girl's heart,—or to destroy a girl's hopes,—without wincing. He can tell a girl to her face that she can go to the—mischief for him. There are so many men who can't do that, from cowardice, though their hearts be ever so well inclined. "I have changed my mind." There is something great in the courage of a man who can say that to a woman in so many words. Most of them, when they escape, escape by lies and subterfuges. Or they run away and won't allow themselves to be heard of. They trust to a chapter of accidents, and leave things to arrange themselves. But when a man can look a girl in the face with those seemingly soft eyes, and say with that seemingly soft mouth,—"I have changed my mind,"— though she would look him dead in return if she could, still she must admire him.'

'Are you speaking of Silverbridge now?'

'Of course I am speaking of Silverbridge. I suppose I ought to hide it all and not to tell you. But as you are the only person I do tell, you must put up with me. Yes;—when I taxed him with his falsehood,— for he had been false,—he answered me with those very words! "I have changed my mind." He could not lie. To speak the truth was a necessity to him, even at the expense of his gallantry, almost of his humanity.'

'Has he been false to you, Mabel?'

'Of course he has. But there is nothing to quarrel about, if you mean that. People do not quarrel now about such things. A girl has to fight her own battle with her own pluck and her own wits. As with these weapons she is generally stronger than her enemy, she succeeds sometimes although everything else is against her. I think I am courageous, but his courage beat mine. I craned at the first fence. When he was willing to swallow my bait, my hand was not firm enough to strike the hook in his jaws. Had I not quailed then I think I should have— "had him".'

'It is horrid to hear you talk like this.' She was leaning over from her seat, looking, black as she was, so much older than her wont, with something about her of that unworldly serious thoughtfulness which a mourning garb always gives. And yet her words were so worldly, so unfeminine!

'I have got to tell the truth to somebody. It was so, just as I have said. Of course I did not love him. How could I love him after what has passed? But there need have been nothing much in that. I don't suppose that Dukes' eldest sons often get married for love.'

'Miss Boncassen loves him.'

'I dare say the beggar's daughter loved King Cophetua When you come to distances such as that, there can be love. The very fact that a man should have descended so far in quest of beauty,—the flattery of it alone,—will produce love. When the angels came after the daughters of men of course the daughters of men loved them. The distance between him and me is not great enough to have produced that sort of worship. There was no reason why Lady Mabel Grex should not be good enough wife for the son of the Duke of Omnium.'

'Certainly not.'

'And therefore I was not struck, as by the shining of a light from heaven. I cannot say I loved him. Frank,—I am beyond worshipping even an angel from heaven!'

'Then I do not know that you could blame him,' he said very seriously.

'Just so;—and as I have chosen to be honest I have told him everything. But I had my revenge first.'

'I would have said nothing.'

'You would have recommended—delicacy! No doubt you think that women should be delicate, let them suffer what they may. A woman should not let it be known that she has any human nature in her. I had him on the hip, and for a moment I used my power. He had certainly done me a wrong. He had asked for my love,—and with the delicacy which you commend, I had not at once grasped at all that such a request conveyed. Then, as he told me so frankly, "he changed his mind!" Did he not wrong me?'

'He should not have raised false hopes.'

'He told me that—he had changed his mind. I think I loved him then as nearly as ever I did,—because he looked me full in the face.

Then,—I told him I had never cared for him, and that he need have nothing on his conscience. But I doubt whether he was glad to hear it. Men are so vain! I have talked too much of myself. And so you are to be the Duke's son-in-law. And she will have hundreds of thousands.'

'Thousands perhaps, but I do not think very much about it. I feel that he will provide for her.'

'And that you, having secured her, can creep under his wing like an additional ducal chick. It is very comfortable. The Duke will be quite a Providence to you. I wonder that all young gentlemen do not marry heiresses;—it is so easy. And you have got your seat in Parliament too! Oh, your luck! When I look back upon it all it seems so hard to me! It was for you,—for you that I used to be anxious. Now it is I who have not an inch of ground to stand upon.' Then he approached her and put out his hand to her. 'No,' she said, putting both her hands behind her back, 'for God's sake let there be no tenderness. But is it not cruel? Think of my advantages at that moment when you and I agreed that our paths should be separate. My fortune then had not been made quite shipwreck by my father and brother. I had before me all that society could offer. I was called handsome and clever. Where was there a girl more likely to make her way to the top?'

'You may do so still.'

'No;—no;—I cannot. And you at least should not tell me so. I did not know then the virulence of the malady which had fallen on me. I did not know then that, because of you, other men would be abhorrent to me. I thought that I was as easy-hearted as you have proved yourself.'

'How cruel you can be.'

'Have I done anything to interfere with you? Have I said a word even to that young lad, when I might have said a word? Yes; to him I did say something; but I waited, and would not say it, while a word could hurt you. Shall I tell you what I told him? Just everything that has ever happened between you and me.'

'You did?'

'Yes;—because I saw that I could trust him. I told him because I wanted him to be quite sure that I had never loved him. But, Frank, I have put no spoke in your wheel. There has not been a moment since you told me of your love for this rich young lady in which I would not have helped you had help been in my power. Whomever I may have harmed, I have never harmed you.'

'Am I not as clear from blame towards you?'

'No. Frank. You have done me the terrible evil of ceasing to love me.'

'It was at your own bidding.'

'Certainly! but if I were to bid you to cut my throat, would you do it?'

'Was it not you who decided that we could not wait for each other?'

'And should it not have been for you to decide that you would wait?'

'You also would have married.'

'It almost angers me that you should not see the difference. A girl unless she marries becomes nothing, as I have become nothing now. A man does not want a pillar on which to lean. A man, when he has done as you had done with me, and made a girl's heart all his own, even though his own heart had been flexible and plastic as yours is, should have been true to her, at least for a while. Did it never occur to you that you owed something to me?'

'I have always owed you very much.'

'There should have been some touch of chivalry if not of love to make you feel that a second passion should have been postponed for a year or two. You could wait without growing old. You might have allowed yourself a little space to dwell—I was going to say on the sweetness of your memories. But they were not sweet, Frank; they were not sweet to you.'

'These rebukes, Mabel, will rob them of their sweetness,—for a time.'

'It is gone; all gone,' she said, shaking her head,—'gone from me because I have been so easily deserted; gone from you because the change has been so easy to you. How long was it, Frank, after you had left me before you were basking happily in the smiles of Lady Mary Palliser?'

'It was not very long, as months go.'

'Say days, Frank.'

'I have to defend myself, and I will do so with truth. It was not very long,—as months go; but why should it have been less long, whether for months or days? I had to cure myself of a wound.'

'To put a plaster on a scratch, Frank.'

'And the sooner a man can do that the more manly he is. Is it a sign of strength to wail under a sorrow that cannot be cured,—or of truth to perpetuate the appearance of a woe?'

'Has it been an appearance with me?'

'I am speaking of myself now. I am driven to speak of myself by the bitterness of your words. It was you who decided.'

'You accepted my decision easily.'

'Because it was based not only on my unfitness for such a marriage, but on yours. When I saw that there would be perhaps some years of misery for you, of course I accepted your decision. The sweetness had been very sweet to me.'

'Oh Frank, was it ever sweet to you?'

'And the triumph of it had been very great. I had been assured of the love of her who among all the high ones of the world seemed to me to be the highest. Then came your decision. Do you really believe that I could abandon the sweetness, that I could be robbed of my triumph, that I could think I could never again be allowed to put my arm round your waist, never again to feel your cheek close to mine, that I should lose all that had seemed left to me among the gods, without feeling it?'

'Frank, Frank!' she said, rising to her feet, and stretching out her hands as though she were going to give him back all these joys.

'Of course I felt it. I did not then know what was before me.' When he said this she sank back immediately upon her seat. 'I was wretched enough. I had lost a limb and could not walk; my eyes, and must always hereafter be blind; my fitness to be among men, and must always hereafter be secluded. It is so that a man is stricken down when some terrible trouble comes upon him. But it is given to him to retrick his beams.'

'You have retricked yours.'

'Yes;—and the strong man will show his strength by doing it quickly. Mabel, I sorrowed for myself greatly when that word was spoken, partly because I thought that your love could so easily be taken from me. And, since I have found that it has not been so, I have sorrowed for you also. But I do not blame myself, and—and I will not submit to have blame even from you.' She stared him in the face as he said this. 'A man should never submit to blame.'

'But if he has deserved it?'

'Who is to be the judge? But why should we contest this? You do not really wish to trample on me!'

'No;—not that.'

'Nor to disgrace me; nor to make me feel myself disgraced in my own judgment?' Then there was a pause for some moments as though he had left her without another word to say. 'Shall I go now?' he asked.

'Oh Frank!'

'I fear that my presence only makes you unhappy.'

'Then what will your absence do? When shall I see you again? But, no; I will not see you again. Not for many days,—not for years.

Why should I? Frank, is it wicked that I should love you?' He could only shake his head in answer to this. 'If it be so wicked that I must be punished for it eternally, still I love you. I can never, never, never love another. You cannot understand it. Oh God,—that I had never understood it myself! I think, I think, that I would go with you now anywhere, facing all misery, all judgments, all disgrace. You know, do you not, that if it were possible, I should not say so. But as I know that you would not stir a step with me, I do say so.'

'I know it is not meant.'

'It is meant, though it could not be done. Frank, I must not see her, not for awhile; not for years. I do not wish to hate her, but how can I help it? Do you remember when she flew into your arms in this room?'

'I remember it.'

'Of course you do. It is your great joy now to remember that, and such like. She must be very good! Though I hate her!'

'Do not say that you hate her, Mabel.'

'Though I hate her she must be good. It was a fine and a brave thing to do. I have done it; but never before the world like that; have I, Frank? Oh Frank, I shall never do it again. Go now, and do not touch me. Let us both pray that in ten years we may meet as passionless friends.' He came to her hardly knowing what he meant, but purposing, as though by instinct, to take her hand as he parted from her. But she, putting both her hands before her face, and throwing herself on to the sofa, buried her head among the cushions.

'Is there not to be another word?' he said. Lying as she did, she still was able to make a movement of dissent, and he left her, muttering just one word between his teeth, 'Mabel, good-bye.'

## CHAPTER 78

### THE DUKE RETURNS TO OFFICE

THAT farewell took place on the Friday morning. Tregear as he walked out of the Square knew now that he had been the cause of a great shipwreck. At first when that passionate love had been declared,—he could hardly remember whether with the fullest passion by him or by her,—he had been as a god walking upon air. That she who seemed to be so much above him should have owned that she was all his own seemed then to be world enough for him. For a few weeks he lived a hero to himself, and was able to tell himself that for him the glory of a passion was sufficient. In those halcyon moments no common human care is allowed to intrude itself. To one who has thus entered in upon the heroism of romance his own daily work, his dinners, clothes, income, father and mother, sisters and brothers, his own street and house are nothing. Hunting, shooting, rowing, Alpine-climbing, even speeches in Parliament,—if they perchance have been attained to,—all become leather or prunella.* The heavens have been opened to him, and he walks among them like a god. So it had been with Tregear. Then had come the second phase of his passion,—which is also not uncommon to young men who soar high in their first assaults. He was told that it would not do; and was not so told by a hard-hearted parent, but by the young lady herself. And she had spoken so reasonably, that he had yielded, and had walked away with that sudden feeling of a vile return to his own mean belongings, to his lodgings, and his income, which not a few ambitious young men have experienced. But she had convinced him. Then had come the journey to Italy, and the reader knows all the rest. He certainly had not derogated in transferring his affections,— but it may be doubted whether in his second love he had walked among the stars as in the first. A man can hardly mount twice among the stars. But he had been as eager,—and as true. And he had succeeded, without any flaw on his conscience. It had been agreed, when that first disruption took place, that he and Mabel should be friends; and, as to a friend, he had told her of his hopes. When first she had mingled something of sarcasm with her congratulations, though it had annoyed him, it had hardly made him unhappy. When she called him Romeo and spoke of herself as Rosaline, he took her remark as indicating some petulance rather than an enduring love. That had been womanly and he could forgive it. He had his other great and solid happiness to support him. Then he had believed that she would soon marry, if not Silverbridge, then some other fitting young nobleman, and that all would be well. But now things were very far from well. The storm which was now howling round her afflicted him much.

Perhaps the bitterest feeling of all was that her love should have been so much stronger, so much more enduring than his own. He could not but remember how in his first agony he had blamed her because she had declared that they should be severed. He had then told himself that such severing would be to him impossible, and that had her nature been as high as his, it would have been as impossible to her. Which nature must he now regard as the higher? She had done her best to rid herself of the load of her passion and had failed. But he had freed himself with convenient haste. All that he had said as to the manliness of conquering grief had been wise enough. But still he could not quit himself of some feeling of disgrace in that he had changed and she had not. He tried to comfort himself with reflecting that Mary was all his own,—that in that matter he had been victorious and happy;—but for an hour or two he thought more of Mabel than of Mary.

When the time came in which he could employ himself he called for Silverbridge, and they walked together across the park to Westminster. Silverbridge was gay and full of eagerness as to the coming ministerial statement, but Tregear could not turn his mind from the work of the morning. 'I don't seem to care very much about it,' he said at last.

'I do care very much,' said Silverbridge.

'What difference will it make?'

'I breakfasted with the governor this morning, and I have not seen him in such good spirits since——, well, for a long time.' The date to which Silverbridge would have referred, had he not checked himself, was that of the evening on which it had been agreed between him and his father that Mabel Grex should be promoted to the seat of highest honour in the house of Palliser,—but that was a matter which must henceforward be buried in silence. 'He did not say as much, but I feel perfectly sure that he and Mr Monk have arranged a new government.'

'I don't see any matter for joy in that to Conservatives like you and me.'

'He is my father,—and as he is going to be your father-in-law I should have thought that you might have been pleased.'

'Oh, yes;—if he likes it. But I have heard so often of the crushing cares of office, and I had thought that of all living men he had been the most crushed by them.'

All that had to be done in the House of Commons on that afternoon was finished before five o'clock. By half-past five the House, and all the purlieus of the House, were deserted. And yet at four, immediately after prayers, there had been such a crowd that members had been unable to find seats! Tregear and Silverbridge having been early had succeeded, but those who had been less careful were obliged to listen as best they could in the galleries. The stretching out of necks and the holding of hands behind the ears did not last long. Sir Timothy had not had much to say, but what he did say was spoken with a dignity which seemed to anticipate future exaltation rather than present downfall.

There had arisen a question in regard to revenue,—he need hardly tell them that it was that question in reference to brewers' licences to which the honourable gentleman opposite had alluded on the previous day,—as to which unfortunately he was not in accord with his noble friend the Prime Minister. Under the circumstances it was hardly possible that they should at once proceed to business, and he therefore moved that the House should stand adjourned till Tuesday next. That was the whole statement.

Not very long afterwards the Prime Minister made another statement in the House of Lords. As the Chancellor of the Exchequer had very suddenly resigned and had thereby broken up the Ministry, he had found himself compelled to place his resignation in the hands of her Majesty. Then that House was also adjourned. On that afternoon all the clubs were alive with admiration at the great cleverness displayed by Sir Timothy in this transaction. It was not only that he had succeeded in breaking up the Ministry, and that he had done this without incurring violent disgrace; but he had so done it as to throw all the reproach upon his late unfortunate colleague. It was thus that Mr Lupton explained it. Sir Timothy had been at the pains to ascertain on what matters connected with the Revenue, Lord Drummond,—or Lord Drummond's closest advisers,—had opinions of their own, opinions strong enough not to be abandoned; and having discovered that, he also discovered arguments on which to found an exactly contrary opinion. But as the Revenue had been entrusted specially to his unworthy hands, he was entitled to his own opinion on this matter. 'The majority of the House,' said Mr Lupton, 'and the entire public, will no doubt give him credit for great self-abnegation.'

All this happened on the Friday. During the Saturday it was considered probable that the Cabinet would come to terms with itself, and that internal wounds would be healed. The general opinion was that Lord Drummond would give way. But on the Sunday morning it was understood that Lord Drummond would not yield. It was reported that Lord Drummond was willing to purchase his separation from Sir Timothy even at the expense of his office. That Sir Timothy should give way seemed to be impossible. Had he done so it would have been impossible for him to recover the respect of the House. Then it was rumoured that two or three others had gone with Sir Timothy. And on Monday morning it was proclaimed that the Prime Minister was not in a condition to withdraw his resignation. On the Tuesday the House met and Mr Monk announced, still from the Opposition benches, that he had that morning been with the Queen. Then there was another adjournment, and all the Liberals knew that the gates of Paradise were again about to be opened to them.

This is only interesting to us as affecting the happiness and character of our Duke. He had consented to assist Mr Monk in forming a government, and to take office under Mr Monk's leadership. He had had many contests with himself before he could bring himself to this submission. He knew that if anything could once again make him contented it would be work; he knew that if he could serve his country it was his duty to serve it; and he knew also that it was only by the adhesion of such men as himself that the traditions of his party could be maintained. But he had been Prime Minister,—and he was sure he could never be Prime Minister again. There are in all matters certain little, almost hidden, signs, by which we can measure within our own bosoms the extent of our successes and our failures. Our Duke's friends had told him that his Ministry had been serviceable to the country; but no one had ever suggested to him that he would again be asked to fill the place which he had filled. He had stopped a gap. He would beforehand have declared himself willing to serve his country even in this way; but having done so,—having done that and no more than that,—he felt that he had failed. He had in his soreness declared to himself that he would never more take office. He had much to do to overcome this promise to himself;—but when he had brought himself to submit, he was certainly a happier man.

There was no going to see the Queen. That on the present occasion was done simply by Mr Monk. But on the Wednesday morning his name appeared in the list of the new Cabinet as President of the Council. He was perhaps a little fidgety, a little too anxious to employ himself and to be employed, a little too desirous of immediate work;— but still he was happy and gracious to those around him. 'I suppose you like that particular office,' Silverbridge said to him.

'Well; yes;—not best of all, you know,' and he smiled as he made this admission.

'You mean Prime Minister?'

'No, indeed I don't. I am inclined to think that the Premier should always sit in your House. No, Silverbridge. If I could have my way,— which is of course impossible, for I cannot put off my honours,—I would return to my old place. I would return to the Exchequer where the work is hard and certain, where a man can do, or at any rate attempt to do, some special thing. A man there if he sticks to that and does not travel beyond it, need not be popular, need not be a partisan, need not be eloquent, need not be a courtier. He should understand his profession, as should a lawyer or a doctor. If he does that thoroughly he can serve his country without recourse to that parliamentary strategy for which I know that I am unfit.'

'You can't do that in the House of Lords, sir.'

'No; no. I wish the title could have passed over my head, Silverbridge, and gone to you at once. I think we both should have been suited better. But there are things which one should not consider. Even in this place I may perhaps do something. Shall you attack us very bitterly?'

'I am the only man who does not mean to make any change.'

'How so?'

'I shall stay where I am,—on the Government side of the House.'

'Are you clear about that, my boy?'

'Quite clear.'

'Such changes should not be made without very much consideration.'

'I have already written to them at Silverbridge and have had three or four answers. Mr De Boung says that the borough is more than grateful. Mr Sprott regrets it much, and suggests a few months' consideration. Mr Spurgeon seems to think it does not signify.'

'That is hardly complimentary.'

'No,—not to me. But he is very civil to the family. As long as a Palliser represents the borough, Mr Sprugeon thinks that it does not matter much on which side he may sit. I have had my little vagary, and I don't think that I shall change again.'

'I suppose it is your republican bride-elect that has done that,' said the Duke, laughing.

# CHAPTER 79

## THE FIRST WEDDING

As Easter Sunday fell on the 17th April, and as the arrangement of the new Cabinet, with its inferior offices, was not completed till the 6th of that month, there was only just time for the new elections before the holidays. Mr Monk sat on his bench so comfortably that he hardly seemed ever to have been off it. And Phineas Finn resumed the peculiar ministerial tone of voice just as though he had never allowed himself to use the free and indignant strains of opposition. As to a majority,— nothing as yet was known about that. Some few besides Silverbridge might probably transfer themselves to the Government. None of the ministers lost their seats at the new elections. The opposite party seemed for a while to have been paralysed by the defection of Sir Timothy, and men who liked a quiet life were able to comfort themselves with the reflection that nothing could be done this session.

For our lovers this was convenient. Neither of them would have allowed their parliamentary energies to have interfered at such a crisis with his domestic affairs; but still it was well to have time at command. The day for the marriage of Isabel and Silverbridge had been now fixed. That was to take place on the Wednesday after Easter, and was to be celebrated by special royal favour in the chapel at Whitehall. All the Pallisers would be there, and all the relations of all the Pallisers, all the ambassadors, and of course all the Americans in London. It would be a 'wretched grind,' as Silverbridge said, but it had to be done. In the meantime the whole party, including the new President of the Council, were down at Matching. Even Isabel, though it must be presumed that she had much to do in looking after her bridal garments, was able to be there for a day or two. But Tregear was the person to whom this visit was of the greatest importance.

He had been allowed to see Lady Mary in London, but hardly to do more than see her. With her he had been alone for about five minutes, and then cruel circumstances,—circumstances, however, which were not permanently cruel,—had separated them. All their great difficulties had been settled, and no doubt they were happy. Tregear, though he had been as it were received into grace by that glass of wine, still had not entered into the intimacies of the house. This he felt himself. He had been told that he had better restrain himself from writing to Mary, and he had restrained himself. He had therefore no immediate opportunity of creeping into that perfect intimacy with the house and household which is generally accorded to a promised son-in-law.

On this occasion he travelled down alone, and as he approached the house he, who was not by nature timid, felt himself to be somewhat cowed. That the Duke should not be cold to him was almost impossible. Of course he was there in opposition to the Duke's wishes. Even Silverbridge had never quite liked the match. Of course he was to have all that he desired. Of course he was the most fortunate of men. Of course no man had ever stronger reason to be contented with the girl he loved. But still his heart was a little low as he was driven up to the door.

The first person whom he saw was the Duke himself, who, as the fly from the station arrived, was returning from his walk. 'You are welcome to Matching,' he said, taking off his hat with something of ceremony. This was said before the servants, but Tregear was then led into the study and the door was closed. 'I never do anything by halves, Mr Tregear,' he said. 'Since it is to be so you shall be the same to me as though you had come under other auspices. Of yourself personally I hear all that is good. Consider yourself at home here, and in all things use me as your friend.' Tregear endeavoured to make some reply, but could not find words that were fitting. 'I think that the young people are out,' continued the Duke. 'Mr Warburton will help you to find them if you like to go upon the search.' The words had been very gracious, but still there was something in the manner of the man which made Tregear find it almost impossible to regard him as he might have regarded another father-in-law. He had often heard the Duke spoken of as a man who could become awful if he pleased, almost without an effort. He had been told of the man's mingled simplicity, courtesy, and self-assertion against which no impudence or raillery could prevail. And now he seemed to understand it.

He was not driven to go under the private secretary's escort in quest of the young people. Mary had understood her business much better than that. 'If you please, sir, Lady Mary is in the little drawing-room,' said a well-arrayed young girl to him as soon as the Duke's door was closed. This was Lady Mary's own maid who had been on the look-out for the fly. Lady Mary had known all details, as to the arrival of the trains and the length of the journey from the station, and had not been walking with the other young people when the Duke had intercepted her lover. Even that delay she had thought was hard. The discreet maid opened the door of the little drawing-room,—and discreetly closed it instantly. 'At last!' she said, throwing herself into his arms.

'Yes,—at last.'

On this occasion time did not envy them. The long afternoons of spring had come, and as Tregear had reached the house between four and five they were able to go out together before the sun set. 'No,' she said when he came to inquire as to her life during the last twelve months; 'you had not much to be afraid of as to my forgetting.'

'But when everything was against me?'

'One thing was not against you. You ought to have been sure of that.'

'And so I was. And yet I felt that I ought not to have been sure. Sometimes, in my solitude, I used to think that I myself had been wrong. I began to doubt whether under any circumstances I could have been justified in asking your father's daughter to be my wife.'

'Because of his rank?'

'Not so much his rank as his money.'

'Ought that to be considered?'

'A poor man who marries a rich woman will always be suspected.'

'Because people are so mean and poor-spirited; and because they think that money is more than anything else. It should be nothing at all in such matters. I don't know how it can be anything. They have been saying that to me all along,—as though one were to stop to think whether one was rich or poor.' Tregear, when this was said, could not but remember that at a time not very much prior to that at which Mary had not stopped to think, neither for a while had he and Mabel. 'I suppose it was worse for me than for you,' she added.

'I hope not.'

'But it was, Frank; and therefore I ought to have it made up to me now. It was very bad to be alone here, particularly when I felt that papa always looked at me as though I were a sinner. He did not mean it, but he could not help looking at me like that. And there was nobody to whom I could say a word.'

'It was pretty much the same with me.'

'Yes; but you were not offending a father who could not keep himself from looking reproaches at you. I was like a boy at school who had been put into Coventry. And then they sent me to Lady Cantrip!'

'Was that very bad?'

'I do believe that if I were a young woman with a well-ordered mind, I should feel myself very much indebted to Lady Cantrip. She had a terrible task of it. But I could not teach myself to like her. I believe she knew all through that I should get my way at last.'

'That ought to have made you friends.'

'But yet she tried everything she could. And when I told her about that meeting up at Lord Grex's, she was so shocked! Do you remember that?'

'Do I remember it!'

'Were not you shocked?' This question was not to be answered by any word. 'I was,' she continued. 'It was an awful thing to do; but I was determined to show them all that I was in earnest. Do you remember how Miss Cassewary looked?'

'Miss Cassewary knew all about it.'

'I dare say she did. And so I suppose did Mabel Grex. I had thought that perhaps I might make Mabel a confidante, but——' Then she looked up into his face.

'But what?'.

'You like Mabel, do you not? I do.'

'I like her very, very much.'

'Perhaps you have liked her too well for that, eh, Frank?'

'Too well for what?'

'That she should have heard all that I had to say about you with sympathy. If so, I am so sorry.'

'You need not fear that I have ever for a moment been untrue either to her or you.'

'I am sure you have not to me. Poor Mabel! Then they took me to Custins. That was worst of all. I cannot quite tell you what happened there.' Of course he asked her,—but, as she had said, she could not quite tell him about Lord Popplecourt.

The next morning the Duke asked his guest in a playful tone what was his Christian name. It could hardly be that he should not have known, but yet he asked the question. 'Francis Oliphant,' said Tregear. 'Those are two Christian names I suppose, but what do they call you at home?'

'Frank,' whispered Mary, who was with them.

'Then I will call you Frank, if you will allow me. The use of Christian names is, I think, pleasant and hardly common enough among us. I almost forget my own boy's name because the practice has grown up of calling him by a title.'

'I am going to call him Abraham,' said Isabel.

'Abraham is a good name, only I do not think he got it from his god-fathers and godmothers.'

'Who can call a man Plantagenet? I should as soon think of calling my father-in-law Cœur de Lion.'

'So he is,' said Mary. Whereupon the Duke kissed the two girls and went his way,—showing that by this time he had adopted the one and the proposed husband of the other into his heart.

The day before the Duke started for London to be present at the grand marriage he sent for Frank. 'I suppose,' said he, 'that you would wish that some time should be fixed for your own marriage.' To this the accepted suitor of course assented. 'But before we can do that something must be settled about—money.' Tregear when he heard this became hot all over, and felt that he could not restrain his blushes. Such must be the feeling of a man when he finds himself compelled to own to a girl's father that he intends to live upon her money and not upon his own. 'I do not like to be troublesome,' continued the Duke, 'or to ask questions which might seem to be impertinent.'

'Oh no! Of course I feel my position. I can only say that it was not because your daughter might probably have money that I first sought her love.'

'It shall be so received. And now—— But perhaps it will be best that you should arrange all this with my man of business. Mr Moreton shall be instructed. Mr Moreton lives near my place in Barsetshire, but is now in London. If you will call on him he shall tell you what I would suggest. I hope you will find that your affairs will be comfortable. And now as to the time.'

Isabel's wedding was declared by the newspapers to have been one of the most brilliant remembered in the metropolis. There were six bridesmaids, of whom of course Mary was one,—and of whom poor Lady Mabel Grex was equally of course not another. Poor Lady Mabel was at this time with Miss Cassewary at Grex, paying what she believed would be a last visit to the old family home. Among the others were two American girls, brought into that august society for the sake of courtesy rather than of personal love. And there were two other Palliser girls and a Scotch McCloskie cousin. The breakfast was of course given by Mr Boncassen at his house in Brook Street, where the bridal presents were displayed. And not only were they displayed; but a list of them, with an approximating statement as to their value, appeared in one or two of the next day's newspapers;—as to which terrible sin against good taste neither was Mr or Mrs Boncassen guilty. But in these days, in which such splendid things were done on so very splendid a scale, a young lady cannot herself lay out her friends' gifts so as to be properly seen by her friends. Some well-skilled, well-paid hand is needed even for that, and hence comes this public information on affairs which should surely be private. In our grandmothers' time the happy bride's happy mother herself compounded the cake;—or at any rate the trusted housekeeper. But we all know that terrible tower of silver which now stands niddle-noddling with its appendages of flags and spears on the modern wedding breakfast-table. It will come to pass with some of us soon that we must deny ourselves the pleasure of having young friends, because their marriage presents are so costly.

Poor Mrs Boncassen had not perhaps a happy time with her august guests on that morning; but when she retired to give Isabel her last kiss in privacy she did feel proud to think that her daughter would some day be an English Duchess.

## CHAPTER 80

### THE SECOND WEDDING

NOVEMBER is not altogether an hymeneal month, but it was not till November that Lady Mary Palliser became the wife of Frank Tregear. It was postponed a little, perhaps, in order that the Silverbridges,—as they were now called,—might be present. The Silverbridges, who were now quite Darby and Joan, had gone to the States when the Session had been brought to a close early in August, and had remained there nearly three months. Isabel had taken infinite pleasure in showing her English husband to her American friends, and the American friends had no doubt taken a pride in seeing so glorious a British husband in the hands of an American wife. Everything was new to Silverbridge, and he was happy in his new possession. She too enjoyed it infinitely, and so it happened that they had been unwilling to curtail their sojourn. But in November they had to return, because Mary had declared that her marriage should be postponed till it could be graced by the presence of her elder brother.

The marriage of Silverbridge had been august. There had been a manifest intention that it should be so. Nobody knew with whom this originated. Mrs Boncassen had probably been told that it ought to be so, and Mr Boncassen had been willing to pay the bill. External forces had perhaps operated. The Duke had simply been passive and obedient. There had however been a general feeling that the bride of the heir of the house of Omnium should be produced to the world amidst a blare of trumpets and a glare of torches. So it had been. But both the Duke and Mary were determined that this other wedding should be different. It was to take place at Matching, and none would be present but they who were staying in the house, or who lived around,—such as tenants and dependants. Four clergymen united their forces to tie Isabel to her husband, one of whom was a bishop, one a canon, and the two others royal chaplains; but there was only to be the Vicar of the parish at Matching. And indeed there were no guests in the house except the two bridesmaids and Mr and Mrs Finn. As to Mrs Finn, Mary had made a request, and then the Duke had suggested that the husband should be asked to accompany his wife.

It was very pretty. The church itself is pretty, standing in the park, close to the ruins of the old Priory, not above three hundred yards from the house. And they all walked, taking the broad pathway through the ruins, going under that figure of Sir Guy which Silverbridge had pointed out to Isabel when they had been whispering there together. The Duke led the way with his girl upon his arm. The two bridesmaids followed. Then Silverbridge and his wife, with Phineas and his wife. Gerald and the bridegroom accompanied them, belonging as it were to the same party! It was very rustic;—almost improper! 'This is altogether wrong, you know,' said Gerald. 'You should appear coming from some other part of the world, as if you were almost unexpected. You ought not to have been in the house at all, and certainly should have gone under some disguise.'

There had been rich presents too on this occasion, but they were shown to none except to Mrs Finn and the bridesmaids,—and perhaps to the favoured servants in the house. At any rate there was nothing said of them in the newspapers. One present there was,—given not to the bride but to the bridegroom,—which he showed to no one except to her. This came to him only on the morning of his marriage, and the envelope containing it bore the postmark of Sedbergh. He knew the handwriting well before he opened the parcel. It contained a small signet-ring with his crest, and with it there were but a few words written on a scrap of paper. 'I pray that you may be happy. This was to have been given to you long ago, but I kept it back because of that decision.' He showed the ring to Mary and told her it had come from Lady Mabel;—but the scrap of paper no one saw but himself.

Perhaps the matter most remarkable in the wedding was the hilarity of the Duke. One who did not know him well might have said that he was a man with few cares, and who now took special joy in the happiness of his children,—who was thoroughly contented to see them marry after their own hearts. And yet, as he stood there on the altar-steps giving his daughter to that new son and looking first at his girl, and then at his married son, he was reminding himself of all that he had suffered.

After the breakfast,—which was by no means a grand repast and at which the cake did not look so like an ill-soldered silver castle as that other construction had done,—the happy couple were sent away in a modest chariot to the railway station, and not above half-a-dozen slippers were thrown after them. There were enough for luck,—or perhaps there might have been luck even without them, for the wife thoroughly respected her husband, as did the husband his wife. Mrs Finn, when she was alone with Phineas, said a word or two about Frank Tregear. 'When she first told me of her engagement I did not think it possible that she should marry him. But after he had been with me I felt sure that he would succeed.'

'Well, sir,' said Silverbridge to the Duke when they were out together in the park that afternoon, 'what do you think about him?'

'I think he is a manly young man.'

'He is certainly that. And then he knows things and understands them. It was never a surprise to me that Mary should have been so fond of him.'

'I do not know that one ought to be surprised at anything. Perhaps what surprised me most was that he should have looked so high. There seemed to be so little to justify it. But now I will accept that as courage which I before regarded as arrogance.'*

# APPENDIX

## THE CHRONOLOGY AND POLITICAL CONTEXTS
## OF THE PALLISER NOVELS

### (i) The internal chronology of the series

TROLLOPE'S Palliser series is rightly seen as one of the greatest English examples of the *roman fleuve*, or group of novels written as an extended narrative sequence. But Trollope did not conceive or plan these books as a sequence. Rather, they became a series gradually, one following another as opportunity and inspiration suggested.

Nor were they written and published consecutively. Trollope published six novels with other topics between *Can You Forgive Her?* (1864–5) and *Phineas Finn, the Irish Member* (1867–9), and five between that and *The Eustace Diamonds* (1871–3). Though this was immediately followed by *Phineas Redux* (1873–4), he produced three novels of other kinds between that book and *The Prime Minister* (1875–6), and two more before starting work on the last novel in the series, *The Duke's Children*, in 1876. In retrospect, he clearly came to think of them as linked. He referred in his *Autobiography* to 'a series of semi-political tales' (not including *Can You Forgive Her?*), and, in a letter written to Henry Howard in 1881, to a 'series of novels' (not including *The Eustace Diamonds*) about 'the family of the Pallisers'. But the books were never published as a named sequence in his lifetime.

As a consequence, though each individual novel is chronologically coherent, the time scheme of the sequence as a whole is a muddle. Trollope introduced Plantagenet Palliser, as a minor character of 'about five-and-twenty years of age', in the 'Barsetshire' novel, *The Small House at Allington* (1862–4). The action here takes place over a period of two years explicitly identified as being in the 1860s ('186—'). Palliser meets and becomes engaged to Lady Glencora in the summer of the second year. Since Trollope began writing the book in 1862, and uses the past tense, it would be reasonable to assume that the years in question were 1860 and 1861.

This sense of immediate, or very recent, contemporaneity would have pleased readers who liked their novels to be modern in setting. The starting date does not, however, allow time for the rest of Palliser's career. By Chapter 72 of *The Prime Minister*, he is 46. Twenty-one years seems a reasonable period in which a man might marry, have four children (the eldest now in his mid- or late teens), serve in Parliament in opposition (twice) and government (three times), rise to Cabinet rank, and spend three years as prime minister. Unfortunately, twenty-one years from 1861 takes us to 1882: eight years after the composition of the novel, and six years after publication. Uneasily aware of this difficulty, Trollope covered his tracks with some contradictory information. In Chapter 62 of *The Prime Minister*, supposedly a year before Palliser's forty-sixth birthday, we are told that Lady Glencora has known him for 'fifteen years'. Since she first met him in *The Small House at Allington* in 1861, this takes us to 1876, makes him 40, and reduces the extent to which the action has been allowed to slip into the future. But it makes his crowded political career improbably rapid and allows too few years for the time schemes of the intervening novels.

In Chapter 20 of *Phineas Redux* we are, for once, given an entirely explicit date, when the unhappy Laura Kennedy heads her letter from Dresden, 'Feb. 8, 1870'. On this basis, there have been nine years since the Palliser engagement of 1861, during which time the events of *Can You Forgive Her?* (three years), *Phineas Finn* (five years), *The Eustace Diamonds* (four years), and the first year of the plot of *Phineas Redux* itself are all supposed to have taken place. There may be an overlap between *Phineas Finn* and *The Eustace Diamonds*. But, on the other hand, there have also been intervals between the novels, in which the Tory administrations of, first, De Terrier and Daubeny and, then, Daubeny by himself are supposed to have taken place. Allowing a mere year for each of these governments would cancel out some of the overlap and give us eleven or twelve years of sequential action in a nine-year time span.

The internal chronology of each individual novel is, by contrast, clear enough. The story told in *Can You Forgive Her?*, for example, occupies three years, from the June of the first year to the April of the last, and these periods can sometimes be linked to an external time scheme by references to contemporary phenomena. Thus, in the first year of *Can You Forgive Her?*, Lady Glencora appears to have been reading Lucy Atkinson's *Recollections of the Tartar Steppes* (1863). But Trollope is not consistent about such details. Though Lucy Atkinson's book was in print while Trollope was writing his novel, it would not have been available to his characters two or three years before.

The use of the perpetual calendar to assign dates such as 'Monday, June 5' to a particular year is also untrustworthy. There are five of these in *The Eustace Diamonds* and four of them confirm the years in which the action seems principally to be set: 1865 and 1866. The fifth does not: 'Wednesday, the 5th of November' (Chapter 37), though supposed to occur in 1865, occurred in 1862. In *Phineas Redux*, in the year for which he gives us the explicit date of 1870 (Chapter 20), Trollope also supplies a 'Wednesday, 19th May' (Chapter 54) which belongs to 1869. Even if one overlooks such local slips, the time scheme of the series as a whole remains elusive.

The problem is that Trollope's realism does not allow for the convenient vagueness employed by (for example) Dickens. His account of the manners, morals, and preoccupations of English society is precise in ways which involve the identification of decades ('186—'), and occasionally even a particular year. A better parallel than Dickens might be the famous 'double time scheme' of Shakespeare's play *Othello*. Here, two different clocks seem to be running simultaneously. According to one, the principal action of the play takes place in less than forty-eight hours. According to the other, it involves months of life in Cyprus, without which there would have been no opportunity for the alleged affair between Desdemona and Cassio. Audiences unconsciously accept both time schemes, enjoying the tragic intensity of the rapid action while also requiring the verisimilitude of the slow one.

Trollope, similarly, has two clocks running in the Palliser series, one of which takes us through the 1860s and 1870s in twenty years, the other of which requires at least twenty-three years to cover the same ground. More precisely, he turns the clock back at the beginning of *Phineas Finn* to give himself (in one time scheme at least) the extra years which he now knows he needs, but had neglected to provide in *The Small House at Allington*. There, and in *Can You Forgive Her?*, the Prime Minister is a Whig, Lord Brock, who resembles Palmerston. But at the beginning of *Phineas Finn* there is a Tory administration, led by De Terrier and Daubeny. This sounds like the Conservative government of 1858–9, led by Derby and Disraeli. As such, it gives the impression that the action of *The Small House at Allington* and *Can You Forgive Her?* had somehow taken place, not during Palmerston's second premiership (1859–65), but during the first one (1855–8), thus providing the extra years required for what Trollope, at this stage, was beginning to think of as a Palliser series.

With the stated starting date of 1861 for Palliser's story, a three-year plot in *Can You Forgive Her?*, and a year for the Tory government of De Terrier and Daubeny, the action of *Phineas Finn* would be set in the five years 1866–71. This is too late, both for the period of composition (1866–7), and for the Reform Bill debates with which it is concerned. With a new, implicit starting date for the series in the late 1850s, *Phineas Finn* can take place between 1863 and 1867. We thereby get, more or less correctly, to that date of 'Feb. 8, 1870' in the second year of the plot of *Phineas Redux*, and from there can trace our way without much trouble to the mid- and late 1870s for *The Prime Minister* and *The Duke's Children*. The past tense of that final novel was not, strictly speaking, appropriate during the process of composition (May to October 1876). It had, however, become so by the time of its delayed publication in 1879–80.

This remains a double time scheme, rather than the substitution of one time scheme for another. The new dating is present only by implication, and Trollope did not change the chronological references in later editions of his earlier novels. He did not, of course, expect his original readers to go back and check them either. If the impression can be given that the Palliser narrative has somehow resumed, at the beginning of *Phineas Finn*, in 1863 rather than 1866, then so much the better. The contradictory accounts, in *The Prime Minister*, of the time that has passed since Palliser first met Glencora could, in this sense, be taken as a graceful acknowledgement of a sleight of hand.

Critics who believe that Trollope was a slipshod writer will see this duplicity as a confirmation of their views. Most readers will find it a satisfactory rectification of a mistake made before he had decided to turn Palliser's story into a *roman fleuve*. But, however ingeniously he handles it, the double time scheme does present problems for a comparison between the political narrative of the Palliser series and the real political history of the age. Which year, after all, is one comparing with which? The best answer may be to accept the implicit rewinding of the clock at the beginning of *Phineas Finn* and to assume that the action of the series runs from 1859 (in *Can You Forgive Her?*) to 1879 (in *The Duke's Children*). The resulting chronology is not flawless. There is only just enough time for Phineas Finn's first marriage and spell in Ireland as a Poor Law inspector, and Palliser is still a few years short of 46 at the end of *The Prime Minister*. But the actions of the successive stories can, on this basis, occur sequentially, and can do so while providing the necessary gaps for four periods of Tory government. Trollope was a realistic novelist, not a historian, and what he offers is broadly correct rather than minutely precise. When, in Chapter 45 of *Phineas Redux*, he remarks that the events of *The Eustace Diamonds* took place 'but a year or two since', he is indicating the degree of exactitude which we can, at the margins, reasonably expect.

### (ii) The external chronology of the Palliser series

These assumptions suggest the chronology on pp. 512–13. Broad parallels here between fictitious and real events, especially in the middle of the series, have led some critics to stress the topicality of the Palliser novels. When Phineas becomes Under-Secretary for the Colonies, for example, in the third year of *Phineas Finn* (1865, in this time scheme), he works on Canadian issues. This is just what his real equivalent would have been doing in the mid-1860s. The American Civil War and the British North America Act made Canada the main foreign policy issue of the period. More substantially, the Second Reform Bill would be both the central concern of British political life in 1866–7 and the key political topic of *Phineas Finn*. Though the internal chronology of the series requires the fictitious Reform Bill debates to be set back slightly into the years 1864–5, Trollope was writing this novel as the real political events unfolded, and presenting a version of them in his story.

At times Trollope is so anxious to locate his fictions in a realistic contemporary setting that he contradicts his own previous novels. Thus, in Chapter 5 of *Phineas Redux*, we are told that the Second Reform Bill has been passed by a Tory government (as, in reality, it was), despite the fact that in *Phineas Finn* it had just been carried by the Whigs. Trollope masks this discrepancy by stressing the 'household suffrage' quality of the Tory Reform Bill, making it possible for readers to believe that the Tory measure had somehow augmented a Whig Bill, rather than defeating and replacing it. Here the wish for topicality and verisimilitude takes precedence over the need for consistency between one novel and another. The incidental detail, too, is often current or very recent. Noting that *Phineas Finn* 'is casually sown with topical references to events of 1865–7', John Sutherland argues that the context is 'recognizably contemporary', and that, 'there is no more misleading remark about the novel than Lord David Cecil's . . . that "if we were wafted suddenly back to 1840, we should find . . . the world of *Phineas Finn*" '.

'1840' is an overstatement. But there remains some truth in A. O. J. Cockshut's less extreme claim that, in the political novels, 'Trollope the recorder of tradition looks back'. Despite the topical allusions to political events of the 1860s and 1870s, in other words, the underlying political culture of the Palliser novels belongs to the 1850s. The most obvious symptom of this is instability. In Trollope's fictional world there are no fewer than ten governments between 1859 and 1879 (Whig, Tory, Whig/Liberal, Tory, Liberal, Tory, Coalition, Liberal, Tory, and then Liberal again). In reality there were four. Rather than reflecting the new politics of the 1860s and 1870s, Trollope is remembering a previous decade in which there had been five governments between 1852 and 1859.

The political instability of the 1850s had several causes. One was the fact that party discipline had not yet taken its familiar, modern form. Another was the Tory split over the repeal of the Corn Laws in 1846. Anxious to bring food into the country at the time of the Irish Famine, Peel had led the party of Church, Crown, and Land into an abolition of agricultural protection. The Tories divided into Peelites and Protectionists. As a result, the Whigs became the natural party of government, though only because they could find support from other parliamentary groups (Peelites, Radicals, and Irish members) in ways in which the Protectionist Tories could not.

This meant that politics in the 1850s was an unstable process of temporary agreements and awkward alliances. At its most extreme, it led to the creation of the only true coalition ministry between 1783 and 1895: Lord Aberdeen's Peelite and Whig government of 1852–5. The coalition led by the Duke of Omnium in *The Prime Minister* (in the fictional years 1873–5) is, of course, a version of this episode from the politics of the early 1850s, not an image of events twenty years later. When the Aberdeen coalition fell, there was a brief Whig ministry, followed by an even briefer Tory one. Tired of such uncertainty, Whigs, Peelites, and Radicals met in Willis's Rooms in June 1859 to create what would come to be known as the Liberal Party. Thereafter British politics settled back into a more or less stable, two-party system.

With hindsight not available to Trollope, it is easy now to see the ways in which political culture changed in the 1860s. Parliamentary parties were evolving into national parties, with proper membership organizations. Governments ceased to be hybrid. Party leaders who had previously needed merely to command the confidence of a majority in the House, became figures who required a wide, popular appeal, and sought it on the stump and in the press. This would be the age of Gladstone and Disraeli, star performers who led alternating but relatively long-lasting administrations. Trollope, whose view of politics had been formed in the 1850s, was slow to recognize these developments. In *The Duke's Children* he remarks, correctly, that 'There had of late been a great Conservative reaction in the country'

| Year | Internal time-scheme 1 | Internal time-scheme 2 | |
|------|------------------------|------------------------|---|
| 1846–52 | | | |
| 1852 | | | |
| 1852–5 | | | |
| 1855 | | | |
| 1856 | | | |
| 1857 | | *The Small House at Allington* | |
| 1858 | | | |
| 1859 | | *Can You Forgive Her?* | |
| 1860 | *The Small House at Allington* | | |
| 1861 | | | |
| 1862 | *Can You Forgive Her?* | | |
| 1863 | | *Phineas Finn (1863–7)* | *The Eustace Diamonds (1863–6)* |
| 1864 | | | |
| 1865 | | | |
| 1866 | | | |
| 1867 | | | |
| 1868 | | | |
| 1869 | | *Phineas Redux* | |
| 1870 | | | |
| 1871 | | | |
| 1872 | | | |
| 1873 | | *The Prime Minister* | |
| 1874 | | | |
| 1875 | | | |
| 1876 | | | |
| 1877 | | | |
| 1878 | | *The Duke's Children* | |
| 1879 | | | |

| Fictional political events | Real political events | Year |
|---|---|---|
| | Whig government (Russell) | 1846–52 |
| | Tory government (Derby) | 1852 |
| | Aberdeen coalition | 1852–5 |
| Whig government (Brock) | Whig government (Palmerston) | 1855 |
| | | 1856 |
| | | 1857 |
| | Tory government (Derby & Disraeli) | 1858 |
| | | 1859 |
| | Whig/Liberal government (Palmerston then Russell) | 1860 |
| 1861: Palliser: Chancellor of the Exchequer | | 1861 |
| Tory government (De Terrier & Daubeny) | | 1862 |
| Whig/Liberal government (Mildmay then Gresham) Palliser: Chancellor of the Exchequer | | 1863 |
| 1864: First attempt at Whig Reform Bill fails | | 1864 |
| 1865 (Aug.) Second attempt at Whig Reform Bill amended but passed | | 1865 |
| | Whig Reform Bill fails | 1866 |
| | Tory government (Derby & Disraeli) 1867: Tory Reform Bill passed | 1867 |
| Tory government (Daubeny) | | 1868 |
| | Liberal government (Gladstone) Church of Ireland disestablished | 1869 |
| 1870: Tory bill to disestablish Church of England fails. 1870: Palliser becomes Duke of Omnium. | | 1870 |
| Liberal government (Gresham) Omnium: Lord Privy Seal, then President of the Board of Trade | | 1871 |
| Tory government (Daubeny) | 1872: Secret ballot introduced | 1872 |
| Coalition (Omnium) | | 1873 |
| Omnium: Prime Minister | | 1874 |
| | Tory government (Disraeli) | 1875 |
| Liberal government (Gresham) | | 1876 |
| Tory government (Drummond & Beeswax) | | 1877 |
| | | 1878 |
| Liberal government (Monk) Omnium: Lord President of the Council | | 1879 |

(Chapter 21). But, in the novel, the resulting Tory government lasts scarcely twelve months. In reality, the Tory administration formed in 1874 would stay in power for more than six years.

Trollope's politicians are also of the old school. Daubeny is not a bad portrait of Disraeli. But Disraeli had been his inimitable self since the 1840s, and Gresham performs aspects of Gladstone's parliamentary role without ever being intended to resemble him as a person. Gladstone started as a Tory, became a Peelite, allied himself with the Whigs, and ended up as a rather radical Liberal. Gresham is simply a Whig, out of the same drawer as the men who led that party in the 1840s and 1850s: Russell and Palmerston. The most conspicuous example of Trollope's 'looking back' is the Duke of St Bungay. Important throughout the Palliser series, he is a fixture in successive Whig cabinets and an indispensable source of shrewd political advice. By common consent he is based on the third Marquis of Lansdowne who died in February 1863, six months before Trollope began to write *Can You Forgive Her?*. Inspired, probably, by a reading of Lansdowne's obituaries, Trollope took a figure from the first half of the century and transferred him, without apology or alteration, into the second.

The political terminology of the Palliser series also belongs more naturally to the 1850s than to the decades in which the novels are set. This is not to say that the vocabulary of politics was suddenly clarified after 1860, or that discussion did not continue about the precise meaning of 'Whig', 'Liberal', 'Tory', 'Conservative', and 'Radical'. As late as 1874 there was a concerted attempt to revive the word 'Whig'. But, in practice, there had been a gradual simplification of the language of politics. By the 1870s there were Liberals and Conservatives, and what those two parties stood for was relatively clear. Tory Protectionists and Ultra Tories had been absorbed into a Disraelian Conservative Party. Whigs, Peelites, and most Radicals had become Gladstonian Liberals.

Back in the 1850s party identity had been more complex, and Trollope's novels reflect that uncertainty. Phineas Finn, without changing his stance, can be referred to by different people as a Whig, a Liberal, and a Radical in the space of a few pages. Trollope can mock the Tories, in Chapter 4 of *The Eustace Diamonds*, and then concede that his target is not mainstream Conservatism but 'ultra-Toryism'. In *The Prime Minister*, Du Boung stands as 'a Conservative' in the Silverbridge election but is 'in possession of four-fifths of the Liberal interests of the borough' and, in that capacity, loses (by 7 votes) to another Conservative. The Duke of St Bungay, in *Can You Forgive Her?*, can observe that he has 'voted for every Liberal measure that has come seriously before Parliament', but 'not been able to get beyond Whiggery yet', while declaring that 'there is nothing' he wants 'so much as to become a Radical'.

If this was confusing at the time, it is even more confusing for modern readers. So it is perhaps worthwhile to try, briefly, to give some meaning to these terms. The Tories, tainted with Jacobitism in the first half of the eighteenth century, returned to respectability at the end of it as the party of monarchy, rather than a particular dynasty of monarchs. In this capacity, they ran the war against the French Revolutionary regicides, an experience which reinforced their belief in tradition, rather than innovation, in constitutional matters. After the Whig First Reform Act of 1832, 'Ultra Tories' argued for repeal of the Act and a return to what Trollope called 'tests and qualifications, rotten boroughs and the divine right of kings' (*The Prime Minister*, Chapter 34). But Sir Robert Peel's *Tamworth Manifesto* in 1835 reinvented Conservativism (as it began to call itself in the 1830s) by accepting the enlarged franchise and committing the party to 'the firm maintenance of established rights, the correction of proved abuses and the redress of real grievances'. The split over the repeal of the Corn Laws in 1846 then broke the party into 'Protectionists' and 'Peelites' and condemned it to opposition, or brief spells of minority government, until 1874. Though the Tories dropped their commitment to agricultural protection, they remained the party of Church, Crown, and the landed interest, seeing the Crown, in an ideal conception, as the protector of the people from the oppressive power of the aristocracy.

The Whigs, by contrast, saw the aristocracy as the protector of the people from oppression by the Crown. Tracing their origins to the Glorious Revolution of the 1680s (and, more fancifully, to the imposition of Magna Carta on King John by the barons in 1215), they had been the 'country' rather than 'court' party in the eighteenth century, and the allies of religious Dissenters against the Church of England. The Whigs split over the French Revolution, when Burke and the Portland Whigs sided with the Tories. This left Charles James Fox the leader of a much-reduced party, committed to peace with France, toleration for Dissenters, abolition of the slave trade, and parliamentary reform: a programme summed up in the slogan 'Civil and Religious Liberty'. The Whigs returned to power in 1830 and enacted their policy of parliamentary reform in the First Reform Bill. By now they were the party of commerce and industry, as well as of Dissent and the liberal aristocracy, and their slogan was 'Peace, retrenchment, and reform'. They supported religious toleration, lower taxes, a free press, and a more humane legal code. Macaulay, in 1834, called them 'the *Centre Gauche*': the centre left.

The term 'Liberal' began to be used, interchangeably with 'Whig', in the 1830s, sometimes merely to describe Whig supporters who did not come from grandly aristocratic backgrounds. But it could also be used to distinguish Whigs who were willing to make further extensions of the franchise from those who had taken a 'Finality' view of the First Reform Bill. In the 1860s, 'Liberal' would replace 'Whig' as the usual name for the party.

'Radical' is the most slippery of these terms, in part because the Radical Members of Parliament were not a party but a miscellany of small groups with diverse views. These included the Manchester School free-traders, the Utilitarian 'Philosophical Radicals', and O'Connell's Irish party. Confusingly, the term was also used of the most 'advanced' members of the Whig party. These 'moderate Radicals' were less restrained than the Liberal Whigs in their attacks on church privileges and military expenditure, and more enthusiastic about further parliamentary reform, usually including the secret ballot. But the difference was relative. In his own eyes, Plantagenet Palliser is not a Radical (*Can You Forgive Her?*, Chapter 23). In the eyes of a Tory like the young Lord Silverbridge (*The Duke's Children*, Chapter 4), he looks rather like one.

In practice, the difference between Tories, Whigs, and Liberals in the politics of the 1850s is perhaps best indicated by the order of priorities in Peel's phrase from the *Tamworth Manifesto*: 'the firm maintenance of established rights, the correction of proved abuses and the redress of real grievances'. There is a great deal of common ground here. But Tories could be said to have seen the first of these things as the most important, Whigs the second, and Liberals the third. Radicals, while sharing the Liberal concern for the redress of grievances, would have reduced the list to two by showing little or no enthusiasm for the 'maintenance of established rights'. By the 1870s, the Radicals had been almost entirely absorbed into the Gladstonian Liberal party, and the party's centre of gravity had shifted somewhat as a result.

Despite the quality of mild archaism which clings to Trollope's account of British political culture in general, there are particular events in the Palliser novels which belong, undeniably, to the 1860s. Most conspicuously, in *Phineas Finn* and *Phineas Redux* he gives his version of the debates in 1866–7 about the Second Reform Bill. When Trollope does present immediately contemporary issues, however, he deliberately distorts them. In reality, Russell and Gladstone introduced a Reform Bill in 1866 which was attacked, from the right wing of their own party, by Robert Lowe. Denounced as an 'Adullamite' (he might, alternatively, have been termed an 'Ultra Whig'), Lowe opposed any alteration of the First Reform Act. With Tory support, Lowe defeated the Bill and the government fell. A year later, in 1867, Disraeli astonishingly 'stole the Whigs' clothes' by introducing a successful Reform Bill of his own.

In Trollope's novel, Mildmay and Gresham introduce a Reform Bill which is opposed, not from the right of their party, but from the left. A Radical, Turnbull, opposes the measure because it does not include provision for a secret ballot. Though Tories could, in reality, support a Whig attack on Whig policy from the right, they cannot, in these new (fictional) circumstances, support an attack from the left. So the Bill is not rejected, and passes into law. So far so good, especially for Whig readers eager to find imaginative compensation for a painful defeat. But Trollope has not yet managed to represent the most dramatic feature of the Reform Bill debates: Disraeli's 'stealing the Whigs' clothes'. In *Phineas Redux*, therefore, he invents another political issue to allow Daubeny to do this. Here, the Tories seek to steal the support which the Whigs had traditionally received from Dissenters by introducing a (wholly fictitious) Bill to disestablish the Church of England. Faced with a choice between opposing a measure which their Nonconformist supporters desire, and allowing the Tories to take the credit for its success, the Whigs fall back on a casuistical 'men not measures' argument. In due course they may themselves introduce such a bill. In the short term, they can vote with right-wing Tory rebels to defeat disestablishment, just as Tories had (in reality) voted with right-wing Whigs to defeat reform.

Trollope is not reproducing the political life of his time, in other words, but creating a credible alternative to it, and these episodes demonstrate the necessary limits of that process. What happens in the major political action of the novels must not be what actually happened, or the books (and their characters) would not be fiction. The outcome of the fictional events, however, must be the same as the outcome of the actual events, or Trollope's parallel universe would begin to diverge from the real world. There has, in fact, been a Second Reform Act, so Gresham's Bill can pass (subject to some correction, at the beginning of *Phineas Redux*, to get the details right). But we are not living in a world in which the Church of England has been disestablished, so Daubeny's Bill must fail. The trick is to achieve the best possible balance between the real and unreal.

Fundamentally, Trollope is creating his credible alternative to the real political world, not for its own sake, but as an environment in which human relationships can be dramatized and discussed. The novels of the Barsetshire series are about people living in a clerical environment, not about religion. The novels of the Palliser series, similarly, are about people living in a political environment, not about politics. Their correspondence to the political events of the 1860s and 1870s needs to be sufficiently correct to make the setting in which the characters exist believable, without being perfect. To achieve this Trollope refracts, rather than reflects, the political circumstances of his time, and does so with a combination of mild archaism and deliberate distortion. In Chapter 17 of *Phineas Redux*, he suggests that his readers need to have 'duly studied the history of the age'. But this is a joke. What such study will reveal, he tells us, is that 'the Duke did make an offer to Madame Goesler'. In novels story, not history, is what really matters.

*Nicholas Shrimpton*

# EXPLANATORY NOTES

THE present editors are grateful to previous editors of *The Duke's Children*, especially Dinah Birch (Penguin, 1995), and to Hermione Lee, who edited the predecessor to this volume for Oxford World's Classics in 1983. Any notes that have been carried over in whole or in part from this edition have been marked '[HL]'.

All references to the Bible (including the Apocrypha) are to the King James Version; references to Shakespeare are to *The Oxford Shakespeare: The Complete Works*, ed. Stanley Wells and Gary Taylor, 2nd edn. (Oxford: Oxford University Press, 2005). References to Trollope's *Autobiography* (1883) are to the Oxford World's Classics edition (1980), ed. Michael Sadleir and Frederick Page, with an introduction and notes by P. D. Edwards. References to the *Oxford English Dictionary* (*OED*) are to the 2nd edn., electronic version.

## VOLUME I

7 *our old friend*: *The Duke's Children* is, of course, the last published of the Palliser novels and the story of Plantagenet Palliser, Duke of Omnium ('all things'), began with his appearance in the 'Barchester' novel, *The Small House at Allington* (1862–4).

*the only daughter*: in *The Prime Minister,* the Pallisers had 'two little girls' (ch. 19), but Trollope seems to have forgotten about Lady Mary's sister.

*Dante*: the 'new kind of life' in the previous sentences anticipates the reference to Dante, whose *La vita nuova* ('The New Life'), written in 1295, includes mourning for the death of his beloved Beatrice.

*the Italian lakes*: popular Victorian aristocratic and middle-class holiday destination.

*Parliament*: Palliser's inheritance of his dukedom meant he could sit no longer in the House of Commons but could sit in the House of Lords. The story of his premiership is told in *The Prime Minister.*

8 *Trinity*: Trinity College Cambridge, one of the grandest of the Cambridge colleges, founded by Henry VIII in 1546.

*was to be found*: despite parliamentary reform, not least the two Reform Acts before the mid-1870s when this novel is more or less set (that is, the Acts of 1832 and 1867), patronage is still envisaged as securing the selection of candidates for some provincial constituencies.

*Matching Priory*: the Pallisers' country house (see *Can You Forgive Her*, ch. 22).

*equality*: a timely reference to the motto of the French state (the Third Republic) formally adopted only in 1870 (though it is usually thought of as a revolutionary slogan): *Liberté, égalité, fraternité* (freedom, equality, brotherhood).

8 *support to him*: see the troubles narrated in *The Prime Minister*.

*Honourable and Right Honourable friends*: Honourable is the title for ordinary MPs; Right Honourable for members of Privy Council and peers.

9 *nearly nineteen*: Trollope has just said that she *was* 19.

*guardians*: see ch. 18 of *Can You Forgive Her?* for the account of the family pressure on Glencora to marry Palliser.

10 *Mrs Finn*: Glencora's friendship with Madame [Marie] Max Goesler, later Mrs Finn, is told in *Phineas Finn*, *The Eustace Diamonds*, *Phineas Redux*, and *The Prime Minister*. There is a deleted portion of the original manuscript of ch. 13 that reminds the reader of Mrs Finn's history at some length.

*ruins of the old Priory*: a glance back at the ill-advised walk Glencora took among those ruins in the earlier days of her marriage in ch. 27 of *Can You Forgive Her?*

*M'Closkies*: in *Can You Forgive Her?*, Glencora's maiden name is 'M'Cluskie'.

*adust*: 'Applied to a supposed state of the body and its humours, much spoken of in the earlier days of medicine, its alleged symptoms being dryness of the body, heat, thirst, black or burnt colour of the blood, and deficiency of serum in it, atrabilious or "melancholic" complexion, etc. *Obscure*. except in general sense, atrabilious, sallow, gloomy in features or temperament' (*OED* 'adust', 3: this sense is still present in 1870).

12 *Lady Cantrip*: wife of a Liberal cabinet minister, she makes appearances in *Phineas Finn*, *Phineas Redux*, and *The Prime Minister*.

*a Mrs Jeffrey Palliser*: Palliser's cousin: he would have inherited the dukedom had Glencora not had children. That indefinite article hints at remoteness between the families.

13 *the Greys*: the relationship, and marriage, of John Grey and Alice Vavasor is told in *Can You Forgive Her?*.

14 *fifteen hundred a year*: Tregear is regarded as a 'commoner without an income' on p. 19: an indication of the modesty of this sum. See also the Note on the Text, p. xxv.

*her own early days*: one of many references to Glencora's decision to abandon the man she loved, Burgo Fitzgerald, in favour of marriage to Palliser (in *Can You Forgive Her?*).

*great wealth*: Burgo, in ch. 18 of *Can You Forgive Her?*, is described as having nearly obtained the hand of a 'great heiress [. . .], on whom the properties of half-a-dozen ancient families had concentrated'.

16 *Lady Midlothian*: Glencora's aunt had, we are told in *Can You Forgive Her?*, 'united herself to a man of bad character, who had used her ill' (ch. 2).

Nevertheless, she had decided she was in a position to advise both Glencora and Alice Vavasor (*Can You Forgive Her?*, ch. 26).

17 *the reader may possibly know*: a nice recognition that the reader may not have read the earlier Palliser novels, or forgotten them. The reference is to Mrs Finn's scrupulously appropriate friendship with the Duke.

*parallel with facts*: a concise self-referential summary of the plots of much of Trollope's mature fiction.

19 *commoner*: Tregear may come from an old family, but it is not a titled one.

*her early life*: another reference to Burgo.

20 *how could she forgive herself?*: Trollope's wry variation on the title of an earlier Palliser novel, all too relevant for Lady Mary's situation in comparison with Glencora's.

21 *Park Lane*: a prosperous residential area of central London.

22 *Eton*: Eton College, founded by Henry VI; by the nineteenth century, a prosperous public school for boys in Windsor. (Public schools in the nineteenth century were distinguished from private schools by having an endowment as a source of income: private schools were those owned and run by private individuals. There were, of course, no state-run secondary schools.)

*Christ Church*: in the Victorian period, the Oxford college most favoured by aristocracy. It was originally founded by Cardinal Wolsey in 1525.

*second-class man*: Tregear has displayed a creditable level of ability, much more than required merely to pass. Arthur Hugh Clough and Matthew Arnold graduated with a second-class degree. Newman, like Ruskin, took a fourth.

*another man*: Burgo again. See ch. 29 of *Can You Forgive Her?*.

23 *tinsel*: the sense of showiness but without substance had been established by the seventeenth century.

*Polwenning*: no real place but Cornish-sounding (as is Tregear).

*Crim Tartary*: no real eastern mountains (and a hint of 'going to the devil'?).

24 *one to bell the cat*: to undertake something risky in an effort to ensure an improvement (a cat's bell is, of course, intended to prevent it from catching birds).

25 *Carlton Terrace*: a fashionable residential area between Pall Mall and The Mall in central London.

*Conservative party*: in spite of the Pallisers' position as central to the Whig aristocracy. Lord Silverbridge, in the Duke's eyes, is betraying the family cause.

*Head of his college*: Christ Church, having Oxford's cathedral as, in effect, its chapel, is headed by a Dean (uniquely in the University).

*my grandfather*: the old Duke, who was his great-uncle, not his grandfather.

27 *'None but the brave deserve the fair'*: from John Dryden's *Alexander's Feast* (1697), l. 15 ('None but the brave deserves the fair'). Trollope returned frequently to this line.

*'De l'audace, et encore de l'audace, et toujours de l'audace'*: this is from the speech of 2 September 1792 by the French revolutionary leader Georges Danton. In Thomas Carlyle's *The French Revolution* (1837), Carlyle records Danton's words: ' "To conquer them, to hurl them back, what do we require? Il nous faut de l'audace, et encore de l'audace, et toujours de l'audace, [It is necessary for us] To dare, and again to dare, and without end to dare!" ' (ch. 3. 1. iv). Tregear is reading *The French Revolution* in ch. 55.

28 *yet had never been claimed*: Marie Goesler had been neither the old Duke's lover nor his wife, and she had scrupulously declined the large legacy he left her: ' "It isn't mine, and never will be" ', she robustly says in *Phineas Redux*, ch. 69.

*awfully cut up*: Tregear's youthful slang is not entirely decorous in this situation.

29 *very intimate*: a Victorian expression: 'good/close friends'.

31 *I . . . happens*: by ch. 55, Trollope has forgotten this, and gives Tregear a sister.

32 *county*: the fictional county of West Barsetshire.

*Liberal*: almost a synonym for Whigs in this novel, which does not police a distinction between the two very carefully. But see also note to p. 50.

*the Radicals*: a clue, of a kind, to Silverbridge's understanding of politics. The 'Radicals' was a general term, often disparaging, for reformists in the nineteenth century, but Silverbridge seems to be using it to refer merely in general to the Whigs/Liberals. He is by no means the only one in the novel to slip between Radical-Whig-Liberal as near or actual synonyms.

34 *Derby*: the Epsom Derby, a flat race first run in 1780.

38 *Cræsus*: King of Lydia (561/560 BCE–*c*.547 BCE), renowned for his wealth.

40 *she-Pandarus*: a woman go-between. Pandarus is the male go-between in, for instance, Chaucer's *Troilus and Criseyde* and Shakespeare's *Troilus and Cressida*.

41 *Good-morning, sir*: it is the evening (certainly after six). Most likely Trollope's slip, but perhaps intended to be an indication of how troubled the Duke is (though Trollope is likely to have made sure the reader did not miss this).

*Beargarden Club*: Felix Carbury in *The Way We Live Now* decides to join a club, and chooses 'the worst'. This was called 'the Beargarden, and had been lately opened with the express view of combining parsimony with profligacy. Clubs were ruined, so said certain young parsimonious profligates, by providing comforts for old fogies who paid little or nothing but their subscriptions, and took out by their mere presence three times as much as they gave. This club was not to be opened till three o'clock in the afternoon, before which hour the promoters of the Beargarden thought it improbable that they and their fellows would want a club. There were to be no morning papers taken, no library, no morning-room. Dining-rooms, billiard-rooms, and card-rooms would suffice for the Beargarden. Everything was to be provided by a purveyor, so that the club should be cheated only by one man. Everything was to be luxurious, but the luxuries were to be achieved at first cost. It had been a happy thought, and the club was said to prosper', ch. 3.

*Carlist army*: those fighting in the Spanish wars of legitimacy on the side of Infante Carlos, later Carlos V. They lasted from 1833 to 1876 and Tifto presumably claims to have been part of what the Spanish call *Tercera Guerra Carlista* from 1872 to 1876.

42 *Had this . . . said about it*: Major is two ranks below Colonel.

*M.F.H.*: Master of Fox Hounds. Runnymede is in Surrey, west of central London and east of Windsor. Its association with Magna Carta, the supposedly founding document of British democracy, makes it perhaps a slightly ironic place for Major Tifto to hunt, given that his own role on the margins of political circles is hardly distinguished.

*How . . . could understand*: Trollope, in his essay 'On Hunting' in *British Sports and Pastimes* (1868), thought the cost of maintaining a pack of foxhounds was £2,700 a year.

*blackballs*: votes against.

43 *painted*: wore make-up.

*steeple chases*: 'horse-race across country or on a made course with artificial fences, water-jumps, and other obstacles. Formerly, a race having a church steeple in view as goal, in which all intervening obstacles had to be cleared', *OED*.

*'deep'*: 'Hard to fathom or "get to the bottom of"; penetrating far into a subject, profound', *OED* 'deep', adj., 6.a.

*Egham*: small town near Windsor (and Runnymede).

*Leamington handicap*: generalized reference to a race. Leamington, incidentally, was a famous UK racehorse (1853–78), who was embroiled in a scandal about manipulated handicaps.

44 *'straight tip'*: name of the horse that eventually wins.

*Newmarket*: the headquarters of British racing, developed by Charles II after the initial grandstand was built by James I. The first recorded race took place on 18 March 1622.

*rubber*: a game of whist, but also cribbage, backgammon, or bridge.

*A dash at loo*: a 'dash' in this sense was a bet; loo was a 'round card-game played by a varying number of players. The cards in three-card loo have the same value as in whist; in five-card loo the Jack of Clubs ('Pam') is the highest card. A player who fails to take a trick or breaks any of the laws of the game is "looed", i.e. required to pay a certain sum, or "loo", to the pool', *OED*, 'loo', n., 1.

44 *blind hookey*: a card game (said in *The Century Dictionary* of 1911 to be 'frequently played on transatlantic steamers') in which the dealer offers the pack to the players and they divide it into several piles, face down. One of these, chosen at random, is the dealer's. Bets are placed on the remaining piles and all are turned face up. The bottom cards of each pile that are higher than that of the dealer's win; those lower, lose. [HL]

45 *claret*: the English term for red wines of the Bordeaux region.

*Sarcinet*: a form of silk.

46 *at the Craven . . . and . . . at Chester*: the Craven Stakes were run in April, and the Chester Cup (first run in 1824) in early May. The Chester Cup was notorious for the heavy gambling associated with it and for the roughness of the course. [HL] These are heavy weights for a jockey. They are now usually between 105 and 115 lb (7½ st and 8 st 3 lb).

*Solomon*: an audacious choice of name for someone who appears to be a betting agent or a respected tipster.

*Adolphus Longstaff*: a character from *The Way We Live Now* (though there spelt Longestaffe and usually known as Dolly). He becomes caught up in the financial collapse of Melmotte.

*Lord Nidderdale*: another character from *The Way We Live Now* (see ch. 4): he is the eldest son of the Marquis of Auld Reekie.

47 *Mdlle Stuffa*: i.e. Mademoiselle Stuffa. There was no singer of this name on the nineteenth-century stage, but the cult of 'nightingales', that is, celebrity singers, was a familiar one in the nineteenth-century British music scene. They included Jenny Lind (1820–87), better known as the 'Swedish Nightingale'.

*overweighted as it were*: an allusion to the heavy jockeys, perhaps.

48 *had one for the last session*: Arthur Fletcher, who wins the Silverbridge by-election in *The Prime Minister*.

50 *Liberalism*: an indication of the ease with which the Duke of Omnium will exchange 'Whig' and 'Liberal'.

51 *Communists*: Silverbridge is somewhat off the mark. Communism had emerged by 1850 following Marx and Engels's *Manifest der Kommunistischen Partei* (1848) as an anti-capitalist ideology. It had hardly penetrated British society by the 1870s to constitute the 'danger' Silverbridge perceives.

*greatest benefit of the greatest number*: an echo of Jeremy Bentham's Utilitarianism. See, for instance, Bentham's statement: 'Ethics at large may be defined, [as] the art of directing men's actions to the production of the greatest possible quantity of happiness, on the part of those whose interest is in view', *An Introduction to the Principles of Morals and Legislation* (1781), ch. 17. The Duke is no Utilitarian (and neither was Trollope), but this allusion confirms the more socially progressive dimension of his politics. His words also echo Trollope's account of Cicero in 1880 who had, he said, 'learned to feel that a man's final duty here on earth is his duty to other men' (*Cicero*, vol. ii, ch. 8).

52 *To endeavour to be just was the study of his life*: a classical guide to life. The definition of the just man was, for instance, of consequence to Aristotle, and central to Plato's moral and political thought.

54 *unlordly, or rather unpeerlike fashion*: it is not wholly clear what Trollope means by this distinction.

*Gatherum Castle*: built by the present Duke's uncle, at huge expense (see *Can You Forgive Her?*, ch. 18).

*spirit of the constitution*: in the absence of a fully written British constitution, the notion of a constitutional 'spirit' was not an unfamiliar one. See, for instance, John Aikin's *The Spirit of the Constitution and that of the Church of England, Compared* (1791) or William Atkinson, *The Spirit of Magna Charta; or, Universal Representation the Genius of the British Constitution* (1841).

55 *cubit*: there was never a single measurement for a cubit, and Trollope rather casually means 'a significant measure' here.

56 *Lucullus*: (*c*.118–57 BCE) distinguished Roman politician, general, and scholar, celebrated for his feasts (and anecdotally careful not to allow others to see when he ate alone).

*seltzer water*: carbonated water.

60 *'In medias res'*: in the middle of things. Trollope enjoys the association between his own fiction, with all its classical touches, and classical aesthetics. Horace used 'in medias res' in his *Ars Poetica* (*The Nature/Art of Poetry*, *c*.18 BCE) to describe epic literature that began in mid-story.

*gold . . . digging for it*: a topical allusion, for there were a number of so-called gold rushes in the nineteenth century, the most celebrated of which was the California Gold Rush of 1848–55.

62 *Belgrave Square*: constructed in the 1820s, this was by the time of *The Duke's Children* a London residential square of exceptional grandeur. It is close to Knightsbridge.

*Seven Dials*: a slum area of central London, near to Covent Garden. The contrast with Belgrave Square is obvious. W. S. Gilbert's lyrics for Act I of the comic opera *Iolanthe* (1882) made the same point: 'Spare us the bitter pain | Of stern denials, | Nor with low-born disdain | Augment our trials. | Hearts just as pure and fair | May beat in Belgrave Square | As in the lowly air | Of Seven Dials!'

63 *Cassewary*: one of Trollope's more amusing names, for it is hard not to think of the ostrich-like bird: 'They stand about five feet high; the wings are of no use for flight, but are furnished with stiff featherless quills, like spines, which serve for combat or defence' (*OED*).

*text*: that is, the biblical passage on which the sermon was preached.

*many Conservatives*: in *The Prime Minister*, Palliser heads a coalition government.

64 *Grex, in Yorkshire*: see ch. 37.

64 *the Beaufort*: an expensive betting club (it appears in the *The Small House at Allington*).

*light that lies in a lady's eye*: this sounds like a line from a song or poem, but does not appear to be.

65 *when the time of eating was at hand*: a slightly cheeky allusion to the Song of Songs 2:12: 'The flowers appear on the earth; the time of the singing of birds is come, and the voice of the turtle is heard in our land'.

*thought it proper to give it up*: Silverbridge is making the best of his father's actions, for pocket boroughs had been ruled out by the 1832 Reform Act so it was hardly the Duke's decision.

*ratting himself*: leaving his own party.

66 *brougham*: four-wheeled horse-drawn closed carriage that comfortably sat two.

68 *'That's nonsense . . .' said Lady Mabel*: Trollope continues the *in medias res* manner, closing in the last sentence of this chapter.

69 *twit*: 'To blame, find fault with, censure, reproach, upbraid (a person), esp. in a light or annoying way; to cast an imputation upon; to taunt', *OED*, 'twit', v., 1.

*Rosaline of his love for Juliet*: Rosaline was loved by Romeo before Juliet (see *Romeo and Juliet*, I. ii and II. iii).

70 *'But you feel . . .' 'I do'*: amusingly apt reference to the Book of Common Prayer's service for matrimony.

73 *She had . . . whole truth*: allusion to the established form of words for an oath in court: 'I swear by Almighty God that the evidence which I shall give shall be the truth, the whole truth, and nothing but the truth'.

74 *The Horns*: Richmond house, which the old Duke gave to Glencora (*The Prime Minister*, ch. 37).

79 *The . . . pity of it!*: *Othello*, IV. i. 191–2: 'Ay, that's certain, but yet the pity of it, Iago: O Iago, the pity of it, Iago!' Not entirely suitable for Trollope's purposes here, but the phrase will just about do for general expressions of regret.

82 *flowering ashes . . . water*: *Fraxinus ornus*, called in the UK 'flowering ash', is often used as an ornamental tree beside water; it does indeed flower in May.

83 *patriotic*: it is perhaps worth stressing that this simply means here 'marked by devotion to the well-being or interests of one's country' (*OED*) without much of the ideological difficulty that surrounds the word in contemporary usage.

86 *great sin*: some readers might have heard an echo of Exodus 32: 30: 'And it came to pass on the morrow, that Moses said unto the people, Ye have sinned a great sin: and now I will go up unto the LORD; peradventure I shall make an atonement for your sin.'

88 *intentional privity*: the word is used in a half-legal sense, referring to privity as 'The fact of being privy to something; participation in the knowledge of something private, secret, or criminal (freq. implying compliance or consent)' (*OED*, 'privity', 6a). It is not merely a synonym for secrecy. Trollope keeps up the semi-legal language for the remainder of the sentence.

89 *Thursday, 12th May, 18—*: in the 1870s, when this novel is set, 12 May was a Thursday only in 1870.

*Grace*: technically, the form of address for Dukes and Duchesses: Silverbridge, of course, is the *son* of a Duke.

90 *sundry politicians,—Mr Sprugeon and Mr Sprout and Mr Du Boung*: *The Prime Minister* gives the story of these three local politicians. Sprugeon supported Lopez, then abandoned him; Sprout, a cork sole manufacturer in Silverbridge, supported Du Boung in the last Silverbridge election. The brewer, Mr Du Boung (born 'Bung' but he upgrades his name when he becomes rich—see *The Prime Minister*, ch. 34), has agreed, as readers will find out soon, not to stand against the Duke's son.

92 *swell*: Silverbridge means someone with wealth and rank, so the slang sense that is *OED* 'swell', n., 9: 'A fashionably or stylishly dressed person; hence, a person of good social position, a highly distinguished person'. He does not mean anyone pretentious or pompous.

93 *George and Vulture*: the odd name of this inn is borrowed from Dickens's *Pickwick Papers* (1836–7), and the 'very good, old-fashioned, and comfortable quarters, to wit, the George and Vulture Tavern and Hotel, George Yard, Lombard Street' to which Sam and Mr Pickwick retire, for the first time, in ch. 26. It is the scene of the courtroom in *The Last Chronicle of Barset*. Dickens's inn is a real tavern, built in 1746, off Lombard Street in central London.

94 *Dr Tempest*: the old Rector of Silverbridge (a Conservative).

95 *Mr Walker*: of the firm Walker and Winthrop, lawyers who look after the Duke's local interests (a Liberal).

103 *one or two things*: cf. Palliser's speech to Phineas Finn (*The Prime Minister*, ch. 68) on his parliamentary beliefs; Trollope's own idea of Parliament in *An Autobiography*, ch. 16, and Trollope's *Life of Palmerston* (1882): 'To do the best he could for English interests, and to do that best in an honest and manly manner, was his object' (ch. 5). [HL]

*paid for doing them*: MPs first received an annual salary only in 1911 (it was £400).

*lightly burdened*: Trollope picks up the language of Matthew 11: 30: 'For my yoke is easy, and my burden is light'.

104 *Mr Monk . . . to the Duke*: 'of all members of the Cabinet the most advanced Liberal' (*Phineas Finn*, ch. 14) and successively President of the Board of Trade, Chancellor of the Exchequer, and Prime Minister.

105 *Sir Timothy Beeswax*: Conservative leader of the House of Commons, partly based on Disraeli (1804–81). See ch. 21.

106 *When I was a child . . . childish things*: 'When I was a child, I spake as a child, I understood as a child, I thought as a child: but when I became a man, I put away childish things', 1 Corinthians 13: 11.

107 *full of chaff*: always teasing.

109 *two pounds more*: the Jockey Club's weight-for-age scale had been devised by Admiral Henry John Rous (1795–1877) and, as is clear, was at this point still subject to some local adjustment: Silverbridge has been persuaded to allow Coalition to carry what has proved an unfair additional weight.

111 *Prime Minister*: HL speculates: 'a horse called The Prime Minister was strongly backed at 7–1 for the 1851 Derby but came nowhere. A famous horse called Plenipotentiary (known as "Plenipo") won in 1834, beating a fine horse called Glencoe. (Could there be an echo of these names in "Planty Pall" and "Glencora"?)'

 *money-lenders*: such as those with whom Trollope was in difficulty as a young man when he was, as he said, 'always in trouble' (see Biographical Preface, p. vii, and *An Autobiography*, 47).

 *conveyed to Epsom*: the transportation of racehorses was a matter of continual discussion through the nineteenth century. Moving horses both by (horse-drawn) vans and, in due course, by train was widespread in the period, but difficult. The latter particularly began to concern the Royal Society for Prevention of Cruelty to Animals at the end of the century.

112 *pundits*: authorities.

 *should do so*: Hansard recorded Palmerston, then Prime Minister, for 15 May 1860 informing the House of Commons that to 'adjourn over [Derby] day is part of the unwritten law of Parliament. I am sure that Her Majesty's Government do not wish to ask the House to depart from so wholesome a custom'.

 *three-year-old*: the Derby is a race for 3-year-olds.

113 *Downs*: Epsom.

 *Leger*: the St Leger Stakes was first run in 1776 at Doncaster, organized by the Marquess of Rockingham, former Prime Minister.

 *Quousque*: presumably a reference to the celebrated phrase from Cicero's first speech against Catiline: 'Quo usque tandem abutere, Catilina, patientia nostra': 'How long, Catiline, will you abuse our patience?'

 *Jockey Club*: the Jockey Club now dates its foundation to 1750: by the time of *The Duke's Children*, it was the leading authority in British racing.

 *crack shire packs*: prestigious country fox-hound packs.

114 *drag*: a four-horse coach.

115 *hansom cab*: a two-wheeled carriage, pulled by one horse.

116 *Liverpool Street*: this station opened in 1874 and was fully operational in 1875. Then as now it was served by the mainline train to Cambridge.

117 *gated*: confined to the college.

*Oaks*: started in 1779, a flat race for 3-year-old fillies (and named after the house in which it was proposed): held in early June, like the Derby.

*Master of Trinity*: it was the classicist William Hepworth Thompson (1810–86) throughout the 1870s, but Trollope did not have him specifically in mind.

118  *sent down*: Oxford and Cambridge expression for 'expelled'.

121  *attaché*: a junior official serving a senior (usually a diplomat).

123  *for . . . as long as the Speaker sat in the chair*: that is, until the day's business is over (and Parliament was not averse to sitting until late at night).

128  *Orlando Drought*: Tory antagonist of the Duke, who resigned from his coalition government (see *The Prime Minister*, ch. 38).

*sugar*: sugar had been heavily taxed in Great Britain. Only as late as 16 April 1874 had Gladstone's Chancellor, Sir Stafford Northcote, abolished the taxation on sugar from 1 May in his budget.

*entail*: a legal limit on the bequest of an estate to descendants.

129  *star . . . parliamentary support*: if Trollope is thinking of anything specific here, he may have in mind the star, pinned to the left breast, that indicates the Order of the Garter, an exceptional honour in the British honours system. It would be quite irregular to wear such a thing to an ordinary dinner, however.

131  *reader . . . assertion*: a small example of Trollope's lifelong readiness to confirm the outcome of a plot in advance.

*Mrs Montacute Jones*: from *Is He Popenjoy?* (1878), a society grandee.

133  *Royal Highness . . . Serene Highness*: the former is a term of address for the British Royal Family, the latter—in the nineteenth century—was in use in parts of continental Europe for royalty.

*"Love your neighbours"*: Lady Mabel recalls Jesus' 'second commandment' in Mark 12: 31 'Thou shalt love thy neighbour as thyself'.

*"Do unto him . . . unto you"*: a commonplace of ancient morality, best known in Christian cultures from Luke 6: 31: 'And as ye would that men should do to you, do ye also to them likewise'.

134  *Conservative reaction*: a recollection of Disraeli's defeat of Gladstone's government in the 1874 General Election.

135  *Attorney-General*: government's chief legal adviser.

*Chief Justice*: Trollope—or Sir Timothy—means Lord Chief Justice, the head of the judiciary.

136  *They who . . . cream of the land*: there is some self-admonishment in this from Trollope himself, after his failure to secure the Beverley seat.

*garters*: the Order of the Garter, see note to p. 129, is the highest order of knighthood, dating from the medieval period.

137  *lick the Russians*: Trollope has in mind the build-up to the Russo-Turkish War of 1877–8, centred on uprisings in the Balkans. In 1877, there was a

danger of Great Britain declaring war on Russia if she invaded Constantinople (Istanbul).

137 *Americans . . . fisheries or frontiers*: the United States Commission of Fish and Fisheries was established in 1871 to investigate the decline of fish stocks in US waters. That same year American subjects had been given the right to fish off eastern Canada in return for permission for British subjects to fish off a portion of the east coast of the US. This was a source of argument until the treaty was overtaken in 1885. On the question of borders more generally, the growing power of the post-Civil War US was always a matter of interest for the British Parliament.

138 *young woman . . . dorsal vertebræ*: an experiment about the allegedly marvellous powers of thought with which, clearly, Trollope has little time.

*Abraham*: the twentieth generation from Noah, Abraham is the iconic patriarch of Jewish, Christian, and Muslim believers.

*a pitt or a Peel*: William Pitt the Younger, Conservative Prime Minister 1783–1801, and 1804–6; Robert Peel, Conservative Prime Minister 1834–5 and 1841–6.

139 *There had been . . . all about that*: Trollope's knowing joke with his reader, as the coalition is the topic of *The Prime Minister*, part, indeed, of the 'political literature' of the day.

140 *Duke of St Bungay*: old friend and adviser to Palliser, the 'very front and head of the aristocratic old Whigs of the country' (*Phineas Finn*, ch. 29). Bungay is a town in Suffolk: St Bungay a fiction.

*Longroyston*: fictional place.

141 *"Solve senescentem"*: that is, 'Solve senescentem mature sanus equum', 'the ageing horse should be put out to grass' (Horace, *Epistles*, I. i. 8).

*Lord Grey*: Whig Prime Minister 1830–4, who took the Great Reform Bill through Parliament.

*emancipation of the Roman Catholics*: the Catholic Relief Act became law in 1829. It permitted Catholics to take a seat in Parliament.

149 *Faint heart*: 'Faint heart ne'er wan | A lady fair' was Burns's version of this proverbial statement (in 'To Dr Blacklock').

150 *duenna*: chaperone of a young woman.

151 *Benedick . . . Beatrice*: from the plot of *Much Ado About Nothing* (though the relationship between Benedick and Beatrice is nothing like that between Tregear and Lady Mary).

152 *heavens to fall*: proverbial, but ultimately from Isaiah 34: 4, 'And all the host of heaven shall be dissolved, and the heavens shall be rolled together as a scroll: and all their host shall fall down, as the leaf falleth off from the vine, and as a falling fig from the fig tree.'

153 *pillar letter-box*: Trollope was instrumental in introducing the postbox to the Channel Islands, and a force in its general introduction in the United Kingdom (see *An Autobiography*, 281–4) and Introduction, pp. xi–xxiv.

*"Noblesse oblige"*: a shorthand way of saying that power and wealth comes with responsibilities.

154 *She had been properly educated . . . to play*: the Duke's sense of an appropriate education for a woman is exactly that which mid-Victorian feminists and sympathizers criticized.

158 *'plunged'*: gone in too deep with a bet.

*book*: a betting book, recording the bets made with others on the outcome of races.

*stud*: when no longer run as a 3-year-old, Prime Minister would become a stud, and as such would retain considerable value.

*Alma Mater*: 'nourishing mother', a phrase meaning an individual's university.

*In the meantime . . . read*: vacation reading parties, led by a tutor, were familiar features of Oxford and Cambridge study in the nineteenth century.

159 *broiled salmon*: that is, grilled.

160 *dura ilia*: from Horace, *Epode* III: 'Oh dura ilia messorum', which Byron gives in *Don Juan*, canto 9, as 'Oh | Ye rigid guts of reapers!'

161 *Ely*: cathedral city near to Cambridge, through which runs the Great Ouse river.

*pot-house*: alehouse.

*public*: public house.

*Not though . . . deep*: an allusion to Horace, *Odes*, III. i, where the poet envisages forms of extreme labour (e.g., 'Fish feel the narrowing of the main | From sunken piles, while on the strand | Contractors with their busy train | Let down huge stones, and lords of land | Affect the sea' [Conington]).

*"Scandunt eodum quo dominus minæ"*: 'sed Timor et Minae | scandunt eodem quo dominus, neque | decidit aerate trireme et | post equitem sedet atra cura', from Horace, *Odes*, III. i: 'but fierce Alarm | Can clamber to the master's side: Black Cares can up the galley swarm, | And close behind the horseman ride' (Conington). The quotation also heads Letter LVI (Mr Lovelace to John Belford) in Samuel Richardson's *Clarissa* (1748). Gerald adds a translation of the last line: his education has not been entirely wasted.

162 *hard work . . . to you*: the Duke's speech concludes with an echo of Carlyle's conviction of the centrality of work to a sense of human redemption.

163 *Sindbad did of the Old Man*: in the fifth voyage of Sinbad the Sailor, Sinbad is ridden by the Old Man of the Sea, who is only thrown off and killed after Sinbad makes him drunk. Trollope's manuscript had 'Sinbad'.

*'You assured . . . as good'*: this is the homely version of the conclusion of Horace's *Odes*, III. i, which has echoed in the chapter: 'why my Sabine vale exchange | For more laborious luxury?' (Conington).

163 *Scotch property*: a portion of Lady Glencora's dowry.

164 *gallery . . . use of peers*: that is, where members of the House of Lords could attend to the proceedings of the House of Commons.

*Irish exaggeration*: a familiar nineteenth-century stereotype.

165 *obligations to Mr Finn*: Finn had defended Palliser against a charge that the Duke had corruptly funded Lopez's election in *The Prime Minister*, ch. 57.

*Sir Timothy was a fluent speaker . . . give him*: Trollope was not always so suspicious of oratory. He was the author of an admiring study of Cicero, after all. But even there he recognized (different) perils. 'A man with such a tongue as that of Cicero', he said, 'will make the listener believe almost whatever he will' (ch. 7).

166 *Royal concert*: Trollope is thinking of a sequence of royal concerts in Buckingham Palace, initially started by Prince Albert, but continued after his death. There was a grand 'State Concert' on 21 June 1876 attended by Disraeli and Gladstone, and many other politicians, ambassadors, military and naval men, and clergy. The programme included music by Donizetti, Mozart, Verdi, and Wagner.

*duel*: see *Phineas Finn*, ch. 38.

167 *bewigging*: literally, putting on wigs, but with an echo, perhaps, of Mr Jarndyce's observation in Dickens's *Bleak House* (1852–3) about the fuss made by the law: 'How mankind ever came to be afflicted with wiglomeration, or for whose sins these young people ever fell into a pit of it, I don't know' (ch. 8).

*Turveydrop and deportment*: Mr Turveydrop runs a dancing academy in *Bleak House* and teaches 'deportment': the point is about style rather than substance.

## VOLUME II

175 *Lord Duke*: an unnecessary doubling of terms—both obsequious and ignorant.

176 *squared*: bribed (slang).

177 *on the square*: military metaphor for 'in public', 'with order/regularity'.

178 *'All vanity . . . spirit!'*: Ecclesiastes 1: 14: 'I have seen all the works that are done under the sun; and, behold, all is vanity and vexation of spirit'.

*certain scenes*: including Lady Glencora's parties at which the Duke was an uncomfortable host (see *The Prime Minister*, chs. 18, 19, 27, and 28).

182 *Queenstown*: now Cobh, where transatlantic liners docked in Cork Harbour (a huge natural harbour) in County Cork, Ireland. It was called Queenstown from 1849 to 1922.

*taffrail*: 'The aftermost portion of the poop-rail of a ship', *OED*.

*tender*: small boat for disembarking passengers from the liner.

*Ascot*: perhaps referring to the Ascot Gold Cup (from 1807), always run in June.

185 *blasées habituées*: lit. 'jaded [female] regulars'.

188 *woman's rights*: the focus of mid-Victorian feminism had included legal issues (including matters of married women's property), education (including higher education), and the range of professions open to women. John Stuart Mill, Emily Davies, Frances Power Cobbe, Josephine Butler, and Millicent Garrett Fawcett were among the prominent feminists in the second half of the century. Trollope was not sympathetic to women in higher education, and was suspicious of organized feminism. Nevertheless, his fiction was often interested in restrictions on women and complicated questions of obedience. See Introduction, pp. xi–xxiv.

190 *The Major is . . . Pilgrim's Progress*: Mr Worldly Wiseman, in John Bunyan's allegory *The Pilgrim's Progress* (1678), lives in Carnal Policy and advises Christian that he need not take so hard a path if he attends to the advice of Legality: Tifto is only like Worldly Wiseman, who offers Christian a modest and happy life, in distracting Silverbridge from the right path.

196 *St James's Park*: the oldest of the Royal Parks, just off The Mall and reasonably close to the Houses of Parliament.

   *position*: Trollope is not usually in the habit of such bad puns.

197 *potential*: i.e., potent, powerful.

198 *Maidenhead*: a town in Berkshire, west of London.

199 *apprehensive*: able to apprehend, perceptive.

202 *flies*: swift one-horse carriages.

   *eighty*: 80° Fahrenheit = 26.7° Celsius.

206 *virile*: manly, masculine (without a specifically sexual sense).

207 *Montague . . . Tybalt*: rather inappropriate allusions to *Romeo and Juliet*. Presumably, this is Mr Boncassen speaking.

208 *Maidenhead Bridge*: as depicted in Turner's *Rain, Steam and Speed—The Great Western Railway* (1844).

209 *ungrammatical*: modern English grammar will accept 'me' here, but for Trollope's age, it is 'I'.

210 *hugger-mugger*: secretly. The choice of marriage partner for the heir to the throne was subject to significant restrictions, including a prohibition on Catholics and commoners.

211 *Erebus*: a proverbial place of darkness between earth and the underworld.

213 *I got to be thinking*: Henry James thought that the speech of Trollope's American characters had 'much more the note of English American than of American English'.

215 *Fifth Avenue*: even by the 1870s, a classy area of New York, leading into the prosperous Washington Square. Edith Wharton's *The Age of Innocence* (1920) described the milieu in the 1870s.

216 *Athenæum*: a gentleman's dining club with distinguished library, founded in 1824 on Pall Mall.

*'Trowsers may be'*: a pun dependent on the fact that duck is a 'strong untwilled linen (or later, cotton) fabric, lighter and finer than canvas; used for small sails and men's (esp. Sailors') outer clothing. In the earlier half of the 19th c. much worn for trousers', *OED* 'duck', n., 3.

218 *Madame Scholzdam*: another opera singer, presumably.

219 *Zoo*: London Zoo opened in 1828.

222 *spontaneous love*: with some recollection, perhaps, of the controversies around scientific efforts to test 'spontaneous generation' involving, for instance, Louis Pasteur in France and John Tyndall in England.

*unencumbered*: not subject to constraining legal arrangements.

227 *ten thousand*: cf. the opening of ch. 1 of *Can You Forgive Her?* 'Whether or no, she, whom you are to forgive, if you can, did or did not belong to the Upper Ten Thousand of this our English world, I am not prepared to say with any strength of affirmation. By blood she was connected with big people,—distantly connected with some very big people indeed, people who belonged to the Upper Ten Hundred if there be any such division; but of these very big relations she had known and seen little, and they had cared as little for her'.

228 *fast*: in the sense of *OED* 10.a: 'Of persons: Living too fast [. . .]; extravagant in habits; devoted to pleasure, dissipated; usually implying a greater or less degree of immorality.'

229 *That unfortunate quarrel*: as we are about to find out, between Phineas Finn and Sir Timothy, over an unspecified matter (the judiciary reforms, presumably).

230 *'I hear men say . . . used to be'*: this discussion scrupulously avoids any suggestion of comment on the controversial 1867 Reform Act, which further increased the electorate and thus the representative identity of the House of Commons.

231 *Twelfth*: the Game Act (1831) had formally confirmed 12 August as the beginning of the (red) grouse shooting season.

*Leadenhall Market*: meat, game, and poultry market in the City of London (the present market building dates from just after this novel, in 1881).

234 *distich*: often a couplet or a few lines of verse that make sense on their own. Here, Trollope is thinking of Jonathan Swift, 'On Poetry' (1733): 'The vermin only teaze and pinch | Their foes superior by an inch. | So, naturalists observe, a flea | Has smaller fleas that on him prey; | And these have smaller still to bite 'em, | And so proceed *ad infinitum*.'

235 *grass-plat*: in the nineteenth century, still a term for grass-*plot*, or turfed area, sometimes with flower beds.

*strap a 'orse*: Victorian slang for 'groom a horse'.

241 *marge*: a distinctive word. Perhaps Trollope has Tennyson's 'Morte d'Arthur' (1833) in mind: 'but at the last it seemed | Better to leave Excalibur concealed | There in the many-knotted waterflags, | That whistled stiff and dry about the marge'. The memory of that heroic scene of Bedevere's irresolution and obedience to the King is a grand backdrop to Trollope's waterside episode in which obedience and being 'trustworthy' are of relevance.

245 *venatical*: of hunting.

    *gillies*: those who 'attend a sportsman in hunting or fishing in the Scottish Highlands', *OED* 'gillie', n., 1.

    *But it never . . . self-indulgence*: self-admonishing words from Trollope, the keen hunter.

248 *crammers*: lies. *OED* gives the first use as 1862.

250 *lawn-tennis*: the adjective is needed at this point to distinguish this new game (from the early 1870s) from real tennis (played indoors).

252 *'When youth . . . flying feet!'*: from Byron's *Childe Harold's Pilgrimage* (1812–18), canto III: 'On with the dance! let joy be unconfined; | No sleep till morn, when Youth and Pleasure meet | To chase the glowing Hours with flying feet'.

    *navvie*: *OED* records the first use of this word as 1819.

254 *He looked . . . alluded*: of course, 'love and war' are meant.

259 *party-coloured*: many coloured.

264 *Ischl*: the Austrian resort of Bad Ischl, with well-known medicinal waters.

265 *Halstadt*: small town about 13 miles from Bad Ischl, and popular with tourists.

266 *'Nervous headaches?'*: several Victorian medical authorities suggested that young women who were frustrated in love were susceptible to migraines, neuralgia, and other forms of 'nervous' ill health.

268 *'Men have died . . . but not for love'*: 'Men have died from time to time, and worms have eaten them, but not for love', *As You Like It*, IV. i. 99–101.

269 *man is born . . . fly upwards*: 'Although affliction cometh not forth of the dust, neither doth trouble spring out of the ground; Yet man is born unto trouble, as the sparks fly upward', Job 5: 6–7.

271 *the Hintersee and the Obersee*: two lakes. These are unremarkable names ('rear lake' and 'high/over lake'), so Trollope may not have specific places in mind.

273 *Richard will be himself*: 'Conscience avaunt! Richard's himself again', Colley Cibber, *King Richard the Third* (1699), in *The Dramatic Works of Colley Cibber*, 5 vols. (London: Rivington, 1777), ii. 367. Cibber's play was an adaptation of Shakespeare's, popular in the nineteenth century.

274 *achieved greatness*: 'Some are born great, some achieve greatness, and some have greatness thrust upon 'em': Malvolio, contemplating 'marrying up' in *Twelfth Night*, II. v. 141–2.

275 *Lady Fawn*: the romantic adventures of her older husband—first in pursuit of Violet Effingham and Madame Max Goesler (now Mrs Finn), then entangled in an engagement to the scheming Lizzie Eustace—are detailed in *Phineas Redux* and *The Eustace Diamonds*.

276 *The great women of the world*: Assyrian Queen Semiramis, legendary founder of Babylon; Pocahontas, Virginian Native American Princess; Ida Pfeiffer, Austrian world travel-writer; Charlotte Corday, French revolutionary and assassin of Jean-Paul Marat.

279 *the pull*: the majority of the betting.

280 *macassar*: hair oil for cosmetic use.

*the Leger distance*: 1 mile, 6 furlongs, and 132 yards.

*duly booked*: Silverbridge is now riskily acting as bookmaker as well as punter, not only backing his own horse to win but 'laying' or taking bets on his rivals to lose.

281 *seventy thousand pounds*: a huge sum, nearly equivalent to the £68,759 7s. 5d. Trollope calculated as his lifetime earnings from literature in *An Autobiography* (p. 364).

*pitch*: 'He that toucheth pitch shall be defiled therewith; and he that hath fellowship with a proud man shall be like unto him' (Ecclesiasticus 13: 1).

*laid*: Tifto too is laying bets, backing Prime Minister to lose.

283 *perspicuous*: lucid.

*frog*: sensitive sole of a horse's hoof, which acts as a shock absorber. An injury to the frog is both acutely painful and a common cause of lameness.

284 *free-school*: Doncaster Grammar School, founded in 1350, but reopened after a period of closure in 1862. By 1869, when it moved to new premises on Thorne Road, it was known as the best school in Yorkshire. In 1879, 'free' did not signal that the school did not charge fees, but that it was not controlled by the Church of England.

*the ring*: the bookmakers.

286 *two thousand five hundred pounds*: presumably the backer of Coalheaver who persuades Silverbridge to lay a bet of £2,400 in ch. 43.

287 *the Jews*: i.e., the moneylenders.

288 *telegraph-wire*: the telegraph network extended itself across the UK during the 1870s, and Trollope's own interest in this new technology is evidenced in his story 'The Telegraph Girl', *Good Words* (1877). To have a telegraph wire in one's own house was, however, an unusual luxury, also enjoyed by Paula Power, heroine of Hardy's *A Laodicean* (1881).

291 *Coblenz*: German city situated at the confluence of the Rhine and the Moselle rivers.

292 *mooncalf*: a foolish youth.

*hecatombs*: ancient Greek sacrifices to the gods.

*Nimrod*: legendary Mesopotamian monarch, described in Genesis 8: 12 as 'a mighty hunter before the Lord'.

294 *I didn't know*: the Duke's ignorance of field sports is the subject of his neighbours' dismay and outrage in *Phineas Redux*.

296 *Lady Chiltern*: Violet Effingham, who married Oswald Chiltern after a flirtation with Phineas Finn. Her father-in-law is Lord Brentford.

298 *salt-mines*: possibly those at Bad Dürrnberg and Hallein near Salzburg, Europe's oldest and most picturesque.

*Again . . . winced*: like Tregear in ch. 4 above, Lord Popplecourt is indecorously familiar in his use of slang.

299 *marker*: a professional scorekeeper.

300 *royalties*: 'a payment made to the landowner by the lessee of a mine in return for the privilege of working it', *OED*, 'royalty', 6c.

*Skald*: any one of a group of Scandinavian and Icelandic poets writing between the ninth and thirteenth centuries. Skaldic verse was written in Old Norse and its dialects, and was highly complex in form.

301 *Lady Rosina de Courcy*: daughter of the Earl of de Courcy and a friend of the Duke's in *The Prime Minister*.

*Moore's Melodies*: Thomas Moore's *Irish Melodies* (1846–52) were Victorian parlour favourites and commonly set to music. Popplecourt's light tastes could hardly impress a young woman able to initiate a conversation about the Skald.

302 *horse . . . colour*: 'My purpose is indeed a horse of that colour', *Twelfth Night*, II. iii. 161.

303 *settlements*: a prenuptial agreement to set up money in trust for the wife to access during her husband's life and after his death. Before the 1882 Married Women's Property Act, any money or property not so settled passed automatically to the husband on marriage.

*in our country*: the New York Married Women's Property Act, used as a model by many other states, had granted married women control over their own property in 1848.

304 *a trap*: a light two-wheeled carriage.

311 *Plantagenet*: the family name of the royal house founded by Henry II in the twelfth century.

*griffins*: heraldic creature with a lion's body and eagle's head.

*Sir Guy*: the history of the Pallisers is told by Lady Glencora in ch. 22 of *Can You Forgive Her?*.

312 *rushlights*: cheap candle, made from dipping the dried stalk of the rush plant in fat.

316 *levanted*: absconded in circumstances of financial dishonour.

*Apollyon*: the king of the bottomless pit and tormenting locusts in Revelation 9: 1–11.

317 *'edge*: to hedge a bet is to make another bet to cover one's losses should the first bet not succeed.

322 *wormwood*: a bitter medicinal herb.

324 *'locus pœnitentiæ'*: literally, place of repentance, and a legal term signifying the opportunity to withdraw from a contract before it is finalized.

327 *Mr Warburton*: the Duke's private secretary.

328 *Barrington Erle*: prominent Liberal and friend of Phineas Finn.

330 *the Brake*: Lord Chiltern is Master of the Brake Hounds (see Ch 62).

337 *pamphlet . . . coinage*: the Duke has been an ardent advocate of decimalization since his twenties, an interest which placed some strain on the early years of his marriage (see *Can You Forgive Her?*, *The Eustace Diamonds*). Although other Trollope characters find the question dull, the topic in real life was pressing enough to prompt the 1856–7 Royal Commission on Decimal Coinage. Its findings were inconclusive.

338 *quints*: fivepenny coin, the Duke's proposed decimal substitution for the sixpence.

   *twelve . . . fourteen*: readers unfamiliar with British nineteenth-century coinage, and imperial and avoirdupois measurement, will want to know that 12 pennies are 1 shilling (and 12 shillings, 1 pound); 12 inches are 1 foot; 12 ounces, ¾ of 1 pound; and that there are 16 ounces to the pound, and 14 pounds to the stone.

342 *King . . . daughter*: a medieval legend about the North African king's love at first sight for a woman begging outside his palace gates. The story also inspired Tennyson's 'The Beggar Maid' (1833), Lewis Carroll's photograph 'Alice as Beggar Maid' (1858), and Edward Burne-Jones's painting *King Cophetua and the Beggar Maid* (1884).

343 *roll a stone*: Sisyphus, condemned to this eternal punishment by Zeus.

   *Sir Guy*: see note to p. 311.


## VOLUME III

348 *convict's granddaughter*: the poet Edward FitzGerald, enjoying reading *The Duke's Children* as it was published, wrote to his friend W. A. Wright on 20 April 1880 to say: 'In Trollope's good Serial in *All the Year Round* (*The Duke's Children*) a Lady Mabel talks of an American "Miss Boncassen" of whom she is jealous, as "A Convict's [Grand] Daughter". Mr B., being a very enlightened American, expected to be chosen President. I knew, of course, that such a phrase was only pitched out in a fit of jealous spleen; still, it was once, as I remember, spoken as serious truth by many English some fifty years ago: and I wrote to Trollope that I wished he would in his three Volumes cancel, or alter, a phrase that could only rouse up disagreeable recollections. I know no more of him than from corresponding with him about Thackeray last year. I am sure he is quite sincere in saying he forgets all the details of his Book, though he remembers the

upshot': *Trollope: Interviews and Recollections*, ed. R. C. Terry (Basingstoke: Macmillan, 1987), 132–3.

*comme il faut*: as it should be, proper, decorous.

349 *younger son*: the elder son would normally stand for Parliament, but he is busy 'investigating the mountains of Crim Tartary' (p. 23).

350 *Polpenno*: the election at Polpenno shares several of the features of the election at Beverley, East Yorkshire, which Trollope unsuccessfully contested in 1868. The episode is described in ch. 16 of *An Autobiography*, 297–306.

351 *elder sister of Frank's*: in Ch. 4, Frank did not have a sister.

*very conservative indeed*: the disestablishment of the Irish Church was a live political issue when Trollope was standing for Beverley.

352 *my governor's ideas*: during this important conversation, Silverbridge realizes how his father's influence has made him a Liberal after all. The passage reflects Trollope's own political theory, further outlined in *An Autobiography*, 290–5.

355 *Parliamentary canvassing*: Trollope's own account of its miseries in Beverley can be found in *An Autobiography*, 297–306.

*buff*: buff and blue were the Liberal colours.

358 *ballot-boxes*: the Ballot Act, an attempt to thwart electioneering bribery by imposing a secret ballot, was passed in 1872, but the practice was not obliterated.

*Salem and Zion and Ebenezer*: popular names for Nonconformist or Dissenting chapels. The use of the term 'Dissenter' was considered old-fashioned by 1876.

*Jacobins*: political radicals—a term derived from the most famous political club of the French Revolution.

363 *cherry brandy*: traditional tipple taken at the start of a hunt. On this occasion, Tifto is the prey.

374 *Pitt's time*: William Pitt the Younger became, aged 24, the youngest British Prime Minister in 1783. He left office in 1801, but returned in 1803, serving until his death in 1806. Although often classed as a Tory, he referred to himself as a 'new Whig', and was opposed to partisan parliamentary politics. His political 'between-ness' offers an intriguing context for Silverbridge.

378 *the top of his bent*: 'They fool me to the top of my bent', *Hamlet*, III. ii. 372.

*the rental*: of the Gatherum lands and estates.

382 *Coldstreams*: Coldstream Regiment of Foot Guards, a Light Role infantry Battalion, first mustered in 1650.

383 *Moreton*: earlier, Morton.

386 *perfect . . . fear*: 1 John 4: 18.

389 *'Bone of my bone'*: 'And the rib, which the LORD God had taken from man, made he a woman, and brought her unto the man. And Adam said, This is now bone of my bones, and flesh of my flesh: she shall be called Woman, because she was taken out of Man', Genesis 2: 22–3.

391 *Trumpington Wood*: the 'Trumpeton feud' between Lord Chiltern and the Duke is described in ch. 75 of *Phineas Redux*. The 'question was [. . .] Is a landed proprietor bound, or is he not, to keep foxes for the amusement of his neighbours?', i.e., to employ a gamekeeper to ensure there are sufficient foxes to be hunted, and refraining from shooting or trapping them.

392 *jejune*: deficient, dull, unsatisfying.

394 *The Brake Country*: these next two chapters permit Trollope to indulge his favourite subject, hunting, which, as he confesses in *An Autobiography*, 'I have dragged into many novels' (p. 64).

   *intimate friends*: Phineas's friendship with Oswald and Violet Chiltern, and his rivalry with Oswald for Violet's affections, are detailed in *Phineas Finn* and *Phineas Redux*, which also describe Gerald Maule's marriage to Adelaide Palliser and Mr Spooner's unsuccessful courtship of Adelaide.

395 *Castle Nimrod*: see note to p. 292.

   *at home*: a sad falling-off for Violet, who is introduced in ch. 10 of *Phineas Finn* as 'great at hunting', her unladylike thirst for adventure outraging her 'dragon' of an aunt, Lady Baldock.

397 *chopped one*: surprised or startled one, as opposed to driving them out deliberately.

   *new-fangled prejudices*: disquiet over blood sports was not pronounced, although there was some opposition, including Bodleian librarian Edward Byron Nicholson's *The Rights of an Animal* (1879), which condemned hunting on moral grounds.

   *Captain Glomax*: Master of the ARU or URU, the Ufford and Rufford United Hunt Club in *The American Senator*.

398 *carpet-bag*: term derived from the American Civil War for an interloper attempting to encroach on territory not his own.

   *'Bell's Life'* . . . *'Field'* . . . *'Bayley's'*: hunting magazines.

399 *great toe*: prime location for an attack of gout, a form of acute inflammatory arthritis associated with alcohol and rich food.

404 *a whip*: a whipper-in assists the Master of Fox Hounds in the control of the hounds.

408 *Hyperion to a satyr*: 'So excellent a king that was to this | Hyperion to a satyr', *Hamlet*, i: ii. 139–40. Hyperion was one of the Titans, gods who were supplanted by the Olympians in Greek religion.

412 *'Facilis . . . Ditis'*: 'Easy is the way down to the underworld; by night and day Dis's door stands wide open' (Virgil, *Aeneid*, vi. 126).

414 *the pips*: the signs on a playing card.

415 'The Fortnightly': in 1865 Trollope was one of the founders of the *Fortnightly Review*, a Liberal periodical edited by George Henry Lewes and later John Morley. It was one of the first publications to publish the names of its authors, and to have an article accepted was a sign of serious intellectual distinction.

416 *craning*: a hunting term, meaning to hesitate or shrink back at a danger, to pull up one's horse and look over an obstacle before jumping it. *OED* records first usage in 1823.

424 *fig*: to fig oneself out is to dress smartly or elaborately: *OED* records first usage in 1825.

*first-chop hands*: first-rate workers. Again, *OED* records first usage in 1823.

425 'come a cropper': more hunting slang, meaning to fall heavily. As the quotation marks suggest, this was a relatively new term: *OED* records first usage in 1858.

*fair*: see note to p. 27.

426 *fail*: *Macbeth*, I. vii. 59–61. As with 'come a cropper', these quotations appear to be haunted by Tregear.

*Mr Roby*: Thomas Roby, Secretary of the Admiralty, Secretary to the Treasury, and Chief Whip: see *Phineas Finn*, *Phineas Redux*, and *The Prime Minister*.

429 *a pint of champagne*: wine, sherry, and port were commonly served in pint bottles or decanters throughout the nineteenth century.

431 *not surprising*: Trollope reveals himself a champion of the reliability of the post office.

432 *Thomas or Abraham*: is she thinking of Thomas Jefferson and Abraham Lincoln, third and sixteenth President of the United States, respectively?

435 *Hebe*: in Greek mythology, the goddess of youth and cup-bearer to the gods.

436 'Clarissa': Samuel Richardson's long and moralizing epistolary novel (1747–8) which, ironically, partly concerns a difference between father and daughter on the choice of a marriage partner.

439 *enter myself . . . you*: another idiom borrowed from the racecourse.

*hook it*: slang for to make off (*OED* first usage 1851).

*the great Asiatic tour*: like Tregear's brother, perhaps.

440 *Mr Gotobed*: Elias Gotobed, the naïve eponymous protagonist of *The American Senator*.

*Ezekiel Sevenkings*: perhaps based on Walt Whitman, whose *Leaves of Grass* (1855) was much celebrated in Great Britain during the 1870s.

444 *Anglican*: Anglophile.

446 *Mildmay*: Whig Prime Minister between Lord Brock and Mr Gresham, prominent in *The Prime Minister* and bearing a resemblance to Lord John Russell.

450  *the Howards*: 'What can ennoble sots or slaves or cowards? | Alas! Not all
     the blood of all the Howards', Pope, *Essay on Man* (1734), Ep. iv, l. 215.
     A leading dynastic family of the English aristocracy, the Howards hold a
     number of titles, including the Duchy of Norfolk.

453  *Islington*: then a rural north London suburb.

455  *Darby and Joan*: a proverbial staid and middle-aged married couple, whose
     domestic felicity is recounted in Henry Woodfall's 1735 ballad and several
     of its imitators.

465  *"There is a tide in the affairs of men——!"*: 'Which, taken at the flood, leads
     on to fortune', *Julius Caesar*, I. ii. 70–1.

468  *caviare to the general*: too good for the popular taste (*Hamlet*, II. ii. 439–40).

470  *Lazarus*: fictional Oxford college also appearing in *Barchester Towers*.

480  *buckram*: a stiff cotton cloth hardened with starch.

481  *suasive*: persuasive.

     *The brewers . . . licences*: the 1872 Licensing Act had been introduced by
     Gladstone's first Liberal government and reduced the number of licences.
     Accordingly, the brewing interest or 'beerocracy' supported the
     Conservatives, and Gladstone blamed the loss of the 1874 General
     Election on the opposition of this interest group.

482  *peculation*: 'The appropriation of money or property held in trust for
     another by a servant, employee, or official; *esp.* the embezzlement of
     public funds belonging to a ruler, state, or government. Also: an instance
     of this', *OED*.

494  *leather or prunella*: nothing of importance. Prunella is a sturdy cloth used
     in shoemaking.

506  *arrogance*: the original manuscript version ended with the Duke thinking
     about Tregear's future, and the hint of a sequel:

>      'Who knows. He may yet live to be a much greater man than
>    his father-in-law. I am certainly very glad that he has a seat in
>    Parliament.'
>      'It will be my turn next,' said Gerald, as he was smoking with his
>    brother that evening. 'After what you and Mary have done, I think
>    he must let me have my own way whatever it be.'